Pieternella, Daughter of Eva

Pieternella, Daughter of Eva

DALENE MATTHEE

translated by
Malcolm Hacksley

PENGUIN BOOKS

PENGUIN BOOKS

Published by the Penguin Group
Penguin Books (South Africa) (Pty) Ltd, 24 Sturdee Avenue, Rosebank,
Johannesburg 2196, South Africa
Penguin Group (USA) Inc, 375 Hudson Street, New York, New York 10014, USA
Penguin Group (Canada), 90 Eglinton Avenue East, Suite 700, Toronto, Ontario,
Canada M4P 2Y3 (a division of Pearson Penguin Canada Inc)
Penguin Books Ltd, 80 Strand, London WC2R 0RL, England
Penguin Ireland, 25 St Stephen's Green, Dublin 2, Ireland (a division of
Penguin Books Ltd)
Penguin Group (Australia), 250 Camberwell Road, Camberwell, Victoria 3124,
Australia (a division of Pearson Australia Group Pty Ltd)
Penguin Books India Pvt Ltd, 11 Community Centre, Panchsheel Park,
New Delhi - 110 017, India
Penguin Group (NZ), 67 Apollo Drive, Mairangi Bay, Auckland 1310, New Zealand
(a division of Pearson New Zealand Ltd)

Penguin Books (South Africa) (Pty) Ltd, Registered Offices:
24 Sturdee Avenue, Rosebank, Johannesburg 2196, South Africa

www.penguinbooks.co.za

First published as *Pieternella van die Kaap* by Tafelberg-Uitgewers 2000
First paperback impression 2000
Third impression 2004

This translation published by Penguin Books (South Africa) (Pty) Ltd 2008

Translation copyright © Malcolm Hacksley 2008
Maps reproduced with permission from Abdul Amien

ISBN: 978 0 143 02583 2

Typeset by CJH Design in 9.5/13.5 pt Lucida Bright
Cover designed by luckyfish
Printed and bound by CTP Book Printers, Cape Town

*The research for this novel was partially funded by a grant from the National
Arts Council of South Africa.*

For Eva

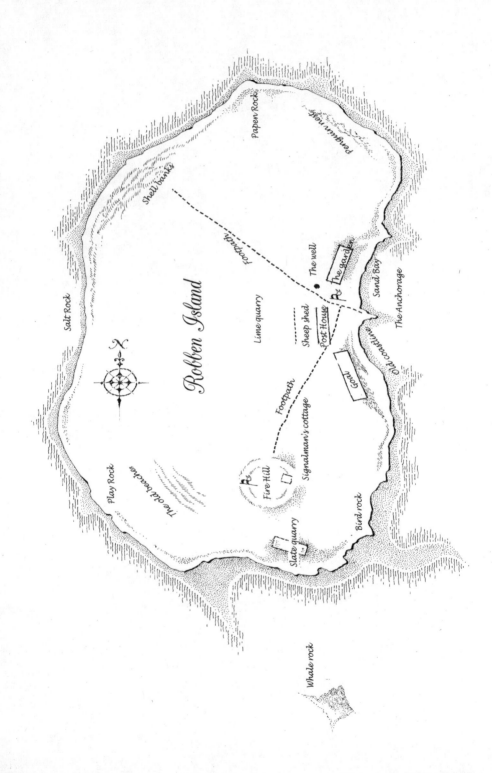

NOTES AND GLOSSARY

of unusual regional and archaic expressions
used in *Pieternella, Daughter of Eva*

Most of the descriptions and definitions below are derived from the
Dictionary of South African English on Historical Principles, *OUP, Oxford*
1996, with the gracious permission of Ms Jill Wolvaardt, the present
editor.

Arita	fine Japanese porcelain
arrack	rough distilled liquor
assegai	spear
aum	liquid measure (approximately 155 litres/35 imperial gallons)
Batavia	Java
buchu	dried, powdered leaves of an aromatic plant of the Rutaceae family
buck	antelope
burgher	Dutch colonist at the Cape
bushbaby	tiny monkey-like animal with very large eyes and a piteous cry
Bushman	member of the San, indigenous hunter-gatherer peoples
Cape, The	colony established by the Dutch East India Company at the Cape of Good Hope in 1652 as a refreshment station for shipping between the Netherlands and its possessions in the East
Castle, The	the star-shaped Dutch fort erected at the Cape between 1665 and 1679, headquarters and garrison of the local administration
Chainouqua	tribe of Khoikhoi people living east of the Cape peninsula
[Chobona	possibly Eva's mispronunciation of Amambo, indigenous peoples living in south-east Africa]
Chorachoqua	tribe of Khoikhoi people living around the Cape peninsula

commandeer	force into military service or for other official tasks
Commandeur	chief employee of the Company acting as Governor of the Dutch settlement at the Cape
Company, The	the Dutch East India Company that occupied the Cape from 1652
Cochoqua	large tribe of Khoikhoi people living north of the Cape peninsula
Corporal	official with supervisory and punitive powers
dagga	marijuana, cannabis
dassie	rock rabbit, hyrax
Dutch East India Company	trading company which placed the first white settlers at the Cape of Good Hope in 1652
fatherland	Holland, the Netherlands
Fiscal	chief legal officer of the Company at the Cape functioning as attorney general, public prosecutor, chief magistrate, customs officer and chief of police
five-stones	children's game played with five stones
free-burgher	former employee of the Company, freed from its control
free farmer	former employee of the Company, freed to farm for his own account
free fisherman	former employee of the Company, freed to earn his living from fishing
Goringhaicona	tribe of Khoikhoi people, also called Strandlopers, living around the Cape peninsula
Goringhaiqua	tribe of Khoikhoi people living around the Cape peninsula
Groote Schuur	great barn and wheat store
guilder	Dutch gold coin
Hamcunqua	presumably a tribe of Khoikhoi people
hartebeest	large antelope
Hessequa	tribe of Khoikhoi people living farther to the east of the Cape peninsula
Hottentot	member of any of several groups of Khoikhoi people indigenous to the Cape
Hottentots-bedding	aromatic shrub, *Helichrysum*
Hottentot fig	succulent plant with edible fruit and leaves, *Carpobrotus*
Huguenot	French Calvinist settler at the Cape from 1688

India	the Dutch East Indies
Juffrouw	Ma'am; Mrs
kabeljou	marine fish, Cape salmon, of the Sciaenidae famiy
Khoi(khoi)	'Man (of Men)', 'Real People'; southern African people of short stature, yellow-brown skin and tightly curled hair
klipspringer	small, sure-footed mountain antelope
kloof	defile, ravine
kraal (1)	enclosure for domestic livestock
kraal (2)	settlement of huts in an enclosure
krantz	cliff face
leaguer	liquid measure (approximately 150 gallons/680 litres)
Lords Seventeen	Board of Directors of the Company in the Netherlands
Mascarenhas	the island of Reunion
morgen	unit of land (approximately two acres)
Master	official Surgeon in service of the Company
mousebird	coly, a small crested bird with a long, straight tail
Mynheer	Sir; Mr
Nama(qua)	tribe of Khoikhoi people living north of the Cape peninsula and in Namibia
Oom	Uncle, respectful form of address to an older man
Ousis	respectful form of address to a woman, usually an elder sister
pandour	member of a Khoikhoi regiment established by the Company to defend the Colony
perlemoen	abalone; large edible shellfish with iridescent shell
puffer	small marine fish with poisonous spines
rixdollar	Cape silver coin
Robben Island	island in Table Bay, used as a prison
sampan	small punt-like boat with a single sail
Secunde	Deputy Governor, or second-in-command, at the Cape under the Company
Seur	Milord
Sergeant	official with supervisory and punitive powers at the Cape

Sick Visitor	minor clerical official and lay preacher employed by the Company to conduct church services, visit the sick and teach children
Sis!	expression of disgust
spoor	tracks
steenbras	marine fish, sea bream
stonefish	small, highly poisonous marine fish resembling a stone
Strandloper	Khoisan coastal fisherman and beachcomber
Tant, tante	Aunt/ respectful form of address to an older woman
-tjie	diminutive suffix
train oil	oil rendered down from seal blubber
trek	relocate, migrate
Tswana	Sotho people living in the west of southern Africa
uintjies	small edible bulbs
Vanger	'Catcher'
veld	open country
VOC	Dutch East India Company (Vereenigde Oost-Indische Compagnie); also its monogram used on porcelain and silverware
waxberry	fruit of a shrub of the Myricaceae family

~ ONE ~

1

She'd pleaded with them for days not to send her away to Mauritius. Kicked and screamed, said the Cape was where she'd been born, it was her whole life. But they took no notice. Didn't care. Early one morning a mounted soldier had ridden up to the Van der Byls' house to announce that the young girl Pieternella van Meerhoff was to bind up her bundles and report to the quay; the *Boode* was preparing to sail.

'I don't want to leave!' she screamed one last time and rolled under the nearest bedstead.

'Pieternella …' Juffrouw Sophia pleaded, 'it's the Church Council that has decided this and you have to obey.' Kindly Juffrouw Sophia van der Tempel, wife to carpenter Gerrit van der Byl, her foster father. One child of their own, Pieter van der Byl. 'Please, Pieternella, come out.'

'No. I'll lie here till I'm dead, I'm not getting on to the ship!'

'Get the bitterness out of your heart, girl. Don't go on so ungratefully pushing away the Almighty's hand of mercy. Go, and be obliging to your new foster parents, Mynheer Borms and his wife. Set an example to your young brother. He went aboard days ago in sweet obedience. *Have faith* that the Lord God will lead you farther along life's path.'

'We never asked for another life's path!'

She'd *told* Salomon they should run away.

'Where to, Pieternella? The Governor will send soldiers after us and then we'll be in big trouble. Jan Vlok is already saying we're bad children.'

'He's lying.'

'He says we're bad children because we're Eva's children. You and I and Jacobus - he didn't say anything about Anthonie.'

'Just stop it!'

'Maybe we're bad children because Mamma was a Hottentot?'

'Stop it, I said!'

He wouldn't. 'But we're not Hottentots, are we?'

'No.'

She and Salomon were sitting on the stone steps in front of Jan Vlok's house. Jan Vlok who'd looked after Salomon on behalf of the Church after the Sick Visitor Juriaan Heere's wife herself got sick and felt she couldn't manage Jacobus and Salomon and the two Willemse children any more. Church Council children, too. Arrived here one day on a ship from Holland. Their mother and three brothers had died on the way. Their dad was supposed to help build the new Castle, to make sure it got finished.

Salomon didn't want to run away. 'We'll have to go together, Pieternella. Oom Bart is a bit fussy about his clothes, but at least he's not nasty. Jan Vlok says Oom Bart is an old India hand. Anyone who's been to the East with the ships and stayed there a long time comes back an old India hand. Don't believe anything he says: he thinks he's wise now. Eats with sticks.'

'I'm very happy with the Van der Byls, we eat with spoons. Juffrouw Sophia won't even let me use my fingers like Tant Barbara Geens and her daughters and the rest do.'

Oom Bart says the ship won't take us on board for nothing and the Church Council hasn't got the money to pay for us, so I'm going aboard as the cook's boy. That will cover our fare. There's a proper galley on the ship, not just a box with sand and stones in it, like on the shell boat.'

'We didn't ask the Bormses to have us.'

Jan Vlok had been receiving money every six months for looking after Salomon. Like the Van der Byls had for her.

'I believe two banished people are also going. Tant Maijke van den Berg and Willem van Deventer, the murderer. For their whole lives.'

'Good. I hope Tant Maijke falls overboard and drowns in the sea.'

'How old are we, Pieternella?'

'You're twelve. I'm fourteen. It's written down in the Church books.'

'How do we know they're right?'

'Mamma said I was born the year after Mynheer Van Riebeeck left and the Lords Seventeen sent that useless Commandeur who was supposed to make the Hottentots more slavish.'

'And me?'

'When we were living on Robben Island. When Dad was the Post Holder there.'

'I don't remember Dad. How old is Jacobus?'

'Older than me. Fifteen or sixteen.'

'Why hasn't he also been banished?'

'We *haven't* been banished! Get that into your head! The Church wants to give us to Oom Bart and Tant Theuntjie because they haven't got any children of their own, and I don't want to be given to them!'

'Jacobus says it's because the Church hasn't got the money to keep us any more, Pieternella. Because Janvos died and they're not getting his slave's wages to share out any more. Jan Vlok's wife says Jacobus is learning a trade. Oom Jac Jacolyn is teaching him to make shoes and the Church Council is paying Oom Jac for it, 'cause that way Jacobus will be useful to the Company. We're no use. But I'm telling you, I won't eat with sticks.'

'Pieter van der Byl says if the Company had bought Janvos before he died, we would have had lots of money, because he was *our* slave. Dad's slave. That Mamma inherited. Then us. Dad bought him long ago from that same Bart Borms.'

'Anthonie also inherited him.'

'Certainly.'

'How old is Anthonie?'

'Don't know.'

'Why don't you want to talk about Anthonie? Because Mamma had him after Dad was already dead?'

'Yes.' She herself never wanted to have children.

'Why is Anthonie's surname Evas? Anthonie Evas?'

'People often call us that, too.'

'When I was little, I thought Janvos was our dad. Then I realised he was a bit too black.'

She didn't mean to laugh. 'Janvos didn't like Anthonie either.'

'What's wrong with Jacobus?' Salomon asked suddenly.

'Sick in the head.'

'But it's not his head that falls down, it's his body. I get scared when he falls over and lies there thrashing about.'

'You're also going to fall over and lie there thrashing about if you don't eat more and get fatter. Look how skinny you are!'

'As though you were any less skinny. The Master gives Jacobus medicine.'

'Doesn't seem to help.'

'There's three ships in the harbour. Which one are we supposed to go on?'

'Pieter says the one nearest to the wall at the anchorage, but I'm telling you I'm not going *anywhere*.'

'I wonder if they'll give me sailors' clothes ...'

Everything had been fine before the evening when the Sick Comforter knocked on Mynheer Van der Byl's door and slapped down the news on the dining room table: 'It hath pleased Almighty God to send good parents to Pieternella and her young brother. Friends of their late father.'

She'd felt the same fright as when one of the cannons on the Castle wall suddenly went off *boom!* like thunder above her head. 'Who?' she asked quickly.

'Don't interrupt, Pieternella,' cautioned Mynheer Van der Byl. Good and strong, like Pieter. He'd once built the Governor a large cupboard that was still in the Castle. Janvos had helped him.

'I'm not going to anyone. I'm staying here.' They'd better *know* it! Janvos always used to say: Pieternellatjie, you must listen to this master and his wife. They take good care of you. And as long as they take care of you, I'll work for you. And for Jacobus and Salomon, too. I promised the Master I would. I said I'd look out for you till he got back.

The Master never came back. The Governor sent him to Madagascar to buy slaves to build the Castle and the slave traders beat him to death. Madagascar is also an island. She'd learnt that at school. And the Master was her dad. The Surgeon.

'Who are these people you are talking about, Sick Comforter?' Juffrouw Sophia asked, surprised.

The Sick Comforter – tall, thin cockroach in his black garb – first lowered his eyes, then said: 'Bartholomeus Borms, Bart as we know him. He and his wife, Theuntjie van der Linde. Decent, childless folk. He used to be a free fisherman here at the Cape. Now he is a free landowner on Mauritius.'

Mauritius? The word fell like a curse from the man's lips.

'I remember Bart well,' said Mynheer Van der Byl. 'They lived for a long time beside the Salt River. Later he bought a house in Tuin Street. His boat was the *Bruijd*.'

'Quite correct.'

4

'I believe he's fairly well-off now?'

'I cannot comment on that. He and his wife are here at the Cape at present. They have asked to take Pieternella and Salomon back to Mauritius with them.'

'I'm not going.'

'Watch your manners, girl. What will Mynheer Heere think of us? And stop scraping your feet across each other like that. Those are your new shoes.'

'I'm staying here.' *Eva, unless your behaviour improves, we will banish you to Mauritius!* That's how they used to threaten her mother. First you are dumped on Robben Island to rid the Cape of vermin, and if you still won't behave, they banish you to the second rubbish pit: Mauritius. A rock somewhere in the middle of the sea where runaway slaves chop you to pieces bit by bit, and the hand of a ghost pokes up out of the water.

'Originally, they wanted to take only Salomon, but now they are prepared to take Pieternella too.'

Fright makes your teeth chatter and you can't speak properly. 'Please, Sick Visitor, I'm happy here with Mynheer Van der Byl and Juffrouw Sophia. I've been to school. I can read and write and make beds and cook rice and everything.'

The first time they banished her mother to Robben Island, she'd gone too. Originally she and Salomon and Jacobus had been given to other people: to Barbara Geens and her husband Hendrik Reynste. But her mother had clung to her so fiercely that they simply let her go along. On the shell boat. She and her mamma and two banished drunken sailors. They lived in the Post House on the island. After a time the Fiscal called for her because she had to go back to school. *O children learn the golden rule: Early to bed and early to school.* Recitation and writing. Nothing but problems with this child, Tant Barbara complained, the Church Council will have to pay more, she keeps running off to her mother, either on the shell boat or on the food boat.

'I'm not going to Mauritius. Please not.'

Her dad had never come back. So she and her mother and Jacobus and Salomon had stayed with the Post Holder who was acting in her father's place, in the Post House on Robben Island. His wife was there too. Most days they would watch secretly for their father's return. Her mother was sure he would come back.

One day they were wandering about on the northern side of the island.

'This is where they left with your father,' her mother said. 'They've got to bring him back before my heart breaks.'

'He will come, Mamma.'

'We mustn't forget the name of the ship. It was the *Westwoud*. The one with trees carved into the wood of the poop.'

'Yes, Mamma.' She often told them that.

Early in the afternoon they returned to the Post House; the food boat was on its way across the water. Her mother walked round to Sand Bay to talk to the boatman, but she had hardly left when she came storming back into the house out of breath, demanding: 'Post Holder Siegfriedt, are my eyes deceiving me?'

'What are you talking about, Juffrouw Eva?'

'The new convict that has arrived looks exactly like Mynheer Hendrik Lacus!'

The new convicts usually came on the food boat.

'It's him all right, Juffrouw Eva. A great sadness.'

So Hendrik Lacus fell down off the highest cliff right into the sheepfold, her mother said later. For stealing. He'd been the Fiscal, then the Secunde, even stood in for the Governor one time. Then he stole wine and brandy and olive oil and everything he could lay his hands on. He lined the ceiling of the new church in the Castle with gunny, but his entry in the books said it was costly linen from the East. He pocketed the money himself. He stole beads from the Company's warehouse and gave them to Bart Borms to barter with the Hottentots for cattle for him. Strictly against the rules: only the Company was allowed to barter with the Hottentots. For every animal, Bart got his share of the money. Close friends.

But it wasn't because of Hendrik Lacus that they'd had to leave the island. It was the fault of Juffrouw Lydia de Paape, his wife. She'd gone crying to Governor Borghorst that it was her earnest desire to suffer on the island together with her husband. Took her little girl along with her. Henrietta. A little smaller than herself, Pieternella.

Before long, Juffrouw Lydia arrived on the island on the food boat. Letter from the Governor in hand. The Post Holder stood around, then called her mother outside. He said: 'Juffrouw Eva, from now on you and your children will have to sleep in the sitting room, because Juffrouw Lydia and her little daughter have to sleep in the room next door. I think it would be better for everybody.'

Her mother said: Post Holder, don't tell me a skunk with a feather in its mouth is an ostrich! I can smell Lydia de Paape under its tail.

Then it emerged that the letter had contained instructions that Juffrouw Lydia was to be most properly accommodated in the Post

6

House and was not to be offered any affront. Her father, Juffrouw Eva, said the Post Holder, was a very prominent clergyman in the service of the Company in the East Indies.

His arse, said her mother. I'm not sleeping in the front room.

Next week the Commandeur sent Juffrouw Lydia six blankets and two bedsheets and soft slippers with open heels that they called mules. And other stuff, too.

That night at table her mother grabbed the Post Holder's wine bottle and put it to her lips. Then she taunted Juffrouw Lydia: I gather your esteemed husband beat you black and blue – does your esteemed father know this?

Juffrouw Lydia sprang up so quickly she knocked over the chair behind her. Kindly require Widow Van Meerhoff to treat me with the necessary respect! she demanded of the Post Holder.

Her mother said: 'I'm not sleeping in the sitting room. I'll sleep on the bed which my husband made with his own hands – hands that wouldn't steal a stone!'

Forbid this Hottentot to address me, Juffrouw Lydia ordered the Post Holder, and tell her to keep her children away from mine.

Then the Commandeur wrote that they were to live in the potter's cottage on the mainland. She and her mother and Jacobus and Salomon.

Barely half a year later Juffrouw Lydia was back at the Fort, pleading in tears to be allowed to leave the island. Heavily pregnant.

The day after her mother was buried, word came from the Castle that the blanket issued to Eva the previous week was to be returned. Pieternella herself went and flung it down at the Gateway to the Castle. The guard on duty commented: 'Oho, just like her ma!'

Juffrouw Sophia remained on her knees beside the bed, first pleading, later threatening to fetch someone else to drag her out. So she crawled out.

The sea chest that Bart Borms had sent up for her and Salomon's clothes and things was already on board. Juffrouw Sophia and Jan Vlok's wife had packed it. Pieter and Mynheer Van der Byl were away round the side of Table Mountain in Leendert's Forest to saw timber for cupboards and chairs and tables and things.

Juffrouw Sophia saw to the bundles. First the mattress. The Church Council had sent an empty mattress cover and Pieternella and Pieter had gone out to gather Hottentots-bedding leaves to stuff it with. Not straw. That you could buy at the warehouse if you wanted to. Salomon would get a straw mattress on the ship because he was a sailor.

A Hottentots-bedding mattress, because Mynheer said it kept the lice and fleas away, and anyway it was more comfortable and softer than straw.

She tore the small grey-blue leaves off the shrubs and flung them down on to a heap. 'I don't want a mattress. I've *got* one!' she shouted at Pieter. 'I don't want to go on board a ship. I've *got* a home on land!'

'It's not going to help, carrying on like this, Pieternella. The bastards have got you caught. Please don't cry so much. Just promise yourself that one day you'll come back.'

'How?'

'On a ship.'

'When?'

'Some day.'

'How am I going to live till some day?'

'Just keep on breathing – and go on picking leaves. We haven't got nearly enough for a mattress yet.'

Perhaps Juffrouw Sophia was secretly glad that the Church Council wanted to take her away. Once she had scolded Pieter and told him not to flirt with Pieternella. She's a girl – but not like other girls from the homeland.

That day she and Pieter had gone out picking waxberries. Later, he and his mother were in the kitchen while she was at the back door snapping kindling for the fire.

'You don't need to worry about Pieternella, Mother.'

'That's not easy. Nature has made her beautiful, and in this wicked world that can be a young girl's undoing.'

'Not while you're taking care of her, Mother.'

'Pieter, I don't think you understand.'

'She's not like other orphans.'

'Well, she's not really an orphan, Pieter. We took her in because no one else wanted to. She was little. She fitted in very well with us, especially after her mother's death. But she's not like us. Believe me.'

'She's always so cheerful, Mother. She sings to the cow while I'm milking and the cow stands quietly and lets down her milk like a tame creature.' Fortunately he didn't mention that she first lifted up the cow's tail and blew into her behind as she had seen the Hottentots doing. Juffrouw Sophia was very proper.

After that he wasn't allowed to go out into the veld with her any more. Because they stayed away too long. Finding enough berries to fill a whole bucket took a lot of searching. More and more branches of the berry bushes had been broken off by woodcutters.

You drop the greasy berries into a cauldron of water. You put it on the fire until the water boils – stirring and stirring – till the grease starts melting and floats to the top so you can skim it off. There's nothing to beat a waxberry candle, Mynheer Van der Byl always said. Then he would read from the Bible till everyone started yawning.

How can you be different from the way nature has made you?

Just a tiny spark of hope was left in her heart when she crawled out from under the bed: that the wind would never blow again. All three ships in the Bay had been lying at anchor for almost a week already, waiting for wind. But not even a breeze.

Everyone and everything that was already on board the *Boode* would rot and stink. Even Salomon. Everyone and everything on the other ships would too.

Pieter van der Byl said the voyage to Holland could take up to five months. A little less if the winds blew you in the right direction. After that the ships lay up for a rest here at the Cape. Exhausted. Then they sailed off again to the East. Also a long way. There they were loaded up with all kinds of things and they came back again, for another rest at the Cape ...

There had been other Church Council children at the Van der Byls'. For quite a while. But she had been there longest and had her own bed.

Juffrouw Sophia was strict. If she left her things lying about, she was made to stand beside the table and recite aloud twenty times: *Wealth begins with tidiness ... Wealth begins with tidiness ...*

Nice and slowly. No gabbling.

Juffrouw Sophia started rolling up the first bundle, the one with the mattress. The leaves of the Hottentots-bedding bush rustled gently. 'Fold the top end back a pillow's width for your head each evening, Pieternella.'

The second bundle. Dark blue quilt, clean dress, clean petticoat, stockings, other clothes. Nightdress.

Juffrouw Sophia had taught her to sleep in a nightie. Not in her petticoat. Tant Barbara and Sara and Maria and Tant Maijke van den Berg all slept in their petticoats. No, you sleep in a nightdress, the dressmaker has made you one.

The Church Council had paid for the cloth and the making of it.

Cheese and bread and rusks and dried fish. A little extra something to eat on board ship.

Her shawl was not wrapped up in the bundle. That was for her shoulders because it was cold.

Two small towels: one for washing, the other for drying with. Two combs: one of bone, one of tortoiseshell; the small mirror that Jannetjie Ferdinandus had once given her as a gift. A pewter plate and a pewter spoon – Bart Borms had said she had to have her own on board ship. A sponge for when next she bled. An extra sponge. She had only bled once so far. A little cloth bag for the sponges.

'Remember to rinse your sponges regularly when you need to use them. And dry them properly.'

Each bundle was bound tightly with a broad leather strap.

Then Juffrouw Sophia's eyes filled with tears. 'We're going to miss you, my girl. Say your prayers every morning and evening as we taught you and take care of yourself. I'll walk down to the quay with you.'

'I'll go by myself.'

2

She hid her two bundles beside the Company's stables where the air smelt of horse piss. Where the foot-and-horse path began to rise towards the lookout hut up in the kloof between Table Mountain and Lion's Head she veered off quickly towards the mountain. Then up along the stream flowing off the mountain, past the brick kilns.

Up past the Company Garden. She greeted the garden slaves quite naturally.

'Morning, Sergeant! Juffrouw Sophia sent me, Sergeant.'

'Oh.'

Everyone had to be constantly watched, Mynheer Van der Byl said, because they're all out to smuggle and steal – particularly when there are ships in the Bay.

She didn't want to smuggle or steal anything. She just wanted to fetch something that was hers. She didn't know why. She simply wanted it.

Ahead of her, above her, the Mountain towered up over everything like a giant stone watchman. Table Mountain.

Fair Ansiela, who had first been a heathen and a slave from the East – smooth black hair and sparkling white teeth – often used to bring flowers in a jar up here for the Spirit of the Mountain. Her mother had told her so herself.

Where did the Spirit of the Mountain live?

Inside it, said Ansiela. Inside everything. Great spirits, small spirits. Many spirits, all actually pieces of the same Spirit. The Mountain's Spirit is the greatest in the whole Cape. Except perhaps the sea's.

Mynheer Van Riebeeck had bought Ansiela from a ship's captain, and when he left he sold her to another man. Then she was freed, because a Sick Visitor had converted her and given her new blood: Christian blood. After that she couldn't take flowers to the mountain any more because that was heathenish.

Then the Fair Ansiela married Mynheer Basson, a white free farmer …

Her mother had also married a white man. In the old Fort, before they knocked it down and put everything in the new Castle. Married with a feast of rice and bread and meat, and wine in the most beautiful goblet, kept specially for weddings. Commandeur Van Riebeeck and his wife had also sat at the table. And other distinguished people, too, because her mother's white husband was an important person. In a beautiful black dress with a snow-white collar and a soft cloth cap just like the ones the Dutch women wore. The Commandeur's stepdaughter put it on her. Ever so pretty. With shiny little beads round the edges of the cap. She married Pieter van Meerhoff, the Master who treated people when they were sick; who cut their gums, or bled their arms into a small basin. Then they felt better.

Her mother had not come from across the sea. She was a real Hottentot. She was born on Robben Island when many, many years ago her tribespeople, the Goringhaicona, had tended sheep on the island for the English ships to stop other Hottentots and other ships' crews stealing and eating them.

Sometimes in the evening, by the light of a waxberry candle, Mynheer Van der Byl would ask her about her mother, and he really listened.

There weren't many Goringhaicona left now. They had lived mostly in the Duintjies – a long way seawards from the town. Often used to beg for food at the Company slaughterhouse behind the old Fort. Tobacco on the quayside. Some carried wood and water to the Castle kitchens in exchange for a piece of tobacco and a small cup of arrack.

Her mother didn't have smooth hair: her hair was short, black and woolly. But you never actually saw it: she even slept with her skin cap on. Only when she was a little drunk and her cap fell off could you see her hair. If she was nearby, she would hastily put her mother's cap back on again. Or the soldiers would, when they picked her up in the street.

She walked all along the footpath to beyond the last hedges of the Company Garden, right to the potter's cottage where they had lived. In her heart she had treasured only the really good days in that cottage – there were some things you didn't want to remember.

Actually, everything you see is stored up in your eyes. Her eyes had had many things in them.

And when you died, you became a bright *//Gaunab*. Or else a pitch-black one. You could stay sitting on your grave or you could go wandering to hear what you'd not been able to hear before, to see what you couldn't have seen before. Her mother's *//Gaunab* wouldn't have gone on sitting on her grave in the Castle church. She was no longer welcome at the Castle.

Her mother would rather have gone back to the potter's cottage. Or to Robben Island. Perhaps. Or else to the Cochoqua Hottentots who had had so many cattle and sheep before the ships came and ate up most of them.

No, the Cochoqua were also angry with her mother.

They say if you take something that used to belong to a dead person, his *//Gaunab* would follow you …

The front door was shattered. Someone had stolen the bolt lock. Perhaps the Company had had it removed. Nothing was allowed to remain idle or useless. Nor were people.

She would not have been useless if they had let her stay. She could do laundry for the people on the ships, she could do needlework, she could cook rice so that it came out just right, not soggy. Vegetables, too. If nobody else wanted her, she would want herself. She would sweep the cottage and fix it up, she would take care of Salomon and look after Jacobus, too. Then they would all live together again.

The Church could give them the money for Jacobus. Or he could make shoes. They would manage.

One of the back shutters was open. She picked up a stick and hooked away the cobwebs before she climbed in. It was cold and murky inside and smelt of damp soil. The second room was the same. She would open all the shutters and let the sun in.

The nails were no longer in the walls …

The Company had had nails knocked into the walls for them to hang their clothes on. Nails were very rare and very expensive. Her mother's other clothes had been kept in the goatskin bag on the floor.

Whenever her mother had gone to the Duintjies, she had put on her skin clothes and draped herself with her strings of beads. Prettily threaded. Most were glass beads. Two red ones, one white ostrich eggshell bead, two more red ones, then another white one. Then a necklace of plain blue ones. Prettiest of all was her mother's skin bonnet. Little beads around the edges, two coins with holes bored in them, and three brass buttons. She worked all kinds of small shells and beads into the hair above her ears, and these would hang down over her ears. The merriest bit was a tiny leather strap with a copper bead that she fastened to a tuft of hair on her forehead so that it hung down in front of her eyes and swung to and fro like a pigtail in front when she walked.

First of all her mother would take off her cloth dress.

She had three cloth dresses. The black one with the white collar that she tied loosely round her neck. Another one that was actually in two pieces: the bottom one wide and pink, the top pale yellow and like a shirt with puffed sleeves. And then the one she liked best: the long loose white one with long sleeves that she called her nightie. All of them hung right down to her feet. The black one she wore only when she had to go to the Castle. Or to church. In stockings and black shoes with heels. One of the shoes had lost its lace somewhere, so it click-clacked as she walked, and they laughed at her.

First she would take off her dress. Then she'd take off her other clothes. She'd knot the under-skin across her shoulders with thin leather straps. Then over it the long top-skin that hung down over her buttocks. When Salomon was small she used to tie him on her back between the two skin garments. Very poor people, like the Duintjies folk, had only one skin.

Next she hung the skin pouch with her pipe and tobacco round her neck. There was only one thing that her mother never took off, that she wore even under her cloth dresses, and that was the pointed skin apron that hung down from above her privates to between her knees and was fastened round her waist with a leather strap.

Finally she quickly removed her cloth cap and put on her pretty skin bonnet. Brass wire earrings hooked into the little holes in her ears. Beads round her body, beads round her neck.

Before her mother became a Dutch woman, she used to wear lots of leather and grass bracelets and anklets. When she became a Dutch woman, she got a cloth apron, a bunch of keys and a tiny pair of scissors with a little mirror, and all the soldiers had to call her Juffrouw Eva.

When she, Pieternella, was small, her mother had plaited grass rings for her arms and ankles, too. When the Church Council gave her and

Jacobus and Salomon to Tant Barbara Geens, the old woman took a knife and cut off all her grass rings and threw them into the fire.

You'd better learn to be white, Pieternella!

I'm white enough.

And less cheeky!

She clambered out through the window again and searched for a stick thick enough to dig with. She had to find the spot where she had hidden the pot that day the Church gave them to Barbara Geens, shortly before they banished her mother to Robben Island the first time.

When they couldn't live on Robben Island any more because of Hendrik Lacus's Juffrouw Lydia, the Commandeur had them brought back in the boat sent to fetch the leftover bricks on the island. Everything belonged to the Lords Seventeen in Amsterdam, even the bricks. It rained very hard indeed that day. Her mother told the Post Holder: I'm not going anywhere, I'm staying here with my children. This is our house. My husband will expect to find us here when he returns.

Sorry, Juffrouw Eva. Commandeur's orders, written on paper: Get aboard!

On top of the bricks, in the rain. The boatman said the Company had found them another place to stay: the potter's old cottage, some distance to the west of the stables, a long way from the Fort and all the other houses.

It was pouring down. Jacobus was carrying Salomon, two soldiers carried the chest. When they got to the cottage it was almost dark. Her mother sat down in the corner, her arms hanging down listlessly, her head on her knees. She didn't want to talk. Jacobus said: Mamma, lift up your head, they've given us two beds as well. With straw mattresses and sheets. And a table and two chairs and a copper pot and a water bucket with a drop handle. And a tablecloth with big thick flowers sewn on it, dark green and brown. Two pewter plates and two pewter spoons. Luckily most of their own things were in their own chest.

Their mother said: Let's go. They walked and walked. It grew dark, but they kept on walking all along the wagon track beside the Liesbeeck River. Right up to the whitewashed house with its reed thatch roof. Tant Maijke van den Berg opened the door, a white kerchief on her head, a candle in her hand. Heavens, Eva, where have you come from at this time of night?

So they slept in the corner of Tant Maijke's dining room, on straw covered with a sheet of canvas. Tant Maijke and her husband, Oom

Thieleman, slept on the bed in the other room. Their elder daughter Johanna, and Cornelia who was still small, slept in the bedroom with them.

Tant Maijke gave her mother some wine. When they woke up early the next morning their mother was gone.

Where's my mother?

Hush, here's some bread. If the guard comes, tell him your mamma didn't come here with you, you don't know where she is.

Then she, Pieternella, cried even louder. Tant Maijke said: Be quiet! I've poured nice milk over your bread. Your mamma has gone up to the kraal on the Windberg, she'll be back soon.

The Windberg was also the Devil's Peak.

Then their mother came back. She and one of Maijke's white servants. With six sheep and a cow. They gave her mother more wine. And an earthenware jar of wine to take home with her. And tobacco. Then they set off along the wagon track back to the potter's cottage, stopping along the way to visit other friends first.

Eva, how strange to see you again! Your children are grown so tall. We hear your husband died.

It's not true, he'll find his way back. He always has.

With his body beaten to death?

Jacobus carried the stone bottle under his shirt, clamped tight under one arm. Her mother had told him to keep it hidden. They had rice and meat to eat with the people they visited. The man gave her mother wine out of a bottle with a cloth stopper and they laughed a lot. Then her mother toppled over and slept for a long while. Salomon was a nuisance. Pieternella walked up and down with him on her hip. Jacobus couldn't take him, he had to make sure the bottle didn't fall out. Then her mother woke up again and they walked on. Her mother did not feel well.

Next day a soldier brought them rice and bread and fish and butter and onions and cabbage and a lantern with a candle in it.

On many days they went out into the veld and dug up tasty roots and bulbs to eat. Uintjies and dune berries and sorrel. Sometimes they picked long greenish bamboo shoots for their mother to boil up at home. Jacobus would fetch water from the river. You weren't allowed to pee in the water; a man on horseback with a whip would thrash you at once. Or they picked the fleshy leaves of Hottentot figs and their mother fried them in butter. With salt and pepper and cinnamon. Lovely! There was nutmeg, too, in their own chest. For fish.

Or they would go out and pick bedding-bush leaves for Salomon to sleep on.

Or up into the mountain for buchu, which their mother dried and ground up fine between two stones. She would store it in a tortoise shell with the holes for the tail and legs stopped up. The hole for the head had only a light stopper so you could easily shake out the spicy powder.

Some of the good women of the town brought her mother a pillow and fish and oil and milk. Sometimes her mother was not at home. Where's your mother? She's coming, she's just gone out for a while. Don't let on that she left yesterday to visit the Goringhaicona in the Duintjies, dressed in her skin clothes.

And don't tell that the soldier had just brought her mother Church money to buy food with. When that happened her mother would often put on her cloth clothes and go drinking at Jannetjie Ferdinandus's tavern. Then Jannetjie's manservant would bring her home slung over his shoulder like a sack of meal and dump her on the bed in the front room. After that she would sleep it off. The next day she would sit on the edge of the bed, shaking and shaking her head. Sometimes she would recite one of her prayers. Very muddled.

I believe in God the Father, the Almighty, Creator of the heavens above our heads and the earth here under our feet and all things visible and invisible, and give us this day our daily bread and forgive us our trespasses as we forgive others their trespasses who descended to earth and ascended up again into heaven and sitteth on the right side of God our Father.

One morning, after a Church-money day, she woke them up before dawn and told them to get ready. 'We've got a long walk ahead of us today. Pieternella must put her shoes on otherwise she'll complain that her feet are too sore.'

Hottentot shoes. That her mother tied on to her feet.

'They're too tight, Mamma!'

'If I don't tie them on tight, they'll slip off.' That morning her mother was impatient. Almost angry.

Actually, the queer shoes were of her mother's making. Two flat pieces of rhinoceros skin without heels or uppers, each with two flat straps to tie them on to the feet.

They walked and walked and walked. But even when they were tired their mother wouldn't stop. She carried Salomon tied on to her back, his head bouncing up and down like your bum on a horse's back. Faster and faster, up and down. She and Jacobus had to trot to keep up with the horse's little brown feet.

First they followed the wagon track for a long way, then veered off

16

towards the Windberg. Her mother knew the way, she didn't stop to think: over the stones, round the rocks, through the streams of water and the bushes that scratched their legs. Rocks. Great silvery rocks.

Luckily, she, Pieternella, had her rhino feet.

'Mamma, my breath is burning!'

She didn't hear.

Jacobus didn't complain.

Up to the Place. Behind Devil's Peak in a ravine at the southern foot of Table Mountain. At first all you saw were the rocks lying around all over, as though they had been ripped out of the mountainside. And the bushes. And the stream.

Her mother took Salomon off her back and handed him to Jacobus. Her breath was racing. She untied the thin strap holding the blue beads that hung round her body, took it off and tied the ends together again so that the beads would not slip off. Then she searched until she found a good stone. She picked it up, drew her top-skin over her head and with one hand held behind her neck took a few steps forward and laid the stone gently on a cairn. Then the beads. After that she crossed her hands over her head and, rocking gently back and forth, she spoke to the stones in stone talk. For a long, long time.

When she turned round again, her face was wet with tears.

Back at the cottage, they found food left at the front door. Rice and bread and fish and cabbage and carrots.

They ate hungrily. Then Jacobus asked: Mamma, who put the other stones on the pile?

Long, long ago, her mother said, before there were any people on earth, the Sun and the Moon lived on the earth. Then they sailed off and went to live up in the sky. The highest of all was *Gounja Tikwa* and just under him *Gounja*, who sends the rain and blows his hot breath across the veld to make the grass and the wild foods grow and to fatten the calves and lambs. *Gounja Tikwa*, who lives higher than everyone, is the All-Best, the One who never hurts anything or anyone and doesn't make anything bad – and who never gets tired.

Were the stone and the beads for him?

Oh no.

For *Gounja*?

No, not him either.

The one you had to be careful of was *Toqua*. Who lived under the ground. The Hottentots regularly had to slaughter their fattest ox or sheep to keep him friendly because in the pitch dark under the ground he would think up all kinds of things to harm them. Like the Hollanders and their ships. They would smear their bodies with the fat of the animal they had slaughtered and shake buchu over themselves. Then they fed one another the meat of sacrifice and told *Toqua* how sorry they were for their wrongdoings – even when they didn't know what they had done wrong.

'Did you give the stone and the beads to *him* then, Mamma?'

No, not him either. 'He doesn't wear beads. The cairn is the place where one of our Forefathers is buried. He was buried in many places, because he died in many places. And rose again. He was a Wizard. Born of the Virgin Mary and rose again – no, I'm getting confused. He was born of another virgin, a young girl who chewed on a particular kind of grass and the sap made her pregnant. The child's name was *Heitsi Eibib*. He could walk though mountains and kill monsters – your dad saw a real monster crawling out of a river one day. At night *Heitsi Eibib*'s spirit comes walking over the veld, and he'll quickly see that Eva of the Goringhaicona came to greet him today, and placed her stone and her beads there in his memory. The stone will tell him: Eva doesn't have any food. The stone will tell him: Eva asks that you please kill the great thirst that lives in her.' The next morning her mother said: Pieternella, we have to make a clay pot. She was wearing her skin clothes because she had washed her shift that morning and hung it out over a bush to dry. She had bartered her pink and yellow dress in the Duintjies for wine and tobacco.

Tant Maijke had lots of pretty gowns, both top ones and bottom ones. She would wear the top dress open from the waist to the floor, so that you could see the one underneath. Sometimes she wore a blue one that she tucked up in a circular bundle round her waist so that the bottom blue one hung out alone. Ever so pretty! With black peasant shoes which her husband always used to make himself. But then he died.

Her mother said they were going to make a clay pot.

Jacobus was not allowed to help, he had to look after Salomon. Only women's hands were allowed to touch the clay, else the pot would be poisonous. Or something like that.

First they had to find an anthill, break it up with a strong stick and crush the clods underfoot. Then they carried the anthill fragments back home on a sheet of canvas and tipped them out on to the flat stones beside the cottage. In the shade. Her mother had pretty little hands, like tiny octopuses. First she picked out all the grains of grit, but left the ant eggs. Then she started adding water and melding it with her fingers till the anthill earth looked like brown bread dough. Then she'd start kneading. Not too fast, for fear of frightening the pot.

'I also want to knead, Mamma!'

'Not yet.'

A dash of water. Knead, knead. Another dash. Knead, knead. Her mother knelt to the task, her long thin tits swinging backwards and forwards in time with the copper bead of the pigtail on her forehead.

'What's a person, Mamma?'

'What do you mean, what's a person?'

'How do people live?'

'By breathing.'

'Where do people come from, Mamma?'

'They grow in a bladder in among the mother's guts.'

'How do you get *into* the bladder?'

'Before you know where you are, you're just there. The clay is ready, you can come and knead now.'

At first her hands wouldn't knead properly. Her mother sat to one side smoking her pipe and laughing in clouds of blue smoke. *Shloff, shloff, shloff.* Brown and smooth, it squelched between her fingers. *Shloff, shloff, shloff.* She wished she also had tits that could swing so prettily.

'Spit in the clay, Pieternella!'

'Why?'

'Spit!'

Chouff!

'Now the pot's got a heart. Otherwise it wouldn't have had a heart.'

Knead, knead, knead. Your arms grew lame. 'Isn't it enough yet, Mamma?'

'Till the sun peeps round the corner.'

'*So* long?'

When the sun came round the corner, her mother lifted the lump of mud-bread dough and slapped it down on another flat stone. There she squatted with her legs spread wide on either side of it, a bowl of water beside her. First she rolled the lump into a ball, moving it round and round. Slowly. Then she began hollowing it out. With her thumbs. It looked as though she was pulling up the sides with her fingers at the same time. Squeeze, pull, turn the lump. Squeeze, pull, turn. Wet your hands. Squeeze, pull, turn. Not too rough and not too gentle. Before their eyes, the pot-bellied vessel gradually rose up out of the clay between her mother's pretty little hands while she sang softly to the pot.

Finally she found a sharp-pointed stone and lay down on her belly to press a row of dots carefully into the neck. Just like little beads.

First the sun had to bake the pot for many days to dry it. Her mother took the stone and pressed the beads deeper into the rim. Lightly. Then back into the sun.

One evening her mother said: 'She's ready for the fire. Tomorrow.'

First a hole in the ground. Dig-dig-dig. Ground is hard. She and her mother. When the hole was deep enough, they made a big fire in the hole. A pot fire. Jacobus had to take Salomon into the veld, they were not allowed anywhere near the fire. And no food, either. Her mother was speaking to the fire. Not Dutch. She only spoke Dutch to the children because they were Dutch children from the Cape. With the fire, she spoke fire-talk. *Click-click-click.* Like gravel being shaken deep inside a clay pot, with snatches of bird-talk in between. Then she raked out the coals, lowered the pot gently into the hole, and cast the embers back into the hollows around and inside the pot.

A soldier brought them rice and butter and oil and collards and carrots and bread. Her mother asked: Where's the meat? He said there wasn't any meat, they were expecting a lot of ships. What's in the hole?

Nothing. Off you go now, and don't let your shadow fall across it.

The hole has to be ice-cold before you scrape it open, her mother said. This is its waiting time. The pot's secret time.

Early in the morning on the next Sunday a soldier came to announce that the Governor had given instructions that her mother was to bring the children to church.

After church, the ash was quite cold.

Bending over the pot as she started scraping out the ash, her mother clucked away just like the mother quail on Robben Island always clucked over her chicks as they crept in under her wings in the evening.

From time to time the Post Holder on the island would send a basket of quail eggs in the food boat for the Governor's table. Or a bunch of fish.

Then her mother would yell after the boat: 'Tell that old blowfly that everyone on the island, high and low, is hollow with hunger!'

'Eva …' the Post Holder would usually warn her that evening after he had read the evening prayer, 'if you don't learn to behave yourself, they're going to banish you to Mauritius!'

That did frighten her mother.

Then, with ash-grey hands, her mother lifted the ash-grey pot out of the hole and carried it down to the river to wash it. So, so pretty! She took a piece of the thin, soft hide that she'd brought from the Duintjies, drew it taut over the rim of the pot and tied it firmly round the neck. Tighter and tighter she drew it.

Put on her skin clothes.

Because now it was a drum-pot, a rumble-drum. Something Jacobus was never allowed to lay his hands on. Only she and her mother. A female pot. For delicate octopus fingers to dance on – drawing the hide still tighter – to *drum-drum-drum-drum* till the pot could sing the right notes late into the night.

Till her mother wasn't quite so sad any more.

When they woke up the next morning she was gone.

When she came back, she had Namtesy from the Duintjies with her; he made Jacobus a reed flute and taught him to play it. Pieternella, was not allowed to touch the reed flute, it was a male thing.

All she could do was practise playing the rumble-drum.

To the moon. She and Jacobus. And her mother would dance. Or Jacobus and her mother would play, while she, Pieternella, was dancing. She alone. Then Jacobus would dance. Then her mother again. Hour after hour.

But the heartache could never be altogether danced out of her mother.

One day, not long after they made the pot, her mother took everything – their clothes, plates, spoons, the cooking pot, their bread – and went off to the Duintjies. She didn't come back.

Salomon wouldn't stop crying. Jacobus walked round and round the cottage with a disturbed expression in his eyes that frightened her.

On the third afternoon she took them to the Fort to ask for food because they were so hungry. There they gave them food and somewhere to sleep and Salomon stopped crying.

The next day the man from the Church came to say that Barbara Geens would take them in, for payment. The Church would give them new clothes.

The first thing Tant Barbara did was to cut off her bangles and anklets and throw them into the fire. She tied her hair back tightly and put a cap on her head. Her mother had gone off with the cap she'd had.

'Your mother is possessed by the Demon Drink and now other people have to struggle with you!' Tant Barbara could hurl words at you that stung like stones.

Her husband's name was Hendrik Reynste, but he wasn't at home.

The Company had sent him to Mauritius to try to make a living there. Not banished. He went as a Company carpenter. He was a tall, gangly man with a cough. Now he was on Mauritius.

She found the clay pot where she had buried it.

She didn't cluck like the quail as she dug it out, she just swallowed the tears that trickled down into her mouth. The pot was shattered. Something or someone must have walked over the hole – it couldn't have been an elephant, no elephants came near the town any more. Perhaps a lion. Perhaps some person. Nothing but shards. Her mother's shards.

She picked out two of the bigger pieces and wiped them on her skirt. One shard showed some of the little bead shapes from round the neck of the pot.

She'd come and buried the pot the day the Church had given them to Barbara Geens. Late in the afternoon, as she was walking back again, she came across two soldiers dragging her mother back from the Duintjies. She was wearing her shift with her top-skin fastened across her shoulders with leather straps. *But that wasn't her mother.* It was a drunken body with a lolling head – like someone who was actually dead.

'Mamma ...' She couldn't hear.

She ran back to Tant Barbara's house, her body shaking uncontrollably. Jacobus was sitting at the table, his fingers drumming on the wood. Maria was playing with Salomon. Tant Barbara was standing at the hearth, stirring a great copper cauldron; Sara was cutting up collards. It was dark in the room, the candle cast a strange weak glimmer over everyone.

Everything was distant. Nothing was real. Tant Barbara spun round, her mouth opened far away and red words flowed out of her mouth: 'Pieternella Evas, where have you been?' Screaming words. 'You're not going to bring your mother's Hottentot tricks into my house, d'you hear? Go and drop them outside in the street or up in the mountain where they belong!'

Hard words. And they wouldn't stop.

Her own mouth opened. She stuck out her tongue at Barbara Geens. The woman strode over and smacked her so hard on the side of the head that it set her ear buzzing. Then everything suddenly sprang back into place.

Slowly, she started walking back to where she had hidden her bundles. She stuck the shards deep into the mattress bundle, like a secret.

When she saw the man approaching on horseback, she knew he was looking for her.

'Pieternella van Meerhoff?'

'What do you want?' she asked sharply when he reined in his horse. It was the same man who had come to call her at the Van der Byls' that morning. She recognised his face. He lived in the Castle. He'd lost most of his teeth.

'They're looking for you. The Corporal is furious. Get to the quay – they've got to get you on board!'

'So what?'

'Van der Byl's wife said you left a long time ago. She's also been out searching for you.'

'I'm on my way.'

'Just hurry up. I've been ordered to see that you get there.'

She tried one last ploy. 'Go and tell them you couldn't find me.'

'What do I get if I tell them that?' With a toothless grin and a gleam in his eyes.

She played dumb. 'I'll give you my quilt.'

'Ah! And then we'll lie on it together for a bit, will we?'

'Get lost.' The horse wouldn't keep still under him.

'Oh no! First I want the quilt and a nice hot thing to lie on it with!' The horse was circling her. She stepped aside and started off again. The horse's hooves came closer.

'Pieternella …'

She pretended not to hear. Tant Barbara had sat her and Sara and Maria round the table one day and said to them: Today I'm going to tell you just how things are in life. You've seen those long pikes with the flat axe-heads that the guards at the gateway to the Castle carry?

Yes.

Dangerous things, aren't they?

Yes.

Now listen carefully, because what you don't know is that every man's also got a pike in his trousers. And a pike is a thing that's always looking for a poke. Night and day. Specially the one in a sailor's trousers. That's what a man has for brains. He breathes with it. For him a woman is nothing more than the thing between her legs. That's all. That's why young girls have to be alert and ready to run, otherwise that pike will leave them with a bun in the oven. Do you understand what I'm saying?

Yes, Ma.

Yes, Tante.

'I said, Pieternella van Meerhoff …' The horse was right behind her. 'Do you want to see my cock?'

She leapt out of the horse's way and snatched up a sharp stone. As she raised her arm to throw, he ducked and kicked the horse in the flank.

She missed.

3

Only one tiny scrap of hope remained to her when she got to the quay: that the wind would never blow again. That they would *have* to let her turn back ...

The other three women who had to go aboard were sitting beside their bundles on the quayside, listlessly waiting. Tant Maijke van den Berg, her red checked handkerchief held in front of her face to hide her tears, though it was too late for tears now: once you were banished, you were banished. Beside her sat Maria, wife of the banished murderer Willem van Deventer, and two of her small daughters. Willem was already aboard, working as a sailor to pay the fares of Maria and the children. Maria's eyes were also red from weeping ...

Probably for Ockert, her manservant. Because Ockert had sneaked into her bed when Willem had had to flee back to Holland after he had shot and killed one of his hired Hottentots one night.

The Hottentot had dropped and smashed the blue-and-white Delft china mug he used to drink his beer out of. He was a Cochoqua and a Cochoqua was someone you stepped round warily. The Company had had quite enough trouble with them already, but it was still embarrassed by the very few cattle and sheep that this once-rich tribe had left. No one was allowed to murder any of them.

Fortunately, by the time the news of the murder reached the Cochoqua kraals beyond Saldanha, Willem van Deventer was gone. The Cochoqua were furious. They weren't allowed to lift a stone or a hand against a whiteskin, they said, but *they* could simply be shot? Hadn't the high Lords beyond the sea forbidden it long before?

Her mother was still alive on Robben Island when the news reached there.

The Company was uneasy.

The Council of the Laws, the one they called the Council of Justice, had met hastily on their big chairs and banished Willem van Deventer from the Cape for ever – even though he had already left on board a ship. The news of the banishment was sent to the Cochoqua by horse, with a word of honour that the man would be condemned to death if ever they caught him. The fleet was on its way, there was a shortage of meat ...

So Maria had two children by Ockert the manservant.

And one day Willem van Deventer arrived back at the Cape, bold as brass, with a letter in his hand signed by the Prince of Orange himself declaring him not guilty. Willem had claimed that he had not realised that the blunderbuss was loaded.

The Cochoqua said: 'Right! He's back here. Hang him now, so we can see.'

The Company was deeply worried. They knew the Cochoqua would not let go until an offence was properly avenged. There was still not enough meat and now they urgently needed draught oxen as well.

So they sent Van Deventer to Robben Island for a while and made him carry shells for four years while they were making up their minds what to do with him. And with the unfaithful Maria, too.

She, Pieternella, was back on the island with her mother. One evening they were sitting in the Post House – Post Holder Wijborgh and his wife and slave and Van Deventer. He wasn't locked up at night like the rest of the convicts, he slept in the Post House. He was sitting darning holes in some of the shell sacks by the light of a candle. The other convicts left all the torn and split sacks for him; the farther he carried them, the more shell grit leaked out.

'You're going to blunt your feet walking, Van Deventer!' her mother shouted at him one morning.

'Go to hell!' he yelled back.

'Fun shooting Hottentots, isn't it?' her mother went on taunting him. Sweat was running down his face like water. 'I hear Ockert Olivier has been sleeping in your bed since you've been away!'

Then he threw down the sack and spun round. Luckily her mother was too quick and the Corporal too close.

The Lawmen eventually decided to banish him to Mauritius for life. Maria and his own two children had to go, too. Her two children by Ockert would be given to her parents to raise.

The third woman with the bundles on the quay was Tant Theuntjie van der Linde, wife of Bart Borms – her and Salomon's new foster mother. Oom Bart was already aboard, working as a sailor to pay Tant Theuntjie's passage.

'Come and sit with us, Pieternella,' Tant Maijke called, her nose bunged up from weeping.

'No.'

'They're watching you.'

'I know.' A soldier with a pimply nose watched her pass. She found a place farther off and sat down by herself.

Seabirds in the air jeered at her with their dry yellow throats.

Birds could fly wherever they wanted to.

On the deep side of the quay a seal raised its head inquisitively out of the water and then tumbled away again in a single black swirl.

Seals could swim wherever they wanted to.

She was trapped. Like the four sheep with their legs tied together, lying jerking on the quayside, kicking against their fate. Too stupid to know they were nothing but shipfood. Fresh food for the voyage. The rest of the cattle and pigs and sheep had already been slaughtered and salted down in barrels, and rolled into the hold the previous day.

Four living Hottentot sheep: two piebald brown ones, a black one and a white one. They were only waiting for the ship's boat to fetch them. Once all the extra barrels of water and bread had been rowed out to the ship, it would be their turn. The other two ships that had been anchored in the Bay had already sailed. Sometime in the early hours there must have been enough wind for them to set sail.

Only the *Boode*, the ship bound for Mauritius, was delayed.

Not enough wind.

Trapped. With her whole life round about her ...

Smoke was rising straight up into the sky from the chimneys in the town.

The smoke from the lime kiln on the beach on the western side of the quay first rose straight up, but then tumbled over and lay across the sea, a trail of white haze. Day and night they burnt Robben Island in that kiln. Sack after sack.

Hundreds of sacks of shell grit mixed with convict sweat.

Her mother was always afraid they would dig and scrape up so much that one day there'd be a hole in the island and the sea would push up from below and swallow them all.

Sand mussels, black mussels, periwinkles, perlemoen, oysters – every kind of shell was smashed on the rocks, spat out and piled up on the island. Deepest at the top end. The storm side of the North-Wester where the wind blew the breath out of your nostrils.

Convicts scraping, a Corporal beating them with a cane to make them work harder. They would shovel the shells into sacks and carry them across the island to Sand Bay, wade into the water up to their necks and tip the sacks into the island boat. The sacks had to be taken back to be filled again. If too few shells reached the mainland, the Governor would get angry and the Corporal would have to beat them even harder.

Most of the convict were sailors who had misbehaved on board. Or sailors who had been involved in knifings in one of the taverns in town. Others were servants who had been caught stealing or something.

They seldom sent Hottentots to carry shells. Except once when they sent five youngsters there who had been up to no good. But they escaped. Her father was in charge at Robben Island at the time, the Post Holder. He fired the cannon to get the message across the bay and the Governor hurriedly sent some soldiers – but the five had got away in a stolen skiff.

Got away for good.

Eventually the shells ended up in the kiln to be burnt to powder. Once the fire was cold, they shovelled out the burnt shell grit and threw it on the sieves. *Shouf, shouf, shouf.* Ever finer, till it was lime. Then the wind would take and blow it everywhere. Coal-black slaves became grey-white ghosts. Arms, legs, bodies, heads. Grey bushes, grey barrows. Grey workers. Grey soldiers. And the whole place stank of rottenness.

The lime was carried in sacks to building sites. When there were lots of sacks, they brought wagons and oxen. Grey wagons. Grey oxen. One sack of lime, one sack of sand. Mix – make a hollow – carefully add water. Just like baking a cake. Then gradually, like magic, and without a single fire-coal, the whole basin of sludge would begin to boil. *Bubble-bubble-bubble.* Then it was building lime that many, many feet had to carry to feed the trowels. Building lime to make stones and bricks stick together. The hellish high stone walls of the new Castle, for protection and cannons so the English couldn't come and grab the Cape for *their* ships. Or the French.

Building lime for the small houses in the short, straight streets beside the sea under the mountain's bowl. Heeren Street, Olifant Street – streets of mud whenever it rained. Sea Street. They dragged Zara's corpse down Sea Street as a punishment for hanging herself. The Company law said explicitly that you weren't allowed to kill yourself. If you did, you'd be dragged through the streets and strung up on the three-man gallows beyond the Duintjies till you dried out. That is, if the wild animals hadn't chewed you up by then or the birds of the air hadn't pecked out your eyes. And so that the sailors off the ships could see the guilty hanging there and know what would happen to them if they didn't listen.

Reiger Street. Berg Street. Cattle dung. Flowers with the sweetest scents.

Building lime for the stables, the slave lodge, the hospital and the corn mill. The canal, the reservoir where the ships' barrels were filled and then rolled *clack-clack-clack* across the wooden quay and lowered into the boats with ropes. Lots of barrels, lots of water. When there was no wind, they had to row. The boatman would shout to get the bodies straining back and forth, the arms in and out again. Evenly. Oars like spoons on long, thin stems.

They never rowed the shell boats. Always waited for the wind. There was wind most days. The food boat with Robben Island's monthly food was not rowed across either. Had to wait for the wind. Food finished. People hungry. Water from the island wells brackish and bitter. Her mother moaning like a puppy without a nipple to suckle on ...

Building lime was one bucket of shell lime to one bucket of sand. She, Jacobus and Salomon were one bucket of yellow-brown sand and one bucket of white sand. Actually snow-white sand. Their father came from a snow country far across the sea. Denmark.

Her own hair was not as woolly as her mother's, but not as smooth as Fair Ansiela's either. She was whiter, though. Jacobus was more yellow-brown like their mother.

She and Jacobus had both been at their parents' wedding, but they were still very small.

Other female slaves that had come on the ships were very black. Not Ansiela's kind of people. And very bad-tempered. Many ran away with the male slaves to try to get back to their own country. If they were caught, they were beaten hard. And branded. Some of the men had their ears cut off. Without ears you are very ugly – just like stolen sheep with the Company's brand, cut off to stop the Corporal thinking they were stolen.

Mynheer Van der Byl said slaves cause more trouble than wealth. Except Janvos. He was a good slave. If he were alive, he would have laid down his life to prevent her and Salomon being sent away.

They hadn't cut Tant Maijke van den Berg's ears off, but she had been branded. Behind her left shoulder. They say she screamed terribly when the hot iron burnt into her flesh. Good! She'd refused to listen.

They didn't brand children. It hurt too much. Many slaves were branded on the shoulders *and* on the cheeks, to tell people they had run away or done wicked things more than once.

The seal's head broke the surface of the water once more, dived under again, as though he was playing. If anyone caught him, he'd be roasted and rendered down for train oil.

There weren't any seals left on Robben Island. All bludgeoned to death for slave meat and their fat. Pelts dried for bedcovers and all kinds of things. The convicts on the island always quarrelled over the dead seals that sometimes washed up on the beaches. If the flesh was not too rank, they would cook and eat it and stretch the skin out over a rock to dry.

Ships.

Often, while they were living on Robben Island, they would go searching for seafood on the landward side. When there was a fleet in the Bay, her mother would bend down and pick up stones and hurl them into the sea at the ships.

'Die! Die, you dogs!'

'Mamma, don't!'

'Leave me alone!'

'Don't, Mamma!'

'Die, die!'

Everything was the fault of the ships. If there hadn't been ships, the world would still have been good, like it used to be, her mother said. The Goringhaiqua cattle and sheep would still have grazed quietly in the basin under the mountains and still drunk the sweet water in the river. Trekked to the rainy side of the mountains in times of drought where the grazing lasted longest, set up their kraal in a wide circle of huts with enough room in the middle for their livestock at night. In the distance, on the side where the sun came up and the Leopard's Mountain stood, all craggy and covered with patches in summer, they would watch the Chorachoqua's fires break out and wonder how many more calves they had gained. How many more lambs.

Far to the North, farther than the eye could see, burnt the fires of the mighty Cochoquas. Too big for just one kraal. Two kraals. Sometimes even three. Thousands of cattle, thousands of fat-tailed sheep. Plenty of milk. Plenty of butter. Beyond the Cochoquas, the Namaquas with their cattle and sheep and *goats*. Things almost like sheep.

And, always, the headmen of the Cape Hottentots had warned her mother: Eva, don't tell the Hollanders anything beyond what they can see with their eyes. Particularly, don't ever tell them anything about the Namaquas. I won't. Or about the peoples who graze their livestock behind the grey-blue mountains on this side. I won't.

Beyond the grey-blue mountains grazed the herds of the Chainouqua. Beyond them, the Hessequa. There were many more tribes even farther away, all the way to that far distant river where black people's kraals began and where the best tobacco, the dagga, could be bartered for fat, shiny cattle.

But the Cape was far from there, no more than the crumbs of the dagga survived all the bartering in between.

Then the Hollanders arrived with their ships and brought different tobacco …

Her mother's people were the Goringhaicona. Pot shards thrown over the walls of all the neighbouring kraals – the discarded ones. Without any cattle or sheep. Only rock pools and everything that washed up out of the sea. Dead seals, great whales.

When her mother was small, her name was Krotoa. The Hollanders made her into Eva and dressed her in their clothes. Her mother's favourite uncle, Autshumao, was the Goringhaicona chieftain. The white people made him into Harry. Even before the Hollanders the English took him on board one of their ships and took him far off to the East with them so they could teach him to speak their language, eat their food and drink their wine. They gave him new white people's clothes and taught him how to barter cattle and sheep from the rich Hottentots for tobacco and copper and cloth and wine. Once they had finished teaching him, they put him ashore again.

That was how her mother's folk had become important people. The shipfolk. The Strandlopers.

At that time they weren't Hottentots yet. They were still *Khoi:* people. *Khoikhoi:* men-of-men. The Dutch said they were Hottentots, and drove away *Gounja* and *Gounja Tikwa*, and built their own Almighty Lord God a church-house.

The Namaqua said they themselves weren't *Khoikhoi*, they were *Nama* folk.

Her mother was never allowed to mention the Namaqua …

All the ships together were the Fleet. The Lords' fleet. Big ships. That came and floated in the Bay under the Mountain. The Hollanders said its name was Table Mountain. Small boats were plying all over the water from ship to ship just like calves going from cow to cow, bringing everything from the shore to the ships that lay rocking on the water with bare masts like trees without leaves. All made of wood. Except the ropes. Floated on the water, didn't have feet like ducks. When they wanted to move forwards, the sailors shook out the sails on the masts. Then they had wings to skim across the water. Like big wooden geese.

Sometimes the ships were so heavy they could hardly get away. Or the wind wouldn't blow them in the right direction. Then they keeled over and were smashed to pieces on the rocks, or capsized and ran aground on the sand. Then they were dead.

Her mother knew the ships. She would just turn her head sideways for a moment, screw up her tiny eyes even tighter to be able to see properly. Then she would say: 'Lying deep. Bellies full.' When the ships lay deep in the water, they were on their way home. Back from the East with the most beautiful rugs for the Lords to hang on the walls of their mansions in Amsterdam. Amsterdam was a big town far across the sea, but not in the East. Knotted rugs made of the finest thread. Hundreds of bales of other kinds of cloth, too. For dresses and shirts and breeches and cloths for their tables and bedsheets. Cloths woven of wormshit that they called silk.

The most valuable of all were the tons of pepper and cloves and nutmeg and mace and cinnamon. Things for special food. White-skinned people's food. Tons of rice. Thousands of rubies and thousands of pearls out of the sea, hundreds of porcelain things, so pretty: little cups and saucers and bowls.

Diamonds like tiny shining stones.

Once there was a Dutchman who had worked and lived for many years in the East. For their Lordships in Amsterdam. The Lords Seventeen. The Dutchman had collected many treasures in the East. When he got old, he sold all his goods and used the money to buy eight or nine little bags of diamonds that he tied round his body with a cord running under his arms. He never took them off. Then he boarded a ship because he wanted to sell them in Amsterdam so he'd be rich for the rest of his life. But English pirates captured the ship on the homeward voyage. They spared his life, because he pleaded so kindly, but they took his diamonds. About eight bags of them. That left him with nothing. So the Lords sent him to the Cape: Commandeur Borghorst. Old and weak and heartbroken. But at least he had a roof over his head again.

Whenever her mother spoke about him, she would get angry. 'He was the one, that blowfly, that gave our room on the island to Hendrik Lacus's Lydia. That had us shoved away in the potter's cottage. I went to the Fort and told him I wished the seabirds would nest in his long locks and peck out his eyes. The two soldiers grabbed hold of me and dragged me outside. Pigs.'

The ships' guts were the sailors that crawled about like maggots.

The ships kept everyone breathing; they were the fire that kept the pot boiling, Mynheer Van der Byl used to say and then pray the words in the book that asked God please to bring the fleet home safely. On Sundays the Sick Comforter prayed the same words in church. Under the lion skin nailed to the ceiling of the church in the Fort. They said it was the very same lion that killed four cattle and a herdsman one time behind the Groote Schuur where they used to pile up the sheaves of wheat. They had shot and skinned the lion. Kept the head whole. Mouth open with the most terrible teeth. Glass eyes. Paws with sharp black claws. A whole flat lion nailed up against the church roof. A flat baboon, too. And a flat rhinoceros, grey-black against the rear wall. Leopard. Wild dog. Elephant tusk. To warn everyone what awaited them if ever they dared venture deeper into this savage country. Particularly any who might take it into their heads to escape. Or the English and the French who were always ready to make war against the Dutch.

The only skin they hadn't yet nailed up, her mother used to say, was a Hottentot's, and she'd spit angrily.

Everyone and everything was always waiting for the ships. Every day the watchers on the back of Lion's Hill on the western side of Table Mountain sat scanning the sea from morning till night. Joy and prospective happiness broke out as soon as a sail was spotted far out to sea. Cannon shots rang out for every approaching ship: one, two, three, four, five, six, seven, eight, nine, ten. Sometimes fewer. Sometimes more.

Then everyone ran around rejoicing – Dutchman, Hottentot, slave and servant alike. Every breathing being on the ships had come to eat and drink, to buy and sell. It was life, it was merriment, news, family, friends. It was harvest time in every tavern, because thousands of sailors were on their way.

The sailors that had survived, that is. The dead had already been thrown overboard.

The sea was all commotion. Big black balls of smoke rose from the cannons on the great wooden geese. The Castle returned the greeting. Twenty-one shots for the happiness of welcoming the returning fleet. At last the wings were rolled up and the anchors lowered – the big wooden bodies brought to rest in the roadstead.

Land boats hurriedly pushed off from the quay. First of all the Fiscal, the bookkeeper, the Surgeon and the man with the hammer and nails who were taken from ship to ship to nail the Company's rules to the masts: *No Hottentot may be beaten or kicked or shoved. Nothing may be bought from Hottentots except ostrich egg shells and fish. No Popish prayers or services.* Wrong God. *No daggers to be drawn.* A man with a loud voice shouted out the rules for all those who couldn't read.

The Surgeon had to examine the sick and decide together with the ship's surgeon which of the sick were to be taken ashore and which should remain on board. Hundreds of sick, usually. They were lowered off the ships with ropes and brought to the quay in the boats. Back and forth. They were carried to the hospital in hammocks or sheets of canvas, like half-dead seals. Exhausted. Mouths open, blue gums swollen over their teeth. Most of the teeth had fallen out already. Scurvy – bloodshit. They couldn't move, just groaned, everything aching. The Master cut out the decayed flesh in their mouths.

'How do they get well again, Mamma?'

'Some die right there on the quayside. Others in the hospital. The rest are fed fresh food that has been cooked soft until they can chew again.'

The best times were when notables on the ships were brought to shore. The boats sent to fetch *them* had a special big red, white and blue flag hoisted on their sterns to say: Get out of our way, we are carrying important people!

The red on the flag was supposed to be more orange, but the dye was never quite right. And the Commandeur was always dissatisfied.

The smartest ladies in the prettiest dresses with fine white lace collars and caps covered in pearls, the points covering their ears and shading their foreheads, caps with the most beautiful jewels on strings dangling down over their pure white necks. Feet in shoes with bows and heels. Fine kerchiefs held in front of their noses when the Hottentots came too close. Milk-white nannies to help carry the children.

Every single Hottentot crowded on to the quay to bow and dance and hold out their hands for a bit of tobacco or a mouthful of arrack or brandy.

The sailors used to wait in a line off to one side. They would pay the female Hottentots to lift up their skin aprons, spread their legs and show their privates.

'Don't you ever lift and show a sailor, Pieternella!'

'I won't, Mamma.'

'Spit on the pigs. They won't mount you, so you can charge more. They say we stink. Just want to gawk and snigger and then head on to the taverns and the slave girls.'

'Yes, Mamma.'

Ships ate up more cattle and sheep than you could count. The more ships, the more meat. Bartered the Hottentots' livelihood out of them for tobacco and beads and copper and little mirrors and brandy or arrack and pieces of iron.

Later, they wouldn't part with the iron any more; the stupid Hottentots were too clever. They beat the iron flat between two stones and made themselves assegai heads …

Different kind of folk. Dutchmen.

The Hottentots, who used to be *Khoikhoi*, only realised their misfortune when they were driven off the best grazing and watering. The Goringhaicona Doman said he'd watched long and carefully: These Hollanders have come to take our land, our water and our livestock and to share out our land to free farmers as though it was theirs. Free farmers, they said, were supposed to plant wheat for bread for the ships, but when next you looked they were also running cattle and sheep. Gave more pipes and tobacco and beads in exchange than the Company did. More arrack and brandy, too.

How are we going to get rid of the Hollanders again? All we've got are assegais. They've got guns that shoot fire …

One day the Commandeur's wife Maria asked: 'Who is that pretty Hottentot child?'

'Krotoa,' said the pretty child's uncle.

'How old is she?'

'Ten calves.'

'Show with your fingers.'

She was dumb. She couldn't speak the English language that the child's uncle spoke. She said she wanted the pretty child to come and live with her and the Commandeur in their house, so that she could teach her about the Almighty Lord God.

At first the Hollanders' houses were made of cloth and called tents. But the wind blew the tents down. Then they built wooden houses inside the Fort with tall walls that were meant to stave off the enemy. Later, they built brick houses – not houses that you could take down and load on to pack-oxen and put up again elsewhere. Houses rooted in the ground. Stupid houses. The dead and the living together in one kraal; some under the ground, the others on top.

A Hottentot takes down his kraal and treks away from his dead. The Dutch say their dead are of the rising-again kind.

They gave the pretty child another name, and a bed with four legs to sleep on in a corner of the handsome room in which the Commandeur and his wife slept.

And a cloth dress.

And the nicest food.

Some of the Hottentots came from far away to see what white people and their things looked like. Most of them quickly took to their heels in fright. Except sometimes when the Commandeur made them sit down in the space in the middle of the Fort and gave them bowls of rice, and tobacco and bread and arrack or brandy. Then he would send a soldier to fetch a musical instrument: the prettiest flat box with things that his fingers ran over, the prettiest sounds.

Not dancing sounds. Listening sounds.

Then he taught the Hottentots to smoke pipes. 'Eva, tell them not to blow into the things. *Inhale.* Deeply.'

The pretty child quickly learnt the Dutch words. Rice. Bread. Please. Thank you. Brandy. Arrack.

She got her own pipe, too.

'Tell them to bring us many cattle and sheep and we will give them plenty of tobacco for their pipes, so that they will be able to smoke a lot. And beads and copper and some firewater to warm their bodies.'

Not warm really, more like jolly and at ease.

She told them, and the good Commandeur gave her, too, a sip of firewater.

Juffrouw Maria was her mother's white mother. She used to fold her hands in her lap and tell the pretty child about Jesus, Son of God. Saviour of mankind.

'Of Hottentots, too?'

'Oh, yes!'

Her mother went to tell Doman: You can stop planning how to get rid of the Hollanders. A different Saviour is coming to help us. *He* will drive them away.

'Eva, Eva!' chided Juffrouw Maria, distress in her pretty face. 'You don't understand. The Saviour is the Light who is coming to drive the darkness out of your hearts!'

She went and told Doman. He said: Eva, the words those people are feeding you are going to end up strangling your own throat. All our throats. Come away from there. Come back to your own people.

No. The Hollanders' food was much too nice.

Please, the wind must never blow again.

Not too long after her mother died, she was walking back from the veld one day, taking a short cut behind the old Fort. Most of the walls had been knocked down already. Only the Governor's house was still standing. And the old kraals where the slaughter stock stood waiting to be butchered. There were ships all over the Bay. In a small pen were two porcupines, an ostrich and two pelicans.

35

'That pelican looks like it's dying!' she called over the fence to the old Hottentot who was feeding bread to the birds. Khonomao. She knew him. He was a Goringhaicona from the Duintjies, one of those who did odd jobs round the Fort in the daytime for a tot of brandy and a piece of tobacco morning and evening and a handful of rice or bread at midday. They say you have to give a Hottentot half his pay in the morning, then he'll work for the rest of the day for the second half. Tomorrow you'll have to agree with him all over again. A Hottentot says he works for nobody – he's a free man.

'Man from the ships asking about you,' said Khonomao.

'What kind of man?' She hadn't done anything and she didn't know anyone on the ships.

'Dunno. Been gone to Ansiela also. Man not from Cape.'

One pelican had squatted down, the yellow pouch under its beak pale and withered. The other bird also looked ill. 'You must feed them fish, Khonomao! *t'Gua*. They don't eat bread.'

'Soldier say *t'gau* belong Company. Must eat *breh*. Going on ships for Prince in other land. Porcupines and ostrich also.'

There were always curiosities for the ships to take along from the Cape for the kings and princes of other countries. They'd even taken a few Hottentots. Mynheer Van der Byl said it helped civilise the little cinnamon people with their peppercorn hair.

When she got home, there was a strange man in the sitting room. His head almost touched the roof beams. Juffrouw Sophia was blushing like someone quite overcome with nerves.

Important man. Long, red-brown hair parted in the middle and hanging down to his shoulders. Hair not quite straight. Big hooked nose. Red-brown moustache, small pointy beard sticking to his bottom lip. Bulging brown eyes that looked as though they saw everything extra sharply – her, too, when she came in.

'Here she is,' Juffrouw Sophia said, folding and unfolding her hands in front of her apron.

'Eva's daughter?' As if to make sure his eyes were seeing properly.

'Yes.' The ringlets dangling down from the cap in front of Juffrouw Sophia's ears were not as tightly curled as usual, they looked rather limp.

The man looked like a governor. Shiny black coat. Pure white shirt with a lace bib, pure white cuffs puffing out of the slashes in the coat sleeves, showy lace points almost covering his hands. Breeches tied with bows under the knee, same cloth as the coat. Black stockings, black shoes with high heels and silver buckles.

How does anyone get to look so smart?

'Pieternella, this is Mynheer Van Riebeeck. He knew your mother. Mynheer Basson's Ansiela told him about you.'

Why was Juffrouw Sophia so nervous?

The man greeted her. 'Good day.'

'Mynheer.' He had known her mother? Then he must be Jan van Riebeeck …

Juffrouw Sophia stepped forward hesitantly. 'If the gentleman would do my house the honour of sitting down at our humble table …'

It was not a humble table. Mynheer Van der Byl and Janvos had made it of yellowwood and other wood, the gleaming table top was polished with berry-wax and the legs were carved.

'Pieternella …' The man repeated her name and sat down at the head of the table. 'Your late father's name?'

'Yes, Mynheer.' It had to be Jan van Riebeeck. 'Are you the commandeur in whose house my mother lived?'

He smiled. 'No. Those were my parents. I am Abraham, the second son. I was born here at the Cape. When I was as tall as you are I was sent to school in the fatherland and then on to higher studies. But I remember your mother very clearly, she always had such a happy nature. A bright little girl who learnt our language very quickly. She spoke it like a born Hollander. She was often my father's interpreter when he needed to negotiate with the Hottentots.'

'Yes, Mynheer.' My mother had to speak the words that would get the livestock out of the kraals. And she would be paid with a tot of liquor and some tobacco for her pipe.

'I was delighted to hear from Ansiela that your mother had a Christian burial.'

'Yes, Mynheer. They buried her in the church in the new Castle, in a coffin that Bart Borms made, and nobody cried.' She looked him straight in the eye as she said it.

Nervously Juffrouw Sophia chided her. 'Pieternella!'

'Your foster mother assures me that you are an obedient young girl.'

'Yes, Mynheer.' If he had asked Barbara Geens, I'd have had it …

'But above all I am delighted to hear that you are going to school and that you fear the Lord. Yesterday afternoon I came across a small kraal on Lion's Head, huts built of sticks and cleverly woven reed mats …'

'My mother taught me to weave, Mynheer. And to make clay pots, too – when they made us live up there in the potter's cottage.'

'Pieternella, stand nice and still when you talk to Mynheer Van Riebeeck.' Juffrouw Sophia was wringing her hands more and more tightly.

The man said: 'When I heard that many of them could understand Dutch, I called the people of the kraal together. I examined them and noted with deep heartache that they know nothing of God and the Bible. How terrifying! Nor about the devil either. They asked me for tobacco; I gave them what I had on me. I tried to tell them about God, but they would not listen.'

'Yes, Mynheer.' They would've for more tobacco. For brandy they would have sat a long time.

'That is why it was so moving for me to find Fair Ansiela in the Faith this morning and to learn that, after the departure of my mother and father, Eva had been baptised and confirmed. That you have also been christened.'

'My mother said we had to have Christian blood, because Christian blood may not be spilt. Only heathen blood. The pelicans behind the old Fort are going to die if they don't get fish.'

That evening Juffrouw Sophia instructed her long and earnestly in humility and submissiveness. When to lower your eyes in the presence of an important person.

Both the pelicans died.

A few days later one of the crewmen of the land boat told Pieter van der Byl that he had caught two chameleons on Robben Island for the skipper of the *Quartel*. For a bottle of arrack. The skipper had sold the chameleons to the same Mynheer Van Riebeeck. For a lot of money. The sailor had been on board the skiff that rowed the important man out to the *Quartel* that evening to fetch them. And back, too. Mynheer was very pleased. He even put the chameleons on some twigs in a little basket. He showed them the wonderful little monsters by lantern light, saying that he wanted to present them as a gift to an important Easterling. The sailor asked him: How are you going to catch flies for them on board ship, Mynheer? The man said the skipper had given him the assurance that the little creatures lived on air.

The wind was never going to come up again ...

They never did banish her mother to Mauritius. Always back to Robben Island. Sometimes they would let her come back to the mainland for brief spells.

38

Like the time she lay down on the floor in front of the soldier on inspection, so as to be able to clutch hold of his feet. She promised she would never get drunk again, begged that the Governor should give her just one more chance, for the love of God.

She, Pieternella, was living with the Van der Byls by then. Mynheer Van der Byl said her mother could sleep in the small room behind the house where the wood was kept - as long as she didn't drink or light a fire or wear her skin clothes. The Company would send her food from the Castle. A soldier came to announce that she was never again to set foot near Maijke van den Berg. Maijke was living in the short street behind the Castle at the time. No, she wouldn't, she was angry with Maijke, because Maijke owed her things.

That was a lovely time. On the first evening Juffrouw Sophia had fetched her mother into the sitting room to hear the Bible reading. Juffrouw Sophia burst out crying because her mother knew just the right words to pray. *Our Father who sitteth high in heaven, may your word be sanctified on earth ...*

'Oh, Eva, your heart belongs to the Lord,' Juffrouw Sophia called out softly.

The ships also belonged to the Lords.

After prayers Mynheer Van der Byl announced that the ship that arrived that afternoon had brought bad tidings: There was war at sea again between the Dutch and the French and the English. The Dutch were very concerned because if the enemy captured the Cape the Lords would have nowhere to rest their ships and let their sick recover.

Next day, when she and her mother went out picking waxberries, they came across a group of flag bearers and cannon haulers high up on the footpath-horsepath. There must have been thirty of them. Most of them strangers, sailors off the ship lying in the Bay. Grunting and groaning in the March heat. Her mother shouted: 'Where are you off to?'

'Top of Lion's Head,' said one of those carrying ropes and picks. He was from the Cape.

'What for?'

'To plant a flagpole. Cannons, too.'

'On *top* of the Head?'

'Right at the top.' The man was dripping with sweat.

Suddenly her mother grew anxious. 'The baboons will stone you, it's their lookout point. It's one of *Tikwa*'s seats on earth!' Her mother was so distressed she kept getting in their way.

'Leave these people alone, Mamma!' She wouldn't listen. She grabbed a soldier by the shirt. He shoved her and she fell.

The man from the Cape helped her up, saying: 'Miss Eva, don't keep looking for trouble! You don't understand these things. This is war! Governor Goske says we have to keep a sharp lookout on Lion's Head for enemy ships. From up there we'll be able to spot their sails on the sea two hours earlier and light our fuses in good time!'

So they planted the huge pole and hung an orange, blue and white flag on it, as big as a bedsheet. The cannons were fixed. The work went on for days. They needed a rope ladder to clamber up the last sheer cliffs.

Blinding lightning struck the pole and split it in two from top to bottom, like a giant axe.

Her mother was trembling like a bulrush in the wind. She picked up her bundle and headed for Tant Maijke's. A few days later Pieter said he'd been down at the quayside; they had carried her mother right on to the shell boat and sent her back to Robben Island.

Blind drunk.

They went up and planted a new flagpole on Lion's Head. The lightning came right back and struck that one, too.

So they had to go up and plant a third one.

When Lion's Head was shrouded in mist, the lookout on Robben Island had to watch from Fire Hill and fire cannon shots to tell the score. And light a signal fire to stop ships running aground on the island. A fire at night. On Fire Hill. Not really a hill, more of a high sand dune. Loose sand. Your legs were utterly lame before you reached the top, because she and Jacobus had had to climb on their own feet. Salomon was tied on to their mother's back. From up there you could see in all directions. Especially when they still used to go up and watch for the ship that had taken their father away.

4

Tant Theuntjie got up, stretched, and came over to *her* side of the quay.

'Why are you sitting there staring at nothing, Pieternella? Are you unwell?'

'I'm just thinking, Tante.'

'About what?'

'About living.' About my mother, about everything …

'What does a silly goose like you know about living? Come and sit over there with the rest of us.'

'I want to sit here, Tante. I don't want to leave.'

'It's time they took us over to the ship. I'm sick and tired of waiting.'

'I'd rather go and stay on Robben Island …' They can banish me there.

'Don't sit there talking rubbish.'

The day after the Church Council gave them to Barbara Geens, Jacobus went to enquire at the Fort where their mother was. He came back to say they had thrown her into the Black Hole. That was a small dungeon under the square stone building against the rear walls of the Fort. Under the hall, under the church. Where they put you to save your soul while you waited to be killed.

She lay quaking all night.

Next morning Tant Barbara gave her the dirty laundry and the soap and said: 'Go down to the river and wash these things, and don't lift your eyes off them for one moment. Hottentots are quick thieves.'

She took the bundle, put it down behind the house and hared off.

All along the shoreline to the outer entrance to the Fort. The Fort was a giant sandcastle on the beach. Four great tall bastions at the corners, two cannons on each bastion. The bastions had names: Olifant, Drommedaris, Walvis, Reiger. The schoolmaster said they were named in honour of the four ships that brought the first Dutch settlers here. Tall thick walls joining the bastions to stop any outside eye seeing into the wide square inside.

A huge red, white and blue flag on a mast at the first entrance from the seaward side. Saying: the Dutch are masters here. More jet-black cannons watching the sea from the top of the two stone towers on either side.

When she got there, soldiers and drovers and servants and slaves were all struggling to get a wagon heavily laden with firewood through the gate. The oxen were worn out. The loose sand clogged their hooves and the wheels of the wagon; soldiers were pushing and shoving on both sides. Another wagon was on its way behind this one. Whips were cracking. People were shouting orders. She slipped through beside the first wagon into the first square.

On the wooden bridge across the canal the first soldier challenged her. She knew his face.

'Pieternella?' he asked, amazed. 'Where are you going?' Behind him was the Gateway. Stone arch. Beyond the arch lay the great inner courtyard. The square was crowded with people and the Fort bell was ringing and ringing ...

'To my mother, please, Mynheer.' She started crying and stood aside because the first oxen had reached the wooden bridge; their hooves tapped like so many heels rattling on the wood and the wagon wheels sounded like barrels rolling across the quay. 'I beg you, Mynheer, I must see my mother. They've thrown her into the Black Hole, they're going to kill her.' She opened her mouth wide and cried as loudly as she could.

'Shut your trap! Nobody's going to kill your mother, we just wish we could. Pass. And tell the Sergeant you've come to ask about her.'

She waited till the wagon was properly inside. The bell had stopped its ringing. Across the inner courtyard, in front of the two sets of stairs rising to the balcony in front of the great double-storeyed stone house where the hall and the church were, a group of people had gathered. The Black Hole was under the stone house. Her mother was in there somewhere ...

A man in black clothes was standing on the balcony. He started reading to the people from a big book about the man who had stabbed another man to death in Jannetjie Ferdinandus's taphouse two nights previously. The man would be hanged that afternoon at two o'clock. All were welcome to attend the execution.

Jacobus had once gone to watch them hanging a sailor. The gallows were not far outside the Fort but you weren't allowed to stand closer than the low stone wall round the gibbet.

She couldn't understand how it could have happened in Jannetjie Ferdinandus's tavern. Every sailor wanting to enter her tavern first had to lift up his jerkin to prove that he wasn't hiding a *kortjan*. This was the dagger that sailors wore in a sheath strapped to their chests under their wide jerkins. Very dangerous with strong drink.

The man on the balcony hadn't finished yet.

'No - I repeat - *no* free-burgher is permitted to barter livestock with the Hottentots. Only the Company may do that. If anyone should be caught engaged in barter, he will be flogged in public and all his goods will be confiscated.' This meant that he would be whipped and his things would be taken for the Company.

Long afterwards she was there on the day they flogged Tant Maijke. Because the old woman had stolen sheep from the Hottentots yet again. And smuggled rice, too. First they tied a sheepskin to the top of a pole and then stretched Tant Maijke's hands high above her head and fastened them to an iron ring just beneath the sheepskin. Then the brute with the cane beat Tant Maijke till streaks of blood showed though her dress. To one side stood a man counting out loud the number of blows. They weren't allowed to give more than the court people had said. Twelve. When they untied her hands, she looked like she was dead.

When a man was flogged, they first stripped off his shirt. Because he didn't have tits. Dutchwomen's tits were not allowed to be bared in public, only Hottentot women's. But they didn't flog Hottentots; the chieftains meted out their own punishments.

She waited till the man who had to read out the laws and the punishment turned round and went indoors. A tall soldier remained standing at the stairs. She circled round to just behind him and began to cry again. Sobbing pathetically. 'Mynheer?'

He said he would ask the Fiscal if she might see her mother. Wait here. She waited and waited. He came back, said she was specially lucky, request granted. But only for a short while. Eva was being very difficult, later in the day they would take her to Robben Island. She was banished.

Stone stairs winding down like the inside of a snail shell – darker and darker, deeper underground. A soldier with a tall axe-head pike let her pass. It smelt of pee. It was cold. Even deeper. An oil lamp glowing over a big iron door full of iron knobs. A big iron key. The door swung open. At first her eyes could see nothing. Then in the faint glow she saw that she was in a tiny stone cell ... there was a wooden bench and a half-barrel. It stank. There was a bundle of blankets on the bench, somebody was in the bundle ...

'She's calmed down a bit,' said the guard.

The iron door banged shut. As if it had been bricked up.

'Mamma?' she cried, and the word echoed off the walls, filling the stone hole.

'Pieternella?' Like the pleading bleat of a goat.

'Mamma.'

Her hands groped till she reached the bleating. Arms clamped themselves round her and began to rock her back and forth. Little stone-words, Dutch words, bird-words, echoing off the walls, round and round. 'Help me out! t'Ka! Help me out! t'Ka! Tiri kalu naha!' A narrow air-hole with criss-crossed gratings took shape in the dark up against the stone roof of the Hole.

'They're going to take you to Robben Island, Mamma.'

''t Danne koha? Bo?' the words shot out of the skinny body like sparks.

'No. Dad hasn't come back.' She deflected the fire.

'*Oro.*'

She was cold. 'Leave me, Mamma, draw the blanket over your head.'

'*Male gu 't nov* and *tabakka!*'

'I'll get you some, Mamma.'

'Tobacco and my pipe, go and fetch them now! *Tabakka, tabakka!*'

Don't shout so, Mamma.

That afternoon when they came to fetch her mother to take her to Robben Island, not one of them could loosen her grip on the poor child she was clutching. The Sergeant said: Take them both. Bring the child back, we've battled enough with the bitch.

'Pieternella!'

'Yes, Tant Theuntjie?'

'Wake up! Get on your feet! There come the boats!'

Two boats. Riding high against the harbour wall because the tide was in. A third boat was approaching from the direction of the ship, boom sail and foresail shaken out. There was a slight breeze on the water after all, though you could hardly feel it.

The last boat curved inwards and tied up on the other side of the quay. This was the one that would take the last of the chests to the ship: Tant Maijke's and Cornelia's two. The old woman still had enough strength left to curse through her tears and threaten to kill them if anyone interfered with her chests or if there was so much as a chip on any of her porcelain. She wanted to go along with her chests to keep an eye on her things, but the boatman just laughed at her. Told her she'd better hop in and they'd hoist her up on board along with the chests.

So she went back to her bundles and went on crying there.

Some of the other sailors came to load the struggling sheep on to the last boat. Sheep with rough bluish tongues hanging out between their rotten sheep's teeth. The boat was called the *Schulp*. She'd often travelled across to Robben Island in it - the boat with the narrow plank deck for transporting animals.

'Women, children and bundles!' called the helmsman in the front boat. Like being called to the slaughter …

Please, I beg …

The same boat, the *Bruidegom*, the same helmsman and pilot that used to take her along whenever there were goods to be taken across or shells to be fetched.

'Pieternellatjie,' the helmsman exclaimed in surprise when he saw her, 'I heard from Salomon yesterday that you're going to Mauritius. I wouldn't believe him!'

'Morning, Mynheer Wyngaardt.'

'Why doesn't Bart Borms just *buy* himself slaves? The old crook has made made quite enough money!'

She didn't like what she was hearing. 'We aren't anybody's slaves, Mynheer.'

He laughed. 'Just what your late mamma used to say!'

There was a sudden burst of activity on the quay. From a distance came the sound of a drum beating – not to summon the sailors from the town; the drums had beaten for them two days earlier, they were all on board already. So were the three free-burghers from Mauritius: Focke Janse, Daniel Zaaijman and Bart Borms. They, too, had to work their passage just like Salomon.

A man with a book in his hand came up. Said they had to hurry, the drum was sounding to announce that His Excellency the Governor was ready to accompany the notables down to the quay for a final farewell toast.

A very important man was coming aboard. Isaac Lamotius, new chief on Mauritius, a learned man sent specially from Holland to solve that island's problems once and for all, Mynheer Van der Byl said. A man with a wife and one small daughter.

Tant Maijke's Cornelia was taken into service to look after the child in return for her own fare. Tant Maijke could travel for nothing, she'd been banished.

The Lamotius man and his pretty wife had been in church with the Governor the previous day. A shortish man. She hadn't actually been able to see them; everyone had had to stand up when the Governor and the officials entered the church, so the shortest couldn't see.

Three musicians arrived on the quay for the farewell. Two slaves, one with a fiddle, one with a great brass wind instrument, and a soldier with another fiddle.

The man with the book was ready.

'Maijke van den Berg!' he read.

Tant Maijke set up a loud wailing as two sailors came up to help her stout body down into the boat. The skiff was rocking on the water, even though it was moored to the quay.

Tant Maijke was aboard.

'Maria Visser, wife of Willem Willems van Deventer, and two daughters, Pietertjie and Daatjie!' the man read out.

Maria also started crying. A sailor came to help with her bundles and the children.

'Theuntjie van der Linde, wife of Bart Borms!'

Tant Theuntjie stepped into the boat without a word. She hadn't been banished. She lived on Mauritius of her own free will. She and Oom Bart. Without children. Now suddenly they'd got two children for free.

'Pieternella van Meerhoff!'

A snail draws its head into its shell if it has no other choice. Not her. She stepped out of her shell and left her body on the quay. Only her bare shell climbed into the boat. Already slaughtered.

She sat down at the far end.

The three musicians on the quay moved into position. They said Governor Goske, the governor before Governor Bax, had himself taught the slaves to play.

Tant Theuntjie thrust her head in the air in undisguised spite. 'Yes,' she said, 'they had a fancy farewell dinner and dancing in the Castle on Saturday night for our Captain and Mister Gentleman Lamotius and now they have to be glorified all over again here on the quay!'

They slipped the *Bruidegom*'s painter and the boat shoved off from the quay. Sails flapped lazily in the light breeze. The musicians on the quay struggled a little to find the right notes, but once they were playing properly their lovely music floated over the water behind the boat, before gently fading away.

Snailshell didn't weep with the others. All she wanted to do was open her mouth and let her powerless hollow shell of a body howl as loudly as ever it could.

It was a long way out to the ship. The ship grew bigger and bigger the closer they got. It wasn't really such a big ship, not like the East Indiamen of the fleet.

With a dull thump, the *Bruidegom* came to a halt against the dark hull of the ship where a rope ladder hung down. A fish beside a whale. Painters were cast upwards to be tied up, while two sailors clambered down into the boat.

First Tant Maijke. A sailor picked up her bundles and tossed them aloft. She stood fixed to the boat, too terrified to climb the rope ladder.

'Then we'll have to rope you and hoist you up, Juffrouw!' Her hands clamped round the ladder, one foot on the lowest rung. Sailors laughed aloud at her hanging there, her legs astraddle over the water. *Climb!* they yelled down at her. Her second foot found the next rung. A sailor gave her a shove under her bum with one hand and climbed up behind her.

'Don't tread on your skirt! Keep your feet free!'

On top there were many hands waiting.

Tant Theuntjie didn't hesitate – she was an old climber.

Maria also hesitated. Like nimble baboons, sailors came to carry her children up on deck.

'Your turn, Pieternella!' the pilot called out. She knew him. Grey beard like the fluff lining a finch's nest, dirty striped cap, dirty canvas clothes, dirty feet. She didn't budge. His hands made as if to take hold of her bundles, but she grabbed them away and stood up. It was the same pilot who'd often come to the island and who'd sneak her mother something to drink where she was waiting for him behind the dune overlooking Penguin Bay. 'Pity you're leaving,' he said. 'That's a nice, plump little body I see you're getting!'

'Leave her be!' the helmsman growled.

A sailor picked up her bundles and carried them up on board.

She climbed up after him.

The first thing she saw was the small sheep pen to one side of the deck. Slatted sides, the undersides made of ankle-high planks. Frightened sheep, their legs untied, on a bed of coarse straw.

She picked up her bundles, walked over to the sheep pen, stopped and went on looking.

Ropes. Masts. Lots of ropes. Three masts. A wooden cabin on the front part of the ship. A wooden cabin on the back side, too, with steps right beside the sheep pen going up to a higher, smaller deck.

She'd never been on a ship before.

An upturned skiff lay tied fast between the front mast and the middle one. Tant Maijke lay with her head on her bundle, leaning against the side of the skiff and pretending to feel faint. Anyone could see that. A sailor – no, it was Willem van Deventer the murderer, in sailor's clothes, carrying a bucket. He splashed some of the water over her face, quickly, as though not wanting to be seen. He looked just like a convict.

Everywhere sailors looked at her in amazement – turned round and looked again. Figures in loose white canvas jerkins and wide yellowish canvas trousers down to their knees. Most of them barefoot, some with soft leather shoes and sloping heels. All kinds of caps on their heads. Caps with short points. Caps with long points. Red ones, blue ones, black ones, striped ones. Short-stemmed pipes in the turn-ups. A few wearing headscarves with knots at the corners.

Where was Salomon?

Cables as thick as a man's waist. Other, thinner ropes were tied to the ship's sides like thick spiderwebs stretching high up to the masts. Through the webs the humps of the mountains across the Bay to the east lay pale blue and cold in the distance. Somewhere there would be the Chorachoquas' kraal. Somewhere their cattle and sheep would be grazing ...

The wooden goose lay floating on the water beneath her feet. She was standing on its back as if she were nowhere. Seabirds wheeled in the sky above.

She clung to the side of the ship, the *Bruidegom* had gone. It was already back at the quayside.

The Mountain was much closer here than from Robben Island. A giant grey rock full of ravines for dassies, rock lizards, bats, klipspringers. A place for leopards. A place for lions. She shut her eyes. Krantzes with the white stripes of bird droppings over the edge of an eagle's nest of sticks. Lion's Head beside it, with the humans' flag on its head. Windberg-Devil's Peak with its crooked head on the other side, its hollow back resting against its Mother-mountain.

Little pictures inside her eyes ...

All the pictures of your life are stuck in your eyes, you never get them out again.

When she opened her eyes, there was a man walking up and down with a length of rope in his hand, flicking it against his canvas trouser leg. It looked like a whip and he was coming straight towards *her*!

'You looking for a nice hot thing, girl?' he asked, his stinking breath almost in her face. Grinning.

Snailshell didn't answer him, just stood stock-still till he walked away. Flick, flick. Just turned her body sideways and kept clinging to the rail. Robben Island was a flat stripe on the water in the distance, the Fire Hill was scarcely even a rise.

'Pieternella ...'

It was Salomon. An odd pale skeleton with a red cap on, in canvas sailor's clothes big enough for three of him.

'Salomon, are you all right?'

'The cook said I could come and say hello to you quickly. I was scared you really might not come; Oom Bart says they don't want any trouble from us.'

'Do they beat you?'

'No. Oom Bart has been told to come and show you where your quarters are – somewhere in the bottom hold at the back, the place where you have to sleep and eat. You aren't allowed in the forecastle where the sailors sleep. That's the plank place up at the front of the ship. I've got to get back to work.'

'Wait! Don't go. Where do you sleep?'

'In the galley. Oom Bart will show you and tell you everything. They're very strict on the ship, please be obedient.'

Then he was gone. One red cap among all the others. It *was* Salomon, but it wasn't like him. She wanted to run after him but knew she shouldn't …

Once, in the Post House on the island, her mother had hauled the Post Holder's Bible out of the cupboard, thrown it down on the table and said: 'Pieternella, lay your hand on this Holy Testament and swear to God you will look after Salomon as long as you live!'

It wasn't long after that that she died. All because of an innocent tale that she, Pieternella, had brought back from the mainland. That the schoolmaster had repeated that Salomon was such a clever child – he and Johannes, the son of Tant Jannetjie Ferdinandus who ran the tavern without a licence and would land up in big trouble yet because of it. It was all true enough, but she was just chattering on with her mother to distract her attention from other things. Then she mentioned the rest of it, never thinking that it would upset her mother that badly! That the schoolmaster had announced that Tant Jannetjie's Johannes was a very privileged youngster because his mother had quietly been putting money aside to send him to the fatherland for a good education.

She'd been helping her mother gather penguin feathers that day. The Post Holder would give her half a cup of arrack that evening for a sack of penguin feathers that he would send to the mainland on the shell boat. The Governor would be very happy because they stuffed them into pillows for the heads of the notables.

Her mother jerked upright, her jet-black eyes shining with fury. 'What did you say? Going to the fatherland to go to school?'

'Yes.'

'But I, Eva, get cast aside? My children, the children of Eva, can be shoved around? Because there isn't any money? Because nobody will tell me what has happened to Pieter van Meerhoff's money? But Jannetjie Ferdinandus can put Johannes on a ship with the money she earns whoring with sailors?' She stamped her feet, her whole body shaking.

'Mamma, listen!'

'Come! Leave the feathers. Come on!'

'Where to?'

'Come!'

They were a long way from the Post House. She had to jog to keep up.

Her mother took the Bible out of the cupboard. 'Lay your hand on this Holy Testament and swear to God you will look after Salomon as long as you live. Swear! Remember, if you swear a lie today, this Book will start spinning before your very eyes!'

'Don't carry on like that, Mamma, I will swear!'

'Say you swear to God!'

'I swear to God.'

It was only very much later that she heard of the Bible on the *Roode Vos* that started spinning around in the name of God …

Suddenly everyone turned to look at the back of the ship. A tall man in soft brown clothes and a pleated white shirt was coming down the steps from the top deck. Right past her and the sheep pen.

'The Captain,' someone whispered. As though he was a person of importance.

She knew his face. It was Tant Barbara Geens's daughter Maria's husband. Broad-brimmed brown hat with a jaunty feather from the wing of an ostrich stuck into the band. He walked past Tant Maijke, who was still lying in a faint beside her bundle.

'Get rid of her.' Abrupt. But when sailors bent down to pick up the old woman, she suddenly staged a miraculous recovery and half sat up by herself to yell after the proud man: 'Captain Wobma, how in the name of the lordjesuschrist can you just walk past a defenceless widow in her sore distress?' There was nothing wrong with her tongue.

'Get rid of her,' he repeated. Without even looking round.

Wobma. That was his name. Cornelis Wobma, she remembered. Pride and joy of Tant Barbara's household. They said it was because *he* was her son-in-law that she had just got the contract to bake bread for the ships. That that would bring in enough money for her to live on without the need to take in Church children.

He stopped at the rail where the rope ladder hung down and looked out across the water.

The *Bruidegom* was returning from the quay, a big blue and white and orangey flag flapping like a floppy tail above the stern.

'Less racket there!' the man with the whip-rope shouted across the deck.

The boat bumped against the ship.

The man in the black clothes was first up the ladder. Halfway up his hat fell off, back into the boat. A sailor brought it up the rope ladder for him later.

The Captain stood waiting to greet the man, his ostrich-feather hat held to his chest. 'Welcome on board the *Boode*, Seur Lamotius! May the voyage ahead prove a prosperous one for you and your family.'

'I thank you, Captain Wobma.' Pompous. Then the delicate lady's head appeared above the rail and he took her hand. 'My wife, Margaretha ... Captain Wobma – you met in the Castle.'

A sailor climbed up with the child on his arm. Behind him climbed Tant Maijke's Cornelia, her fat cheeks just like her mother's. In pitch black, mind you, with a white pinafore and a thin cap without any lace or beads. The nanny.

Everyone remained standing till the Captain disappeared through a door into the rear part of the ship. As into the Forbidden. Cornelia followed with the child.

'Pieternella, come and help with the children and our things,' Tant Theuntjie called from the other end of the deck. 'Oom Bart is going to show us our place.'

Snailshell wouldn't budge. Snailshell wouldn't speak.

'Pieternella!'

She bent to pick up her bundles. Willem van Deventer was there with Oom Bart, he could carry his own children.

First through a big hatch on the poop deck, then down a wooden staircase into the bowels of the ship. Bodies, bundles, feet, people breathing – hollow sounds in the half-light of a wooden well.

'Mind your heads!' warned Oom Bart.

Tant Maijke was the first to bump her head.

Then Maria.

Then she, Pieternella. Sore.

'You have to duck!' Willem van Deventer scolded them. He was carrying the two children.

She suddenly wondered how deep a ship lay in the water. Whether they were under the waterline. She wanted out!

Dark, narrow passage.

No, they weren't under the waterline. The first door to the right was open; it was a small room with a sleeping bunk, a tiny cupboard against the wall and an open wooden hatch. Outside was still outside – just a little nearer the water.

'This is First Mate Berks's cabin,' whispered Oom Bart respectfully. 'Remember, he is next in importance to the captain, so don't worry him. His proper place is above your heads but he had to surrender it to our new Chief.'

Across the passage was another door. A closed one.

'Second Mate Lubbert's cabin.'

She wanted to go up above again!

Right in front of them was another door. Oom Bart pushed it open and waited for all the bodies and bundles to squeeze past.

'Keep stooping, don't bump your heads! This is the steerage hold where you – women and children – will eat and sleep for the duration of the voyage.'

A hold? The breadth of the ship. Dim, even though there was an open hatch at either end. Thick beams up against the deck, curved wooden ribs arching up all over from the side walls. The roof and walls painted dark brown, the floor scrubbed white. Only the children could stand upright, the rest had to stoop. A lantern with a candle in it hung from a beam on a string. Dead candle. Two tin chamber pots were tied to iron rings in the floor with long ropes through their ears. The rest of the rope was neatly coiled. Not cut off. A wooden bucket with a rope handle. A smaller barrel. Piled up against the back wall were chests, with ropes passed round their bodies and tied on to their sides. The bottommost chest was hers and Salomon's.

If she stood up straight between the beams, she just managed to fit

…

'How are we supposed to keep alive in this place?' demanded Tant Maijke anxiously.

'You wouldn't moan if you could see what Daniel and Focke and Willem and I have to put up with!' Oom Bart rebuked her.

'Cornelia is working for an important man! If he could see where we have to sleep …'

'Calm down, Maijke. There isn't any other place and just you leave Cornelia where she is. Under no circumstances are any of you allowed anywhere near her. She's on the deck above this one. All the important people are up above your heads, so you'd better behave yourselves down here. Lamotius and company are in the cabin immediately above you. Captain's cabin, the Surgeon's one. The small deck right at the top is the poop deck. Don't you dare set foot on it either! On this ship the tiller – the steering beam that has to steer us in the right direction all the way there – runs across the upper deck to where the First Mate stands. D'ye hear me? They're all forbidden places. The hold beneath your feet is packed with provisions and tools for the island.'

'What's under that?' Pieternella, asked. She wanted to know how far down it was to the bottom of the ship.

'At the front is the cable well where the anchor cables are rolled up.

Then there are the bread rooms and the space where the extra sails are stored. The powder house is right underneath.'

'God-a-mercy!' cried Tant Maijke in fright. 'Are you telling me we're lying on top of a death trap?'

'Oh, don't be so obstructive, Maijke!' Willem van Deventer was thoroughly annoyed. 'We're all in this together.'

'I won't be able to live like this,' Tant Maijke persisted. 'My back is broken already. I can't even stand upright.'

'Well then, sit!' said Oom Bart. 'It's better anyway.'

'Sit where?'

'On the deck.'

'On what?'

'On your arse! Like Theuntjie.'

Tant Theuntjie had already sat down. Back against the wall, skirt between her legs. Willem van Deventer was crouching on his haunches.

The place smelt of something …

Tant Maijke groaned as she sank down on to the floor and started weeping softly.

'Pieternella,' Oom Bart said, 'you'll have a great deal of responsibility in the steerage hold. You could say that you'll be earning your own fare in here.'

'Salomon's working for our fare.'

'What a cheeky little madam!' Tant Theuntjie exclaimed, shocked. 'How can you speak to a grown-up like that?'

I don't want to speak at all. I want to go back to the sheep. On land.

'Miss Cheeky will be taken to the Captain,' Oom Bart threatened. 'He doesn't play around with brats! Did you hear what I said, Pieternella?'

The smell was vinegary. 'Yes, Oom.'

'This hold has to be tidied every morning. Mattresses rolled up and tied in the corner next to your chests. There's a rope for it. Untie your bundles and bring out your mattresses now so I can show you.' All the mattresses were dragged into the corner. Oom Bart piled them up and tied them to the wall with a running knot. 'Nothing is allowed to lie around loose, this is a ship!' he said. 'The floor has to be swept clean and you're the one that's going to do it, Pieternella.'

'With what?'

'With a broom that you'll find beside the mainmast up on deck. And a piece of sailcloth to sweep the dirt into. Rubbish is thrown over the side and everything else is put back neatly where it belongs. Don't let an officer count the brooms and find yours is the one that is missing! The floor down here doesn't get washed. It would never dry. The Captain will say when it's time to sprinkle vinegar.'

'How long before we get there?' Snailshell needed to know how long she would have to breathe like this.

'Thirty-eight days, more or less, depending on the wind and whether the Captain takes us along the western current. That way we don't sail, we fly!'

Thirty-eight days? Crammed in there with all the others? She'd prefer to crawl in with the sheep in their pen!

'Tell them about meals,' the murderer suggested.

'Breakfast. Lunch. Supper. Sailors will bring in a table and stools for you, and take them away again afterwards. Pieternella, you'll fetch the food from the galley; it comes dished up in one basin. You eat off your own plates. A whistle will blow when the food is ready to be fetched, but because it will be difficult for you to hear it down here, the officer of the watch will send a sailor to call you. Early. Four o'clock. For the rest, whistles blow for everything and you'll soon learn which whistle is blown for what. Just remember, when the whistle blows for meals, you jump. The cook won't wait.'

'Tell about the meetings.'

'Before breakfast and supper a whistle blows the tune for prayers. Then everyone stands in the waist; that's the first deck, where the sheep pen is. Stand respectfully and keep the children quiet. The Captain speaks from up on the poop deck.'

'Where's the privy?' Maria wanted to know.

'You go in the pisspots and they have to be cleaned every morning,' Oom Bart explained. 'That's also your job, Pieternella. Tip them overboard and watch the wind if you don't want the muck blowing back into your face. The ropes through the ears are for lowering them into the water to rinse them out. Don't complain that your pot has landed in the sea.'

'Tell about the water.' Willem van Deventer.

'The bucket with the rope handle is for fetching water from the Steward's well up at the front every morning. That's the hatch beside the foremast. The water is for drinking *and* washing. Pour the drinking water into the small bucket. The pitcher is for the three tankards of beer that you're entitled to – for as long as the beer holds out. It saves drinking water. Just remember: what you get is all you'll have. Not a drop more if it runs out during the day. The Steward knows how much has been allocated to your hold. You, Pieternella, will go and fetch the water and the beer each morning.'

'Yes, Oom.' She wanted to get out …

'You'll see where the others are waiting for their water. Don't get chatting to the sailors. They're a randy lot. Keep your skirts and your knees together. D'ye hear me?'

'Yes, Oom.' She had to get out!

'The nails in the beams are to hang your clothes on. If you need anything out of your chests, make sure they're stacked up and secured again afterwards.'

'What are they doing to Salomon, Oom?' She wanted to know.

'Leave him be. Cook says he's a good worker. Because today's water and beer were shared out early this morning, I arranged with the Steward that I could get yours later. Only half, though. It's an exception. Cost me a hefty bribe, too – else you'd have had to wait till tomorrow for water.'

'What do they say, when will we set sail?' Tant Theuntjie wanted to know. 'I'm in a hurry to get home now.'

'As soon as there is a wind. If any of you meet Lamotius on deck, be very respectful. Remember: he's our new Chief – the man with his hand on his the handle of the knife. Even on board this ship, his word comes before the Captain's.'

Willem van Deventer got to his feet, still bending. 'As Bart says, behave yourselves quietly and decently. This isn't a boarding house, it's a ship and every ship is a small and important cog in the mighty wheel of the United Dutch East India Company. Don't forget it.'

She didn't quite understand what he'd said. Tant Theuntjie snorted: 'What are you saying, Willem? I thought you hated the Company just as much as the rest of us!'

'Careful, Theun – planks have seams and ears.'

Oom Bart continued. 'Don't get in the way when you go up on deck. The officer of the watch – he's the man who is the master of the men on duty – won't stand for a foot out of place or on a rope.'

'Who's the man with the lash?' she asked.

'The Bosun,' Willem van Deventer replied. 'Swine. Same as the Corporal on Robben Island that had to chivvy the shell carriers. Except this one's got a rope instead of a cane and he chivvies the sailors.'

He's not allowed to hit Salomon.

Then a man in smart clothes arrived. Writing book, inkwell, quill pen, all on a one-legged table. He made a list of all their names. Bending low under the beams.

When he'd left, Oom Bart explained that he was a clerk from the Castle who had to write down the names of everyone on the ship. He would go back in the last boat that returned to the mainland. In case the ship was lost at sea and the Company wanted to know who had perished.

'Oh-my-God,' cried Tant Maijke in dismay. 'I've just had an awful premonition in my heart.'

'Don't invite trouble, Maijke!' snapped Maria. 'Things are bad enough as they are!'

It was better up on deck.

Someone had thrown a sheaf of green fodder to the sheep. Stupid man, didn't know frightened sheep wouldn't simply eat. Wooden water trough. If she, Pieternella, crept into the farthest corner of the pen, she wouldn't be in anybody's way.

For thirty-eight days?

She smelt the sheep, closed her eyes and clung to the warm smell.

She didn't want to be on the ship!

She didn't want to be shoved down into a wooden hole!

She sat down with her back to the side of the ship and leaned over hard against the slats of the pen. She would even be able to squeeze her mattress in here …

'Why are you sitting crouched in here, girl?' The voice was scolding her but it wasn't angry. When she looked up, she recognised him, though she couldn't remember his name. It was the tall strong man with hair like a jackal's who sometimes used to visit Tant Barbara Geens, the one who told the story about the hand sticking out above the water near Mauritius. Striped cap with a long point, almost like Mynheer Van der Byl's sleeping cap. Sailor's clothes. Barefoot.

'I'm just sitting, Mynheer.' Don't chase me away.

'You can't sit here much longer.'

'Why not?' She wanted to cling to him like to the smell of the sheep.

'Because it's not the place for a young girl. Even less so when it gets dark.'

'I'll look after myself, Mynheer.'

'That's what you think. You're in the same hold as Maijke and company, aren't you?'

'Yes, Mynheer. Do you know my little brother? Salomon van Meerhoff. He works for the cook.'

'Bart Borms is keeping an eye on him.'

'They mustn't beat him.'

'Cook will clobber him if he needs it.'

'The man with the rope whip mustn't beat him.'

'Bosun's blows don't kill. Who's fetching supper for your hold tonight?'

'Me, Mynheer.'

'It's nearly time. See that you get into the queue as soon as the whistle blows. But before the supper whistle, there's the whistle for evening prayers.'

'When does this thing start moving forward, Mynheer?'

'It's a ship, not a thing. Depends on whether the night wind is strong enough to take us out on to the open sea.'

He walked off towards the front part of the ship.

The wind isn't going to blow again, please, the wind is never ever going to blow again!

Whenever the Fleet was in the Bay, sailors would come to eat and drink and laugh in Tant Barbara's house. They'd give Tant Barbara money and tell the most exciting stories. The next day she, Pieternella, and Tant Barbara's two daughters, Sara and Maria, would have to sweep and tidy the house and do the laundry, because Tant Barbara would be tired out. Jacobus chopped the wood and kept an eye on Salomon. When they had to go to school, Tant Barbara's manservant looked after Salomon. The Church had said they *had* to go to school. Later, Salomon also started going to school.

One night a sailor told the story of the ghost on the water off Mauritius. Gospel truth. Tant Barbara's Sara was quite sweet on the sailor. Tall and strong with nice thick yellow hair like a jackal. Down to his shoulders. Crooked cap with a long point. Sara said he wasn't really a sailor but a barrel-maker. A cooper. Tant Barbara said: Leave the man alone, he could have been your father!

The jackal-haired man told the very best stories. Long before the Cape was at the Cape, he said one night, the Cape was actually at Mauritius. But there were no cattle or sheep there, because there weren't any Hottentots. It was just an island. Without people. About the only food was tortoises and fish and dodos – birds that couldn't fly, but their flesh wasn't very nice. Very tough.

'My mother says there used to be lots of tortoises on Robben Island, too, Mynheer,' she told Sara's barrel-man. 'But they've all been eaten up.'

Everybody laughed. Tant Barbara poured more wine. The man said, 'No, girlie, not little tortoises like those. Different tortoises ... But because the fleet needed food and rest during the voyage,' he went on, 'the island of Mauritius meant relief, because the ships' crews were dying in droves at sea. Often, by the time the ships reached Mauritius, the water in the barrels was so stale – if there was any water left – that you had to suck it through your teeth to sift out the worms.'

'Oh no! *Sis!'* cried Jacobus. He didn't want to be a sailor when he grew up.

So the Lords in Amsterdam started a food-place-rest-place at the bottom end of Africa. Then the Cape was the Cape. And Mauritius was deserted again – just a bunch of runaway slaves that had fled into the forests.

'Where's the ghost?' Tant Barbara's Maria wanted to know.

'Patience, the ghost is still coming.'

The Cape hadn't been the Cape very long when the homeward-bound fleet left the East on its return voyage to Amsterdam. Jam-packed with goods. Many ships. An enormous amount of stuff. A man by the name of De Vlamingh was the master of the fleet, he was the Admiral. They held *two* church services before they left, praying hard that the fleet would reach the Cape safely. Particularly that they would sail past Mauritius without mishap, because that was where the worst storms always lay in wait for the ships. Cyclones.

'Worse than the Cape storms?' asked Tant Barbara.

'Much worse.'

Admiral De Vlamingh's best friend in the East was the Hollanders' famous lawmaker-man. His name was something like Maatsuiker. Every night, for weeks after the fleet sailed, he had special prayers said for the ships.

He was happily lying asleep one night when he dreamt that his friend, Admiral De Vlamingh, was standing on the water waving at him. Off Mauritius. He woke up in a terrible fright and sat bolt upright in bed. Was it a premonition? No, it couldn't be. He didn't believe in such things.

He went back to sleep.

And dreamt De Vlamingh was now up to his neck in the water and waving straight at him, Maatsuiker himself! Again he woke up in a panic. He called to the sentry outside his door and said: Our fleet is in trouble, there's a terrible cyclone off Mauritius!

How can you know that? asked the sentry.

I dreamt it, soldier!

The sentry gave him a little water to drink. It was a nightmare, Your Honour. Perhaps from that tasty roast venison you had for dinner? Go back to sleep.

Maatsuiker had scarcely dropped off again when the dream came once more. Now De Vlamingh had disappeared completely, only his hand was visible waving above the water.

It all happened a long time ago, but to this day the sailors of the homeward-bound fleet feared the hand above the water off Mauritius, because anyone who saw that hand would never see home again.

She remembered the story well. All night. The candle flame in the lantern slowly lengthened, and then suddenly shrank again, and with it the shadows on the white-washed walls. Tant Barbara's green eyes shone yellow in the candlelight, like lion's eyes. Outside the wind was howling; one of the sailors had fallen asleep with his head on the table.

'And then?' asked Sara.

'The lookouts here at the Cape waited and waited for the fleet to appear. Nothing. The Governor sent out small boats, with rags soaked in train oil and set alight, to patrol the approach to the Bay all night, in case the fleet might miss the entrance in the dark. Extra wood was sent to Robben Island to keep the signal fire burning high.'

Then at last the watchers saw a sail. In rags and tatters. A crippled ship. The cook was the captain; half the crew were dead, the rest almost all prostrate with scurvy. They brought the news that the fleet had lost its biggest ships with all the most valuable cargo in a cyclone off Mauritius. De Vlamingh was one of the many who drowned.

So the Lords in Amsterdam said: Go forth and man Mauritius again. Keep the English and the French away, watch out for any of our ships that get into difficulties on the return voyage. Save them. Collect all the cargo that washes ashore. Take care of the sick. Give them food. Most important of all: stop any pirates from setting up safe havens there and lying in wait for our fully laden ships.

And cut plenty of wood for us on the island. We'll send ships from the Cape to fetch it.

Sara married another man, not the one with the jackal hair. Maria married Captain Wobma. One day she, Pieternella, was going to marry Pieter van der Byl ...

If only she could get off the ship!

The forbidden top deck stuck out a little over the lower one. She could swear she heard some fowls. Somewhere. On the other side of the deck. She got up to have a look.

The fowls were in a coop made entirely of laths and tied under the overhang of the upper deck on the inner side of the ship. At least they wouldn't get wet if it rained. Ten speckled fowls and two pea-hens. Luckily. No peacock would be able to spread his tail feathers in *that* coop.

The ship was lying with its back to the land and its nose facing the open sea.

The water had to be fetched from the front hatch.

She started walking carefully along the fowls' side of the deck. There was a tall thick mast pole more or less in the middle of the ship. How did it stay upright? An upside down skiff in the middle. To row to land in, probably. Then a short, thick pole with holes in it. Another mast. Sailors everywhere. Don't hear what they say. Just walk slowly. The last hatch was beside the front mast. A big hatch, with a lid like a big wooden griddle over it. You could look down into the ship through it. Down below was a ship's room full of barrels.

Galley. Barrels stood all round in the galley, too. Some lay on their sides in big wooden cradles. Probably to stop them from rolling. Two open half-casks on a table. The galley was an upright hutch built of tiny bricks under the overhanging deck of the foremost upper deck. Open in front. Wide flat hearth, irons with huge soot-blackened copper cauldrons hanging from them. Smaller saucepans. To one side something that looked like a small bread oven. Salomon, busily packing firewood piece by piece into a box, hadn't noticed her. A big fat man was stirring a pot, his cap a kerchief knotted at the corners. He looked round and saw her.

'Are you looking for cock or for trouble?' he demanded. Uncouth boor.

'I'm looking for my little brother.'

'He's not here.'

It must have been the cook. His face was red and ugly and he openly thrust her away with his eyes.

Salomon looked round, frightened.

'Pieternella, you mustn't come here.' Pleading.

'Oh so?' mocked the cook-man. 'So this *is* your sister? You didn't tell me she was ready for sailorfood!'

'Pieternella, please leave.' Asking urgently.

The sheep were still huddled together, trampling around anxiously, when she crept back into her place beside the pen again.

There was something about the cook that made her nervous.

She laid her head on her arms and felt the tears prickling in her nose. A most terrible fear had taken hold of her body ...

Salomon said Oom Bart said he didn't want to take Jacobus as well. Jac Jacolyn had complained to the Church that Jacobus would finish only one shoe and then refuse to start on the other one. Just wanted to sit and stare.

She was glad her mother hadn't made her swear for Jacobus, too.

Suddenly the whistle blew. Shrill. Like a long silver thread stretching and shrinking, stretching and shrinking. The whistle-man stood beside the middle mast, opening and closing his hand round the whistle. A small silver tube.

People started coming out of wooden holes all over, the deck was covered with bodies. Hands took off caps and pressed them to chests. Sailor bodies suddenly took on human form. Black heads, red heads, brown heads, grey heads. Long hair. Curly hair. Straight hair. Matted hair. Bald heads. Plenty of bearded faces turned up towards the upper deck where there wasn't anybody.

She knew she had to stand up too.

Ahead, above the nose of the ship, the golden patch of sunlight glittered on the water.

Please, please, I want to get off!

'Pieternella, come out from behind the sheep pen!' It was Oom Bart. Cap on his head, his big round belly making the yellowish canvas jerkin bulge.

She stepped forward. Tant Maijke's head came out slowly through the rear hatch. Then Theuntjie and Maria and the children. They pushed open a space to stand among the others.

The whistle gave a long blast.

The gentleman Lamotius and his wife appeared at the railing on the top deck. He nodded his head graciously to the upturned heads below. He and his wife were equally tall. She held on to the railing but he didn't. Cornelia was standing behind them with the child on her hip.

The Captain appeared beside Master Lamotius. A much taller man. Book in hand.

It was dead quiet.

'Headgear off!' the Captain ordered. His voice was loud. Like in a deep cave. Everyone who still had their caps on quickly removed them.

The top of Oom Bart's head was bald, just yellowy-grey rat's tails hanging down to his shoulders.

'We read from the Word of God, from the book of Amos, chapter eight.' Every word fell clearly on their heads. On the heads of the sheep, the fowls and the peahens. '*And they shall wander from sea to sea, and from the north even to the east, they shall run to and fro to seek the Word of the Lord.*'

I don't want to run to and fro, Mynheer, and I'm not seeking the Word of the Lord either. I just want to go back to where my body is waiting for me on the quay. I beg you.

With his eyes open the Captain prayed words out of a book.

Mynheer Van der Byl used to say we should guard against false teachers and lost souls and only trust what was written down for simple Christians. The Captain wasn't a lost soul. He asked God in a loud voice to preserve all the voyagers sailing under the compass of the Lord's holy Providence, to preserve them from storm and wrack, from attacks by enemies and all such misfortune. To give each one a thankful heart ...

My heart will be so thankful, Mynheer, if I can stay with the Van der Byls I will be obedient for ever and ever.

'... that, after our voyage across the stormy seas of this life, we may attain unto the harbour of everlasting bliss. Let us pray together – Our Father, which art in Heaven ...'

The waist became a rumble of reciting voices. Most with eyes closed and heads turned up to heaven. Some with eyes open and mouths closed. Like Oom Bart. Probably all the old India hands. The one who recited the highest and loudest was Tant Maijke, standing there with a trembling voice and her head twisted sideways, crying aloud as if to make sure she'd be heard.

Amen.

The whistle gave two long blasts. Caps back on heads, feet hurrying towards the galley.

'Pieternella,' Oom Bart called, 'get into the queue and fetch your food. Hurry up!'

Bodies bumping and shoving. Hot breath blowing filthy words in her neck and ears. Two galley sailors scooped big ladles of food out of the pots and plopped them into the wooden basins each one held out. Focke Janse showed her where to find the basin.

The red-faced cook watched over everything.

Peas with small chunks of meat and lots of butter. And bread. And Salomon wouldn't look up. He was sitting beside a tub of sand scouring a copper pot that he could almost have fitted into.

As she walked back across the deck, small bunches of sailors were sitting around cross-legged, eating out of wooden bowls. Most with wooden spoons. Some with flat shells. Her spoon on Robben Island was always a pretty pink shell with tiny blue ridges. She used it to eat off her mother's plate.

The man with the jackal hair was sitting alone, eating out of a porcelain bowl with a narrow green pattern round the edge. He must have noticed her feet passing because he looked up.

'Are you managing, girlie?'

'Yes, Mynheer.'

'Remember to come and clean the basin when you've all finished.

There's a barrel of water beside the galley. It'll save you using the water from your own hold.'

'Yes, Mynheer.'

Down in the sleeping place there was hardly enough room to set your foot because someone had carried in a small table and three folding stools. It was cold and dark. The hatches were closed. The candle in the lantern was lit. Maria's children were whimpering.

'Why have you taken so long with the food, the children are hungry!' Tant Theuntjie scolded her. 'What are you standing there for, put it down!'

Tant Maijke was complaining about her chest that was fastened to the wall. Her plate was in the chest. What was she supposed to eat out of?

'You can use my plate, Tante, I'm not hungry.'

'You can't go without food,' said Tant Theuntjie and asked where the plate was.

She crawled over to her bundle on all fours and pulled it out. Not the spoon. Tant Maijke always ate with the fingers of one hand. Always had lots of napkins.

She had to get back on deck ...

The children were troublesome; Tant Theuntjie shared out the food. 'Please, can't we open one of the hatches?' Pieternella, asked.

'Do you want to be thrown overboard?' Tant Theuntjie snapped. 'The Captain said to close them; if the wind comes up tonight, we'll set sail.'

'Just one hatch. Please.'

'If the Captain says the hatches are closed, they're closed! Here's your food, eat out of the basin.'

She sat down on the floor to eat. The food wasn't nice. The bread tasted better.

She wanted to go home. Juffrouw Sophia made tasty food.

'Here, have a mouthful of beer, Pieternella,' offered Tant Maijke. 'Bart says we must use the beer to save water.'

'I don't want any beer. I have to go and wash the basin when we've finished eating.'

'It's almost dark outside. You're going nowhere. I'll go and wash the basin myself,' Tant Theuntjie interrupted. 'Maijke, we'll open the chests tomorrow and get out your plate and things.'

She wanted to go and sleep with the sheep. Please. Anyone, please.

'I want to go outside for some fresh air.'

'What?' exclaimed Tant Theuntjie angrily.

'I want to go to the sheep.'

'You stay where you are!'

'I want some fresh air, please.'

'You're going to have trouble with her, Theun,' Tant Maijke warned, pretending concern and shoving great lumps of food into her mouth. 'I watch and I listen carefully – she's getting more and more like her late mother.'

How does one really die?

'I think she wants to go after the sailors!' said Tant Theuntjie. 'I think she wants to get up to tricks! She doesn't realise she'll get her skull smashed in!'

'Quieter, Theuntjie!' warned Tant Maijke. 'The Captain and the notables are right above our heads.'

'Well, let them hear! Let the new Chief hear what kind of scum Bart Borms wants to drag along to Mauritius!'

Close your eyes. Be dead. She'd always done that when her mother wouldn't calm down. When she'd wanted to rip Robben Island apart because they wouldn't give her anything to drink, or when the food boat hadn't arrived, or when they wouldn't let her go back to the mainland ...

If a mountain gets in your way, you can climb over it. If people hem you in, you're stuck.

Someone banged on the door with a flat hand; two sailors came in to fetch the table and chairs. The ship had to be tidy.

'Untie my bedding and roll it out,' Tant Maijke ordered one of them.

'Listen, old girl,' he said, 'you're not on land now. If you haven't brought your own servant along, you do it yourself!'

When they had taken the things away, Tant Theuntjie told her, Pieternella, to untie the mattresses and roll them out. In her heart she said: I'm not your servant, and pretended not to hear.

'Pieternella, I'm speaking to you!'

In the yellow-brown dusk she crawled into the mattress corner and tugged the cord to let the bundles and bags tumble down. Pushed everyone's mattress across the floor and crept back with her own one right to the door. Quickly drew her other bundle closer.

'Gor!' mocked Tant Theuntjie. 'I see the godly Van der Byls were too mean to shell out a bean for straw for your mattress! Hottentots-bedding costs nothing.'

She said nothing. But she thought in her heart that Tant Theuntjie didn't know that she, Pieternella, knew that she was once banished to

Dassen Island for six weeks for lying and scandalmongering. She'd gone all about the town sweetly spreading the tale that Hester Weyers, wife of Wouter Mostert, had had two children in the fatherland and had killed one of them. Eventually no one would even tread on Hester's shadow, that's how thoroughly Tant Theuntjie spread the story.

So Hester took Tant Theuntjie to court. Tant Theuntjie argued, said she'd never said any such thing, but witnesses lined up to say she *had.* So the Fiscal ordered that Theuntjie van der Linde should stand in a public place for one whole day, wearing a placard round her neck stating that she was a scandalmonger and a backstabber. *And* she had to apologise to Hester.

Tant Theuntjie refused, said she would do it in hell first. The Fiscal said: In that case I hereby banish you to Dassen Island for six weeks to contemplate your sins, and if you come back and still refuse to apologise, I shall send you to scrape up shells on Robben Island.

They say that after ten sacks of shells you begin to crack, after a hundred you'll sing anything they play.

'Pieternella?'
  'Yes, Tant Theuntjie?'
  'Come and help Tant Maijke with her mattress!'
  'Yes, Tant Theuntjie.' Backstabber.
  Her mother said that meant you crept up on someone and attacked him from behind.

Namtesy had taught Jacobus to make a bow and arrows. But Jacobus never hit anything. Her mother laughed and said: It's because you've got no patience in your head! Patience to wait till the heat of the day when the buck lies down in the shade in the forest.

But Jacobus said: I didn't want to shoot a buck, Mamma, I wanted to shoot a mouse.

And her mother said: Buck, lion, Dutchman, mouse, no matter what – if you don't learn his secret ways, he'll get the better of you.

Only patience was going to get her out of that wooden hole. And cunning.

'Maria,' she suggested, 'lay your two mattresses beside mine, so I can give you a hand with the children tonight. It'll be better if Tant Maijke and Tant Theuntjie lie up against the chests.'

Rats in a hole, wriggling and milling around. And straw mattresses that kept creaking. Hottentot-bedding creaks differently. Not as deadly dry.

'Pieternella, untie the pisspots. Put one here for me and Theuntjie and keep the other one over there with you.'

'Yes, Tant Maijke.'

'And no one is to kick over a pot in the night! Maria, make sure your children go before you put them down.'

'Yes, Theuntjie.'

Maria had two mattresses, one for herself and one for her two children.

'Pieternella, get me a drink of water.' Tant Maijke.

'Yes, Tante.'

'Pieternella, draw your mattress closer to the front wall, Maijke's taking up a lot of space back here.'

'I'll do so, Tante.' She said it in her most obedient voice and dragged the mattress a tiny way closer to the wall. Not too much, she needed enough space to roll over on to the floor before she got up.

Tant Maijke sat on her bedding and took off her shoes and stockings and her top dress. There were deep rings under her knees where the stockings had been pinching her all day. Like in fully risen white bread dough. 'Pieternella, come and hang up my dress.'

She crawled, creaking, across one mattress after another, felt up for a nail in a beam, took the dress and hung it up. A big black shadow that made the dark even darker.

'Pieternella, come and put the pot here on my side, I don't want to stumble over Maijke if I have to get up tonight.'

Patience took a long time.

Till all the dresses were hanging from the beams like dried seal skins. A cap beside each dress. Till everyone had used the pots and bumped their heads, and Maria had finally settled the children. Till Tant Maijke had stopped complaining that the stuffing in her mattress was too thin.

'It's your body that's too fat, Maijke!'

Patience till Tant Theuntjie and Tant Maijke had stopped bickering.

'Pieternella, what are you fiddling with the door for?'

'I'm tying to see if it won't shut more tightly, Tant Theuntjie. There's a cold draught creeping in on to the children.' The swivel would turn easily …

It was cold. She put on her nightdress and wrapped her shawl about her shoulders.

'Pieternella, blow out the candle in the lantern.'

'I'm coming, Tant Maijke.' The thing was hanging almost immediately above the old woman's head, but *she* had to crawl over everyone and creak back again in the dark.

Dark as hell.

Cold. Which made her decide to snuggle in under her quilt while she waited for everyone to fall asleep. Then she would pretend to be turning over, but roll out on to the floor and flee.

She thought she could hear the sea outside against the ship's sides. Footsteps walking above her head. Her bedding smelt of the veld and the river and rain ...

'Mamma, something's biting me.'

'Lice. Go to sleep.'

'Mamma, I'm cold.'

'I've already got Salomon lying against my back.'

'Mamma, I'm frightened.'

'Of what?'

'What's that groaning?'

'A lion. He says he wants a juicy young cow to gobble up!' Her mother laughed in the pitch black darkness.

'Is he going to come and gobble us up?'

'Not him. The fences are too strong and too tall.'

That was her Hottentot mother. Her lovely mother. Not her Dutch mother.

'Mamma, the darkness is too frightening.'

'Close your eyes, then you won't see the darkness.'

Hottentot-bedding smells like a reed hut ...

The first time she heard they were going to the Cochoqua was on the evening in the Post House when her mother told the Post Holder that she had to go to her people.

'You can't just leave the island when you feel like it, Miss Eva. The Commandeur still has to decide about you and the children.'

'I'll decide for myself. Jacobus has to stay here, his foot is still too sore with the cuts from the sea rocks. Oedasoa owes me a whole lot of cattle and sheep; I'll have to go and fetch them myself, because his ears don't hear my messages.'

'Oedasoa's kraal is way over beyond Saldanha. That's too far for the children, Miss Eva.'

'There's a drought. Oedasoa and Gogosoa's kraals have moved to Rietvlei. I've seen their fires burning over there for the last two nights now. It's a day's walk – if the shell boat takes us across early.'

'Sorry, the Commandeur first has to give his permission for you to leave the island, Miss Eva.'

Her mother carried on like a caged animal until the permission paper eventually arrived. The shell boat landed them on the quay one afternoon. Her mother said the light would still last a good while, they would start walking. It was summer.

At Salt River a fisherman rowed them across in his boat. Once across the river, her mother put on her other clothes and tied Salomon on to her back between two skins.

All along the beach. The sand was still warm from the heat of the day. They walked and walked, to where a tall wooden house loomed up on the beach in the twilight. Her mother said: Don't look. It was an observation post, where soldiers had to watch for Hottentots and free-burghers trying to pass by with stolen or bartered cattle and sheep. And for runaways. And ships in danger of running aground.

Two soldiers came walking across the dunes from the observation post to ask her: Where are you going to, Eva?

To my people and my late sister's children.

Oh.

They laughed and one said: Anyone can see you must have fucked a white man to get two such white children!

Her mother spat in his face and the other soldier had to step in quickly to stop spittleface from attacking her mother.

When it grew dark, her mother scooped out a sand bed for them under a shrub with yellow flowers and gave Salomon some of the sheep's milk in the little bottle. And bread and fish for her, Pieternella. Next morning her mother picked little black berries off the bush for them to eat and gave Salomon some more of the sheep's milk.

The Commandeur had once sent a message to the island to say Eva was not to milk the sheep. The milk was for the lambs. So Eva sent a message back: I'm not letting my children die.

Before the sun was up, they were walking again. Past the spot where great big chunks of a dead ship stuck up out of the water. 'How did it get there, Mamma?'

'The wind blew its feet out under it and the tide just came and tipped it over here. Long ago. I must have been about as big as you. They were Hollanders. Most of them made it to shore. My uncle Autshumao went and told them: You can't come and build shelters here, this is our place. We were still *Khoikhoi* then. They said they only wanted to pick up the things that washed up and to wait till another ship came by.

'They waited out twelve full moons. When the ship came, there was a man on board whose name was Jan van Riebeeck. Without his wife. Autshumao saw him clearly. Then they loaded all the goods on to the whole ship and left.'

They walked and walked. After a while her mother said: 'Then, one day, they came back again. The Hollanders. We ate their food and drank their wine and enjoyed ourselves, thinking in our stupid hearts that they would stay only twelve full moons.'

Tant Maijke and Tant Theuntjie both snored. One high, the other low. The children were asleep – but not Maria. You could hear by her breathing that she wasn't sleeping.

If you keep your eyes closed, you won't *see* the darkness around you!

Then they reached the kraal. Lots of huts like big round tits made of plaited rushes tied round bent staves driven into the ground. In a wide circle. So beautiful. Fences of branches running from hut to hut. Her mother was cautious, you could see. Squinting through the branches till they found somewhere they could enter.

Suddenly there were many men-of-men all round them, speaking stone talk. It sounded as though they were cursing her mother and trying to drive her away. But her mother stood stock-still and held her ground. She clung to her because the men-of-men's children were wanting to crowd around her, looking at her as though she was bewitched. It sounded as though they were driving *her* away, too. A woman tugged her by the hair; she screamed because she was afraid they were going to cut off her head! Others took hold of her dress. She screamed again. Then her mother told her just to stand still.

Suddenly, a path opened up between them for a man of the men-of-men wearing a leopard skin round his shoulders. The chief. Other men, too. And the chief spoke to her mother for a long time. Fierce or angry-like. Then her mother sank to her knees and touched her head to the ground and Salomon's head slipped down into her neck. She, Pieternella, fell flat out of sheer fright.

A Hottentot kraal.

Then the man said something. Her mother stood up and said: 'Get up, Pieternella!'

For three days they stayed in the kraal. She wasn't frightened in the daytime, only at night when the lions roared.

They made her a *Khoi*, too. A Hottentot. First they took off her dress and smeared her whole body all over with animal fat. They sprinkled a handful of grey-green buchu over her. Plastered all her hair flat against her head.

'Mamma, help me!'

Her mother told her to sit still, they were making her pretty for the moon.

Then they tied a little skin apron in front of her private parts and fastened it round her body with a thin strap. They hung strings of ostrich eggshell beads and seashells round her neck and body and arms and legs.

'These are just on loan,' her mother told her. 'You have to give them back again.'

There were some huts that they weren't allowed to stand near. Something was happening in one of them, because women were going in and coming out of it, as serious as for church. But her mother said it wasn't for church, there was a girl in the hut who was bleeding for the first time.

In another hut a woman was giving birth to a baby.

Lots of milk, that the women pulled out of the cows and poured into pretty clay pots. Flat wooden dishes with bright yellow butter that they smeared all over their bodies with their fingers. On her, too.

The men ate on one side, the women and children elsewhere. Never allowed to eat together, her mother said. Sometimes, a place where women had eaten was poisonous.

Living in the kraal was more and more fun. She went out into the veld with the children, played five-stones with them. Drank milk.

An old woman with a wrinkled face, long wrinkled tits and a wrinkled body on huge, flat buttocks sat in the sun with Salomon on her lap, smearing him from head to foot with sloppy wet cattle dung; her hands and legs were covered in dung. He looked too odd for words and every time he tried to wriggle free, she would sing him a stone song. Over and over. Then he'd lie still again.

When the dung had dried, she started lightly rolling it off with the palms of her hands, till it came away in long rolls.

Then he was white-red and clean. But everyone sitting round the old woman shook their heads, as if not at all satisfied. So the old woman took butter in one hand, mixed it with soot that she scraped off a clay cooking pot, and smeared him gently and evenly till he was shiny brown and beautiful. At that everyone laughed, satisfied. Now he was beautiful.

Lots of flies.

The men-of-men sat bunched round her mother. Pebbles came rolling out of her mouth in streams and her hands talked along with them. They listened in amazement, lowered their heads, looked up again, clapped their hands, leant over backwards, sat up straight again. The chief sat a little apart, listening attentively, his eyes screwed up small from all his watching. His fly-switch had the tail of a wild cat attached to it.

It looked as though he was still angry with her mother.

In the middle of the afternoon the cattle came back to the kraal in a cloud of dust, ready for the night. Lowing. Flocks of sheep bleating with trembling voices. The gap in the thorn fence behind them was stopped up to keep out the hungry lion lying in wait somewhere outside.

When it was almost dark, *Gounja*'s face hung in the west like a shining sickle. The fires burnt high. With their knees bent, the reed-flute players began their hop-hop-hopping dance in a dusty circle like rabbits, round and round and round. The women, in a wider circle, danced with smaller hops, clap-clap-clapping their hands and sing-sing-singing a long trilling song.

With Salomon shaking on her back, her mother joined in the dancing.

And she, Pieternella, fell asleep beside a strange fire.

5

'Pieternella, wake up!' Tant Theuntjie's voice. 'You've got to take the bucket and fetch the day's water. They've been knocking on the door to tell us to get up!'

She realised immediately that she had fallen asleep by mistake on a Hottentots-bedding mattress in a dark hole in the insides of a ship.

Please. Somebody, please.

The candle in the lantern had been lit again.

'Pieternella, go and empty the pots before the children step in them!' Tant Maijke got up and bumped her head.

'Pieternella, why are you standing there looking stunned?' Tant Theuntjie. 'Don't forget the beer pitcher.'

The water and the beer.

As she went up the steps to the deck, she trod on the skirt of her nightdress and stumbled. The early morning air was as cold as night and the boards of the deck were damp and slippery underfoot. Burning lanterns swung from the masts as the ship rose and fell on the tide. Sailors were standing in a line at the front hatch in the greyness. The galley was a red-hot glow with dark bodies moving about rapidly and big copper pots shining. Spoons were knocked clean against the rims of pots. Shivering seamen leant against the warm bricks of the galley. Filthy words poured out of sailors' mouths like steam.

Salomon was using a long-handled pot to scoop up water from an open barrel and carry it with both hands towards the fiery glow.

'Pieternella, is that you?' It was Cornelia behind her. A black body with a white apron for a tummy and a white cap for a head. Black shawl round her shoulders. Buckets in her hands. 'Aren't you cold?' she asked.

'Yes. I forgot my shawl.'

'What's it like down there where you are?'

'Cramped.'

'The Lamotius-man and his wife are very kind. They say we ought to be able to sail today. Has Ma calmed down?'

'Yes.' The queue shuffled forward.

There was no sign of the day breaking yet, stars were still glittering in the sky.

A water sailor stood at the hatch, a bundle of rope at his feet. He knotted her bucket to the end, put the pitcher in the bucket and lowered them into the hole.

'For how many people?' came a voice from deep inside the ship.

'The Steward wants to know how many people you're fetching water for,' said the water sailor.

She didn't realise that the man was speaking to her. 'For six, Mynheer,' she shouted down the hatch.

'Who are they?'

'Maijke van den Berg and Oom Bart's Theuntjie ...'

'How many children?'

'Two, Mynheer?'

'Have you counted yourself?'

'Yes, Mynheer. No, Mynheer.'

'Make up your mind, you're wasting time!' A hollow voice.

'Three grown-ups, two children and one half-grown.'

The water sailor hoisted up the bucket, untied it and lowered a coil of the rope at his feet for the beer pitcher.

'Out of the way!' he shouted.

The bucket was so heavy she had to drag it out of the way with both hands. 'Please, would you take care of the pitcher for me? I first have to take the bucket down.'

'Why do they send such a slip of a girl to fetch water?' he demanded angrily, but promised to look after the pitcher. 'Tomorrow morning you'd better send someone with arms!'

Oom Bart suddenly loomed up out of the darkness and took the bucket from her. She picked up the pitcher. 'Come,' he said.

The steerage hold was all a jumble with Maria's children whining and Tant Maijke on her knees trying to get her mattress rolled up. Tant Theuntjie had been searching for one shoe and bumped her head. Maria had also bumped her head.

Oom Bart put down the bucket in the doorway. 'You'd better get this place tidy!' he scolded. 'Just look at it! They'll be bringing down the table for breakfast any minute now.'

'It's Pieternella's fault for dawdling with the water,' whinged Tant Theuntjie, adding: 'Hurry up, girl! The pisspots are in the way – and they've got to be cleaned!'

Oom Bart turned on his heel and walked off.

The pots. One at a time. They stank – there was more in them than just piss.

Up on deck she knotted the end of the rope on the first pot round her arm, threw the pot far overboard and let it sink away properly before she hauled it up again.

Back down again to fetch the second pot.

'If that pot had been a bucket,' said the jackal-haired man suddenly, speaking to her as she was hauling up the second pot, 'and this ship was under full sail, it would have pulled you clean overboard, rope and all. Don't ever wind the rope round your arm.'

'No, Mynheer.' Just then the whistle blew. 'What is that whistle for, Mynheer?'

'For cleaning the fo'c'sle.'

Back down again.

She rolled up her mattress and put on her dress.

'Now you all see what I've done, don't you?' Tant Theuntjie announced. 'I've poured the drinking water into the smaller bucket, so don't you go dipping your hands or cloths in it. Use the jug.'

Maria bumped her head.

Pieternella crawled to the washing water to wet her facecloth and to wipe where she had to.

'I want things out of my chest!' Tant Maijke kept on nagging. 'Come and help me loosen the ropes, Pieternella.'

'Later, Tante. First we have to get the mattresses tied up in the corner like Oom Bart showed us.'

'Why are you sulking?'

'I'm not sulking.'

'Theuntjie, you're going to have a hard time with this girl!'

'No, Maijke, I won't take any nonsense from her. I'll soon slap her into shape.'

I won't let you slap me. Scandalmonger.

Maria helped her with the mattresses and knew how to tie a running knot.

She fetched the broom from the mainmast. Day had broken, the sea was grey and flat, no sign of a breeze. The *Bruidegom* was on her way from the mainland, twelve men rowing. A shining wake trailed longer and longer behind the boat.

They were bringing more bundles of firewood.

Broom. Piece of canvas.

Please, she wanted to go back to the mainland on the boat ...

'What are you standing around for, Pieternella?' Oom Bart called across from the chicken coop side. 'You'd better hurry. They're going to scrub the deck soon and before that all the brooms and things have got to be put back.'

The sheep's eyes were full of fear, their ears drooping.

She swept the wooden hole, but couldn't see properly in front of the broom for the tears in her eyes.

'Sweep properly, Pieternella!' Tant Maijke scolded and crawled out of the way of the broom. 'Seems to me you haven't ever held a broom before. Sophia van der Tempel with her stuck-up nose never taught you to sweep, I see. The story goes that you had a right royal time with the Van der Byls!'

Leave me alone.

When she heard the whistle blow, she snatched up the broom and canvas and ran upstairs, shook out the canvas over the side and got the things back to the mainmast just in time.

Sailors hauled buckets full of water, long ropes tied to their handles, up out of the sea and splashed them over the deck, while others scrubbed away with long brooms. The water ran off through the holes at the sides of the deck.

She lingered at the fowls' side of the deck. She was hoping to slip past to the galley to see where Salomon was, but a gush of water swirled round her feet and splashed her dress.

The man with the rope whip yelled at her: 'Get out of the way, girl! Get below decks and stay there!'

She took fright and scurried over to the sheep's side of the deck and crept in beside their pen. The man didn't see her.

She didn't want to go back down again. Next to her was the companionway that led up to the forbidden deck. If she scrambled up there quickly ...

There wasn't anybody on the top. She pressed her body tight against the side of the ship where the backmost spiderwebs of ropes were tied. Didn't move.

Nobody looked up from below or noticed her.

Three sailors were crawling on all fours across the bottom deck, rubbing the boards with what looked like cakes of soap. Another was walking backwards after them, strewing sand from a bag round his waist. Like sowing corn. Four other sailors with their backs to the sower walked backwards scrubbing and scrubbing with brooms.

Then two more sailors came from the fo'c'sle side, dragging something that looked like a big flat stone with a hole in it for a tow-rope – it *was* a stone. And sitting on the stone was a shrunken human bundle clutching the tow-rope with both hands. The human bundle was Salomon! They started dragging him and the stone the whole length of the waist while he seemed to be clinging on for dear life.

When they'd finished dragging him, the buckets were lowered over the side for water for the final wash.

She was halfway down the companionway when the whistle blew for prayers. No one had seen her.

As on the evening before, bodies came into the waist from holes all over the place. Up out of the sleeping hole as well, Tant Maijke first of all.

Master Lamotius and his wife were on the poop deck, the Captain behind them. Cornelia with the child. Lamotius opened the Book and called down: 'Headgear off!'

It was as though the caps came off more slowly than on the evening before. Perhaps they hadn't heard clearly, the man had to shout loudly to be heard.

He read about a king who did what was right in the eyes of the Lord for forty-one years and then banished all the sons of shame from the kingdom. Something like that.

Tant Maijke seemed to have lowered her head. Perhaps she was thinking that she was a daughter of shame who had been banished from the land.

One day her mother had shouted at Tant Maijke: Maijke van den Berg, many's the day I'd have given you my soul for sheer shame!

It happened on Robben Island, the first time they banished Tant Maijke from the Cape.

It sounded as though Master Lamotius was angry about something, for he was hurling the words ever more fierily at the heads below him: 'As the God-fearing King Asa encouraged his subjects, so also the Government should follow his example and likewise use its authority and power to encourage its subjects to seek the face of God!'

Then he prayed out of the book that the Heavenly Father should bless the State, for that the State was parent unto us all, and that the Heavenly Father should preserve the State from strife and temptation, and that we, the children of the State, should honour and obey our parent.

After that everybody had to recite the Our Father together.

Salomon was standing on the other side of the waist next to Willem the murderer, solemnly praying with everyone else, his cap held to his chest.

Her mother used to say: he's just like his dad, Pieternella: as finely spun as a silken cloth. Don't let him and Jacobus ever forget that their white grandfather lived far over the sea in a real castle. And don't let them forget that their fearless Hottentot grandfather bore on his cheek the scar of a man who had killed a lion single-handed!

6

Breakfast was barley, boiled with prunes and butter. And bread.

When she got back with the food, the table and stools were already in the hold. The hatches had been opened again, the ropes round the chests untied. After breakfast she had to help Tant Maijke get into her trunks. Almost enough for a whole house inside. Dresses, shoes, cups, saucers, fine porcelain plates. Pewter plates and pewter spoons, two big kitchen forks. Cloths. Stockings. Foot-warmer. Candles. Tablecloths. Copper pan. Copper pot. Meat hook. Pie dish. Bottles. Quilts and bedsheets. Napkins.

Cushions. Aprons. A spade. Cloaks. Caps. A bathing slip. A dismantled table.

Their sleeping quarters began to look like a provisioning shed; Tant Theuntjie had fled out on to the deck with Maria and the children.

Then everything had to be packed back in again. Everything except one pillow, a plate and a spoon, some serviettes, two cloths and a candle.

'Just in case we need light in the night and the lantern's one has burnt down,' Tant Maijke said. 'You never know what might happen to you. Keep a couple of pairs of extra stockings out for me, too, and pack the rest back neatly.'

'I always pack neatly.' She had to get out ...

'Don't answer back. I'm telling you, God will punish them for what they have done to this poor widow. Barbara Geens may think as highly as she likes of her son-in-law the Captain – *I* don't think much of him! Put the candle back again, I'm not going to burn up my stuff for the Company.'

'Please, Tante ...'

'To think that our lives on this ship are in the hands of Wobma. I tell you, I have a peculiar feeling coming over me.'

'Hold on to that side, Tante, so that we can get the chests back in their place. I need to go up on deck.'

'Don't you rush me. My life has been destroyed. I'm heading for the dark. I'm glad my poor Thieleman – God rest his soul – was spared this bitter cup.'

'It's just a pity that you didn't think twice before you put that cup to my mother's lips, all for a sheep and a cow!' She said it because it had been sticking in her throat for a long time; she just hadn't been able to find the right words to say it before. She saw the old woman get furious, draw herself upright, bump her head ...

'Goddammit, what did you say?' she screamed. 'D'ye want me to lose my temper? *I* put the cup to *your* mother's lips? You're asking me to shove my fist into *yours*, you black-arsed mongrel Hottentot, you!'

'Better than a banished old Dutch bitch and a thief and a tell-tale of a murderer!' She knew she was leaping off a cliff; she didn't care. Snailshell couldn't care.

When Tant Maijke struck her, she fled up on to the deck and crept in beside the sheep pen where her breathing gradually slowed down.

She was in trouble.

The sky was blue, the sun shone down warmly on her and the sheep.

There wasn't a breath of air.

After some time Maria came to say: 'Pieternella, Theuntjie wants you.'

'No.'

Sailors everywhere in the sun. Some were mending their clothes with needle and thread. Others were painting the spiderweb ropes with tar, or hanging over the side to scrape the outer hull of the ship. Some were looking out as if watching for something. The Bosun walked slowly up and down, flicking his rope. Down in the fo'c'sle someone was playing a fiddle. Like heartache.

A grey-haired old man was sitting flat on the deck next to the upside down skiff, a thick bundle of sails folded on his lap. He opened them an arm's length at a time and examined them carefully. Everything about him looked crusty with sea salt.

Tant Theuntjie and Maria and children sat on the chicken-coop side of the deck pretending not to see her.

The jackal-haired man came from the direction of the galley and stopped right in front of her. 'Girl?' Like one bringing a rebuke. 'I saw what you did this morning. If they catch you on that top deck, you'll be up to your neck in trouble.'

'Yes, Mynheer.' She was in trouble already.

'Don't you do it again.'

'No, Mynheer.' He turned round but she stopped him. 'Mynheer ...'

'What is it?'

'How does one get off this ship?'

'Jump overboard.'

She'd thought he was kind-hearted.

Sit. With her back to the ship's side. Legs drawn up, arms round her knees, head on her arms ...

Nobody cared.

She wouldn't go down below again; Tant Maijke was too furious and Tant Theuntjie was surely just biding her time ...

If there were really serious troublemakers on board, they waited till night and then quietly threw them overboard off the ship's stern. Tant Maijke was a serious troublemaker all right, they should toss her overboard.

Been taken to court how many times already. In gaol, too.

They said she'd been a skilful Dutchwoman when she arrived at the Cape. Her husband, Oom Thieleman Hendricks, was much younger than she was. Her mother used to say the Hollanders' old cows came to the Cape to find themselves young bulls.

One day they caught Oom Thieleman calmly driving a herd of Hottentot cattle to his place. When there were ships in the Bay, he would secretly sell meat to the sailors at night behind a sand dune or some scrub bushes. Illegally. On the first three days only the Company was allowed to sell.

So they caught him and took him to court. He actually got up in court and swore at Governor Borghorst, the poor old man who lost his diamonds. He shouted out at the top of his voice: 'Be damned to the devil in hell, Borghorst, you and all your henchmen in the law!'

So they threw him in gaol. To get out again, he had to pay a whole lot of money, and as an extra punishment the Company took some of his best cattle and sheep.

Tant Maijke was furious. She'd hatch a plan.

Janvos was coming along the wagon-track from where he'd been cutting wood for Mynheer Van der Byl. When he got to the house he said: Pieternella, your mother's back on land. I've just seen her on the road, on her way to Miss Maijke.

She hadn't been to see her mother on the island for a long time because she was cross with her. Juffrouw Sophia asked her one day: Pieternella, what is troubling you? Something in your heart is not as it usually is.

She couldn't tell Juffrouw Sophia because she didn't know the words to say it with. Just that there had been a wedge of pitch darkness somewhere in her head since she'd last visited her mother and it wouldn't go away. She'd found her mother that day above the high-water mark gathering feathers from the penguin nests. She looked, and saw that her mother was carrying something hump-shaped on her back in pieces of an old flag ...

It turned out to be the ugliest little baby.

'Whose is it, Mamma?'

'Mine. I've told the Commandeur I have to go to the mainland. The child has to be christened because he's got to get Christian blood.'

She was so shocked she spun right round and ran all the way to Sand Bay, got straight back into the food boat and returned to the mainland. Her mother had called her, but she just kept running.

Jacobus and Salomon were still living with Sick Visitor Juriaan Heere and his wife at the time. Jacobus was busy outside taking the day-frames off the window and putting up the shutters for the night.

'Mamma's got another baby.'

Jacobus got so angry he punched a hole right through the oilcloth in the frame.

That was when Janvos announced that he had seen her mother on the road.

The next day she and Pieter were walking to the Fort for school. She told Pieter she wasn't going to school, she was going on because her mother was at Tant Maijke's. Pieter pleaded, he said, 'Don't stay away from school, you'll upset your mother. Rather go after school.'

The baby was lying on straw in a wooden box under Tant Maijke's dining room table. And her mother had come from somewhere with a whole lot of sheep and cattle. Tant Maijke laughed aloud, her mouth agape, she was paying her mother with wine and tobacco and promising to tell the church about the baby that had to be christened, to arrange for witnesses ...

Everyone was in church on Sunday, the Commandeur and all the bigwigs had already taken their places and the reader was getting ready to open the Book when suddenly all fell silent as her mother came walking into the church. A black dress, no lace collar, leather shoes of Tant Maijke's on her feet, and the baby in her arms. To have him christened. Swaying drunkenly up the aisle right to the front of the church to where all the others were waiting for their children to be baptised.

The child's name was Geronimus. He later died. Fortunately. The first one, Anthonie, was somewhere with people in the town.

After church she just walked into the veld, kicking stones with her new shoes, and crying and crying, letting all her painful pent-up words escape.

Now Tant Maijke had the same number of cattle and sheep in her kraal as the Company had taken from Oom Thieleman. It was Eva who had bartered for them.

All the old woman still needed was the money the oom had to pay to be let out of gaol.

There was a pandour named Arent and his friend Frans Cuiper, a soldier. They absconded. They knew they'd land in the most terrible trouble but they absconded anyway.

'Stupid things,' said her mother.

The Company sent out a troop of soldiers to search for them. No luck. Again. Still nothing. Then they nailed up a poster proclaiming that the Company would pay a handsome sum to anyone who caught them. Dead or alive.

Less than a week later, Tant Maijke went to tell the Fiscal that her servant had seen them at the Witteboomen, starving. Her servant had promised to bring them food the next day; she had the food all ready: salted hippo fat and bread. Oom Thieleman would take it there himself.

Next day the two were sitting happily beside Oom Thieleman's wagon eating the food when the soldiers caught them, right there.

Jacobus went to watch them hang Arent. He said the hangman climbed up the ladder and put the rope round Arent's neck. Arent pleaded till the spit was trickling down his chin but it didn't help.

The other one, Cuiper, was a big strong man. They flogged him and sent him to Robben Island in chains and for twelve years he had to scrape up shells for punishment.

And Tant Maijke went to the Fort and collected the reward – exactly the right amount to have Oom Thieleman let out of gaol.

Her mother said not even the devil could knock Maijke van den Berg over.

Tant Theuntjie came walking across the deck from the chicken-coop side.

'Pieternella,' she asked, her lips drawn tight, 'why did you not come when I sent for you? Do you want to be slapped right off this ship?'

'I was scared.'

'Since when does a hussy like you speak to a grown-up as if she was your equal? Tant Maijke is in deep distress down in the hold and it's your fault!'

'I didn't banish her.'

'Jay-sus!' Tant Theuntjie was white with rage. Luckily the whistle for the midday meal blew just then and brought a moment of respite. Everywhere sailors were jumping up and hurrying off towards the galley. 'Lift your arse and fetch the food!' shouted Tant Theuntjie.

Something made her look towards the land while she was in the food queue. A fresh worry shot through her body: there were thin wisps of cloud over Lion's Head.

That meant the wind was getting up.

7

One moment it was a dead wooden goose floating on the water.

Then suddenly a roughness began to show on the surface of the sea behind them – a deeper blue swell growing stronger and stronger.

The wind was coming.

It reached the ship – and a shudder jerked through the wooden body like something suddenly catching its breath. A creaking. A groaning. Every seam, every sinew suddenly started coming alive. A dead animal slowly coming to life.

The breath passed over its nose making it rock back on its anchor cable as if to pull away from the hindrance shackling it.

Breath that blew into sailors' bodies. Mouths shouting orders. Loud. Urgent. Feet running from one side of the ship to the other. Feet and hands nimbly clambering up the spiderwebs hand-over-fist up the masts to hang on to the yards, their feet in slack ropes.

The wind had come.

The smoke billowing from the galley chimney fell flat on its back. Ever more groans, more creakings; bodies hurrying faster and faster to keep out of the way of the Bosun's whip.

Long, narrow pennants, like the tails of mousebirds in flight, dancing red, white and blue at the tops of the masts.

'Shorten anchor!'

A man was shouting from the poop deck. It wasn't the Captain's voice but the Captain was standing beside the man.

She crept in deeper behind the sheep pen and put her hands over her head. She could feel her heart beating in her ears. She would have fled downstairs but she was trapped – there were too many bodies in the waist and the deck hatch she would have to use was closed.

Hands picking things up, changing their grip, shifting and tightening.

In front of the upside down skiff in the middle of the deck sailors were sticking poles into the thick, heavy drum and walking round and round it, pushing hard to reel in the anchor cable, thick as a man's waist. No, not reeling it in; they were pulling the ship forward by its anchor cable.

'Brace for a luff to larboard!' the words thundered down from the top deck. On one side of the deck sailors ran to untie a cable and let it play out; on the other side a line of hands grabbed hold of another cable and began to pull, bodies straining, feet stepping backwards, slipping ...

The Bosun getting in his first lashes.

Sailors turned the long yards on the two front masts sidelong, one at a time. Two sailors to a yard. The rearmost mast was shorter and its yard was set sideways. Only two men were needed to untie its sails and let them unfurl.

'Shake out the foresail!' *Whup!* Monkeys lying across the yards to untie the ropes and release the bundles of sail. 'Shake out the mainsail!' *Whup!* Monkeys up in the mainmast yards. *Whup! Whup!*

Woodgoose grew big square grey-white wings that hung down from the top corners on long ropes tied to the body of the ship.

And a tail wing.

Ropes were being drawn tighter on one side, played out on the other. Ropes spinning off wooden reels, screeching *chee-chee-chee*. Sailors shouting to one another, their bare feet slapping the wooden deck as they ran.

Masts groaning like old trees in the wind.

All over under the caps were faces that she knew. Bart Borms at the cables. Next to him the murderer. The jackal-haired man hanging on to a mast up above. Focke Janse clambering down the rigging.

The old sailmaker stood with his hands cupped over his eyes against the midday sun, carefully watching each sail unfurl.

Even the cook was hanging on to a rope somewhere. Only Salomon was nowhere to be seen. Perhaps he was hiding beside the fire.

'Weigh anchor!'

'Winch home and set!'

Moments. Then slowly woodgoose started gliding across the water, taking her with it like a hawk with a mouse.

A cannon shot rang out in greeting from a side hole and the body of woodgoose quivered. A second shot, from the other side. Cannons from the Castle replied – one, two, three, four. Usually they only fired one shot – unless there was some notable on board the vessel that was leaving.

She stood up and clung to the railing. The sheep were milling around restlessly, pissing again and again. Fright piss.

She felt the wind blowing cold against her. The nose of the ship had swung towards the strip of white sand on the other side of the Bay where the old wreck lay ...

She saw the Bosun coming towards her, whip at the ready, eyes wide open.

'No!' she screamed, thinking he was about to lash out at her.

'What are you doing here, you little cunt?' he shouted, aiming a blow at her.

'I'm trapped, Mynheer! Please, don't hit me!'

'Get below!'

There was a short rope on the outside of the hatch cover that she could pull to open it and climb down into the hole. She waited, crouching, for her eyes to get used to the dark.

The door to the hold was open. The candle in the lantern was lit because the outer hatches were also shut. Tant Maijke was sitting with her legs splayed out, her back to the chests. Maria had her back to one wall, Tant Theuntjie had hers against another.

'I *thought* they'd chase you away up there,' sniffed Tant Theuntjie.

She crawled over to Maria's side and got hold of one of the wooden ribs because the ship was rolling and throwing her across to one side. Tant Maijke snatched at the ropes round the chests and held on for dear life. Maria grabbed the children who had tumbled into each other, screaming.

'Oh Gawd!' Tant Maijke cried out in fright, ducking to avoid the lantern swaying above her head. 'What's going on?'

'They're lowering the sails on the other side,' said Tant Theuntjie stolidly and calmly leant over as the ship listed again. 'Tacking. The ship's sailing into the north-west wind at the moment.'

How did the old woman know that?

'How are we going to survive the whole way at a slope like this?' Tant Maijke called out in alarm.

'Oh, don't pretend you're stupid, Maijke van den Berg!' Tant Theuntjie berated her. 'Is this supposed to be the first time you've ever been on board a ship?'

'When last was I on a ship, do you think? A hundred goddamned years ago when I went aboard in the fatherland! I was young, I was hopeful. I believed their promises – Oh Gawd, we've had it!'

'Just let your body go slack, we'll tack a few more times before we turn out of the Bay over towards Rietvlei,' Tant Theuntjie said. 'Pieternella, stop clinging to that beam and get a grip on the pisspot before it slides over to my side!'

'I can't, the ship's going to topple over!'

'Oh, don't be ridiculous! Let your body go slack and let the ship roll you as it wills!'

She couldn't. She couldn't budge, she couldn't swallow, there was no spit in her mouth.

'Pieternella, get hold of the rope on the pisspot!'

She caught the rope between her toes. The entire hold was slanting; if she let go, she'd slide down into Tant Theuntjie. Clinging to the rib with one hand, she reached out with the other to get a hold on the rope. Before long the ship started creaking all over again and listed to the other side. Her body was suddenly squeezed between two wooden ribs while the pot began sliding over towards her like a snail on a slimy foot. She stopped the pot with her foot, pushing Maria's Pietertjie back to her mother at the same time. Tant Theuntjie was now sitting high while Tant Maijke hung on the ropes, wide-eyed, her body twisted halfway round. 'Oh Gawd!' she kept on crying out in anguish, 'Oh Gawd!'

The lantern was tilting alarmingly.

At the third tacking roll, Tant Maijke cried out in fright: 'When is it ever going to end?'

'It's a long way to Rietvlei if you have to tack back and forth,' said Tant Theuntjie, as if there was nothing to it.

She closed her eyes and abandoned herself to her fear. The world had suddenly been turned upside down and inside out: she was in a place where she shouldn't have been, and where she belonged was outside somewhere and passing away from her.

How many times hadn't she and her mother sat in the sun on the rocks on Robben Island, watching the ships in the distance as they started on their journeys out of the Bay. One, two, three – sometimes twelve. Gorged. Fully rested. In the winter months they usually had to turn just short of Rietvlei. A little way this side, a little way that side – like things trying to find their way. Always closer and closer to the old wreck.

Then her mother would yell: 'Keep going, keep going! Don't stop! Go and join your dead brother over there!'

They would laugh.

But always, just before the ships reached their dead brother, they would suddenly swerve out one by one and head for the open sea. Still tacking back and forth.

Sometimes, just as they were opposite the island, the wind would drop and the sails would flap like the wings of a fledgling losing heart on its first flight from the nest.

Then she and her mother would jump up and clap their hands.

One day the wind from the landward side dropped completely just as the ship with a full load of sheep on the deck was passing by the top end of the island. Just as though the island was holding up a giant hand in front of the wind. The sheep had to be offloaded to graze on Dassen Island because there was a drought at the Cape. It was summer, and hot. The wind died. The ship lay becalmed. Breathless. Dassen Island wasn't very far, but Dassen Island wouldn't float any nearer! The sheep were bleating. You couldn't hear them, the sea was making too much noise, but her mother said they would have bleated their throats hoarse by evening.

The ship dropped anchor to halt it from drifting. All day long ...

'Oh Gawd, stop it! We're going under!'
'Maijke, now just stop your panicking.'

The sheep ship lay unmoving.

Nearer and nearer, a small black dot was coming across the Bay. It was the *Bruidegom* with a load of fodder for the sheep. Twelve men rowing, and her mother fell over backwards laughing.

Rietvlei.

'Are we near Rietvlei yet, Tante?' she cried as the ship tilted them over again for the umpteenth time.

'Not yet.'

'Is it late yet?'

'The sun ought to be touching the water in the west by now. Lord knows when we'll get anything to eat tonight.'

Rietvlei. Somewhere out there the Chorachoquas' cattle and sheep would be wending their way towards the water to drink. Behind them the herdsmen in their skins, sticks in hand. Without haste because it was *thoukou* – the dark of the moon.

There wouldn't be any dancing tonight.

She didn't want to be here!

Her mother wouldn't have wanted her to be here either!

But the wooden goose kept floating onwards across the water with her in the dark hole down below. She saw the pictures before her eyes: the Mountain as it looked from the island. Lion's Head with its cloud cap on. Windberg-Devil's Peak. Castle, huge five-pointed Dutch kraal. The cottages. Whitewashed reed-roofed cottage with green shutters beyond the stables where Pieter would now be carrying in the firewood ...

'Wave the flies away, Pieternella!' Juffrouw Sophia would call several times a day.

On her last evening she had gone to help Pieter with the wood.

'Guess what?' he said.

'What?'

'They say there are terribly big tortoises on Mauritius. You like tortoise meat.'

'Tortoise meat's arse!' she shouted and threw a piece of wood at him.

He ducked. 'Pieternella, stop being angry at Father and Mother and me! We're not the ones who want you gone, believe me.'

She didn't believe him. She didn't believe anything.

'Are we opposite Robben Island yet, Tant Theuntjie?' she asked, clinging to the beam, her eyes still tight shut.

'We're not even at Rietvlei yet, stupid!'

When the sun sank behind the sea in the west, the shell bearers had finished for the day and they could walk back, tired and sore, to their sleeping quarters in the old sheep shed behind the Post House. Under a reed roof. Not a single window. Only a door that was locked with a big lock at night after evening prayers and supper. Sealskins stretched between four poles for beds; sealskin screens like rigid barriers between the beds.

Her mother never slept in the convict quarters when she was banished. Only in the Post House.

And always, in her remorse after she had been very drunk, she would tell them about the churlish Commandeur who had written, in ink, on paper, that she, Eva, was a skilful and good Post House wife on Robben Island. Their father had read it out to them with his own mouth.

'The day a boorish man says you're good, you can take it as true. I'm telling you.'

'Yes, Mamma.'

The watcher on Fire Hill would see them zigzagging as they tried to leave the Bay. He'd be sitting under his shelter of planks with the firewood beside him, ready for lighting. The Company's latest stinginess law laid down: no more tarred wreaths to be lit for smoke signals by day, no more wood fires at night. They cost too much. If a ship wanted to know how to reach the island's anchorage at night, it could ask for it with a cannon shot. If it was still astray, it could fire a second shot to ask for a fire to be lit in front of the Post House as well. Best would be for it to wait outside on the open sea till daylight ...

'There we are!' Tant Theuntjie called out when the ship came out of the next roll. The heaviest one. 'I think we've just turned away from Rietvlei for our run for the open sea.'

'My whole body's just one purple bruise, I tell you. I'm in a very bad way.'

'That's because you keep resisting, Maijke! As soon as we're away things will be better because then we'll have the wind behind us. But whether we're going to get anything in our stomachs tonight, I don't know. They're not going to be able to light a fire. With zigzagging like this, the water usually rushes back and forth across the foredeck in streams.'

'What if Salomon washes overboard, Tante?'

'Bart will show him where to hold on.'

'Which way are we heading now, Theuntjie?' asked Maria. She didn't sound scared, just disheartened.

'Straight for the open sea.'

That meant that the sand dunes at the Duintjies lay to the left of the ship's nose. The three-man gallows on the highest point. Janvos in his grave not far from there.

Mynheer Van der Byl went with her and Jacobus and Salomon to Janvos's funeral. Not really a funeral. Just a hole. Because Janvos had never wanted them to give him Christian blood, even though he did sometimes come and sit in the doorway when Mynheer was reading from the Bible.

Mynheer Verhage was also at the funeral. Janvos worked mostly for Mynheer Van der Byl, but sometimes the Church sent him to work for Mynheer Verhage as well.

Mynheer Van der Byl was good to Janvos. Sometimes, when he went to pay over Janvos's hire to the Church Council, he would say that the slave needed a new pea-jacket or blanket, he'd worked hard and faithfully. Better than most Dutch menservants.

Whenever she'd been sitting beside Janvos as he ate his meals or sawed wood, Juffrouw Sophia would say afterwards it was not proper for a young girl to sit chatting to a slave. 'Janvos has a good heart for a slave, Pieternella, but I don't think you should get so close to him.'

'He doesn't stink.'

'I didn't say he did. Besides, that's a nasty word. Nice girls don't talk like that.'

One day she was sitting beside Janvos again. She asked: Janvos, where are your mother and father? He said: Far across the sea on an island. Don't you long for your mother and father? No, he said, longing is a snake in your head that you have to pluck out, else longing will make you desert or pine away till you die. Pass the chisel.

'Janvos, is it true what Jacobus says, that all the money you earn is given to the Church to pay for our board and lodging?'

'Yes.'

'Do you wish us dead?'

'No.'

'Why not?'

'I promised the Master. He was my mother and father.'

'And Bart Borms? You spent a long time as a slave on his fishing boat.'

'We never spoke.'

Before there were many slaves at the Cape, most of them were bought from the captains of the homeward-bound fleet and other important people. Slaves were not allowed in the fatherland; white people had to do the work themselves. That's also how Oom Bart got Janvos.

'What do you want most, Janvos?'

'That you all grow up nice and obedient so that the Master won't come back and say I didn't look after you.'

'Do you still believe my dad will come back?'

'I can't always keep that feeling fixed in my heart any more.'

'What do you want most for yourself?' Like when you want to give somebody something because you feel sorry for him. Your little mirror, perhaps.

'Shoes,' he said, 'or a red cap like the farmers wear.'

She waited till Mynheer had finished reading from the Bible that night, then she said: 'Mynheer, Janvos would really like a pair of shoes and a nice red cap.'

'My word!' he laughed. 'A slave with shoes on?'

'May one pray for shoes for a slave?'

'Pieternella!' Juffrouw Sophia stopped her. She was very pious. Though actually she wanted to laugh. You could see.

When next Mynheer went to pay over Janvos's money, he came back from the Fort with a pair of shoes *and* a red cap for Janvos. He was very pleased. The day they lowered him into the hole, the shoes stuck out at the bottom end of the canvas sheet and the red cap at the top. Mynheer Van der Byl said that was the way it had to be.

Then the Sick Comforter arrived to announce that Mynheer Van der Byl should not forget to bring Janvos's last earnings and that the Company had had to pay for the bottle of wine that Janvos had asked for on his deathbed.

'Theuntjie?'

'Yes, Maijke?'

'Why do I feel this ship is moving differently now?'

'We're on the open sea.'

'Why does my head feel so dizzy?'

'Don't be a nuisance, Maijke, there's no room here for getting sea-sick.'

'It's not seasickness, it's my head. A weird feeling.'

'It starts in the head. Pieternella, go up above and see if there is a fire in the galley. Ask if we're getting supper or not. I'm hungry.'

'But what if the ship swings round when I'm up on deck?'

'It's finished its swinging. Go and find out what's happening.'

It was pitch dark outside. Lanterns swayed from masts. When she climbed out through the hatch, the ship rolled under her and pitched her accidentally up against the first mast, which she had to cling to with both arms. She didn't dare take a single step farther. The mast creaked – it was going to snap! The ship kept pitching from one side to the other, as though something was lifting it up high and then dropping it down low again ...

There wasn't any fire to be seen in the galley at the front of the deck. She couldn't get there – she'd be killed on the way!

The figure of a sailor loomed up out of the dark. 'Sailor!' she called out in fright.

'Pieternella! What are you doing here?' It was Focke Janse's voice; there seemed to be a line of sailors at the water hatch.

'Oom, Tant Theuntjie wants to know if we're getting food?'

'No, you'll have to eat your own provisions. They sent me to tell you.'

'Oom, why is the ship rolling so?'

'It's on account of the swell that keeps overtaking us from behind and lifting us. You'll have to get used to it, it's going to carry on for a long time yet.'

'Where are we, Oom?'

'Almost directly opposite Hout Bay. Bart said I was to ask how you are all doing down there.'

'I don't know, Oom.' Don't go away. 'You haven't seen Salomon, have you, Oom? He's my little brother, the cook's boy.' She couldn't hear his reply, the wind was making too much noise in the rigging and in her ears. So was the sea. 'I can't hear!'

'He's somewhere down in the fo'c'sle. You'd better get back down into the hold.'

How? 'I'm frightened, Oom!'

'Of what?'

'The ship keeps pitching and rolling so, how am I going to get the hatch open again?'

'Give me your hand.'

His hand was like grace and mercy helping her down through the hatch.

Each one ate something out of her own bundle. On the floor.

Nailed in.

She struggled to swallow. It was as though all her fear had gathered in her throat. 'Why is it so noisy, Tant Theuntjie?' she asked.

'What do you think? How much seawater is running past us on either side of the ship?' talking with a chunk of bread in her cheek.

Tant Maijke kept putting her hand over her heart. 'I'm not feeling well, I tell you.'

'Eat. Get something in your stomach,' said Tant Theuntjie. 'And don't you get seasick, d'ye hear? Maria, wipe Daatjie's mouth.' She kept on talking and started quarrelling with Maria. 'It's not that I want to go poking my nose into your affairs, but if the Governor didn't say Ockert's two had to stay behind, we'd have had a fine time of it down here in the hold.'

Maria didn't reply.

Tant Maijke complained for the umpteenth time: 'People, I really don't feel well!'

'Have a swig of beer,' suggested Tant Theuntjie.

'You just don't understand, Theun. It's not just my body! On top of it all there's the heaviness in my heart from having my face trampled on by that impertinent Pieternella wench! Many a day, when no one at the Cape had a good word for her mother, I was the one who took her in and even fed her children. And look at the way I get treated now!'

'Pieternella, ask Tant Maijke's forgiveness.'

I won't.

'Pieternella, I'm talking to you!'

No. I can't swallow my food. The ship is creaking as if every plank is trying to break its nails.

'Hell's child, I'm talking to you!'

'I ask Tant Maijke's forgiveness.' Quickly. Anything. Just as long as they didn't talk to her! It was like being buried alive in a wooden hole; you couldn't dig yourself out, because then you'd drown because you couldn't swim!

Tant Maijke gave something like a cough but it wasn't a cough.

'Maijke!' cried Tant Theuntjie in fright.

'Pot!'

'Pieternella, pass the pot before it's all over the floor! Lord have mercy on us if she gets seasick! Pass her the pot!'

She crawled across the floor with the pot. Behind her Tant Theuntjie was shouting to her to push it in under the old woman's chin so she wouldn't miss. She'd already missed. Maria seized a cloth and cast it over the puke; it was one of Tant Maijke's towels. Pieternella grabbed the towel, dropped it in the pail of washing water, wrung it out, wiped up, wrung it out again. Oom Bart had said the floor was not to be wet!

The children went on crying.

Tant Theuntjie wouldn't stop scolding. 'It's because you wouldn't hold the pot the way I told you! Who do you think is going to sleep on that patch? Roll out her bedding so that she can lie flat! And the other beds, too.'

'Hatch, open a hatch, I'm going to faint …' pleaded Tant Maijke.

'Have you lost your mind, Maijke van den Berg?' exclaimed Tant Theuntjie, shocked. 'Do you want the whole ocean in this ship tonight and the Captain off his head?'

All night long. She slept, but didn't really sleep. Her hands did as Tant Theuntjie ordered: Wipe her face! Lift up her head! Take away the pillow under her head!

Meanwhile the ship went on climbing and rolling and plunging. Or perhaps it rolled first and then climbed? You got confused after a while. If only day would come so that she could go up on deck, even if it meant she had to hang on to a mast all day long! Anything. Just to get out.

Woodgoose was rolling them around in its belly. Time wasn't passing. Time had no end at all. No Castle bell to sound the hours of the night. Louder as day began to break.

It was terrible to be flogged. Terrible to be hanged. Or beaten to death.

To be caged in a wooden coffin, under the eyes and tongue of a cantankerous bitch and puking seasick old woman, was another kind of terrible.

She buried her head in the Hottentots-bedding mattress and ate the scents of the veld and the soil …

Someone came knocking on the door with a wooden spoke and roared, 'Awake!' beyond it.

'Pieternella, get up and go for the water! See that the bucket is properly rinsed.'

'Yes, Tant Theuntjie.'

'Hurry up! The pots have also got to be cleaned, they're just about running over!'

The deck hatch was open. It was still night. Cold, but it was a breath of fresh air. The ship didn't feel as if it was listing quite so much, it just went on rolling. The deck was wet, slippery – how do you get to the foremast without falling down?

Patches of lantern light.

'Use your hands, girl. Hold on and keep to the starboard side.'

'Where's that?' It was the jackal-haired man.

'Your writing-hand side. Better to walk on the higher side. Sheep's side.'

'Thank you, Mynheer.'

Grope. The ship's rail was damp under her hand ... sheep pen ... round the pen ... the sheep smelt of wet and piss ... lantern on the foremast. Sailors' bodies were pale yellow shapes as they wove through the light of the lantern without legs or feet. There was nowhere to hold on to to get across to the mast and the water hatch. Let down the bucket, drag it along like an anchor ... wait for the roll ... let go of the rail!

She couldn't help it, she grabbed hold of the back of the jerkin on the last sailor in the row to stop her feet slipping. He turned round and asked if she wouldn't rather grab hold of the front of his trousers?

The others laughed.

'Pieternella?'

'Morning, Oom Bart. Tant Theuntjie asks if you could please rinse out the bucket. Tant Maijke puked a lot in the night.'

'Have you got a rope?'

'No, Oom.'

He took the bucket. 'Stay in your place. I'll get one quickly.'

Tant Theuntjie hadn't said who had to rinse the bucket.

When it was her turn at the water hatch, she herself called down who she was fetching water for and asked them please not to fill the bucket too full, it was too heavy. She'd rather come again. The Steward yelled back: *The man who is keen straight shoulders the load; the lazy young slob must be pricked with a goad!*

She'd knotted the beer pitcher in a corner of her shawl and half dragged, half carried the bucket downstairs.

'Has the thing been rinsed?'

'Yes, Tant Theuntjie.'

'Go and clean out the pots.'

'Yes, Tante.'

First pot. It stank. Too dreadful. Careful now ...

It was like climbing up the cliffs to the eagle's nest. She and Jacobus. You have to think with four heads, one for each hand and foot, else you come tumbling down and your mother says you're never to climb up there together again.

Her head told her to empty the pots over the lower side and let them down into the sea from there. Chicken-coop side. The pot was heavy. Grip with one hand, walk slowly ... first round the chicken-coop ... it smelt of feathers. One foot at a time ... out from under the upper deck ... a little way farther. Don't wind the rope round your arm, roll it once round your hand ... quickly tip the pot overboard.

Day was breaking. In the east the morning star was twinkling in its nightie.

Second pot.

'Roll up the beds, Pieternella. Not Maijke's, she'll have to stay down.'

Sweep up.

The best would be to go for the broom along the same way as she'd gone for the water. To see if she could see where Salomon was. Think. Slowly. Wait for the ship to come out of a roll. Small steps to the foremast, pick up the broom, use the broom handle as a walking stick to cross the deck to the galley.

Salomon was standing on a sawn-off tree trunk stirring a copper cauldron with a wooden spoon held in both hands. Round and round.

'Salomon?'

Beside him the cook was stirring another pot.

'Pieternella, I can't talk now.' He didn't look round. 'Go away.'

She was startled. Why did he sound so different? 'Do they beat you, Salomon?'

'No.'

It felt as if her heart had suddenly started beating inside her head. They've done something else to him. She could hear it. His 'no' was like a hand held in front of his mouth.

'Salomon?'

The cook finished knocking out his spoon and turned round. She told herself: Don't let him see you're frightened. Look him straight in the eye, his bulging swollen eyes, but speak to Salomon. 'The Captain is married to Tant Barbara Geens's daughter Maria,' she said quickly. 'He sent a message that we're to come and greet him so he'll know how we're doing.' She spoke the words loud and clearly. Lying. She didn't quite know why, but something in the cook's manner told her her lie had hit home.

She tried to keep her body still, not to start shaking. Her eyes warned him: I'll murder you with your own knife, Cook.

It was growing light.

She stood with the broom beside the sheep pen, waiting for her breath to stop racing. Suddenly she realised she couldn't see land anywhere. Nothing but sea. She shuddered and gripped the rail. Where was the land? The back end of the ship rose each time a swell caught up with it and rolled under its belly. Then sank again while the next swell rolled in.

Something inside her began to feel different. All the while it was growing lighter. At least she wasn't trapped down below in that wooden hole. No. Something else. Her fear was a fire that had burnt out because there was no more wood left inside her. It was her and the ship and the sea and the strangest furious rage rising within her to crush these skunks, all of them!

Except the worry about Salomon gnawing in her head ...

Wooden goose creaked. Masts creaked. Rigging. Wood-goose's wings billowed in the wind.

'Don't sweep over the wet patch!'

Think.

'I said: don't sweep over the wet patch!'

'No, Tante.'

'Answer properly when I speak to you.'

'Yes, Tante.'

'What were you doing, taking so long with the brooms?'

'I went to the galley to see how Salomon was.'

'You don't need anything in the galley. You keep out of the sailors' quarters, I don't want any trouble from you.'

'Yes, Tante.' Salomon. He had refused to look up. On purpose. 'Tante, the other man who came from Mauritius with you and Oom Bart and Oom Focke, the one with the coarse reddish hair ...'

'Daniel Zaaijman. What about him?'

'I just wanted to know what his name is.' Now she knew: Daniel Zaaijman. She stored the name in her head.

But Tant Theuntjie wasn't satisfied. 'Don't let me catch you getting randy about some old man, d'ye hear!'

'I just want him to keep an eye on Salomon. The boy isn't well.'

'Bart is looking after Salomon. He doesn't need anyone else.'

Tant Theuntjie was sitting flat on the floor pulling on her stockings when the sailor bumped open the door.

'Can't you wait for permission before you come barging in?' the old woman scolded, drawing down her skirt. 'There are women in this hold. We're getting dressed!'

'*Ag*, old dame,' he laughed coarsely, 'anything worth seeing that you ever had withered away a long time ago. I haven't got time to waste!'

'Scum!' Tant Theuntjie snarled at him. 'I'll report you!'

Tant Maijke struggled to get up. 'This is the end of me,' she groaned. 'My will's in my trunk – the little that's left after the Company robbed me.'

'Lie down, Maijke. This isn't your final hour! You need something in your stomach. Pieternella, come and help us open Maijke's chest to get her a clean petticoat.'

Stupid woman. 'If we undo those ropes now and the ship rolls, the chests will tumble down on to the table and Tant Maijke's head.'

'She's dirty. We've got to do something. Go and call Focke or Willem, they can come and help.'

'They're still scrubbing the decks, Tante. I'll tell them when I go for the food.'

'Don't stand there telling me what to do!'

I'm not standing, I'm sitting.

Up at the hatchway the whistle blew for prayers.

She made sure she was first up. She went and stood beside the sheep while the deck filled up.

She searched for Daniel Zaaijman's face …

Tant Theuntjie and Maria were clinging to the middle mast, the younger child on Maria's arm, the older one round her legs. Prayers were compulsory for anyone who could stand.

Second whistle.

The Captain himself was standing up at the rail to read the lessons and prayers.

Daniel Zaaijman was near the chicken-coop.

She would wait till after the Amen, when the breakfast whistle blew. She didn't know what she would say to him. Just knew she had to.

Caps off. Feet shifting under rocking bodies. Salomon was standing next to the galley, looking down at his feet.

Master Lamotius was standing beside the Captain. His wife and Cornelia and the child weren't with him.

'Our Lord, to whom the winds and the waves are obedient ...'

She didn't know what made her look up. She didn't know whether it had been there since first light. All she knew was that she had suddenly stopped breathing, because in the air above the ship, right above the topmost pennant, hung the biggest bird she'd ever seen in her life. Without moving a feather. Without falling out of the sky. Dead still above the ship it hovered, like a watcher with wings longer than any arms could stretch. Pure white, with just a thin black edge round the wings. Black tail tip.

Had her eyes tricked her? Did no one else see the bird?

No. They were praying.

Long reddish hooked beak. Made it look as though it was smiling. Jet black eyes. The most beautiful, the strangest thing!

Salomon did not join in the prayers.

Amen.

She found him with another man, rolling over and examining a barrel.

She waited. He picked up a mallet and a blunt-nosed chisel and tap-tap-tapped lightly along the edge of a hoop. As if he was trying to knock the hoop off.

When he noticed her, he came straight over.

'Yes, girl?'

'Mynheer?' How should she say what she wanted to say? 'Mynheer ...' Woodgoose felt like quicksand beneath her feet.

'What is it, Pieternella?'

He remembered her name! 'Mynheer, did you perhaps know Captain Frooij?' she asked quickly. He looked at her with sudden urgency, fright in his eyes.

'Why do you ask?'

The quicksand was going to swallow her up. 'Mynheer ...'

'Why do you ask me that? What is worrying you?'

He knew. He was clever. 'My little brother is the cook's boy.'

'I understand.' He knew. 'I'll keep an eye on him and have a chat with him.'

'Please, Mynheer.' Thankyouveryverymuch. She had to wipe away the

words. 'The biggest bird is hovering over the ship, not moving a wing
…'

'It's an albatross.'

'Mynheer?'

'It's actually come rather early. I was only expecting it tomorrow,
farther south.'

'Albatross?'

'Yes. Once it's chosen a ship, it stays with it. You'll see. Now go and
fetch your food.'

She stood in the queue but kept looking round. The bird had still not
flapped a wing; perhaps the wind was blowing it forwards?

The second man in front of her was Willem van Deventer. She tugged
at his sleeve from behind. 'Tant Maijke's sick. She wants to get into her
chest. Could one of you men please come and help make sure the chests
don't fall down?'

'I'll ask the officer of the watch to send Focke.'

'Thank you.'

Barley with prunes and bread. Tant Maijke wouldn't eat. All she would
do was lie on her mattress.

'You've *got* to eat something!' scolded Tant Theuntjie. 'Even if it's just
the bread. Sit up straight. Hold on to your plate.'

Maria was sitting in one corner on a quilt with her children. She was
very unhappy, you could tell.

'There's the biggest bird hovering above the ship.' She was actually
speaking to Maria, but Tant Theuntjie seized on it.

'Yes,' she said. 'It's a *malmok*.' Uninterested.

'Somebody said it was an albatross.'

'Same thing. When you've finished washing the bowl, you come back
here and you sit with Tant Maijke. D'ye hear me?'

No.

'I'm speaking to you, Pieternella!'

'I heard.'

'Good God, what possessed Bart Borms to take this child?' As though,
she, Pieternella, couldn't hear her.

'Why *did* you take me?' she asked pointedly.

The old woman looked down before she answered. 'Go and ask Oom
Bart.'

If the edges of the bird's wings are black …

'Pot!' groaned Tant Maijke.

'Pieternella, pass the pot and hold it properly so she doesn't miss and puke all over everything again! It must be the bread wanting out now.'

Sis. 'Yes, Tante.' Perhaps the bird's back is black ...

'Wipe her face.'

'Yes, Tante.' She had to get out of there. 'Maria's husband said he would send Focke Janse to help with the chests as soon as the table and things are out of the way.'

'We're waiting. Take and wash the basin, and don't make me come looking for you!'

8

She rinsed the basin in the tub on the deck just in front of the galley.

Salomon was sitting next to the galley, having his breakfast. Again he wouldn't look up when she tried to talk to him.

It was cold.

The bird was still floating above the rear mast. Even more beautiful. Whiter even than the little clouds in the clear blue sky. If it wanted to, it could fly away ...

Sailors all over, looking out across the water on all sides. Foulmouthed. They could walk firm-footed, hands free, no matter how badly the ship pitched and rolled. She was the only one who had to hold on and plot every step forward. The Bosun strode up and down with his whip. On top of the foremast, above the sails, there was a sailor sitting on a small platform. Probably to be able to see far into the distance.

The strangest thing was looking up, because then the ship seemed to be still while the little clouds went scudding past.

A sudden loud banging.

A sailor was beating on the foremast with a wooden spoke, beside him a man in black clothes that would actually have been smart if they weren't so creased. At his feet a wooden box decorated with brass scrolls. She didn't know the man but somewhere in her mind she recognised the clothes and the box ...

The sailor began to shout: 'Come forth to the mainmast, ye halt and ye blind, come for the Master to heal you and bind!'

The man was the Surgeon. Except that her father always wore a wide white apron as well. Then the sick would come to him and while Jacobus held the small basin to catch the blood, he'd quickly make a tiny cut in their arms or hands with a sharp shiny little knife. Sometimes her mother held the basin.

She remembered her father's long yellow locks hanging down to his shoulders. But the picture of his face wasn't firmly fixed in her eyes. Only sometimes, just for a moment.

A sailor with an injured foot came limping out from under the fo'c'sle. Behind him two more, holding on to each other. They looked like fever cases.

Red medicine for fever, she remembered.

'Pieternella, Theuntjie says you must come!'

Maria had stuck her head out of the back hatch to call her.

'I'm coming.' She didn't want to go below, it was too stuffy down in the hold. But she had to. 'The Master's up on deck,' she said. 'I'll help get Tant Maijke to him.'

'He can come and see her on her bed, if necessary. The Company's paying him,' said Tant Theuntjie bluntly.

Sit. Tant Maijke kept on groaning. Maria and the children were sitting between two of the ribs against the side. Maria was weeping quietly into a blue striped napkin. Tant Theuntjie was half sitting, half lying up against the opposite wall. She, Pieternella, had to sit beside Tant Maijke and keep wiping her forehead with the damp cloth.

Another thirty-seven days of this?

'Tant Theuntjie, did you know my father?' Just to break the nerve-racking silence.

'How could I not have known him? Good-looking man. Handsomest man at the Cape. Biggest arse-licker, too.'

She shouldn't have asked. Her mother used to say that the Dutch bitches were rotten with jealousy because he had married *her*. 'Perhaps we should give Tant Maijke a little of the barley and prunes that you have dished up for her.'

'No. Looks like she wants to sleep. Maria, the children's blood is going to curdle if they don't get some exercise. Take them up on deck and get them moving.'

'It's cold, Theuntjie.'

'Pieternella, cover Tant Maijke's shoulders. Don't you care at all?'

'I need to go up on deck to get my body moving, Tante.' Please.

'Sit down!'

'Please!'

'Sit! You're not going anywhere.'

This was another kind of terrible …

'Arse-licker, your father. Believed everything and did everything that came out of the mouth of our Noble Commandeur. When they didn't get the cattle out of the Hottentots' kraals as Wagenaer had hoped they would, he thought if he could get a female Hottentot into the Hollanders' kraal, the cattle would follow by themselves. He told your father: If you could have two babies by her, you could marry her, too.'

She should never have asked.

One thing she swore to herself, without the need of a Bible: she would not spend the rest of her life with Theuntjie van der Linde and Bart Borms!

She would run away.

Tant Theuntjie said: 'The Lord probably took your father away when He looked into the future and saw your mother getting up to her old tricks again.'

It was a lie.

Tant Maijke looked very poorly, she was having a bad time with her seasickness.

Mynheer Van der Byl came home one day and said he wondered who the rice smuggler was that the Company was so keen to catch. All the pots in the town were full of rice, cooking away, but very little was being bought from the Company's stores. Someone was smuggling. Wonder if it isn't Maijke? No, said Juffrouw Sophia, Maijke's been converted, she's changed her ways.

Soldiers dug up three sacks of rice in Maijke's sheep kraal, ten more sacks that she'd hidden somewhere else. Neatly got the boatmen bringing the rice ashore from the ships to steal it for her and throw it over the kraal wall during the Sunday sermon.

They flogged her and branded her on the back with the sign of the gallows. When they did that, they meant they really should have hanged you. Instead of hanging her, they banished her to Robben Island for three years and ordered the Post Holder not to give her any food at all. She could have rations sent to her from her own house on the mainland. The Company confiscated all her goods except her house and stables behind the new Castle. Jan Mostert, who had been lending her money for years, bought her farm and the Fiscal got the money.

Tant Maijke had to help cook and wash and scrub on the island.

So did her mother.

One day she, Pieternella, got a lift to the island on the *Schulp*. Janvos had to walk down to the quay with her. Juffrouw Sophia said that if a child wept for wanting to see how her mother was, it was a child's heart that was weeping.

But when a grown child wept because she didn't want to go aboard a ship, that didn't count!

Tant Maijke had also been on the boat. Along with the sweet potato runners and seedling cabbages.

The skipper said: Pieternella, sit with the seed-tray on your lap and hold on tight, the sea is rough. To Tant Maijke, he said: Your day has come, Maijke van den Berg, crying and swearing isn't going to help. When they reached the island, her mother was sitting on the stone in front of the Post House.

'Yes, Maijke,' she said, 'who could have known that you and I would be banished together? You for stealing and me for drinking. Have you brought me anything?'

'Cover Tant Maijke's feet, Pieternella.'
'Can't I just go up on deck for a breath of fresh air, Tante?'
'No. Sit.'

Her mother once died on the sea – and then came alive again.

Long ago. Before her father was the Master at the Cape.

The chief of the Dutchmen, Jan van Riebeeck, had her mother's uncle Autshumao held on Robben Island to stop him interfering with Hottentots who wanted to bring their livestock to barter at the Castle.

It was while her mother was living with Mynheer Van Riebeeck and his wife for the second time. Just one wife. Her uncle Autshumao had two wives. One was as deaf as a post. Her mother's uncle said: Eva-Krotoa, your ears are good. Listen carefully what this Hollander chief says. You understand their language very well. We must get them muddled and really afraid so that their ships will come and take them away. And send me rice and bread to the island.

One day her mother heard that the boat would be taking food for the shepherds and the shell carriers. And grass to plant, to make the island green. And a duiker ewe with a little one in her belly so that the island could have game to shoot.

This was the prelude to the story of her mother's dying. It was always Salomon's favourite. The story about the Hottentots' war against the Hollanders was the one Jacobus liked best.

102

The dying story: the sun was still high on the day the boat set off. A light breeze from behind filled the sails. On the island in the distance, the smoke from Fire Hill was blowing over backwards like a puffed-up bundle of pitch black curls. (Here her mother would usually light her pipe, with obvious enjoyment.) In a bag, the little ewe, its feet tied together, lay dead still.

Then – all at once – the wind seemed to gather force and shout in rage: Now I'm going to blow that boat with those rags on sticks right over the edge of the sea till it falls off the other side of the earth. The sail man took fright and jerked down the mainsail, the helmsman hung on to the tiller, her mother screamed: What's happening?

All they shouted was: Eva, hold tight!

The wind blew. The helmsman said: We're not going to be able to cross in front of the island to reach the sand bay on the side, the waves and the wind will capsize us. We'll first pass by and then try to make it through from the top end between the mainland and the island and reach Sand Bay that way. But for fear of the rocks he stopped too wide of the side of the island. The waves and the wind at the top end of the island were just as strong. He still couldn't risk cutting across the wind.

So the wind blew them clean past the island and right out to sea.

By nightfall no one could see either the mainland or the island.

All night long. The wind blew. Her mother said she was soon lying with her head on the little ewe in the bag, she could feel the animal's heart beating. The helmsman yelled: Puke over the side, Eva!

The whole of the next day.

When night fell, her mother felt death swimming alongside the boat like a big white duck. When day broke, the duck climbed over the side and she breathed her last.

The next thing she heard was the helmsman saying to a shell carrier from somewhere far away: Don't ask how far out the storm drove us. If the wind hadn't swung round, we'd have been blown into eternity. Give us a hand here. The little ewe is still alive but Eva's dead.

At that she got such a fright she came alive again.

Long afterwards the Commandeur told her mother he'd already written in his journal: The Lords' costly boat has perished.

Her mother always got confused with the Lord and the Lords. The Lords in Amsterdam were actually a bunch of important gentlemen: the Lords and Masters. The other Lord was up there in heaven.

They said if you died on board ship, they threw you overboard …

'Pieternella, what are sitting there sleeping for? Cover Tant Maijke's shoulders!'

'I'm not sleeping, Tante.' She had to get out of there! 'I just want to go and see how Salomon is ...'

'You're not going anywhere. Sit down. Wet her face again.'

Whenever she took the boat to visit her mother and the wind was blowing off the land she would be scared that they'd be blown past the island. But when the wind was blowing from across the sea, she was afraid they'd be driven on to the rocks ...

'Pieternella!' She nearly fainted when Oom Bart suddenly pushed open the door of the hold. 'You've got to come!'

'Has Salomon fallen overboard?' she asked in fright. That was her first thought. 'Has he, Oom Bart?'

'No. Lamotius wants to see you. He's waiting outside. Come!'

At that she panicked.

'What does he want to see her for?' asked Tant Theuntjie.

'I don't know. He simply asked if I was her guardian and told me to fetch her.'

'Most likely because of all her disobedience!' declared Tant Theuntjie rudely.

The air outside was crisp and clear.

The Lamotius man was standing beside the barrel where the jackal-haired man was tapping a hoop more firmly into place. *That* completely terrified her. She must be in trouble. The jackal-haired man must have blabbed about her asking if he knew Captain Frooij. Juffrouw Sophia had said she never wanted to hear the name Frooij in Pieternella's mouth again. That was the silent sin that not even grown-ups spoke about.

She would say she knew nothing about Captain Frooij, that Pieter van der Byl had said ...

Lamotius turned round. 'Ah, Free-burgher Borms!' he called out cheerfully.

'Greetings, Commander!' Oom Bart called out even more cheerfully. 'I hurried straight off to fetch my ward as soon as I received your message. Her name is Pieternella, Commander.'

'Free-burgher Borms,' said the man with a chuckle, 'I am only the Commander *Designate*. I shall not be the Commander until I have been duly sworn in on the island. Address me as Monsieur Lamotius.'

'For me and for the other free-burghers on the ship, you are already our honoured Commander, our only hope of salvation.'

'I shall not disappoint you.'

She stood there quietly. The man looked her up and down, then turned to Oom Bart again and said: 'Thank you, Free-burgher Borms.' As if to say: Dismissed.

'It was my privilege, Commander. I shall hasten back to my duties now – if you will excuse me.' He gave an elegant bow and left.

She just stood there.

'Kindly come with me,' said the Commander Designate, walking on ahead, through the forbidden door under the poop deck. She was sure he could hear her heart beating. *Thud-thud-thud.*

A short passage, with doors closed on either side. Light. A door straight ahead. The pretty lady was sitting at a real table with the finest real chairs. Against the wall there was a cupboard with small doors of clear glass in tiny frames, just like little windows. Behind her, on the seaward side, were *three* proper windows with clear glass in them! Almost like a room in a house, but smaller. And the roof was lower. In the cupboard were porcelain plates and earthenware pots and salt and pepper sets and shining jugs with lids. More shining jugs with knives and forks and spoons stuck upright in them. Books. Pictures in frames on the wooden walls. The prettiest porcelain-like pot covered with porcelain pictures was just standing on the floor. The ship rolled but the pot didn't fall over. Was it full of sand?

'Girl,' said the Commander Designate, taking his place at the table. There was an iron ring in the floor; underneath the table was a rope to fasten it to the iron ring. Probably for when the ship pitched badly. 'Petronella.'

'*Pieter*nella, Mynheer.'

'*Monsieur.* Do you have any experience with children?'

'Yes, Monsieur. My little brother, he's called Salomon and he's the cook's boy.' Don't! 'Yes, Monsieur.'

'Good. This is my wife, Juffrouw Margaretha d'Egmont – address her as Juffrouw Margaretha.'

'Yes, Monsieur.' The lady looked exhausted.

'Our child minder is very ill. She tried bravely to carry on with her task, but she is too sick. Seasick. After consultation it has been decided that you and she should change places until she has recovered.'

'Yes, Monsieur.' Could she have heard correctly? Tant Theuntjie would have a fit ...

The lady smiled. 'It would be good if you could stand in for her. I assume you are perfectly well?'

'Yes, Juffrouw Margaretha.' Her mother had taught her never to grovel before a Hollander. If you grovel, you make it easier for them to tramp on your back. But she would willingly bow to this Dutch lady, just as long as she could stay up here. 'I am very well.'

The monsieur stood up. 'Juffrouw Margaretha and the cabin boy will inform you of the necessary rules governing this section of the ship.'

Then he left.

'In the evenings, after supper, and after the cabin has been cleared,' the lady explained, 'a screen will be placed in that corner for you. Our little daughter, Andrea, sleeps with us in the sleeping cabin next door.'

Tant Theuntjie was going to have a fit ...

'Where is Cornelia, Juffrouw?' This was better than dreaming.

'I have allowed her to rest for a while in our cabin,' said the lady. 'Monsieur will arrange for her to be assisted to the steerage deck; we are extremely sorry for her. Come and greet her and then go and fetch your things. It is a pity that her clothes will not fit you – Monsieur likes orderliness.'

Cornelia was lying on a straw mattress on the floor like a black mountain of dough, shoes on her big feet.

9

Better than dreaming. She couldn't believe it.

She was lying in Cornelia's place on her own Hottentots-bedding mattress, behind a screen that a sailor had come and put up in the front cabin. Like a thin wooden wall. She couldn't sleep, she didn't want to sleep.

She wanted to *see* the dark. When she turned on her back, there was the reflection of the three framed glass windows. Not stars. Sea spray had made the glass too grey. Under the windows was a bench with something like a mattress that you could sit on.

Much smarter windows than Jannetjie Ferdinandus's one old glass window that she got off a ship. It didn't fit properly in its hole, and one of the little panes got smashed in the struggle to make it fit, so now it had three glass panes and one linen one soaked in train oil that Janvos had fitted into the hole for her.

One day when one of the soldiers of the mounted guard rode past on his horse, stones shot up under the horse's hooves and another glass pane was shattered. Jannetjie yelled at the sentry on the nearest bastion at the Fort: Did you see how that horse of the Company's broke my window?

The sentry shouted that he hadn't seen anything.

Now Jannetjie had two linen squares and two glass panes in her window, so most of the time she kept the shutters closed.

One evening, one of Barbara Geens's sailor guests told a story about when he was on board a ship coming back from the East. There were two horses tethered on the deck, specially sent to the Cape to hunt Hottentots. But they found themselves becalmed in the middle of the ocean and there they lay. And lay. Their food was all salty and their thirst past bearing. The water levels in the barrels were dropping. The Captain ordered the Steward: Don't make the tankards more than half full. That was hardly more than a cupful. The sailors grumbled, asking: What about the bloody horses that have to drink their fill day after day just to be kept alive? Why don't we just throw them overboard? The Captain said the horses were urgently needed at the Cape, the Hottentots were in revolt, he had to do everything possible to keep them alive.

Eleven sailors' corpses went overboard before one of the horses died and the wind began to blow again.

Luckily there were no horses on the *Boode*. That would have caused trouble on deck, especially during prayers and scrubbing. And no elephants, either! Once an English ship had docked in Table Bay; the Captain asked only to have his barrels filled with drinking water. They filled his barrels for him, friendly enough, and off he sailed, straightaway – without even firing a single cannon shot in gratitude or greeting. Churlish. The Governor wrote to the Lords in Amsterdam, giving the name of the ship so they could inform the skipper never to expect such a friendly reception at the Cape in future.

Eventually a letter came back. From the Captain. He said he was very sorry; it was never his intention to be discourteous; it was just that he didn't dare fire a cannon because he had an elephant on board. An Indian one. For the English king.

She was allowed out on the forbidden upper deck.

Starboard was right; sheep-pen side. Larboard left; chicken-coop side. The lookout's little platform high up on the mast was called the crow's nest. Anthonie was teaching her. He was the cabin boy and about the same age as Salomon. Pity about the ugly name, though.

Yes. But if a storm blew up, the waves got so high the lookout had to

107

duck or he'd bump his head on the sky!

Really?

The helmsman – no, the tilllerman – who has to stand beside the tiller that steers the ship gave a great belly-laugh and told Anthonie to tell her about the stinking fright in the lookout's trousers when a storm started thumping him from *below*!

Juffrouw Sophia had warned her they were loud and silly.

An ordinary seaman was hanging on to the tiller behind the helmsman: one man was too light to steer such a heavy ship. In a storm it took up to four to hold on and push, so Anthonie said.

For supper they had leftover roast chicken and rice with currants and carrots and cabbage. And they shared what was left of the jam fritter, too. Lovely!

Anthonie took a sip of wine on the sly and wanted her to take one, too. But she said no.

Pieternella, swear on the Bible and by the Sun and the Moon and all the eyes of the dead who are looking down on you from the stars that you will never allow a single drop past your lips.

I swear, Mamma.

Secretly though, she opened Juffrouw Margaretha's pretty little glass perfume bottle and sniffed it. It smelled like the tiny blue flowers in Juffrouw Sophia's garden – but sweeter.

She would lie on her tummy among the little flowers and Juffrouw Sophia would say: Do you like them, Pieternellatjie?

Yes, Juffrouw.

She didn't mean to long for home. She didn't have a home any more. Just a ship-house.

It was better than dreaming.

Foremast in front. Mainmast in the middle. Mizzenmast behind. Poop deck steerage hold was where Tant Maijke and Cornelia were probably lying puking. Another steerage hold under the fo'c'sle. The sailors' privy was right at the front on the ship's prow so that the sea could wash away all the muck. As long as Salomon didn't get knocked off there.

Yards were the cross-bars on the masts that the sails hung from.

From the poop deck you had a good view down on to the galley. Salomon knew she was up there, he'd waved to her twice. He was looking better.

Somewhere in her head a plan was swelling like a fig on a twig; as soon as it was ready for picking she'd lay it at the feet of the jackal-haired man.

The last thing Cornelia said on the morning that the two sailors held her arms and helped her down the narrow passageway was that she'd be coming back. That Pieternella was not to think she could just come and steal her job.

The last thing Tant Theuntjie said when she went down to fetch her things was that she would go and tell Lamotius with her own lips that she wasn't going to be stuck down below without any help, like some beggarly pauper! In any case he was still only an ordinary *Seur* – a long way yet from being Commander.

She couldn't care what he was. Until Cornelia came back or Tant Theuntjie came up and caused trouble, she was going to enjoy every turn of the hourglass.

Ship time was hourglass time. Not clock time, like Mynheer Van der Byl's pocket watch. Nor Castle time. The hourglass was in a small wooden cage on the deck beside the First Mate. Every half-hour, when the sand had run out, they stuck a wooden peg in a board full of little holes and turned the glass round again. The other thing in the cage was a compass.

The cabin boy knew about everything. Or nearly everything. He slept in a gangway next to the Captain's cabin. Actually, it was where he served out the food into the bowls before taking it through to the stateroom, and where he did the washing up.

He said the Lamotiuses had taken over the First Mate's cabin and that the First Mate was highly annoyed because he'd had to move down below decks. The Surgeon's cabin was next door to the Lamotiuses'.

Andrea slept beside Juffrouw Margaretha in a narrow wooden cradle with a little straw mattress. Only just enough space. The cabin was very small, but the hatch was sometimes left open during the day. A sailor would go out and close it in the late afternoon.

And the child was the prettiest little girl baby you could imagine. Little pink cheeks, blue eyes – a real little doll. Tiny clothes just like a grown-up's. A cap with tiny beads, and points over the little forehead and ears, just perfect. Tiny shoes. Even though she couldn't walk yet.

She, Pieternella, didn't have to go for the food. That was Anthonie's job. But she did have to fetch the Lamotiuses' water.

First Anthonie spread a snowy white cloth and laid the table with the porcelain plates and knives and forks and spoons out of the cupboard against the wall. Table napkins. The prettiest wine glasses. A pot-bellied wine flask with a broad flat base; let the ship roll, the wine flask would not topple over.

And Anthonie fetched the food from the cook himself, because the important people got much nicer food. The Captain's table: the First Mate and the Surgeon and another man and the Lamotiuses all had their meals with the Captain.

Everyone on board had to eat at the same time except her and Anthonie. They ate later.

While the Captain and his table were having their meals, she would look after Andrea in the Lamotiuses' cabin. Wipe her down with warm water which she had to fetch specially from the galley. Dress her in her little nightie and put on her sleeping cap. Wrap her little shawl round her and tie the tassel-ends together. All so lovely.

'You're amazingly skilful, Pieternella,' Juffrouw Margaretha said early in the afternoon.

After lunch she could go out on the top deck – the poop deck – while the baby was asleep. Up a narrow stepladder out of the cabin to the upper hatch. Then you were out on the deck. High up. The men at the wheel stood beside the tiller in the middle of the deck. You weren't allowed to get in the way.

She couldn't yet walk without holding on. She didn't know how the sailors managed it.

Anthonie was sitting in the sun beside the rail, mending his clothes.

The bird hung in the sky above.

She shouted to the bird: 'Look, I live up here now!'

The front tiller man standing with the beam under his arm, laughed. 'Were you just talking to that bird?' he asked, amazed.

'Yes.'

He laughed some more. 'Has it got ears?'

'Yes. Under its feathers, on the side of its head.' She'd simply thought it out for herself. Where else would a bird's ears be?

'Oh, I see you're a person of learning, too!' He was deliberately teasing her. She could tell. It was like a game.

'Oh yes. I went to school at the Cape. I can read and write and do sums and sing psalms *and* I've been instructed in Piety so that I won't be a blind heathen like a Hottentot. Only half of me is blind heathen.'

The man laughed himself helpless. 'Oh really?' he said.

After a while she asked him: 'Mynheer, how do you know which way to make the ship go?'

'It's got its own eyes, girl. Just like the bird's got its own ears!'

Just teasing.

It was the most beautiful bird. Such gentle eyes, with tiny pitch-black feather-stripes for eyelashes.

'Where does the bird go at night, Mynheer?'

'It sits sleeping in the galley, nice and snug.'

'Helmsman is lying to you, telling you a lie-joke,' Anthonie called across from the rail. 'Skipper says the bird catches its food at night – any fish that swims up to the surface.'

'What does an albatross's call sound like?'

'Albatross only talks in his nest when he has something to say to his wife,' the helmsman laughed. 'Keeps his trap shut while he's in the air. That way he doesn't get into trouble.'

Then he opened the wooden cage and turned the hourglass over …

A swell rolled up from behind and lifted the ship; as it rolled underneath them the ship dipped down again. How many swells are there in the sea?

Cornelia should please not get better soon. Anthonie said you could stay seasick for ten days – after that you didn't get sick again. Usually about five days. Some people never stopped being seasick …

Shipping lesson.

Sailors are divided into watches. Each watch is on guard and must keep alert for any danger; after four hours, they are relieved. The rest clean the ship and take care of the sick sailors. When the yards have to be turned, or when there is a storm, then everyone has to leap into action and help. There is no resting till after supper.

Anthonie says storms are terrible.

The Bosun is actually the Porvostmarsel – was that the right word? – the man in charge of prisoners. But if she thought *he* was rude, said Anthonie, she should wait till she met the Second Mate. Lubbert. Always wanting to show everyone he's not afraid of anything or anyone. Even curses heaven during a storm.

But don't think the helmsmen can simply steer wherever they like; the First Mate tells them which way. Or the skipper does. When the First Mate is resting, the Second Mate takes over.

Salomon wasn't a proper sailor.

She was glad they'd never banished her mother to Mauritius. She couldn't have stayed alive for thirty-eight days on the sea.

She wondered why Sara, Barbara Geens's daughter, married Adriaan van Brakel the carpenter. She'd have done better to marry the jackal-haired man, he's so kind and strong. Sara's wedding cap had had little reddish straw flowers all round the brim. Awfully pretty. Anthonie said one day he wanted to be a skipper like Captain Wobma. He only had to look at a sailor and the man trembled to the soles of his feet. He never shouted.

Better than the best dream. She didn't even want to think about the steerage hold down below. *That* was another dream.

Swells come up, swells pass by ...

She woke up with Anthonie tugging at her foot.

'Get up, Pieternella, we've got to fetch the water!'

She bounced upright, she was wide awake, she was on the top deck.

'Take your shawl.'

It was terribly cold outside, she was sure her ears were going to freeze off, and her nose, too. The ship seemed to be listing more to the chicken-coop side. Anthonie could walk with his hands free but she still had to go the long way round, groping her way past the sheep pen. It was the coldest she'd ever been in her life. Something about the ship really did feel different, it wasn't rolling nearly as much any more. It felt almost as if there was fine rain in the air, but it wasn't rain – there were stars in the sky ...

She thought it might be the wind that was blowing differently. Perhaps she was just imagining it. It wasn't a sailor standing in front of her in the dark at the water hatch, it was someone in a dress. Maria! With the bucket from the hold. She couldn't tell why but she suddenly wanted to turn and run and hide. She hadn't wanted Maria to come and fetch water; it felt like it was *her* fault.

'Maria?'

'Pieternella.'

She sounded as if her teeth were chattering. 'I didn't mean you to come for water. I'm sorry.'

'It's not your fault.'

'How is Cornelia?'

'Poorly. She cries and cries about her work. And Theuntjie had to go out last night to empty the pots and rinse them out.'

Juffrouw Sophia often said you must never be glad when someone else suffers. It was just that she was glad that Maria didn't have to wash out the pots as well.

'And Tant Maijke?'

'Bad.'

'Who fetches the food?'

'Me.'

'I'm sorry.'

'You don't have to be. What's it like up there?'

'Fine. Do you think Cornelia's going to get better soon?'

'Not very soon. At least Maijke isn't puking quite so much any more, but she's really very sick.'

The Lamotiuses' bucket was just as big as the steerage one, but she thought they put less in it. And no beer.

She called down the hatch to ask about the beer. He shouted up: Top dogs don't drink sour beer, you stupid thing!

Breakfast was thick slices of smoked pork and eggs with onions, and bread and sweet biscuits with butter. There wasn't any buttermilk left for her and Anthonie to share.

The hot water for the baby could be fetched from the galley only after breakfast.

Anthonie said everyone below decks got fish four days a week, bacon on two days and meat just once. With barley or beans or peas. Prunes for breakfast, to stop their guts clogging up. And hard tack.

Sailors were always hungry. They'll catch that bird out of the sky yet, just wait and see.

The bird wouldn't allow himself to be caught.

That's what *you* think. They put a hook in a little fish, tie the fish to a length of plank and drag it along behind the ship on a long line. The bird dives down *Swoop!* at the fish, hooks its beak, and they've got him. Just wait, you'll see.

No!

Then they hang it by the neck in the galley, cut all round the crop to loosen the skin, and pull off the skin whole, feathers and all, like taking off your trousers. Easily as much meat as six or eight fowls.

She wondered if the Captain could stop them catching the bird ...

It was cold. Terribly cold.

She rolled up her mattress and quilt and tied them up in Anthonie's narrow passageway, as he'd shown her.

'Don't forget the pot.'

She had to clean out the Lamotiuses' pot and tidy their sleeping quarters. *But not before the door had opened!* Why not? Ship's law. Never open a closed door.

The funniest of all was the privy. She just couldn't help laughing. Top people only use a pot at night. For daytime there were small steps leading down the side of the stateroom to a wooden hutch painted green. There was a narrow green bench with a round hole in it, and a wooden lid. In the hole was an iron bucket. At first she thought that the sea was underneath the hole, that your bum hung out over the water, because the hutch stuck out from the ship. There was even a little glass window as well, decorated with carved wooden curls. And she was allowed to use it, too. So weird, hanging out over the water.

It was Anthonie's job to clean out the iron pot. And the Captain's night pot, too. All the pots up there were made of porcelain. The Lamotiuses' one was blue and white and breakable.

She wanted to be a top person one day and have a porcelain chamber pot.

Morning prayers were not nice. She had to stand in front with Andrea, holding on to the rail. When she looked down she saw Tant Theuntjie and Maria and the children down in the waist, and when Tant Theuntjie looked up her face was taut with fury.

Daniel Zaaijman, the jackal-haired man, must have spoken to Salomon because he didn't look so crestfallen. Or perhaps to the cook man. When she went to ask for the baby's hot water earlier that morning, Salomon was plucking a freshly slaughtered fowl. 'Salomon, are you well?'

'Yes, Pieternella. I see you're in Cornelia's place.'

'Yes. It's lovely, I hope she stays sick the whole way.'

The bird was still floating above the ship. He was made of feathers.

Her mother hated horses. Always said they were foreign things that came on the ships to frighten the Hottentots. Before the horses came, no Dutchman could run down a Hottentot.

Mynheer Van Riebeeck had a stump-tailed horse that he sometimes used to frighten the Hottentots. But that horse couldn't run more than a short distance before it grew faint. After that it would have to rest in the stable for days.

She felt like going out on to the upper deck for a bit, but there was something happening on the ship because both the Captain and the First Mate were standing with the helmsmen, looking into the wooden cage. They had rolled out a thick paper and were talking very seriously ...

The yards with the sails had been turned skew and the wind and the swells were now coming more from the side.

Anthonie said it was because the wind was turning; if the ship didn't swerve aside before nightfall, they would run into the icebergs down south.

Icebergs?

Like mountains of hardened snow. Before they got there the ship would have to be turned towards the rising sun.

Is that when you get to Mauritius?

No. First southwards, like now – he pointed with his arms – then east, then north.

It sounded like rather a roundabout route, like groping for your way.

Anthonie said you didn't just sail and sail and suddenly reach the island. Oh no. It was more like searching for a rock sticking up out of the wide open sea. Only Captains and First Mates knew how.

Or perhaps Second Mates did, too.

Juffrouw Margaretha had given her an extra shawl to cover her head too, when she had to go out. And Juffrouw Margaretha went for a walk every afternoon. *A walk.* All along the edge of the lower deck. Round and round. So that her blood would keep moving, she said.

Then she showed her, Pieternella, how to rub Andrea's little legs and arms and back so that the baby's blood would also keep moving. On the bench under the glass window in the stateroom.

The Captain came down from above, greeted her and tickled the baby's chin.

Then he said: 'Years ago you were a foster child of Juffrouw Barbara Geens's, weren't you?'

'Yes, Mynheer.' Or should she have said Captain …

'I gather your young brother is also on board, the cook's boy?'

That gave her a nasty fright. 'Yes, Mynheer.' I swear, Mynheer, I didn't say a word, Mynheer.

Then he left. Luckily.

The jackal-haired man wouldn't have said anything, would he?

Long after it was dark she wanted to go out and see whether the bird flew above the ship at night, too.

The folk at the Captain's table were all still eating, Juffrouw Margaretha had come into the sleeping cabin to check that all was well with Andrea, so Pieternella asked if she might go up on deck for a moment. The child was fast asleep. She wanted to look for the bird.

'Just for a little while, Pieternella, and not through the stateroom.

Take the companionway out of the waist.'

'Yes, Juffrouw Margaretha.'

The sickle moon hung in the west. Like a broad smile in the sky, just for her. It was dark, but the stars were shining brightly – everything was so clear. Not a veld moon, not a dancing moon. A sea moon. A water moon. A bird moon. Her throat ached from swallowing back the tears of longing for her mother. She was sad, too, because the world was nothing but water, and she was on a ship that just went on sailing – where to, she didn't know.

It was fine up on deck; it was just that she didn't want to be on the ship at all. That she was scared of Mauritius.

She wanted to turn back, to fetch the potshards in her bundle so she could show them to the moon, but just then the man who'd been standing beside the helmsman in the middle of the deck came asking if she didn't feel like a quick fuck. It was the Lubbert fellow with his grinning yellow teeth. She got such a fright she nearly fell down the companionway in her haste to get away.

10

She didn't know what a desert looked like. Only what her mother had said other people had told her who had walked very far to go and see for themselves. Far beyond the Namaquas – whom her mother wasn't allowed to mention.

A desert is just sand.

The sea is a water desert. Just water.

How the Captain could tell which way the ship had to go over the wide ocean, she didn't know. That morning Anthonie said that they had swung eastwards during the night and were now heading straight into the sun. The sun did come up over the ship's nose that morning. Maria had again come for the water and said Tant Maijke was a little better but that Cornelia was still very sick.

And just when she was learning to go short distances without holding on, the ship seemed to be pitching and rolling worse than ever. Some time in the night they had straightened the sails a little and the waves seemed to be coming at them from behind again.

All day long the sea and the sky were almost equally blue. But the sheep were restless, ears pricked, heads in the air ...

Andrea had been troublesome in the night, so Juffrouw Margaretha had woken her to look after the child so that she could get some rest. Monsieur had lit the lantern. His sleeping cap was made of the same stuff as his nightshirt. He had long white feet, like things that had never been in the sun.

So she sang quietly to the child, lay her down on the Hottentots-bedding mattress and tickled her back. She chortled too prettily!

Some time during the night someone must have come to fetch the child because when she woke up the lantern had been blown out and the baby was gone.

After breakfast Juffrouw Margaretha said she was not to put the child down on her mattress again. 'Go down to the galley and ask for more hot water, then wash her cap and nightie and bootees thoroughly with soap. The Captain has granted permission for them to be hung out to dry in the rigging.'

They looked like children's tiny flags when they were hung out.

But she waited for her moment. When they took the child out into the sun a little later, she told Juffrouw Margaretha that Hottentot's-bedding didn't have lice.

Oh, she said.

The first sign of a storm brewing was an abrupt burst of wind that shook the ship and made the sails go *whup, whup.* Suddenly there were sailors everywhere, hanging on ropes or scrambling up the rigging to shorten sails. The wind came rushing through the shrouds as through thousands of reeds. Whitecaps appeared all over the water and made the ship list to the sheep-pen side while the spray kept blowing over the chicken-coop side. Luckily the child's washing was on the sheep side.

The sheep stood with their backs to the wind.

By bedtime that night all her fear was back and her whole body was full of it. She asked Anthonie in the passageway: 'Are we perishing?'

'Not yet.'

The sailor had not come to put up the screen for her to sleep behind. She lay down but kept rolling off the mattress. After the umpteenth time she drew the mattress over her and lay on the bare boards. She couldn't tell if it was the cold or her fear that made her shiver so. The noise and the rolling and the creaking seemed to be all round her. She heard the child crying above the noise of the wind and crawled to the

Lamotiuses' cabin but the door was closed. And there was a bundle lying in the passageway; she thought it was Anthonie.

Wilder and wilder, right through the night.

At rising time Anthonie came to say she had to wind her clothes tightly round her head and body and hold on to him so they could fetch the water.

There was no outside. Nothing but water and wind and rain like fine hail in your face, and all of it was a dense white haze with dark bits of masts and rigging and creatures in between. Perishing wasn't quick, perishing was slow – as if the storm first wanted to torture everyone on to their knees. Each time she fell Anthonie would grab hold of her shift and help her up again. Everywhere bodies were bumping into other bodies and clutching at one another – one of them was Maria. Somebody had actually lit a fire in the galley, she couldn't believe it!

'There's no water coming in over the fo'c'sle,' Anthonie shouted in her ear as he held on to her in the water queue.

Salomon, where was Salomon?

In the dark it looked as if the ship no longer had sails. Perhaps they had been ripped off and blown away in the night?

Sailors were running like drunken shades through the ghostly gleam of the swinging lanterns, their eyes pieces of dead glass in wet faces under sopping caps. Voices shouting orders …

'Pieternella!' It was Maria. 'Things are pretty bad down in the hold.'

The wooden griddle-thing wasn't over the hatch, but there was a fixed wooden door instead. A sailor grabbed the bucket out of her hand and lowered it hastily. Back it came. Everything in a haze of rain and wind – against her body, in her eyes, her teeth that wouldn't stop chattering. Somewhere in that hell she'd lost Anthonie …

She started half carrying, half dragging the bucket across the deck when a hand gripped her forearm and helped her to the door under the poop deck. It looked like the Captain's face.

The Surgeon's cabin door was open; the feet of the man whose head he was bandaging stuck out into the passageway. Blood was seeping through the bandages. Another sailor was sitting on the floor, cradling his arm, his face twisted with pain. She stepped over their legs and as the ship rolled she fell against the wall, came upright again, stumbled once more and spilt some of the water over the man.

She didn't want to be on the ship when it sank!

Someone had already rolled up her mattress and lit a second lantern. Juffrouw Margaretha was on her knees laying a long sandbag in a circle round the child on the floor. The entire ship was banging and creaking as though some demonic force had caught it and was shaking and shivering it.

'Put on some dry clothes!' Juffrouw Margaretha shouted above the noise.

How was she supposed to put on dry clothes? Monsieur Lamotius was sitting at the table with the Bible open in front of him and the lantern in his hand. His knuckles were as white as bone.

'Go and change in the sleeping cabin!' said Juffrouw Margaretha, as though she had heard what she was thinking. 'Then come and help me with Andrea.' Every time the ship came out of a roll, the child fell over, and she had hardly managed to squirm her little body upright again before she would fall over with the next roll. The sandbag caught her each time.

Hourglass after hourglass after hourglass. If only there was another hourglass as well!

Nearly two full days and two whole nights.

Anthonie was the messenger between the storm and the cabin:

Four men were wrestling with the tiller, but they could hardly last for two hours – they got too tired and then four others had to hang on to the tiller.

Steering the ship where?

Don't know.

Where's Salomon?

Don't know.

Every time Anthonie had to go outside, he put his wet clothes back on again. When he got back, he put on Monsieur's dry nightshirt that Juffrouw Margaretha had given him for indoors.

What's happening to the sheep?

Not drowned yet. But very wet.

The fowls and the peahens?

The three that looked worst have been slaughtered.

Where's the bird?

Don't know. You can hardly see the tops of the masts, how could you see a stupid bird?

Salomon was still alive. Anthonie found him down in the galley. Sopping wet.

Some time during the storm it had become night again. And day again. One sailor had fallen from a yard into the sea and been lost. Juffrouw Margaretha wept for him, saying that he had a mother somewhere in the fatherland. Monsieur tried to comfort her, putting a hand on her shoulder, but the ship pitched him off his feet. He had shiny black shoes on his feet. She saw that one had a hole in the sole.

Bread. Cheese. Slices of smoked pork. It wasn't possible to light a fire in the galley any more. Anthonie served the food on pewter plates and poured wine for the grown-ups, who kept spilling.

Day and night sailors had to keep pumping water out of the ship's bilges. A canvas snake fed the water away over the side in a steady stream. Bilgewater, said Anthonie, was water that had leaked in through the seams between the planks. If they didn't keep pumping, the water would rise higher and higher and drown them from their feet to their noses!

And if the pump broke?

They'd sink.

Wind, rain, water. Fear.

The Captain wore a leather jerkin. Every time he climbed in through the hatch, a bundle of wind and rain came in with him. Then Anthonie spread butter on a biscuit for him. He stood eating it as the sea pitched and rolled.

She, Pieternella, searched the Captain's face for any sign of fear and found not a trace of it. In her moments of greatest fear, she clung to that.

She spent most of her time sitting with Andrea in the sandbag circle, because then the little body didn't topple over so much. Feeding the child small pieces of bread and fish that she first soaked in water to get rid of some of the saltiness. Falling asleep beside the child inside the circle. Juffrouw Margaretha on the floor next to the sandbag. Monsieur in the cabin. The Bible in the cupboard.

On the second morning Anthonie was trembling as he sliced the meat. She asked if he was scared; he said a sailor wasn't ever scared.

The Captain wasn't scared ...

The decks were not scrubbed. Anthonie said the sailors were so tired they just lay down in their wet clothes and fell asleep.

There was no food whistle. No prayers whistle. Only the wind and the water and the rain and the ship ...

Juffrouw Margaretha forbade her to go outside; she didn't have any more dry clothes. Only the ones in her chest down in the hold.

120

A storm doesn't just suddenly stop. You begin to sense that the wind is getting tired, the rain is running out. Somewhere in the night while the ship was wrestling the waves to keep afloat and the child was falling asleep up against you ...

Not like when her mother died.

That was a God-storm.

Mynheer Van der Byl asked her about it one day. Gently. As though trying to establish that it was no more than an accident. The Cape knew all about storms.

She didn't think he knew the whole storm. Perhaps he did. Grown-ups don't tell children all the words.

She'd been in the very middle of that storm, but she didn't know the right words either. Only the storm had the right words – to be ragingly furious with.

Everything always washed up on Robben Island. Dead fish, dead whales, pieces of dead ships, creels of woven cane, sail ends, scraps of cloth. Seaweed. Dead shells.

And all the news from the mainland.

That afternoon the food boat brought the news that Captain Frooij would be rowed out the next morning to one of the ships in the Bay. The *Marcken* was ready to sail for Mauritius with food and tools for the people there. The previous ship had had to turn back with the stuff; the skipper and his mate couldn't find Mauritius.

She was sitting with her mother in a corner of the sitting room. The food boat's boatswain and the Post Holder were sitting at the table drinking wine. The Governor had sent her mother a quilt on the boat; the Post Holder had written to ask for one. It was a cold winter.

Captain Frooij also sometimes called in at Barbara Geens's when his ship was in the Bay. The *Helena*. Or at Jannetjie Ferdinandus's tavern. One night, on a day when the soldiers had brought her mother's food money, she, Pieternella, had had to go searching for her in the town. Found her at Jannetjie's tavern. Captain Frooij said: Girl, I'll ask someone to help you get her home, but have something to eat first, I'll pay for it.

A tall man with a black beard and bone-white teeth. Kindly eyes.

The tastiest hot meat and vegetables and sweet cinnamon dumplings. He sat watching her eat; waited till she had finished, then asked: 'What is your name?'

'Pieternella, Mynheer.'

'I'm Captain Frooij. I don't want to upset you, Pieternella, but your mother seems to have got worse lately.'

She didn't want him to talk about her mother. Everybody was always going on about Eva, Eva, Eva! 'It's late, Mynheer, I must get my mother home.'

'Your mother was always a very special person, but it seems as if, deep inside herself, she has fallen asleep.'

'She always falls asleep when she's drunk too much, Mynheer.' She was deliberately playing dumb.

'One day when you're older, you'll understand. Come, let me get a soldier to help you with her – and be kind to her.'

'I am, Mynheer.'

Then the boatswain told the Post Holder about Captain Frooij who had appeared in court in the Castle. A dirty business, he said, and whispered: For the silent sin. Two young slutboys, too: one fifteen, the other twenty. Sailors.

The first one testified that he was the cabin boy on the *Helena*. Captain Frooij and the bookkeeper had already gone to bed when the skipper called for him to blow out the lamp. When he got to the skipper's bed, Frooij said: Come here, boy, I want to feel your bum. The bookkeeper was fast asleep and snoring. The cabin boy told the skipper: No, I won't allow that. So the skipper chased him out of the cabin.

Then the second one testified. He said he was on board the *Helena*; they lay at anchor in Hout Bay for ten or eleven weeks, cutting wood for the Cape. He and Captain Frooij were walking in the dunes when the Captain asked him if he, Klaas Jacobs, couldn't find a Hottentot girl for him. He asked the Captain where he was supposed to find a wench thereabouts? In that case, said the Captain, he, Klaas Jacobs, would do just as well. He told the Captain: Skipper, just remember, there's a God in Heaven looking down on us. So the Captain said: Well, let's just forget it, then.

The Fiscal didn't believe them. He ordered them to be taken to the torture chamber to hear what they would say in the agony of torture. They were so terrified that, before the soldiers could even seize them, they abruptly started singing a different tune. The first one, Joost Jans van Schoonhoven, admitted that he had once, in the cabin in the half light of evening, let himself be used by the skipper for the shameful act of sodom-something-or-other, but it was only once – O God, be merciful unto me.

The second was trembling so badly his teeth chattered, but he admitted that he and Captain Frooij had gone for a walk in the dunes one day when the captain asked him to play with his male tool – so he'd taken the captain's prick in his hand, and then – and then – and then – he swore it only happened that once and never again – Oh please, dear God, be merciful unto me!

So Captain Frooij and the two youngsters were sentenced to be thrown into the depths of the sea the next morning, so the water could drown them dead.

Early one morning her mother said she wanted to go outside. Down to the sea rocks. There was some cloud in the sky but everything was dead calm. Not a blade of grass was moving. It was in the twilight before dawn.

'Mamma,' she asked, because she was troubled by what the boatswain had told the Post Holder, though she hadn't understood all the words. And didn't know how to ask them, either. So she just asked: 'Mamma, what happens when you die?'

Her mother sat on the rocks with her new quilt wrapped tightly round her shoulders, a skinny little bundle with its head in a skin cap. Only here and there was there still a bead or a small shell left on the edge of her cap, her forehead-pigtail just a teased-out tuft of hair like a thin little horn.

'Mamma?'

'You just get born again behind the hills.'

They were still sitting there like that when a storm blew up – so abruptly, so fiercely, as though the wind had been corked up somewhere and had just escaped and was set on breaking everything asunder. She grabbed hold of her mother, afraid the wind would blow her into the sea. As she felt the bones through the quilt, she was scared the wind might smash her mother to pieces!

They had to cling to each other as they made their way, one step at a time, back to the Post House.

'It's a dreadful storm!' shouted the Post Holder when he caught sight of them. He was shoving his full weight against the shutters to thwart the wind. 'Get your mother under cover!'

It lasted three days. The shell boat couldn't set out, the sea was too rough. The shell carriers were bent double like trees twisted in the wind; for every ten steps forward they were driven one step back, standing like a row of chameleons before they could hobble onwards again. The lookout whose turn it was to go to Fire Hill was blown back to the sheep shed twice.

'I don't know how far this storm is raging,' said the Post Holder anxiously, 'but there'll be very few masts left upright today.'

She fed her mother sips of brandy from a mug with a spoon. The Post Holder gave it to her because she couldn't stop shaking.

Her mother said something but there was so much noise they couldn't make out what it was.

'What is it, Miss Eva?' asked the Post Holder.

'It's an angry storm.'

'Give your mother some bread and milk, too, Pieternella. It looks as though her mind may be wandering.'

The first night. The second day. The second night. The third day broke and part of the roof of the convict quarters blew off.

She fed her mother spoonfuls of milk, but she couldn't swallow properly, it kept trickling out of her mouth.

'Mamma, you've got to eat something!' It was terribly cold. She rubbed her mother's arms and legs through the quilt. Her mother liked that. She smiled. In the morning light her eyes twinkled brightly in their bed of wrinkles …

And suddenly her mother was gone. Just gone. And just as abruptly, the storm outside ended. The two things happened together; but they wouldn't match up in her head …

She heard the Post Holder going out through the door.

'Mamma?' She blew in her face. 'Mamma?' She took fright, leapt up and ran to the door. The Post Holder was coming back in again. He said: 'Never in my life have I experienced anything like it! One moment there's nothing but destruction, the next it's all over.'

'My mother is dead.'

She saw the fright he got. His mouth fell open, but he couldn't speak. He just stood there, shaking.

'Pieternella?' It was Juffrouw Margaretha, standing with the child on her arm. 'Why are you crying? The storm has more or less blown itself out now. Listen.'

Juffrouw Margaretha could have been Juffrouw Sophia's sister. 'I only cried a little.'

'Don't worry, it doesn't matter. Sometimes one has to have a little cry. Take Andrea up on deck. The sun is out, she should get some fresh air.'

The sea was grey and muddled, there were still clouds on the eastern horizon but the storm was over. Sails hung from the yards again and only two men were needed at the tiller, with First Mate Berks beside them to say which way the ship should go.

There the bird was, floating behind the ship again. So peaceful.

The ship was a wet old elephant full of drenched sailors busily cleaning its body. Scrubbing decks. Lighting the fire to cook on.

Salomon was chopping wood on a tree stump.

One day, long after her mother died, Pieter van der Byl told her about the storm. He heard it with his own ears from the sailors aboard the *Marcken*. The sailor said: Before dawn that day, Captain Frooij, the two slutboys, the Fiscal and the Sick Comforter reached the ship. They had to take them on board first so the Fiscal could take down their wills and the Sick Comforter could read the Bible and pray for them. Then they raised the red flag from the ship's stern and all the sailors had to gather on the deck to witness the punishment. Some climbed up the rigging for a better view.

Then Captain Frooij and the boys were lowered into the land boat again and rowed round to the ship's stern where they had to be forced into a big canvas bag. The bag was drawn up to their heads and tied at the top, and they were thrown overboard to drown. The moment they sank beneath the waves, the storm burst. 'Strues God, that storm broke over them right then. One of the sailors on the poop got such a fright he wet himself.

She was still playing with Andrea in the sun when all at once the whistle gave a different blast.

'What now?' she asked Anthonie as he came out through the hatch. 'It's not time for lunch yet.'

'No. It's for church 'cause it's Sunday.'

'But we've had prayers already this morning.'

'Doesn't matter. On Sundays we have church as well.'

Juffrouw Margaretha was wearing a nice clean dark-red dress with a pure white underdress full of frills. A different cap, too. Beside her, his arm ceremoniously through hers, Monsieur stood at the railing in front and she, Pieternella, had the child on her arm. The Captain himself preached the sermon. Down in the waist stood the tired sailors, still damp, their damp caps held to their chests. Some looked as though they were too tired even to look up.

'*If Thou dost chasten us with tempests ... that shall not diminish Thy compassion ... Bless Thou this voyage ... may the Light of Thy Gospel illumine our path and deliver us from iniquity that sin may not gain the mastery of these our mortal bodies ...*'

Some of the crew looked up with weary eyes, like supplicants pleading

125

for mercy. Salomon was standing between Daniel Zaaijman and the murderer. Tant Theuntjie …

But it was *Cornelia* standing there beside Tant Theuntjie! Her face was still pale, but she wasn't sick any more! Behind her Tant Maijke was leaning against Bart Borms' shoulder.

This was like bad news staring her straight in the face. She wanted to cry. She wanted to run and hide. She didn't want to go back down again. Please not.

'Our Father which art in heaven ….

She closed her eyes, falling with the ship over the swells, falling and falling.

When the prayer was done, the Captain made them all sing a psalm together.

Between the shadows of the masts and rigging lying like dark spider-webs across the deck and the bodies, the bird's big flat shadow moved gradually forwards. And hung there …

Psalm 146.

All the sounds together – the psalm, the wind in the rigging, the creaking of the masts, the water – blended into the strangest song. Deep and wide.

When it was over, the Captain stretched out his arms and his shadow formed a flat cross down on the deck behind the bird. His words fell clearly on the faces below: *'The Lord bless you and keep you; the Lord make His face to shine upon you and give you grace and peace.'*

Church was over.

The food whistle blew.

She sat playing with Andrea on the bench under the three glass windows in the stateroom, while Anthonie went for the food. The Captain and Monsieur Lamotius were standing in the passageway just outside the door; from the Monsieur's voice it sounded as though he was reprimanding the Captain about something. Seriously. 'I repeat, Captain Wobma: only a properly ordained minister has the authority to pronounce the Blessing. Not a Sick Comforter or a Captain!'

'I am fully aware of the ordinances, Monsieur Lamotius, but I repeat: my crew have just survived a severe storm; they deserve the Blessing!'

'Notwithstanding, Captain, it is not permitted for you to pronounce it. You are authorised only to close with: "Go forth in the peace of the Lord".'

Her mother would have said they were making a thunderclap out of a fart. That's what it sounded like.

126

Luckily they had to get out of the way so that Anthonie could pass with the food. Roast peacock and cabbage and carrots and sweet potatoes and onions and jam puffs.

Later that afternoon, when she went out on deck with the child again, Juffrouw Margaretha also came up the companionway.

'Pieternella, you probably know that Cornelia has recovered.'

'Yes, Juffrouw Margaretha.' I'd rather go and stay in the sheep pen.

'It was a pleasure to have you with us as her replacement. The best would be for you to change places again tomorrow morning. After breakfast. Only make sure that the stateroom is tidy first, because there is to be an important meeting of the ship's Council early in the day.'

I'll go and live with the sheep. 'Yes, Juffrouw.' Please say that you'd rather have me than Cornelia! Please!

'So that is settled then.'

It was settled.

The bird had fallen back and was now gliding quite a long way behind the ship. Still without a single wing beat. Sometimes, though, he would tilt his body slightly, as if in play, or showing off, so that one of his wing tips almost touched the water.

The old moon lay on its back in the west, shining white.

'What are you looking so down in the mouth about?' asked the mate at the tiller. He was the kind one.

'I have to go back down into the hold again tomorrow. Cornelia's coming back.'

'Don't let them trample on you down there, girl. Don't.'

'Grown-ups don't look where they're treading, Mynheer.'

'Oh, really? You're almost grown up yourself. One of these days you'll be doing the trampling.'

'You don't understand, Mynheer.'

'Don't make me take off my cap and show you just how grey I am from understanding!'

'Is it still a long way to Mauritius, Mynheer?'

'It's a long way to the East, girl. Mauritius is only halfway. Only one more storm, if we're lucky.'

'I have to go in now. I've got to fetch hot water to wash the child and get her ready for the night.'

11

Tant Maijke was sitting with her back to the chests. Maria was on a blanket in the corner with the children, Tant Theuntjie leaned against the starboard wall. One hatch was open.

'Well, well, well – look who's fallen out of the sky!' Tant Theuntjie; she didn't sound altogether unhappy.

'Good morning, Tante. Morning, Tant Maijke. Maria – Pietertjie, Daatjie.'

She put her things down in the corner.

A sailor came in with the table and the folding stools for lunch.

'Yes,' sneered Tant Maijke, 'you'll miss the fleshpots above our heads, won't you?'

'When was the hatch opened?'

'Skipper sent a sailor down this morning,' Maria replied.

It was much better than having it nailed shut. She sat down beside her bundle. The meeting Juffrouw Margaretha mentioned began just as she was leaving. The Captain, Monsieur Lamotius, First Mate Berks and one more.

Anthonie said it was all about an ugly thing that happened on the ship during the storm and a man got sent down into the hell in irons for it. The hell was a narrow wooden hole without a hatch, at the front of the ship beneath the waterline. No light. Hardly any air. Apparently the Bosun had cut the man's back open with a single lash because he wouldn't move up the rigging fast enough and the man had spun round and hit the Bosun in the face so hard that four of his teeth were knocked skew. The Surgeon had pushed them back into place but he still couldn't really chew.

Anthonie didn't know who the man was. Luckily it couldn't have been Salomon; he didn't have enough strength in his fists. And luckily Jacobus wasn't on board.

'Where were we before Pieternella came?' asked Tant Maijke.

'We weren't anywhere,' snapped Tant Theuntjie. 'You were trying to pick a quarrel with me about my Bart's character! You, the last one to talk! Bart has worked for what he's got.'

'I was only asking …'

'You lie. You're exactly like the whole darned lot of them at the Cape; can't take it when a poor man manages to do well for himself!'

'Why was *my* stuff confiscated, and not Bart Borms's? Why was Bart given a second chance? Supposedly banished to Batavia for being a danger to the Cape ...'

'Bart was never banished! He chose to go of his own accord, and I chose to go with him. Don't go adding to your lies.'

As long as Tant Theuntjie and Tant Maijke were squabbling, they would leave *her* alone ...

She'd once had a beating from her mother on account of Bart Borms's secret wine. Jacobus had come home; they were still living in the potter's cottage at the time. He said Oom Bart was back from the East. *What!* exclaimed her mother. Yes. He'd bought himself another house at the Cape. And a boat, too. He was an old India hand now. He said Mamma should send a bottle for a little something, he'd got plenty from the French.

Was he getting mixed up with the French again? asked her mother and said, Pieternella, take the bottle and run, before they catch Bart Borms a second time. The previous time he'd almost been thrown in gaol. This time they'd send him off to carry shells – or hang him.

The little something her mother sent her for turned out to be nothing but wine. She poured it out behind a bush on the way home because as it was her mother drank too much wine. She'd say Oom Bart wasn't at home. Her mother sniffed the bottle and said: That's one big lie you're telling me now, Pieternella! She picked a switch from the nearest milkwood tree and chased her round and round the cottage, beating her.

Then she had to take the bottle back and tell Oom Bart what she'd done.

Before long the tale had spread throughout the town: Bart Borms had been summoned to appear before the Governor and the Fiscal a second time. He was in bigger trouble than last time when they'd found the two vats of French wine and all the other goods in his house. Cloths and bowls and strange silver coins. And where did you come by *these*, Free-fisherman Borms? Picked them up at Saldanha Bay, Your Worship. They washed up on the beach.

Ah! Not according to eyewitnesses!

'Even gave your dad a little of the wine,' said her mother.

Neatly allowed himself to be picked up by a French ship and then pointed out to them where all the freshwater springs were, and the narrows and the deep places and the shallows and the best anchorages in the great lake at Saldanha. All round, even up and down the coast. For weeks. Ate with them, drank with them, showed them where the

Cochoquas' kraals were, how much they would need to tender in barter for an ox or a sheep. Where the best wood could be cut. The lot.

'Your father told him: Bart, you're looking for a noose round your neck.'

No, he said, he knew what he was doing.

Even though he *knew* the Lords in Amsterdam were deeply anxious because the French had designs on the Cape for *their* ships.

Just like the English. Every burgher, without exception, was forbidden to approach even one of them. Weren't even allowed to tell which side the sun came up if they were asked. And he, Bart Borms, went and *showed* them? That was treason! said the Governor and the Fiscal.

'Your Honours,' he swore, 'Bart Borms would not betray his own blood for those Papists. Never.'

So he sold all his goods and he and Tant Theuntjie took ship for Batavia. That was an island somewhere in the East.

'He sold his slave, Janvos, to your father,' said her mother.

A few years later, when the waters were calmer again, he and Tant Theuntjie returned. Dressed in silk. Silk hangings on their walls, with the strangest pictures on them. Ate with sticks. Never set foot in the Church. An old India hand. Said he'd seen the delights of the East – all a man needed was enough in his pocket!

One day her mother met Tant Theuntjie in the street and said: 'Theuntjie, why are you walking with your toes turned out like a hen ostrich?'

Tant Theuntjie was angry and said: 'Eva, don't let your mouth speak about things you know nothing about. Go and talk to the baboons up in the mountain, perhaps they'll understand your lingo.'

Her mother crouched down on her haunches and lifted the hem of Tant Theuntjie's dress. She burst out laughing so loudly that the ever-so-proper Juffrouw Droes, Elbert Diemer's wife, came out of her house to see.

'Juffouw Droes!' called her mother – not letting go of the hem for a moment – come and see what Theuntjie's got on her feet! Shoes with heels in the middle!'

Eastern shoes. Under the most beautiful long gowns of red silk, with pictures and gold thread woven into them, almost like the wall hangings.

This happened not long after they had killed her father on Madagascar.

So Bart Borms hurriedly sold up all his goods a second time and said he'd decided to be a free-burgher on Mauritius. Had always wanted to farm anyway.

'What's it like on Mauritius, Theun?' asked Tant Maijke on the day that Cornelia went back upstairs again. You could hear she was really just wanting to smooth out the wrinkles between her and Tant Theuntjie. 'You've been there a number of years now.'

'Well – how shall I answer you? My Bart always says where the Company's breathing down your neck, trouble runs down your back.'

'Are there any Hottentots over there?'

'Oh, don't be daft, Maijke! It's a different kind of wild place from the Cape. A jungle full of strange creatures. Bats bigger than your head!'

'Oh, God have mercy! You're lying, aren't you, Theun?'

'Just wait. We'll soon see who's lying. At that time, you remember, when the Hollanders closed down the island because it was an additional expense to the Dutch Lords to maintain both Mauritius and the Cape as stations on the way to the East, my Bart was one of those called upon to assist with the closure.' She made it sound important. 'Their instructions were: Burn down the Post House, destroy the vegetable gardens, pull up the fruit trees – not a thing was to be left that might be of use to a French or an English ship. Slaughter the cattle and sheep and pigs – bury what you cannot salt away. Shoot the rest. Catch the fowls. All the things that the Hollanders had taken there down the years. Deer, too. The creatures fled into the jungle, didn't catch half of them.'

'What a waste of good money.'

'Yes. And – it's strange the peculiar twists that life takes – one of the commanders on Mauritius, shortly before it was closed down, was a certain Por. Great friend of Van Riebeeck's. He died on the island. And who did Van Riebeeck marry when his own Maria died of smallpox in the East? The late Commander Por's widow Maria!'

'Well I never!' Tant Maijke was sitting with her head on one side and her mouth open, drinking in every word. 'As you say: life certainly takes odd twists and turns with us mortals.'

'For a number of years after that the island was left to go back into its own wildness. Till the home-bound fleet was caught in a cyclone just off Mauritius one day and the Lords Seventeen ordered: Take back the island and, if this happens again, salvage whatever washes up on the shore. The Cape was barely able to support itself and now it had Mauritius round its neck as well.'

'Madness.'

'Exactly. One day Wagenaer sent the ship to take the island its annual provisions and to fetch wood and stuff. Arrived there – Commander Nieulandt had been dead goodness knows how long. Brandy and rice finished ages ago. Settlers going savage, living off wild deer and palm wine they made for themselves.

'There you have it!' said Tant Maijke, laughing. 'You'll always find a way!'

'The Dutch Lords said: Get free-burghers on the island, give them land so they can sow and plant. The question was: Where were the free-burghers to come from? *That* was when the Company took it into its head to send all the riff-raff – every layabout, drunken farmer, quarrelsome bitch – off to Mauritius!' *Ha-ha-ha-ha*, laughed Tant Theuntjie. 'And here you are, too, Maijke van den Berg!'

'What about you and Bart?'

'We were among the few volunteer free-burghers.'

'So you say. I'm not so sure.'

'Are you trying to besmirch my husband's reputation? Do you want to land up in court?'

'Stop it!' cried Maria. 'You're frightening the children with all your bickering.'

'We're not bickering, I'm just telling you the facts. So you'll know what's waiting for you.'

She and Salomon had to get back to the Cape …

'Perhaps they'll give me a piece of land …' Tant Maijke hoped aloud.

Tant Theuntjie didn't seem to hear her. 'After Van Nieulandt, the next Commander was Wreede. Had a new lodge and sheds built; not very good, but still. Sent for ten or so skilled craftsmen and better equipment from the Cape, had ox wagons built for getting the wood out of the forests. After him, it was Smiendt, if I remember correctly. He had fruit trees planted. Pumpkins, sweet potatoes and cabbage. Locusts and caterpillars and rats ate the lot. Managed to send some ebony to Holland to pacify the Lords. Arse-licker. Wife, too. Then they sent Wreede back to Mauritius. Where he drank like a fish while everything fell apart around him. In the end he drowned when one of the island boats ran aground on a reef. He was drunk as a lord but apparently got down to help shove. Imagine. This very same Daniel Zaaijman of ours was on the boat as well.'

'The place sounds cursed!'

'You can say that again, Maijke.'

'And then?'

'Then the so-called Political Council of Three governed the island. The only one of the three who amounted to anything was Col. At least he tried to stop the mutiny by the free-burghers and soldiers. A good man. He wrote to the Cape in plain terms saying that the island should be shut down, that it was no place for mortal men. The Lords Seventeen replied that all Mauritius needed to contribute to the profit and prosperity of the Company was a competent Commander. A strong man. A fierce man.'

'So that must have been Hugo,' Tant Maijke chipped in.

'The same.'

'I heard he was such an attractive man,' said Maria.

'The devil often prowls around in the guise of an attractive man – which I certainly don't have to tell *you*. Hugo was a pirate. Got all his treasures by plundering pilgrims along the Red Sea. Went buying slaves and elephant tusks for the Company on the African coast. Fearless. Thought *he*'d be able to turn a profit on Mauritius. But then his only daughter and Col fell in love, so instead of governing the island, he tried to govern them by keeping them apart.'

'Why?' Maria wanted to know.

'An assistant corporal was apparently not what he had in mind for his daughter. Lived like a princess, she did. Marya. Not exactly a beauty, but when she fell in love with Col her pirate father turned into a sea-monster father. Had her nailed up in her room in the lodge for six weeks.'

'Really?'

'Yes. But love doesn't allow itself to be boarded up – as you, Maria, ought to know. Love letters slipped through the cracks in the boards, letters with their names signed in blood. Hugo was going out of his mind. He tortured poor Col almost to death, but they refused to give in. You haven't heard the food whistle yet, have you, Pieternella?'

'Not yet. But perhaps we didn't hear it, I'll go and see.' She wanted to get out.

'No. Sit down.'

'So what happened to them?' asked Maria, her eyes filled with tears.

'She was eventually put on a ship to Batavia, supposedly to an aunt there. Heartbroken.'

'And Col?'

'Someone once saw him in a tavern at the Cape. He was a bookkeeper on one of the ships of the fleet. They say the welts raised on his ankles where the leg irons had chafed him – chains which Hugo put him in to keep him away from her – were scars he would bear lifelong, in her memory.'

'That's terrible.' Poor Marya.

'In the mean time, what with misery and wretchedness, all the free-burghers on the island were being destroyed. At last we wrote to the Cape ourselves, saying that things were going from bad to worse under the pirate. All Governor Goske did was inform us that we should direct our complaint to Batavia.'

'What happened to Hugo?'

'He's still on the island. They say he hasn't heard a word about Lamotius being on his way to expel him.'

'Goodness gracious! What are you telling us?' cried Tant Maijke, most interested.

'Yes. He is a merciless man. One day a good-looking young sailor missed the land boat by a few minutes. Hugo bound him to a stake so he could fire off a bullet just above his head to give him a fright. The laid-down penalty was the loss of one month's pay. The bloody soldier shot so badly that the poor boy's head was blown off.'

'Ohmygod!'exclaimed Tant Maijke in fright.

'Yes. Hugo's ruthlessness was one of he reasons why Bart and Daniel and Focke decided to go to the Cape in person, to give eyewitness accounts of what was going on on the island. The only hope left to us now is Lamotius.'

At that, like a deliverance, the food whistle blew.

While she was in the queue Anthonie came past to fetch the food for the captain's table. She asked what had happened to the man in the hell, and how Cornelia was.

'The meeting had already been adjourned by the time I got a chance to try and eavesdrop,' he said. 'Cornelia's fine, but we miss you up there.'

They were missing her.

Fish cooked in white beans with lots of butter. And bread.

Then one of the senior sailors knocked against the mainmast with a wooden spoke and announced: 'Everyone in the waist at a quarter to four to attend the execution of justice that will happen at four o'clock.'

Like announcing for church.

It was better now in the hold, with the hatch open.

When she went to wash the bowl after the meal, she decided she would put on both her shawls and go and sit beside the sheep till darkness fell. Juffrouw Margaretha had said she could keep the shawl. Cornelia said the Monsieur had asked her to look after the child on the island, too.

The sheep were calmer, they were eating a bit better each day.

Tant Maijke was not content. While they were eating, she told Tant Theuntjie in as many words that she had no intention of keeling over and dying on Mauritius. A year at most, then she would apply to be a free-burgher. Focke Janse had promised to help her; he said there were plenty of wild cattle on the island, all you had to do was drive them into a kraal.

Tant Theuntjie gave a loud laugh. Like a dog barking. 'Focke's just passing wind, Maijke. The first bullock you slaughter is registered as credit on the book at the lodge. Not a guilder ends up in your pocket. Ask for a tool or a quilt and you're told: Sorry, stocks are low and we don't know when the next ship from the Cape will arrive bringing more supplies. Furthermore, you are given land where it pleases the *Commander* to grant it, not where you yourself would like to live. The best always belongs to the Company – like everywhere else!'

'Focke says deer are good eating.'

'Right. But Hugo has forbidden us to hunt: deer belong to the Company! We are forbidden to cut wood: wood belongs to the Company!'

'But how are you supposed to make a living?' Tant Maijke asked, now deeply concerned.

'Well, you at any rate don't have any worries, Maijke. You've been banished, so they have to give you food and shelter.'

'That's not what they're planning to do with Willem,' said Maria. 'The order says that he has to farm for a living. The island urgently needs wheat and he's one of the few who knows anything about growing grain.'

Tant Maijke chewed attentively for while and slowly licked her plate clean with her finger. 'Do you think – how shall I put it? – do you think one could open a tavern?'

'Before the door is open, they'll have nailed it shut. All liquor is bought from the Company's store at the Lodge.'

They sometimes called the Post House on Robben Island a lodge ...

'Sounds a lot like the Cape to me.'

'Worse,' Tant Theuntjie warned. 'And beware your soul on any day that you try to sell as much as a loaf of bread to an English or French ship, to make yourself some pocket money. *That* is the worst of all sins.'

'Heavens, Theun, where is it you're taking me?' Tant Maijke asked, really worried.

'Not to heaven, *that* I promise you.'

Sitting beside the sheep pen was better than being in a wooden hole full of old wives squabbling.

The bird was at its post behind the ship, looking peaceful and happy …

The sheep were not happy. Their pen was cleaned every morning, and fresh straw was spread for them, but their bodies were full of brown patches from lying in their dung at night. Tails caked with muck. Keeping four Hottentot sheep on board a ship was as bad as putting Juffrouw Margaretha in a hut of reed mats in a Hottentot kraal …

One day one of the shell carriers on Robben Island had thrown down his sack halfway to Sand Bay and sat down right there on the prickly grass. She and her mother were gathering penguin feathers. Her mother sent her to tell the man to get up; the Corporal would come and beat him in moment, he'd just quickly gone back to the Post House.

She walked over to the man. He was one of the new convicts who hadn't been there long. She came up and looked at him, sitting there with his two blue eyes rigid in his head, staring at nowhere.

A handsome man.

'Shell carrier?' she called. He just went on staring. 'Shell carrier, my mother says you mustn't sit down, the Corporal will come and lift you up with his cane.'

He turned his head towards her. She was frightened. The man looked like someone sleeping with his eyes open. 'Who are you?' he asked.

'Eva's Pieternella.'

'What day is it?' Completely befuddled.

'Saturday.'

As if he didn't care about anything.

'Are you tired?'

He shook his head slowly.

She'd seen many shell carriers come and go on the island. Many were sentenced to stay there for ever. When they started carrying shells, they cursed and swore, some cried; but most eventually became resigned and just kept trudging on. At first they had been required to scrape up five sacks a day each. Then the Governor heard that they would start from early morning, hurrying to get the required number to Sand Bay so they could then lie among the bushes and rest. So he said: Now you will carry eight sacks a day.

Big sacks. That they had to make themselves out of the canvas sent from the mainland. Along with canvas thread and needles.

But she'd never seen one like this who just sat and stared. He wasn't even scared of the Corporal!

'Shell carrier,' she tried again, pressing his shoulder, 'what is it with you?'

'Nothing. I'm just living because I'm not dead.'

The sheep were also just living because they weren't dead.

'Pieternella?' It was Salomon. 'The cook said I could come here to you for the time it takes him to smoke half a pipe.'

'How are things?'

'You just have to hurry all the time, like they say, then they can't grab hold of you. The storm was terrible. I was really scared.'

'I've got a plan. We've just got to keep living.'

'Pieternella, please, don't cause trouble.'

'I'm not going to cause trouble. I'm just busy with the words of my plan.'

'What words?'

'The right words.'

'Won't help, we can't turn back. Oom Bart says everyone's deliverer is now with us on this ship – Monsieur Lamotius.'

'One of his shoes has a hole in the sole.'

'Perhaps he's poor.'

'His foot's probably cold.'

They laughed.

Shortly afterwards the whistle blew a tune it hadn't blown before. *Teeeeeeewhiiiiiii*. A long blast.

'Everyone to the waist to watch the punishment!' the whistler called. *Teeeeeeewhiiiiiii*. 'Everybody! To the waist! To the waist!'

Sailors came tumbling out of the fo'c'sle; most looked half asleep. Juffrouw Margaretha and Cornelia and the child also came and stood in the waist. Juffrouw Margaretha looked grim. Worried. Tant Maijke and Maria and the children, Tant Theuntjie …

Daniel Zaaijman stood with arms folded at the upper end of the upside down skiff. She was relieved. She had wondered whether he had not perhaps been the one to be locked up in the hell-place. He looked like someone who would hit back. Who wasn't afraid of anything.

It wasn't another church service. Commander-designate Lamotius and First Mate Berks also came down into the waist. Only the Captain was up at the rail. A sailor with a red flag on a pole appeared beside him and gave her such a fright that she leapt upright. A red flag on the stern meant they were going to cast someone overboard to drown!

Sailors carried the grid that was sometimes placed over the front hatch up to the stern and leant it against the wooden wall beyond the chicken-coop. Right in front of everyone in the waist.

The whistle blew again.

Two sailors came out of the fo'c'sle, leading a man without a jerkin. Chains round his wrists and ankles. The chains between his feet *clink-clink-clinked* over the wooden deck. The man didn't look up. He was either very unhappy or sick. They led him to the grid, undid the chains and stretched him out on the grid like on a cross, his hands and feet tied with ropes through the holes.

Her mother had never liked being in church when the minister preached about a man being nailed to a cross ...

As punishment, men caught for knifing often had their hands skewered to a pole at the Fort with the very same knives they had used. For a whole day. On those days her mother would always hurry past.

The man stood with his back to the people, his face against the grid.

Were they going to throw him into the sea like *that*?

The Surgeon came down from the upper deck and took up a position a short distance from the man. He looked worried.

The bird moved forwards ...

Her heart started beating in her throat because she suddenly realised what they were going to do to the man. They weren't going to cast him into the sea, they were only going to flog him. The Bosun took his place behind him. He had a rope in his hand that looked as if it had been unravelled and then smeared with tar or something.

The Bosun's mouth was badly swollen.

'Sailors!' declared the Captain on the upper deck. 'Assistant carpenter Klaas Dirkse maliciously resorted to violence against one of my officers. Such insubordination is mutiny and mutineers go overboard! If a man lifts his hand against an officer, he lifts it against the Captain and against the Lords Seventeen themselves. At a plenary meeting of the Council of this ship it was decided to flog this mutineer with three dozen lashes. Let this be a warning and a lesson to all present. Insubordination is mutiny! Boatswain, commence!'

No, please not ...

When the first *ssswhip* landed on the man's back, it sounded like the broom handle beating the dust out of Juffrouw Sophia's wall-hanging in the yard outside.

Ssswhip!

Second blow.

Someone was calling out the tally. *Four ... five ... six ...*

They were going to beat him to death.

Nine ... ten ... eleven ... twelve ...

The corporals on the island were taught how to flog correctly. Slowly, and the blows had to fall downwards.

Sixteen ... seventeen ... eighteen ...

The man didn't utter a sound.

Twenty-one ... twenty-two ... twenty-three ... twenty-four ... twenty-five ...

'Boatswain!' the Surgeon cried out abruptly. 'Lay the blows across the shoulders not the kidneys!'

Twenty-six ... twenty-seven ...

All over, caps were coming off sailors' heads. As though for prayer.

Daniel Zaaijman just stood, not removing his cap, his face impassive. Watching each blow. Stone jackal.

Thirty.

Tant Maijke was crying. She'd had only twelve lashes.

The man's back was a mess of bloody weals, one on top of another. Some of the blows had fallen across his buttocks, blood was showing through the cloth of his trousers.

She clung to the side of the sheep pen, her body ready to collapse.

Thirty-four ...

The man's head lay limp against the grid.

Thirty-six ...

The flogger stepped back, you could clearly see his chest heaving, panting.

Two sailors hauled up a bucket of sea water on a rope over the side and splashed it on the bleeding stripes.

That was when the man cried out for the first time.

She crawled in beside the sheep pen with her back to the deck and pressed her head against the side of the ship. Tighter. Screwed up her eyes to squeeze out all the pictures of her life, to silence all the sounds in her ears. She didn't want to be a human being any more. People were no good. Not Dutch people, not *Khoi* people. No people.

All she wanted to do was cry and cry.

Because she was frightened.

Jacobus had run out into the veld one day and when he came back, his knees buckled under him, his eyes rolled over in his head and he started foaming at the mouth. They said it was the falling sickness.

She didn't want to have the falling sickness!

Jacobus had run away into the veld after someone had been beaten to death.

Gonnema and Oedasoa of the Cochoqua had said again and again that the Dutch farmers should stop shooting the hippos in the river with their guns. The hippos belonged to the Hottentots for when the droughts wouldn't break and hunger crept in through the cracks. The farmers wouldn't listen. So Gonnema's men surrounded eight of the hippo hunters and killed them. One of them was Tant Maijke's husband, Oom Thieleman. Soldiers then marched out of the Fort to shoot all Gonnema's Cochoqua Hottentots. But the Hottentots saw them coming from a long way off and fled. The soldiers took thousands of cattle and sheep and drove them back to the Fort. The Government was very grateful for the livestock.

Then one day some of the Cochoquas' enemies came to the Fort to exchange four Cochoquas for tobacco and rice and arrack. Two of the exchanged men admitted they had been among the killers, but the other two denied being involved. Because the law said Hottentots had to punish Hottentots and Hollanders Hollanders, the Fiscal turned the four over to a hundred of the Cochoquas' enemies to beat them to death with knobkerries.

On the beach, in front of the Fort, on Sunday, after Church.

Most people coming out of church turned aside to watch the killing, Jacobus among them. Mynheer Van der Byl said: Sophia, take the children home.

Jacobus said later that the hundred Hottentots had first sat down in a circle round the captives. The Fiscal and his friends looked down from the wall above the Poort, laughing and waving their arms.

Then the oldest Hottentot in the circle got up and delivered the first blow with his knobkerrie. Then the next one. And so they went on, each in turn, beating and beating – slowly, so the four wouldn't die quickly. Without a drop of blood being shed. Just beaten to pulp.

That was when Jacobus ran away.

After that all the Company's draught oxen landed up in the Liesbeeck River and drowned.

Each and every soldier had to help skin and salt the carcasses. Few realised they would be paid with that same meat instead of money, so the Company could try to make up the loss. The food boat brought a load of the meat for the hungry on Robben Island. Her mother said she wouldn't take a single bite of it.

She was afraid to look and see if the man on the grid had been untied. She didn't want to have the falling sickness!

12

'Mynheer?'

'Yes, Pieternella?'

'Morning, Mynheer Zaaijman.' He was wearing a big leather apron while he opened a barrel with a hooked iron thing.

'Why are your eyes so swollen, girl? Did you sleep badly last night?'

'Yes, Mynheer.' Not much. Tant Maijke and Tant Theuntjie had snored terribly. Maria couldn't sleep either.

'What is it, Pieternella?'

She had the right words ready. 'Have you lived on Mauritius for a long time, Mynheer?'

'Eight years.'

'Have you got a house?'

'Yes.'

The next words were the most important ones. 'Have you perhaps got a room for my little brother and me?' She saw the surprise on his face and the frown forming between his eyes. Her mother used to say that your strength lay in your stomach. Her stomach felt strong. 'We can pay you some rent, Mynheer.'

'You've been placed in the care of Bart Borms.'

'We'll take care of ourselves, Mynheer. We won't be a nuisance. We'll work.'

'Wait a moment ...'

'I'll do laundry for the people on the ships, my brother can look after livestock, and write and read and all kinds of things. We can keep your house tidy, Mynheer, Salomon can chop wood ...'

'Hang on!'

Please, Mynheer. 'I'm asking nicely, Mynheer.' I won't cry.

'Pieternella, hang on!'

'Yes, Mynheer.' Her stomach must just not start getting that hollow feeling!

'You can't just walk out of Bart Borms's care as you please. How old are you?'

'I'm fourteen and my brother is twelve. Please, Mynheer.'

'Don't cry!'

'I won't, Mynheer.' But the tears wouldn't stop coursing down her cheeks. 'It would only be till we can get a berth on a ship back to the Cape.'

He shook his head and put down his hammer. 'Girl,' he said, 'waiting for a ship to take you back to the Cape would be just as good as climbing up to the top of a mast and waiting for the albatross to alight on your shoulder.'

'But we haven't been banished.'

'There's not much difference.'

'That's not true!' Why did he say that? 'It's just that I don't want us to get stuck with Tant Theuntjie and Oom Bart. My brother's not going to be an unpaid manservant and I'm not going to be an unpaid housemaid!'

'I admit, your position is not ideal, but then whose is? Besides, going by what your brother says, it sounds as though he's looking forward to farming with Bart.'

Her stomach gave a sudden lurch and all at once nothing felt right any more. 'Then I just don't know, Mynheer.' She had been so sure he would help them!

'It's still a long way to Mauritius, Pieternella. Don't get yourself wound up even tighter by digging in your heels.'

Then her mouth said something which she had not meant to say! 'The Second Mate in the cabin just in front of the steerage deck grabs me in the dark when I have to go past.'

'And?'

'I bite and kick, and then he lets go.'

'Good!' he laughed. 'Sometimes you *have* to bite yourself free. But just remember, Lubbert's type don't easily give up. You might have to bite harder next time.'

He didn't want them.

Her clever plan lay like a rotten fig under the tree.

13

It didn't matter how many days had passed, Mauritius was still a long way off.

It felt as though the sand in the hourglass was trickling through grain by grain; never-ending, rolling swells from dawn till dark. Rise, fetch water, rinse pots, sweep, fetch food. Bad food. When Tant Theuntjie and Tant Maijke weren't gossiping, they were squabbling. Maria was sure they were going to come to blows before the voyage was over.

Maria spent her time looking after the children.

She, Pieternella, sat beside the sheep pen, staring at the deck planks in front of her. The sky, the bird, the water. How the sails trapped and held the wind. Sails drawn taut on the yards. The ship ran on and on and on, a long trail across the water.

The sailors were beginning to look more and more like flotsam fished up out of the water each morning to tighten the sail ropes. Scrub the decks. Watch. Those who were resting lay or sat around in the sun – coughing, smoking, spitting over the side, sleeping, coughing. Sitting with their legs stretched out round circular wooden boards full of small holes, moving little wooden balls around on them. Coughed, spat, yawned, scratched. Some seemed to be hunting for lice.

Vinegar days. When everything had to be carried out on deck to be sprinkled. All bedding taken out into the sun to air.

It looked like a rag ship.

Sailmaker – the ship's mother hen always about its cloth wings. Not the tiniest threadbare patch where a sail had chafed against a rope missed his eye. And then his hands mended it.

Day. Night. Day. Night.

When a Hottentot woman has a baby inside her, each new moon she cuts notches in one of the slats that the reed mats are fastened to. Nine notches. Then the baby comes out of her, down below.

She wished she had a knife, so she could cut a notch in one of the spars of the sheep pen for every day on the water …

Planks are dead, wet bits of tree. The whole ship was once trees full of leaves that had to be cut down and sawn up. Long planks, tall trees. High masts, very tall trees. What if the masts and planks began to sprout again – the whole ship would be covered in leaves …

Schoolmaster Valkenryk once told them you needed to cut down two thousand trees to build one big ship. The fleet was in the Bay: seven great East Indiamen, five smaller big ships. They had to work out the sum. Jacobus asked how many trees for the smaller ships. The Schoolmaster reckoned a thousand ought to be enough. The first one to get the answer had to put up his hand.

Jannetjie Ferdinandus's Johannes was the first to put up his hand. This fleet had taken nineteen thousand trees.

That afternoon she and Salomon were walking home from school when Salomon asked: 'Pieternella, how many is a thousand?' She didn't know. A thousand was a thousand. She asked Juffrouw Sophia; she said if you picked up a hundred pebbles and made a pile of them, you would need ten piles to make a thousand.

She and Salomon were playing in the veld, piling and piling up pebbles. It was fun. On the third day, Salomon came out to her in the veld, breathless from running; he was laughing so much he could hardly speak. He said Sick Comforter Heere had come from a meeting of the Church Council and announced that the Hottentots were engaged in some pagan witchcraft; one of the soldiers had come across piles of pebbles in rows in the veld above the town. So they summoned one of the Hottentots, who carried wood for the kitchens and understood Dutch fairly well, and questioned him. But he fell to trembling and ran away. They had to pray to the Heavenly Father to protect them from the wicked ways of the heathen.

She and Salomon rolled around laughing. Juffrouw Sophia scolded her for getting soil all over her frock; she said she was sorry but she and Salomon had had such fun in the veld.

She went to the island to visit her mother, she said: Mamma, Salomon and I had fun doing witchcraft! She tried to tell her mother about the pebbles but her mother wasn't really listening. She didn't laugh either.

It was one her mother's *walkabout* days. When she wouldn't stop walking about, staring eyes rigid in their sockets, not looking where she was going. Straight across bushes, right through penguin nests, over rocks, through pools.

'Mamma!'

You could call, you could plead. It was as though something was gnawing away inside her, and driving, hurrying, her small brown feet under the dirty gown.

By then she didn't have her skin clothes any more. Somewhere they had got lost. Only her skin cap. The Company sometimes had a dress made for her, paid for out of Janvos's wages, but when next they looked the dress would be gone. Or torn.

'Mamma!'

All day long. Sometimes round and round the island. Just walking and walking. Past the stone quarry where they came to prise off slabs of blue stone with chisels and crowbars to build stairs in the new Castle and hospital. For a freshwater dam to fill the ships' barrels from. For paving stones, grave stones. Lizards fled, rainwater collected in the holes, the island sheep came there to drink.

The big stones for the walls of the Castle they broke out of a hole on the mainland at the tail of Lion's Head. The hole just grew bigger and bigger.

Her mother didn't care about the Fort or the Castle any more. It was a long time since she had been welcome there.

'Why not, Mamma?'

Sometimes, when her mother was in a good mood, she would first give a little laugh and then say: 'Because at the Governor's beautiful dining room table, with all the high and mighty people off the ships present, I let off a stinking fart.'

At other times she just shook her head. That was when she was too sad. Didn't care about the difference between living and dying, like the shell carrier that day who had sat down next to the sack. Sometimes she drew lines in the sand with her fingers and said *that* was her name. Krotoa. Her real name. Like a snake trying to slither back to its cast skin to put it on again.

She followed her mother all day. Suddenly her mother sat down flat on the ground and the words began pouring out of her mouth like puke when your stomach is too full.

Not the same as seasickness.

'We did bewitch them,' she shouted. 'We bewitched them properly and the spells kept their force for a long time!'

'What are you talking about, Mamma?' she asked cautiously. She didn't want to startle her into starting her endless walking again. 'Why did you bewitch them?'

'To get back the place on earth that had always been ours. To get them to go back across the sea the way they came. Asking politely didn't help; asking rudely didn't help! So we bewitched them. You don't go walking into the forest where the lion lives that catches your cattle; you send your biggest, strongest oxen, the ones with the longest horns, into the forest ahead of you in a wide half-moon, and you shoot your arrows over them. Lion doesn't see you, lion thinks these are just tasty little oxen coming nearer.'

'But how did the Hottentots bewitch them?' She wanted to know.

'Crow's heart first. Hemoao Khatimao, the best fowler of all the Goringhaicona, killed the crow in flight. Gogosoa, chief of the Goringhaiqua, cut out the heart, chopped it up fine and sowed it into the wind – as the Hollanders would blow away again in the wind with broken hearts for the lovely land that the Hottentots would no longer allow them to take.'

'And then?' Like sticking a finger down her throat to make sure the words kept coming out.

'Then the *!gai aob* of the Chorachoqua came down from behind the Lion's Head – the best wizard among all the enchanters. He'd never touched a drop of cold water that could wash off his powers. He gathered a bunch of his magic roots and set it alight. He let the wind blow the smoke towards the enemy to keep them deeply asleep when the rustlers came to steal their livestock, and the rustlers would be far away before they woke up in fright – and so they would choose the wrong tracks to follow after them.'

'Don't stop.'

'Hottentots didn't have guns, just cunning in their heads and eyes that spent long hours carefully observing the lion's habits. If lion doesn't eat, he lies down and dies. If Dutchman doesn't have food for his ships, it's no use dropping his anchors here. Hottentots' land would mean nothing to the Hollanders. The chiefs of the nearest tribes gathered together, they said: It's easy, we take their food – their cattle and sheep and oxen that draw their ploughs and wagons. We set fire to their wheat. Hottentots' law of war says you don't burn down a man's hut, but Hollanders are not Hottentots. If you have to burn down his huts, then burn them.

'The best days for the rustlers would be wet, rainy days. Hollanders' fire for their guns doesn't burn right in wet weather. Best of all: no Dutchman can catch a Hottentot, our feet are too quick for them.' *Choof!* Her mother spat in the sand.

'And then?'

'Your plans have got to be as sharp as the points of your arrows. Before the lion can get up, the livestock and the kraals and the women and the children and the old ones and the young ones must all be hidden far away, so nobody gets hurt if the lion decides to pounce.'

She sat there, looking far out over the sea, but her eyes were not seeing the water.

'Tell,' Pieternella prompted her gently.

'Ha! Then the first animal was driven in between the lion and the forest: me. Eva. Krotoa. Because I had learnt to speak the lion's language and knew his habits. My uncle Autshumao, chief of the Goringhaicona, was cast aside, stuck on Robben Island to keep him out of the way of the mighty Oedasoa of the powerful Cochoqua at Saldanha, in the hope that the mighty Oedasoa could be enticed to the Fort so they could get their hands on his cattle and sheep for their ships.

"You, Krotoa-Eva," said the chiefs of all the Cape Hottentots – "you, Krotoa, must go to Oedasoa to ask for places to set up our kraals for the time they have to stay hidden."

'Hottentots' law says you have to *ask* to water your stock at another man's waterhole, *ask* before you trek across another's pastureland, *ask* to stay with him till the danger is past.'

'It's a good law.' Just to keep her mother talking.

'Yes. And I was pretty, too. Your father couldn't stop looking at me. Then he'd say: Eva, you're the first beauty in the world.'

'Really?'

'Yes. Then I became the woman with two heads. One was Eva, one was Krotoa. You have to be clever to be a woman with two heads. You need to learn to glide like a snake so as not to waken the lion!' Her mother rolled over and lay on her stomach, pretending to glide over the ground. Stuck out her tongue and went *le-le-le-le-le*. 'To speak with two tongues.' Got up again and sat down. 'To learn to soothe the lion with the words his ears want to hear, because then he rewards you with an extra finger-length of tobacco, an extra sparkling glass of wine, an extra porcelain bowl of rice. You know that his heart is bubbling with the desire to make friends with the mighty Oedasoa of the Cochoqua. You say: Mynheer Van Riebeeck, I want to go to my sister among the Cochoquas, my heart is sore with longing for her.'

'Your *sister*, Eva? Among the Cochoquas?' Like one who cannot believe his ears.

'Yes, Mynheer, chief wife of Oedasoa, their highest chieftain.'

'I didn't realise you had such important relatives, Eva. I grant permission for you to go to your sister as soon as possible. Bear my greetings to Oedasoa and invite him to come to the Fort soon, so we can conclude the most binding bonds of friendship.'

'I'll give him the message just like that, Mynheer.'

At that, her mother got extra tobacco and wine, and even more to take along with her.

It was a long walk to Saldanha where the Cochoquas' kraals were. Her mother's sister was overjoyed to see her. Oedasoa listened closely and carefully to the messages from the chiefs. He summoned the elders of the kraals to meet. Gonnema, head of the second Cochoqua kraal, sat at his right hand; he asked her again and again about the plans of the Cape Hottentots.

She said Doman of the Cape had thought of a plan. Without cattle and sheep, the Hollanders wouldn't have any slaughter stock; without slaughter stock, they wouldn't have any food for the ships. Without oxen, they wouldn't be able to draw their wagons piled with loads and loads of firewood for their houses and kilns and all the ships. Without oxen, they couldn't plough up the ground – ploughs pulled up the grass where the pastures had been. Without oxen, they were a lion without claws. Without cattle and sheep, a lion without teeth.

Doman's plan was to steal all the Hollanders' cattle and sheep and oxen and to drive them deep into the valleys. But before Doman and his men could begin, the kraals had to be hidden far away – without Van Riebeeck noticing anything.

Doman had been on a ship to the Hollanders' other place in the East, where the people of that country had also tried to drive them away. With fires and sticks and things.

Doman said: We have to be cleverer.

First he would have to test the heart of the Dutch chief about the Cochoquas. He was going to go to Mynheer Van Riebeeck and tell him that he would attack the Cochoqua if he was given twenty soldiers with guns. That he would bring the Hollanders uncountable numbers of cattle and sheep, and all he asked was that a few of them should be pushed towards his side.

Brilliant plan, said Mynheer Van Riebeeck, and poured the wine of rejoicing. Fetch Chora of the Chorachoqua and Gogosoa of the Goringhaiqua and Trosoa whom Harry appointed to oversee the Goringhaicona while he was stuck on the island. Let's talk this out properly.

Oedasoa ordered Eva to go straight back to the Fort and cast sand in the eyes of the Dutch chief so that he wouldn't notice that the kraals round the Cape were disappearing. She should cast the sand slowly because they would need time to make places for their kraals and to seek out watering holes.

Only Doman and the robber bands were to remain at the Cape. Not a calf or a lamb was to be left for the Hollanders. Not a Hottentot to fetch wood for the Fort's kitchens or to draw a single bucket of water for them. The Hollanders would have to fetch their own wood and water and do their own dirty work, so they would be tired out when they went to bed at night.

14

'Pieternella, why are you sitting here sleeping beside the sheep? The day is almost over!'

'I'm not sleeping, Oom Bart, I'm thinking.'

'You must get away from here. Before sundown they're going to come and slaughter one of the sheep for the Captain's table. Your clothes will be spattered with blood!'

'How long is it still to Mauritius, Oom?'

'Depends. Focke says First Mate Berks reckons we might run past on the south and then swing north – and pray that we find the island. Daniel Zaaijman says some of the water barrels are leaking, and that could be serious. Some of the barrels of salted meat are also leaking. The Steward is cursing and swearing about the barrels loaded on board at the Cape.'

'What does that mean?'

'That we'd better hurry to get to Mauritius. Tant Theuntjie says you're very disobedient down in the hold.'

'I never wanted to be on the ship.'

'What?' Shocked.

His anger was different from Tant Theuntjie's, she wasn't afraid of him. 'I never wanted to go to Mauritius!'

'Well, where did you want to go to, then? The Church Council couldn't afford to support you any longer, because what happened to your late father's estate only the Orphan Chamber would be able to say and their books are sealed. You should be grateful that I took pity on you, else you would have had to stay at the Cape and end up like your mother!'

'Leave my mother out of this.'

'What?' More pretended shock.

His cap was dirty, his jerkin was dirty, his trousers were dirty. One eye had a spot of red in the white. 'My mother never did anything to you.'

'Who abandoned you and ran off?'

'She did. Because she didn't know what else to do any more.'

'Don't you shout at me, girl!'

'I'm not shouting, I'm saying.'

He threw up his arms. 'Now I see what Theuntjie means! In taking you on, I've hung a chain round my neck!'

The bird was floating high above his head. The sky was blue.

'Which sheep are they going to slaughter first?' She felt like being deliberately defiant; like reminding him that she was the daughter of the woman with two heads! She felt like kicking, screaming. 'Which sheep?'

'How should I know? Go and ask the cook.'

'Do you believe in witchcraft, Oom?'

'What?'

'Witchcraft.'

'Good God, what's got into your head, girl?'

'Do you really think the Orphan Chamber's still got some of our money?'

'Of course they must still have some of your money.'

No one had ever mentioned a word to her about it. 'How much?'

'How am I supposed to know? I intend to get the new Commander to write and enquire as soon as we get there.'

So that he, Oom Bart, could get his hands on it? 'Do you think he will? The new Commander.'

'Of course he will. It's his job. A kindly man, decent and highly educated, they say he knows Latin and everything.'

'Do you believe in witchcraft?'

'Good God! Why are you going on about witchcraft again? What on earth has your mother put into your head? Everybody warned me, said you're just like her. You kept on creeping under her wings! Pieternella, I don't like that look on your face, I don't want Hottentot blood in my house!'

'My mother taught us never to bow and scrape to a Dutchman unless you want him to trample on you.'

'I'll have you thrown off this ship!' The blood was pulsing red in his neck.

'Do you know about the Bible that spun round of its own accord one day, Oom?' She'd been wanting to ask him that for a long time. Just to hear if there really was a God who listened when you asked …

'No, 'strues God, now I've had enough of what goes on in your head!' He turned round and stumbled away.

The nicest new fig had unexpectedly started swelling on the twig.

If the Orphan Chamber still had some of their father's money, they'd have to give it to them so that she and Salomon would have the fare to buy themselves a passage on a ship back to the Cape. Cornelia must get sick again so she could go back and look after the child, so that she would get to Lamotius first. Before Bart Borms.

The whistle blew for prayers.

The Captain read and prayed. Monsieur Lamotius stood next to him, Juffrouw Margaretha and Cornelia with the little dolly a little farther off. Cornelia looked the picture of health.

'Headgear off!'

Salomon was standing beside Bart Borms like a motherless lamb with nowhere else to stand, his cap meekly pressed to his chest.

What if the Orphan Chamber had enough of their father's money for her to be able to send him to the fatherland like Jannetjie Ferdinandus's Johannes …

The Cape was their fatherland. Their mother country.

'*As the hart panteth after the water brooks, so panteth my soul after thee, O God. My soul thirsteth for God, for the living God: when shall I come and appear before God?*

The heart of a crow, chopped up fine. Were there crows on Mauritius?

'*It is for this reason that holy men have no fear of death, nay rather that they long for it exceedingly ...*'

The man who was flogged lived for another three days.

The supper whistle.

Barley and prunes left over from breakfast and the rest of the vegetables and bacon from lunch. And bread.

The hatch on the wooden hole had already been closed for the night; the Captain always sent a sailor to do it late in the afternoon. So it felt as though they had been nailed in again. Bundled up with the sound of the water and the creaking of the wood, Maria's children's whining and Tant Maijke and Tant Theuntjie's endless bickering and snapping at each other.

'Pieternella, roll out the bedding before I really lose my temper with this Theuntjie of Bart's.'

If she kept her eyes closed, she wasn't so aware of the dark. If she pressed her face deep into the mattress, she could smell the mountain. If she held the pot shards, cupped in her hand, to her nose, she could smell her mother ...

Oedasoa of the Cochoqua must have been a wise man. A different kind of wise from an old India hand in silk clothes. He tasted the wine which Commander Van Riebeeck gave her mother for him only once, then he said: the fire in our honey-beer is a lukewarm fire; the fire in this white man's wine is a red-hot fire that will burn to death.

And he never drank wine again.

Her mother was burnt out by the heat of that fire.

The woman with two heads. Who had to stand between Hottentot and Hollander so the livestock and the kraals could slip away quietly and be safely hidden out of harm's way ...

The messenger.

From Oedasoa to Mynheer Van Riebeeck.

From Mynheer Van Riebeeck to Oedasoa.

Doman sent to say that the Dutch chief had decided it would be better to forge links with the mighty Cochoqua for all their livestock. That Oedasoa had sent a message to say that he was keen to establish bonds of friendship with the Dutch.

All over the Cape the kraals were secretly broken up and loaded on to the oxen …

Just as secretly, Doman and his robber band began to steal the cattle and sheep by night. Soldiers were sent out in the morning light to search for them but couldn't pick up the spoor.

This was powerful witchcraft.

The woman with two heads. The messenger. Back and forth.

'Mynheer, my sister's husband says you need not soil your smart clothes by bothering with the Goringhaiqua or the Chorachoqua or the Goringhaicona – unless they really cause you a lot of trouble. If that happens, you can attack them and he, Oedasoa, would not take offence. All he desires is deeper friendship, and to be able to trade with the Dutch.'

Back to Oedasoa.

With a pack-ox back-breakingly laden with gifts for this good Hottentot. Soldiers, Sergeant Harwarden and his fiddle.

'What can I send to Oedasoa to keep his heart warm towards the Hollanders, Eva?'

She thought quickly. Rice and tobacco and small mirrors and a cloak and a comb, and some pepper and nutmeg and cinnamon, and perhaps a bottle of Mynheer's nice arrack brandy. A porcelain bowl with designs on it, and Mynheer's music box, because my sister's husband is very fond of music.

Along the road somewhere, she would tell one of the soldiers to share the wine between her and themselves.

'Unfortunately not the music box, Eva. It's a clavichord and very difficult to replace. But I'll make sure that Harwarden takes his fiddle along to play for Oedasoa.'

'That would be good, Mynheer.'

'However, the most important task that you have to perform, Eva, is to persuade Oedasoa himself to come to the Fort.'

That was the last thing that Oedasoa would want. Speak the road full of thorns, Krotoa, he told her. I don't want Dutchmen in my kraals and I'm not going into their kraal! Tell Van Riebeeck I am of noble birth, I don't walk into lesser kraals.

That evening her mother waited until Juffrouw Maria had sat her down on the chair in the smart room in the Fort to teach her more prayer-words. Goose feather cushions covered with shiny material under her bum. The cloth was almost the colour of copper when you rubbed it hard. Some of the same material hung from poles all the way round the big wooden bed where Mynheer Van Riebeeck and Juffrouw Maria slept at night. Just like a long shiny dress. Carved wooden frames round painted pictures on the walls; birds with long tails, sitting on branches; angels with half their bodies hidden in clouds; the most wonderful flowers in a vase with patterns on it. When her mother saw it for the first time, she secretly touched it with her finger to feel if it was real ...

'Juffrouw Maria,' she asked, 'is Mynheer a high-born man?'

'Eva, Mynheer is a lowly man of God who wants only the best for everybody.'

She went to tell Oedasoa: Mynheer is a high-born man; he's related to God himself, and he asks that you, Oedasoa, bring your kraals closer to the Fort so that you and he can become good friends for ever, and if you would please come and attack the Cape Hottentots, because they are the most terrible stock thieves. The fleet is on its way and there is not enough meat.

Back to the Fort. Harwarden was with her. He said Oedasoa had received them wonderfully well, he'd had to play his fiddle almost all night long.

Mynheer Van Riebeeck was thoroughly dissatisfied. He reproached Harwarden: You come back and tell me of all the Cochoquas' thousands upon thousands of cattle and sheep, but all you bring back here are three old cows and thirteen sheep with worn-down teeth?

He asked her mother: Eva, did you give Oedasoa my message?

Yes, Mynheer, he says he's very sorry that he cannot move closer to the Fort at this time. There's not enough grazing here. Also, he can only attack the Cape Hottentots if they harass *him*. But he won't hesitate if that becomes necessary; the Goringhaiqua have caused him great loss and injury in the past. They are his enemies. So are the Chorachoqua and the Goringhaicona. Great enemies.

Back to Oedasoa.

Harwarden and his fiddle, soldiers and a wagonload of trade goods.

Oedasoa was furious.

'Krotoa, I told you to keep the Dutchmen away from my kraal! Why have you brought them back here again?'

'My feet are worn out with walking, husband of my sister. I don't know what to say to Mynheer Van Riebeeck any more to keep him satisfied. He wants livestock. Urgently. Any number of cattle and sheep have been stolen and one free-burgher has had his house burnt down. And they can't trace the spoor of the culprits.'

'I'll send him some animals to calm him down and allow the second group of Chorachoqua to get through safely to their hiding places.'

Two hundred sheep, twenty-five cattle, seven draught oxen.

Harwarden said that was hopelessly too few.

Her mother did not go back to the Fort with them.

Not before the following full moon would Oedasoa send her back.

'Mynheer, Oedasoa has been mauled by a lion, he cannot come to you.'

'Eva, once before, long ago when I needed cattle and Harry kept stalling the other Hottentots to stop them coming to the Fort, you mentioned a rich tribe somewhere in the hinterland.'

She'd actually made up that story. To stop Mynheer Van Riebeeck being so angry with her uncle. She couldn't now remember all the lies she made up then; her two heads were getting muddled; her tongues were tripping each other up. 'They were the Chobona, Mynheer.'

'Where do they live?'

'I just want to stay in the Fort with you and Juffrouw Maria and to learn to read and pray more, even if Doman laughs at me.'

'Where is Doman?'

'They say he's at Hout Bay.' Doman was helping the Chorachoqua move off to Oedasoa.

'Where do the Chobona live?'

'Very far away, Mynheer.' It wasn't all lies; it was just that she didn't know much about these black people. She'd only ever heard bits and pieces about them.

'We've got to get livestock urgently, Eva. The Chainouqua from behind the mountains to the south do occasionally bring a few cattle and sheep to barter for the tobacco that they have learnt to desire, but they are far too few. We have to find other sources and you have to help us.'

'The Chobona live a very long way away.'

'Who are they?'

She made up all kinds of words to hide the fact that she was suddenly growing uneasy. If Oedasoa heard that his real enemies the Chainouqua were bringing animals to the Dutch, there would be trouble. 'They are a very rich, whitish people, Mynheer, the Chobona. They live in stone houses with black walls and they have lots of gold and pearls and churches that they pray in, just like the Hollanders.'

His eyes stretched wide, his mouth fell open. 'They must be the people of Monomotapa!' he cried. 'At last! Tell me everything you know about them, Eva!'

'I'm too tired now, Mynheer.' So he poured her a big glass of wine. Sweet and lovely. 'I'm feeling a little better, Mynheer.'

'The Chobona. Tell!'

'They've got long hair. Lots of cattle and lots of elephant tusks, but they don't have any red beads. They've got pitch-black slaves that don't run away like the Hollanders' slaves ...' The woman with two heads had to think ever harder to say the words properly: her tongue was thick and loose. 'What they actually want is copper and brass, like the Namaqua have.'

'Namaqua? Who are the Namaqua?'

It had slipped out! Oedasoa had said she was never to mention the wealthy Namaqua, north of the Cochoqua, because what if the Namaqua moved south after the Hollanders' trade goods? What if the Namaqua became friends with the Hollanders?

'Who are the Namaqua?'

'Different kind of Hottentots. Not Khoikhoi. Khoi. Different sheep, different skin clothes, goats that look almost like sheep. My tongue is lame, Mynheer, and my arms and legs, too ...'

She woke up the next morning in her bed and couldn't remember how she'd got there.

'You've got to go back to Oedasoa for me, Eva. Tell him we are being plundered and pillaged by robbers. I have good reason to believe that most of them are Goringhaiquas and that Doman is misleading them. Our greatest problem is that all of a sudden we cannot find their kraals. Only the traces of where they used to be. I'm sending Harwarden with you again. You have got to find out whether Oedasoa would be prepared to send us spies to find the kraals for us.'

'Oedasoa has trekked deep into the hinterland, Mynheer. I wouldn't know where to look for him.'

'But you said he'd been mauled by a lion.'

'Yes, but ...' She'd forgotten about the lion! 'He's much better now.'

'How do you know?'

'I heard from one of the wood carriers.'

'When?'

'Yesterday.'

'Eva, why are you telling lies? The wood carriers, the water carriers – all disappeared without trace two days ago!'

'I'm not telling lies, Mynheer, I just can't bear seeing you so full of anxiety. One day I went to Oedasoa and he wasn't there ...'

'Eva!'

'Yes, Mynheer?'

'Do you believe in God the Almighty Father?'

'Yes, Mynheer.'

'Go and tell Oedasoa we dare not put off destroying the Cape Hottentots any longer. The blood of God's people is being spilt! A free-burgher was bludgeoned to death last night by Hottentots after he had used up all the shot in his musket firing at them!'

'Mynheer, if you send me to Oedasoa, I'll never see you again. I've learnt to love the Dutch people; it's just that this country is going to be full of war now.'

Back to Oedasoa.

'Why are you shaking so, Krotoa?'

'Mynheer Van Riebeeck is so anxious he's at me day and night to tell him where he can find animals, where the Chobona live and where ... He asks you, my sister's husband, to send him spies to track down the kraals so that he can destroy the Goringhaiqua.'

'I hear a bunch of soldiers have set off on foot from the Fort to search for the Namaqua?'

'No.' She began to tremble even more.

'Who told him about the Namaqua?'

'They'll never find the right way; there's a drought; their water will run out on the way; wild dogs will eat them up; the Bushmen will shoot them with arrows.'

'Who did they hear about the Namaqua from?'

'I don't know.'

'What does that soldier standing next to you say?'

'It's Harwarden. He wants to know why you are shouting at me. I haven't done anything.'

Back to the Fort.

She and Harwarden and fifty delegates from the Cochoqua, to tell Mynheer Van Riebeeck that Oedasoa was sorry he was unable to compensate for the gifts which had been sent to him, that he had to trek far into the hinterland in search of better grazing for his stock because his animals were very lean ...

'Eva, the expedition sent out to search for the Namaqua have found no sign of any such people.'

'I don't understand it, Mynheer.' Thanks be.

'Yesterday sixteen oxen were stolen from free-burghers.'

'I don't understand it, Mynheer.'

'Harwarden says it sounded as though Oedasoa was also displeased with you. Why?'

'Because … because I don't want to marry the man he has chosen for me, Mynheer.'

'You said a while ago that Oedasoa regarded the Goringhaiqua as his enemies.'

'He hates them Mynheer, and they hate him.'

'Yesterday soldiers saw a kraal with a group of Goringhaiquas and Chorachoquas together near the Leopard Mountain, and they saw you and Harwarden and the fifty unarmed Cochoquas pass close by them without any sign of hostility. How do you understand that?'

'It was because the soldier was there. With the shooting stick.'

She could see that he didn't believe her.

So she took her things and ran away to Gonnema's kraal among the Cochoqua.

Then the real war broke out.

All the free-burghers' work at the Cape came to a standstill.

Mynheer Van Riebeeck called for reinforcements from a ship anchored in the Bay and started criss-crossing the whole area with over two hundred soldiers, searching for the kraals that had disappeared. At Salt River they caught a Chorachoqua. They sent for Harry on Robben Island: he and the Chorachoqua were to show them where the kraals lay hidden in the valleys. They searched and searched and found nothing. Harry pleaded, he didn't want to go back to Robben Island. Mynheer Van Riebeeck said he had to.

They took the Chorachoqua to the torture chamber in the Fort; tied his legs together; blindfolded his eyes; hoisted him up by his arms with a rope, up and down, up and down. He cried, he said he knew nothing. They placed him on a wooden bench with his arms and legs stretched out and tied him down; then they turned a wheel fastened to him with ropes. Gradually they began to stretch him longer and longer. One stood at his head with a heavy iron bar. They said if he cried out too much in pain, they would give him a death blow on the head, for mercy's sake.

They turned the wheel, they turned the wheel …

He screamed. He told them Oedasoa and Gogosoa were hiding everybody. The group of Cochoqua that came with Eva had not returned, they had gone to give Doman a message from Oedasoa – the lion was arising.

'Pieternella, wake up! What are you screaming like that for?'

It was still night. Someone had lit the candle in the lantern.

'Secure the pisspots, we're in for another storm!' shouted Tant Theuntjie.

A storm. The second one. The First Mate said ...

'Pieternella!'

She tied the ropes of the pots to the cords holding the chests; the mattresses were covering the floor rings.

The clothes on the nails were swinging to and fro, the ship creaked and grumbled. It was cold.

As she crawled, she searched for her shawl in the half dark, felt the pot shards and pressed them in under the overlap of her mattress. Maria's Daatjie started crying.

'Shut that child up!' ordered Tant Theuntjie. 'There's enough noise in here already.'

'Open a hatch, I'm gong to faint.' Tant Maijke began to pant.

'Do you want the whole sea inside the ship?'

'I've got a dreadful feeling in my head again.'

'It's nothing, you're not going to get seasick again. Lie down. Pieternella, cover Tant Maijke's feet and pass my bundle. I want some of my cheese to eat, I'm hungry.'

'Oh Lordjee, we're capsizing!'

'Relax your body, Maijke! Pieternella, hold on to the pots, they're not tied on tightly enough. If those things spill over tonight, there's going to be one hell of a mess, let me tell you!'

She struggled to reach the pots, the ship seemed to be bumping and pitching at one and the same time.

'I'm telling you, we have sailed into Doomsday!' was Tant Maijke's uneasy prophecy.

'Doomsnight,' Tant Theuntjie mockingly corrected her. 'This is nothing. The storm is still just gathering its forces at the moment. Once Bart and I were coming back from Batavia. The ship we were on ran into a storm off Mauritius. The mainmast snapped clean off like a twig. Bart said it was the end of us, but we limped along on one leg all the way to the Cape. If your time has not yet come, Maijke, your time has not yet come!'

'Aren't you afraid of death, Tante?' Pieternella asked.

'What does a snotty nosed kid know about death? Wait till you've had the life behind you that I've had. Hold on to those pots!'

'Shame on you, Theun,' said Tant Maijke, clinging to a wooden rib. 'What you've had behind you is nothing. Wait till the day comes when you – a proud woman – are branded like a convict! Then your only comfort is the knowledge that God will call them to account yet.'

'Do you think God is not going to call *you* to account as well?'

'I wish you two would just stop it,' shouted Maria, holding on to the children and throwing a quilt over their heads.

'Doesn't help getting the shits about everything.' Tant Theuntjie flopped over loosely with the ship's next roll, but went on hacking off a chunk of cheese. 'The day of reckoning comes, whether you want it or not – as Pieternella is going to find out tonight if she lets those pisspots spill over!'

'The pots are too full. Someone has to go and empty them!'

'I'll come with you,' offered Maria. 'Theuntjie, come and sit with the children.'

'Since when am I your nursemaid?'

It was like hell out on deck.

With the damned everywhere dressed in sailor's garb. Rain and wind and creaking wood.

They had to hold tight to the pots and each other, she and Maria. The wind was from the larboard side. In the dark the pots tumbled into the sea on the starboard side – only one came back, the other one's rope jerked out of her hand.

'Can't you even hold on to a pisspot?' yelled Tant Theuntjie above the noise of the storm. 'What's the use of one pot among the six of us? What do you think is going to happen?'

A spoke beating on the door. 'Get up!' shouted the sailor.

'I'll go and ask for another one.'

'Who will you ask? This isn't a goods shed. This is a ship in the middle of the sea!'

The ship gave a severe list; Tant Maijke called out for the umpteenth time: 'Gawd, Theun, are we going under?'

'Not yet,' Tant Theuntjie shouted back. 'Not before our bladders burst from keeping it in, because how do you think we're going to manage with only one pot? Go and fetch the water, Pieternella. And throw the water bucket into the sea, too, while you're about it.'

Anthonie and Cornelia were just ahead of her at the water hatch. 'How is my mother?' asked Cornelia above the noise of the storm.

'Just scared.'

When the sailor took the water bucket, he handed back the beer tankard. 'Beer's finished.'

There wasn't any fire in the galley either.

Breakfast was cheese and hard tack and dried salt fish.

When she was taking the basin back, she noticed that there were only three sheep left in the pen. Almost no sails on the masts. She didn't want to go back down again, but she had to, because it was cold and raining hard. Tant Theuntjie was still swearing about the pot and the beer that was finished and Maria's children.

She had to get out.

'Where are you going, Pieternella?'

'I'm going to sit in the passage in front of the door.'

'Don't you give me any of your sulks! I'll smack you right through that hatch!'

Keep quiet, just keep quiet, she told herself and sat down in the farthest corner.

Day outside. Night within.

She sat with her back to the wooden body of the ship and closed her eyes. The ship could bounce her all it liked, the ship could founder, she didn't care any more.

People didn't care about people either.

'I tell you, there's going to be one hell of mess with only one pot!' Tant Theuntjie, never-ending.

'Well, it's lucky the beer is finished,' said Maria defiantly.

The war.

Her mother often said the witchcraft would have gone on working if the ships hadn't brought these new things, horses.

And dogs.

First they hunted down Doman with the horses and shot him. And three of the others, too. But when they went back to cut off parts of the bodies as proof, to be able to claim the reward, the dead had disappeared.

What a loss ... There was a large reward on Doman's head.

They caught one of the wounded who had fled and took him back to the Fort so Mynheer Van Riebeeck could make him talk and tell where the rest of the robbers were hiding.

They put his thumbs in screw-like iron things: he told them a bunch of Goringhaiconas – the water drawers and wood carriers – had a kraal in the valley at Hout Bay. That was where they left from to steal the Hollanders' livestock and burn down the free-burghers' houses at night.

They then released his thumbs.

'Why are you people doing this to us?' asked Mynheer Van Riebeeck in despair.

'To make you go away.'

The soldiers leapt back on to their horses, but when they reached the valley, the kraals were gone. They found the tracks and followed them for hours, almost to where the Cape sticks its point into the sea, and there they trapped forty of her mother's people, the Goringhaicona, who fled into the bushes in terror. Soldiers pursued them, shot two dead and caught poor old Trosoa, who had always been Harry's best friend. Trosoa flung himself down on the ground, kicking and screaming, saying they could shoot him but he wasn't going to be dragged to the Fort!

So they shot him. Because the soldiers couldn't load him on to a horse, the horses were too small. And they didn't feel like *carrying* him over the mountains; it was far to the Fort. A third Hottentot tumbled over the cliffs when the shot struck him.

To claim the reward, they cut off the top lips.

A few days later one of Oedasoa's spies brought the news to the kraal: Van Riebeeck was now so angry with the Hottentots he was having poles cut for a paling higher than the tallest Hollander's head. They were fixing them into the ground all the way from the Salt River, right round the free-burghers' farms along the Liesbeeck, to above Forest Hill up against the mountain. The best land and water had now been fenced off for the Dutch. Worst of all was that no ox or bullock or sheep could now be stolen and driven off because a cursed gate of poles was going to be put up through which everyone had to pass in and out.

Soldiers with guns at the gate.

They wanted to plant wild almond trees all along on the outside of the palings. Wild almonds you could trample down, or you let your stock trample them down, but what to do about the fixed poles? Any Hottentot that wanted to set foot inside the pale first had to prove his peaceableness by waving a small white flag. Flags obtainable from the lookout posts.

Lion was too cunning. Witchcraft didn't work any more.

And Doman wasn't dead, he was with Oedasoa and the Cochoqua. One arm had been shattered by a ball lodged in his shoulder.

Oedasoa sent her mother to Mynheer Van Riebeeck with a little white flag and a bunch of the Cochoqua to accompany her.

'Mynheer, Oedasoa has sent me to ask you please to forgive the Goringhaiqua. They will bring back the plundered cattle that have not yet been eaten, and Oedasoa will send the rest.'

Mynheer Van Riebeeck was no longer the same man. Deep down in his heart he was far too angry. Specially with her mother. He didn't offer her even a small glass of wine.

'They ought to offer to repay us twice the losses!' he snarled at her. 'Go and tell Oedasoa I'll consider the matter, but he will have to come to the Fort in person to speak to me.'

She asked if she might just first take her greetings to Juffrouw Maria. No. Juffrouw Maria was resting.

A few days later a whole horde of Goringhaiconas arrived at the Fort, waving little flags. They had heard that Oedasoa had asked for peace for the Goringhaiqua; they had come to ask for peace for themselves. These were some of the wood bearers and water carriers and pot scourers who had always lived around the Fort. They would start work again straightaway if Mynheer would take them back. The war was all Doman's fault, *he* was the one who had said they should rob the Hollanders to drive them out of the country.

Fine, they could fetch their huts and put them up again near the Fort.

The Post Holder on Robben Island sent an urgent message that Harry had disappeared off the island. A rotten old skiff that had lain on a sand dune near Sand Bay without any oars was also missing.

'Never mind,' said Mynheer Van Riebeeck. 'Now at last we're rid of Harry, too – the sea was too rough, he'd never have made it to land.'

The war was over. Except that Doman and the other Cape Hottentots were too scared to risk going anywhere near the Fort. In case Mynheer Van Riebeeck was still too angry about the stolen stock and burnt-out houses, and might order them shot. So they stayed in hiding near Saldanha. So did her mother's uncle Harry, because he hadn't drowned.

'I'm telling you, there's going to be a hell of a mess in here with only one pisspot. Pieternella, go and tell the Captain you threw the pot over the side so that he can deal with you.'

'There's a storm on, Theuntjie!' chipped in Tant Maijke. 'You can't have the child go bothering the skipper about a pisspot!'

The horses' hooves had trampled out the witchcraft.

Day after day, everywhere in the forests around the Cape, the axes were felling trees for the paling. Stinkwood and yellowwood. The ends were sharpened, burnt black with fire and then embedded in the ground. Fencing as far as the eye could see. Teams of sailors off the ships were called in to help fell and plant the poles.

Eventually Mynheer Van Riebeeck said he would consider making peace with the Hottentots. And, yes, Eva could come back and stay in the Fort, but it wouldn't be the same as before. She had betrayed the Hollanders who had been so kind to her. She could earn her food and wine and some clothing by acting as an interpreter whenever the Cochoqua brought livestock to barter. When Oedasoa eventually came.

Her mother went and told Juffrouw Maria she wanted to be baptised and confirmed so she could have Christian blood, but Juffrouw Maria said she had first to find forgiveness for her sins.

On the day that the Son of God ascended into Heaven Mynheer Van Riebeeck summoned everyone to the square in front of the Fort: the Hottentot chieftains, the lesser chiefs and the elders. He told her mother: Eva, ask them if there is anyone who has anything to say before we reach an agreement.

Harry was there, too. And Gogosoa, and Choro. Not Doman. He'd been too grievously wounded.

'Yes,' said Gogosoa.

'Eva, interpret his words and interpret them correctly. Not your own version again!' Mynheer Van Riebeeck cautioned her.

'You have come and taken our very best land,' said Gogosoa. 'We want to know if you would have let us do that in *your* fatherland.' Mynheer Van Riebeeck didn't reply. 'We are the oldest owners. Who should now leave – the rightful owners, or the foreign invaders?' Mynheer Van Riebeeck let him speak. 'The wild almond trees are ours, now you have taken them for your hedge. Their roots in the ground are our winter food, now you're taking it from us with the hedge!'

Mynheer Van Riebeeck stood up and said: 'You lost the land in warfare. You did not return the stolen cattle which you wrongfully stole from us without any reason.'

Then the soldiers came and placed copper and beads and plenty of food and lots of brandy and arrack in the middle of the square and the Hottentots got roaring drunk.

Her mother, too.

Then the new Commandeur arrived and Mynheer Van Riebeeck told him not to believe anything that Eva the Hottentot said. And he should not allow wheat to be sown beyond the hedge because the Hottentots would drive their cattle into it. They'd had plenty of difficulties with the

Hottentots. Always keep them wanting tobacco, it was to the advantage of the Company.

15

She was standing at the front hatch waiting for the water bucket.

'Salomon says you were looking for me yesterday?' Daniel Zaaijman, the jackal-haired man, came up through the hatch from below, the bucket behind him. He looked like someone who'd been working all night, his hair in rat's tails, his face unsmiling in the light of the lantern.

'Yes, Mynheer.' He untied the bucket for her and moved it out of the way. The storm was abating. 'They say you're a cooper.' Her lips were stiff with cold as the words steamed out. 'I wanted to ask you if there wasn't an old barrel that you could saw in half and put a rope handle on to.'

'Why?'

'I lost one of our pots over the side. Tant Theuntjie goes on simmering about it, she goes at me right into the middle of the night ...'

'I'll see what I can do.'

'Thank you, Mynheer.'

He picked up the bucket and carried it to the rear hatch for her while she struggled round the sheep pen on the starboard side. The deck was slippery and she had to hold on wherever she could. The man with the jackal hair walked without any difficulty. 'Mynheer,' she asked when he put down the bucket beside the hatch, 'how many days have we been on the water?'

'Twenty-two. We ought to turn northwards tomorrow or the day after. It'll get warmer then.'

Twenty-two. 'Is that when we get to Mauritius?'

'No. Madagascar.'

There had to be a mistake somewhere. 'Madagascar?'

'Yes.' He turned round and walked off.

Maria was rolling up the mattresses. Tant Theuntjie was sitting against the wall with her legs stretched out, Tant Maijke next to her. They had their dresses on already and both looked equally sheepish.

'Where've you been all this time?' Tant Theuntjie scolded her.

'There were lots of people needing water.' Madagascar. She didn't want to go to Madagascar.

'Has anyone lit a fire?'

'Yes, Tante.'

'Go and empty the pisspot!'

'Yes, Tante.' The old woman had the pot on the brain!

Somewhere there'd been a very big mistake ...

The storm was abating; the ship was tired, like something that had been beaten too much.

'Salomon?' She found him next to the galley, piling wood on to his arms in the half-light before dawn.

'Pieternella, come and stand against the bricks, you're freezing.'

'The ship's going to Madagascar.'

That made him jerk upright. 'Madagascar?'

'Yes. Daniel Zaaijman says so.'

'I don't want to go to Madagascar.'

'Nor do I. I just wanted to tell you.'

'Why are you looking so bedraggled, Pieternella? Where's your cap? Look how tangled your hair is.'

'I've come out to clean the pot.'

'Are you all right?'

'Yes. And you?'

'Yes. Why are you crying?'

'Tears just run out of my eyes by themselves.'

'Meerhoff!' thundered the cook from down below somewhere.

For the first time in three days there were prayers again. Her ears heard the words, but she didn't.

Breakfast was barley and prunes floating in butter. And hard tack.

And the wind couldn't make up its mind which way to blow. It would gust for a while, grab hold of the sails, then drop again abruptly. Sailors were chased up the rigging to shake out the sails, shouted down again, chased up again to shorten them.

'Helmsman, keep your eyes on the sails.' Lubbert's voice. 'You're sailing too close to the wind!'

The sea was grey and muddled.

She sat down beside the sheep pen, but the cold drove her downstairs again. At some time during the night when she had to go out and empty the pot again, Lubbert's door had been open. A lantern swung above the wooden bunk he was lying on.

'Prettiest wench!' he called when she came back. 'Come in here and

I'll warm you up.'

She scurried past.

The hold stank. It was a long time since the Captain had allowed anyone to open a hatch. Maria said it was Tant Maijke's feet, too.

'The ship's going to turn towards Madagascar. Tomorrow or the next day.' She said it so that everyone would know.

'Fasten that pot, the ship is going to roll violently!' was Tant Theuntjie's response.

Tant Maijke had heard. 'Madagascar? Funny that – right till the end your mother went on hoping he would come back.'

It wasn't true.

'Yes,' Tant Theuntjie chipped in with a sneer. 'If Pieter van Meerhoff had lived, Eva might not have taken to booze the way she did.'

That wasn't the whole truth either. Nothing, it seemed, was the whole truth.

'Theuntjie ...' Tant Maijke shifted her body to a more comfortable position, 'how did it happen,' she started prying, her voice the voice of the snoop, 'that you all had to appear in court that time over the jar of Spanish wine but Pieter van Meerhoff was not called to give evidence?'

A hoary tale. Her mother used to say it was a bone that the dogs had long since sucked the marrow out of, but everyone who came by took another lick at it. She tried to kick the bone aside: 'One day my dad saw a real monster.' They ignored her.

'Yes,' sniffed Tant Theuntjie, crossing her legs. 'That's life for you. Everybody was summoned, but Pieter van Meerhoff was too high and mighty to bow his head in a court – except when they gave him a Hottentot to marry!'

'Don't say that, Tante.' Horrid old woman.

'It doesn't help disputing the truth, Pieternella.'

'Well, you tell us what really happened, Theuntjie,' prompted Tant Maijke.

They wouldn't let it alone.

'One afternoon I walked over to Barbara Geens's. Bart was on the boat to Saldanha. By then he had his own boat. The new Commandeur said he didn't want only fish, he wanted salted penguins to feed to the slaves as well. And birds' eggs. More seals, too, so they would have more oil to burn since more and more lamps were swallowing oil. I can still see all the empty barrels stacked up on deck as they sailed out that morning.'

Tant Maijke nudged her: 'Get to the Spanish wine!'

'My dad saw a proper monster once.'

'He must have had too much to drink!'

They didn't want to hear about the monster.

'As I was saying, I walked over to see Barbara. You know, she had a very tough time of it after Jacob van Rosendal died so suddenly.'

'I didn't know Barbara was a widow when she married Hendrik Reynste,' Maria exclaimed in surprise.

'Not just a widow, a pregnant widow! Her Machteldjie, that we call Maria, the one married to Captain Wobma, was born well after Jacob's death. Poor as church mice. Jacob had been the Company's master gardener but when he was gone, he was gone. She had to take in the Church's charity children just to keep herself alive. So I walked over to see her one afternoon; Jannetjie Ferdinandus was also in her sitting room. Not long, but there came a knock on the window and a voice called: "Barbie, are you home?"'

'It must have been Beselaar,' Tant Maijke interrupted excitedly.

'Don't take over my story! The Company's butler, Martin Beselaar with his red beard and fat belly – and a jar of Spanish wine under his jerkin. Barbara said: What are you hammering like that on my window for? The oilpapers are still soft, I oiled them only yesterday.'

Tant Maijke butted in quickly: 'I hear she's having glass put in now.'

'Yes, of course, she bakes bread for the ships now. That's what happens when you have a skipper for a son-in-law.'

'And then?'

'Barbara set out the mugs, Beselaar poured. It's not every day that a nice bottle of Spanish wine falls in through your doorway. We'd hardly lifted our elbows when there was a knock on the door. Pieter van Meerhoff. Barbara had sent for him to check whether her eldest, Sara, hadn't caught the smallpox. She had a rash that didn't look good. She didn't want to take the child to the Fort to be looked at, because of the danger of infection. He looked at the child and asked: Have you fed her any pork? Yes. He said it was the pork that was causing it.'

Hottentots never eat pigs, no matter how hungry they are. Not wild pigs, not tame Dutch pigs …

'Beselaar said: Give the Master something to drink, too. Barbara took a glass from the wall cupboard. Beselaar poured. We drank. Beselaar poured some more. We drank. You know what they say: the sweeter the wine, the sweeter the bliss. Soon Jannetjie undid her bodice to help her breathe. Bosom bulging like risen loaves in a bread pan. Beselaar kept wanting to touch with his finger, Jannetjie would smack his hand away and laugh. Master Pieter's pale face began to get some colour in it. Beselaar poured. We drank. I was the first to say that things were doing somersaults. Jannetjie kicked off her shoes and didn't smack Beselaar's hand away until after the third squeeze. I got up and walked over to the bed; I felt I had to lie down because everything was spinning. Beselaar poured. The jar seemed bottomless. The second one to fall on to the bed was Barbara. Her head was rolling, her cap had come off. Jannetjie was next, though she only just made it as far as the bed. Then Beselaar. Last Master Pieter. Each one as drunk as the next. I don't know how we all fitted on to that one bed but we did. Bodies all in a muddle. Woke up before dawn in misery.'

'Heavens!'

'Disentangled our bodies only with pain and difficulty.'

'But when did you hear that Beselaar had stolen the wine from the Fort?'

'The week after. It all came out that he'd long been a thief. They went around looking for witnesses. But not Master Pieter. O no, he'd only gone to examine the child.'

'You say: all on one bed?'

'Yes.'

'Well,' Tant Maijke said with a laugh, 'I wouldn't refuse a little comfort if a bottle of Spanish wine fell in through this door. Stolen or not stolen. Feels as though I've been pickled in a barrel of brine.'

It wasn't a bottle of Spanish wine that came in the door, it was Daniel Zaaijman with an iron bucket.

'I hear you lost a pot, Theun.'

'We didn't. Pieternella did. It's a pity you've brought the bucket, she was learning a lesson.'

'That's your business.' At the door he turned round and said: 'Pieternella, remember the bucket will exert more force on the rope than a pot.'

When he'd gone, Tant Theuntjie said to Tant Maijke: 'Now *there's* a mystery wrapped in a very dark cloth.'

'What do you mean?'

'Bart says Daniel's father was the very best cooper in the fatherland. At Flushing. In the ship-building yard. You could say Daniel was born with a cooper's chisel in his hand. Then one day he just disappeared – Daniel, I mean. A few months later he arrived at the Cape. Not long after that, he turned up on Mauritius. Makes you think. They say he's pretty quick to pull out a knife ...'

'Hang on a moment,' Tant Maijke interrupted her, 'you remember that so-called soldier – Hans Christoffel, if I remember right – who pitched up at the Cape one day and who wasn't a soldier at all but a woman disguised as one?'

'Yes! Now that you've dug it up again, wasn't she also from Flushing, or was that the ship's name?'

'I was told the truth was,' Tant Maijke leant forward eagerly, enjoying the news, 'that she had run away to follow this same Daniel Zaaijman!'

'Right, I remember! Wore a strap with a big buckle under her clothes to make it look as though she had a whatyoucallit.'

'Imagine! The thing must have rubbed her raw!'

'Perhaps that's what made Daniel lose interest!'

Ha-ha-ha-ha.

'You two really are the worst scandalmongers ever born!' Maria burst out abruptly. 'Daniel Zaaijman is a decent man, anyone can see that, but you two have to smear every decent thing to make yourselves look a little cleaner!'

'Oooh, look who's talking!' Tant Theuntjie sat up. 'I don't need to smear Daniel Zaaijman, he'll do it himself one of these days. Because *there's* a dark horse for you. Not one of us free-burghers can make a decent living on Mauritius – one after another, the damned commanders have always seen to that – but somehow or other Daniel Zaaijman does pretty well. They just haven't caught him at it yet!'

She covered her ears and drew the quilt over her head.

Her father was the first white man to see the monster in the Olifants River. Before him, only a few Hottentots had ever seen the thing and they went in deadly fear.

Her mother had told them the story. Monsters appear out of the water only to certain people. They stick out their snouts to breathe; can't breathe under water.

That was before her father and mother were married. Jacobus was still a tiny baby. Mynheer Van Riebeeck said: Pieter van Meerhoff, I'm sending you, as a person of authority, with another search party to find the Namaqua and their flocks and herds. The animals from the Chainouqua and the Cochoqua are coming in too slowly.

Mynheer sent for her mother and poured wine for her. 'Eva, these Chobona and Namaqua, are you lying to us about them?'

'No, Mynheer, you heard Harry say I wasn't lying.'

Not about the Namaqua. Harry himself had said they were true.

A group of about ten men, five pack-oxen with all the goods, and two Hottentots who had a smattering of broken Dutch as interpreters. Plenty of tobacco and liquor for when they found the Namaqua, to teach them to smoke and drink liquor, so they would get a taste for them and bring lots of cattle to trade for more. Pen and ink and paper, because each day her father had to write everything down.

No, Eva, you're not going to tie the child on to your back and go with them. You're staying in the Fort. The Cochoqua could send people to trade here any day and then we'd be stuck without an interpreter.

Harry was too old and decrepit by then. Doman was only half alive: the side where they had shot him was quite numb, and in any case he was too filled with bitter hate for the Dutchmen.

So her father's party set off to find the Namaqua. They'd searched for them the previous year, too, but found nobody.

Northwards. Walking and walking and walking. Day after day. Not too far at a time, to spare the oxen.

Lots of lions along the road. And ostriches and wild antelope. Thousands of hartebeest and rhinoceros and Bushmen. They said they knew nothing about Namaquas. Nor where they lived.

The leader, Cruythof, said: 'Eva's lied to us again!'

Her father said: 'She wouldn't lie to me. We'll find the Namaqua yet.'

Walking and walking and walking. Days on end. Her father would scout out ahead to make sure they kept going in the right direction. One day the two Hottentots were following him secretly when a lion leapt out from behind a bush and went for them. They yelled: Master Pete, he gonna bite! When the lion saw the white man, it got such a fright it simply ran away. So her father shot a hartebeest and loaded it on to an ox. For food.

The next day a party of Bushmen came to tell them: The Namaquas are going to kill you. Her father told the interpreter to ask them to show them where the Namaquas' huts were; he would give them tobacco and beads. No. Never. At that, the interpreters also wanted to turn tail, but her father promised to protect them.

Walking and walking and walking. The next afternoon one of the previous day's Bushmen came back. He asked her father how much he would give him for taking him to the Namaquas.

A roll of tobacco as long as a musket, one bar of copper, a copper chain and a whole handful of beads as well – but first the Bushman would have to show where they could get through the mountains with the cattle that they were going to barter from the Namaqua. The Bushman said he would. Hand over the things.

Her mother always laughed happily at this point. 'Your dad was too cunning for Mister Bushman! He wouldn't give anything in advance. When next they looked, Bushman was gone with the wind.'

Walking and walking and walking. Another day, and another. Through rivers, through ravines. All along they came across deserted Bushman shelters, as though they had fled in haste.

At last they reached the beautiful river: the Olifants River. For three days they trekked alongside it. Suddenly a few more Bushmen appeared out of the bushes; they said the rest had gone ahead to warn the Namaqua that the Dutch were coming. The Namaqua said: Let them come, we'll kill them.

Her father said he wasn't afraid.

He took his gun and walked a little way along the river to try to shoot a bird for the pot. Suddenly a frightful monster rose up out of the water: a thing with three heads, like cats' heads, a long body and three long tails. And then it disappeared again, just like that. Her father came back to their campsite and told them what his eyes had seen. Everyone was dumbstruck, because they knew her father was not a man to tell lies. The two Hottentots were trembling so badly, they shook from head to foot. They said it was the *Cham-ouna* that lived under the water and told *Toqua* where your feet would walk so that *Toqua* could plan how to thwart you and hurt you. They would have to slaughter one of the pack-oxen immediately, to placate *Toqua*, and smear the fat all over their bodies.

Her father told them: Christian people don't believe in such things.

And then they found the Namaqua. And taught them to smoke and drink brandy.

When her father returned to the Cape, he told Mynheer Van Riebeeck: 'Eva was telling the truth. The Namaqua really are different from the Cape Hottentots. Even our interpreters had difficulty understanding all their words. They say they are *Khoi* – not Hottentots. The skins they sit on in their huts are so white, and tanned to such a softness, they're like bed linen. They have thousands of cattle and sheep and goats. But they cannot move closer to the Cape because between them and you lie all Oedasoa's kraals, and Oedasoa and Akembi, the king of the Namaqua, are sworn enemies.'

Then Mynheer gave a big banquet and her mother was also invited to sit at the table and was given wine. 'You sent our travellers in the right direction, Eva! Pieter van Meerhoff has at last managed to make contact with the Namaqua.'

The next day brought the news that Oedasoa was very angry with her mother. She was a traitor and a deceiver; if ever she set foot anywhere near a Cochoqua kraal again, she would be stoned to death!

One day her mother was sitting in the sun beside the Post House on

Robben Island. She, Pieternella, had been gathering shells that morning at the head of the island and was arranging them in patterns on the sand. Most of them were scallops with the ridged side on the back – in reds and blues. Shining and smooth on the inside.

'Pieternella?'

'Yes, Mamma?'

'You must go to Jannetjie and get me something to drink next time you come. I'm dying of thirst.'

'They'll give you a tot tonight, Mamma. The feather bag is full. Smoke your pipe.'

'You're a good child, Pieternella.'

'I'm glad.'

'Don't ever let a Dutchman take your goodness out of you, for the Lords' sake.'

'Which Lords?'

'The ones across the water, the ones everything belongs to. That steal everything they want from the Hottentots. Before he died, your great-uncle Harry, who used to be Autshumao, said the Dutchmen were going to take all the pastureland yet, and the rivers and the valleys as well. We Hottentots would have to flee into the mountains and crawl in with the Bushmen. As many are already doing. Don't you go living in the mountains, though – that's the home of baboons and leopards and Bushmen.'

'I won't.'

'Jacobus has a restlessness in him. He's my Hottentot child because his father gave him to me in the veld when he and Cruythof were sent off on their first expedition to search out the Namaqua for the Lords. Hottentot children are made on the ground in the veld, white children in beds – ground never touches them.'

'What about me and Salomon?'

'You are my white children with Hottentot feet.'

'Why only our feet?'

'It was a short bed, my feet were touching the ground.'

'Oh.'

'*Oh Lord God, if only they'd give me something to drink!*'

She went into the Post House kitchen for a cup of water and stole a little sugar to melt in it.

Lunchtime. Green peas with bits of meat in among them.

'The food's beginning to taste mouldy!' Tant Theuntjie cursed.

She went out to scrub the wooden bowl and stayed up on deck beside the sheep.

The bird was peacefully floating along behind the ship.

Don't you ever get tired, bird?

Daniel Zaaijman came past. 'Thank you for the bucket, Mynheer.'

'That's fine.'

She was glad Maria had stood up for him. It didn't matter what he'd done, she hoped they'd never catch him.

Maria, too, came up on deck with the children. The murderer went over to chat to them. You could tell Maria didn't like him. It must be dreadful to be married to someone you don't like.

Monsieur was very fond of Juffrouw Margaretha. And Mynheer Van der Byl of Juffrouw Sophia. Her father had been really fond of her mother. And Pieter van der Byl of her, Pieternella ...

Maria made her way slowly across the deck towards the sheep pen.

'Do you also long for the Cape, Maria?'

'With all my soul.'

'What's going to happen?'

'I don't know. As you don't know either, Pieternella.'

'Are you scared of Mauritius?'

'Yes.'

'So am I. And I'm not going to stay with Tant Theuntjie and Oom Bart, I promise you.'

'Don't imagine the impossible. It just makes the pain doubly sore afterwards.'

'Salomon and I are going back to the Cape. You'll see.'

'Bart Borms reckons Willem is going to get the piece of land just opposite his. So you and I might be neighbours.'

But only until their money arrived from the Cape ...

16

Some time on the twenty-third or twenty-fourth night they must have turned north because, when she went up on deck before dawn to fetch water, something was different. She couldn't tell what it was, she just felt it. Something like a restlessness.

The hollowed out old moon was hanging in the east with the big bright star just under it. The rest of the stars were scattered all over the sky …

She had almost reached the front of the water queue when all of a sudden she realised what was different. The ship wasn't moving! Or almost not. All the sails were unfurled on the masts, but they hung like things struggling to catch their breath.

'Has the ship come to a standstill?' she asked the sailor in front of her.

'Not yet.' Grimly.

The sailor behind pinched her bottom through her shift and laughed when she jumped out of the queue. 'Wait till it's really becalmed – you'll jump right over the side, and I'll jump after you!'

The one in front said over his shoulder: 'It's because we've turned north out of the current.'

'Thank you.' He was decent.

Morning prayers.

The bird was gone.

Breakfast. Barley with prunes floating in butter.

Both the hatches had been opened. The sea was two grey-blue squares on either side. The ship was still barely moving.

'Yes,' said Tant Theuntjie, 'one day the wind rips you apart, the next day it disappears. Can leave you to drift and drift all the way to hell without a drop of drinking water. The food already tastes off.'

Tant Maijke was also uneasy. 'Gawd, people, we're not moving forward at all! They say your life passes before your eyes when your end is approaching, but on these waters life just comes to a halt.'

'Oh, this is nothing. When you need to beware is when the wind has been quiet for long enough and the sailors start coming down with dysentery. Bart knows of one case where the *wives* of the skipper and the mate had to climb up the masts. The sailors that hadn't died were lying at death's door!'

'Don't sit there making me scared! I'm not clambering up any of those ropes.'

'Bart says Wobma should have stayed in the current.'

'I wouldn't know,' Tant Maijke said. 'All I want to know is what *they* are eating, the high-ups above our heads. What do they get to eat, Pieternella? You've eaten with them.'

'Smoked ham and eggs and onions and bread and roast chicken and all kinds of things.' She added in a few extras for good measure.

'The first thing I'm going to do when I get home is put rice and meat on to cook,' declared Tant Theuntjie. 'Bart's got to slaughter a bullock.'

'Oh, please think of me, too, Theun. Gawd, but I'm hungry.'

'Luckily you're pretty well covered, and you've still got enough cheese and dried fish in your chest,' Tant Theuntjie said nastily, adding with a sneer: 'It's the starvelings like Pieternella that are going to keel over first if the wind doesn't get moving soon.'

'Why are you so skinny, Pieternella?' Tant Maijke wanted to know. 'Didn't that stuck-up Sophia van der Tempel feed you, or what?'

'She did.'

'Tasty food, too, I'll bet.' Tant Theuntjie was prying again. 'The Van der Byls were paid to have you, but Oom Bart and I have to give you *and* Salomon food and clothes – and not get a blue bean for doing so.'

'Oom Bart says there's still some of my father's money in the Orphan Chamber.'

'Exactly. And Bart Borms isn't going to leave it there either, that I can promise you.'

'If it's true, then that money belongs to Salomon and me. It's not Oom Bart's.'

Tant Maijke uttered one long 'Ooooooh ...'

'What did you say?' It was like a shout from someone who had just had a fright.

'That money's Salomon's and mine.'

'Don't make me take the name of the Almighty in vain today!' Tant Theuntjie screamed and hurled the spoon in her hand across the room, just missing Maria's head and splattering barley porridge on the wall behind her. 'Little snotnose trying to force me to do *her* will? Others get paid to look after you, but Bart and I have to take you on and not charge anything for doing so?'

'All I thought was that then we'd have the fare to get back to the Cape.' She couldn't turn round and wish the words unsaid!

'There's nowhere for you to go at the Cape.'

There *is*! 'Or else we can look after ourselves, then you and Oom Bart will be rid of us.'

'*Jay-sus!*'

She'd crept in behind the sheep pen again. She had to think, she didn't know what ...

There was an uneasiness on the ship, you could feel it. The Captain was striding up and down, so was Monsieur Lamotius. The eyes of the sailors on the watch were different – scared. Like they were trapped.

Where was Salomon?

Scouring pots.

The bird was still missing. Perhaps he'd fallen into the sea because there wasn't any wind. Or perhaps he'd turned back.

The sails drooped from the masts like unstarched linen.

The Church at the Cape had alms money in the poor-box for people who really had nothing. But if a woman was getting alms she wasn't allowed to starch her dresses. That way everyone could see she was too poor.

The ship's sails hung slack so everyone could see there was no wind.

Her mother didn't get alms and she didn't care about starched dresses either.

Zara, who had hanged herself, always had dresses that spread out beautifully wide with starch. White people had raised Zara from babyhood to be a Dutch child, so Zara wanted nothing to do with Hottentots. Then she took paid employment with Fair Ansiela and her husband, Mynheer Basson. They said she did the finest needlework, like Ansiela, and cooked superbly, too. Her young man, too, was Dutch, Frans Schanffelaar. Then he married Tryn Roos and Zara hanged herself with the belt of her dress.

They say people who kill themselves don't want to live any more.

That's not the whole truth. Many people don't want to live, but they go on living just the same, on and on and on …

Like the shell carrier who sank down next to his sack of shells and said he was only living because he hadn't yet died.

One day when she arrived on the island, the Post Holder said her mother had left early that morning with the feather bag. She found her at the water's edge, sitting on her haunches beside the very same man. Drawing closer, she asked: Is he sick, Mamma?

'Yes, of despair.'

'What's that?' As he sat there, the man's neck was drooping.

'It's when your insides squeeze into each other from heartache but you can't breathe out. You just keep breathing in. I've told him to get up and walk into the sea so the water can smother his breath but he won't.'

'But, Mamma, how can you sit there and say such a thing? It's against the law! You saw what they did to Zara!'

'The law's arse. And all the Dutchmen's arses, too. See what the man looks like! They've beaten him to a pulp, they've cursed him up and down, but he hasn't got any better for it!'

'How long is his sentence?'

176

'Twenty-five years, and hardly one has passed so far.'

'Mynheer Van der Byl says the Governor says it's terrible that they have to punish people so severely, it doesn't really deter them.'

Once, when Salomon was still living with Sick Comforter Heere and his wife, they made him write out fifty times: *Disobedience leads to misfortune.* Because he'd refused to do the laundry, said it was women's work. So for a whole day they made him go without food, except rice water. Without salt. And Sick Comforter Heere read out of the Bible book that he who will not work shall not eat. Or something like that. Then he had to write lines *and* do the laundry.

The shell carrier was another who had refused.

On the first day of the month the soldiers who had to help build that hellish Castle did not have to fall in again after lunch and the midday break. That was when they were paid their food wages and their rice ration.

So, as usual, they all lined up. The Sergeant then came up, saying there was a need for haste, the Castle had to be finished, they had to go back and fall in. Till four o'clock. They said they were tired, they wanted their money and rice, as was the custom.

The Sergeant said: If you don't fall in immediately, you're mutineers.

They wouldn't budge. They wanted their money and rice.

The corporals arrived. They hauled a couple of the malcontents out of the bunch to make an example of them and whipped the rest back to the stones and the building lime.

The four hauled out were sentenced to Death or Life. The Fiscal wrote out four slips: two for DEATH, two for LIFE. He made them draw lots. They fell on their knees, they prayed aloud for mercy; the Fiscal said: Draw!

The two who drew DEATH were hanged. The two who drew LIFE were shackled and sent to Robben Island to carry shells for twenty-five years.

The despairing shell carrier was one of those who drew LIFE. That's why he was living because he wasn't dead.

'Pieternella, are you sick?'

When she looked up, the jackal-haired man was standing there. 'Yes, Mynheer.'

'What's wrong?'

'I'm in despair, Mynheer.'

'You're in *what*?' He seemed ready to laugh.

'Oom Bart says the Orphan Chamber at the Cape still has some of our father's money; he says he's going to get the new Commander to write and ask for it, and claim the money for himself. I say the money belongs to Salomon and me. I'm getting into more and more trouble for arguing. They say I'm just like my mother, but my mother wasn't really bad, Mynheer.'

'Girl, if you're going to sit and mope in the hope that someone will feel sorry for you, you're going to spend the rest of your life crying beside a sheep pen.'

'I'm not going back down again, Tant Theuntjie is too angry with me.'

'Stop bumping up against Tant Theuntjie, learn to live your own life.'

'Yes, Mynheer.' He didn't understand. 'How long are we going to lie here without wind, Mynheer?'

'The wind will get up towards evening.'

'Tant Theuntjie says Oom Bart says the skipper shouldn't have turned north so soon.'

'The skipper knows what he's doing. Get up and walk about a bit and get some fresh air into your head.'

Rude.

She got up and started walking. She didn't *have* a life of her own! Others were living her life, throwing her on to a ship …

'Come here, girl, and sit on my lap. You can feel what a nice cock I've got!' Sailor mending a rent in his trousers.

Walk past.

'Pieternella!' Oom Bart was unrolling a coil of rope at the foremast. 'What are you walking up and down like this for? Are you looking for trouble?'

'I'm getting my blood moving.' I want to live my own life!

'Be careful, I'm watching you.'

Willem van Deventer was standing next him. 'Don't forget: she's full of Hottentot blood, Bart,' he laughed. 'It's wild blood. Though Salomon seems a little less wild.'

'Never mind,' Oom Bart bragged. 'Don't forget I'm a man who could tame a quagga in my day!'

Yes. So he could flog the animal to the French as a curiosity. And the quagga died of misery. Her mother saw it in the animal's eyes.

When the sun went down, the wind got up. They slaughtered the second sheep and there the bird was, suddenly, following the ship again.

She lay on the Hottentots-bedding mattress and pretended she was asleep.

Where *is* your life actually?

Not in your legs. Once one of the soldiers carrying blocks of stone from the tail of Lion's Head down to the Castle slipped and his leg was trapped under a block that fell off the barrow. The leg was crushed to pulp. The Surgeon had to saw it off at the knee. The man got compensation money for being maimed in the service of the Company. But only half, because he didn't lose the whole leg. They paid more for a right arm than for a left. Her mother once went to the Fort and hammered on the door yelling: chop off my more expensive arm and give me the money, I want to go to the tavern! A soldier said: Eva, you better run before they chop your head off!

Maria wasn't sleeping, she was crying ...

Once, soon after they had moved into the potter's cottage, the Governor invited her mother to dine at his table in the Fort one night. She put on her black dress, attached the white collar, put on her proper shoes – the bow on one of them was still missing – put on her cloth cap and became her Dutch body. The soldier who brought the message said the Governor said she had to dress smartly, there was an important man who wanted to speak to her.

It was a clear moonlit night. A warm night. She and Jacobus sat outside beside the cottage. Salomon was asleep.

They heard their mother coming from a long way off when she was on her way back; heard her cursing the two soldiers escorting her.

She was drunk, but not very drunk. Just very angry.

'You ought to be ashamed of yourself, Miss Eva,' one soldier scolded her as they reached the cottage. 'Commandeur Borghorst was only trying to restore your honour, but you Hottentots don't *have* any honour!'

'What kind of honour do you white-arses have? Bunch of thieves, bunch of murderers, bunch of liars!'

The second soldier joined in: 'You're the biggest liar of all!' He'd been at the Cape a long time. 'Thought you Hottentots could rob and trick and sweep us Hollanders away with all the lies out of *your* mouth. I don't know why the Commandeur even bothers with you any more, why he ever invited you!'

'Do you see that moon, soldier?' her mother asked and ripped off her lace collar. 'Do you see his eye? Do you see all those eyes looking down on you from on high? Do you *see* them?'

'I see the moon and stars, not all kinds of rubbish with heathenish eyes like a Hottentot!'

'They're watching you. Just wait.'

'Don't take any notice of the Hottentot,' said the other one. 'You heard the Commandeur say he's had enough of her now.' Then they left.

Her mother threw the white collar on the ground and stamped and stamped on it, trampling it into the earth, and then went and sat on a rock in the moonlight.

'What have you been saying in the Fort now, Mamma?' Jacobus wanted to know.

'I didn't say anything, I just had to answer questions from the holy preacher man. On his way from the fatherland to the East to go and preach there; sat at the table deep in mourning and misery about the frightful laws of the Hottentots that he had had to encounter here at the Cape. Stuffed himself with all the nice food, drank almost a whole bottle of wine. Folded his arms across his chest. Said: Miss Eva, if you don't help us tell these Hottentots about the true God, they will be condemned to the everlasting fire! Have you heard of the terrible happening in our midst yesterday afternoon? I told him there are so many terrible happenings here at the Cape he should rather pour me some more wine!'

'Mamma!'

All because some of the fine young ladies of the town had gone out walking the previous day and had come across a Hottentot funeral at the Duintjies. Sama's funeral. Who had died three days after her baby's birth. The child was still alive but was being buried with Sama, according to their age-old custom. The fine ladies were so horrified they rushed back to the Fort; they brought back soldiers and had the child dug up again and washed clean – they themselves wouldn't touch the lousy child. The Church called in Barbara Geens and asked her to take the child. They would pay and provide a sheep ewe for her to milk.

The preacher asked: 'Eva, are the Hottentots people or are they animals?'

'I've often asked Hollanders the same question, Preacher,' said her mother. 'Hottentot law says: a newborn child rests with its dead mother. Dutch law says: Bind the godless slave girl alive, in a sack, and drown her in the sea ...'

At that, the Fiscal sprang up and said: Yet again, Eva, you've drunk too much!

When the Church sent her and Jacobus and Salomon to Barbara Geens, the dug-up baby was lying whimpering in a small box under the kitchen table. Baptised and all. Florida was her name.

They woke up one morning to find her cold and stiff.

So the Company sent a soldier to fetch back the sheep, because it belonged to the Lords.

17

'How far are we from Madagascar, Mynheer Zaaijman?'

'We're running before a very favourable wind, we ought to see land by tomorrow. Watch, as soon as we're nearly there, you'll see over the nose of the ship how clouds will be forming in the distance over Madagascar.'

'How many days have we been on the water, Mynheer?'

'Thirty-seven, Pieternella.'

'But then we ought to reach Mauritius tomorrow!'

'No. Madagascar.'

'But they said it was thirty-eight days to Mauritius!'

'Who said so?'

'Oom Bart. And some of the others, too.'

'At this time of the year? Never.'

Somewhere she'd been cheated and lied to!

The Steward said that from the next day they'd be getting less water ...

The bird had turned back. She'd been standing on the top deck that afternoon, talking to Cornelia. Juffrouw Margaretha said she might.

'Your bird with ears is going to turn back!' the helmsman teased her.

'He won't. He's coming with me.' The bird was still peacefully hovering behind the ship.

'Silly child. Can't you feel it's getting warmer? It's a cold-weather bird! Its feathers are too thick.'

The next morning the bird was gone.

'It said I should say goodbye to you!' the helmsman laughed.

Don't cry, she told herself, you don't cry over a bird.

You cry because you can't get away!

The evening after the bird turned back, with the sickle of the new moon hanging shiny and white on the larboard side in the west, she closed her eyes and danced in her heart beside the sheep pen on the deck, but the dance didn't go right.

Only the black sheep was still alive, because it hadn't been slaughtered yet.

There were three fowls left in the coop.

Learn to live your own life. Silly words, but they did help to prevent the disobedience from falling out of her mouth.

The previous day Tant Theuntjie had sneered and said to the others: 'It looks as though Pieternella is being broken in. Perhaps she's realised Theun van der Linde won't allow herself to be messed around by a brat!'

The thing that worried her mother most of all was the Bible that spun round. 'I ask you, Pieternella, whose hand made that Bible spin? The Lord's or the devil's? I asked Juffrouw Maria. She said it was the devil's. The devil is like *Toqua* – he can give you great devil powers in exchange for your heart.'

All this because of a First Mate's gold ring.

Because one day, on board the *Roode Vos*, Captain Kes arrived back from Madagascar. He complained that on the voyage his crew had done a terrible thing.

All because of the First Mate's gold ring that disappeared. He used to take it off during the day and put it on his finger each evening before supper in the stateroom. To show off.

Then suddenly the ring was missing. He searched and searched, said someone had stolen or hidden his most valuable possession.

Later, in desperation, he took a Bible, placed the key of the chest where the ring was kept inside it, and asked the first person he suspected: Did you take or hide my ring? If you lie, this Bible will turn over in the name of God.

The man said no, he hadn't taken or hidden the ring. The Bible lay still.

Second one: Did you take or hide my ring? If you lie, this Bible will turn over in the name of God.

No, he hadn't taken or hidden the ring. The Bible remained motionless.

Captain Kes sat to one side, watching the whole business.

In his distress the First Mate asked: Captain Kes, I'm shattered. Was it not perhaps *you* who took or hid my ring?

No, said Captain Kes.

182

And the Bible flipped over.

The first suspect got such a fright he called out: Mr Mate, it's not true, you could have made that happen by force of willpower!

The Mate said: Then I'll ask again. Watch carefully. Captain Kes, did you take or …

The Bible turned over again.

The second suspect jumped up, he said he'd pay a lot of money never to have witnessed such a thing!

The Mate said: You are all witnesses to who has been implicated. But who will have the courage to make it public?

The Captain waited till they got to the Cape. He told the Commandeur his authority had been undermined, his officers had done a terribly irreligious thing.

The Council in the Fort summoned the men to a hearing. They asked: What exactly happened?

One after another, they told the same story. The Council was furious. They sentenced the Mate to fifty lashes in public for doing such an unchristian thing to God and Captain Kes.

One day her mother stole the Bible out of the cupboard in the Post House, hid it under her shawl and said: 'Come, children! Today we're going to make the Bible spin round.'

It was a windless day on the island, just a week after the *Westwoud* had brought the news that black people on Madagascar had beaten Pieter van Meerhoff and eight others to death on the island.

Her mother set the Bible down on a flat blue stone; she took one of the keys off her bunch and placed it inside the Book. She shifted the Bible about a little to make sure there were no cracks or seams in the stone that would prevent it from turning over.

She said: In the name of God, I, Eva, ask if my handsome husband, the father of my children, Pieter van Meerhoff, has truly been beaten to death on Madagascar. If it is so, this Bible will turn over.

The Bible remained motionless.

She did it again.

She did it a third time. The Bible lay dead still.

'Now did you see?' she said. 'They're lying. Pieter van Meerhoff has not been beaten to death!'

'Ask if he's going to come back, Mamma,' said Jacobus.

She asked three times. The Bible didn't budge.

They went back to the Post House; the Post Holder who was acting in her father's place asked: 'Eva, have you seen the Post House Bible?'

'What would I want with the Bible? I can't read.' She had already slipped it back quietly into the cupboard without the man noticing. 'The Bible is there in its place.'

'The Bible is not in the cupboard ...' Then he saw the Bible. His eyes stretched wide. That night he told the convicts: Signs and wonders happen before our very eyes.

Day. Night. Day. Night.

There were days when Tant Theuntjie and Tant Maijke hardly exchanged a word because they were so cross with each other. Or perhaps because they couldn't think of anyone else at the Cape to slander.

Sometimes they lay awake till late at night chewing on old bones.

'Maijke,' said Tant Theuntjie one night, 'I hope I'm not imagining it, but the new Governor – Governor Bax – his neck seems to be full of sores.'

'On the backs of his hands, too,' said Tant Maijke. 'Wears his shirt cuffs much longer, to hide them, I suppose, but I looked closely. Leprosy. I'm telling you.'

'Leprosy? But that's dangerous, he could infect everybody!'

'What would the Lords Seventeen care? As long as the ships keep unloading luxuries in the fatherland. The other day a man was telling me they've now put up poles in the streets in Amsterdam with lights burning on them all night. Have you ever heard anything like it? And hundreds of fine churches, too. People walking about in only the most elegant of clothes. The ships don't unload much for the poor mortals at the Cape, though!'

It wasn't nearly as cold now that they had turned north. She could go for water in the mornings without wearing her shawl.

The thirty-eighth day.

At daybreak the clouds lay like billows of smoke in the distance. The rest of the sky was blue. She had the strangest sense of unease inside her; it felt as if the ship was running over her father's footprints ...

A father whom she could only partly remember. Some parts were clear, but most were blurred, like glass windows covered with sea spray.

Salomon couldn't really remember their father at all.

One of the clear parts were the shoes her father had made her. Of wood. He hollowed them out with a sharp kind of iron thing and she had to put her foot in and say where it pinched. In the sun on the steps in front of the Post House, or at night under the lamp. And he'd sing them a godsong with strange words, something like *oploft did syn, o kristen sjel*

- she didn't know what they meant, that's all she remembered.

Sometimes Janvos sang along; he knew some of the words very well. So did her mother.

Salomon said three sailors were down with dysentery.

The whistle for prayers.

'We read in the Gospel according to John that a man came to Jesus to ask him to heal his son who was dying. Jesus said unto him: Unless you see signs and wonders, you will not believe.'

What made the Bible turn over?

'For that we are creatures of sin, our bodies are subject unto all manner of diseases and even unto death; wherefore should we the more take refuge with the Heavenly Physician and pray that Thy divine strengthening may come upon us, that we may be restored to health and holiness ...'

Dysentery's got nothing to do with sin; they say it comes from too little exercise, the blood builds up inside the veins.

Her father healed the sick ...

She was glad when she could flee the hold after breakfast to wash out the food basin.

Daniel Zaaijman was leaning up against the side of the ship, looking out attentively over the sea, a chisel in his hand.

'Are those Madagascar's clouds, Mynheer?'

'Yes, my girl.'

'Is the ship going to stop there?'

'No. As soon as we sight land, we'll swing out eastwards. That ought to be in a couple of hours' time.'

'My father died on Madagascar.'

'I know.'

'Did you know my father, Mynheer?' Tell me something about him, please.

'I saw him a few times, but I didn't know him.'

'What did he look like?'

'A lot like Salomon. A little like you.'

Sometimes the food boat brought her father a canvas bag of oatmeal. Then he'd bake them flat round loaves and pile them up high, one on top of another. They would last them a long time.

Sometimes he had to pull convicts' teeth.

When there wasn't a soldier to tend the sheep on the island, she and her mother looked after them. They saw to it that they didn't get into the patch of wheat or the vegetable garden. The middle of the island was covered with yellow flowers with flat green leaves. Her mother would drive the sheep into them and shout: Eat them up! Get yourselves as fat as butter! The ships are coming!

And the sheep's mouths and noses would get all yellow with pollen.

If any sheep died, it had to be buried as proof. So when the inspectors came from the mainland to count the sheep, they could check whether the Post folk or the convicts might not have stolen one.

The convicts would dig up the dead sheep and cook the meat. Then there'd be big trouble.

In the evenings, after her father had gone out to lead prayers for the convicts and locked them up for the night, they would all sit round the table by the lamp. The wind would blow. They'd hear the noise of the sea. Her father would be reading his books while her mother sewed strips of cloth together for flags: red and white and blue. They would all laugh because she stuck out her tongue each time she pushed the needle through.

The wind could blow all it wanted to, the sea could make as much noise as it liked: inside the house it was safe and warm. Her father would tell them stories about brave kings who went out to fight real dragons, and Jacobus would listen with his mouth hanging open. Or about snow. *Those* were the best. About horses with bells round their necks drawing the sleighs. A sleigh is a thing like an ox wagon without wheels that glides over the snow. Her father and his brother and their little sister would go in the sleigh to visit their grandmother. *Ting-a-ling, ting-a-ling, ting-a-ling.* His mother would cover them with blankets and thick coats *and* then put a bearskin on top – and the cold still got through. *That's* how cold snow was.

A bear was like a calf, but more woolly. And very dangerous.

Then her father would pour a small mug of wine for himself and her mother.

She couldn't remember that her mother drank much at that time. Jacobus said he remembered what happened the night his mother fell off that short bench, but she, Pieternella, could only remember the blood and how she'd screamed. They'd all been sitting in front of the house that evening; it was still light. Her mother was sitting on the bench beside the low stone steps, just sitting looking out over the water at the Mountain and the other mountains, bronze in the evening sun.

Suddenly Janvos shouted: Master, come!

Jacobus said two convicts had stabbed each other in the sheep shed; their father had had to hurry out to stitch up the stab wounds and he'd left the jar of aniseed arrack on the table instead of locking it away in the cupboard, as he usually did.

Her mother got up and put the jar to her mouth and drank and went on drinking because it tasted so good. Then she fell over. Fell off the bench and cut her head open on the stone step. A nasty hole in her forehead just above the eye.

And there she lay. She wouldn't wake up. Her father came and put a cloth over the wound and carried her indoors. But she just wouldn't wake up. Janvos went down to the sea's edge for a bucket of water to pour over the blood. Her father said: Pieternella, don't cry, Mamma isn't dead, she's just sleeping very deeply.

She remembered how her father had paced up and down, up and down, his hands clasped behind his back. Then he would bend over her mother again and call and call to her. But she went on sleeping.

Salomon was also asleep. Jacobus had run away.

Very early the next morning her father sent one of the soldiers on the island in a skiff to tell the Governor he needed a second surgeon immediately to come and attend to his wife. The fleet lay at anchor in the Bay.

They came back with one of the surgeons from the fleet in another boat, one that could skim much faster across the water. The strange man and her father both bent over her mother. They tried to hold her in a sitting position but her head kept lolling forward. She wouldn't wake up. They bathed her with cloths dipped in cold water. They tapped some blood out of one hand.

She called and called to her mother. Her father picked her up and walked with her down to the sea's edge. He said: Your mamma will wake up again. It's just that she hurt herself *too* much.

And her father called her by the other name he sometimes used – Pirternilla or something like that. She couldn't quite remember it any more.

The next day her mother's eyes started waking.

But for a long time after that, she was still very weak.

Soon afterwards they sent her father to Madagascar to buy slaves to help with building the new Castle.

The lookout in the crow's nest at the top of the mast suddenly cried out: 'On deck! Land straight ahead!'

The words shivered their way right down inside her.

The Captain replied from the top deck: 'What do you see?'

'There's a mountain, Skipper, with small clouds. Very hazy.'

'Keep it in your sights, I'll send up a telescope with one of the men bound for Mauritius. Where is Cooper Zaaijman?'

The jackal-haired man scrambled up nimbly with the glass while everyone waited. The eyes of all the sailors on the watch were fixed on the horizon.

She didn't want to see Madagascar …

'Crow's nest, what do you see?' shouted the Captain.

Daniel Zaaijman shouted back that the south-west corner of Madagascar was visible, and some other words as well. The Captain asked him what lay ahead, whether he knew these waters.

'Yes, Skipper, they're clear all the way to land!'

She hadn't wanted to see Madagascar, but her feet climbed the companionway to the upper deck as if on their own. She went up and stood cautiously at the rail and trained her eyes on the horizon.

A long dark hump-backed stripe rose up out of the water in the distance in front of the ship's nose …

Land.

Madagascar.

Like a little piece of her dad.

Her body started trembling, as if with cold.

Down on the deck the whistle blew loud and urgently. From all over, sailors hurried to the deck, scrambled up the rigging to turn the yards so that the ship would swing out towards the east.

'Pieternella?' It was Salomon calling to her from down at the sheep pen.

'I'm coming.'

'We're not going all the way there,' he said when she stopped beside him. Comforting. Or scared.

'I know. But now at least we know where the place is.'

'Yes. I just wanted to tell you.'

'Yes.'

'Don't cry, Pieternella.'

'No.' But the tears that had been bottling up inside her since early that morning were streaming down her cheeks. A different kind of crying. A helpless scream against everything she didn't understand. She covered her eyes with her hands and went below to fetch one of the pot shards from her bundle in the hold, ran across the water and put it down somewhere on land for her dad, so he wouldn't be left there all alone any longer.

A small piece of her mother.

The slaves from Madagascar were the blackest black of all the slaves at the Cape. Once she and her mother and Jacobus and Salomon were walking along towards the Duintjies. Some of the Malagasy slaves, in leg irons, were breaking stone out of the tail of Lion's Head. Her mother stopped and screamed: You black-arsed murderers!

Jacobus took her by the arm and pulled her away: 'Mamma, the slaves don't understand you, they don't know what you're talking about.'

She jerked free and cried: 'They *know*!'

Her mother hated the slaves; the Goringhaiqua hated her mother – because of the slaves. Because someone had knocked a lie into their heads so firmly that no one could ever get it out again.

'Jacobus and Pieternella, listen carefully to what I'm telling you ...' Salomon was still too small. They were living in the potter's cottage. 'Innocence is a terrible thing when you're innocent and no one believes you! Worse than real pain!'

One day a big Dutch ship arrived at the Cape with a cargo of slaves from a Portuguese slaver they had raided. Slaves from Angola. That was a place a very long way from the Cape.

Slaves, because the Hottentots wouldn't work for the Dutchmen.

Like bunches of terrified naked animals the slaves were brought ashore in boats. Many had died on the way, but there were still plenty left. Men, women and children. One or two more died almost every day.

The Lords Seventeen said: Send the best ones to the East.

Mynheer Van Riebeeck split the rest among the officials and sold a few to the free-burghers.

Then the slaves started running away.

It made no difference how kind or harsh the Dutch were to the slaves, they wanted to go home. They didn't want to be slaves.

Mynheer Van Riebeeck sat in the Fort fuming. He said the Hottentots had either killed the slaves or hidden them. He summoned Harry and said: There's food here and plenty of drink for you, go and find the slaves! Harry searched but found nothing. Mynheer called for Doman. He said: Go and find the slaves, my soldiers are tired of searching. Doman said he had no idea where to start looking. Mynheer called Eva: Eva, more and more slaves are deserting into the veld; one of these days it's going to be like Mauritius where the runaway slaves in the forests conduct a reign of terror over the whole island. What is happening to the slaves?

'I don't know, Mynheer.'

'I suspect the Hottentots are hiding them.'

'I don't know, Mynheer.'

'I have a good plan for bringing them back.'

'How, Mynheer?' Doman had told her to listen very carefully. Some of the slaves were with the Chorachoqua, others had sought refuge among the Goringhaiqua. As soon as the time was ripe, they would take them to the Cochoqua so the Cochoqua could send them on to the Hamcunqua who lived far beyond the Namaqua and planted dagga. From there to the goat people, the Tswana – and so on farther and farther up country till they got to the place where they had come from. 'How are you going to bring them back, Mynheer?'

'Do you remember the famous man from the fleet who had dinner here about a year ago when you and Harry were also at the table?'

'Which one, Mynheer?'

'Commissioner Van Goens. He said if the Hottentots won't return the stolen cattle, we should simply catch some of them and lock them up till the cattle return.'

Her mother was badly frightened; she knew what that meant. 'The Portuguese often caught Hottentot children and locked them up – till they found the cattle and sheep they wanted,' she said. They must just not catch her uncle Harry and lock him up!

'Really?'

'Yes, Mynheer.'

So Mynheer Van Riebeeck had the sons of the chief of the Goringhaiqua kidnapped and locked up. And the story spread throughout the kraals that she, Eva, had told him to do it. She said she did say but didn't *tell*.

The Hottentots' heads were confused. They thronged in front of the Fort; they couldn't understand why people who hadn't done anything should be in gaol.

Mynheer Van Riebeeck said they were hostages. Until they surrendered the slaves.

What if the slaves aren't there?

Mynheer said that for every slave they brought back, he would pay just as much copper as for an ox.

So they began to bring back the slaves.

Doman asked Mynheer Van Riebeeck: Why don't you catch Harry and one of the Choroqua and lock them up, too? Why only the Goringhaiqua?

So Mynheer Van Riebeeck enticed Harry to the Fort and caught him.

190

And Jan Cou and Boubo, too. And sent them to Robben Island.

The Cochoqua and Chainouqua sent a number of cattle in exchange for Jan Cou. Mynheer took the cattle and sent to the island for Jan Cou. The Post Holder sent word that the Hottentot they called Boubo was pining to death on the island. What should he do?

Send him back to the mainland without delay. He might die soon and the Hottentots will say we killed him.

That left only her mother's uncle on the island. She begged, she pleaded that she had no cattle to exchange for him – no Goringhaiqua had any cattle to exchange for him, they lived off the sea. Please, Mynheer!

No. Harry has done us enough harm. Leave him on Robben Island.

Then Mynheer Van Riebeeck had the blacksmith forge lots of chains and he put the slaves in irons so they couldn't run away. The women and children and old men were not shackled. But the slaves still ran away. Chains and all. Made a small fire, sat with their legs wide apart over the fire so that the chains hung into the flames. They battered the hot chains between two stones until their legs were separated. Dragged the two pieces with them round their ankles.

Some slaves surrendered and grew tame.

Janvos never deserted.

And you could pine to death on an island ...

By the time the sun sank into the sea behind them there was no longer any sign of Madagascar. The ship was running differently. More slowly. Billows kept breaking over the fo'c'sle; they couldn't light the fire.

Down in the hold Tant Maijke and Tant Theuntjie were still moaning about the food that was not being sent down to them. 'Our own is running out!'

Maria had made her children rag dolls out of cloth from her chest. Worked eyes and mouths in black thread. So pretty.

Before the mattresses were unrolled for the night, she and Maria went out to clean the bucket and the pot. They dawdled a little out in the fresh air.

The sails on the yards had been hung differently again, the ship was now listing to starboard.

'You can feel we're moving in a different direction,' said Maria.

'Yes. Almost as if the ship is getting tired and weary.'

Maria gave a little laugh.

The moon was almost round, its shining path stretched out across the sea.

After a while Maria said: 'I sometimes wish we'd never reach Mauritius.'

The sailors on the watch walked up and down, looking out across the water.

'I never realised the sea was so big,' Pieternella said. And, a little later, 'You can smell the moon.'

'Oh, don't be silly, Pieternella, no one can smell the moon!'

Perhaps not everyone can smell equally well. 'Listen ...'

The sound of a fiddle was floating out from under the fo'c'sle. Like thin strips of copper that stretched out for a while and then curled over in the sky. A rumble-pot made red spots that hopped all over the bushes. A reed flute made yellowish sounds.

'I'm longing for my children,' Maria said, tearfully. 'My other children, Dina and Cornelis.'

'The Cape is getting farther and farther to long for.'

'I wonder if I'll ever see them again.'

'I wonder if I'll ever see my brother Jacobus again.'

'I wonder if I'll ever see my mother and father again.'

'I don't have a mother and father any more.'

'I just can't imagine that.'

'I'm not going to stay with Tant Theuntjie and Oom Bart.'

'We don't have any say, Pieternella. Like this ship underneath us doesn't have any say. The Company says where it has to go – the Captain and the Mate say, on behalf of the Company, which way the sails must hang. The Company says everything. The Company can wrench your heart out of your body if they feel like it.'

'What does it mean to live your own life?'

'It means you're dead and gone to heaven!' Maria shouted out the words.

'We have to go down again.'

'Yes.'

Lubbert was standing at the hatch where they had to go down.

'Aah! Two at once!' he said, deliberately blocking their way. 'Which one wants to be fucked first?'

'Is your cock bothering you?' Maria asked him to his face. 'Give me your knife and I'll cut it off for you.'

'Bitch,' he said and stood aside. As she, Pieternella, came past, he groped at her chest. 'Lovely soft little figs already!' he said and laughed.

'I thought you'd dropped the bucket overboard as well and jumped in after it! What kept you so long?' Tant Theuntjie wanted to know.

She waited till everyone was in bed. 'Tant Theuntjie ...'

'Yes, Pieternella?'

192

'How many people live on Mauritius?'

'Too many. The officials booze and live high on the hog – the free-burghers struggle to breathe. About a hundred, I suppose. Altogether.'

A hundred. 'Is the island bigger than Robben Island?'

'Oh, don't be so stupid!'

Tant Maijke wanted to know if Zacharias, the former Post Holder on Robben Island, hadn't also been banished to Mauritius. 'The one that married the slave.'

'Company practice was to put all its officials that married lesser breeds well out of sight on Robben Island. Woutersz, Zacharias, Van Meerhoff ...'

'Is he still alive? Zacharias?'

'Yes. And still drinking like a fish. And he was one of Hugo's lying witnesses that helped keep Col in chains.'

A ship almost ran aground on Robben Island one night because Zacharias had not lit the fire beacon. Too drunk. Then his wife fell ill on the island, but he was too scared to call for help because the Commandeur had once roundly cursed him for firing the emergency cannon for a sick slave girl. Many people on the island were sick. From hunger. Just like on board ship. They swelled up terribly because of all the water in their bodies. They say Zacharias's Maria swelled up to double her size with the dropsy. Or something like that. Then she died.

After that two convicts stole a skiff on the island and rowed to land. They reported at the Fort that Post Holder Zacharias was selling the Lords' sheep and rabbits to the ships. So they banished him to Mauritius.

'Zacharias has become an important person on Mauritius,' said Tant Theuntjie in the darkness. 'Hugo's even put him on the island's Council. Walks around all day swigging from a jug of arrack. Just shows you what a crook can do – see, there's hope for you on the new island, Maijke!'

'God will punish you, Theuntjie van der Linde!'

Days. Nights. One after another.

Then they turned the ship's nose northwards again.

Oom Bart said they were now heading straight for Mauritius – *if* they were on the right course. There was a strong likelihood that they would sail right past the island. The ship should have been turned a day sooner.

'Mynheer Zaaijman, is Mauritius bigger than Robben Island?'

At first he laughed but then he thought for a moment. 'Let's say: if you took about three hundred and twenty Robben Islands and stuck them together you ought to get one Mauritius.'

Three heaps of a hundred pebbles plus another twenty …

That was a lot of islands, she couldn't get them all joined up.

Cheerful dolphins, their mouths open and laughing.

Two dead sailors were wrapped in sailcloth and made to slide overboard from a plank. Dead because they weren't living any more. The Captain conducted the funeral himself.

Salomon said it was just as well they weren't still in the current, else the corpses could have gone on drifting alongside the ship for days.

It was hot. Even stuffier in the hold. Tant Maijke and Tant Theuntjie spent most of the day sitting out on the deck. So did Maria and the children.

'O God my Father, why are You punishing me like this?'

'Don't blame God, Maijke! You've been banished for being dishonest.'

'I can't take it any longer. My health's starting to crack.'

'It's not your health, Maijke, it's the ship you're hearing. Sounds to me as though the thing is breaking apart!'

One morning Tant Theuntjie woke up with a new bee in her bonnet.

'Pieternella, have you used the sponge since we left the Cape?'

'No, Tant Theuntjie.' If she'd known the old woman was going to make such a scene, she'd have lied.

'Not been on the sponge yet?' her eyes rigid with fright. 'You haven't bled yet?'

'No, Tante.'

'Oh-my-god! Have you been with the sailors?' she asked fearfully.

'No, Tante.'

'Leave her alone, Theuntjie!' Maria tried to stop the old woman. She'd grabbed Pieternella by the hair and started bashing and bashing her head on the floor between her legs …

'Tante, stop it! I haven't done anything!'

'Done nothing? Damned little whore, just like your mother! I'm not going to raise a whore in my house!'

'Theuntjie, leave the child alone!'

'You shut up, Maria!'

At that Maria grabbed Tant Theuntjie by the shoulder and jerked her away. 'The child's only been on the sponge once before. She's not regular yet. Leave her alone!'

'Maria's right, Theun!' Tant Maijke was also shouting, to get her to calm down.

Just then they brought the table and stools for breakfast. 'Hey, what's going on here?' laughed the sailor. 'Give her to me, I'd enjoy spanking her!'

Tant Theuntjie let go of her and grabbed at the sailor. He said: You keep your paws off me, you old witch!

Maria went for the food.

The sheep pen had been taken apart. It was like sitting out in the open without any shelter.

'What happened to your forehead, Pieternella?'

'I fell, Mynheer.'

'That didn't happen in a fall.'

'How far is it still, Mynheer?'

'What are those two raw patches on your forehead?'

'It's where the planks … Mynheer, how far is it still?'

'Why are you crying like this?'

'Tears just run out of my eyes, they won't stop.'

'Who bashed your head against the boards?'

'Tant Theuntjie.'

'What had you done?'

'Nothing.'

'Don't lie to me.'

Standing behind him, Maria said: 'Theuntjie went off her head, Daniel. Pieternella did nothing at all.'

Night.

Day.

She was going to fetch the broom from beside the foremast to sweep the hold. The day was breaking, a pale pink glow in the east, and again the ship seemed not to be moving …

Then suddenly she saw it.

Across the ship's nose, in the distance. Dark humps and peaks like chunks of mountain rising up out of the sea in the early light of morning.

It was land!

The air smelt of soil!

She stood there with the broom, unable to move. Everywhere there were sailors busily cleaning the ship …

Could this be *Mauritius*?

Hundreds of Robben Islands stuck together. No. Not Robben Islands stuck together – just lots of bits of funny-shaped mountains ...

❦ TWO ❦

1

'Pieternella?'

It was the umpteenth time that he had called to her in a whisper in the dark. Salomon. Like putting out a hand to feel if she was still there.

'Try to sleep,' she whispered back.

'I'm trying to but I can't. Is your body also trembling all by itself?'

'No, not any more.' It was just the earth that wouldn't keep properly still, as though everything was still rolling with the swells as it had on the ship.

'Pieternella?'

'Yes, Salomon?'

'Do you also feel so terribly far from home?'

'We haven't got a home, Salomon.' The words had spoken themselves; but she added: 'Except, at the moment, this tool shed below Oom Bart's house.'

Plough. Shovel. Thongs. Saws. Lengths of wood. Poles. An opening without a door. Roof of leaves. Walls of leaves that didn't quite reach the roof. While it was still light, it looked as though the layers of leaves had been sewn together, the long string stitches running over and round wooden laths.

Luckily it wasn't cold.

An insect that sounded rather like a Christmas beetle was shrilling somewhere in the roof. Endlessly. A night beetle. When you turned your head the shrilling suddenly came up out of the gap.

She had the one bed: a wooden frame nailed to four poles, with a mat woven of leather thongs. Her own mattress on top. A Hottentot's-bedding mattress that smelt of damp and the steerage hold.

Salomon was lying under his quilt on a length of canvas. Oom Bart said as soon as there was time they would make him a bed and a mattress.

'What's going to happen to us, Pieternella?'

'Tomorrow I'm going to go back to the place where we landed, to the Post House – the Lodge they call it here. I'm going to knock and ask to speak to Monsieur Lamotius and I'm going to ask him to write for our money.'

'Will Tant Theuntjie let you go?'

'I don't care.'

'Don't go looking for trouble, please don't.'

'Go to sleep.'

'Do you think it's nearly morning yet?'

'No. It's the middle of the night.'

'Oom Bart's got a funny house, hasn't he?'

'Yes.'

'Quite nice furniture.'

'Yes.'

'All the cloths on the walls.'

'Yes. Some look like carpets.'

'Pretty lamps. The bowls they eat out of and the table with the carved chairs probably all come from the East.'

'Probably.'

'And they really do eat with sticks! Do you understand it?'

'No. It's just as well we've got our own spoons. Now go to sleep.'

She didn't feel like talking. Just holding on to her other name for a little ...

Pernilla.

To play with it. To wrap the pot shards in it and put it under her head, because *that* was the name her father sometimes called her. The name she had forgotten.

But then somehow that strange man, Master Sven, knew it.

'Master Sven,' Mynheer Zaaijman called him over that afternoon. Everybody was ashore already except a few of the sailors. 'Guess whose daughter this is?'

'She looks like a damned starved locust.' Crude and unconcerned.

'Not a bad face.'

'It's Pieter van Meerhoff's daughter.'

You'd have thought a blow from someone's fist had stopped him in his tracks. *'Gut!'* he cried. 'Peder van Meerhoff's daughter?'

'Yes.'

'Peder's daughter?' as though trying to make sure before he believed it.

'I swear.'

'With the Hottentot?'

'Yes. Pieternella is her name.'

'Peder's Pernilla?'

'That's my name!' she cried, she couldn't believe it. That was her name! Like stretching out your arm and suddenly catching a bird in flight. 'That's the name my dad called me!'

'Hello, Peder's daughter. What are you doing here?' The bluest of blue eyes, looking at you as though you were a ghost. A wrinkled brown face like a piece of leather that had been left out in the sun too long. Yellow-brown hair down to his shoulders. Hair pickled in brine. No cap. 'I asked what you're doing here.'

'I don't know, Mynheer.' He was half tipsy. She could see, she could smell it.

'Yes, you're Peder's daughter. I see him.'

'Did you know my father for long, Mynheer?'

'Small together, grew up together, went to hell together.'

'Master Sven,' Daniel Zaaijman took him by the arm and pushed him to one side, 'I think the Secretary is waiting for her, you can chat later.'

'Secretary's arse. How does Peder van Meerhoff's daughter land up on this goddamned island?'

'My young brother is here, too.'

'The younger one? Did the other one die?'

'No. He's at the Cape.'

'Cape's arse.'

'Secretary Van Hoeven is waiting for you, Pieternella.'

The strangest man.

'Why is he like that, Mynheer?' she asked the jackal-haired man quietly as they walked away.

At first he laughed, but then he said: 'He's actually a fish in human dress. Perhaps a shark. Don't take any notice of him.'

'Where does he live?'

'He's supposed to live at the Lodge, but sometimes he simply sleeps in the forest. Come.'

Pernilla.

She'd seen him that morning.

Everyone was up on deck. Tant Theuntjie, Tant Maijke, Maria, the children.

The ship was edging its way in slowly like an animal searching for a gap, because they were in the oddest stretch of water: on one side the deep grey-blue sea, then a white strip of foam, as though a long wall under the water was trying to stop anything getting to land …

'It's the reef, stupid.' Tant Theuntjie knew.

Between the reef and the land – island – the greenest, bluest, oddest stretch of flat smooth water. Patches of dark blue in between …

'Why is the inside water blue-green?'

'Fish piss,' said the nearest sailor, with a grin full of rotten teeth.

All round the big island were smaller islands. Browner. Barer. Some greener and forested. A big brown island on the left, like part of this reef-thing.

Then a gaff-rigged boat came across the inside water, weaving a path through the reef up to the ship. They lowered the rope ladder; a man climbed up out of the boat on to the ship. His clothes were tattered, his feet bare.

Sven Telleson. Tant Theuntjie knew.

'I hope he's sober,' she added. 'Otherwise we'll run straight into the reef today, that's for sure. He's the pilot, he'll take us through to the anchorage.'

'Why should *he* have to come and do it?'

'He knows the way through the reef. Skippers don't know the way.'

The island was made of all kinds of green. Dark green, light green, grey-green. Bits of blue mountain in the distance. At the foot of the nearest mountain, on the shore of the first bay, there were some buildings. The Lodge. And the mountain looked like a big fat cat without a tail, lying on its belly. Green. Hind leg up.

'That mountain looks like a cat!'

'Hmf. You've got sharp eyes. It's called Kattiesberg.'

A stretch of pure white sand on one side where the trees came down almost to the water's edge …

The Bosun yelled to them to get off the deck, they were in the sailors' way. The seamen were running and shinning up the ropes to turn the yards this way and that to keep the sails in the wind as the ship veered back and forth to make it through the gap. Sven Telleson was issuing the orders.

When she and Tant Theuntjie and Tant Maijke and Maria and the children came up on deck again, the ship was lying at anchor in calm water not far from the land. The big brown island they had seen from out at sea was now three islands next to one another.

And Tant Theuntjie got in a final dig at Tant Maijke. 'Watch out, Maijke! You could say that the middle island is Mauritius's Robben Island. Tobacco Island. Where they banish you if you can't behave yourself, with nothing but a can of water and a fishing line to feed your own stomach with. I just thought I'd warn you ahead of time.'

'God have mercy on me.' Tant Maijke's eyes were red with weeping. So were Maria's.

The pilot boat lay alongside the ship. Someone raised a big red, white and blue flag on the stern to show that important people were on their way. Monsieur Lamotius, Juffrouw Margaretha and the little dolly. Sailors helped them down the rope ladder.

Lastly, Cornelia, the nursemaid.

Three more gaff-rigged boats came over.

Along with the first, three more strangers from the land came aboard. Back went the heavy coffer with the money, the Captain, First Mate Berks and Sven Telleson. All the steerage folk were let down into the third boat with their bundles and taken to the small quay below the Post House.

When she took her first step on dry land again, the earth gave way under her and she grabbed at Maria and Maria at her.

Sand, not firm ground. Not proper sand either. Coarse white stuff that looked like sand, with little branches of greyish sand in between.

'What's this?'

'Coral, stupid.' Tant Theuntjie herself was stumbling as she walked. A sailor had Tant Maijke by the arm.

Black pebbles on the seabed. Bright green, smooth seaweed. Brown, dead seaweed …

Her eyes were looking but her body felt squashed, like something still waiting to be unfolded again. Actually, her body wasn't there at all. She'd left it on another quay: *this* was only her snail-shell.

Everyone was queuing up at the half-moon-shaped fence of tall, thick poles in front of the long, whitewashed Post House. Many more fence poles were lying around. Wooden outbuildings. All the roofs made of dried stuff like thin leaves. Then she noticed that the Post House was actually just parts of buildings joined together, with a roof made of leaves. Black with age in some places, brownish elsewhere. Small windows with black shutters.

At the entrance there was a flagpole. Great big red, white and blue flag, just like at the Cape.

A bell frame with a bell on a rope.

And the earth wouldn't stop rolling.

They bunched together in front of the door. A man with papers in his hand came out and called up into the air: 'First the banished! Maijke van den Berg and Willem van Deventer!'

'He's still on the ship.'

'Then we'll wait.'

They could sit under the trees on tree stumps and wooden benches.

The man with the papers came out again. 'The two Van Meerhoff orphans!'

'One is still on board the ship.'

'Then we'll wait.'

'We're hungry and thirsty!' Tant Theuntjie snapped at him angrily.

'The food bell will ring for mealtime. There's water in the stream.'

'Come!' Tant Theuntjie knew where that was. 'Leave your bundles. Just bring your mugs.'

Clear water in a narrow streamlet with high green banks. Strange crabs. Slippery banks. The place to draw from was a little higher up. Steps made of logs, a big flat stone.

'Scoop some up and pass it on, Pieternella!'

Sweet water. Fresh. As much as you could drink. To wash your arms in, your feet, your legs.

'Come away there, Pieternella, you'll be sick tonight!'

'I'm coming, Tante.'

The earth wouldn't stop moving.

And the oddest-looking trees in among the ordinary ones. Actually not like trees at all. Tall, straight trunks without any branches, just bundles of leaves like green ostrich feathers waving off their tops. Big, yellow-gold bunches of fruit in among the feathers. Others with green bunches.

'Coconut palms, stupid.'

'Can you eat them?'

'Hard as rocks. Their meat and milk are inside – where are you off to, Pieternella?'

'I'm just looking …'

Beyond the Post House there were gardens with the same feather-leaved trees planted in long rows. Finer leaves. Smaller trees. With pumpkins trailing between them.

Gaff-rigged boats plied back and forth from the small black stone quay and the wooden goose. The water in the anchorage looked bluer, deeper. The blue-green started lower down.

Another gaff-rigged boat with their chests.

A gaff-rigged boat with Daniel Zaaijman and Focke Janse, Oom Bart and Salomon and the murderer. All of them wearing their own clothes again.

'Pieternella?'

'Salomon.' He seemed to have grown taller.

Tant Maijke and Willem van Deventer were called in first.

Focke took a bottle out of his bundle, pulled out the cork and took such a long swig his Adam's apple moved up and down. He passed the bottle along from mouth to mouth, right to Tant Theuntjie who took the bottle in both hands.

Sven Telleson came out of the Post House. Daniel Zaaijman stopped him and took her to him.

Pernilla.

A soldier came to ring the bell and a slave brought them two basins of food. Fish with rice and carrots and cabbage and pumpkin. Fresh food. And beer for Tant Theuntjie and Maria and Oom Bart and Focke Janse. Daniel Zaaijman wasn't there.

After they'd eaten she and Salomon had to go into the Post House where their names were written in a big book with a white quill pen. She wondered where the albatross was ...

The writing man sat at a big table. Black jacket, black breeches, white shirt with a pleated collar. You could see they were old clothes: they were tight on his stout body. Black and grey hair down to his shoulders.

Two carved chairs, the rest plain and rickety. Bare patches on the wall where the plaster had fallen off. Thick walls, low windows in black frames. Wooden floor.

'Mynheer ...' She tried to ask it in her politest voice. 'Please may I speak to Monsieur Lamotius?'

The man finished writing. 'Monsieur Lamotius is resting after his exhausting voyage.'

'Could you please tell us, Mynheer, where Tant Maijke van den Berg is? She's the one who was banished.'

'Why do you want to know, girl?'

Just because. 'I just wanted to know. My brother and I have known her since we were small.'

'She's been taken to her cell.'

'Is she in gaol?'

'Not completely.'

They had to go and wait outside again.

Oom Bart had gone to one of the sheds to buy provisions.

'Our expenses are doubled now, because we have you to feed,' Tant Theuntjie said reproachfully.

Four soldiers and two slaves came to help carry the chests for them. Focke Janse walked alongside them, his own chest on his shoulder, his head to one side.

Everything felt as though it was happening in a delirious dream.

Black soil, smooth footpath. Lots of trees. Everything green.

Dense forest. Everything strange. The air smelt different and heavy as you breathed in.

Birds flapped their wings in the thickets, but you couldn't see them. Somewhere a dove-like bird was cooing – a different cooing from a real dove's.

The footpath kept giving way under her.

A shaky wooden bridge across a deep narrow stream.

'The Molens River, tributary of another river,' Oom Bart told Salomon. 'Half an hour farther up is Hugo's water mill and saw mill, but the mill is standing idle. The last blade broke a year ago.'

A long way on, the forest cleared abruptly and the bearers set down the chests for a rest. Everyone rested. Only Tant Theuntjie carried on walking. As though she was in a hurry.

Down in the distance the wooden goose lay on the still surface of the water without its wings. A long strip of foam where the reef-thing was.

'Oom …' Salomon asked hesitantly once they were all on their feet again and the forests were closing in on them. 'Oom, aren't there lions and things here, Oom?'

Oom Bart and the soldiers laughed fit to split their sides. 'No, there aren't any "things" here.'

They came to a swiftly rushing river and followed the slippery footpath upwards along its edge into a dense ravine that gradually opened out and became wider. The river grew narrower and narrower.

'Orange Tree River,' said Oom Bart.

Pieces of green mountain loomed up whenever there was an opening in the trees. A mountain on the opposite side of the river on the left.

Were they really on an *island*?

'This is what we call the Orange Tree Flats,' said Oom Bart. 'This here is the Orange Tree River. The mountain opposite is the Orange Tree Mountain. The orange trees were planted by one of the old fleets. They bear pretty well. The Company's trees. But Focke always pinches a few each year for us to make a little wine.' Salomon was trotting to keep up and not miss a word.

Lots of feather-leaved trees. Grey-green ones with leaves that looked more like giant combs. Not even a sign of a trunk; the comb's teeth simply sprouted out of the earth in a big tuft.

'Is that a *tree*, Oom?' Salomon wanted to know.

'Water palm. Make a hole underneath one of the leaves and it will yield clear drinking water'.

After a while Salomon asked: 'Oom ... Oom, is this place still on the same earth as the Cape?'

The two soldiers at the back, the two carrying the heaviest chest, almost dropped their load laughing. 'Yes, Salomon,' Oom Bart said. 'The earth is the earth, we haven't fallen off anywhere.'

Focke Janse had to put down his chest to stop laughing.

The soldiers were battling with the chests; the footpath was too narrow for them to be carried cross-wise.

Some way farther up the river they came to the ford. A narrow part of the river with a path of black stones laid across it to the other side. You had to tread carefully, the water was still running between the stones. And the earth still kept rolling beneath her feet.

Beyond the ford the footpath wound its way up a slope to where another footpath veered off to the left.

'Well then, Bart ...' Focke Janse put down his chest. 'I'll say goodbye here. Let us join in hoping that the wind has finally turned in our favour, that we'll be able to get somewhere on this island now.'

'I'm confident that Lamotius is going to turn things around. The man is on our side.'

'We believe so.'

Focke continued along the footpath that went straight on; they turned off with Oom Bart and their chests on the one that split off.

'Oom Focke's land lies highest up in the valley on this side of the river.'

'And yours, Oom?'

'You're already on my land, Salomon. The first farm above mine is Free-burgher Pieter van Nimwegen's. Beyond him is Oom Focke. Straight across the river from me is a good piece of ground that a man just abandoned when he absconded with his wife and child on an English ship two years ago. Beyond him is Laurens Gabrielse and beside *him*, right opposite Focke on the opposite side, is Daniel Zaaijman.

Absconded on an English ship ...

'Do English ships often call here, Oom?' She wanted to know. They had to get back to the Cape, no matter how.

'They only come when they need food or water or repairs, but the Company doesn't want them here. That's why most of the English ships cast their anchors secretly on the far side of the island. They cut timber illegally and hunt, and by the time the news reaches the Lodge, they've already weighed anchor.'

The Lodge was the Post House. She had wanted to ask if it was far to where the English ships anchored in secret but just then they got to the clearing in the trees. The weirdest leaf-house. Where Tant Theuntjie was seated on a log, her gown spread across her knees like a sail filled with wind.

'Why have you been dawdling so? Open up, Bart.'

Palm-leaf house. Palm-leaf roof. Dried brown feather-leaves. Wooden door, big lock. Two small windows in front, one little window behind. Black painted frames and shutters. Inside it was cool and dark and smelt of strange leaves and things.

Oom Bart opened the shutters.

'What are you standing there gaping at, Pieternella?'

The most beautiful furniture. One long room: sitting and dining area on one side, sleeping area on the other. The most beautiful bedstead with red curtains round it. Cloths on the walls, pictures in frames ... 'I'm just looking, Tante. I was wondering how the pictures and the cloths stay on the leaf walls?'

'With nails, stupid! Start carrying out the loose things, we've got to get this place tidy. It's been closed up for months.'

'How do the walls stay up?' Salomon asked this one. He was just as amazed.

'On a wooden frame of poles and laths,' Oom Bart explained and took a bottle of wine out of a cupboard to pour the soldiers each a mugful. Not for the slaves.

The kitchen was a smaller leaf-house, a little farther away. The hearth and chimney were built of small black stones.

There was a tool shed below the house.

2

Housemaid.

She, Pieternella.

Salomon, farm labourer.

She realised this when the sun came up the next morning and Tant Theuntjie called them into the house.

'First of all I'm going to teach you to make tea, Pieternella. Do you know what tea is?'

'Yes, Tante.'

'Oom Bart and I have tea first thing in the morning. With our rusks.'

'Yes, Tante.' Salomon had had to go down to the river the night before to draw water.

'And you and I, Salomon,' said Oom Bart, 'have to go and fetch the cow and the young ox that I left in Laurens Gabrielse's care.' Oom Bart was still in bed, the curtains open and fastened at the sides. 'Late this afternoon we'll have to slaughter the young ox.'

'Yes, Oom.'

Tant Theuntjie was up already but still in her shift. 'Pieternella, go and lay the fire and put the tea water on to boil.'

'Yes, Tante.'

'After breakfast you'll have to hurry and tidy everything, there's a lot of laundry to be done.'

'Where, Tante?'

'Down at the river, of course!'

She had to get to the Lodge ...

She and Salomon would get back to the Cape; she swore it in her heart and blinked her eyes quickly to stop the tears.

'Where is the *Boode* going when it leaves here, Oom Bart?'

'Back to the Cape. They ought to start tomorrow, loading ebony and whatever else there is for the Cape.'

'How long will it take to do that?'

'A couple of weeks. It depends.'

Tant Theuntjie wasn't stupid, she was immediately suspicious. 'And what do you want to know all this for? What have you got in your head?'

'Nothing, Tante. I just wanted to write Juffrouw Sophia a letter to say we're here.'

'Bart Borms, I'm telling you, I don't trust this girl. She's going to write a pack of lies. Now just you forbid her to put her hand to paper!'

'You're not to write, Pieternella!'

'I won't, Oom.' Monsieur Lamotius will write …

'Salomon, listen to me. Believe me. Look at me!'

They also had to have some of the tea and rusks for breakfast. Outside. Next to the leaf kitchen.

'Pieternella, I get frightened when *you* look scared like this, because that always means you're up to something!'

'Do you want to go back to the Cape or don't you?'

'I do want to go back. It's just that I don't want you to push us into even more trouble.'

'I've got to get to the Lodge, that's all.'

'How? When? Tant Theuntjie won't let you go.'

'I'll let myself go. While you and Oom Bart are fetching the cow and the ox and I'm supposed to be washing the laundry down at the river. All you have to do is make sure you take as long as possible getting the two animals back here. Get the cow or the ox to run off into the forest to cause yourselves trouble. Tant Theuntjie might come and look for me at the river, but she will send Oom Bart to search if it's any farther. I must have enough time because I'll surely have to wait to see Monsieur Lamotius.'

'What if they beat you when you get back?'

'I don't care.'

'Will you find the way?'

'Of course.'

But it wasn't easy. Fear attacked her from all sides when she set off on the path back to the Lodge. She prayed out loud. God our Father – *Gounja, Tikwa* – anything that lives in heaven, I'm scared a runaway slave might leap out of the forest and grab me! She ran faster and faster. It was farther than she thought.

Green. Everything was green. Green air, green breath.

She'd hidden her blue dress and her clean shift and her knickers in among the laundry. Down at the river she first washed herself. Juffrouw Sophia had made her two pairs of knickers for when she bled. Cornelia didn't have any knickers; she just squeezed her sponge between her fat legs and it didn't fall out.

Hottentot women in the kraals died if they touched cold water when they were bleeding. Dutch women living in houses didn't die of it.

Hottentot women lived far across the sea.

She soaped the laundry and packed it on a stone so she need only rinse it out quickly when she got back.

Salomon and Oom Bart had gone to fetch the animals.

'What are you looking so frightened for?' Oom Bart asked him.

You could always read the boy's heart in his eyes; he could never hide anything. 'I'm just wondering how we're going to get the animals here, Oom.'

'They've got legs! We're not going to drag them!'

'Yes, Oom.'

Wooden goose in the roadstead. Abandoned.

Sailors were sitting in the sun in front of the Lodge on fallen fence poles. Some were smoking pipes, others were just sitting.

'Pieternella!' One of them had seen her. 'Come and sit here beside me and play with my willy!' To make the others laugh.

She walked past.

Three grown children came round the corner of the Post House, swinging blue cloth bags in their hands – the kind you take to school ...

'Is there a school here?'

'Yes. Master Steenwyk's school. Are you also coming?'

'No, but maybe my young brother will.'

'What's his name?'

'Salomon.' Somewhere there was a strange noise ...

There was a soldier on sentry duty at the entrance. The door was open. The children greeted him and he let them through.

Don't look scared, she told herself. 'Mynheer, I have come to speak to Monsieur Lamotius about an important letter that he has to write.'

'Down the passage, first door to the left.'

It was where their names had been taken down the previous day. And the same man was sitting at the table.

'Yes, girl?'

'Mynheer, I have to speak to Monseiur Lamotius urgently. He knows me.'

'Young lady, you must not come and make a nuisance of yourself here. Monsieur Lamotius is extremely busy.'

'Please, Mynheer.' Somewhere there was a noise, it sounded as though someone was screaming too terribly.

'Put your case to me and I shall decide.'

Say I may sit on one of the chairs, my legs are lame. 'I very much want to see Monsieur Lamotius. Some of my and my brother's money is at the

Cape in the Orphan Chamber and he must please ...'

A soldier came hurrying in with a paper in his hand. 'Seur Jongmeyer,' he said excitedly, 'all these items have suddenly come to light as well! Commander Hugo asks that you add them quickly to the existing list with a view to reclamation.' He passed the paper across the table and the writing-man's eyes scanned it rapidly. He whistled softly though his teeth and began to read aloud.

'One hundred and sixty pounds of nails! Thirty-four pounds of gunpowder and sixteen pounds of lead musket balls!' Another whistle, as if in amazement. 'Two muskets, six axes, fifty-four pounds of pork fat, one earthenware basin, eight canvas bags! Corporal, this is beginning to look as if Free-burgher Beer and his heathen henchmen were planning a proper revolution! Has he let on yet which island they were planning to occupy?'

'Kronenburg, right opposite the Groot River.'

'Miss Van Meerhoff, you may return home.'

'But, Mynheer ...'

'Don't argue, this is an important outpost of the Dutch East India Company, not a place for social calls.'

'I'll wait outside.'

'What does she want?' asked the soldier.

'Monsieur Lamotius,' she answered for herself.

The soldier just laughed.

She stood outside the door not knowing whether to wait or to leave. The same soldier came by and stopped when he saw her. 'You arrived on the *Boode* yesterday?'

'Yes, Mynheer.'

'You and your young brother are in the care of Bart Borms and his wife?'

'Yes, Mynheer.'

'Why do you want to see Commander Lamotius? Do you want to lay a charge? Has Bart Borms been trying to fiddle with you?'

'No, Mynheer. I only want to ask him to write a letter to the Cape for me about my and my brother's money that was left behind there.' The noise was clearer when you were outside; it was coming from one of the outbuildings. 'We want to use it to go back to the Cape, to pay our fare.'

'You'll have to come and ask him another day, he's engaged in very serious matters at the moment.'

'Why does it sound as though someone is screaming somewhere?'

'Torture chamber. They are stretching Free-burgher Beer a little to loosen his tongue.'

'What has he done?' She wanted to cover her ears, she didn't want to hear! 'Why are they doing it, Mynheer?'

'Grown-ups' business. You go home now.'

She shut her ears and ran and ran. At the second river she met Daniel Zaaijman with an ox on the footpath, the ox with its back piled high with green feather-leaves. Jackal-hair had a long cleaver in his hand.

He pushed the ox out of the way so she could get past, but stuck out his arm, knife and all, and blocked the footpath. 'Pieternella,' he asked suspiciously, 'where have you come from?'

'Please let me pass.'

'Why are you crying?'

'They're torturing a man.'

'What have you been to the Lodge for?'

'His name is Hans Beer. Please let me pass.'

'Why did you go down to the Lodge?' His eyes were fierce.

'I wanted to ask Monsieur Lamotius ...'

'To write for the money.'

'Yes, Mynheer. Please, Mynheer.' You're not my keeper!

'Did you have Bart and Theun's leave to go?'

'No.' He was green, everything was green. Even the ox. A different kind of ox. Short silly little horns. Drooping ears. Not a Hottentot ox with long horns and straight ears. Jackal-hair pulled a bundle of leaves out of the leather straps and threw it down beside the footpath.

'Sit down.'

'I have to get back to the river to do the laundry, Mynheer.'

'Sit.'

She sat down because her legs were so tired; she wanted to close her eyes and sit till everything had melted away. The ship, Mauritius, the man in the torture chamber, Daniel Zaaijman. Everything. 'We want to get back to the Cape, Mynheer. My brother and I, that's all we're asking for!' Could nobody *hear*?

He sat down with his back to a tree on the opposite side of the path. A real tree. The ox was half covered with leaves. 'The Cape, Pieternella, will not grant the required permission. You have been entrusted to Borms.'

'Then we'll stow away on a ship!' She shouted it. She wanted to pick up stones and throw and throw! Hard! 'We never said we wanted to come here! We're not anybody's unpaid servants!'

'I know. But unfortunately there *are* times in one's life when decisions are taken *for* one.' He filled his pipe, his hands covered in scratches as if from thorns.

'Our home is not here, Mynheer! This is a wilderness where we are going to be smothered because no one here cares about us!'

'That's why you'll have to learn to care about yourselves.'

Grown-ups' words, airy words. 'You can't care about yourself if you're pushed around and thwarted wherever you go!'

'Hans Beer also tried to climb over the Company. Robbed a storage shed to get hold of provisions; made plans to burn down the Lodge in the hope of erasing his tracks. Was going to steal a boat and sail to one of the islands with his slave friends … and there build himself a kingdom for ever and ever. Stupid man. The Company doesn't allow anybody to climb over it.'

'We don't want to climb over anybody! We just want to go home.' Didn't he have ears? 'If it's true that there is some of my father's money left, then it's ours, Mynheer!'

'Right. But how long do you think a letter will take to get from here to the Cape? How long will it take the Company to go into the matter? How long for a letter, with or without the money, to get back here?'

'How long?' It felt as though a rope was being wound tighter and tighter round her.

'A year, if you're lucky. In the mean time you live on hope. And hope, Pieternella, is a treacherous thing. It keeps you hanging in the air until you realise it's not going to arrive - and then you fall all the way down to earth again.'

'Are you saying we shouldn't hope for the money, Mynheer?'

'It would be stupid. Hans Beer hoped for years for his own kingdom.'

'Well, how are we going to get back to the Cape then?'

'Start living in hope - or swim.'

She jumped up, she wanted to kick him and scratch him and spit! 'Tant Theuntjie says you're a dark horse, Mynheer, and one day the Company's going to catch you out!'

'Go and do the laundry, girl.'

The two cattle were in the kraal.

At the door lay a bunch of carrots and a cabbage, and a strange woman was sitting at the table with Tant Theuntjie.

'Pieternella, where have you come from? We've been worried sick about you!'

Who was this woman? 'I'm sorry, Tante.'

'Oom Bart went to look for you. You weren't at the river. Where were you?'

'I heard … there was something in the forest, I got so frightened I grabbed the washing and ran and hid. I waited for a long time and then I came out.'

'It was your imagination!'

'You say she's fourteen, Theun?' the woman asked, looking at her with a frown. Stringy grey curls above her ears under a brown cap. Not a single bead anywhere. 'She looks a bit small for fourteen.'

'It's because she's slight.'

'Is she taking an interest in men yet?'

'That was the problem the whole time on the ship!'

As if she wasn't standing right there in the doorway with a cake of soap in her hand. 'The washing is spread out to dry on bushes in the sun, Tante, like you told me. What shall I do now?'

'Your food is in the kitchen. When you've eaten, go down to the garden and help Oom Bart and Salomon.'

Garden. Which was where?

Rice and fish and nutmeg, and a narrow-bodied bee on the pumpkin.

'We're stuck.'

The garden was a piece of cleared forest on a slight slope down in a valley. More weeds than garden. Sweat was trickling down Salomon's face and hanging from the ends of his hair like dewdrops on blades of grass.

'Did you see Monsieur Lamotius?'

'No. They were too busy torturing a free-burgher. You could hear his screams even outside. I met Daniel Zaaijman with an ox and a load of leaves on the footpath. He says you can't climb over the Company. Gave me a whole long sermon. He says we mustn't hope for the money. I'll hope for the money as much as I like!'

'What are we going to do?'

'I don't know.'

'Don't cry.'

Oom Bart was lying on the slope, his head supported on one hand, a dead pipe in his mouth. 'Less talking down there!'

'Your arse, old man!'

'Pieternella, he could have heard you!'

'I don't care. Who's the woman up there with Tant Theuntjie?'

'Laurens Gabrielse's wife. Her name's Magdalena.'

'Just my luck she was there.'

'Her husband's still on his way. He's going to help slaughter the ox because they want to share the meat.'

'Less talking, I said!' Oom Bart had got up and was slowly making his way down to them. 'You and I are going to plant tobacco here, Salomon, like this island has never yet seen. I've told Hugo how many times: Forget the wheat the Cape goes on gnawing at us about. Rather encourage the free-burghers to plant enough tobacco.'

'Where will the seedlings come from?'

'The Company will supply.'

Along with the Gabrielse man came a pitch-black slave with chains round his ankles and downcast eyes. Gabrielse leant over forward as he walked, as though there was something wrong with his behind.

The slave's name was Moses.

'Watch carefully how we work with the meat,' said Oom Bart. 'Next time we may have to do it without help.'

'I'm going to be sick.' She really was nauseous.

'From what?' Tant Theuntjie asked quickly, like someone who has had a sudden fright.

'From the ox with its throat cut.'

'Are you sure?'

'All the blood.'

'Put more water on to boil, the tripe and the feet need to be cleaned before dark. After that they'll still have to boil for a long time. Early tomorrow morning, before church, they will have to go on cooking. There'll be plenty of eaters.'

The Magdalena woman was waving away the flies with a small switch while the slave skinned the ox and Oom Bart and the other man held the legs. The head had been laid aside.

Groaning, they hung the skinned animal with a leather thong from a beam in the tool shed. The stumpy neck almost touched the ground. The grown-ups went into the house for some wine, and had bread and chunks of cheese to eat, with dried fish.

She and Salomon and the slave got the leftovers from lunch, but first they had to clean the tripe and the scorched feet on the sloping table next to the kitchen. Moses soaked the feet in boiling water and pulled off the hooves like shoes. Salomon mostly just waved the flies away. She had to scrape the feet with the sharp blade of a broken knife, while the slave scoured the tripe. The insides of his hands were pink. His feet were as rough as a tortoise's. He didn't speak, didn't look up, didn't even wave away the flies that settled on his face.

'Can you speak?' she asked. He didn't answer. Perhaps he was deaf. 'Where do you come from?' He was definitely deaf.

'Leave him alone, Pieternella.'

'I think he comes from Madagascar.'

'Do we have to sleep in the shed with the dead ox tonight?'

'Where else? The carcass first has to hang before you can cut off any of the meat.'

'Do you think they'll take us to church with them tomorrow?'

'Probably not. I wonder what the slave is thinking.'

'Forget it, Pieternella!' After a while Salomon said: 'The Gabrielse man told Oom Bart they're going to hang one of Hans Beer's slaves at the Lodge on Monday morning, one that helped cause the trouble. He wants to go and watch.'

She was deliberately watching the slave. If he did hear anything, he didn't seem to care.

The slave got his food on a piece of canvas and took it, dragging his feet, *clang-clang*, round to eat behind the house in the dark. She and Salomon sat eating on either side of the door, in the reflected lamplight in front of the house. To be able to see and to hear what was being said inside. Her mother used to say that the truth rolled more easily off a loosened tongue.

There was definitely something wrong with the Gabrielse man's backside because he didn't sit on his chair like everybody else. He half leant on the table to eat, with only one hip supported by the chair.

At first it was nothing but Cape gossip. Stale news. Like about Hugo who was sure to become a pirate again now; after all, he still had his black pirate ship. Somewhere.

Eventually, the Magdalena woman said: 'You've struck it lucky with the two orphan children, haven't you?'

'Yes,' said Oom Bart.

'Not so sure about the girl,' chipped in Tant Theuntjie. 'Bit cheeky, but I'll get her right.'

'The problem is,' said the woman, 'that as soon as you've got her properly trained to your hand, along comes a swain and all your trouble goes down the drain. Those young soldiers at the Lodge are a randy lot.'

'Let them come,' laughed Oom Bart. 'I'm going down to the Flats on Monday or Tuesday to fetch my dogs from Ewijk.'

Dogs?

The dead ox was a black patch hanging in the middle of the tool shed in the dark, like a gown on the beam in the steerage hold. Salomon had dragged his canvas sleeping mat to the back of the room and fallen asleep mercifully quickly, so he didn't keep calling to her.

Oom Bart was supposed to see to it that he got a bed and a mattress, he couldn't just go on sleeping on the earth. Salomon said Oom Bart said he was going to build them a room of their own as soon as the nails that he'd ordered arrived. Nails were scarce and expensive.

A star was shining in the gap between the top of the leaf wall and the leaf roof. The eye of a dead someone. A tiny fleck of comfort looking straight at her. We are trapped on a strange island, she told him in her heart. Told *her*. Perhaps it was a maiden-star. It wasn't her mother's star, her mother's star wouldn't be able to shine *this* far.

The pot shards were wrapped up and in the chest.

And meanwhile the slave could hear perfectly well and speak Dutch, because when the Gabrielse man and his wife left, they called him to carry the lantern, and he asked them without looking up whether he should walk in front or behind them.

In front.

How do you learn to care about yourself?

They all had to go to church. The Commander wouldn't countenance any absence from the Sunday preachments.

'Salomon, go and fetch water.'

'Pieternella, lay the fire. The tripe and feet need to cook for longer. Add more water. It still has to get salt and pepper and nutmeg. And a cup of vinegar. Move the hook to the middle of the fire. Hang the cauldron on it. No, the pot isn't too heavy, it's your arms that are weak!'

Salomon, why is the bucket only half full?

Pieternella, come and make the bed.

Salomon, go and help Oom Bart get a sack over the ox to keep the flies off, and go for more water.

Pieternella, get on and sweep in front of the door in the mean time.

Go and take off your shift and put on your blue dress.

Pieternella, where's your cap?

Salomon, where are your stockings?

Salomon, put on a clean shirt.

Come on, we've got to hurry!

Oom Bart in front.

Tant Theuntjie behind him.

Then Salomon.

Then her, Pieternella.

Beyond the stone ford they caught up with the Gabrielse man and his

216

wife and their two stripling sons. Focke Janse and his wife and little boy were behind them. Focke's wife was shy; the child had shiny little shoes and was trotting along beside her.

Molens River.

The Lodge.

The church was beside the Lodge. Two blocks of pews, one on either side of the aisle. Women one side, men the other. Just like the Cape. In front of the pews were two rows of chairs. Right at the front, a high-legged table covered with a deep red cloth with golden flowers. On it, the Bible. The roof was a whitewashed linen ceiling, the walls unevenly plastered and also whitewashed.

Juffrouw Margaretha sat on one of the chairs, Cornelia with the little dolly just behind her. Two more ladies. Elegant, like Juffrouw Margaretha. Chair-people.

About twenty or twenty-five pew-people. A good half of those on the men's side were lewd young soldiers without caps. Some lounged back, bored, others sat up straight, expectantly.

A group of slaves dressed almost like sailors sat at the back on the floor. Three slave women in mobcaps. Most with coal-black faces. A few brown ones with straight hair like slaves at the Cape who had come from the East. Like Fair Ansiela.

It was hot.

Two windows on one side, two on the other. Open.

Dolly wanted to clamber over to her mother.

Daniel Zaaijman sat in one of the front pews right on the aisle. He wouldn't tell that he'd met her on the path the day before, would he?

Tant Maijke and the murderer came in with Maria and the children. Tant Maijke wearing her pretty red gown with the black lace collar and a black underdress. Seed pearls all along the edges of the flaps on her black cap. Head held high and amused.

Maria meek in dull yellow.

Suddenly there was a noise like someone beating on a door with the flat of his hand. Like a signal. All the pew-people stood up straightaway, rustling, as the eminent people processed down the aisle.

In front, a young gentleman kept his eyes fixed on the floor in front of him.

'Hugo's son,' whispered Tant Theuntjie.

Then someone who looked like an important soldier. Behind him, First Mate Berks of the *Boode*, then Secunde Van Hoeven, then Captain Wobma. Writing-man Jongmeyer. Monsieur Lamotius, his hat under his arm, his shoulder askew, like one afraid of treading on his own feet.

217

Perhaps he was afraid of the creature behind him, the oddest fat dog waddling in on its short legs, round fat face, bottom teeth protruding queerly.

'Hugo's English dog,' whispered Tant Theuntjie.

Then the handsomest, tall, dark man in black breeches and coat, the whitest of shining white shirts with a fine collar, delicate lace under his sleeves. Big black hat with a snowy white ostrich feather pressed to his chest.

'Hugo.'

She couldn't remember ever having seen such a handsome man. Behind him two tall men.

'His bodyguards.'

All chair-people.

First, Hugo's son went up to the table and read out the notices. That from the following Sunday, there would be regular services held every second week on the Flats. Other matters.

Then his handsome father went up to the table.

Curly black hair down to his shoulders, eyes that looked as though they were hiding deep in his head. A fierce man. You could tell.

She jerked upright in fright when the first words fell from his lips.

Once a huge rock had come tumbling down from the cliffs on Table Mountain and rolled right down into a ravine, dragging its own droning thunder along behind it. Her mother threw herself flat on the ground and cried: *O God, the Mountain has spoken a great word!*

'We shall read a Psalm of David. Psalm Twenty-three.' The Hugo-man was not looking at the Bible, he was reciting it out of his head, and the words were like rocks tumbling down a mountain. 'The *Lord* is my shepherd.' As if to say: Not you. '*I* shall not want.' He stopped after every sentence, to allow the rock to stop falling. '*He* maketh me to lie down …'

Biting. Unhurried.

As he reached 'Though I walk through the valley of the shadow of death', Sven Telleson came swaying in through the door and padded along looking for a seat. Drunk.

Her hands felt sweaty. She wiped them on her dress, raised her eyes to the roof – there was no flat lion pegged out on this ceiling, no one stopped her mother coming into church here with Tant Maijke's shoes on her feet and Geronimus on her arm …

Daniel Zaaijman got up and took Sven Telleson by the arm to lead him outside.

At the table in front, the handsome man's rocks suddenly stopped rolling. 'I call upon Master Lamotius to come forward and read the prayer assigned.'

Monsieur Lamotius went behind the table and coughed a couple of times to clear his throat. *'When the day shall have fallen on these our earthly lives and the night of our death shall be upon us … do Thou remain beside us with the staff of Thy Spirit so that in the dark vale of death we shall have no cause to fear calamity, but that we shall come through that dark valley unto Thee and into the light of eternal life.'* Cough, cough.

Outside, after the church service, a woman declared to Tant Theuntjie, with her nose in the air: 'Theun, this Lamotius is not a gentleman. He's only a Monsieur. Hugo is a gentleman.'

The people didn't go straight home afterwards. They stood about in small groups in the shade under the trees, chatting to one another. Monsieur Lamotius and Juffrouw Margaretha moved from group to group, shaking hands with everyone. Even the children.

To Oom Bart and Tant Theuntjie and the Gabrielse man and his wife Magdalena. 'Ah, Free-burgher and Mistress Borms!' Shake hands, shake hands. 'And who are this gentleman and this lady whom we have not yet had the privilege of meeting?'

Oom Bart said this was Free-burgher Gabrielse from Orange Tree Flats and his wife. Juffrouw Margaretha greeted them and then turned round to her, Pieternella. Salomon was standing right beside her.

'Pieternella! How good it is to see you again!' It sounded as if she really was glad. 'How are you?'

'Well, thank you, Juffrouw Margaretha.' Tant Theuntjie was standing slightly to one side behind them, her hands folded across her stomach, listening.

'And *this* is your young brother.' She put out her hand to Salomon and said in just as friendly a tone: 'Our hard-working cook's boy!'

She, Pieternella, nudged Salomon to put out his hand; he was standing there as if dumbstruck. Behind Juffrouw Margaretha, Monsieur Lamotius came up to greet them as well. 'Pieternella, our faithful substitute for Cornelia!' he said heartily. 'How are you, young lady?'

'Fine, thank you, Monsieur Lamotius.'

'I hear from Secretary Jongmeyer …'

No!

'… that you came to ask to speak to me yesterday. Unfortunately I was occupied.'

She glanced up first to see if Tant Theuntjie had heard. She had!

There was fury in her eyes!

They weren't blows. More like thumping and shoving every few steps the whole way home, with Salomon behind one moment, then in front again, crying and pleading.

'Leave her alone, Tante!'

'Shut up! Don't you come trying to sweet talk me. You also lied!'

Thump-shove *thump!*

I'll show you, I won't cry ...

'She only wanted to go and greet Monsieur Lamotius and ask ...'

'Blasted little brat! Think you can mess around with adults! Who do you think you are?'

'She just wanted ...'

'Shut up! Go and find Oom Bart!'

Thump-shove *thump!*

'Ungrateful creature! Trying to sully my and Bart Borms's good name before the new Commander, and after all we've had to suffer on your account!'

The *Lord* is my shepherd. She said it in her heart like the Hugo man said it, in mockery, to stop herself from crying.

The next thump-shove was more of a blow. She stumbled forwards and nearly fell.

'Thought Lamotius would take any notice of a little shit like you!'

Another blow.

'You're going to injure her back, Tante!' shouted Salomon.

'Didn't I tell you to go and see where Oom Bart is!'

I'll run away. I swear it.

'Thought you could go and plead for pity with your skinny arse!'

'She only wanted to ask the monsieur to write to the Cape about our money, Tante. Please!'

Only when the old woman lifted her hand to hit Salomon did she shout: 'Stop it! Tante, I'm sorry. I beg for your forgiveness!'

That helped.

They hadn't been back at the house long when the Gabrielse man and his wife and the slave returned to help with the meat. Sawing and chopping and cutting; the wife seeing to the flies.

She, Pieternella, at the fire with the cauldron of tripe and ox feet.

'Put on the rice!'

'Yes, Tante.'

'Just wait till these people have gone today. Oom Bart will take you

220

in hand!'

'I said I was sorry.'

'Don't you answer me back with your sulky face!'

She would run away. If she knew where to, she'd do it the moment it grew dark.

'Wait till the rice is almost cooked before you put on the cabbage, I don't want limp cabbage. Put more wood on the fire!'

The *Boode* was going back to the Cape ...

Salomon went for more water. Then he chopped the blocks of wood into smaller pieces. While he stood there, sniffing, she realised she could never run away and leave him behind.

'All the time she was thumping and shoving you, Daniel Zaaijman was quietly following us.'

Don't care.

The slave didn't have a head. You could see. His hands were doing the work on their own. His head was just there to hold his eyes.

Mynheer Verhage - Janvos sometimes used to work for him as well - once told Mynheer Van der Byl: 'A slave, Gerrit, isn't tame before the deserting demon has been driven out of him. Before that he lives only for the chance to get away. I warned Jan Louw.'

Jan Louw was a Cape farmer. One night all four of his slaves ran away. People laughed behind their hands because Jan Louw had been very kind to his slaves; the best two actually ate at the table with him each day. And *they* were the very first to abscond. Her mother laughed: Perhaps the food wasn't nice enough! Then it emerged in the torture chamber that they had actually planned to sneak back and cut the throats of Mynheer Louw and his wife. So they hanged them and had them dragged with the nooses round their necks all the way to the Duintjies where the birds of the air could consume them. Just like Zara.

The other two slaves were only flogged and then had their ears cut off and their cheeks branded with the sign of the gallows.

She waited till they had sent the slave from the tool shed up to the kitchen for more salt. Then she asked him: 'Moses, would you run away if you could?' She nearly died of fright when he turned round and looked her straight in the eye, with a hate as hot as the fire under the cauldrons. She knew: he wouldn't just abscond, he'd cut her throat as well.

Oom Bart and Tant Theuntjie knew that white slaves didn't cut people's throats.

But white slaves could abscond! But first she had to work out a plan, she swore in her heart.

The plan came by itself. The miracle. Right up to the door. Right to the table.

Afterwards, she lay on her bed, unable to sleep, because the joy and the fear were too much for her to contain. Sweet water and seawater mixed in one cup.

It was after sundown by the time they had finished cutting up and salting the meat. The Gabrielse people had gone home. The tool shed and the kitchen and the house were all tidy, the two wine bottles had been rinsed and placed upside down outside the house to dry.

Then Oom Bart called her and Salomon into the house. He wanted to speak to them. They had to stand against the wall – opposite the big dark red cloth with the golden-winged birds on the leaf-wall facing them. Next to the framed mirror. Oom Bart and Tant Theuntjie were seated at the table in the lamplight. The birds at the edges had been cut off and hemmed. Fine branches for the birds' feet to cling to.

'You saw the leather thong the ox hung from?' was how Oom Bart 'took them in hand'.

'Yes, Oom,' Salomon answered cautiously.

'Pieternella?'

'Yes.'

'Don't let her cheek you, Bart!'

'Yes, who?'

'Yes, Oom.'

'Good. Now, before I'll allow this farm to be upset by two wretches like you, I'll whip that thong to tatters on your arses!'

'Salomon didn't do anything, Oom.'

'He knew you'd gone to Lamotius!' screeched Tant Theuntjie.

'I told him not to tell.'

'What did you go to Lamotius for?'

'To ask him to write for the money which you said was left behind for us in the Orphan Chamber.' She rattled it off quickly. Tant Theuntjie had taken the collar off her dress. Where her neck and chest met, there was a deep fold. The string of pearls she wore fitted just neatly into the cleavage.

'Whose roof are you living under? Whose food are you eating?'

'Yours, and we're working for you.'

'Don't let her get smart with you, Bart!' Each time Tant Theuntjie moved her head forward, the cleavage completely closed over the pearls. They stuck out a little only at the edges.

'Salomon is an obedient child, you're the one that is the no-good, Pieternella! Elder Basson told me with his own lips back at the Cape that they were afraid you were going the same way as your mother!'

Leave my mother out of this. 'Oom, Salomon's knees are giving in, he's exhausted.'

'He can go to bed as soon as Oom Bart has finished speaking!' said Tant Theuntjie.

'Salomon can't go on lying on the hard earth at night, Tante, he's got to have a bed.'

'*Jay-sus!* If I get up out of this chair tonight, I'll knock you right out through that door!'

They didn't see him coming because they were sitting with their backs to the open door. Daniel Zaaijman. He was standing in the doorway in the twilight. Bending, because he was too tall for the door.

'There's someone at the door,' said Salomon.

Then they saw him.

'Evening, Bart. Evening, Theun.'

'Neighbour! Why are you standing there in the dark? Good evening. Come in, have a seat.'

'Thank you, Bart.'

He was still wearing his Sunday clothes. Big smart brown cap. Brown jacket, brown breeches and a pale yellow silk shirt without any lace but with deep cuffs folded back. White stockings.

'Theuntjie, bring us a bottle, it's not every day that Daniel pays us a visit. Pieternella, Salomon, get yourselves off to bed.'

'No, let the children stay,' Daniel Zaaijman interrupted him. 'I haven't come on a visit.' As though there was something wrong somewhere. He took off his cap and dropped it on the floor beside him. Jackal hair. 'I've just come to say I'll take them. The children.'

'Good God!' exclaimed Tant Theuntjie out loud, at once both startled and angry. Oom Bart's eyes stood out on stalks. She, Pieternella, got the shakes, as she always did when she was very frightened. She didn't look at Salomon. She waited for Daniel Zaaijman to say them again. Those words.

'What did you say?' As if Oom Bart couldn't believe it either.

'I'll take them. I'm enlarging my house, I'll need a day or two longer.'

'Have you taken leave of your senses, Daniel Zaaijman?' The flames in Tant Theuntjie's neck made the pearls shine pink in the lamplight. '*You* take them?'

'Yes.'

'For what?' Oom Bart wanted to know.

'Because here with you things are going to turn nasty for them. For the girl, particularly.'

'You can say that again. But nobody invited you to stick your nose into my domestic affairs!'

'I'll talk to Hugo tomorrow. He's still the Commander.'

'What? Do you want me to knock the hell out of you in my own house this night?'

'Oom Bart,' she chipped in quickly, 'Oom Bart, one day on the ship I asked Mynheer Zaaijman if he wouldn't have us.'

'O God have mercy! Give me some water, I'm going to faint!'

'Scoop up some water for the tante, Pieternella! You'll be the death of her yet tonight!'

She spilt two splashes of water on the table, her hand was shaking so and trembling. With joy. With fear. Salomon was standing up against the wall, pale with fright. She scooped up a cup of water for him, too, and held it to his lips, then turned round and said straight to Oom Bart's face: 'Please, we'll go and stay with Mynheer Zaaijman.' I'll crawl there on my knees ...

'Be quiet, Pieternella!' Tant Theuntjie shoved her finger almost into Daniel Zaaijman's face as she said: 'The Church at the Cape entrusted these children to *us*.'

'So it did, Theun. But this island's Commander can oppose it if an application is made with sound reasons supporting it. I'll do that tomorrow.'

'And *we* will oppose it!' screamed Oom Bart in a rage.

'That would be stupid. I heard this afternoon that during the church service this morning they caught one of the sailors from the *Boode* with a bag full of stolen nails. He said one of the free-burghers on the ship had bribed him to steal them.'

'Who was it?' asked Oom Bart quickly.

'They'll try a little persuasion in the torture chamber tomorrow to get him to say who it was. Klaas Visserman. You and he were great friends on the ship ...'

'Goddammit!' Oom Bart leapt up like someone in terrified panic. 'I'll take you to court for defamation!'

Tant Theuntjie was also frightened. She was twisting the string of pearls around and around. She said: 'Sitting here screaming at one another isn't going to help.'

Like a savage dog that had stopped jerking at the rope round its neck.

Oom Bart's hands were trembling so he could hardly fill his pipe.

When Daniel Zaaijman got up, she pleaded in her heart: Please, Mynheer, don't leave without us.

But he did.

Just said he'd be back the next morning. 'To hear what Pieternella and Salomon have decided.'

When day broke the whole farmyard was filled with unease.

It was in everybody.

Unease in *her*, for fear that Daniel Zaaijman might not come back.

In Tant Theuntjie, sitting on a log in the shade beside the house, there was a storm brewing. 'Pieternella, look where you're sweeping!'

In Salomon, leaning bent over the bucket as he struggled up the slope from the river.

'Pick up your feet!' Tant Theuntjie shouted at him.

Salomon said Oom Bart said he knew nothing about stolen nails.

Oom Bart was still in bed, he had a headache. Salomon had had to take him his tea and rusks that morning.

'Pieternella, stop watching the cursed footpath. Go and see to the meat on the fire!'

'Yes, Tante.'

'Wash the sweet potatoes and peel them – put them on top of the meat in the pot.'

'Yes, Tante.'

'And put more wood on the fire!'

Salomon said Oom Bart said he would inherit both the land and the cattle one day. Cattle that he would buy as soon as the Lodge lowered their prices, because he was not prepared to pay twelve guilders for any animal. Salomon said Oom Bart said Daniel Zaaijman was nothing but a two-faced swine who was interested only in getting his hands on their inheritance money. The moment he had it in his pocket, he'd throw them out. And while Hugo might still be the Commander by the book, Lamotius was the one who had the law on his side.

The first blast of the storm burst abruptly out of Tant Theuntjie's mouth. 'Daniel Zaaijman mustn't think I don't know the difference between a turd and a turnip! He needn't think he can drop one on my doorstep and think I won't look where I'm walking!'

'Must I peel all the sweet potatoes, Tante?'

'Yes.'

Four sweet potatoes that Oom Bart had dug up in among all the weeds in the garden.

What was the time?

Why hadn't he come yet?

Why wouldn't Salomon talk to her? Kept saying he was thinking big thoughts.

'But I'm ready for him! Let him come. *If* he still has the cheek to look Theuntjie van der Linde in the face this morning. Scum.'

He would come. Please.

'What thoughts are you thinking, Salomon?'

'Don't ask me, Pieternella, I've got to let the cow out and take her down to the river, and fetch more water.'

She was standing at the sloping table, peeling the sweet potatoes. When she looked up, Daniel Zaaijman was standing there, watching her attentively. Her heart leapt into her mouth; joy and fear raced through her being together and made her drop both knife and sweet potatoes.

Tant Theuntjie had also seen him and was waiting for him with a sneer. 'Rinse that sweet potato you've just dropped, Pieternella!' she called. 'I won't have dirt in my food. It's bad enough to have dirt walking on to my yard. Bloody cheek!'

'Morning, Theun.' He wasn't scared of her at all, you could see he wasn't.

'Get lost, Daniel, go and rub yourself against a pole. There's no unpaid whore-child for you here!'

'Don't talk rubbish, Theuntjie. I've come to hear what Pieternella and Salomon have decided.'

She placed the sweet potatoes on top of the meat in the pot and wiped her hands on her apron. Her breath just wouldn't come evenly.

'There's nothing to decide, they were entrusted to us!' Oom Bart had appeared in the doorway in his nightshirt and sleeping cap. 'You can clear off.'

'We *have* decided, Oom!' she, Pieternella, interrupted quickly. She wanted to run and cling to Daniel Zaaijman and cry: Take us with you, Mynheer, please!

There they were, like three dogs spoiling for a fight: Oom Bart in the doorway, Tant Theuntjie on the log, Daniel Zaaijman a little way off – each one ready to bite.

Daniel Zaaijman didn't take his eyes off Tant Theuntjie as he asked: 'What have you decided, Pieternella?'

'We've decided yes, Mynheer,' she said. But Salomon suddenly appeared round the side of the house, he must have been there the whole time waiting to speak his thoughts.

'I've decided it would be best if my sister went with you, Oom, and I stayed here with Oom Bart.' Like one who had had to scrape together every drop of his courage to say it.

An axe that split her in half with a single blow. 'Salomon, no!'

'Shut up, Pieternella!' shouted Oom Bart. 'Salomon has taken his decision. If you want Daniel Zaaijman to make a child whore of you, Pieternella, it will be my Christian duty to take you to the Lodge and get Lamotius to set the law on you!'

An axe that had chopped her to pieces.

'You're making a mistake, Bart Borms,' Daniel Zaaijman said coolly. 'I've just come from the Lodge. I have no intention of making Pieternella into a child whore. I want to marry her.'

'Godalmighty!' was all Tant Theuntjie could cry before she snatched up a piece of wood and hurled it at him in fury.

He didn't dodge, just stood perfectly still.

She missed.

3

Twenty-three days. It had taken the *Boode* fifty-two days to sail there, but now twenty-three suddenly felt longer. Like never.

Company law was Company law: for three successive Sundays the banns had to be published in church.

Banns saying that Daniel Zaaijman and Pieternella van Meerhoff were to be married.

While her being was split in half and the pieces were being pulled apart day by day!

'Please, Salomon, I beg you on my knees. I promised Mamma on the Bible I would look after you!'

'Daniel Zaaijman's land is just up here in the valley, you'll still see enough of me.' A tough branch that wouldn't break!

'You can come and stay with Daniel and me and still come and help Oom Bart each day.'

'No. I'm staying here. I'll come if Oom Bart and Tant Theuntjie chase me away or something. *You* are the one that has to get away urgently before Tant Theuntjie murders you.'

Getting married.

She knew what getting married was like. You lay with a man on a bed and so on, and then you had children. You cooked the food and kept the house tidy.

But she didn't want to think about that yet. Just about the escape that was filling half her being with joy while Salomon lay on the other half like a dead weight.

Twenty-three days.

Beyond the privy in the forest she plucked twenty-three leaves off a branch and laid them out in a row. Took one away each day.

Tant Theuntjie started early in the morning and didn't stop before evening fell. Cursing. Or making weird little barking noises in her throat and saying: 'You, Pieternella, are going straight to hell with Daniel Zaaijman, mark my words. And you'll spend more time on your back than on your feet, because a randy old man having trouble with his cock has only one thing on his mind!'

She asked him herself if he was very old, that day they went down to the Lodge to see Secretary Jongmeyer and register their desire to be married. So the Secretary could inform the Commander. So the banns could be published – so anyone who had any objections to the marriage could raise them.

If no one raised any objections, they could be married. On the first Wednesday after the last calling, on the thirteenth of October.

It was just before the narrow wooden bridge over the Molens River that she asked him. 'Mynheer, are you really very old?'

'Oh, yes!' he laughed. 'Twenty-seven! Which means that when you were born I was about a year older than Salomon is now.'

That wasn't old!

But then a bad thing happened. Two soldiers came to the house to fetch Oom Bart away because of the nails. Tant Theuntjie cursed and swore without stopping: Bart Borms didn't need a single nail of the Company's; he had sacks full of nails; he was a wealthy man!

Late that afternoon Oom Bart came trudging back up the slope like a worn-out old man. Sweat was pouring off his face and making damp patches on his shirt. 'Bastard!' he swore as he pulled the cork out of the wine bottle. 'Almost got me into serious trouble.'

'What did the swine say?' Tant Theuntjie asked anxiously.

'Fortunately he couldn't remember if it was me or Willem van Deventer who had given him the money. So we had to stand there while he looked and decided.'

'And then?'

'First he said it was me, then he said it was Willem. I think all the torture had got him muddled. Fortunately Secunde Van Hoeven was there, he knows the law. A man has to say straight out, not stand there dithering. And Hans Beer died this morning.'

'I heard him screaming,' she told Salomon that night when they were in the tool shed. 'The one that died.'

'Do you think it was the torture?'

'Certainly.'

'Would they have flogged Oom Bart if the sailor wasn't all muddled?'

'Certainly.'

'And branded, too?'

'Not for nails.'

'Pieternella, did they ever flog or brand Mamma?'

'No.'

'It must be terrible to be beaten like that.'

'Yes. The law says the Surgeon has to see to it that you don't die while they're flogging you. Swear to me that you'll never steal.'

'I swear.'

Next day Oom Bart stayed in bed. Tant Theuntjie said it was from the previous day's anxiety. Salomon had to tether the cow on a long leather thong down at the river so that she could graze. Then go and dig in the garden.

She, Pieternella, took him his midday meal: meat and rice and cabbage and bread. Oom Bart told her to take the second spade and help dig.

'Salomon, why have you got those cloths on your hands?'

'For the blisters.'

'You can't dig up this whole piece of land on your own, you're already looking overheated.'

'Oom Bart's going to come and help me tomorrow.'

'He'd better.' She turned a few sods and straightened up. 'Salomon, now that I'm going to get married, I don't know if I'll ever get back to the Cape. But if you go and ask to become a sailor ...'

'I don't want to be a sailor, I want to be a schoolmaster. With lots of books.'

'If you come and live with me at Daniel Zaaijman's ...'

'Stop it!'

Salomon was growing up.

When it was time for him to go and fetch the cow, she wrapped the cloths round *her* hands.

And when they turned the last sod in the strip, there was the new moon, shining brightly above those strangely shaped mountains. The sun was setting. The hem of her dress was covered in brown mud. She leant on the spade and looked at the moon, searching and searching for the picture of a rumble-drum, and Jacobus with his reed flute ... her mother's hands clap-clap-clapping. Her small brown feet step-stepping in the dust.

But the pictures would only come in little bits – like the pot shards in the chest in the tool shed.

It was far to think all the way to the Cape.

This was a different moon. A green moon, that couldn't dance the dance of a Hottentot girl.

A half-Hottentot girl ...

She overheard Tant Theuntjie asking Daniel Zaaijman if he wasn't scared out of his crazy mind to want to make babies with this half-caste Hottentot. What would they look like? Was he blind? You could see she was white, but not white like white ought to be. Why didn't he send for a wife from the fatherland? Even an English one – after all, he had plenty of contact with English ships?

'Don't you worry about my business, Theun,' he said. 'And don't keep making out that Pieternella is a child because she's small and dainty. She's not.'

'Her mother was a full-blooded Hottentot!'

'I know.'

He knew.

What are you if you are a half-Hottentot?

Somewhere deep inside her there was an ache that hadn't been there before ...

Once her mother had put a ridged limpet shell on a rock and started bashing it to pieces with a stone. Furious.

'Mamma, what are you doing?'

'Filthy mongrel with his hooked beak of a nose!'

'Mamma!'

'Goes and tells them at the Fort that he got such a fright when he stepped ashore off the ship. Thought the Hottentots on the quay were monkeys with smoke coming out of their noses!'

'Who?'

'Preacher Hoffman, on the big ship in the Bay. Never seen a Hottentot before, never thought you could blow smoke out through your nose and have some in your head, too!'

'Last night Mynheer Van der Byl said an important man of God had arrived from the fatherland.'

'Man of God, my arse!' Bashing and bashing the shell finer and finer; sweeping the little heap of grit into a ball. Moving to another rock, picking up a perlemoen shell and starting to bash that to pieces as well.

'He's actually on his way to the East, Mynheer said, but he'll be taking the service on Sunday.'

'They sent for me with the food boat, I had to go to the Fort because the holy man wanted to learn monkey language and I had to go and say the words for him. Wanted to write them in a book. I sat down. I said I wouldn't talk till they gave me some aniseed arrack. A soldier brought me a drop in a mug. The preacher asked what the word was that Hottentots used for their god. I said: Hollanders came and drove out the Hottentots' god; now we're godless and nameless.'

'Mamma!'

'Shook his head, said it had pleased Almighty God not to make all His creatures the same. I told him Hottentots thought so, too. Lion and leopard don't wear the same coat, but mince them fine and there's no difference. Same with people inside. He called the soldier, said they could take Miss Eva back to Robben Island.'

By then she had two little piles of shell grit. And you couldn't tell the difference.

She started walking back to the leaf-house.

She didn't want to be a half-caste Hottentot. Just a person.

When the sun went down, darkness fell swiftly on Mauritius and the forests became a black-green wilderness. Her feet wouldn't walk fast; she wanted the twilight to wrap her round like a quilt. To hide her.

A big dark bird suddenly flew out of the trees in front of her. Then another one. And another. A swarm of them!

Night birds. No! They weren't birds, but the most frightful bats! As big as your head!

She stopped dead. The quilt folded tighter and tighter round her, the sliver of moon grew ever brighter. Excitedly, she placed her hands on her small breasts and gradually let them slide down her body to the little bulge in her knickers.

She *was* a person!

A whole person. A real person.

Bats aren't birds.

She wasn't a child. There was a someone inside her body. She herself.

That made her happy, made her scared …

She wiped the table, spread the cloth, laid out the two little porcelain bowls and the sticks beside them. Broke the bread. Scooped out some more butter from the keg.

'Don't come crying to me if he beats you!' Tant Theuntjie was sitting on a chair against the wall; the light of the lamp made her face look yellow. Oom Bart was sitting on the bed, his head in his hands. Salomon crouched on his haunches in the doorway. 'I'll chase you straight back to him, I'm telling you!'

'I won't come crying at the door, Tante, I'll only come to see how Salomon is getting on.' Her words suddenly sounded different in her own ears. Felt different.

'You're not going to come here and keep Salomon from his work!' warned Oom Bart from the dark side of the house.

'I won't, Oom.'

'Acting all grown-up now, are you?' said Tant Theuntjie. Ill at ease.

The morning after she had removed the fourteenth leaf, Tant Theuntjie was sitting waiting for her with the announcement that on the next day she was going to have a bath.

Like a challenge.

Because it meant that afterwards she would take to her bed to ward off the danger.

'Seven days. I have to take care of the life in my body.' Juffrouw Sophia never spent more than three days in bed after she had had a bath. 'Get my bath shift out of the chest and give it a good shake. You'll have to see that Oom Bart and Salomon get their meals, that the house is tidied, kitchen and all. I don't want to lie there worrying myself to death.'

Dutch women's bodies died of fright when they bathed.

'Can't you wait till after I've gone, Tante? Tant Magdalena is making me a gown, she said I was to come for another fitting,' she said.

'She came here to take your measurements, she came here for the first fitting. She can come here for the last one as well. I'm bathing tomorrow.'

A green gown.

'Why a green gown?' demanded Tant Theuntjie when Daniel Zaaijman said he'd asked Magdalena to make her a pretty gown. The day the banns were first published. There was good material for sale in the store. He would pay for it.

'Thank you, Mynheer, but I already have a proper blue gown to wear.' Juffrouw Sophia had had it made for her. And other clothes, too. The Church Council had paid for them.

'Doesn't a girl want a new dress to get married in? Magdalena is very skilful with her needle, she regularly sews for Secunde Van Hoeven's wife.'

Then it had to be a green dress. Thank you.

So the island would not take fright at her. She didn't say so, she just knew it.

Because after church that Sunday, when everyone else was setting out for home, Daniel Zaaijman had taken her and Salomon down to the small bay below the Lodge for a while. He drew a map of the island on the sand for Salomon. Crumbly sand. Because Salomon had asked: 'Mynheer, what does this island look like? It feels like proper land.'

So Daniel Zaaijman picked up a stick and drew Salomon a map. She took off her shoes, bunched up her gown and waded cautiously into the clear water. Between the black pebbles and the seaweed there were the prettiest shells. The water wasn't *cold* cold, and something was very strange – she just couldn't work it out!

Salomon kept calling to her. Urgently. 'Pieternella, come and see!'

'No,' she called back. 'Take off your shoes. Come and feel the water and look at all the funny shells!' Strange pale white crabs on long thin legs. Almost transparent.

'Sailors often come and pick up the prettiest shells here, usually early in the morning,' Daniel Zaaijman told her when she went back to them. 'They take them back to the fatherland to sell.'

Salomon remained on his knees, studying the map on the sand. Daniel Zaaijman was crouching on his haunches with the stick. And Salomon's face was beaming with happiness; her mother would have said: My clever boy, his father's child. 'If this island was a clock, Pieternella,' he said excitedly, 'the Lodge would be more or less at half past four. Here. He poked a hole in the sand with his finger. 'Orange Tree Vale, where Oom Bart and the others live, is just a bit farther inland. Everything we have seen so far is only a little patch of the whole island.'

'What's at twelve o'clock?' She just wanted to know.

'Bight-Without-End,' said Mynheer Zaaijman; he seemed to be enjoying his 'schoolmastering'. 'It's a great deep bay with plenty of flamingos and little ducks and turtles.'

'Who lives there?'

'Nobody.'

'Oom Bart says this damned island is bewitched.'

'Salomon!' At the Cape, the punishments for swearing were severe. They would be on Mauritius, too.

'Oom Bart says first the island bewitches all the Commanders and then the people. He says we're also going to be bewitched. The new Commander is already getting bewitched.'

Jackal-hair laughed a great happy open-mouthed laugh. 'No,' he said, 'the island isn't really bewitched. It's just that it's not really a people-island. Never was. I think the island just can't get used to all of us.'

That made her uneasy. 'What sort of island is it if it isn't a people-island?'

'Just an island.'

'Are there baboons here, Mynheer?' He told her not to go on Mynheering him, but she hadn't quite managed it yet.

'No. Only bushbabies that the Portuguese released here.'

'Who came and released the people here?'

'The Hollanders.'

'How would you know if an island has got used to you or not?' she asked.

He looked out attentively and for a long time across the calm water to where a ship was bobbing up and down near the strip of foam. Then he said: 'I think you just know it – deep inside yourself.'

'Has the island got used to you, Oom?' Salomon was the one to ask.

'Most of the time.' With a sly little laugh.

And all at once she knew what felt so strange! It was the silence. There wasn't a single seagull as far as the eye could see; not along the shore, not in the air in search of something to dive for – no shrieking squabbles over some bit of carrion.

Even the noise of the sea was a distant roar far beyond the reef.

'Mynheer, where are the seabirds? There's not even a seagull in the air.'

'You don't get them here. And no penguins or seals either.'

She thought her and Salomon's mouths hung open equally far. No seagulls, no penguins, no seals? Not even on the islands behind the reef? No. Are you sure, Mynheer? Quite certain.

Arm in arm, Monsieur Lamotius and Juffrouw Margaretha came walking slowly along the beach. The hem of Juffrouw Margaretha's gown trailed over the grains of white sand. Behind them came a soldier with a musket over his shoulder. The bodyguard. Because Monsieur Lamotius was now the official Commander, sworn in and all.

He and Juffrouw Margaretha would stop every few paces and stare out across the water. Come a little closer, stop again. The soldier kept pace behind them, aping their movements.

'Cooper Zaaijman!' Monsieur Lamotius greeted him in surprise when he noticed them. Daniel got up off his haunches. 'How pleased I am to have found you here.' Salomon had also risen to his feet and dusted the sand off his hands and knees.

Juffrouw Margaretha nodded and smiled.

'The boat out there behind the reef,' Monsieur Lamotius pointed towards the reef. 'I note that it has no sail, no oarsman – yet the boat seems to be moving to and fro. Is there an explanation?'

'Sven Telleson, Commander. Lying on his back while he waits for the shark on his hook to get tired of the game.'

'Really?' Completely taken aback. 'Master Sven, our master woodsman?'

'Yes. You could safely add: master shark catcher, too.'

'Really? Is it deep out there?'

'Yes. It's actually open sea, even though it is still part of the southeast trough, where the ships are brought through from the sea. Hunting grounds of our biggest sharks.'

'Give me more detailed information, Cooper.' His voice had changed since he had become the Commander. More important – more authoritative.

'There's not much to inform you about, Commander. Master Sven usually sails out early in the morning, attaches a big chunk of venison to the hook the smith made specially for him. The hook is on a chain, the chain on a strong line. Then he begins to trail the bait back and forth. For two days, sometimes. A shark will come and play with it like a cat with a mouse. The moment one swallows it, Sven tugs it tight and goes to sleep because that's when the shark starts dragging the boat. That's what's happening out there at the moment. *That* can also take two days.'

'Incredible! And then?'

'Sven brings it to land. He could comfortably render half an aum of oil out of it. It's the best lamp oil there is. And if you boil it even longer it becomes the best possible grease.'

'And I cannot help perceiving immediately a healthy source of income for the VOC. One that ought to be exploited!'

'Not before the island's large boats have been repaired or a new one built, Commander. You cannot tackle shark-catching in a skiff.'

'What boat is that out there?'

'The *St Hubert*. But *I* would never risk taking it out. It leaks quite dangerously.'

'Why was it not repaired long ago?'

'There's no pitch to caulk it with.'

'Cooper, I regard it as quite providential that I should have encountered you here today. Without free-burghers like yourself, I shall never be adequately informed about everything that I need to know to perform my task as Commander properly. The *Boode* will take all the necessary requests to Governor Bax. No wonder there are so many problems here!'

'As you say, Commander.'

'I am inviting a few of the neighbouring free-burghers to come and have a drink with me at the Lodge tomorrow evening – we need to get to know one another. I hereby invite you, too.'

'Thank you, Commander.'

'And my sincere felicitations upon your forthcoming marriage, Cooper Zaaijman. May you and Juffrouw Pieternella receive the blessing of our Heavenly Father.'

Juffrouw Pieternella.

Like a crown on her head. A testimony – even if she didn't know to what. Perhaps that she was a real person.

When Lamotius walked on, the words came bubbling out of Salomon's mouth – about the shark and the hook, and where Master Sven could possibly have got venison from, and how much is half an aum, Oom?

A smallish barrel, about knee height.

Please could they wait there till the shark was spent and brought in?

No, that could take till the next morning. 'I told Bart I wouldn't bring you back too late.'

Oom Bart had been cross anyway when Daniel Zaaijman arrived there that morning. She'd asked Tant Theuntjie earlier whether they were going to church, and she said Oom Bart said he would never again set foot in church with that bunch of hypocrites. She wouldn't either. Finished.

Salomon reckoned it was because of the nails.

Then Daniel Zaaijman arrived and said she was expected to be in church on the days when her banns were published. It was customary.

Tant Theuntjie said she wasn't going to be disturbed, the whole marriage affair was all a farce anyway. Who did he think was going to take the slightest notice? And in any case Pieternella was still in her shift, and she had work to do.

Daniel Zaaijman stated flatly: Pieternella is coming. Finished. Salomon said he had promised Sick Comforter Heere he would go to church every Sunday on Mauritius so that he would never turn into a heathen. In that case, said Daniel Zaaijman, Salomon is coming, too.

Monsieur Lamotius read the banns. Very formal. 'It is hereby publicly announced that Daniel Zaaijman, bachelor of Flushing, and Pieternella van Meerhoff of the Cape, minor spinster under the guardianship of Bartolomeus Borms of Woerden, intend to enter into the state of matrimony. If any knows just cause or impediment why these two should not be joined together in matrimony, let him report to the office with his evidence. This is the first time of asking.'

State of matrimony. It sounded so grand.

The words sent a momentary shuffle through the church. Afterwards Tant Maijke and Maria and the murderer and some of the other people came to look at her in astonishment and to congratulate her. When did this courtship begin? On board ship? What did Bart and Theuntjie have to say about it?

'Thought there was something up,' sniffed Tant Maijke condescendingly. 'Knew you weren't constantly going up on deck for nothing. I just didn't want to upset Theuntjie any further.'

Faces she didn't recognise, that Daniel Zaaijman put names to for her.

On the walk back to Orange Tree Vale he mentioned the gown.

When she woke up the next morning she knew it had to be a green one. The island would get used to her more easily if she wore a green dress.

A few days later Willem van Deventer's Maria arrived unexpectedly at Oom Bart and Tant Theuntjie's place – actually just wanted to come and say hello, she said. A decision about the fate of Willem and Tant Maijke had finally been taken. Willem would have to farm on the Flats, which were somewhere north of the Lodge, on behalf of the Company. For equal halves. With wheat. They would give him two slaves, twelve oxen and a plough. And seed. The Cape was no longer prepared to supply Mauritius with wheat.

And Tant Maijke?

She had also been placed on the Flats, to work in the Company's garden with the slaves.

When Tant Theuntjie had to go to the privy, she and Maria were left alone for a while.

'How are your little girls, Maria?'

'You can't always tell how children are feeling. Pietertjie is still rather listless. Daatjie at least does play a little. I didn't want to bring them along – I actually wanted to come and ask if there is anything I can do for you.'

'It's kind of you to offer.'

'Perhaps I could make you a dress, I've brought lots of material from the Cape with me.'

'A woman up here in the valley is making me a gown. But if you perhaps do have a piece of green material, I'd be very glad if you would keep it for me till our money arrives, then I'll come and pay you.'

'I've got some very pretty green cloth. I'll make you a dress as a gift.'

Then she'd have *two* green dresses! 'Thank you so much. I hope I'll be able to do something for you, too.'

'You did enough for me on the ship. Actually – actually I wanted to ask if you understand things, Pieternella. You're still so young, and you haven't got a mother to ask. About being married.'

'I think so.' She wished Tant Theuntjie would come back, she didn't like Maria talking like this.

'Being married isn't easy, Pieternella. Daniel Zaaijman seems a good man, but once they've got you ...'

'You needn't be worried.'

'Has a man ever had his thing inside you, Pieternella?'

Don't ask such things! 'No.'

'Just open your legs wide and let your body relax. The first time is usually over quite quickly.'

She wanted to stop her ears. She didn't want to know!

Luckily Tant Theuntjie was coming back.

It was Friday. The next Sunday would be the second calling of the banns. The third of October. The church was full, not for the publication of the banns – it was the farewell service for the *Boode*. The wind was set fair, the wooden goose would depart straight after the service. The Captain was in church, so were the Mate, Second Mate, Surgeon, officers, soldiers. Anthonie, the cabin boy, too. And the cook.

Daniel Zaaijman and Salomon sat in one of the pews near the door at the back. She was across the aisle from them, on the women's side. It was stuffy with so many people in there. She wanted to go out.

Free-burghers, their wives and children. Servants of the Company, the schoolmaster, the wainwright, the blacksmith, the Company's handful of raggedy soldiers. The Company's bald barber.

She wanted out!

Commander Lamotius read the banns and then the sermon and prayers. *'Bless all seafarers and all those who travel by the compass of Thy Divine Providence, that they may be preserved from shipwreck, seizure by enemies, and all such calamity ...'* Just words being read off.

She'd known the wooden goose would leave again. Bound for the Cape. But deep in her heart it was a cable anchoring the Cape in the calm water and waiting to take her and Salomon back together. But she would have to think through the right plan first. She and Salomon would just have to sit it out for a while and be patient – till the banns had been read. Hold on to Daniel Zaaijman.

She stood up with the others for the singing of the psalm; she'd forgotten the words ...

After church, Tant Maijke stood crying down at the shore when most people gathered to wave goodbye and laugh and send greetings and shout wisecracks at the departing land boats.

'He and his two sons were taken out to the ship early this morning,' said Tant Maijke.

'Who?'

'Hugo. Didn't even come and say goodbye on the beach. He was in the little lodge on the Flats where I also have my room. A broken man. I got a lift on the boat. Shook him by the hand.'

Sven Telleson was also taken out to the ship by boat, to pilot it through the reef and out on to the open sea.

At last the drummer came down to *drrrrr-drrrrr-drrrrr* on the quay with his drum ...

On the end of the quay, Lamotius, Captain Wobma, Secunde Van Hoeven and Juffrouw Margaretha raised a last glass of wine.

When the wooden goose shook out its wings and slowly began to move its body, the most dreadful sense of desolation came over her. Like when your mother takes everything and leaves, and it's just you and Jacobus and Salomon alone in the potter's cottage ...

Crying didn't help them.

The *Boode* mustn't leave!

Being left behind alone was painful.

A cheer went up around her. Caps were thrown in the air, caught and thrown up again.

'*There*, my friends,' a man cried out, 'goes all our hope!'

'And crooked Hugo, too!' added another.

A single cannon shot thundered out of the ship's side and a small pitch-black cloud disappeared into the air above it. Behind them, a single shot from the Lodge cannon returned the greeting.

Salomon was standing beside her: 'Pieternella, don't cry so.' She noticed that he was also crying.

Like walking on and not looking back ...

And for a moment Daniel Zaaijman's eyes were full of compassion.

On the way back to the Orange Tree Flats, at a bend in the Orange Tree River where the green forest world opened up for a space, Daniel stopped so they could look back. The ship was through the reef and out on to the sea under full sail.

'I'm feeling sick.' The weeping inside her had turned into nausea.

'Sit on your haunches and keep your head down,' jackal-hair said, and rested his hand for a moment on her shoulder. That helped.

'Oom,' Salomon asked anxiously, 'why did that man say that was all our hope? The ship?'

'The broken saw-blade is on that ship; the Commander is asking for new ones. Timber is this island's only hope, but the small quantity of ebony loaded for the Cape is hopelessly too little, because just how much can you cut *and* saw with nothing but soldiers' sweat? The instructions from the Lords Seventeen in Amsterdam to our new Commander are wood, wood and more wood.'

'What else is on the ship?'

'A little over three hundred barrels of lime.'

'Do they scrape up shells here, too, Oom?'

'No. This lime's made of coral. The stuff Pieternella says looks like sand twigs. It's better than shell lime. The whole seabed under this water is coral; the Company has it broken out and burnt for lime.'

'What else is on the ship?' She was still sitting on her haunches.

'The Commander's reports on the state of things he found here; that he has taken over from Hugo; important requests, like asking the Cape to send pitch to caulk the boats with; the letter that he promised to write about your money.'

Salomon's hope.

'How long do you think it will be before it comes back, Oom?'

Daniel Zaaijman didn't answer Salomon.

'How long?'

'Not tomorrow or the next day. The *Boode* has not left for the Cape, Salomon. She's bound for the East first. Batavia. To put Hugo ashore, and other things. Then she turns and heads back to the Cape.'

The ship would not come by them again, then. Ships from the East

240

passed by on the other side of the island, more on the Madagascar side. Cheated again. The *Boode* wasn't going home.

That night Oom Bart had a good laugh, said he wondered if they'd found who was hiding down in the hold yet.

Who?

'Ready to make a court case for a few nails but too inept to count how many men are rowed aboard and how many return!'

'Who?'

'Jan Zacharias. They say he's taken a good supply of arrack along for the trip.'

Zacharias was serving his second term as Post Holder on Robben Island when they were forced to leave and go to the potter's cottage on the mainland. He was sent there in place of Post Holder Siegfriedt. He would pour a cupful of arrack and pretend to pass it to her mother, but just as her face lit up he would snatch it away and drain it himself. Laughed in her face. So did Hendrik Lacus's Lydia. Her mother would scream: You Dutch pigs!

The morning of the fourteenth leaf was the day for the bath.

First, all the shutters had to be closed. Salomon had to carry in the water. Oom Bart had to drag the copper bath up from the tool shed. She, Pieternella, had to heat the water in the old dented copper cauldron. Put the meat for the midday meal in the smaller pot and hang it over the fire. Lay the bath shift over the chair. The towels. The soap. Oil in the lamp – Tant Theuntjie needed to see to bath.

Clean sheets on the bed for the seven-day lie-in.

And there on the bed sat Tant Theuntjie like someone preparing for impending peril.

Oom Bart came to help carry the hot water and pour it into the bath. Bath at the foot of the bed. Bucket of cold water to add.

'Bart, light the lamp and close the door tight as you leave. Pieternella, first comb out my hair and wash it.'

The tortoiseshell comb traced footpaths through the thick bush of greasy hair. Yellow hair, with some grey in it. White people's hair.

Don't!

'If Oom Bart and I hadn't taken pity on you – and then you go and defame us!' All the old reproaches all over again. Till she had to kneel beside the bath and the water was streaming out of the pewter jug. 'Slowly! Are you trying to drown me, girl!'

'Don't jerk back, Tante! It's running down into your neck.'

'You're doing it deliberately!'

She washed. 'It's so dark, Tante, I can't see properly. If I could only open the door ...'

'Are you trying to kill me?'

Not really. 'No, Tante.' Soap.

'I'm not a piece of laundry!'

'Sorry, Tante.'

'Just wait. You'll get your reward under Daniel Zaaijman's roof!' Her voice sounded hollow against the water. Like gargling. 'Dry my hair properly. If I catch a cold in my head ...'

Towel round the head. 'It's done, Tante.'

'Pass my shift and turn your head away from my nakedness until I call you to scrub my back.'

To do that, she had to slip her hand under the thin cloth of the shift. The old woman's buttocks were great lumps of kneaded dough. Bulges everywhere. Lots of loaves.

One of the first things Barbara Geens did when the Church Council gave them to her was to ask Jannetjie Ferdinandus's tavern boy Jeronimus to come and bath Jacobus and Salomon. Soap and hot water. Clean! She wouldn't have a louse in her house. She herself would get the girl clean.

With water so hot it felt as though her skin was being scrubbed off! She screamed. Tant Barbara scrubbed. Tant Barbara said: Shut up! When it was all over she had to go out and sit in the sun, wrapped in an old quilt. She crept back into the house and dug a handful of butter out of the tub. Back in the sun she began to smear herself from top to toe – not her hair – like her mother used to do. Tant Barbara came round the corner, covered her head with her hands and let out one long yell.

Then she was scrubbed all over again. And got a tongue lashing, too. 'Just imagine! Sitting outside in my yard, stark naked and bare-arsed like a Hottentot child! Here you are a white child and you'll learn to behave like one!'

Only once Tant Theuntjie was tucked up safely under her quilts could the door be opened again. But the shutters had to stay closed. Just in case there was a draught near her bed. Oom Bart came to help carry out the bath: dragging and spilling as they went.

Seven days.

It was hot. An easterly breeze brought some cool air in the afternoon, but the sweat was already dripping off her at the fire, at her broom; from running to obey whenever Tant Theuntjie called. From running down to the garden with Salomon's breakfast, his lunch.

At midday she found him with the cow in the forest beyond the garden. Different kind of cow. Not a Hottentot cow, an Indian cow. It lowed in another language. Oom Bart was dissatisfied because he had to do the milking himself, morning and evening. Salomon didn't milk properly, could get hardly any milk out of the cow.

'I don't understand it,' she said to him one morning. Oom Bart kept on complaining about his back that couldn't endure the milking. 'You used to help Jacobus milk at Jan Vlok's.'

'Well, I don't milk here. I've got enough other work. You can see for yourself, Oom Bart digs just a couple of spadefuls, then says he's too weak!' A certain defiance on his face, just like a young cockerel that suddenly wanted to show his spurs. His hair was full of light streaks where the sun had bleached it, his skin was tanned brown.

She said nothing; she was just glad about the slight sense of reassurance that she felt rising within her suddenly. Salomon wouldn't simply allow himself to be squashed by Bart Borms when she was no longer there.

Each evening Focke Janse's slave-without-chains came to fetch away most of the milk. Focke's wife made lovely white cheese with it and shared half-and-half with Tant Theuntjie. And good yellow butter, too.

In the afternoon she found Salomon in the forest below the garden, sitting peering up into the trees.

'What do you see?'

'Look.'

'I can't see anything.'

'Look at the balls of brown stuff hanging from the branches.'

All of a sudden one of the balls spread its wings and flapped rapidly while still clinging to the branch with its feet. It was an upside down bat! It folded its giant wings neatly across its body, like cloth arms, and hung there, dead still. 'I've seen them flying!' There were more balls hanging on branches everywhere.

'Oom Bart says they flap their wings to cool themselves. And if you have six in a pot you've got quite a lot of food.'

'No! I'll never eat bats.'

'He says as soon as Tant Theuntjie is up and about again, he's going to go down to the Flats to fetch his dogs, and then he's going to go hunting deer. The law of the island says dogs have to have wooden sticks round their necks to stop them going hunting in the forest on their own.

There's a hefty fine for any dog caught without a stick round its neck.'

'Where are the Flats the people talk about?'

'On the three o'clock line, but farther inland. I mean, island. Daniel says so. He's been here looking for you twice while you've had to sit in the room with Tant Theuntjie.'

'I wish to goodness she'd get up.'

'Why does she keep shouting at you?'

'It's almost over. Four days more.'

'Are you glad you're going to marry Daniel Zaaijman?'

'Yes.'

'Do you love him like married people do?'

'I don't know.'

'He says you don't call your brother-in-law Oom. So now I call him just Daniel. The Flats where Tant Maijke lives are actually the Noordwyk Flats, where lots of other free-burghers also live. The best way to get there is by boat, the shark boat, along the inner reef – that's between the island and the reef – to a big river, the Groot River. Then farther on foot. The Company's got a lodge and garden and things on the Flats as well; Oom Bart says he'd like to buy a few cattle and perhaps move there. And sell meat. Did you know Daniel's got his own boat?'

'No.' She didn't actually know anything about Daniel Zaaijman.

'He and Oom Bart built it. It's called the *Zeemaat*. Daniel says it's his best friend.'

There was something she wanted to know from Salomon. *Had* to know. 'Salomon, will you go back to the Cape if you can?'

'Yes.'

'Why?'

'Because it's my fatherland. Yours, too. Oom Bart and Tant Theuntjie and most of the rest come from Holland. That's their fatherland. We're not Dutch people.'

'No.' We're half-caste Hottentots. Don't! She couldn't understand why the thought kept coming up in her. 'Jannetjie Ferdinandus worked out a plan to send Johannes back to Holland – I'm going to find a way for you to get back to the Cape. I promise.'

'What about you? Would you go back to the Cape?'

'Don't ask me.'

'Would you?'

She couldn't lie to him. 'Yes. The Cape is a people-place. I'm scared this island won't get used to me.'

She was afraid Daniel Zaaijman wouldn't get used to her.

4

On the morning of the last leaf she woke up with the strangest scared feeling. Her wedding dress was hanging from the same beam that the dead ox had hung from. The prettiest green dress with a gathered skirt and a square white lace collar. With an upside-down V opening up from the waist down to the frill at the hem where a green underdress showed through. A green cap with little white pearls round the edges.

Was it really her *wedding day*?

Once, on Robben Island, she saw a convict walk into the sea and start swimming. They said he was trying to escape. He got caught up in a current, waved his arms, struggled to get back, but the current sucked him deeper and deeper in. He drowned.

She felt that *she* had been driven into a current – that she would just have to float in the flow and hope that somewhere her feet would touch the bottom again. From the shore Tant Theuntjie was shouting that she should turn back, that Daniel Zaaijman only wanted her for a bed-wench. On the other side, Tant Magdalena urged her on saying, as she fitted the new gown, that this marriage would be her salvation.

Somewhere in the current alongside her was Salomon. She cried out to him: Hold me tight! But he wouldn't.

Tant Theuntjie had left her bed, but said the night before that she wasn't well, she didn't think she would make it to the Lodge for the wedding. Daniel Zaaijman said Tant Theuntjie and Oom Bart were coming, even if he had to tie them on to an ox to get them there. They were her guardians, they had to give her away.

'Didn't Theuntjie even offer to give you a wedding feast?' Tant Magdalena enquired several times. Fishing.

'Tant Theuntjie is in bed. She's had a bath.'

'Convenient time to choose.'

Salomon would get her bed and mattress when she was gone. And her quilt. She would just need to borrow the quilt to tie up her things because Oom Bart wouldn't let her take the chest.

She washed all her clothes down at the river and ironed them on the sloping table next to the kitchen. Nice and neatly.

On the previous afternoon she'd gone down to the river to wash herself, too. Nice and clean.

Ten o'clock. They had to be at the Lodge at ten o'clock. It was an hour's walk. Daniel had said he'd be there at half past eight.

'It's really very odd,' said Tant Theuntjie in bed one day, 'that he's never even invited you to come and look at his place.'

'Tant Magdalena says he's working on his house.'

'We hope so. It was so cramped you could hardly turn round in it.'

Salomon first had to pick green fodder for the cow before he was allowed to go down to the wedding with them.

She, Pieternella, had to lay the fire and put on the water for tea and their breakfast. Start the meat for the midday meal. Make the bed in the house.

'It's getting late, Tante!'

'There's time enough.'

'Please, Tante, I still have to dress.'

'You'll be a proper sight in that dress, I don't know what got into Magdalena.'

'It's a beautiful dress.'

'People are going to think *I* made the thing. Surprised Daniel didn't ask her husband to make it instead!'

'Her *husband*?'

'Yes. Laurens Gabrielse. Professional tailor, worked for the Company for years and years. But on this island any monkey can become a free-burgher just as long as he signs on for fifteen years.'

'Oom Laurens is a *tailor*?'

'Yes. And now I hear Jan Yser, the Company cobbler, is also going to take his freedom and move to the Flats. Not to farm, though, but as a free shoemaker. It's a blessing his wife and children stayed behind in the fatherland else they'd be boiling up shoe soles for food before long – like what is going to happen to you when they catch Daniel.'

Don't say that!

At least it wasn't raining. The footpath was dry.

Daniel led the way. Then she herself. Then Salomon. Then Oom Bart and Tant Theuntjie. All in a line, without a word spoken. Except the green sounds of a bird call now and again.

Something else was happening at the Lodge when they arrived. Sven Telleson was there. Juffrouw Margaretha and Cornelia with Andrea on her arm. Focke Janse and his wife. The Gabrielses. Tant Maijke and Maria. And other, unfamiliar, folk as well.

'What are they all doing here?'

'They've been invited to your wedding, Pieternella,' said Daniel Zaaijman, taking her by the hand.

Invited?

'Pernilla!'

'Master Sven.' He was sober. 'I'm so glad you're here.'

'For Peder van Meerhoff and for nobody else on earth would I pinch my feet into shoes on a day like this.'

'Thank you so much.' Her whole body was all a-tremble, she had to hold Daniel's hand tighter and tighter. All of a sudden she was dreaming a dream – with her eyes wide open!

Claas Wieringa, the carpenter, and his wife.

Two soldiers with sabres at their sides.

Another couple. 'Pieternella, this is Willem van der Hoeven and his wife Grieta. Van *der* Hoeven, the Secunde is only Van Hoeven. They're our neighbours. They live on a parcel of land of Focke Janse's.'

A jolly woman with a wide mouth and small teeth. The man was tall, with a bush of unruly light brown hair under his cap. 'Well, then!' said the woman. 'At last I get to see Daniel's darling! But you're still a girl!' She took Daniel saucily by the arm: 'You dark horse, you! Choose yourself a child bride and tell us nothing!' Her husband just watched, saying nothing; his eyes were fierce, but he gave her a friendly greeting.

Another unfamiliar man. Pieter van Nimwegen. Also from the Orange Tree Flats. On his own, slightly bashful. Cornelia, without the child, pushed past him to come up and greet her.

'My word, Pieternella! To think it's your wedding day! You're very good at keeping a secret, aren't you? I hear this has been going on ever since the Cape.'

She wanted to say something but Daniel squeezed her hand. Like a signal. So she just said hello.

The bell rang and everyone started walking round to the side of the Lodge. To the church. Tant Theuntjie had said the marriage would simply be conducted in the secretary's office. There was no minister, so it couldn't happen in church.

Suddenly it was turning into a real wedding! Everyone stood aside to let her and the jackal man pass and go in ahead of them.

The Commander didn't take his place behind the preaching desk as he did on Sundays, but behind another table. He nodded his head graciously and indicated that they should come and stand before him.

Juffrouw Margaretha emerged from somewhere with a posy of speckled orange lilies bound together and surrounded with delicate green leaves, and placed it in her hand. Barbara Geens's Maria had also had a bouquet when she married Captain Wobma.

A real wedding! She just couldn't stop trembling. Please, from somewhere, could her mother just look down and *see*! This tall handsome man beside her. She'd always said: Pieternella, one day you must find yourself a good Hollander to marry.

She didn't find him. She didn't even know if he was good. All she knew was that she was standing beside him. The hand holding hers was hard and rough, and her feet weren't really touching the ground.

'Since there are a good many people present here today,' announced the Commander, 'it was decided to conduct this as an official meeting in the church.'

Then the wedding began. He stated that the banns of the couple about to be married had been published on three successive Sundays and that no just impediment had been adduced. All present were witnesses. *'Holy matrimony is an honourable estate, instituted by God himself,'* he read from the book, *'for the mutual society, help, and comfort, that one ought to have of the other, both in prosperity and in adversity ...'*

Her beautiful green dress.

Daniel must have been afraid she would fall over because he hooked her arm through his, holding a stylish ostrich feather cap to his chest.

'Thirdly, God hath ordained matrimony in order that the natural instincts and affections, implanted by God, should be hallowed and directed aright, that all unchastity and evil desires may be avoided, and that we may live with a good and peaceful conscience. To avoid wantonness, each man should have his own wife and each woman her own husband ...'

She didn't like the way the Grieta woman had touched Daniel's arm, didn't like it at all. Self-righteous.

One evening Jannetjie Ferdinandus had brought Juffrouw Sophia a loaf of bread. She'd then sat down at the table and started getting coquettish with Mynheer Van der Byl. So Juffrouw Sophia put the bread back in its cloth wrapping and said to her, very properly: 'Get thee gone, Satan!'

'Wherefore the husband shall know that God hath set him to be the head of the wife ... and, you, woman, shall conduct yourself towards your husband according to the Word of God, you shall love him, honour him, and in all things lawful obey him ... you shall not exercise authority over him, but conduct yourself meekly, for Adam was created first and thereafter Eve ...'

Somebody was sniffing back tears. It sounded like Tant Maijke.

'Therefore I ask you, Daniel Zaaijman, and you, Pieternella van

Meerhoff, do you understand this and do you desire, before this congregation here present, to enter into this state of matrimony?'

'Yes,' replied Daniel and squeezed her arm.

'Yes,' she said.

'Then give each other the right hand. Daniel Zaaijman, since that it is your desire to take unto you Pieternella van Meerhoff to be your lawful wedded wife, do you here promise never to leave her, ever to love her and faithfully to support her?'

'Yes.' In a clear voice.

'Pieternella van Meerhoff, since it is your desire to take unto you Daniel Zaaijman to be your lawful wedded husband, do you promise to obey him, to serve him and never to leave him ...'

Her mother came back from the Duintjies one day and sat next to the house for a long time, saying nothing. Jacobus asked her: Mamma, what's troubling you so much? She said: They beat Nakakoa to death with knobkerries this morning. She had dishonoured her husband and lain with another man. Now I can't get her pleadings out of my ears because the Dutch have stolen my ears.

'... that you be a godly and faithful wife to your husband, as you are enjoined by the holy Gospel to be?'

'Yes, Mynheer.'

'Then I hereby declare you man and wife together, and may the God of all mercies grant you His blessing.'

They were married.

It wasn't her imagination, but all of a sudden she felt different. As though a different Pieternella had got into the green dress, into her shoes. Strange. Scared. Happy.

Outside people were laughing, congratulating them, bringing greetings; most started walking back in the direction of the narrow wooden bridge. Once across, Focke was the first to draw the cork out of a bottle – Laurens Gabrielse a second, and so on down the line to Sven Telleson at the back, who had taken off his shoes, tied them together and hung them round his neck. Blue stockinged feet, his legs blue up to the knees.

'Here's long life to Daniel and his wife!'

'Long life to Daniel and his wife!'

Three soldiers from the Lodge led the way: one with a fiddle, one with a flute and the third, a small dark man plucking the most beautiful skipping sounds from a pot-bellied lute. Jacomo Baldini was his name.

All along the footpath to Daniel's house. Jollier and jollier all the way.

Somewhere in the crowd Daniel let go of her hand. Somewhere in the crowd Tant Theuntjie laughed and Oom Bart wiped the wine off his chin with the flat of his hand.

'You didn't know Daniel had planned a party!' Tant Magdalena cried, waving a bottle in the air.

'No.' A *wedding* party?

'Grieta and I had to help with the preparations, but we were sworn to secrecy. Theun should feel ashamed of herself!'

Behind Tant Magdalena the Grieta woman was dancing about as she walked, her dress spinning. Behind her Salomon was laughing, mouth wide open, and stepping like a soldier in time to the music. Behind him came Cornelia and the shy man. Tant Maijke behind them, her cheeks red, exclaiming when she saw her standing in the undergrowth: 'Lordy, child, where's your bridegroom? Why are standing here amazed on the edge?'

'I'm so glad they let you come, Tante.'

'A man with a kind heart, our new Commander!'

Like dreaming. Better than dreaming.

Carpenter Claas Wieringa and his wife – Betta was her name.

Last of all came Sven Telleson singing himself a song of his own with words that sounded like *oploft did syn, o kristen sjel ...*

'Pernillatjie!'

'Master Sven.'

He walked past her like someone blest and in a world of his own.

She wanted everyone to have passed so she could slip down to the river to give the lilies a sip of water. They were so pretty.

'Put them in a little water as soon as you get home,' Juffrouw Margaretha had told her when they said goodbye.

Monsieur Lamotius told Daniel that Tant Maijke and Cornelia had to be back at the Lodge before sunset. She couldn't understand why he'd said it; she hadn't known about the party then.

A party that was disappearing into the forest as the footpath wound its way along.

The river was running, smooth and calmly, over a bed of brown and black stones, before tumbling over a protruding rock a little way farther down. A dove-like bird was cooing its strange coo – *caroo-coo-coo, caroo-coo-coo*. Accompanied by the shrill chirping of little sharp-beaked birds.

It was all so lovely, so strange ...

And she was married.

'Pieternella!' Daniel Zaaijman was calling anxiously somewhere.

'I'm at the river!' she called back.

'You gave me a fright,' he said when he reached her.

'I just came to give the lilies a drink, Mynheer.'

He laughed. Happy.

She shook the water off the stems and took the hand stretched out to her. 'Please see that Salomon doesn't drink any wine, Mynheer.'

'I told Bart to keep an eye on him.'

'I feel like I'm dreaming, Mynheer.'

'I'm glad. And tomorrow, when the sun comes up, I'm Daniel.'

'Yes, Mynheer.'

Long before the sun came up, she was awake.

She and the little sharp-beaked birds and the dove-bird and some other feathered creature that uttered long kirrr-sounds.

And when she went outside the old moon hung in the west.

Sven Telleson was in a dead sleep outside next to the wood-place, work-place. Six completed barrels, two half-finished ones, under a roof on poles. With a rear wall of planks hung with cooper's axes, strange planes, bundles of bamboo leaves, saws and hammers and chisels. A wooden lean-to for the slave, Thomas. The door was open; there was no sign of the slave. He was also shackled, like Moses.

The jackal-hair's slave.

His yard, his world. That she had walked through barefoot, like treading cautiously on strangeness.

His land. The last of the small properties on the Orange Tree Flats – almost at the top of the odd-shaped mountains. Not flats at all really, more of a forest vale straddling the river.

He would be here somewhere.

She was married to him.

On the cleared yard stood the new two-roomed, green-leaf house with its green-leaf roof. Attached on one side was a three-walled kitchen built of black stones. Two windows with green shutters. Two windows in the front room, two for the room on the left. Green shutters that were open.

Four chairs round a table, the posy of wedding lilies in a bottle in the centre. Pretty, and fresh again.

He wasn't in the house.

Daniel.

In the kitchen copper pots hung above grey ash. Water buckets. Crumbs and bits of bread on the table. A wooden basin with dirty crockery and spoons stacked up in it. Pewterware. Tant Magdalena had used two pretty green and white porcelain bowls to serve the food for her and Daniel only.

The tastiest white meat from something called a *dodo*. Turtle flesh with onion in a butter sauce with salt and pepper and nutmeg. And rice. Not like the turtles you sometimes found in the Cape marshes. Sea turtle. Huge, said Tant Magdalena. In the copper pot was the flesh of two of them.

'You will learn yet, Pieternella.'

'Yes, Tante.' She still had many things to learn, but she wasn't scared any more.

In the bedroom was a big bedstead made of polished brown wood with a snowy white quilt and pillows to match. They didn't look as if anyone had ever slept on them. Shelves. Two chests for clothes and bed linen and things. A corner curtain in front of a hanging space with wooden pegs in the wall. Late in the afternoon she had come in here to take off her wedding gown when Salomon and the shy man – Pieter van Nimwegen – arrived with her stuff from Oom Bart's. Daniel had sent them to fetch it.

It *was* a party!

She didn't notice when Oom Bart and Tant Theuntjie left; they were among the keenest dancers. Or any of the others either. Except when Tant Maijke and Cornelia came to say goodbye.

'I have to maintain my reputation with the Commander,' said Tant Maijke. 'I'm going to ask him to write to the Cape for me to have a piece of land of my own on the Flats. It's good soil, a little stony, though.'

Tant Maijke – filled with new hope.

And Cornelia, shamelessly clinging to Pieter van Nimwegen, who had offered to walk with them.

'Widower with two children,' said Tant Magdalena. 'I helped bring both of them into the world with my own hands. But the mother wasn't tough enough for this island.'

Some time during the night, while the old moon was coming up over the island, she went and lay down on the bed in 'Salomon's room'. A brown-leaf hut below the new one.

'That's my old house,' Daniel told her, 'but now it's ready for Salomon for whenever he wants to spend the night or to come and stay for good.'

Privy nearby, behind the old hut.

She'd only wanted to rest for a bit. And look at the wedding presents that Daniel had put there the night before. A purse with ten rixdollars from the Company; tobacco and a keg of beer; a bolt of red and white cloth from Tant Magdalena and her husband. Two pewter mugs. A small, pure white figurine of a woman - a gift from Master Sven - carved from a narwhal tooth. A writing book covered in sharkskin and decorated with the prettiest silver curlicues - from Claas Wieringa and his wife. They said he'd been a silversmith before becoming a carpenter. An important carpenter who had to assist the new Commander to improve the sawmill for when the new blades arrived ...

She didn't wake up till the next morning.

The slave came shuffling in his chains from the forest behind the work-place, axe in hand, a load of kindling on his back.

She waited till he'd passed Sven Telleson before speaking.

'Thomas, where is the master?'

'He said the yard must be quiet, the Juffrouw must not wake up. He's gone to fetch her present.'

Present?

Gift.

'Clean out the hearth, we've got to make the fire.'

'Thomas does not go inside the master's house, Thomas is an outside slave. Not master's slave either, he's just hired from the Company.'

'Then fetch me a broom and something to scrape out the ash. Don't disturb Master Sven, let him sleep.'

'I'll do so. But the master said the Juffrouw must also sleep.'

'You don't sleep once you're awake.'

Hired from the Company. At least he could hear and speak and answer her. And he brought her a useful spade with a broken handle to scrape out the ash and a shallow flat box to put it in. He thought the broom would be somewhere in the house.

Gift?

The water buckets were full. There was a box full of wood and enough food left over from the feast.

She cleaned the hearth. Laid the fire. Hung a pot of water over it to wash the dishes. Everything was greasy.

She cleared the table. There were four smallish kegs under it ...

What kind of gift?

Maria had made her another green dress, as a present. Almost like a night shift. It would be very comfortable to wear.

There were nails to hang the dishcloths on. Somebody had thought of everything. Even Tant Theuntjie admitted that she was surprised.

When she went outside again, Master Sven had turned over but was still asleep. The slave was hoeing down in the garden in a bed of what looked like onions. She walked to the edge of the garden and asked him what he usually got to eat in the morning.

He said the master gave him food.

Salomon had drunk wine. She knew. Before the day was over she would have words with him about that!

It really *had* been a party!

The Grieta woman had danced a lot with Abraham Steen, the Company's wainwright, and you could see quite clearly that her husband didn't like the way she pressed her body against him.

Jackal-hair danced only with her, Pieternella.

She didn't know where he'd slept.

She hung the leftover food over the fire and scooped some rice into it to heat up.

There was a cupboard with slatted doors in the front room. An earthenware pot of brown sugar, another with salt in it, a third with pepper. Cloves, nutmeg, rusks, some kind of grainy stuff she didn't recognise, a wooden box of washed sweet potatoes. A tub of flour ...

Daniel Zaaijman had thought of everything.

What kind of gift?

When she looked out of the door she saw Master Sven was sitting up with his back against one of the poles supporting the lean-to, his head drooping.

An old picture flashed into her eyes – how many times had she not seen her mother just like that? And then wiped her face, her hands, her feet. Helped her up. Sometimes just covered her, when she wouldn't get up. All she wanted then was more to drink. Eventually you don't even plead any more. You see that she gets something in her stomach.

'Master Sven.'

'Go away.'

'Lift up your head, you need to eat something.'

'Don't come and mess me around!' He was being difficult. She wet one of her own cloths to wipe his face with. His breeches were wet in front; she'd call the slave to help him down to the river.

He struggled, but she held his head tightly as she wiped his face. 'It's not going to help trying to push me away, Master Sven. You smell

254

horrible!'

'Your arse!'

'Keep still!' She wiped his shirt. His neck. The worst was always when her mother threw herself down on the ground and started kicking. Then she'd shout for Jacobus to take Salomon out of the way so she could rub her mother's back and soothe her until she calmed down. Captain Frooij said she was sleeping deep within herself.

She didn't know who was sleeping in Sven Telleson. All she knew was that it was something that moved her deeply. Perhaps because she wanted him to be a part of her father.

'I said: leave me alone!'

'I've finished. Come, eat up now – or must I feed you?' Sternly, as with a child. 'You've got to *eat*, Master Sven!'

Eventually, he took hold of the bowl with feeble hands and angrily shoved the spoon into the food.

There were no wall hangings in Daniel Zaaijman's house. Only one picture in a frame: of the countries of the earth. Very like the one that had hung in the schoolroom at the Fort. The Cape. Madagascar. A speck for Mauritius.

After their arrival Salomon had stood looking at it for a long time.

'We're a long way from the Cape, Pieternella.'

'Yes.' Salomon wasn't really on Mauritius. As soon as their money arrived, he would have to go back to the Cape alone. That she had already firmly decided.

Daniel Zaaijman's world. But she didn't feel unwelcome in it; perhaps it was the green-leaf house that had been awaiting her. When her things came, she wrapped the pot shards in a cloth and put them under the clothes chest. Like something you hide.

She looked round and saw Daniel coming up the footpath from the direction of the river – with a woman shuffling along a little way behind him. An old black dress down to her ankles. A bundle on her head.

Thomas the slave was leaning on the hoe, staring.

'Morning, Pieternella.'

'Morning, Daniel.' She looked past him at the woman who had stopped a short distance away, taken the bundle off her head and thrown it down at her bare feet. A strange woman. Who folded her arms brazenly across her chest and stared up into the blue sky. As if to say: I don't see you.

'I'd hoped you'd still be sleeping,' Daniel said.

'Who's the woman?'

'Anna. I bought her from the Company last week – my wedding present to you. Your own slave.'

I never wanted a slave. 'Daniel ...'

'She's very capable. She'll teach you all the things I can't.'

No. 'I *can* cook, I *can* keep the house tidy.'

'I know. But you're not my slave girl. And Anna will be here when I'm not at home, so you won't be alone.'

'I don't know what to say.' She didn't want a slave. 'Can she speak? I mean, can she speak Dutch?'

'Yes. There's a bed for her in the room with Thomas; he'll show her where to put her stuff.'

'Where does she come from?'

'Madagascar. But she's been on Mauritius for many years. She's worked at the Lodge. She knows the island's ways, things you'll simply have to learn if you want to survive here.'

'Like what?'

'Just trust me for now – and give her something to eat.'

Anna.

Tall. Thin. Brown bonnet-cap with a frill down to her neck.

Black otter's eyes that said: I'm looking down at you from a height.

Master Sven came round the lean-to, saw the woman and stopped abruptly: 'What the hell, Daniel!' he said. 'What's this crazy woman doing here?'

'I bought her for Pieternella.'

Her own slave.

Who padded silently through the house, like a cat in a strange place, first sniffing at everything. Touching everything with purring fingers. Feeling at the kegs under the kitchen table.

Without uttering a word.

She went to tell Daniel: 'She won't talk to me.' He was busy in the lean-to, edging round and round and round a barrel, tightening a hoop round its body with a blunt-nosed chisel. Like an iron tune played over and over: *tap-tap-tap, taptap. Tap-tap-taptaptap.* If you let yourself relax, your body could dance to the chisel's tune. 'She won't talk to me.'

'She will.' He put down the tools and wiped the sweat from his face. It was hot. 'Thank you for giving everyone food.'

'Where's Master Sven?'

'He's gone back to the Lodge. Come and sit here with me for a while.'

She sat down on a small rough wooden bench. He sat opposite her on a log, his knees touching hers. 'Trust me about Anna. In a week or so the strangeness you feel will have worn off.'

'I never wanted a slave!'

'If you tell me in a month's time that you still don't want her, I'll sell her.'

'Promise?'

'Promise.'

'Thank you. For everything.' Jackal-haired man. With the handsomest of faces.

'These barrels are an order from the Lodge. The *Boode* has sailed away with their entire stock. As soon as they're finished, I'll be free for a while and then I'll take you up along the island to the Groot River in my boat. From there we can go on foot to the Flats.'

'Will I see Tant Maijke?'

'Yes. And possibly Maria, too. Lamotius has asked me to investigate the possibilities of starting sweet potato farming up there – for distilling arrack. The new Commander is an expert on distilling and expects to make large profits from it. The Cape has said that the island has to provide its own arrack as soon as possible, enough to export, too.'

'Are there taverns here?'

'No. They're illegal. Every free-burgher is entitled to buy four cans of arrack each month from the goods store at the Lodge. Company servants and visiting sailors also buy some. It could become an interesting island industry – if Lamotius manages to catch the clandestine distillers and palm-wine makers.'

He had the nicest laugh. And specks in his eyes that made their blue look grey. And he spoke to her like an adult; took her hand and played with her fingers. 'It's important to me that you should be happy, Pieternella.'

'I am.'

'It's still too soon to tell. Master Sven always says Mauritius rolls heaven and hell together for you into one bundle – more hell than heaven. Promise me you'll tell me if anything bothers you. Or makes you unhappy.'

'I will.' I'm scared of Anna.

Jannetjie Ferdinandus had once brought her a cap to the Van der Byls' house for a present. A purplish one. But she told Jannetjie she didn't want it, it smelt like an old person's hair.

Afterwards Juffrouw Sophia told her it was very ugly to tell someone you didn't like his gift. Yet not long after that she herself gave Jannetjie back her bread …

'Why is Thomas shackled?'

'Because he'll flee into the bushes if I release him.'

'Why isn't Anna on a chain?'

'Anna comes back on her own when she absconds. So they assure me.'

5

The man emerged from the thickets above the house, not from below along the footpath.

A wild man. His clothes, his hair; his feet in dilapidated shoes.

Daniel knew him, because he got up immediately. 'Hendrik!'

'Daniel.'

The man had come to say that there was an English ship at the mouth of the Black River that urgently needed a cooper-carpenter. And meat.

Where's the Black River?

At eight o'clock on the clock-face, between the most inaccessible mountain ravines, but I can't take you with me, Pieternella. If anything happens to me, dig under the bed in the old house till you come across a small wooden chest. In it are all my papers and enough silver to keep you for a while.

I'm scared.

When I get back, I'll go down to the Lodge and have a will drawn up and attested.

I am afraid.

You don't need to be, the slaves are here. Thomas will bring back the ox.

He rolled two small kegs out from under the kitchen table, attached them with ropes on either side of the ox's back, fastened his tools and bundle on top. Musket. Folded sail for the boat. Whose boat? His. Where's the boat? Drawn up on the beach at French Church. Where's that? At the mouth of the Orange Tree River. Is there a church there? No. It's just a narrow spit of land that sticks out into the sea like a thumb. They say a French ship came and buried its dead there long ago and spent a whole day holding a church service. Probably just a story. Is the place haunted?

I don't believe in ghosts. What's in the kegs? Salted meat. There's another one under the table for you to use while I'm away. If the slaves or anyone else wants to know where I am while I'm away, tell them I've gone to trap turtles. Why? Because you're not allowed to help English ships. Why not? The Company's law. Then why are you going to help the English? They pay well. Aren't you scared they'll catch you? I live my own life.

Where did you sleep last night?

Beside your bed in the old house.

Heaven and hell rolled up in one bundle, and with them the little geckos that were all over the walls and in the roof, like tiny lizards.

'Geckos don't worry you,' said Anna, unconcerned.

Wrapped up in her own bundle.

On your own on the bedstead under the sheet and the quilt, till it gets so stuffy that you feel your way in the dark to the clothes chest and put the quilt in it. Feel your way back to the sheet that smells of sun and soap. The strangest stuffing under you in the mattress – not straw or Hottentots-bedding. Thin wiry hair that creaks softly as you move.

All the shutters tightly closed and firmly tied with thin leather thongs on the inside. The door bolted.

Completely, totally, utterly alone in a green-leaf house that breathed gently and clattered softly. Then a louder creak! Was that someone at one of the shutters?

Night beetle's unending shrilling through the leaves – faraway, nearby, faraway. Teasingly.

How much longer before it was day again? How would she *know* it was day?

Can geckos see in the dark?

Once Daniel and the Hendrik man and Thomas had left with the ox, she put on her shift to go and see Salomon.

'Anna, I'm going to my brother at the Bormses. 'The slave was sitting with her legs stretched out in the shade of the house. Didn't move. 'Anna, did you hear me?'

'Got ears.'

'I won't be away long.'

She had ears.

Just before the footpath that turned off towards Oom Bart's land, the ox came walking back slowly – Thomas seated comfortably across its back, shake-shake, shackled feet folded across each other. He didn't see her. Only when the ox realised she wasn't going to give way, and stopped, did the slave look sideways and quickly slip off the animal's back, embarrassed.

'Juffrouw Pieternella, I was just resting a bit!'

'Has the master left?'

'Yes, Juffrouw. Sailed off on a good stiff breeze. He and the other man and the stuff.'

'I'm on my way to the Bormses, I won't be gone long. See that the ox gets home.'

'Yes, Juffrouw. Thank you, Juffrouw.'

The door was open. But Tant Theuntjie and Oom Bart were still taking their afternoon nap on the bedstead in the cool dim house. At first she thought it was a green cap the Tante had on her head but then she saw it was a cabbage leaf.

'God in heaven only knows what Daniel Zaaijman gave us to eat last night but I haven't had a headache like this for ages!'

'Afternoon, Tante. Afternoon, Oom.' She remained standing at the table.

'We *did* expect you back but not *this* soon!'

'I've just come to see Salomon.' Don't ask where Daniel is …

'And Daniel lets you out if his sight *so* soon? Is the man all right?'

'Yes, Tante. Is Salomon in the garden?'

'Yes, but don't you go and get in his way!'

One strip was freshly dug, the spade was sticking into the ground at an angle. The cow was tethered a little lower down, grazing, and Salomon was lying under a tree even farther down, fast asleep. Without his shirt. Without his cap. Without his shoes.

'Salomon!' He sprang up as though he'd been hit by a stone. 'Wake up, I want to talk to you!'

'Pieternella? Has something happened?' Confused.

'Not yet. Just your luck it was me that caught you sleeping here and not Oom Bart!'

'Where's Daniel?'

'Where he is. I've come to ask just why you want to fall apart on this island!'

'What are you talking about, Pieternella?'

'How much wine did you drink yesterday?'

'Only … only … '

'Only how much?'

260

'I don't know. Only a few mouthfuls. They passed me the bottle and I just took a little swig for your happiness. Don't look so angry, Pieternella, please.'

'I'm not angry, just afraid!'

'Everybody was drinking the wine. It was your wedding, Pieternella! Everybody said it was a special occasion. I didn't intend to make you afraid.'

'A very clever Hottentot man once said the fire in our honey-beer is lukewarm but the fire in the white man's wine is a fire that burns you to death.'

At first he just looked at his feet; when he lifted his head, his big blue eyes were full of unease. 'Pieternella, why are people saying, behind your back, that they don't know what got into Daniel to marry a half-white wife?'

It struck *her* like a blow.

The thumping on the door woke her with a start.

'Who's there?'

'Me.'

It was Anna. When she opened the door, the dawn light streamed into the house like life.

The strangeness was wearing off. The house, the yard, Daniel's work-place – that smelt of him, felt like *him*. The fear and misery of the night had disappeared with the darkness, the ox was grazing below the brown-leaf cottage.

She wished she could ride on the ox's back. Before Oedasoa became so angry with her mother, he sometimes sent her back to the Fort on one of his riding oxen. Hottentots allowed only important women from the kraal to ride on an ox ...

No. She didn't want to call up old pictures. Only the now-picture. Green pictures. And make new pictures.

The slave wasn't in the garden.

Smoke rose out of the chimney and blew away on the wind. Westwards? Yes. The sun was rising on the other side. She made a game of it, turning her body so that the sun shone on her right cheek. When the sun shines on your right cheek, your nose points northwards. When it shines on your left cheek, your nose points south. Her mother had taught them that ...

The shutters on the house were open. Anna was in the kitchen. A small copper pot was hanging over the fire, the flames licking round its body. A bigger pot beside it. Higher. Small pieces of meat were soaking in a basin of water on the table to get rid of the saltiness.

'Where'd you find the meat?'

'In the keg under the table.'

One month, then Daniel would have to sell her. This was *her* kitchen. *Her* house.

She drew back the covers on the big bedstead. What kind of stuffing had they put in the mattress? She fetched water from the kitchen and poured it into the washbasin; took off her night shift ...

What was white?

What was half-white?

Where was the little mirror that Jannetjie Ferdinandus gave her?

Somewhere in the clothes chest. Her combs, too.

Mirror with a handle.

She'd forgotten what she looked like. You don't *know* what you look like, you just feel how you are. She *was* white. Her whole body was white. Excepting only her little black-haired privates. Why were they asking behind her back what had got into Daniel to marry a half-white wife?

Half-caste Hottentot. Tant Maijke said it.

Was that something seriously wrong?

When she turned round to put the mirror away, Anna was standing in the doorway of the bedroom staring fixedly at her nakedness.

'There's too little of you,' the slave said, frightened, and held out her hand for the mirror. 'The food is on the table. You must eat.' She took the mirror and brought it slowly to her pitch-black face, looking and looking. Then she said: 'It's me.' Proud. Content.

She put on her green shift and sat down at the table, the bowl and spoon in front of her. Boiled grainy stuff.

'What's this?'

'Sago. Sago porridge. Eat.'

Strange and sweet and nice.

'Where is Thomas?'

'At the river.'

'What's he doing there?'

'Catching river fish. We eat them.'

'Did the master say he must go?'

'Master's not here.'

'I know!' She didn't mean to be impatient but the woman drove her to it. 'Who sent him fishing?'

'I did. Anna. You must put on an old dress. We have to make new brooms, these ones are worn out.'

'What brooms?'

'For the house and the yard.' Otter's eyes that look at you as though you're an idiot child!

'Where do we pick the broom stuff?' She and her mother used to pick broom grass on the mountainside. Her mother would tie it in a tight bundle and beat out the seed heads on the ground.

'In the forest.'

In the forest.

The forest surrounded the yard on all sides. She didn't want to go into the forest, she didn't want to put on an old dress, but after breakfast Anna came and stood in the doorway with a long cleaver and a bundle of thongs over her shoulder, waiting for her, Pieternella, to give in and put on an old dress.

The dress with little yellow flowers that the Church Council had had made for her by Sick Comforter Heere's wife. Without an underdress that stuck out.

'Come.'

Down the footpath to the river, through the river and up a slope without a footpath on the other side. Pushing with their bodies to break their way through the green thickets. Thickets of great knobbly trees that shot out knuckled arms like old tree-people.

'Anna, wait for me!' Following a crazy slave who pretended she couldn't hear! 'Broom grass grows in open spaces on the mountain, I know broom grass! Anna, wait!'

It was too hot. When branches had ripped off her cap for the umpteenth time, she stuck it down the front of her dress and pushed on up the slope behind the black-clad figure, stopping again and again to wipe the sweat out of her eyes with the hem of her dress.

'If a snake bites me today, the master will kill you!'

'There aren't any snakes here.'

'How do you know?'

'No snakes on the island.'

'And tree snakes?'

'No snakes in the trees.'

Thorny things trailed and caught and tore. Greenstuff hanging like hair high in the branches of trees.

'Why can't Thomas come and pick the broom grass?'

'Chained feet can't walk in thick forest.'

Down a short ravine. Up the other side. Trees. Bushes. Trees. On a tree trunk a fat, grass-green lizard as long as a man's hand. She could have touched the thing! Jet-black eyes. Blue and red flecks on its body. Flat toes.

'Come, it won't harm you!'

Suddenly they were out of the forest and with a blue world before them. Open. The sky. The sea, far off in the distance. The white foam strip of the reef like a necklace all round.

No sail on the water.

'Where's the Black River?'

The slave pointed with her arm in the direction of the mountain behind them. Like towards nowhere.

Down another slope to the bottom, getting more and more humid, till they reached a clump of ostrich-feather trees with golden yellow bunches of fruit. As though Anna knew they would be there. She began to shove aside the undergrowth at the base of the trees and came up with a roundish hairy brown thing in her hand.

'What's that?'

'See those yellow things in the trees?'

'Yes?'

'This is what you get if you pull off the yellow stuff. Coconut.'

Coconut. As hard as rock.

'Shake it.'

It sounded as though there was water in it.

'Look at its face.'

'What face?'

'Monkey's face. Look.'

A clear monkey-face on one side. The underside. Little round eyes. Mouth. Flat forehead, hair laid back, rubbed smooth.

'A proper monkey-face, I see.'

'The tree's eyes. Doesn't grow properly if it can't see the sea.'

Then the slave split the head open with one hard knife-blow and nimbly stopped the white milk from spilling. Put one half to her mouth like a bowl and drank with obvious enjoyment. Gave the other half to *her*.

'Drink. It will make you clever.'

Cautiously at first. Just tasting. Sweet milk. Stone milk. Different kind of nice. Strange. Like everything here. Except the old flowered dress that still hung like a piece of bygone times on her body!

'Eat.'

She started scraping out the white flesh inside with her fingers and licking them. It tasted like milk. But thick.

'Is it still far to the broom grass?'

'We're there already.'

Where?

Anna stood up, clenched the cleaver between her teeth like a huge moustache sticking out on either side of her face, and shinned up the nearest palm tree, one foot flat, the other crosswise, hand over hand – a black-clad tiger cat! She started hacking off a feather-leaf branch and dropped it with a swish on to the ground. Then another one. A third.

Up the next tree.

'Anna, what are you doing?'

'Broom stuff. To teach you, like the master said I must.'

6

The next morning, when the house had been tidied, breakfast eaten and the filleted silver-black river fish were salted and hanging from a beam in the wind, Anna made her come and sit beside her, legs stretched out, in the shade of the work-place roof.

With the oxload of palm leaves between them.

Except that it wasn't an ox that had carried the bundles there but she and Anna, through the thickets, on their backs.

Because Daniel Zaaijman had left her behind with a crazy woman who thought you made brooms out of palm leaves!

'Does this perhaps look like a palm leaf to you?' she challenged the slave when she got home, drop-dead-tired, the previous afternoon, brandishing one of the twig brooms in her face.

'Yes,' said Anna carelessly.

She didn't have the strength to argue.

So Anna sat her down, legs stretched out and, without a word, began to 'magic' the stalks out of the palm fronds.

First she stripped the long sharp-pointed leaves of the green-feather branch away from the central core. Each sharp leaf had its own thin core in the middle, which Anna split off *rrrip* down one side and then *rrrip* down the other with her nails – to make the long thin core into a long thin stick. A broom twig. Just like the old broom's.

Palm-leaf school.

Leaf by leaf, till she began to get the knack of it and the pile of twigs on *her* side began to grow.

'I see you sleep scared at night. Shutters closed.'

'Yes.' She'd got up a few times the previous night to open a shutter just a crack and to see whether day had broken yet.

'You can leave them open. Thomas is chained.'

'Is it true that there are lots of runaway slaves hiding in the forest?'

'Not here. Far away.'

'How do you know?'

'Anna knows.'

'What is the stuffing in the mattress on the bedstead made of?'

'Monkey's hair. Coconut hair. Leave the coconuts in the river for six weeks for the hair to soften, then pull them apart like thick thread. I'll teach you.'

Palm-leaf school. Coconut school.

Anna was not crazy. She was just good and evil wrapped up together in one bundle. Good at tidying the house, good at cooking, good for teaching you all kinds of things, good at doing the washing. But deep down in her eyes and her soul was evil anger because she was your slave. Great anger. Like hate. No matter what you said or did, it was always there.

A few days later, though, she, Pieternella, did manage to surprise her with something …

When the bundles of twigs were ready for Thomas to bind them on to broom handles, Anna laid the stripped leaves in water and said: 'I'll wait till tomorrow to teach you more, because I see Master Van der Hoeven's wife, Juffrouw Grieta, is on her way up here for a visit. Don't ask her to stay for supper.'

'I came up yesterday to see how things were going with the bride and groom – to see if everything was going well!' the Grieta woman said and winked with one eye.

'Things are going well with all of us.' Luckily she was wearing her pretty green dress. Grieta was all dressed up.

'But the slave said you'd gone off into the forest!' A wink with the other eye, laughing with her mouth wide open. 'You try everything when it's all still new! Not that that's all much of a novelty to Daniel any more, of course!'

'What is sago?'

'What's that?'

'Sago. Anna makes the loveliest porridge of a grainy kind of ...'

'You scrape it out of the inside flesh of the trunk of a palm tree. Odd question. Didn't you have sago at the Cape?'

'Not that I ever saw.'

'And palm trees?'

'Not that I ever saw; perhaps deeper inland.'

'How old are you?'

'Fourteen.'

'Well at your age you don't know much anyway. But don't worry, Daniel will teach you!' Laugh-laugh-Laugh. How do you chew with such blunt little teeth?

'And you, Grieta, how old are you?'

'Old enough to be your mother! Tell your slave to bring me some water to drink. Where's Daniel?'

'He's coming.'

She waited till dusk, said she wanted to ask Daniel something. To ask him how it was possible that Willem van Deventer got not only land on the Flats, but oxen and a plough and wheat seed as well. While she and her husband had been pleading for land on the Flats for ever so long. Had Willem van Deventer not been banished, after all? Supposed to have shot a Hottentot – not that *that* could have been such a terrible thing. Oh, forgive me, I forgot, they say your mother was also a Hottentot – was she?

Yes.

Luckily you didn't inherit much of the black! Ha-ha-ha. Luckily you're very white but you can see not completely.

Hottentots aren't black.

How come?

You wouldn't understand.

You should see how the little half-castes creep out of the Lodge, more blackish than white. The results of the fun officials and soldiers have with slave wenches. The law expressly forbids it, but I've yet to hear of a law that can keep a man's breeches where they belong! Ha-ha-ha. They say the new Commander now has the slave women locked up early each evening. What does Daniel say about him, about Lamotius? The men are dissatisfied, they say at least Hugo was a pig with some stature, but all this one's got is a pretty wife. Did you hear, they say old Drunk-Jan Zacharias stowed away on the *Boode* and Lamotius is furious. But he's only beginning to feel the head wind gathering against him.

Poor old Schoolmaster Steenwyk is a broken man. Conducted evening prayers himself all these years, and read the lesson in church. The old man's pride and joy. Now Lamotius has relieved him of the task; says he prefers to do it himself. Steenwyk says he's going to ask to go back to the fatherland. What did Daniel go and buy you this stupid slave for?

When dusk began to fall, she went home. Luckily.

Anna cooked some of the river fish, with sweet potatoes on top. She, Pieternella, ate indoors by candlelight, the slaves outside with their own lantern.

Slept all night with the shutters open. Cooler. She and the frogs and the crickets and the night beetle, now shrilling here, now there, in different places.

Next day she and Anna were sitting long-legged in the shade again because Anna wanted to teach her to plait palm leaves into a mat to lay beside the bedstead.

Anna had scarcely finished plaiting the wet leaves into her first row when Pieternella started plaiting a braid of her own. A flat braid, like her mother taught her. Anna sat back astonished.

'Where did you learn that?'

'From my mother.'

'Where's your mother?'

'Dead. She was a Hottentot.'

'What's that?'

'A man-of-men.'

'Like a Dutchman?'

'No. A real person.'

'And your father?'

'They beat him to death on Madagascar.'

'Slave buyer?'

'Sort of.' Anna knew about things.

'What have you come here for? To Mauritius?'

'Nothing. I never wanted to come here. Daniel says it's not a people-place.'

'Except if the island gives you some of its blood.'

'What kind of blood?'

'Secret.' Like the lid of a chest snapping shut and the lock clicking.

'Christian blood?' she pestered. But Anna wouldn't answer. 'I *have* Christian blood, I've been baptised and confirmed, too.' Anna still wouldn't say. 'What kind of blood could an island have, after all?' she challenged.

Anna's hands just folded the wet leaves back, faster and faster, folded round, folded back, folded round …

Seven days. She began to get uneasy because Daniel had not come back.
Then dig under the bed in the old house.
No.
He would come.

On the ninth day the soldier came. 'Juffrouw Van Meerhoff – wife of Daniel Zaaijman?'

'Yes.' She was frightened …

'Commander Lamotius wishes to speak to you urgently.'

'Why?' He would surely not have sent for her to look after Andrea again. 'Why does he want to speak to me?'

'That I cannot tell you, Juffrouw. But you must go to the Lodge immediately. I have come to accompany you.'

Then she was deathly scared. Accompany sounded like guard, so that you couldn't run away …

She ahead. Soldier with the sabre behind her. After the ford she asked to walk behind because going first felt too much like being driven. While one frightened thought after another kept running through her head. Why had the Commander sent for *her* and not Daniel? Because they had caught him and thrown him in gaol?

No, that just didn't *feel* true.

Because Salomon was in trouble and they wanted to flog and brand him – and she had to witness it so that she knew what would await her if she didn't behave herself?

By the time they reached the narrow wooden bridge over the Molens River, her legs were ready to give way under her.

Secretary Jongmeyer was standing in front of the Lodge chatting to the wainwright, Abraham Steen. They greeted her in surprise. Probably because of the soldier. He took her right down the passage to a door and knocked.

It wasn't an office, it was the Lamotiuses' parlour. Smart, padded, dark-red velvet chairs with red and gold tassels round the edges of the cushions. Lots of blue and white plates in a cupboard with glass windows; the most beautiful silver plate on the walls, each piece with a silver snuffer and a candle. Crooked. The walls were too uneven. The roof had sagged in the centre. A dark wooden bench with the most beautiful carved back – curled leaves and deers' heads. Cornelia said the

Lamotiuses' furniture had come with them, in the ship's hold.

Monsieur Lamotius got up out of one of the chairs and nodded to the soldier to leave.

'I appreciate your coming.' The Commander. Importantly.

'Monsieur, the soldier said it was urgent. My heart is terribly worried.'

'Be at ease. No charge has been laid against you or your husband. Address me as Commander.'

'And against my brother?' She had to know.

'No. May I offer you a glass of wine?'

'No, thank you, Commander.' Offer me a chair to sit on!

He began to walk up and down with his hands behind his back. 'To be a Commander, Pieternella, is like driving a wagon drawn by a hundred oxen – without anyone leading the front ox. In other words, your ears and your eyes have to be everywhere. Because sometimes one is forced to use the whip to make everyone pull together and prevent the wagon from leaving the track, there will always be a few oxen that object to censure and correction. That will not cooperate. That even desert.'

'You will need a long whip, Commander.' She didn't really know what to say.

'Because I have to drive this wagon on behalf of the mighty Dutch East India Company, and have to assume the greatest responsibility in the name of the Company, there will always be people who will try to bring me into disfavour. If, however, they cannot find or invent accusations to lay against *me*, they will attempt to do so through my good wife!'

She would just sit on the very edge of the chair ...

'Now a serious charge has been laid against Juffrouw Margaretha and consequently also against me. We are deeply disturbed by this. We need to take you into our confidence in our search for an urgent solution.'

The room was squeezing the breath out of her; the Commander had spoken too many words! 'I don't understand what you are saying.'

'You were in the same cabin as Juffrouw Maijke van den Berg during the voyage.'

No cabin, just a wooden hole. 'Yes, Commander.'

'Can you recall whether Governor Bax was ever discussed during that time?'

Governor Bax ... 'The days were long, Commander. They talked about many people.'

'Tell me the truth, Pieternella.'

'I won't lie to you, Commander, it's just that I'm a bit muddled now.' You use too many words.

'Annie Bruyns – the widow Verhagen, her husband was a soldier in the service of the Company here on Mauritius – currently lives on the Flats at Noordwyk. According to her, Juffrouw Maijke says that Juffrouw *Margaretha* is spreading the story that Governor Bax is a leper. If the island gossips were to send such an outrageous lie to the Cape, it would have serious consequences for me as Commander.'

'Tant Maijke is lying. *She* was the one who told Tant Theuntjie on the ship that Governor Bax was full of sores, that he was a leper.' All of a sudden the whole business had fallen flat. All her fright, the whole way there, had been groundless!

Lamotius halted in front of her; his cheeks working like someone grinding his teeth. 'Thank you. Your evidence is of the utmost importance to us.'

Evidence? She wanted to go back. 'Please, may I now return home?'

'The soldier will accompany you there.'

She deliberately walked faster and faster, pretending not to hear the soldier telling her to go slower! He was rather stout.

On the fifteenth morning Anna said the master would be home by evening.

'How do you know?' Happy and scared gripped her body from either side.

'His shadow is coming closer.'

On the floor, on each side of the bedstead, lay a palm-leaf mat. A palm-leaf mat in the slaves' room. Two new brooms and a scrubbing thing. Altogether, they had brought in three loads of palm leaves; who was the slave and who the mistress was barely perceptible.

'My fingers haven't got any skin left on them, Anna!'

'The master said I had to teach you.'

'He didn't say I had to know everything before he got back!'

'Wait till the coconuts have soaked enough …'

Two sacks of coconuts were soaking in the river. Sacks dragged back on leather thongs till the sweat was pouring off her. She lay down in the water alongside the monkey-face things and threatened to go on lying there for the rest of the day!

'Crabs will eat you.'

Big black-brown crabs with big yellow pincers. They lived everywhere in the mud in round holes that Anna dug open with a stick. If the crab was at home its shell went one way and its white flesh landed in her

271

stomach!

'*Sis!*'

'You've never been hungry, Juffrouw Pieternella, you've never been a runaway slave that had to keep alive.'

'Why don't you run away, Anna?'

'I go when I have to go. Now get up out of the water!'

Thomas caught big eels in the river. Anna skinned them and cooked the fishy flesh in a flat pot that she stood on four flat stones over the coals. Salt and pepper and nutmeg, tastily fried in butter and oil from a bottle. Coconut oil. ·

'Once we've got the husks off the coconuts, I'll teach you how to render oil out of the shells.'

That was on Sunday.

Salomon came for lunch.

'Why weren't you and Daniel in church?' he wanted to know.

'We couldn't go.'

'Pieternella, when you turn your head away so quickly, you're fibbing.'

'Daniel has gone off to catch turtles; I didn't want to go to church alone.'

'Why are your hands and arms all covered in scratches?'

'Palm leaves. How are things with you?'

'Oom Bart says the tobacco won't grow properly on the land we're preparing now, it's too far to carry water all the way there. He says we're going to move to the open land on the other side of the river. When is Daniel coming back?'

'Tomorrow, probably.'

'Is he good to you, Pieternella?'

'Yes. He's even bought me a slave.'

'Tant Theuntjie kicked up an awful fuss when she heard that. Now Oom Bart is trying to buy her one, too.'

'And you're the other slave.'

'I suppose so.'

'You can come and stay here with Daniel and me.'

'It's not just about coming to stay; the church law appointed Oom Bart as our guardian. You could get out of it, because Daniel married you legally, but I can't.'

'When the *Boode* comes back and if there really is enough of our money left ...'

'That's why I'm sticking it out. I don't want to stow away on a ship like

Zacharias to get away, because what do you tell people when you have to get off on the other side?'

'We must believe *firmly* that the money will come.'

'I just can't get used to this island, Pieternella.' Like someone caught in a vast fearfulness.

'I'll go and speak to the Commander, tell him well ahead of time that you must go back to the Cape.'

'Cornelia was in church with Pieter van Nimwegen; she says you've got her mother into deep trouble. What have you been up to, Pieternella?'

'Nothing.'

'She wouldn't just have said a thing like that. We've got to keep our names clean, Pieternella!'

'Salomon, I promise you, I won't make any mark on our name that could possibly do you any harm.'

What kind of trouble?

On the previous Monday Anna had set off on a different course to cut palm leaves. First up the river on a footpath for a while but not through the river, just straight into the thickets towards the nearest mountain peaks.

Until they heard axe blows falling and Anna stopped in her tracks. They would have to take a roundabout way, she said. Why? Woodcutters. Who? Master Sven and his axe-men. Pigs.

'I want to go there.'

'No.'

'Please.'

'No!'

She took no notice. Just walked on towards the sound of the axes, pretending not to hear Anna's scolding.

Five woodcutters and Master Sven. Two were chopping, two were sawing logs into great slabs of wood. Master Sven and the soldier who had summoned her to Lamotius were working a long saw, sawing slabs into planks. A slab had been laid across a pit. A two-handled saw. Mynheer Van der Byl also had saws like that. Master Sven on top, the soldier in the pit below, covered in sawdust. All with their shirts off. Just trousers on, barefoot and wet with sweat.

They hadn't seen her.

'Master Sven?' They didn't hear her either. 'Master Sven!' Louder.

He stood upright. The axes at the tree stopped chopping. The saw at the trunks stopped.

'Pernilla! What do you want here?' he asked fiercely and walked across the trunk to a fork where he could climb down to the ground. 'Anna, what are you doing here with the juffrouw?' he panted.

'She wouldn't listen!'

'Pernilla?'

'I just wanted to come and see, Master Sven.'

He shouted at the others to take a break and took her aside. 'Where's Daniel? Why have you come here?'

'We were going to fetch palm leaves when we heard you all, so I told Anna I wanted to see if you were here, Master Sven.'

'Where's Daniel?'

'He's gone to catch turtles.'

'Shit. There are probably English somewhere in the bay again, so he leaves his wife alone with a crazy slave!'

'She has to teach me. He said so.'

'If the wild pigs in the forest get your smell, they'll knock you over and eat you up!'

'Anna knows where to go.'

'Master Sven,' called out one of the big-mouth axe-men, 'Daniel's not giving her enough cock, so she's come here for more!' Great guffaws from the others, blue clouds of smoke puffing out of their mouths.

'Come!' scolded Anna. 'It's not the wild pigs that are going knock you over, it's the tame ones!'

Deep into a ravine and up the other side, past a clump of short-stemmed palm trees with blue-green peacock-tail leaves. Palmyra, said Anna, and carried on. No, she would not climb a palmyra. Why not? Men's job to climb them. Men chopped off the tree's head and hollowed out its neck to let the sap collect in the hollow so they could scoop it out and make wine. Or they distilled it for a little arrack. Tree for sailors to climb. And runaway slaves. Already many hundreds of dead palmyras on the island. Specially the smaller ones. Just like humans: died if you chopped their heads off.

Yes, you could make brooms with their leaves. Harder brooms. Harder leaves.

'Palmyra's real place is on the other side of the island near the Black River, where the master has gone to help the English.'

'How do you know that?' Daniel had expressly said that the slaves were not to know.

'I feel where the shadow falls. Thomas hasn't got the feel, he thinks the master has gone after turtles.'

Anna chose a different route for their return and brought them out again at the Molens River. Where Carpenter Wieringa and a few soldiers or sailors were working on a dead sawmill. You could see it was a clever place to have built a mill: in a narrow gorge between a small island in the river and the high bank on the other side. There was a dam from where a wooden chute spat out the water over a wooden wheel – except that there was too little water to get the wheel to budge, even.

'Wait till the rains come,' Anna came to defence of the streamlet, 'then that wheel will run so fast the saws will be screaming to high heaven!'

Except that the saw blades were broken.

The *Boode* would bring new ones.

The next day the Grieta woman came visiting again. Where was Daniel? Gone after turtles. Seems he leaves you alone rather casually? Is something wrong? Have you heard about Pieter van Nimwegen? He's courting Cornelia, nursemaid with the Commander and his wife. Probably looking for a nursemaid for his own two. I hear Cornelia's mother was banished for theft. Did you know her at the Cape?

'Grieta, I was raised by very decent Dutch people. Juffrouw Sophia wouldn't stand for gossip.'

Which offended her, so she got up and left.

Then Tant Theuntjie arrived, head in the air, to ask Anna whether she knew Katriena. A slave Henk Karseboom was selling; had earlier worked at the Lodge. All that she'd really come to say was that she was getting a slave.

'I hear Daniel has gone out in his boat again?'

'He's catching turtles, Tante.'

'I want some of the meat. Oom Bart hasn't got the energy to trap turtles any more. And the tortoises you get on land are so scarce hereabouts that even if you do find one you have to leave it alone if you don't want to pay a fine. I'm telling you, we're going to have a lot of trouble with this new Commander. Wants every word of the law carried out, every jot and tittle! Call Anna to come and tell me about the slave!'

Anna stood in front of her and played dumb, said she didn't know Katriena.

She was deliberately being cussed. Because when Tant Theuntjie left, she was talking to herself in the kitchen at the top of her voice about Katriena who gave herself such airs because the white-arses couldn't get enough of her at night.

'Anna,' she said later, 'you seem to know about everybody and everything.'

'Anna's got eyes.'

Tant Magdalena and Oom Laurens also called in one afternoon. She and Tant Magdalena sat indoors; Oom Laurens wouldn't sit down, he stood under the roof of the lean-to, smoking his pipe.

'Why are you so pale, Pieternella?' the tante wanted to know. Is there some trouble? Why have you and Daniel missed church for two Sundays in a row?'

'There's no trouble, Tante. Daniel's gone off to catch turtles.' She didn't dare say how scared she was getting because he hadn't come back!

And the oom just stood there under the roof, just stood. His pipe had gone cold long ago.

When they left, Anna said: 'Of course, Laurens Gabrielse can't sit.'

'What do you mean?'

'For years he was the Company's tailor. The clothes that Thomas is wearing are some that he made. Soldiers' uniforms, too. All the sitting pushed his tailbone through his flesh. They say it looks like a little white horn sticking out above his bottom.'

When she was small, she thought the tailor at the Fort didn't have legs because he always sat cross-legged on a table, working away and covered with cloth. Sailors' clothes, slaves' clothes, soldiers' clothes. Jacobus said the tailor was really only half a person; her mother said Jacobus was telling a lie.

That evening she and Anna were sitting in front of the house in the moonlight. Thomas had already gone to his room.

'And he's got piles as well.'

'Who?'

'Laurens Gabrielse. The only thing that helps is the shark oil that Master Sven renders down for him.'

'What is the new Commander like?'

'Better than the old one. But he's got a wrong kind of cleverness in his head for the people of this island. They want a king without a head who won't notice when they lose interest. Just want to sit in the shade and wait for hunting days and for the sweet potatoes to come out of the ground. Specially the bunch on the Flats. You'll still learn, Juffrouw Pieternella. You don't know anything yet.'

'Where is the island's blood?'

'Your young brother's heart is dying; his body's here but his heart is far away. You must get to bed, the master will come back.'

'When?'

'His shadow isn't coming closer yet.'

'Where does Thomas come from?'

'Also Madagascar. But not from my people. Different king. Many kings on Madagascar, many people. Sell their people to the ships.'

'What's it like to be a slave?' She hadn't meant anything nasty by asking, she just wanted to know. But Anna sprang up straightaway, furiously angry, and walked off towards the river. Like pride in a dark dress. She called after her, but Anna wouldn't turn back.

Left her just like that, all alone in front of the house. Her fear came creeping up gradually out of the moonlit forest, scattering spectral patterns all over the yard till her hands clenched together in cramp. A wave of misery came over her, making her suddenly yearn for home – for a home long gone. Potter's cottage. Like yearning for the old trails you used to walk on. The real moon, the real earth under your feet, your real mother. A rumble-drum.

Between the potter's cottage and the green-leaf house lay the most terrible ocean waiting to swallow her, because there were no stepping stones to hop from one to the other. This was a different kind of fear. Of belonging nowhere.

Why was Daniel Zaaijman not coming back? Because he didn't really want her?

Barbara Geens hadn't really wanted her either. Nor had Juffrouw Sophia. Nor Bart Borms.

She got up, went and lay down on the bedstead in her clothes, just as she was, and cried and cried till at last sleep made her go numb.

The next morning Thomas came to the door to say that Anna had not slept in the room the night before. 'You'll have to go to the Lodge and report it, Juffrouw, so they can send out soldiers to look for her. She's not right in her head. I told the master he should put her in chains.'

'Anna will come back.' Daniel said so.

The daylight drove the spectres back into the forests and put new hope into her.

She laid the fire and hung a pot of water over it; shook in some sugar and cinnamon to make the grainy porridge like Anna had taught her. Took hard tack out of the barrel to add to the slave's portion.

She hadn't wanted to have Anna. Now she did want her, to have someone to cling to when her fears started stalking her again.

She gave the slave his breakfast.

Made the bed. Washed and dressed herself.

Set off down the road to Salomon.

Katriena was sweeping the yard …

There was a slave woman at the Cape who spent the whole day, from morning till night, sweeping the inner courtyard in the Fort. Day after day, year after year. She and Jacobus would sometimes tease her. But Fair Ansiela scolded them and said: Watch out! Slaves are God's own children of pity.

'Is Juffrouw Theuntjie here?'

'She's gone on the boat from the Lodge to visit the banned woman on the Flats.'

Tant Maijke. 'And Oom Bart?'

'Him, too. He's gone to visit the banned man, Willem van Deventer.'

'And Salomon?'

'He's digging. He looks after the cow.'

'Salomon, I think my slave has deserted.'

'Now what?'

'I don't know. I'm scared.'

'What does Daniel say?'

'He's not back yet.'

Salomon jabbed the spade hard into the ground to make it stand. 'Pieternella, how can Daniel still not be back yet?'

'I don't know.'

'Oom Bart says he left on the *Zeemaat*. He could have drowned and be lying washed up somewhere!'

'Don't say that! You've got to come and help me find Anna.'

'Where in this wilderness are we going to look for her?'

'I don't know. What am I going to do?'

'Pray.'

'I don't know how.'

'Say the Our Father. It helps.'

'Is that what you do? Why are you still digging here? I thought you said Oom Bart wanted to move to another piece of land?'

'He says I have to carry on here for now. Perhaps your slave is back home already and you're worrying for nothing.'

She was.

Scraping out the fire and laying a fresh one.

'Anna!' She was so happy.

'Leave me alone. The master's on his way, got to get food in the pot.'

'How do you know?'

'His shadow's starting to come closer. A soldier from the Commander was here, came to look for the master. The Commander wants to see him.'

'What did you say?'

'I said he wasn't at home, he'd come tomorrow.'

Our Father which art in Heaven, hallowed be thy Name and let Daniel please come home and thank you that Anna has also come back.

Not supposed to pray your own words.

'Peel the sweet potatoes, Juffrouw Pieternella, it's not going to help sitting watching out for him all day. Master's still far away.'

'Anna, if you're telling the truth today, that the master really is on his way back, you can have my little mirror.'

'I don't want your mirror. I don't want anything.'

He was dirty and tired, without his cap or shoes, stripes of caked salt on his shirt and breeches.

But it was Daniel Zaaijman, with his shining eyes and his broad smile, who came striding into the yard late that afternoon and picked her up and swung her round for joy and foolery. Who sent Thomas off to French Church with the ox to fetch the rest of his things. Hendrik was waiting with the boat.

And the prettiest little silver spoon in his breeches pocket for *her*. Tiny patterns on the stem. A small knotted black pouch with something in it that sounded like money or buttons and that he put away in the brown-leaf cottage.

Then he meekly went off to wash in the tub in the lean-to because Anna said a dirty man gets no supper.

7

Anna.

Who brought her a bucket of warm water the next morning and set it down without a word on the chest at the foot of the bedstead.

She was still in bed. Daniel had left to see the Commander.

Anna had never heated washing water for her before.

She got up, washed and put on her green shift. Ate her grainy porridge at the table using her pretty silver spoon.

Casually walked down to the river.

Green was the colour of happiness.

With dancing specks of light everywhere on the leaves and the ground. Little silver splashes glittering on the river water. The wings of a bird going *shouff-shouff* as it settled beside its mate on a branch overhanging the river: two big, pinkish doves with long red-brown tails and wings, small heads on reddish necks, rubbing their beaks against each other in a kissing greeting. They were *caroo-coo-coo* birds and this was the first time she'd seen them.

A flock of sharp-beaked little birds with cheerful whistles and tiny green bodies came hopping out of the thickets. Funny little things hanging upside down on their tiny black claws. Tame. They came almost right up to her. White borders round their eyes.

Her body kept trembling as she breathed the green air deep into her lungs ...

She was married to Daniel Zaaijman.

Yesterday she was still a speckled egg in a quail's nest. During the night the shell round her broke open and out she crept.

Beautiful – the fine mistiness lying over everything and rejoicing in everything, right up into the blue sky above the trees. Beauty in the shining body of the crab. The pebbles under water. The shoal of little grey fishes, all with their heads into the current, flapping their tiny arms to stay in one place.

A golden-green butterfly. And another. A third. A butterfly dance over the water right in front of her!

Long-legged flies on crooked feet making dimples on the still water at the river's edges.

Her whole body and everything all round her was filled with living.

She heard him coming from afar. Whistling. She knew it had to be Daniel on his way back from the Lodge.

Living was in his eyes as he saw her sitting beside the water.

Commander Lamotius had said that, as a matter of urgency, he was to go up to the Flats and look out the best land for cultivating large crops of sweet potatoes. To distil arrack. He could stay in the lodge on the Flats, provision had been made for visitors.

Daniel had agreed, on condition that he could take his wife with him.

Granted.

She tied up a quilt, two pillows, two sheets, her nightdress and washcloths and things in a bundle.

Anna packed bread and salted fish and cheese and some of the leftover cooked meat. Two plates, two mugs, two spoons. A small earthenware pot of butter. Another earthenware pot of sugar, for the nasty stuff Daniel had brought back from the English. Coffee. That you steep in boiling water like tea. Anna said it tasted better if you stirred sugar into it.

And the English gave him the prettiest dress materials as well, one with little green flowers on white cloth, and another four bed sheets, and four pillows, too.

'May I give the brown one with the stripes to Anna?'

'As you like, Pieternella.'

Blue-painted sailing boat at French Church, name branded on the stern: *Zeemaat*.

She and Daniel and their bundles, the small spinnaker billowing in the wind, over the pretty greeny-blue water all along the shoreline of the green forest island, the foam reef on their right, the open sea safely distant. Stone cat mountain above the Lodge. Pointed mountains, long low mountains, forested green foothills with the odd cleared plot like a small garden. Like dreaming you're in heaven and two eyes are not enough to see with. Clear water. Golden bars of sunlight on the sandy bottom as far as the boat sailed. One moment so shallow she was scared, then deeper again.

Don't look down!

Mountain island. Balls of white cloud against the blue sky.

Daniel, calm at the tiller, had a broad smile on his face as though it was fun to watch her happy surprise at everything. Little green islands, like breakaway children of the big one.

Then the scary water again. A deep blue sailing channel running like a road through the reef in from the sea.

'Eastern Gap,' said Daniel, 'where a ship can pass through without a pilot if it wants to.'

Before them a large green-forested island reared up out of the water. The whitest of white sand where the water was shallower. Palm trees bending low over the sand.

'Look!' She could see right down to the sea bed. The strangest little hump-backed fish with blue-stripes and a long thin horn on its head swam alongside the boat for a brief moment.

'That's nothing,' said Daniel.

A shoal of small grass-green fishes.

The wind in her ears, the creaking of the mast, the ripples on the water passing on either side of the boat.

Quivers running through her body if she closed her eyes for a moment.

Living was better than even the best of dreams ...

Gradually the water began to change. Grew rougher. Yellower. The island flatter, the mountains farther and farther away from the edge. Daniel turned the prow landwards. Even scarier water. Broad and browner.

'There's the mouth of the Groot River. Where we have to leave the boat and carry on on foot.'

A mooring pole on the opposite bank, where he picked her up out of the boat and carried her to the footpath before setting her down. His mouth tasted of salt, his body bore the smell of freshly chopped wood. The footpath smelt of mud. And he wouldn't let her carry either of the bundles. She ahead, he behind. Dense forests with many clearings where trees had been felled, the stumps like broken teeth.

At first the footpath followed the river, but gradually climbed higher as the river found its course down along a deep crack in the earth. High banks of black rock whenever there was a clearing where you could look down.

Then the hissing started ... At first she thought it was something in her ears. Till the noise became that of falling water. Nearer. Stronger and stronger. Beside them. All round them. Overwhelming, but the thickets still prevented her from seeing where it came from ...

Daniel put down the bundles, took her hand and started climbing down the slippery wet slope, planting his feet crosswise as he went. Showed her how to hold on to the bushes so she wouldn't slip ...

Then she saw it. The gorge between the cliff faces, the river tumbling down, booming and foaming – with a force that made her feet seize up because her body refused to go any closer. A waterfall. A whole river falling over the rocks! This wasn't a people-place! It was a wild-place, a fright-place. But Daniel wouldn't stop going closer.

'No!'

He wouldn't *listen*!

Right to the rock on the edge where the frothing yellow-brown water started thundering down, trying to take her with it into the hellish abyss! Spray like fine rain in the air. The worst was knowing that she was right inside all this mighty tumult – just one step away from her death. Clinging to the jackal-haired man standing there without fear on the rock beside her.

'I never want to go down there again!' she told him several times back on the footpath as the booming gradually faded away behind them.

The footpath led through the dense wet forest with here and there a clearing where trees had been felled.

In one of the clearings they sat down to rest and have something to eat.

'Are you happy, Pieternella?'

'Oh, yes!' She was too shy to ask him if *he* was happy.

'And if the *Boode* comes back tomorrow and Captain Wobma says you can go aboard and head back to the Cape?'

'No. I'm staying with you. But he must please just take Salomon back with him.'

It was shortly after they had started walking again that they saw, standing in a clearing, the weirdest creature. Her mother would have said: Tell me if my eyes are seeing straight!

From behind Daniel whispered to her to stand still.

A great big bird with white feathers and a thick body on short yellow legs and flappy yellow feet. It looked stuffed. Her mouth wanted to burst out laughing, because it really looked as if the thing had a feather bonnet on its head, and out from under the bonnet stuck a black face with a spout that became a big hooked beak. A flat brown point like a nose. It couldn't be true! Surely nothing like this could exist! Scratch, scratch in the leaves around it, rake, rake with the beak. Clumsily. Something must have pulled its tail feathers off and left only the little tuft of curly feathers at the base. Small wings, like fish fins, folded flat.

'Dumbcluck,' whispered Daniel.

The thing certainly looked dumb. 'What is it?'

'A dumbcluck.' Was that really its name? The size of eight fowls.

Then Daniel startled it and chased it into the thickets.

'Can it fly with those little wings?'

'No. It's a dodo. The old seamen called it the loathsome-bird because its flesh is so tough and loathsome, but Jan Harmse's wife – they live on the second bay this side of the Lodge, and also distil arrack for the Company – pounds the flesh between two stones to get it tender, and cooks it up with salt and pepper and cloves.'

A monster bird. That had made a picture in her eyes that her head wouldn't believe! 'Do you find them on the Orange Tree Flats as well?'

'Not any more. Hugo started warning a long time ago that the things

283

were going to die out altogether because people could catch them so easily. Food for runaway slaves. Though the wild pigs are actually their greatest enemies.'

'Master Sven says the wild pigs will knock me over and eat me up.'

'They don't *eat* the birds, but they go rooting for the eggs, and a dumbcluck lays only one egg a year ... Where did you see Sven?'

'When Anna and I went to cut palm leaves.'

'How is Anna behaving herself?'

'She's not crazy, just strange.'

'Do you still want me to sell her?'

'No. When will we reach the Flats?'

'We've been on the Flats for a long time already. It's not far now to the lodge. Would you like another rest?'

'No.'

Flat. More and more open patches. Fewer mountains, just chunky hills, unconnected, with wide spaces in between. The real mountains far in the distance. Not like an island at all. Lots of rivers, some hardly more than streams. Stony. They crossed the Groot River at a ford, far above the waterfall. Knee-deep, not shallow like the one through the Orange Tree River. Once on the other side, she asked if there wasn't a *road* from the Lodge to the Flats.

Yes. A wagon track. Bad road. First across the Bamboo Mountains, then over the White Mountains and then northwards through a col. A full day's walk. Hugo, in his furious period on the island, had the soldiers round up all the layabouts and made them cut the road.

Along the river, the way they had come, was only half a day – counting the walk. There was another wagon track from the Flats down to the river mouth for taking out the wood. Or bringing lime up from the mouth, when the Lodge had a few barrels to spare. Transport for supplies.

A dodo ...

The very first whitewashed cottage with a leaf roof they came to was Willem van Deventer's and Maria's place. Palm-leaf kitchen with a small room a little farther away. Rough wooden outside table.

Maria burst out crying for happiness at seeing them. Daatjie clutched her, Pieternella, round the legs, but Pietertjie sat in front of the house and didn't get up.

'Is she sick?'

'I don't know. Willem took her to the Surgeon; he says she's pining for her granny at the Cape.'

Maria didn't look well either. One-roomed cottage. Chairs but no table. One bed on legs, one without legs. Mattresses without sheets. Daniel looked around outside before he, too, came inside.

It was a little while before Willem arrived, musket over his shoulder and a bunch of green-necked pigeons tied by the neck.

'Tell Annie to pluck them.'

Annie?

Annie Bruyns who lived in the room next to the kitchen. Whom Lamotius had mentioned ...

Suddenly she wished they could leave. Go home.

Willem opened a bottle of wine and poured a glass each for himself and Daniel.

'What brings a cooper to the Flats?' Willem wanted to know. He wasn't very friendly. 'Or has Lamot sent you to come snooping around?'

Lamot. That must be Lamotius.

'I've come to see how suitable the area might be for a sweet potato farm.'

'Waste of shoe leather. Bastards shove me up here on this stony plain that you have to plough twice before you can get a single seed into the ground, and then still expect half the crop as well. Willem van Deventer isn't cracked in the head! I asked Lamot: And if the harvest fails, are you going to take half the loss as well? No answer.'

'Have you started ploughing?' Daniel wasn't particularly friendly either; his eyes looking at the man were hard.

'Plough for what? They can send for the plough and oxen themselves. Battled to get the things here, not going to battle to get them back as well. One rotten slave I've already sent back and had him taken off my book. The other one is heading the same way. They'd better come and get him before I drown him.'

'I thought you had a contract to sow wheat?'

'Master gardener at the lodge here on the Flats says the moment the first wheat blade shows above the soil, you won't see anything for rats fighting to eat it.'

'What are you going to live on?'

'I'm expecting a man from the Cape on the next ship; I'll get him to plough. Meantime there's enough to be made from hunting and fishing.'

'We saw a dodo on the way.' She just wanted to say something.

'Shot three last week. Luckily Annie knows how to make the things edible. I don't know where you're heading for, but I haven't got food or a place for you to sleep, I'm telling you now.' Rudely.

'I wouldn't ask you for food or shelter,' said Daniel, even more rudely, got up and threw the remaining wine in his mug out through the door.

Maria tried to cover up by saying that it was unfortunately so that Annie Bruyns lived in the outside room, otherwise they could have arranged something.

Willem said the Company shouldn't think he was going to put up their dead soldier Verhagen's widow for nothing! They would have to pay.

It wasn't far from there to the lodge on the Flats. Lots of trees, lots of shade. With a high bridge over a pretty stream, and from there down an avenue of banana trees laden with bunches of green fruit ...

There were banana trees in the Company garden at the Cape, too. One day her mother asked the gardener: How many more alien things are you Dutchmen still going to dig into the soil here? Later on the Governor once added a few bananas to her pay, along with the handful of tobacco and the mug of wine, when she had had to go to the Fort to interpret for Cochoquas that had come to barter.

'Pieternella, these are banana trees,' Daniel said behind her.

'Yes, I know.'

A narrow footpath of flat rounds cut from tree trunks led up to the first plastered building with low walls and a leaf roof. A slave greeted Daniel by name. Another tree-trunk path to the next long building: two plastered buildings, really, with a palm-leaf section in the centre.

Everything looked even more neglected than at the other Lodge. As though it was tired.

A tired soldier at the door. Yes, the Sergeant was in, and Juffrouw Maijke was in the coconut garden over there.

Daniel went in to see the Sergeant, she walked over to the garden.

Coconut garden, a stone's throw from the lodge. Hundreds of small feather-leaf trees planted in a long narrow arc. Only the leaves visible above the ground. No stems yet. And Tant Maijke and two slave women hoeing between the trees. Old dress gathered up and tied with string, barefoot and lost in thought.

'Good afternoon, Tant Maijke.'

When she looked up, a sudden hatefulness shot into her eyes. 'Pieternella?'

'How are you, Tante?' The old woman came closer, wiping the sweat from her face with her arm.

'If you've come to see if I'm having a bad time, you can go back where you came from.' Spiteful and with all her old arrogance in the set of her head. 'Thought you could go and blacken me to our Commander!'

'That's not true.'

'I told Lamotius. I said: Mynheer, Eva almost lied us Hollanders right out of the Cape with her made-up stories, and now that girl of hers wants to blacken *me*!'

'On the ship you *did* say that Governor Bax was a leper, Tante.' Her whole body was shaking. 'The Commander sent for me. He said you were going about spreading the story that it was Juffrouw Margaretha who had said so.'

'Hugo said she said so.'

'I don't believe it.'

'Believe what you will. And I asked Lamotius straight out: And what about all the half-caste children popping out of the slave women here? Were they put on the mother's book or on the father's? He said: On the mother's. Like you will be on your mother's book as a Hottentot for all eternity. And I, Maijke van den Berg, will not be kicked over by any Hottentot! So get lost.'

She turned round.

She wanted to go home. To hide.

All at once she felt altogether alone within herself – something apart. A human dodo.

A strange man had come to the potter's cottage one day; he was telling Jacobus that he caught butterflies and all kinds of flying things when she and her mother came round the house and his mouth fell open and he stared and stared at her mother. He stretched out his arms like a preacher and said: Earth Woman, I greet your divine appearance before my face!

Her mother asked if he'd been drinking. He said yes, with his eyes, the nectar from Adam's rib!

Her mother said: No, she preferred aniseed arrack.

She waited outside the lodge till Daniel came to look for her.

By the next morning the sore place in her heart felt better. All night long in the dark, Daniel had held her tight in his arms on the narrow bed in the spare room behind the lodge.

After breakfast he took her with him to have a look at the gardens. With them went the Sergeant and one of the free-burghers from the Flats. Michiel Romondt was his name, a tall, surly man. Long plots of tilled earth ran from the lodge down to the cow byre. Flat. A plot of wheat. A plot of barley. A plot of rice. No more than a sprout here and there. Too many rats, said the Sergeant. The new Commander said he had to dig a deep moat round the garden and fill it with water from the river so the rats would fall in and drown. Where was he supposed to find the men and slaves to dig such a hell of a moat?

An elderly slave was working manure into the soil. A plot of young orange trees on the lower end and a few small leafless grape vines on the upper side. Only one green plot, with thick, upright grass. Sugar-cane, Daniel said. For distilling arrack.

About four horses were grazing down at the bottom of the garden. Hugo had them sent here, the Romondt man said. To do his inspections faster so that he could get back the Lodge to look after his daughter.

When they got back to the lodge, Tant Maijke and the two slave women were carrying buckets of water from the river to the young coconut trees.

On the afternoon that they got back to the boat, she told Daniel, please, she never wanted to live on the Flats.

8

You don't suddenly grow up when you're fourteen and you get married.

Like the green-leaf house that Daniel had made for her was slowly turning brown, because that was what leaf houses did, she was learning, one step at a time, to live her own life on this strange island.

Sometimes, when sitting dead still beside the river or when she had to spend the night alone on the bedstead in the dark, she would feel inside herself: goodperson, badperson. Now and then the urge to take out and hold the shards of the clay pot would overtake her, and then she was white and brown in one body. Who could close her eyes and smell the cold ash of the potter's cottage ...

Who could hear her mother laughing.

She was sitting in the shade under the roof of the lean-to with Daniel one day while he chipped away, shaping curved staves for a barrel to make them fit, edge to edge, into the round hoops.

Curious, he asked her: 'What do you think about when you sit looking so far away, my love?'

'I sometimes wonder: What is a person?'

He laughed. 'What do *you* think a person is?'

'I don't know. I haven't managed to think it properly and that makes me scared. What do you say a person is?'

'Pieternella, every person is really just in search of something to be happy with.'

'Really?'

'Yes.'

Then it became a game. 'What does Thomas want to be happy?'

'A magic axe to chop off his chain with a single blow so that he can flee into the forest.'

'What does Tant Theuntjie want?'

'I don't think even she knows.'

'What do you want?'

'You.'

'You've got me.'

'I'm not so sure about that, my love.'

'Why do you say that?'

'Because I don't know how deep your yearning to be back at the Cape is.'

'My yearning is for Salomon, not for myself.'

'How sure are you?'

'Because *you* are my happiness.'

That made *him* happy.

So she asked Anna. But Anna pretended not to hear her.

The day after that she asked Sven Telleson. He said a bloody saw-blade was the only thing that would make him happy – apart from a bottle of good palm arrack.

'I'm not making them saw any more, Daniel,' he said. 'They're just felling now. It's sawing the trunks into planks that breaks the men and makes them rebellious. And then they go off into the forest and booze. The day the saw-blade arrives, they'll take heart and get going again. I know. This island's salvation lies in its ebony; the Cape will need to send a big ship to fetch all the wood. The fatherland can just as well stop its yapping.'

'I see you've been felling a lot up here beside the river.'

'Wait till you see what we're felling above the fourth bay. Lamotius is going to send the *Europa* to Groot River for the load of trunks.'

'The *Europa* needs to be hauled up and careened so it can be cleaned and caulked.'

'I know. The *Boode* better get its arse into the wind and bring us pitch.'

A year.

Then shortly after daybreak one morning a soldier hammered on the door, breathless with the news that the *Boode* was anchored out beyond the reef, waiting for a pilot to bring her into the roadstead. Master Sven and his team were felling up near the Groot River; the Commander had asked that Daniel come urgently to help the ship through.

Apart from Sven, Daniel was the only one who knew the passage through the reef.

When she heard Anna come in, she got up and went into the kitchen.

'Anna,' she asked, 'is it going to be my time today?'

The slave turned and looked at something *round* her, not at her swollen belly. Like at something in the sky.

'No, not today. Many days still.'

That was all she wanted to know.

She wanted to go the Lodge, to the quay.

The *Boode* was the hope that had finally arrived. For many.

The saw-blades.

Salomon's hope of deliverance, because Lamotius had promised Daniel that he would give favourable consideration to sending Salomon back to the Cape if money came for them from the Orphan Chamber.

In the course of the year, Oom Bart had moved from across the Orange Tree River to the nearer side. And back again. Each time more forest had to be cleared and new gardens made for the tobacco that was eventually going to deliver the crop and the miracle. New leaf house, new tool shed – each time that much more rickety than before. Each time new promises of a room to be added on for Salomon – as soon as there were nails to spare. Meanwhile he still had to sleep behind a partition in a corner of the tool shed; Katriena the slave slept in another corner.

Katriena had been taken to the Lodge twice to be beaten. Owners themselves were not allowed to beat slaves. It was because Katriena had stolen meat and once threatened Tant Theuntjie with a log of wood.

Bart Borms had forbidden *her*, Pieternella, his yard umpteen times.

'Salomon is working himself to death, Oom!'

'No, he's not working himself to death. It's you that's putting that idea into his head. Get out!'

'Look what he looks like, he'll scare the birds away!'

'If you expect him to work in church clothes, go and ask the tailor at the Lodge to make him some, and pay for them yourself while you're about it.'

Salomon didn't go to church any more; he'd outgrown the clothes the Church Council had had made for him at the Cape. His hair was caked with sweat, the dirt so ingrained in the cracks in his feet that no amount of washing could remove it. It sometimes looked as though only his eyes were still alive.

'I'm going back to the Cape, Pieternella. I'll work my fingers to the bone there, I swear. I can't belong in this place. I understand that you feel content, but you've got Daniel. People are saying you have all the luck.'

'Your bed is ready for you, Salomon. How many times has Daniel told you to come and stay with us?'

'No. That will create the impression that I'm also content. I'll wait for the ship.'

She walked slowly. It would take a while to bring the *Boode* into the roads ...

The countryside was very dry.

All that remained of the Orange Tree River was little more than a streamlet; the Molens River at the Lodge had dried up months ago - only a few stinking pools for the fish, where the slaves from the Lodge went to draw water for the kitchen. Drinking water was brought in in barrels.

Daniel had made the most beautiful rocking cradle for the baby ...

No, she didn't want to go back to the Cape. Never again. The island had accepted her early in the year, because Anna had made her eat some of its blood. This was now her place, her fatherland, her mother country.

She knew the blood wasn't really blood, it was like being baptised or married. *Something*. But you felt different afterwards.

And Daniel wasn't stupid, he noticed it that same evening. 'Are you happy, Pieternella?'

'Why do you ask?' They were sitting at the table; the slaves had already gone to bed. Daniel read to them each evening from the Bible or the book of Home Sermons. Thomas on the threshold, Anna just inside the door on the floor. Then they all had to repeat the Our Father aloud. 'Why do you want to know?'

'There seems to be an extra glow about you tonight, and it's not just the lamplight.'

'Yes, I am happy.'

'You warm my heart, my love.'

'I'm glad. And my body's making us a lovely child.' She couldn't tell him anything *more*: there are feeling-words and saying-words, and feeling-words are not saying-words.

She didn't tell him, either, that, a long time back, Tant Theuntjie had come to ask for some onions one morning. Daniel had gone to help a French ship at Northwest Harbour. While they waited for Thomas to pull the onions out of the roof of the work-place, Tant Theuntjie suddenly looked at her suspiciously and asked: Pieternella, are you expecting? That was in February, she was hardly showing yet. Yes, Tante. Then you'd better start praying that it's not going to be too much of a little Hottentot. When is your time?

The end of August.

Oh Gawd.

When Tant Theuntjie had left, Anna wanted to know why she was lying on the bedstead crying. She said she was afraid the master wouldn't be happy because the baby might not be to his liking.

'Then you've got to get the blood, so the child can have the blood. Come, get up, we've got to go.'

'Where to?'

'The island only bleeds every second year. It bleeds out of the white-bark trees and now's the time.'

They walked a long way.

The nearest white-bark trees had all been felled, but Anna knew of a good few down in a narrow ravine behind the Kattiesberg beyond the Lodge.

'Spared because they'd be too difficult to haul out of there.'

'What white-bark trees? Why white-bark trees?' she asked impatiently when Anna simply walked on, making promises about the trees. It was hot.

'You'll see. We're nearly there.'

A small patch of black ebony trees. Then white-barks – upright, with twisted trunks. A whole little townful of trees. Branches with narrow green leaves for shade which fell like a blessing on them – tired and sweaty and thirsty. All over, under the trees, in among the fallen leaves and scraps of bark and twigs, lay little ripe, black-purple fruits like fat little fingers.

'Pick up and eat.' Like the words of the Holy Communion. 'Eat the blood of the island so the child will also have the blood.'

Sweet and tart. Strange.

Only the blood was she to eat, not the peel or the seeds.

A branch creaked. A bird gave a bubbling call. A rustle. Green. It didn't taste like blood. Tasted like island. Like a mystery trickling quietly down into your body and lying there.

Like a comfort. Her mother said only her and Salomon's feet were like Hottentot feet ...

The *Boode* would be bringing Juffrouw Margaretha's porcelain that the Commander had ordered from the Cape because Hugo had gone off with all the Lodge porcelain. Secretary Jongmeyer said it did belong to him, after all. Secunde Van Hoeven said that wasn't true, and it was beneath the dignity of the Commander and his fine lady to eat off and drink out of pewter.

'It is my desire, Pieternella,' Juffrouw Margaretha said after the leprosy business, 'to present you with a pretty Japanese bowl or plate as soon as the ship with the provisions arrives from the Cape.'

Daniel had brought her six porcelain cups and saucers that he'd got from the English. Anna held them up to her ear, one after the other, and then said the language they spoke was a foreign one. She held them to her cheek, caressing them gently.

That's when Daniel said the woman was really crazy.

The English had the prettiest fabrics. They said that was why they could barter so many more slaves on Madagascar than the Dutch. Their cloth was prettier. Daniel knew now it had to be green cloth, and Tant Magdalena made her another two dresses. And a brown striped dress for Anna - which she never wore because she'd wanted a black one.

No, you don't suddenly grow up when you're fourteen and you get married ...

Only *after* the blood did the island accept her, in secret - and she the island. She didn't tell anyone, not even Daniel; one day, all of a sudden, she just knew, with the strangest kind of knowing, that the island had accepted her.

Anna kept on nagging for a palm tree trunk until Daniel took the ox and the tools and went to chop one down. It had to be one of the pot-bellied palms. Down on the south of the island, high up in the bed of the Hout Bay River. At about six o'clock on the clock face.

Almost a half day's walking, but it was really enjoyable. She and Daniel and the ox. Slop-slopping through places in the marshes where the trees grew up out of the water on crooked roots. Mud squeezing up between your toes, the reef in the distance, the sea still farther. Daniel held her hand almost the whole way.

Then he led them farther inland. Where it was drier. Blue mountains far off to the west. Black River mountains, Daniel said. Very inhospitable, very densely wooded, and where most of the palmyra palms grew. They distilled arrack from them.

'Anna told me that.'

'What does Anna know?'

Plenty.

They walked and walked, along a faint footpath through thickets of scrub bush. Daniel in front, then the ox, then her. Till Daniel suddenly stopped and beckoned to her to come to him ...

The most unbelievable giant tortoise was trudging across a patch of grass. Her eyes saw it clearly, but her head just wouldn't believe it! As with the dodo. Daniel climbed on to the tortoise's back; the creature just went on walking till Daniel lost his balance and had to hop off.

She and her mother and Jacobus had once come across three elephants beyond the Salt River. Jacobus wanted to turn round and hare off; her mother said: The wind is on our side, they won't smell us. Come! They were on their way to the Chorachoqua at the Leopard Mountain; Salomon on her mother's back. They crept quietly past the elephants ...

That was when the chief of the Chorachoqua chased her mother away.

And the tortoise's back feet looked exactly like the elephants' back feet. She could swear. Daniel laughed, said he'd never examined an elephant's back feet, but he believed her. Perhaps they were elephant tortoises.

It was incredible.

Not far from there they came upon a smashed tortoise. Chopped open. Insides scraped out and baked dry. Millions of flies.

'And this?'

'Now you'll understand why Lamotius asked in church on Sunday that the destruction of God's gifts on the island should cease.'

'Why was this tortoise destroyed like this?'

'Tortoise fat is the nicest butter on earth. Sometimes they'll chop it open for the fat alone.'

Her heart wept for the tortoise, because *someone* had to weep for it, as Juffrouw Margaretha had wept for the dead sailor that time on the ship.

The island was not a people-place. The people on the island grew angrier and angrier the longer they waited for the ship which didn't arrive. Ever more dislike of the Commander. He wouldn't allow them to go sea-fishing out of sight of the Lodge, or to go hunting in the forest on more than two days of the week so they wouldn't neglect their farming. Farming that had to produce food for the handful of VOC soldiers and sailors and officials who had to man this island of succour. Tobacco, wheat, rice and sweet potatoes. Vegetables. Everything had to be delivered to the Lodge for credit on the book. Not a farthing in your purse.

Cattle farming was much better, because salted meat in a barrel and an English ship on the other side of the island at Northwest Harbour at least meant a little money in your pocket.

'Just ask Daniel! He knows what we're talking about, even if he pretends he doesn't hear!'

Lamotius had expressly forbidden them to sell fresh victuals to English or French ships. If foreign ships required refreshments, they could ask for them at the Lodge at Southeast Harbour. And pay for them.

One day an English ship came limping in. The Commander sent a pilot to bring it through. Allowed the English to go hunting with the Company's hounds, let them cut wood, provided them with meat and all kinds of supplies from the Company's shed – but the free-burghers were always told that stocks were low, they should wait for the next ship from the Cape.

Angry people growing angrier still.

Fortunately the Company didn't know that at the same time there were *two* English ships being refreshed at Northwest Harbour. Daniel spent almost three weeks helping them with their barrels and masts and things. Took them hunting, too.

Anna taught her to wash sago out of the grooves of the palm tree trunk. Then to scoop out the sediment carefully and let it dry on the piece of canvas. For making palm meal to bake bread with. There was no more wheat flour to be had from the shed at the Lodge; the supply ship had still not arrived.

9

They'd got it through the reef. Wooden goose. Three full wings on its tired body for the last stretch. Tears coursing down her cheeks as great billows of remembering came adrift inside her: smells, noises, the deck planks under her feet, the darkness in the steerage hold, chamber pots on long ropes ...

She wanted to reach out a hand and touch it. Greet it.

Yesterday and the day before are pictures in your eyes for ever. Tomorrow and the next day are living that is still waiting to become pictures. Somewhere among the old pictures were fifty-two days on board the body of that wooden goose – and a jackal-haired man.

'Heavens, Pieternella, what are you doing here, with a little one that could pop out at any moment?'

'Morning, Tant Theuntjie. Where is Oom Bart?'

'Here somewhere. Every living thing seems to be on the shore this morning.'

'Where's Salomon?'

'He'll come as soon as he's finished his work. Thinks they're going to let him aboard ahead of time. Oom Bart says he doubts there'll be a blue farthing on board for you.'

Woodgoose folded its wings. Woodgoose dropped anchor.

'Morning, Pieternella! I see you're still walking!'

'Morning, Grieta.'

'I wonder if there are any new exiles? I well remember how confused you all were when you arrived here last year.'

'We were never banished.'

'You're carrying low, your time must be near. Where's Daniel?'

'On the ship.' You keep your hands off him.

Twice Grieta had come, beaten and bruised, to her and Daniel for shelter. They'd let her sleep in the small house. Tant Magdalena said Van der Hoeven beat her for playing around with the Company's wainwright, Abraham Steen. He'd caught Free-burgher Gerrit van Ewijk from the Flats with her, too.

Commander Lamotius and Juffrouw Margaretha were waiting on the quay for the first land boat that was on its way from the ship. Cornelia was holding Andrea by the hand.

There was something wrong with Cornelia. You could see. An unhappiness.

Soldier Hans Pigt, Lamotius's bodyguard with a musket over his shoulder, stood straight and proud, watchful. It always seemed to her a bit overdone – this everlasting bodyguard, as if anyone would try to steal a commander!

Attractive man, Hans Pigt. They said Gerrit van Ewijk beat him to a pulp one day when he caught him with his slave girl, Maria Mooy. The next week Pigt bought Maria Mooy from Van Ewijk and three weeks later they were married.

Captain Wobma, First Mate Berks and Daniel and the money coffer were on the first boat from the ship.

She moved in behind the others so Daniel wouldn't see her. He didn't want her even to go as far as the river alone nowadays.

Woodgoose resting. Sailors all over the deck.

They said papers from the Cape are always locked in the money coffer.

'Pieternella …' Salomon touched her shoulder.

'I'm glad you could come.'

'You shouldn't be standing around here like this, Pieternella.'

'It's not my time yet.' At least he was washed and clean for a change. His hair was nice, too. 'The *Boode*'s arrived.'

'So I see.' As though both relieved and confused.

Another sail was approaching from the top end of the island, between the reef and the land. The *Europa*. Sven and the woodcutters with the wood.

'By God, Daniel, you'd better pray for rain so we'll have water for the mill! When the saw-blades come, we'll have to get stuck in!'

Daniel said there weren't nearly enough planks for a load. But there were plenty of barrels of lime to send to the Cape. He could hardly keep up, making barrels for the Company's lime kilns – barrels with bamboo hoops, because no cooper wastes iron hoops on barrels for dry-goods.

She had to get home.

A lot of lime. Smoke rising day and night from the ground across the bay below the Lodge. Mud Bay. They didn't burn coral in a big round kiln here, like they did with the shells from Robben Island; they burnt it in a hole in the ground. Greyish slaves, greyish spades, greyish shrubs and grass. The same stench. Except that these lime slaves had greyish cloths wound round their hands and arms and legs so the sores wouldn't sting so much. Daniel said they were given to them because coral lime had more salt in it than shell lime.

They used long poles to break out the coral under the water and then tipped it out on the sand to dry in the sun.

If Sven Telleson had shark blood, Daniel Zaaijman had seawater blood. She sometimes thought he only came ashore to draw breath.

Daniel's water world frightened her ...

Apart from the *Zeemaat* he also had a small, flat-bottomed surf boat that he called his little sampan. He would stand on the back and wiggle-waggle it forward with one oar. It wasn't the same as rowing. He said it was called *sculling*. It had two narrow thwarts. And a mast for a sail when you wanted to take more than two people on board. Luckily you couldn't go out to sea on it. Only on calm waters.

One day he said he wanted to take her to show her something. He nailed four posts to the corners of the boat, stretched a sail across them as an awning and said it was for shade for her.

Wiggle-waggle southwards from the Lodge. All she could see was the lower half of his body and his legs. The rest of him was above the awning. Nearer and nearer to the green water while she held on tight to the sides, nervous because she was so close to the surface of the water.

Wiggle-waggle farther and farther away from land. Sculling. At times the water was shallower, clearer than the clearest glass. Yellow shafts of sunlight quivered on the sandy seabed below.

'We're far from land, Daniel!'

'Don't be scared, Pieternella. *Look.*'

She didn't want to look, she wanted them to turn back.

Closer and closer to the reef where the water grew deeper again and the real sea behind the reef was coming closer, dark blue with great rolling waves.

'We've got to turn back!'

'There's no danger, Pieternella.'

The anchor was a big stone tied to a rope. He lowered it over the side and crept in under the canvas roof beside her.

'The boat's going to sink!'

'No, it isn't. Look down into the water. Look at the fishes.'

Not real fish like kabeljou and steenbras and other fish you ate. Little play-play fishes. Fishes with all kinds of silly bodies under the clear water, and the strangest pointy pebbles: red, white, pink. Almost like colewort.

Prickly round things. Starfish. Little brown and orange branches swaying under water like miniature trees in the wind. A shoal of tiny greenish fishes with long noses and little black eyes. Then more finger-length orange fishes with pure white stripes painted across their bodies. Grey fishes with black spots. A flat-bodied fish as round as a plate, blue and yellow and with a long, thin horn on its head ...

Wearing only his breeches, Daniel slipped into the water and became a long dark shadow on the sea floor. Deeper and deeper into the water world.

'Come back!' she pleaded, too late. She was alone and scared in the boat so far from land. She couldn't swim.

Suddenly Daniel came up out of the water beside the boat, a wet-bodied, wet-haired merman with a huge orange and brown speckled shell in his hand, thrashing foot withdrawing into the shell ...

A living shell. A real shell. Not an empty hull washed up on the shore. Wonderment drove the nervousness out of her body for a moment, but each time he disappeared under the water again she was terrified that he would lose his breath or that a shark would tear him to pieces.

A big striped shell like a horn: white, brown, dun. The snail's body shrank back into the mouth of its long white shell.

'Take off your dress and come in with me, Pieternella.'

'Never!'

'I'll hold you.'

'No. Please not. I'm afraid of water.'

'Don't worry, one day I'll teach you.'

She didn't want to be taught!

Another horned shell: pure white and covered in rows of little knobs.

A branch of pale coral.

A black and white speckled shell.

A Daniel she didn't know. Fish man, water man, with the most beautiful, the happiest of faces.

At other times he went walking with her along the water's edge below Mud Bay so she could gather 'dead' shells. The most incredible colours and shapes – big ones and small ones. He would carry them home for her in a bag and Anna would take them and throw them back into the sea.

'But I *want* them!'

'Don't belong here.'

'I want to send some of the prettiest ones back to Juffrouw Sophia when Salomon goes back to the Cape.'

'Don't belong in the Cape.'

'Daniel, speak to Anna!'

'She's *your* slave.' Teasing.

10

The *Boode* arrived on the twenty-fifth of August.

It was a Wednesday.

By Friday the unease had begun to spread across the island like a thick cloud ...

The saw-blade had not arrived.

'This is bloody disastrous news!' said a thoroughly drunk Master Sven to Daniel, rocking on his feet under the roof of the lean-to. 'I'm telling you, the Cape doesn't give a damn about this island!'

She kept asking: 'Why haven't we heard if the money has come or not, Daniel?'

'It takes time to go through everything, Pieternella. Believe me.'

The plough that Focke Janse was waiting for hadn't come either. 'How does Lamotius expect a man to get beans and tobacco into the ground with no more than his own two hands? Go and complain and he throws at your head how many acres a man in the fatherland will dig in a day – forgetting that here there are forests to be cleared away first, that we don't have the soft earth of the fatherland under our spades. Ask to move to Batavia and he waves the fifteen-year contract that you signed under your nose!'

Laurens Gabrielse came up from the Lodge, said he'd heard from Secretary Jongmeyer that the Cape had sent word that the Commander and his wife would have to be content to eat off pewter dishes because the Cape didn't have any porcelain to spare.

And the man from the Cape that Willem van Deventer was waiting for to help him with the farming wasn't on board either. The next day Lamotius sent three soldiers to confiscate Willem's hunting firearms and his fishing boat, to force him to get stuck in and farm himself.

Willem took the wagon-track down to the Lodge. When Maria followed, to try to stop him, he shoved her out of the way. She was also pregnant. Willem went and stood at the door of the Lodge and shouted at Commander Lamotius at the top of his voice that he had just asked the devil to save him from this godless, damned island; that he'd rather carry shells on Robben Island for five years than spend one more day here!

Thirty lashes. At the stake in front of the Lodge.

Tant Magdalena went to watch; she said Willem bellowed like an ox but never stopped cursing.

They flogged Oom Bart the next day. Salomon said Tant Theuntjie threw every piece of firewood stacked up next to the kitchen at the soldier who came to fetch him away.

Katriena had to go and bring it all back again.

Because of nails. He'd bribed one of the *Boode*'s sailors to steal a lot of nails for him on the ship.

Twenty lashes. They said he fainted.

The sailor was thrashed on board ship.

Annie Bruyns was called to the Lodge from the Flats for the order from the Governor of the Cape to be read to her: that, in exchange for food and clothing, she was to manage the Company's dairy and creamery on the Flats. She flatly refused. Told the Commander to his face she'd quite enough work of her own to do. The Commander said he was giving her one week to report to the lodge on the Flats.

Willem van Deventer and Oom Bart went together to see Lamotius to ask him if they could go to Batavia together on the next ship ...

On Sunday after the church service the Commander told Daniel he wanted to see him and his wife at the Lodge at ten o'clock the following morning.

The storm clouds had blown all the way up into the Orange Tree Flats ...

It could mean anything at all.

She kept wandering about in the yard. Anna helped her with the food and setting the table. Not she, herself, just her hands. In the afternoon she went to see Salomon, found him in the shade of the tool shed.

'We must be brave,' she told him, without a drop of courage in her own heart.

'It feels as if everything has just come to a stop, Pieternella.'

'Willem van Deventer's Maria says Commander Lamotius has agreed that she can send her Pietertjie back to her parents at the Cape. The child is pining away here on the island.'

'The ship won't take the child for nothing.'

'Maria has a little money that her father gave her before she left; she says it's just enough. If our money hasn't come, I'll ask Daniel to pay for you.'

'I'll *work* my passage there! All they need to do is let me aboard.'

'How's Oom Bart?'

'Bad. He and Tant Theuntjie are both in bed.'

'It was a stupid thing he did.'

'Yes. He says it's your fault.'

'What?'

'Because you kept on and on about an additional room for me. That's what he wanted the nails for.'

'Do you believe that?'

'No.'

Ten o'clock on Monday morning.

The Commander was sitting at the head of a long table.

'Good morning, Cooper Zaaijman. Morning, Juffrouw Van Meerhoff.' He looked tired. Black jacket, white shirt with puffed sleeves and broad lace. 'Do sit down.'

Her body was very tired. All along the way Daniel kept telling her to banish her unease, it was bad for the baby inside her. If the money hadn't arrived he would find Salomon's fare himself.

Lamotius cleared his throat. 'Cooper, clear proof has arrived from the Cape that you have apparently been incorrectly informed about your wife's capital. The children of the late Pieter van Meerhoff have already consumed their entire inheritance. What is more, the various expenses for their maintenance down the years were considerably higher than the value and interest of the inheritance.'

'The wages of our slave Janvos were used for our maintenance!' She was so nervous she had difficulty breathing.

'The Church Council's receipts for expenses are here and open for your inspection.'

Daniel took the paper that was passed across the table to him.

'I wasn't hoping for the money for myself, Commander, but for my brother who is wasting away in the care of Free-burgher Borms. He has to go back to the Cape.'

'To whom?'

The fatal question. 'The Church always placed us with people ...'

'Juffrouw Van Meerhoff – Pieternella – the Church placed you and your brother in the care of Free-burgher Borms. In the mean time you have got married and all I need to do is see to it that Salomon is not maltreated.'

'My husband is prepared to pay his fare back to the Cape.' I beg you, on my knees!

'Unfortunately I may not grant permission for that. He is twelve years old, if I remember rightly ...'

302

'He's thirteen now.' Please. 'We have an older brother at the Cape, Jacobus, who can take care of him.'

'In that case I shall write to the Cape and ask if he may be placed in the care of his brother.'

'It could be a year before an answer comes.'

'That we all realise. In the mean time I shall ask Free-burgher Borms to raise the child properly.'

'You don't understand, Commander ...'

'Unfortunately I cannot grant you any more of my time.'

A rock that fell out of the sky and only just missed you!

Salomon had been struck full in the back and turned to stone beside the spade, on the plot of dug-over black-brown island soil.

Daniel stood aside, arms folded across his chest, feet set wide apart, tall and strong and unconcerned, just like that day on the ship when they flogged the man.

'Help Salomon!' she shouted and grabbed him by his shirt.

'Calm down, Pieternella. Salomon can fetch his things and move in with us. Give him a chance to get over the shock.'

A second rock, one that was taking her by the hand and leading her home as though she was a blasted child! Telling Anna to pour some water into the tub so Juffrouw Pieternella could cool her feet in it.

'I don't want to put my feet in water! I want to go back to Salomon!'

Daniel the Rock had no ears. He made her sit outside in the shade with her feet in the water while he bathed and bathed her face and neck with a wet cloth.

'I promised my mother I would take care of him!'

'And that's what you're doing. But you can't breathe for him. Hold your head still.'

Master Sven came striding up from the direction of the garden and sank down beside them in the shade. 'Has she got lice?' he wanted to know.

'No,' Daniel laughed. 'Just severe rebelliousness.'

'For that she'll need something stronger. And so will I. Worry is eating me up.' He was already tipsy.

'Master Sven, the Commander says there's no money left in my father's estate, it's all been spent on our upkeep. I don't believe it, because we had a slave that brought in an income for us.'

'Slave's wages and your father's credit on the books couldn't patch the holes for ever, Pernilla.' As though he wanted to help to get her to calm down. 'The Company is a cruel master, but the Company wouldn't have stolen your money. I know your brother wants to go back to the Cape, but the Company's not going to let an orphan boy wander about wherever he wants to. I'm sorry for him … Doesn't a man get anything to drink here, Daniel?'

She went and sat down apart, on a log, her head in her hands. No one was listening, nobody cared! Salomon only wanted to go home, like a bird to its nest, an ox to its kraal. Mauritius was not his home.

Daniel came over from the house with a bottle of wine. 'Anna is heating a little milk for you.'

'I don't want any milk!' Daniel had gone and bought a stupid cow. And a bunch of fowls.

'Oy, oy! Isn't Pernillatjie fierce?' laughed Master Sven. 'Pernillatjie is going to have a cross little baby!'

'Leave me alone!' Anna brought the milk in one of the pretty cups. On a saucer.

'At the right time, Salomon will find his own way back to the Cape. Trust me. Your father's blood was strong.'

'How well did you know our father, Master Sven?'

'Very well. Like good friends. Arrived at the Cape together on the *Princess Roijal* – easily twenty years ago. A couple of nights later we had dinner with the Secretary of the Council, Hendrik Lacus and his wife – her name was Lydia, if I remember rightly. Poisoned food. Because that night we were roaring like lions, top and bottom. Peder said: Sven, we're dying! When the sun came up, I agreed and said goodbye to the earth. The same Lacus came and wrote our wills.'

'Wills?'

'Your father was too sick to doctor himself, never mind concern himself about me. The Surgeon General came, and he pulled us through. I went on to Batavia, your father stayed behind. I met your mother many times. The prettiest little Hottentot with small, narrow eyes that were always laughing. You dad was quite sweet on her already.'

'What wills?'

'Your dad named his father, Aug Ede, as his heir. I named my brother Olaf. Don't even know if he's still alive.'

'But why did my dad's father have a different name?'

'Aug Ede was one of many Edes. Peder adopted the name of his ancestral land. Meerhoff.'

'My dad owned *land*?' Like new hope falling from his lips!

'Yes, but he bequeathed it to his father in his will, and a will is something that the law has to enforce. These are yesterday's things, Pernilla. At the right time Salomon will get back to the Cape.'

After supper, when Daniel took out the book of Home Sermons to conduct evening prayers for her and the slaves - more for *her* than the slaves - her rebelliousness was threatening to reach boiling point. In her mind she mimicked and hated every word from Daniel's lips. *That our bodies may rest in peace and quietness*, he read. She didn't want to rest in quietness, she wanted to fight to get Salomon on to the ship! *Lighten the eyes of our understanding, that we may see Thee alone as our Redeemer in all misery ...* Lighten Lamotius's understanding! *Though we come to the end of this day with great sins which we have committed against Thee, we pray that Thou wouldst cover our sins ...*

If a boy wanted to go back to his home, that wasn't a sin!

Daniel and the slaves recited the Our Father aloud; she only mumbled.

He waited till the slaves had gone to their room, and then started preaching to her, not from the book. 'Pieternella, one's courage can be broken only to a certain point - then one gets fresh courage. At the moment most people on this island are living in fearfulness, but somewhere new strength will arise. You'll see. For Salomon, too.'

'All he wants is to go back to the Cape.'

'Lamotius is a man of his word; he will write for the necessary permission.'

'That will take too long! I'm afraid Salomon's courage will be smashed to pieces and that he'll start drinking too much wine. He's got to go back to the Cape on the *Boode*!'

'That's impossible. You know it, but you keep dancing around on the same spot and carrying on like a wild thing. Let go. Let Salomon regain his courage for himself, you can't do it for him.'

Zacharias had stowed away on the *Boode*. 'Is the ship going from here to Batavia again, like last time?' She had to know.

'No. It's going back to the Cape - with hopelessly too little wood for a load. The Cape sent word that they have no record of the kind of saw-blades granted to Mauritius earlier; we have to send more details. So now Sven has suggested that I carve one out of wood to send back.'

She couldn't care less about the saw-blade; they didn't care about Salomon ...

But Daniel was right about fresh courage.

That shot up, after the sermon on the following Sunday, like a spark from an old fire. Most of the congregation were standing around in the shade under the trees, like things whose dissatisfaction had knocked all the stuffing out of them. Commander Lamotius's reputation was in tatters; Secunde Van Hoeven's kicked into the ash because he had not come up for the free-burghers; they couldn't stop whingeing about Hugo, who had at least been a better class of swine.

Then Henk Karseboom said: 'Good people, let's lift up our heads. I was chatting to Captain Wobma yesterday. He says the Cape is in a wretched state, and as they weighed anchor, Governor Bax was dying. For most of the time a certain Crudop was acting.'

'What difference does that make to our misery?' came a voice out of the crowd.

'Wait. One of Crudop's biggest problems is to stop the free-burghers at the Cape from planting tobacco, because they're bartering it for honey and ostrich feathers from the Hottentots and that undermines the Hottentots' dependence on the Company's tobacco. They are bartering fewer and fewer cattle at the Castle. Wobma says the Mauritian free-burghers are not prohibited from growing tobacco. I'm telling you, this is our chance. We must get stuck in and get tobacco into the ground for the Cape.'

'Does Wobma really think that?' asked Willem van Hoeven seriously.

'Yes. The Company is importing barrels of tobacco by the shipload from foreign colonies; they can't barter for livestock without it.'

'The Company wants ebony, not tobacco,' Master Sven argued, his tongue thick. 'We need saw-blades.'

'We can't plant saw-blades!' Henk Karseboom.

'We should sow beans as well, the Company needs dry beans for its soldiers and its ships,' added Tant Magdalena.

'What about arrack?' enquired Focke. 'Why is it that Jan Harmens can have the sole contract to distil for the Company?'

'And get free rice for his family because he's supposedly too busy to farm at the same time?' Grieta added rudely. Jan Harmens was sitting just behind her.

'You're forgetting that Commander Lamotius is urgently looking for free-burghers to plant sweet potatoes on the Flats to distil arrack,' Daniel reminded them. 'But so far, every vegetable that comes out of the ground has landed up in your cooking pots.'

'People, you're not hearing me!' cried Henk Karseboom impatiently. 'We've got to plant *tobacco*.'

'Saw-blades, tobacco, sweet potatoes. You're all forgetting one thing!' said Laurens Gabrielse uneasily. He was standing with his back leaning against a tree trunk. His seat in the church was on the aisle in the back pew, so that he could half-sit with just one haunch on it. 'You're forgetting that everything needs water to live, and at the moment only the fish in the sea have got enough. There's a drought on.'

Someone said: 'Old Schoolmaster Steenwyk says a curse has fallen on the island since Lamotius snapped the Bible shut in front of his face.'

'Steenwyk's mind is wandering. Though I don't know what got into Lamot to go and appoint the old man to oversee the soldiers now.'

'You may just as well ask if Daniel's crazy slave woman isn't showing signs of rain!' laughed Grieta.

'What signs?' Pieternella wanted to know.

'You mean they haven't told you yet?' said one of the others. 'She was always the Lodge's storm signal. Whenever there was a cyclone in the offing, she knew about it ahead of time.'

'How?'

'No one can tell. But the day Anna disappears into the forest and stays away, there's heavy weather to come. The wench is bewitched.'

It wasn't true.

11

She waited her chance. Impatiently.

Till a week later when Daniel and Laurens Gabrielse went deer hunting.

'Where are you off to, Juffrouw Pieternella?'

'To the Lodge.'

'If the master comes home and finds you're not here, I'll get the blame.'

'I'll be quick.'

'The second lot of coconuts is ready to come out of the water, we've got to tease out the coir for Salomon's mattress, I've got to teach you to twist rope ...'

'That can wait.'

She stopped in the bushes on the near side of the ford to retrieve the canvas bag of shells that she'd hidden from Anna. She had a plan.

When she arrived at the quay below the Lodge, one of the land boats was taking on a load of cabbages and pumpkins and two barrels of meat.

'Are you wanting a lift to the ship, Juffrouw Van Meerhoff?' asked one of the island's sailors. 'I don't think Cooper Zaaijman would be very pleased.'

'I'm wanting to get a message to the ship. To Anthonie, the cabin boy. Tell him Pieternella wants to see him urgently. He must come back with you, I'll wait here.'

'I'll tell him.'

She took off her shoes and walked up along the shore towards the gardens so she could watch the land boat unobserved ...

Row upon row of green feather-headed coconut trees had been planted on her left. Daniel said the heads had to fill out before the stems began to grow and they became proper palm trees.

The boat had nearly reached the ship.

Tant Maijke had arrived at their house on the previous Monday after nearly killing Pieter van Nimwegen in his own house. Cornelia was pregnant and Pieter wasn't planning to marry her.

'I need something to refresh me, Daniel,' she said as she stumbled across the yard, breathless. 'I've had it! Plunged into shame and disgrace by my only relative on this island. There I sit, abandoned on the Flats; I had to hear the news from our honourable Commander himself when he came up there to hold a church service for us poor mortals yesterday. That Cornelia is a walking disgrace.'

'What now, Tant Maijke?' she asked while Daniel was pouring the old woman a glass of wine. Everybody had known about Cornelia for ages.

'Just about smashed his skull in. Van Nimwegen's. Thinks he can get away with it. Commander says he's nailing up the banns on the church door this very day; but they need to go and see him first. Emergency. Lord, Pieternella, you say it's almost your time and you're hardly showing even! It's not just a growth, is it? Your mother had two after your father's death.'

She hated the old crone.

The land boat had reached the ship.

She turned round and slowly started walking back. Black pebbles. Slippery green seaweed; slippery brown seaweed; a shard of blue and white porcelain ...

She saw his feet first. Black shoes with bows, brown stockings to the knee where the puffed black breeches began. Lubbert. Just this side of the quay. He stood there waiting for her with mocking eyes and a disdainful attitude.

'Aah! I see Daniel got in before me! Little pretty-wench's already got a bun in the oven!'

'Leave me alone.' She wasn't afraid of him, just filled with disgust.

'And still so fierce, too. I like that. How are you, Missy?'

'Fine. Let me pass; the land boat is on its way back and I have shells to give to Anthonie.'

'I'll let you pass if you promise to let me put the next little bun in the oven another time when I come by.'

'Leave me alone.'

'Once you've tasted me, you'll never want to let go.'

'Please.'

He stood aside.

Anthonie was on the boat and very pleased to see her.

'Pieternella! I hear you're married and all! Captain Wobma said I could come and say hello to you. How are you?'

'I'm very well. I have a good husband. It's only my brother who is so unhappy.' She looked round to see where Lubbert was but he had gone. 'I just wanted to ask if you would give these shells to Juffrouw Sophia, Gerrit van der Byl's wife, when you get to the Cape. Tell her they're from me.'

He took the bag and peered at the shells inquisitively. 'They're really pretty! She *will* be pleased. Shells from Mauritius are a real curiosity in the fatherland, they mount them on silver stands with curly legs.'

'I'll collect shells for you, too.' She struggled to find the words that she really wanted to say.

'I'd be glad.'

'Actually, I wanted to ask you what happened to Zacharias who stowed away on board the *Boode* when last you called here.'

'Did you know him?' he asked in surprise.

'Yes. Did he get to Batavia safely?'

'With dysentery, and his body all swollen from being down in the bilges too long.'

'Do you ... do you think Salomon could stow away on the *Boode* till it reached the Cape?'

'Zacharias died soon after we got there.' Like cutting her short. 'Salomon mustn't even think of trying it. One of the cook's boys died on the voyage out; they're looking for someone to take his place. Perhaps he should rather ...'

'Never mind.'

She'd thought it all out so carefully. The food, the water, the clothes, the quilt she would pack for him. The letter to Jacobus to tell him to take good care of him. Suddenly it had all come to nothing. Her last hope shattered.

Daniel and Thomas were skinning a big brown deer beside the house in the shade.

There was no resistance left in her eyes to help her lie or argue when Daniel washed his hands and, with a firm hand on her arm, pushed her into the house.

'Pieternella?' The worry on his face made her drop her eyes. 'Where were you?'

'Please, don't make me tell.'

'You've *got* to tell me.'

Anna was standing in the doorway with her arms folded, listening, like someone who was glad to see a child being punished.

'I went to give Anthonie a bag of shells to take to Juffrouw Sophia.' When he took her head in his big hands and forced her to look him straight in the eye, a bottomless heartache began to wash over her. 'I'm sorry.'

'Tell me the truth, so you won't have a stone getting heavier and heavier inside you.'

'I wanted him to help Salomon stow away on the ship.' The stone rolled out of her mouth on its own.

Daniel picked her up and laid her down gently on the bedstead as though she was a doll, and Anna came to take off her shoes and stockings, mumbling all the while. 'Without even a cap on her head! Walks off with her head naked in front of all the people. Disgraceful.'

Daniel lay down in his dirty clothes beside her on the white quilt and held her till she stopped crying. Let one hand play over her belly, soothing the kicking baby to sleep.

'You're a good man, Daniel.'

'You're settling deeper and deeper into my heart, Pieternella van Meerhoff.'

Saturday afternoon, the tenth of September, and the *Boode* left for the Cape. Master Sven was too drunk, so Daniel had to pilot her through.

'No, my love, you can't go down to the quay.'

'I'm begging you, as nicely as I can. Please.' He was tightening a master hoop on a barrel when the soldier brought the news. She and Anna were sitting in the shade, tangling out the coir off the nuts.

'No, Pieternella.'

'It's not her time yet,' said Anna curtly and got up. 'She can go and wave to the ship. I'll go along to keep an eye on her.'

'Anna,' Daniel's voice was raised. 'I told you last week to know your place in this yard!'

310

'Please, Daniel. It will be a long time before the *Boode* comes again.'

He gave in.

Down at the shore it was different from when the ship had left after the church service almost a year before. Then many people had come to wave or weep or call out after it. When Hugo was aboard and the new Commander ashore.

Now only a handful had come to bid the ship farewell, waving with limp arms as the ship approached the reef.

Salomon stood beside her. Moody. His hair was dirty again and too long, under one of Oom Bart's old striped caps. His eyes were fixed on the ship. The Commander's letter requesting permission for him to return and be placed under the care of his brother Jacobus was also on the ship.

'By this time Jacobus will be a free-shoemaker and have his own place,' reckoned Salomon. Fresh courage …

Anna stood behind them. Watchful.

Juffrouw Margaretha came along from the quay holding Andrea by the hand. Behind them, the new nursemaid. A fat, black slave in Cornelia's clothes. The same thin cloth cap without any lace or beads.

'Good afternoon, Pieternella,' Juffrouw Margaretha greeted her cheerfully. 'How are you?'

'Very well, Juffrouw. Andrea's getting big.'

'Yes. And a bigger joy to the Commander and me with every day that passes. How is Cornelia?' Sincerely concerned.

'She's also well, Juffrouw Margaretha.' Cornelia and Pieter van Nimwegen had been married in the Lodge after church on the previous Sunday. Without any wedding feast.

Willem van Deventer's Maria was standing to one side. Confused and heavily pregnant, her two daughters on either side of her, clinging to her dress. There was no one on board who could look after the child Pietertjie all the way back to the Cape. The old schoolmaster Steenwyk and his wife would have taken care of her as far as that, but then the Commander wouldn't allow him to leave because he had nobody else to entrust with the welfare of the soldiers.

Willem said that was fine, he would straighten out the child's problems himself.

Beyond the reef the wooden goose had swung its wings around for the cross-turn and the run into the open sea. On the orders of *her* Daniel. *Her* husband. *Her* pride.

A land boat shoved off from the quay to fetch him back off the ship.

No, this time she didn't want to be on the *Boode*. The Cape was no longer her home. The island was her home now, its blood was running warm in her body.

Sven Telleson, clinging drunkenly to a pole on the shore, was shouting orders across the water: 'Damn it, Daniel, you're going too far over! You should have swung round sooner!'

'Master Sven …'

'You shut up, Pernilla. Get into bed and have your baby. That hooker's going to run on to the reef today!'

Sven Telleson's fresh courage was also on board the *Boode* somewhere. Daniel had made a wooden copy of the saw-blade – a model that looked very like Mynheer Van der Byl's double-handed saw, perhaps just a little longer. The Commander had asked that *eighty* of the blades be forged at the Cape and sent on the next supply ship. 'Ebony, Cooper Zaaijman, is this island's gold, just waiting to be properly exploited. When the blades arrive, we'll be sawing night and day.'

It was to be hoped that the Molens River would have water in it when the supply ship next arrived. The rain couldn't stay away for ever.

Many of the Company's servants at the Lodge were sick. The Surgeon, Master Walrand, said it was from the stagnant water in the pools. Putrid.

'We've got to get home, Juffrouw Pieternella.' Anna was growing impatient. 'The darkness is going to overtake our feet and there's got to be food on the fire when the master comes in.'

'Where's Salomon?'

'The Commander is talking to him. Come!'

Master Walrand hadn't recognised her when she first arrived on the island.

Not until later.

'Heavens, they tell me you're Eva's daughter! You're still small but when last I saw you, you were nothing but a little bundle of bones in a long dress always hiding in your mother's skirts.'

He was the Surgeon appointed in her father's place at the Cape.

Before long he was spending more time drinking and gambling in Jannetjie Ferdinandus's tavern than caring for the sick. Sometimes for days on end. The Company warned him, but it didn't help. Juffrouw Sophia said: Once drink and gambling have taken hold of you, Satan has built his nest in your head.

So they banished him for twelve years to Robben Island to carry shells. Her mother had already been banished there. One day she said:

Master Walrand, you're not going to make it; the shells are going to kill you. He said: Eva, pray for me. Her mother walked back and forth with him all day, reciting the Our Father for him over and over.

Soon afterwards he heard they needed a surgeon on Mauritius – he could serve the rest of his sentence there.

Her mother always said it was *her* praying that saved him.

They had gone some distance up along the Orange Tree River before Anna made her sit down for a rest.

'I'm not tired!'

'It's not whether *you're* tired or not, Juffrouw, it's to let the baby rest.'

'I'm scared, Anna.'

'Of what?'

'I don't know. When the ship sails away.'

'Ship goes, ship comes. That's the island's fate. Sometimes it doesn't come.'

'What then?'

'Nothing. Waiting.'

The first bats flew silently out of the trees, turned round and went back to hanging among the branches again. Rag wings stretched across twigs.

'Come, or the master will catch us up.'

'Am I near my time, Anna?'

'Not many more days now.'

The *Boode* left on the tenth of September.

Catharina was born on Tuesday the twenty-seventh. Before dawn.

A little white Dutch girl baby with fine reddish brown hair.

Daniel sent Anna to fetch Tant Magdalena, as previously agreed, and stayed with her the whole time. Holding her, wiping her face with a damp cloth.

Tant Magdalena gave her a ball of cloth to bite down on. She bit, to stop herself from screaming at them to go away and leave her alone with Anna. Bit to stop herself from calling for her mother. Her mother used to say Dutch women didn't know how to have babies properly. A woman should lie on the ground on her side, her head on her mother's legs. She'd helped more than one Post Holder's wife give birth on Robben Island. Drove the Post Holder out of the room and told her, Pieternella, to heat the milk, stir in finely shredded tobacco and salt and, at the right moment, to hold it to the woman's lips. To make her throw up. Because that was what made the baby come out all by itself.

But Tant Magdalena wouldn't hear of her lying on the floor in front of the bedstead. Tant Magdalena would drive Daniel away ...

Before dawn.

Tiny. A little milk-white worm, once Tant Magdalena had wrapped her up tightly in the swaddling clothes and pinned them firmly in place.

Next morning Daniel had to go out and shoot some doves because Anna kept nagging about the pigeon soup she needed, to give her milk the necessary strength for the baby.

Teeny little mouth too sweet for words. Daniel himself taught her to suck. Great lion's paw cupping the tiny head.

'What was your mother's name?' she asked him.

'Catharina.'

'Then *that* is her name.' Because all of a sudden she wished she had some gift to give him. Just because. As a thank you.

He was so happy.

And Anna went on nagging about the doves.

Only once he had disappeared into the forest did Anna come to the edge of the bedstead with the truth. 'You'd think it was the master who had had the baby! No, a man mustn't keep hanging around a woman's bedstead.'

She picked the little worm up out of the rocking cradle and wrapped her in another little quilt.

'Anna, what are you doing now?' Suddenly, she was uneasy.

'The child has to go outside so the sun can see her, so her blood-land can greet her.'

'Please, don't take her away!'

'Don't be frightened. Anna will take her only as far as the door. Anna knows.'

She took her only as far as the door.

Like a baptism.

Came back and laid her gently in her cradle.

'Now I'll make the caudle.'

'Do you know how?'

'How would Anna not know the Hollanders' whims?'

Whenever there was a birth in a home where she was still in any way welcome, her mother would put on her Dutch clothes and go in to wish them well – though it was really because she knew there would be caudle to drink ...

Anna brought her the first little taste. 'There's wine in it, I don't want any.'

'Drink! The wine has boiled away.'

'What else did you put in it?'

'Hot wine, hot milk, lovely sugar and egg yolks, with cinnamon. Drink!'

That afternoon Tant Theuntjie called. 'Luckily, she throws back to Daniel's blood. I hope you saw to it that your slave made caudle.'

Salomon came the next day. 'Why is the baby so small, Pieternella?'

'She's perfectly formed.'

'The Commander sent for Oom Bart. He says Oom Bart isn't allowed to go moving around all the time. So now we're back where we started. Has the child got a name?'

'Catharina.'

'Must you stay in bed for long?'

'I get up on the sly. Then Daniel just about has a fit.'

Grieta came.

'Willem digs from morning to night, preparing land for planting tobacco - says when the *Boode* comes back, he wants to have a number of bales already rolled. Willem knows about tobacco. Was the birth hard?'

'Yes.'

'How long do you have to keep to your bed?'

'Tant Magdalena says twelve days. My mother used to let the Post Holders' wives lie for seven days.'

'Lucky the baby's white, isn't it?'

'Would you like a cup of caudle?'

'I was hoping I'd get some.'

She was up and about already when Anna burst in from outside one afternoon like a creature possessed. She started taking the porcelain cups off the shelf and hurried off to the kitchen with them.

'Luckily we've got tea leaves,' was all she said.

Only the day before Daniel had been quarrelling with Anna because she had gone off into the forest and picked fine branches to lay across the baby in the rocking cradle. With a dove's feather as well. 'We've got to get rid of this mad woman, Pieternella.'

She was sitting on the edge of the bed, hemming another little sheet for the baby's cradle. 'I'd struggle without her, Daniel.'

'I'll buy you another slave girl.'

'Anna's just different, she's not mad.'

When she looked up Juffrouw Margaretha was standing in the doorway. Alone. The bodyguard with his gun behind her.

She'd brought Catharina a pretty little quilt, and also some baby dresses and capes that Andrea had outgrown.

Anna chased the soldier out of the house.

Juffrouw Margaretha sat at the table, amazed at how spacious the house was, and admired the cups and saucers and the carving of a woman that Sven Telleson had whittled from the tusk of a narwhal.

'Thank you, a little bowl of caudle would be lovely.'

She picked Catharina up out of her cradle and held her against her shoulder, comforting her with gentle clucking noises. A beautiful baby, she said. The Commander had just submitted a request to the Cape to send a minister to the island on the very next ship so the island's children would not have to go unbaptised any longer, nor the young people remain unconfirmed.

12

Catharina was almost a year old when, towards evening one day, the supply ship next folded its wings in the roadstead. The *Boode*. Battered and exhausted. Two sailors had been lost, blown off the yards in the most dreadful storm. Seven others had fallen ill and died.

Including Anthonie, the cabin boy.

The island itself was still reeling after the cyclone; everywhere there were thin scabs covering its sores. In some places the sores were still raw ...

Every living person near the Lodge turned out on the waterfront to watch the *Boode* come through. Most of them looked battered, too. The news of an approaching ship had run through the whole island well before midday, but the *Boode* had been struggling against contrary winds to get to the Gap.

Fortunately Master Sven had been informed early, so he was sober enough to be taken out. Daniel was at the Black River mouth on an English ship. In the afternoon Salomon had come to tell her there was a ship arriving. Possibly the *Boode*.

A candle flame in Salomon's private darkness.

The cyclone had come.

Thomas came to the door before dawn to report that Anna had disappeared during the night.

The haste with which Daniel came back into the bedroom and dressed, the unease on his face, were strange.

It was the end of February.

Catharina was five months old and almost too big for her rocking cradle. The wood for a bigger cradle was drying. A sweet-natured, friendly little creature. The joy of her and Daniel's life. Of Anna's life.

And Salomon's, too. 'It's a pity I won't see her grow up.' Only Salomon's body was on the island; most of the time his head was already back at the Cape. 'I'm going to be a free-burgher, Pieternella, you'll see. I'll write to you.'

'Didn't Anna say anything?' she asked Thomas when she went outside.

The slave gave no answer, just looked at Daniel.

'Pieternella, Anna has a habit of disappearing into the forest whenever there is a cyclone in the offing.'

Cyclone. It was only a word. The storms round Mauritius that the home-bound fleet so feared. The hand above the water ...

'How does Anna know?'

'Nobody knows.'

'Does she come back again?'

'Usually.'

Cyclone.

She laid the fire and put the water on to boil so she could start the breakfast; but she kept looking out to see if Anna wasn't coming across the yard, because surely she wouldn't simply walk off into the forest without saying anything?

Daniel and the slave climbed up on to the roof of the house to fix more bracing struts in place. Threw ropes and leather thongs across the roof and knotted them to iron anchors in the ground. Took all the tools off the back wall of the work-place, piled them up in a heap under a canvas sheet and packed stones on top. Took down the wooden wall and laid it flat, strengthened the cottage with planks and ropes ...

'Daniel, why are you doing all this?' she asked, half uneasily.

'Just in case there is a cyclone about to hit us.'

So did they all believe Anna then?

In the afternoon Daniel and Thomas went to French Church to make sure that his boat was properly secured and to haul his sampan up out of the water. Then Daniel sent Thomas to the Lodge with a note to say

Anna had disappeared into the forest, they should ask Sven Telleson what that meant. On the way back he stopped at Oom Bart's and Laurens Gabrielse's to tell them about Anna. Oom Laurens should get the news to Pieter van Nimwegen and Focke.

They rolled two extra water barrels down to the river and filled them. Smaller barrels of dried fish, bread and cheese. An earthenware basin of meat for her to cook. The cow was milked and untethered so she could walk into the forest.

'Daniel, isn't all this a little unnecessary?' If you'd grown up at the Cape you knew what storms were like …

'No, it's not unnecessary, we need to be ready. Don't worry, I'll protect you and Catharina with my life.'

Oom Bart arrived late in the afternoon. 'Your yard looks as though a cyclone has struck it already, Daniel! Jongmeyer down at the Lodge says Anna disappears into the forest whenever the devil gets into her; it's just coincidental that it sometimes happens before a cyclone. About the rest, I'll keep my thoughts to myself.'

'What rest?' Pieternella, asked. She wanted to know.

'What Katriena, Theuntjie's slave says. Black slaves are full of superstitions.'

'What does Katriena say?'

'That Anna goes into the forest to summon the wind.'

'I don't believe it.'

'No, you wouldn't.'

Before sundown the sky was full of small snow-white thunderclouds. She didn't really believe in her heart that there was any actual threat.

Whenever a storm passed over the Cape her mother would say: Open your mouths, children! Let its strength blow into you!

Night came, the island tried to sleep in the sultry heat. She and Daniel and Catharinatjie. The slave outside somewhere.

'What side will it come from?' she had asked Daniel earlier while they were having supper.

'Possibly from the top end of the island. Once Hendrik and I were helping a French ship up at Northwest Harbour on the other side of the island. Barrels, mastheads. The ship was very conveniently anchored far up but in deep water, a freshwater stream close by. Our work-place was a kind of half-island, we just called it Cooper's Island. We were standing there one day, sawing away in terrific heat; the next thing I noticed was a wave rolling in like I'd never seen in my life. Huge, soundless, like something stalking you. I shouted to Hendrik: Get a grip! I ran to the nearest white ebony tree, he for a liverwood. I heard the watch on the ship shouting. With my eyes I measured our chances of keeping our heads above water, then saw that the wave had almost reached the bank. We were quite a few feet up; that wave wasn't going to break on the bank, it was going to roll right up the bank and wash over everything in its path – waist-high over Cooper's Island.'

'And your tools and things?'

'Gone in the backwash. Hendrik's sampan, too. I told him: This is just a forerunner; there's something big coming. When the sea started coming in at high tide, I saw it was no ordinary tide. I asked the interpreter to tell the captain to batten down everything he could and strip the masts. When the first wind rose, Hendrik and I ran for shelter on the south side, behind one of the heads above the harbour. A cyclone.'

'Luckily we're not close to the sea.'

'No. And the Bamboo Mountains ought to afford us a measure of protection. At first. But you can never tell, every one is different.'

Before they went to bed, Daniel walked round the yard one last time. She went only as far as the door. The clouds were building up, from time to time a waning moon broke through. She wasn't really scared.

Not even when the first gust broke over them at daybreak like a dog that gives only one warning bark.

'Is this it?'

'Not yet. But we'd better get up. The slave must be fed, we've also got to eat – but don't light the fire. As soon as it's necessary, I want you and the baby under the table in the front room. I'll pack things on top of it and bring in a piece of canvas.'

The strangest sense of anticipation that made her stomach feel hollow, as with excitement. Like waiting for an invisible monster coming from somewhere – but nobody had told her it would arrive with the most terrifying roaring!

Not a storm at sea trying to smash a wooden goose to smithereens. Not a Cape south-easter that first spread its white cloud-sheet gently over Table Mountain to say: I'm coming to blow you off your feet. Not the north-wester that made the ships at anchor in Table Bay cling tight to avoid being ripped up and smashed on the shore.

No. This was different.

As though an unearthly force somewhere far away and deep under the sea had been waiting for the right day, and had then arisen, wrapped itself in the densest, darkest clouds, and started rolling in blind rage across the waters, ever faster and faster, sweeping everything out of its way. Crumpling. Smashing. The whole green-forested island in its path. Its body filled with water to pour down in streams.

It ripped the first piece out of her pretty home – a gaping hole between the kitchen wall and the outside door – to clear a path of wind and water straight across the bedstead and then kick out a piece of the back wall as well.

Daniel drew the sail down over them.

No, not scared. Her body shrank as she curled slowly into Daniel's arms, like standing with your back bent to the blows. The baby between them. Blows that she endured with the strangest meekness.

The island was not a people-place.

Then the 'eye' – that Daniel had said would come. Sometime in the afternoon. So still outside that a candle-flame would hardly have flickered. Time to assess the damage ...

'Stay in the house, Pieternella, don't look!'

She wanted to see. All that was left of the cottage was a bamboo skeleton. Miraculously, Salomon's bed was intact, though the mattress and the quilt were cast up somewhere among the banks of debris.

Mud.

Ditches through the garden so deep a man could stand in them. Not one tobacco plant, not a single sweet potato vine.

The slave under his canvas sheet, shivering beside the heap of tools.

'Get yourself round to the other side, Thomas, it's just turning round.'

'Master ...' Pleading.

'We'll pull through. The damage is not too serious.'

Trees were lying uprooted all over the edge of the forest.

There was a different roaring in the air. 'Is that the river?'

'Yes. It's burst its banks.'

The monster waited till dusk before striking again. Broke an even bigger hole in the wall behind the bedstead.

Threw down a riverful of water out of the sky till the drenched leaf-roof between the table and the kitchen gave way.

No, not scared. Beaten.

It was a full month before the footpath down to the Lodge was clear of all the fallen trees and branches and debris.

The front half of the Lodge had collapsed. Books and papers were spread out to dry like bleaching laundry. Quilts, chairs, tables, mattresses, clothes. Outbuildings completely destroyed.

'We are grateful that no human lives were lost, Pieternella,' said a brave Juffrouw Margaretha.

'I'm glad you and the Commander still have a roof over your living quarters.'

'Yes. And the slave quarters behind the Lodge lost a piece of only one wall. In the mean time, it has been nailed up with boards.'

The Sunday preachment, for those who could get there, was held under the trees; the church was still too wet inside.

The most urgent task was repairing the quay. Master Sven reckoned it had been under water to a depth greater than the height of a man, *that's* how high the sea rose. The sawmill weir had broken, but miraculously the mill itself had not suffered any irreparable damage.

The Lodge gardens had all washed away. Of all the rows of feather-leaf trees only the odd broken stem was left sticking out of the mud. Almost all the palm leaves on the whole island had been stripped bare by the wind. Daniel had to struggle for days on end to gather just two oxcart loads of leaves, barely enough to patch the hole in the roof of the house.

The Flats had been worst hit. Focke Janse had been out to see and said it looked as if a war had swept over them.

Tant Maijke got permission to move in with Cornelia and Pieter van Nimwegen for a bit while they were fixing her room. Cornelia had had a little boy.

Cows had drowned in their stables.

Mercifully, most of the free-burgers' tobacco crops had been gathered in, fully dried and baled in rolls. Most of the beans, too, were dry and stored in barrels.

The low stone steps were all that was left of Willem van Deventer's house. They were living in the kitchen.

Salomon had built himself a shelter of planks he'd picked up on the beach. One of Tant Theuntjie's beautiful wall hangings was found beside the sea at French Church.

Anna came back three days after the cyclone. Mud on her body and her dress. Said she'd walked through deep places.

Very hungry.

But she wouldn't say where she'd been, and didn't want anyone to ask.

She ate and went down to the river to wash; put on the old black dress that Thomas had spread out to dry in the sun with his own things, and started helping with the clearing up.

Four months.

Then the old brown-leaf cottage was a new green-leaf cottage, while the main house was a mixture of brown and green. The work-place was back on its feet again and Daniel had fitted the head to his first new barrel ...

All over, new life was sprouting again like tender shoots, and whispers had it that Juffrouw Margaretha was expecting.

The *Boode* arrived in early August that year. Six months after the cyclone.

She and Salomon and Anna, with little Catharina on her arm, waited with all the others at the shore for the arrival of the first land boat from the ship. With their eyes fixed on the wooden goose that had come to rest in the roadstead three stone throws away from the shore. A milch-cow with an udder full of hope for orphaned calves somewhere on a green island in the middle of the ocean.

Island of succour. In case the wealth-laden return fleet from the East ran into a cyclone near Mauritius. A salvage corps to gather in whatever washed up on the beach after the storm, a bunch of listless soldiers, a few sailors for the boats and a number of foot-dragging slaves. The free-burghers and exiles who had to provide food and till the island soil for the benefit of the Company were the salvagers' only salvation. Mostly in such heat that they sought shelter for their tired bodies in the shade. Heat that in rainy weather made the earth steam and bodies sweat rivers.

Free-burgher saviours who wound sweet potato vines in wreaths as wide as a man's outstretched arms measured in a circle from fingertip to fingertip, and covered them, leaving just a few small leaves sticking through the soil.

Waited in the shade for the earth fruits to swell. Hoping that no cyclones would wrench the crop out of the ground.

'Pieternella, I just can't go on any more.' For every wreath Oom Bart wound, Salomon had to wind six, and plant them. 'This is no place for people!'

Hope was always the ship from the Cape; living was surviving from ship to ship.

Certain people, here and there, lived with their own willpower in their hearts. Like her Daniel. Oom Laurens. The Commander.

'Cooper, if only the men would deliver enough sweet potatoes for us to distil arrack! What use is my knowledge of distilling if it isn't properly exploited?'

'The problem is the stills, Commander. Up at Jan Harmens' it barely drips out of the coils.'

'Those are Company stills; I'll send them back to the Cape on the next ship, so they can be repaired.'

For her the arrival of the ship was Salomon's only hope. She had a feeling deep within that like a kindly stepmother the island was accepting her - making her a child of its own. But not Salomon.

Juffrouw Margaretha, too, was among the notables from the Lodge waiting on the new quay. Whispering was no longer necessary; she was clearly pregnant. She had a gentleness in her eyes - especially when she looked at the Commander. Andrea was babbling excitedly and dancing about, her hand held by the slave. The first land boat was coming.

There was a *woman* in the boat ...

It was Tant Barbara Geens's Maria, with her husband Captain Wobma. A feather from the wing of a Cape seagull had blown all the way to her!

'Look, there's Maria!' she told Salomon. He wasn't interested.

Also in the boat was a strange man who was warmly welcomed by the Commander. And the money coffer and Sven Telleson.

'Master Sven?' She touched him lightly on the arm as he passed.

'Pernilla?'

'Who's the stranger?'

'Renier Drijver, the new Secunde. Where's Daniel?'

'Looking for turtles.'

'Under the tail of an English ship, of course! Wobma needs a cooper. The *Boode*'s one died at sea.'

'He ought to be back by tomorrow.' Anna had said that his shadow had started veering homewards ...

Maria stepped off the quay with Juffrouw Margaretha and stopped on the sand when she saw *her*.

'Pieternella!' she cried, delighted, stretched out her arms and ran across the sand to her. They hugged and cried and kissed like sisters who had long forgotten about each other.

'Maria, I can't believe it!'

'I thought I was going to die before I got here. We came through the most dreadful storm, and now I hear you were struck by a *cyclone*.'

A soldier came up and announced curtly that Captain Wobma's wife was being waited for.

'I'll come and visit you. I've got a letter for you from Sophia van der Byl.'

A second seagull feather from the Cape.

That was brought right up to her on the Orange Tree Flats the next afternoon by a rested but sad Maria.

'I couldn't wait any longer to see where you live, Pieternella.' The soldier accompanying her sat down under the awning.

Anthonie had taken the shells to Juffrouw Sophia, but he had died at sea soon after the storm. They found the letter among his few things. Aren't you going to open it? Later. I need to wake up first and stop dreaming that you really are sitting at my table, Maria.

'I can't believe it myself. You've got a very attractive house, and your little girl is quite lovely.'

'Daniel had to battle to get the house repaired again. We've all got leaf-houses on the island ...' Not that she was ashamed of the house, but it wasn't as pretty as the clay or brick houses of the Cape.

'The Commander says you and Daniel are among the very few upright citizens on the island. Honourable. Your mother would have been so proud of you, Pieternella.'

'Did the Commander really say that?' It was good to hear.

'Oh, yes. He complains about the many layabouts. I believe Willem van Deventer got a beating, so he's calmed down a bit.'

'We don't often go up to the Flats where they live. But I feel sorry for his Maria.'

'And Tant Maijke? Is there anything here for her to smuggle?' she asked teasingly.

'No, she has to take care of newly planted coconut palm seedlings.'

Anna brought them a pot of tea she had brewed and Pieternella poured it into her pretty cups. Then each of them also had a pancake with butter and sugar, served on the pretty plates Daniel had got from the English ships the time before.

Maria said several times: 'You're lucky to have a slave of your own. One can see that Daniel is good to you.'

'Very.'

Like two sisters on a visit. Enquiries and sadness. Governor Bax died last year, poor man. Hendrik Crudop is acting in his place, been doing it for a long time actually. More and more bent by the day from all his worries, poor man – if it isn't the drought, it's the taverns selling liquor on Sundays during church services. Jannetjie Ferdinandus has been fined twice. And poor Crudop is at his wits' end with the whoremongers carousing in the slave quarters at night. He nails up bigger and stricter posters every week, threatens worse beatings. It makes no difference. There are half-caste brats crawling about all over the Cape.

How are things on Robben Island?

Still a burden on the Cape. Bernewitz is the Post Holder, and he and Crudop are constantly at loggerheads about the amount of shell being sent to the mainland. Because of the drought all the sheep were taken off the island. After the rain Bernewitz asked: When are the sheep coming back? Crudop said it was too dangerous; if England or France attacked the Cape to wrest it out of Holland's hands, as they want to do, they'll first take Robben Island and launch their attack from there. There mustn't be a single sheep for the enemy to eat.

What she most wanted to hear was news of Jacobus, but she didn't have the courage to ask, not until Maria was about to leave because the soldier was parading up and down in front of the door, as if signalling.

'My brother, Jacobus, do you ever see him?'

Maria looked away quickly.

'Was he still with Jac Jacolyn when you left?'

'No. He'd just been placed with Barent Backer.'

'Is he still there?'

'Yes. But he's not well, Pieternella. Surgeon Ten Damme does what he can; he says Jacobus is like someone whose blood has stopped flowing. Come to a standstill or something.'

'Is he still having attacks?'

'Yes. I'm sorry. Your little brother, Anthonie Evas is still with Cornelius Adriaans. The Church Council pays Cornelius and his wife extra to look after him. The child has turned six already but still has to wear a nappy at night.'

She didn't want to know about Anthonie! Suddenly all she wanted was for Maria to leave and take the dust from the Cape away with her. So she could shut up the house tightly and sit dead still in the darkness with Catharinatjie till Daniel came. Till the Cape ghosts were gone and the *Boode*, too.

And somewhere there was another uneasiness. It had been hanging round Anna like a gauze shift ever since she'd come back from the Lodge that morning with the supplies she'd been sent to buy. Flour and sugar and soap and hard wax candles. Pieternella had sent her because she wanted to be at home when Daniel got back.

There'd been nothing wrong with Anna when she set off. There was when she got back. Before Maria came.

'Why do you look so frightened, Anna? Was there something on the path that scared you?'

'No. I sent Thomas to fetch the ox out of the forest, because when the master comes it'll have to go to French Church.' Curt.

'Anna, answer me!'

'Anna doesn't answer anybody. If a black cloud hangs, then it hangs.'

'What black cloud? Is there another cyclone on its way?' It felt as though the gauze of unease round Anna was suddenly sticking to *her*. 'Tell me!'

'Cyclone isn't black cloud, cyclone is white cloud.'

'Is something going to happen to my husband?'

'The master will get home safely, I don't know what the black cloud means.'

'Where is the black cloud?'

'Somewhere above the Lodge.' Frightened words.

She was reading the letter in Juffrouw Sophia's beautiful hand when Daniel walked in. Dirty, tired and as happy as always to see that everything in his yard and house was still in such good order.

'My love, my longing for you and Catharinatjie has become an ache!' He smelt of the sea, of tar and tobacco. He was her handsome husband! Her breath. Her new body, her new life. 'But why are you crying, Pieternellatjie?'

'The *Boode* has arrived. Tant Barbara Geens's Maria is here with her husband, Captain Wobma. She brought me a letter from Juffrouw Sophia.'

She felt his body tense up. He held her at arm's length. 'What letter?'

'To say thank you for the shells I sent her; that she is thankful to know that I haven't forgotten her and Mynheer, and she is happy that I am so content.'

'And are you really content, Pieternella?' Like someone deeply uncertain.

'I am, really and truly, Daniel.'

'Would you like to go back to the Cape?'

'No. Never. Mauritius is where I live now. With you.'

That made him very, very happy.

That was a Tuesday.

By Friday she no longer found it strange that Anna had seen a black cloud above the Lodge.

The saw-blade had not arrived. They said Master Sven had disappeared into the forest with a can of arrack.

The still which Lamotius had sent to the Cape had not come back. The

Cape had sent it to Batavia, the Cape could not repair it.

Nor did the Cape have a minister to send on the *Boode* to baptise the children and confirm the young people.

The Orphan Chamber had sent word that under no circumstances was Salomon to return to the Cape. His brother Jacobus was a layabout.

Salomon just turned on his heel and walked off. Daniel stopped her from running after him.

'Worst of all, Cooper Zaaijman,' Lamotius complained confidentially to Daniel after church on Sunday, 'is that the *acting* governor Crudop has taken me to task, me, the Commander, because I had that deportee Van Deventer thrashed for his flagrant and churlish behaviour.' Daniel didn't like Willem van Deventer either. 'His instructions are that I should treat and lead the island's men with a gentler hand. Not circumscribe their freedom any further. Allow them to hunt as much and as often as they like and with as many hounds as they like. Catch as many tortoises as they like - all this, in spite of the fact that I had reported to the Cape that almost three thousand tortoises had been destroyed in the last two years!'

All Daniel would say that night was that he was glad he wasn't Isaac Lamotius.

'Does this mean that you're now allowed to help the English ships if they need you?' she asked.

'I doubt it!' he laughed.

It wasn't a joke. Every time that Daniel went to help an English ship, she was afraid he would be caught. Oom Bart said straight out one day: 'If they catch Daniel on an English ship, they'll strip him of all his possessions and throw him in gaol. Conniving with the enemy is treason. Do you know what that means?'

'Daniel has gone to hunt turtles, Oom Bart.'

'I'm not stupid, Pieternella.'

'Daniel has gone to hunt turtles, Oom Bart.'

'I'm not stupid, Pieternella. *You're* the one that is.'

On Monday Willem van Deventer went to the Lodge to ask for his slave and slave girl back, and got them. Plus twelve cattle, on credit. Once he'd paid his fine for all his illegal fishing, he could have his boat back, too.

Tant Maijke had come down from the Flats with Willem and had gone on, with official permission, to Cornelia on the Orange Tree Flats. But first she called on her, Pieternella. Daniel was on board the *Boode*, repairing barrels.

'Willem's Maria is getting ready to send Pietertjie back to the Cape on the ship. To her mother.'

Tant Maijke was sitting in the shade under the lean-to with her legs stretched out in front of her. Anna had brought her milk and bread and cheese. 'Secunde Van Hoeven and his wife will take responsibility for the child on board ship. It's better that way. Pietertjie is going to pine to death in this hellish place.'

'How is Cornelia's little boy?'

'Fat as a suckling pig. I was telling the Commander only this morning that the Company could at least have given us down and outs a leg-up after the cyclone, to help us get on our feet again. Poor Cornelia is still stuck in a house with half its walls blown away. You might at least send your slave woman over to help her for two or three days a week.'

'Anna cannot help rebuild a house and Anna is not for hire.'

'Don't you come cheeking me! I'm old enough to be your grand-mother!'

'Was the food my slave brought you at least edible?'

'You're insolent! D'ye think because you landed under Daniel Zaaijman by accident that you can come over all high and mighty with me!'

'That's not true.'

'You've forgotten that you crawled out from under a Hottentot! I hear they're going to tighten up the laws on all half-castes. Declare them all slaves. You got sent to Mauritius just in time.'

'Hottentots are not Dutchmen's slaves. They never were.'

'My family are important people in the fatherland,' she said and got up to leave. 'If they were to hear about the misery I've been dumped in here, there'd be big trouble. I told the Commander so, too. He promised to try again to have me unbanned so he would be free to grant me some land. They say Daniel has regular contact with foreign ships on the other side of the island. He must please tell them that one of these days I'll have meat for sale. If we don't start working out our own salvation on this island, we're done for, I'm telling you.'

'Yes, Tant Maijke.'

Master Sven arrived at the house that same afternoon. Dirty, tattered – but honestly sober.

'I know Daniel isn't here, Pernilla, but it's not Daniel I want. It's you I need to talk to.'

'Sit down. Anna will bring you something to eat.' How many times had she not seen her mother in a sober moment hopelessly trying to straighten up, to shake herself awake again. At such times she would always take her mother's hand and walk along the beach with her.

'One day, Pernilla, this island will admit that Sven Telleson was the one who saved it. With ebony. I'm off to the Cape.'

'To the Cape?'

'Yes. On the *Boode*. Daniel's got to carve me a new wooden saw-blade; I'm going to go and *fetch* us blades! This toing and froing has got to stop now. I've already spoken to Lamot. He says I'm his right hand as far as wood is concerned, he couldn't get by without me, but without saw-blades we're not going anywhere at all. The Lords Seventeen want wood, they say Mauritius has to pay its own way, urgently.' He was like a man who had suddenly found new strength. 'And while I'm at the Cape, I want to find myself a wife, too. You've got to tell me where I should go looking for her.' In the kitchen Anna burst out laughing. 'Tell that mad wench she's looking for trouble!'

'She's not mad, Master Sven, I myself feel like laughing! *You*, getting married?'

'What's wrong with that? Daniel's been strutting around like a peacock since he's been married. Quite forgets to fold his tail-feathers and put them away now and again. I hear your little one's crawling already?'

'She's been crawling for a long time. I've just got to step in and stop Daniel taking her out on the sampan to show her the fishes and shells along the reef.'

'I want a wife who can still have babies.'

Anna brought him a plate of stewed duck on rice with currants, leftovers from the midday meal, heated up. She stopped in blank amazement, the plate in mid-air. 'Not much use if the woman can have babies when arrack has burnt the bee's sting off,' she said out loud and put the plate down in front of him.

'Anna!' she scolded. 'If the master was here now, there'd be trouble.'

Master Sven was just as angry. 'Time they put your mouth in chains!'

Anna just laughed and turned round. At least she had laughed again. From the time she came back from the Lodge with the black cloud in her head, it was as though some wildness had possessed her.

'Don't take any notice of Anna, Master Sven. Rather tell me if you're serious.'

'As serious as if my hand were on the Bible. The tailor's making me two new shirts and new breeches; I thought perhaps you and your crazy slave might take a look at my old clothes.'

'Of course we will. Daniel says the *Boode* is in a hurry to leave …'

'Time enough. The bitterest complaint against me, the master woodsman, is that there isn't enough wood to take on board. The Company doesn't care where it's supposed to come from, doesn't care how it's supposed to get sawn. Doesn't care if Lamotius repairs the mill; but a mill without blades means nothing. Not much shell-lime either, the slaves were too sick to burn and sift it. Surgeon says it was because of the stagnant water during the drought. Don't know when last I had such a nice plate of food.'

'I'm glad.'

'Are you sure you haven't got a sister somewhere at the Cape?'

'No. Just a brother. I'd be pleased if you would take him a letter from me.'

'Jacobus. Peder sent word to me.'

'How old are you, Master Sven?'

'I haven't worked it out for a long time.'

'Estimate.'

'Your dad and I were the same age.'

'Estimate.'

'Somewhere in the early forties. If that bad-mannered slave thinks I haven't got a sting ...'

'Never mind. The problem is going to be where to find a wife at the Cape. All the women are snapped up.'

'I'd be happy with a good Hottentot.'

'The best Hottentot women are carefully looked after in the kraals to stop them stumbling across white men. They never really forgave my mother for doing so.'

Daniel got home after dark. That was on the Tuesday. They had supper; with Catharinatjie on his lap, he read to her and the slaves from the Bible and led the prayers.

Some time in the middle of the night she woke up with Daniel leaping out of bed and grabbing for his clothes in the dark.

'What is it?' she asked. The baby began to cry.

'I'm lighting a candle. Something's wrong.'

'What?'

'There was a cannon shot.'

The word was hardly out of his mouth when the next shot rang out in the air like a distant *thud.*

'What does it mean?' She lifted the baby out of her little bed.

Outside the front of the house Thomas called: Master, did you hear?

'Yes,' Daniel was outside speaking to him. 'Get me ropes and a lantern!'

'What could it mean, Daniel?'

'I don't know. But the shots came from the *Boode*.'
In the middle of the night?

Pieternella settled the baby on the bedstead beside her and once Catharinatjie was asleep again she went outside. The east wind, which had risen the previous afternoon, was blowing fiercely, but it didn't have the feel of a cyclone wind.

Between the house and the work-place there was a tall thin shadow, blacker than the night.

'Anna?' Deathly silence. 'Anna?' After the third call the figure started moving towards her. It *was* Anna. 'Why are you not asleep?'

'Those were cannon shots. Thomas says it's for war. Maybe we should take the baby and go and hide in the forest.'

'Don't talk like that, it just makes me more uneasy.'

'You can't flee on an empty stomach. Anna is going to light the fire.'

'Flee where to?'

'Anna knows. It's the black cloud, it's arrived.'

'Please, don't talk like that!'

Anna made them crumbly porridge with sweet milk and sugar.

'I'm not hungry, it's still night-time!'

'Eat. The day's not far off now.' Catharinatjie woke up just before dawn. Anna gave her some of the porridge too. 'Child must have something in her tummy.'

Like being nailed up in the darkness; you don't know what's going on outside. Just the wind blowing ever more fiercely.

Thomas came to the door for the pail and went out to milk the cow – the new one. The other one had washed up on the shore at French Church after the cyclone.

Pieternella had known she would break out.

Anna didn't try to stop her. Just said the child had to stay inside the house, the wind was too fierce. 'The cloud has passed,' she added, 'but be careful: there could be fallen branches that have blown down.'

Twice she had to clamber over branches lying across the footpath.

At the ford she imagined she could smell smoke on the wind. Just before the narrow wooden bridge across the Molens River she heard voices. Many people.

Beyond the bridge was the most incredible picture her eyes had ever had to take in. There was no Lodge any more. Just a black and white ruin with the odd wisp of smoke blowing off it like morning mist ...

She wanted to tell her body it wasn't true. She wanted to turn round and run away. Everywhere people were huddling together in disbelief, everyone's clothes clung limp and damp and dirty on their bodies, as though they had been too near a fire. Torn. Wooden buckets, iron buckets. Jacomo Baldini just stood there, dismayed, with his lute pressed to his chest as though that was all he had left to cling to. A woman was sitting on the ground while the Surgeon bent over her. There was no cap on her head – just scorched hair. It was Secunde Van Hoeven's wife. Henk Karseboom was there. Secretary Jongmeyer with bundles of papers in his arms, his eyes staring wildly ...

She felt sick.

A man turned round – a dead man, Commander Lamotius. His eyes were no longer alive. The skin on his hands and arms had been singed off. Someone tried to take him by the shoulder but he jerked free. Someone tried to wrap a quilt round his shoulders but he shook it off in fury.

'Pernilla?'

'Master Sven, what happened?'

'Daniel is down by the water. He's burnt his hand badly, too; there was nothing we could do ...'

She wanted to be sick. She heard herself asking: 'Master Sven, did anyone die in the fire?'

'Yes. Juffrouw Margaretha and Andrea and two slave women.'

'Oh God, NO!'

Master Sven later said he could see she was going to faint, so he caught her and laid her down on the ground.

When she came to, she got up and started walking. Jacobus had run into the veld. She began to run. She didn't want to catch the falling sickness, she ran faster and faster and in her head the ceaseless screaming: Oh God NO! Oh God NO! Oh God NO! If she could get far enough away, it wouldn't be true. Telling herself: Don't think. Don't make pictures. Just run. Don't see the flames!

Somewhere near the Orange Tree River she ran into Oom Bart and Tant Theuntjie. Tant Theuntjie asked: 'God, Pieternella, what's going on? Has something happened to Daniel?'

She shook her head, ran on.

Anna was standing in the front room with Catharinatjie on her arm. She grabbed the child from the slave and squeezed her tight. The child tried to wriggle free; she just squeezed her tighter and tighter. When the child started screaming, Anna pulled Catharina out of her grasp. Her hands empty, she cried and cried, then grabbed the earthenware bowl of butter off the table and flung it out of the door, splattering brown and yellow all over the earth.

Then she walked into the forest. In the direction of the Bamboo Mountains. She wanted to get away. The more densely it closed in all around her, the more her dress got caught in the undergrowth, the harder she had to force and push her way through thickets, the better. The harder she fell, the more painful, the better. Her arms were scratched and bleeding. She needed something to break till the rage within her had broken. The helplessness. So that the flames that went on and on rising up before her eyes to trap three women and a child could die down.

The slope under her feet became ever steeper, the forest sparser. The stones and rocks bigger and bigger. Her breathing louder.

When a stone gave way under her feet and she fell forward for the umpteenth time, she didn't get up. She could feel her heart beating against the earth.

The cyclone was spent.

But not Daniel when he came walking back into the yard.

His right hand was wrapped in bandages, a hole burnt in his shirt, his shoes covered in muddy ash. His face frightened her badly. Fury and fear in a single bundle.

'Daniel ...'

'Start carrying everything outside! The kitchen must be built separate from the house. From tonight the slaves sleep chained to weights.'

He stumbled across the yard and fetched two club-like hammers from the lean-to, shoved one into the startled Thomas's hands and then went round to the back of the kitchen and struck the first terrible blow against the black stone wall.

'Daniel!' When he lifted his arms for the next blow, she got between him and the wall and stopped his arm. Calmly, she announced: 'It stays where it is.'

'God, Pieternella!'

'Come.' *His* strength was suddenly in her. 'Come, Daniel.'

He sank down on the tree trunk before the door, his head hanging low. She melted some sugar in a cup of water, poured a little brandy from the earthenware jar into it, and gave it to him to drink.

The slaves stood watching in fright. Even Anna.

'The fire,' he said, 'started around midnight in the slave lodge just beside the servants' barracks and from there the wind threw it on to the roof of the Commander's living quarters. At daybreak it emerged that two slaves deserted last night. They set the fire to give themselves enough time to get away.'

13

The *Boode* stayed only for two days more.

Most of the people on the beach were clad in deepest mourning. No drum sounded. Not a wave of a hand, not one unnecessary gesture. Not even a cannon shot as a farewell greeting when the wooden goose spread its wings on its way to take the most mournful tidings to the Cape.

Master Sven was on board. Working by the light of two lanterns under the lean-to at night while the two slaves were asleep in their beds as usual, Daniel had hurriedly made him a second wooden model of a saw-blade. Daniel would have to get the weights to which to chain them at night from the Lodge.

'If you're going to chain up the slaves at night, you're going to have to chain me up, too.' She *said* it.

'Pieternella, don't contradict me.' Persuasion and warning in one.

'I mean it.' She turned round and went indoors to finish Jacobus's letter by lamplight. Asked him not to damage their reputation any further; said that Salomon wanted to return to the Cape, that they were all well – that he should live thankfully for being alive.

Maria and Willem van Deventer's Pietertjie was also on board, in the care of Secunde Van Hoeven and his wife, her short singed hair covered by a thick cloth cap.

Captain Wobma's Maria came over the quay to say a quiet goodbye to Pieternella and to take the letter for Jacobus.

'It's so awful, Pieternella.'

'Yes, Maria.'

'I feel desperately sorry for you who have to stay behind.'

'Yes. I wanted to send your mother a few pretty shells …'

'We were only supposed to leave in two weeks' time, but now we've got to get the news to the Cape.'

'Give your mother my love.'

A little coral lime. Some ambergris. No wood.

In a chair on the quay, above everything, *over* everything, sat Commander Lamotius. His hands and feet wrapped in bandages: a greyish stone face, dead eyes staring fixedly at the ship. A slight hand gesture brought two soldiers forward to pick up the chair and carry it away with him in it.

They carried him past her. He even looked her straight in the eye for a moment, but she didn't think his eyes could see. They were just cold pieces of blue glass.

They took him to one of the outbuildings that was still standing, a half-burnt leaf building a little farther off. There were tents everywhere.

Slaves, the men all shackled, were shovelling debris from the ruined Lodge on to canvas sheets to tip into the shallow ditch below the garden. Two soldiers brandished canes at anyone who dared to stumble.

On the footpath back to the Orange Tree Flats, just where the forest opened up and you could look back for a moment at the sea, Salomon stopped. The *Boode*'s white wings were carrying it away across the water.

'If I had parents, I could have had Anthonie's job all the way to the Cape. But because I'm an orphan, the Company is my master!'

'You're alive.' She didn't raise her voice. Just said it.

'You can't live on this island, Pieternella, you can hardly even breathe!' The words came from his mouth in both a high and a low pitch, a boy's voice and a man's at once. He was angry. 'I wanted to be on that ship!'

'You're *alive*, Salomon! Stop looking back to the Cape and be happy.'

'It's easy for you to talk, you're not Bart Borms's slave labourer! You don't have to sleep under a bush because your sleeping place was blown away by a cyclone. You don't have to …'

'You're not listening to what I'm saying, Salomon!' Now she herself was angry. 'At least you're *alive*! And you *chose* to sleep under the bush so they would feel sorry for you and send you back to the Cape!'

He looked at her strangely. 'What's got into you, Pieternella? Why are you talking to me like this?'

'You think you can go back and take refuge with Jacobus. What you don't know is that Jacobus can't provide you with any because Jacobus is turning into a layabout! If you don't crawl out from under Bart Borms's bush, *you're* going to go the same way! Cornelia tells me you join in when they pour wine.'

'I'm working myself to death, Pieternella!'

'Do you reckon wine is going to bring you to life again?'

'You're not like you used to be …'

'Yesterday and the day before are not like tomorrow and the day after. Even a sweet potato sends down roots and makes new leaves. Daniel has said you are welcome to come and stay with us, but you won't.'

'This island isn't my home, I'd rather carry shells on Robben Island!'

'You know nothing about Robben Island, you always ran away when I wanted to take you to see Mamma.'

'It wasn't pleasant being beaten over the head each day with the fact that your mother was a Hottentot.'

'She was a *Khoi* – a true person.' In her heart she used to tell herself the same thing. 'Half our bodies are made of the true people. And *we're* not lying in a grave, burnt to death!'

Old Schoolmaster Wouter Steenwyk conducted the burial service under the trees. Just one coffin. Juffrouw Margaretha and Andrea. The two slaves were buried without funeral rites, they didn't have Christian blood. The Commander was carried to the service on a chair but he didn't once open his eyes, didn't weep, only kept his jaws firmly clenched together.

And Daniel didn't let go of her hand even for a moment.

The new Secunde, Renier Drijver, was the one to dig fresh courage out of the ruin for the mourners at the graveside. After Lamotius had been borne away. She and Daniel stood around, as disconsolate as the others, when Mynheer Drijver set it down among them like a comfort.

But Henk Karseboom was the first to break the mourning silence. 'I'm telling you, this Mauritius is mowing us down. Take one step forward and it throws you two steps back. The only thing the supply ship from the Cape brings is dissatisfaction because we don't have anything for it to load and take back. Or else they whinge about what we ask *them* to send us.'

'Yes,' added one of the women from the Flats, 'and the rice they send us is full of weevils!'

'Do you think,' Laurens Gabrielse wanted to know, 'that the Governor of the Cape would be content to lay down his head at night under a rotten roof? Like this Lodge's one was?'

'No!' came a chorus of voices.

'But a fine Christian lady like Juffrouw Margaretha had to – may she rest in peace.'

'People ...' It was the new Secunde. Stout body, serious face. 'We stand gathered here in black crêpe, but the Word says we should be faithful. I believe that help for Mauritius is already on the horizon, because the man in the fatherland who has been appointed as the new Commander at the Cape was born on Mauritius.'

Astonishment was clear on everyone's face. 'Born on *Mauritius*?'

'Yes. And lived here till his seventh year because his father was one of the first commanders on Mauritius.'

'Born *here*?'

'At sea, actually, while his worthy father and mother were still on their way to the island. His name is Simon van der Stel.'

Heartache mixed with fresh hope was like weeping with one eye and laughing with the other.

Hendrik, the wild one, was sitting under the lean-to waiting when she and Daniel got home from the funeral. There were two English ships at the mouth of the Black River, in urgent need of help if 'Mister Zyman' was still on the island ...

Both were ships Daniel had helped before.

'Tell them I'll need a couple of days to get there because I'm not coming without my wife and child.'

'Daniel?' She didn't want to go; she and Anna were plaiting new coir mats, they still had sago to wash out, the palm tree trunk lay waiting ...

'I'm not leaving you alone with the slaves, Pieternella, and I'm not even prepared to discuss it.'

'But you always say it's untamed jungle at the Black River. What about the child, where are we going to stay?'

'There's a hut. We'll manage.'

There was a hut.

Made of planks and palm leaves, on a flat-topped hill, in dense forest overlooking the river, higher than the reach of any floodwaters. A hut with signs of recent repairs after the cyclone; the thickets on the seaward side had been cleverly thinned to allow a lookout just enough space to keep an eye on the sea for the first sign of a sail. There was a narrow passage in the reef to the wide mouth of the river ...

'How would a ship know there was help in these thickets?' she asked Hendrik. Daniel was already down at the anchorage with the ships.

'Skippers tell other skippers, they write it down in their books. A cannon shot asks: Is there anyone who can help? Then I spy through the glass to see if it's a friend or a pirate, and I answer with a smoke signal of wet leaves.'

'And if they're pirates?'

'If they're badly hit, I'll answer. Luckily they very seldom come here, their hideouts are in the bays of Madagascar.'

A little way off, an open cooking place built of stone.

Still farther back in the thickets a second surprise: a low three-walled palm-leaf shelter with six narrow bunks in a row.

'Sick bay,' explained Hendrik, embarrassed. '*Very* sick sailors have to be brought ashore.' Bunches of dried yellow-bush leaves hung upside down from the roof. 'It grows on the edge of the forest, I make tea of it for sick stomachs. An old slave taught me.'

'Where do you get fresh food for them?'

'Quite a few free-burghers have gardens on the sly near Northwest Harbour. And a couple of cows. But the bastards steal my ambergris, I'm going to shoot holes in them yet!'

Besides being an unlawful lookout on the west of the island, Hendrik was also the ambergris king on that side. And on the north side as well. Daniel used to say there wasn't a dog anywhere to match Hendrik when it came to smelling out the nasty blackish-grey lumps along the water's edge. Particularly after a storm. The biggest lumps of all washed up after cyclones.

Not long after the cyclone, Daniel came home one day with a lump of the stuff and set it down on a plank under the lean-to to harden. Anna and Thomas kept fiddling with it, almost with reverence, and pleading for a piece. Daniel had to keep warning them: 'Leave it alone!'

Ambergris.

He was supposed to take it to the Lodge to exchange for a bottle of arrack and a little credit on his account. The Secretary usually weighed it and determined the reward according to the prescripts laid down by the Lords Seventeen in Amsterdam. Once, years earlier, Carpenter Joosten had picked up a large lump. They gave him *two* bottles of arrack, a hundred guilders in his pocket and a further two hundred guilders' worth of credit as well. Daniel laughed, saying that after that Gerrit van Ewijk, who was supposed to plant wheat on the Flats like Willem van Deventer, had left his fields just like that and gone off in search of ambergris.

But then one day Captain Frooij came out with it: the Lords Seventeen had sold Joosten's lump of ambergris in the fatherland for more than three thousand, four hundred guilders. This was shortly before Frooij's death.

Anna came into the house to plead with *her*, Pieternella. 'Ask the master for just a little bit for each of us.'

'It's disgusting stuff, what do you want it for?'

'Ooo ...' Anna folded her hands in front of her chest, as if in prayer. 'A little piece in a mug of water and a strength draws out of it into the water that gives your body the force of the biggest waves breaking on the reef. The stuff on that plank, Juffrouw Pieternella, is whole barrels of sea-foam compressed into one lump.'

She pestered Daniel till he gave the slaves what they wanted. No, he had no intention of exchanging it, he was keeping it for Hendrik. It was *his* livelihood. The English ships bought it off him and paid well – the French ships even better. They melted it down and mixed all kinds of fragrant flower petals in it to make perfume. No, he didn't believe the sea-foam story. The old sailors used to say it was whale vomit. No one really knew what it was.

Black River. Another strange piece of the island at almost half-past eight on Daniel's clock-face on the beach.

'Don't wander off into the forest, Pieternella. Stick to the path laid out with tree stumps down to the river; there's a good place to play there and shade for you and the child.'

The work-place was not far from the river mouth, and also cleverly hidden in the thickets. From the look of it, not the kind of work-place where barrels were made. A lot of wooden pegs with bundles of old rope hanging on them. Others that looked like long strings of rope that had been washed and teased out – just like thick flat bunches of hair. Dirty iron buckets full of black pitch or something. A mountain of bundles of short twig brooms, tightly bound with coir string. Mallets. Blunt-nosed chisels. Other, unfamiliar things ...

Two fine large ships were lying at anchor on the inner side of the reef. Much bigger than the *Boode*. More like the great East Indiamen of the fleets at the Cape. You could hear voices from the decks.

One ship looked crippled, like a wooden goose on one leg.

'There's no man anywhere that can dive like Daniel to see what's going on under the water. The English all know him.' On their first morning Hendrik walked down with them to the start of the long sandy bay. Yellowish grainy sand – washed up yellow sand coral twigs.

She turned round and began to walk back along the river.

'Where are you off to now?' Hendrik called after her.

'I want to see something.' Yellowish sand growing gradually blacker towards the centre – higher up, to where the river of clear water ran over a pitch-black bed. 'Is *that* why it's called Black River?'

'I think so. The sand is black the whole way till it runs in between the hills. Pitch-black water in the pools. The best bathing pool on the whole island when the sun has been melting you all day is just an hour's walk from here, but it's not for women.'

'You don't have to keep following me, Hendrik.'

'Daniel said I had to keep an eye on you. Work will only start tomorrow, today they're just checking and fixing a price.'

Many, many palm trees. The tall peacock-tail kind that she and Anna passed one day on their way to pick feather-leaves. Blue-green.

'Are these the wine-trees?' she asked Hendrik.

'Oh, I see you've learnt that already!' he laughed. 'Listen carefully and you'll hear the sailors' axes chopping off the heads to make the wine. The drunkard's heaven. They may as well chop today, tomorrow Daniel will have them sweating!'

'Palmyra,' she remembered the name Anna had used. 'They hollow out the head, the sap dams up and then it's wine.'

'Not quite *that* easy. It has to ferment first. But a bunch of thirsty sailors like this crew can do terrible damage to get at the sap.'

'The tree dies when its head is chopped off. Anna told me.'

'Weird wench that, I'm scared of her.'

'There's nothing wrong with Anna.'

A broad expanse where the river joined the sea. Silly silver fish jumping out of the sea. High, green-forested hills on the opposite side, with blue-green patches of palmyra everywhere in between.

It was hot.

Catharinatjie fell asleep on her little quilt in the shade above the yellow-sand bay. She dozed off beside her.

She was missing Anna, but was strangely relieved to be away from it all for a bit. Orange Tree Flats. The burnt-out Lodge. Tant Theuntjie, Oom Bart – even Salomon.

Daniel said he'd show her the most beautiful spot on the whole island on their way back. There hadn't been time on the trip round to Black River.

The *Zeemaat* with her and Daniel and Catharinatjie and the equipment had come all along the inner edge of the reef and round below the island. Daniel had tied a rope round the child's body and secured the other end round one of the thwarts. They tied Anna's palm-leaf hats on their heads to shade their faces. In places the reef broke *so* close to the shore that she was afraid it would be too shallow for them to get through, but Daniel knew all the ways. Every sailable channel.

Then the reef would be far off again.

Pretty water, green water, blue-green water, green island, green forests on the mountains ...

A whole day long.

Only when the sun was beginning to colour the clouds in the west did they turn the corner of the island. The strangest rocky headland. As though some giant had dug out the biggest chunk of mountain rock somewhere and stood it up squarely for a beacon as if to say: Here endeth the island's underside! Turn your ship!

'Quarrel Hill, I call it,' laughed Daniel, because one says this is Pieter Both's head and another says Pieter Both's head is the conical hill with the little stone cap on it above Northwest Harbour.'

'Who's Pieter Both?'

'One of the old Dutch seafarers, long before the Cape, who came to grief here. He was Admiral of the return fleet. Hollanders stopped here for refreshment; planted oranges and lemons, peas and beans as well. Left fowls behind to catch on their next voyage. Even the maritime maps disagree about which head or bay it was that he named after himself. In those days the English and French were just as ready to take on refreshment here; they came cutting loads of ebony for the European market.'

'I wonder how Master Sven is getting on at the Cape.'

'I hope he gets the saw-blade and gives up the wife-taking.'

'Are you sorry you took a wife?'

'You've become my life, Pieternella.'

Hendrik came and woke her and Catharinatjie. Lunch was ready. Eel and hard tack.

'From tomorrow, I'll see to the food,' she said.

'In the daytime, you'll only need to see to yourself and the child. Daniel and I usually get ship's food when we start working.'

'When will Daniel get back?'

'Before dark.'

He only came back in the dark of the night.

Tired out, but cheerful and content.

'Sorry, my love, but that's the way it goes on the first night on the ships. From tomorrow there won't be any time for being sociable.'

'Will we have to careen the ship?' asked Hendrik anxiously.

'Yes. They're already repacking and unloading. The tide will be right at noon.'

Another Daniel.

Not the one she married, not the one who made the very best barrels, not Catharinatjie's dad, not the free-burgher from the Orange Tree Flats ...

Daniel the shipman. Fearless tamer of the wooden goose.

'The wives of both the Captain and the First Mate are on board, and three or four children, too,' Daniel explained before dawn. 'A canvas shelter will be put up for them under the trees above the sandy bay; there's no room on the other ship. I told them my own wife and child are on the shore; that you can't speak their language but that you might also go there in search of shade. You can't stay cooped up here alone in the hut all day.'

It was pleasant alone in the hut. Just her and Catharinatjie, without Hendrik, who kept wanting to tail along behind them. She laid the fire and hung washing water over it for herself and the child. Spread butter on the sweet biscuits that Anna had packed for them. Thin strips of dried fish. Put on her oldest green shift and tied the child on her back in one of her little quilts ...

She had walked over to visit Salomon one day with the child on her back like this and come across Tant Theuntjie and Grieta on the way. 'God-a-mercy, Pieternella!' The old woman stopped, shocked, her hand on her heart. 'Don't go publicly announcing your Hottentot blood like this! Carry the baby on your arm.' Grieta stood there laughing brazenly, all her little teeth showing.

'What's wrong with carrying the child on my back?'

'Have you ever in your life seen a Dutch woman carrying her baby like that?'

From then on she only put the child on her back when she was going places alone with her. Or else she took her off before reaching the Lodge ...

She didn't turn down towards the sea but walked slowly up along the river and across to the other side. A kind of footpath. Wet, shiny black stones. Dry, dull black stones. Where it got too muddy, she took off her shoes and walked through it, or looked for a way round it through the thickets. Craftily. Because before long she would come across Hendrik or somebody's old footprints in front of her. Secretly. Like a game.

More butterflies than she'd ever seen. Yellow, blue, brown; brown and orange; white. White and green. Black and white. Singly or in pairs. Colours all mixed together. Like little river fishes on the wing.

Birds. Mates for the Orange Tree River's little green ones, *Caroo-coo-coo* doves. Strange other birds ceaselessly singing their gargling song. A small kestrel with brown feathers ...

A wide forest bowl among the hills. Green. Blue sky with wispy white clouds here and there.

She walked and walked, ever deeper into aloneness ...

To where the river unexpectedly became two rivers because the prettiest little river of blue pebbles came cheekily trotting down from the thickets on the south side and ran into the other one. Shallow. She could easily cross on the stones. On the coarse white sand on the opposite bank she found more old footprints.

But the walking wasn't so easy now. In places the thickets closed over the stream so densely that she had to go bent double along the pebbles in the water. In a bend where the sandy bank widened again she slipped Catharinatjie off her back. She felt she was right inside a big green world full of thin yellow sun stripes. All alone and lovely.

Cool.

She let the child drink water out of her cupped hands like a little animal; took off her little shoes and watched how her tiny white feet curled as the coarse sand tickled them.

Moving deep within her being was the happiest happiness ...

When she looked up, a snow-white bird with two long thin tailfeathers was gliding round and round against the blue. Gliding in a wide circle, round and round. She stretched out her arms and waved to him.

By midday she was back at the hut to feed the child and have something to eat herself. And have a nap. Then she took the child on her arm and walked down in the direction of the yellow-sand bay at the river mouth.

Voices and noise. She walked faster. Stopped dead in her tracks because the most dreadful accident was happening before her eyes! That huge ship was lying cross-wise against the bank while hundreds of sailors hung shoulder-deep on ropes tied to one side of the ship. They were pulling it over on to its side like an ox about to have its throat cut.

The whole yellow-sand bay was in turmoil. Piles of stuff tied up in bales lay above the high-water mark. Piles of chests. Piles of barrels. Rows of bundles. The ship's innards shaken out all over the sand.

A great cheer went up: the ox had tilted! Water was streaming off its wooden belly over greyish-white barnacles ...

Woodgoose dead.

Lines of dripping wet sailors came up out of the water. The first fell in at the belly and started scraping off the barnacles with long flat iron things. A bosun's rope lashed open the first bleeding cut.

It was hot, the child in her arms was fidgety.

Above the sandy bay, at the forest's edge where the shade began, canvas shelters hung limply from the trees. She went closer, slowly and in a wide arc. There was no sign of life or movement, only more bundles and chests and barrels and big coils of rope ...

They were lying against some of the bundles like people washed up on the shore. One in a blue dress, one in red, another in a black one. A girl was lying on her stomach with her head on her arms. Another lay on her side with her legs drawn up like someone feeling the cold. A chest of drawers. A table with pretty chairs standing crookedly on the sand. Cloth mats. Mattresses. A big wooden bucket full of dishes ...

The woman in blue sat up slightly, like someone aware of being watched. But she didn't turn her head far enough round to see her there. Sank back again and dozed off.

She shifted Catharinatjie on to her other hip and turned round. The woman was exhausted. One exhausted woman among other exhausted women and children.

The air smelt of the tar smoke billowing out of iron cauldrons beside the listing ship in thick grey-black clouds. They were burning the ship's bottom clean with bundles of burning brooms.

Sometime in the night Daniel crept in behind her, his body damp, and fell asleep almost immediately.

At first light he was away again.

Hendrik was at the fire. He'd got fish and sweet potatoes in the pot already.

'We ought to be able to finish cleaning one side today so that we can caulk it tomorrow. Plug the seams with tarred rope. Fortunately I'm always teasing out and boiling up old ropes; you never know when you'll be lucky and have a ship with a serious leak come limping in here. Daniel says this one wouldn't have made it much farther – pumping out water day and night with only one pump.

What was it Anthonie said? That the water rises higher and higher from below, up through the boards and drowns you off your feet. When the pump breaks, you sink ...

'I saw the prettiest bird gliding in the sky. As though someone had tied two long thin white ribbons to its tail.'

'I just call him old straw-tail – looks as if he's got straws on his tail. Always gliding here above the forest.'

She went back to the sandy bay.

The woman in red was walking up and down, dragging her feet through the sand, her arms folded tightly across her chest. A pale boy under a grown-up's hat was sitting drawing lines in the sand. The woman in black was sitting on a bundle, her head hanging down; the one in blue a little farther off. On one side a tattered sailor had made a fire and was hanging pots over it.

They didn't notice her standing just inside the thickets watching them.

Like people who'd lost hope, waiting for the wooden goose to straighten up again so they could climb back into its body. She never wanted to be trapped inside the body of a ship again. Mauritius was where she belonged. With Daniel. Willem van Deventer and Oom Bart had said they would slip off to Batavia under Lamotius's nose, just wait …

Daniel said they weren't moving anywhere.

The girl came out of the thickets behind her and stopped in amazement to see her standing there with Catharinatjie. Called out to the others. Urgently.

The three women in their blue, red and black dresses, the boy, a second girl beside the first one, all came and stood staring at her with tense faces and astonished eyes, speaking a foreign language.

They had the prettiest caps on their heads. Not like Dutch women's caps; more like high bonnets with lacy edges and long ribbons tied in bows under the chins.

'My name is Pieternella, I'm Daniel Zaaijman's wife and this is our baby,' she said in Dutch. Her mother used to say if a Dutch woman scares you, just smile with your best friendliness. She wasn't scared of these strangers. The red dress was a pretty woman, her hair curled in ringlets. The girl was her own age …

So she smiled.

And they smiled back.

Three very strange weeks.

While the wooden goose lay hauled over first on one side, then on the other. Bamboo rafts to stand on when the tide was in. Never-ending *tap-tap-tapping* as the hammers knocked the tar-drenched oakum into the seams. Pitch on their hands, pitch on their feet, pitch on their clothes. Pitch smoke.

Sailors lying like flotsam at the water's edge.

She would sit with the women and children. They played with Catharinatjie in a strange language, trailed along behind her, Pieternella, up to the hut. All along the river. A little farther each day. To where the river of blue pebbles ran into a dam under overhanging black cliff faces: deep, cool, black frightening water. She wished she could tell them about the monster that her dad had once seen.

That night Daniel laughed out loud.

'Why are you laughing?'
'They think you're a beautiful *wild island girl.*'
'A what?'
'Born on the island.'

Three unfamiliar free-burghers crossed the river in their sampans, nervously bringing carrots and cabbages and pumpkins and onions and palm wine and eels and fish and meat and tobacco. Huge turtles on their backs in a sampan, their flat flippers swimming in the air. They'd been caught in the shallows, grazing under water. It took two men to turn the heavy, slippery bodies upside down and lift them on board.

And oily water trickled out of the turtles' eyes. Like tears.

Oom Bart and Pieter van Nimwegen preferred to trap turtles when the moon was at the full and they came out to lay their eggs in the sand. They'd carry them home in a hammock slung between two poles, the turtles weeping all the while.

They usually cooked them in their shells over the fire, just like that.

Jan Dirks, Jan Muur and Jan Lodewijks were the names of the three free-burghers.

'How did they know there was a ship here?' she asked Hendrik.

'Oh they'd know. Their sampans are always ready hidden in the forests across the river – just in case.'

'Do they have wives?' she asked Hendrik.

'Yes. Elisabet and Willemina and Aaltjie. They eat their porridge as life serves it up, work like slaves in the gardens, hunt on their own to fill the barrels with salted meat for the foreigners, climb up the palms themselves like monkeys for the sap. Haven't been near the Lodge for years, no matter who the Commander is. They put two of the older girls on an English ship the year before last, hoping to get them back to the fatherland. Hoping to get away themselves in the same way.'

Late in the afternoon of the Thursday in the third week they untied the ropes. Slowly the wooden goose righted itself in the water. Like being healed. Happy.

They started loading all the stuff back on board the next morning.

Jan and Jan and Jan brought the last boatload of vegetables and meat and palm wine.

On Sunday the minister on board the ship held a service in the shade beside the seashore and baptised Catharinatjie. Daniel asked him to. The minister wore the smartest robe, read from the Bible, and sprinkled

Catharinatjie with christening water from a pretty little silver bowl.
Pieternella didn't understand the words but they sounded right.
The women cried when they said goodbye to her.

14

Anna and Thomas were waiting at French Church with the ox when they got back.

Anna with a sour face, like one trying hard not to look happy.

'Child's had too much sun!' Simmering on ahead with Catharinatjie on her arm. 'Probably left to sleep under a bush like the child of runaways!' The whole way home.

She let the slave carry on because, really, she wasn't back with her feet firmly on the earth of the Orange Tree Flats yet. She wanted to go on clinging to a dream so it wouldn't vanish; to sit dead-still so the pretty butterfly on her hand wouldn't fly away.

Once the ships had left, Daniel and Hendrik tidied up the sandy bay and the work-place. The ships left without a pilot; the skippers knew the reef at the Black River Gap.

At first light on Monday they started carrying the things that had to go back on the *Zeemaat* down to the beach and taking them out to the boat on Hendrik's sampan. He rigged up a sailcloth roof for the sun, and finally came for her and Catharinatjie.

When Daniel hauled up the anchor, he had about him the contentment of a tired but happy man.

He gave Quarrel Hill's sandbanks a wide berth because the tide was out. Poison Bay lay in the hollow of the mountain's back as they turned eastwards. Daniel had taught her: 'Poison Bay' because almost all the sailors on a ship had died there from eating stonefish that they had trapped in the pools. Some of the most poisonous fish in the sea. Black and white with fins like wings stuck with quills.

'Very like the puffer in the Cape waters, but bigger.'

All round the heel of the island, homewards between the reef and the shore. She and Daniel and Catharinatjie and the wind and the water and the foaming reef and the big blue sky above their heads. Nosy dolphins smiling and playing, doing somersaults on either side of the bows.

Catharinatjie, her little legs stiff and straight with excitement, holding her hand out the side to see them.

Peaceful. Hour after hour. The high brown-stone mountain thrusting into the sea above the boat like a big craggy dragon. Making her eyes search for a way round it ...

'Daniel, could you walk right round this island on foot along the shore?'

'I knew you'd ask. Hendrik usually walks along the shore to get to the Orange Tree Flats.'

'How does he get round that mountain?'

'He can't. Nobody can. You have to climb *over* it. It's called Climb-up Mountain – it's been the death of a number of runaway slaves that tumbled over it. Hugo tried twice to walk to the Black River mouth but couldn't get past it.'

'And you?'

'I've been over it a few times. You have to know your climbing, though. Lamotius asked me to walk round the heel of the island with him and a few soldiers; he wanted to do a survey of the rivers and arable land and woods.'

'Poor Lamotius. He probably won't want to stay on the island much longer now.'

'If I were him, I wouldn't be able to.'

Orange Apple River. Just another name for Orange Tree River, really. Turtle Bay. Because it's usually crawling with turtles. Above Northwest Harbour there was another Turtle Bay.

Gradually nearer and nearer to the shore as the reef drew closer. Barely more than the breadth of the boat in places, with the waves breaking ever more loudly in your ears.

'I'm scared, Daniel!'

'We came through here on the trip out, Pieternella. Let your body relax.'

'Now I'm even more frightened!'

'It's not much farther.'

'Farther to where?'

'To the most beautiful spot on the island. The most beautiful place I've ever seen in my life on earth.'

Apple Tree River.

Quietly, slyly, Daniel steered the boat's nose up into a secret place. Away from the sea. Away from the reef. Into the body of the island, where a small waterfall cascaded down in silver strands over yellow-brown rocks almost into the sea on the eastern side of the mouth. On either side, dense green forest bent low over the dark water, its reflection clear in the deep water mirror.

Not a talking-place.

A feeling-place.

Not a human place.

Wide at first, then narrower.

Narrower still ...

Shallower. Brown pebbles on the river bed below.

Was that an eel? *That* size?

A grass-green bird with a red beak and a necklace under its chin. Another one. And another. Green parrots.

Daniel gave the boat a brisk turn, lowered the sail and let the *Zeemaat* glide gently along the edge of a small grassy cove in the dense moist forest.

That's when she saw them. The blossoms. Like bunches of soft pink and white butterflies hanging from all the branches.

The most delicate sweet scent in the air.

'I reckoned they would be in bloom.' Daniel was speaking quietly, it was a place for whispering. He let down the anchor carefully on the deep side and stepped over the nose to swing the boat straight.

Apple blossom.

He lifted Catharinatjie off first and put her down on the grass. Then her.

Four old apple trees among the wild trees, garlands of blossoms woven through the branches ...

'She chose her spot cleverly.'

'Who?'

'Maria Scipio, Commander Por's wife. They say she was little more than a child when old Por married her in the fatherland and brought her to Mauritius. Long before the Cape. A lady with a heart of compassion for sick and starving sailors. She had fruit trees planted in the bays and up along the rivers all over the southern side of the island. On the hillsides. On every ship to the East, old Por had to send a letter asking for more saplings.'

Maria Scipio's apple-tree place. Hidden place. Secret place.

She and Daniel and Catharinatjie.

'Tell me more.' Her handsome barefoot Daniel who had tied the child to a long rope so she couldn't get more than her feet into the water. Who sat holding her, Pieternella, tight in the hollow of his body ...

'I don't know much more. Except that she was furious when a ship once brought a load of reed-like plants instead of fruit trees. It turned out they were the first sugar canes sent to poor Por to plant on the island. And the rats ate the lot.'

'Many years later Maria Scipio was Mynheer Van Riebeeck's second Maria.'

'How did you know that?' he asked, surprised.

'My mother knew about Por.'

'Of course, he was a friend of Van Riebeeck's.'

'Are we going to sleep under Maria's apple trees tonight?'

'No. We'll sleep on this side of the waterfall.'

She and Daniel and Catharinatjie on the *Zeemaat*, on mattresses under the sail he had rigged up. After he'd caught a big fat eel and grilled it for them; after they had bathed their naked bodies in the silver water in the moonlight ...

Her tall strong Daniel.

'Child's not the same,' Anna carried on nagging and kept on looking and looking at Catharinatjie. Stood back a bit, looked again.

'I don't understand what you mean, Anna! There's nothing wrong with her.'

'Anna didn't say the child's gone wrong, Anna said the child is different. Like different breath.'

'She's been baptised.'

'Baptised?'

'That means a holy man sprinkled water on her head.'

'Yes.' All at once like someone satisfied. '*That's* the difference. It's round her head.'

The house was neat and tidy. Coir mats on both sides of the bedstead. In front of the cradle. In the dining room. The yard had been swept. The garden was bursting with food, strings of salted fish hung in the lean-to.

'How is everyone?'

'You're not the same either, Juffrouw Pieternella.'

'What do you mean?'

'I'm just saying. And your brother's not well. You'd better go and see.'

'I'll go tomorrow.'

Salomon was hoeing between rows of beans in the new garden below Oom Bart's old-new house. Wearing only trousers. The weals on his back were not fresh, most of the scabs had already peeled off.

350

He hadn't seen her coming.

'Salomon!'

'Pieternella!' Glad and scared and relieved.

'Who beat you?' Oom Bart was coming down from the house.

'I ... I ran away. You weren't here. I went to the Flats, to Oom Willem van Deventer.' He spoke quickly, as though to tell her everything before Oom Bart reached them. 'I wanted to go and work for him, but he tied me up and sent word to Oom Bart that the runaway was at his place.'

'Who beat you?'

'I did.' Oom Bart said it himself standing in front of her challengingly. 'Because Bart Borms has battled enough with the Company's rubbish that I took upon my back in all good faith for the sake of this cursed bloody island!' The old man's rage was the barking of a frightened dog. She looked him straight in the eye for a moment and then turned on her heel and walked away, leaving him shouting after her that she was never to set foot on his property again!

She knew what she had to do.

They were building and thatching a new Lodge; half of the roof was still only a skeleton of poles. A palm-leaf lodge. Exactly where the old one had stood. Soldiers, slaves and sailors trimming branches to thatch the roof – wheelbarrows, ladders, coils of rope, hammer blows, orders ...

On one side the new schoolmaster, Herman Paskij, was sitting with a little class of children in the shade.

Secretary Jongmeyer approached her. They were saying he'd already fathered a whole bunch of children with slave girls ...

'Good afternoon, Juffrouw Van Meerhoff.'

'I need to speak to the Commander urgently, Mynheer.'

He nodded his head in the direction of the nearest outbuilding.

The shutters were open, there was a hole in the leaf-roof; if it rained, it would leak on to the table Lamotius was sitting at. Piles of paper, inkpot, off-white quill.

Lamotius in the same clothes she'd seen him in last time. His hands covered in burn scars.

All at once it occurred to her that there was a person living inside you. One day it wasn't the same person any more. As though a stranger had moved in.

The trembling started in her legs ...

No greeting. Just his eyes full of derision or disgust – something. Hate.

'What do you want?' Curt. Rude.

'Mynheer Borms is not raising my little brother properly. He beats him and makes him sleep under a bush.' I didn't want to complain, at least my brother isn't a burnt-out wreck …

'Granted that he be placed in the care of Cooper Zaaijman and his sister.' He rattled it off, indifferent. 'As an apprentice cooper and under thorough supervision.'

'Thank you, Mynheer Commander.' She couldn't believe it.

'Dismissed.'

Daniel himself went to fetch him from Bart Borms.

And after supper he read to her and Salomon and the slaves from the Bible about the prodigal son, and prayed from the book of Home Sermons: *'… for Thou, O Lord, hast commanded us to call upon Thee in all our need, and from out the depths of Thy unspeakable mercy … '*

'He'll need other clothes,' Anna interrupted.

'Silence!' Daniel snapped at her angrily, and continued. *'… from out the depths of Thy unspeakable mercy hast Thou promised to hear our prayers, not for our deserving but for the righteousness of our Lord Jesus Christ. For this reason we forsake all other help and succour …'*

'And better manners, too. Look how rudely he eats, look how badly he's sitting on the chair!' Anna chipped in again.

Daniel was furious. She, Pieternella, had a loud fit of coughing so he wouldn't notice that she was trying not to laugh!

He wasn't stupid, though. 'Your lack of respect, the pair of you, is an insult to God that I will not countenance in my house!'

'Yes, Master.'

'Sorry, Daniel.'

Salomon just slouched down even further in his chair, his voice barely audible as he recited the Our Father with them.

But as the days and weeks went by, Salomon straightened up more and more.

'He's clever and he's got a feel for wood,' Daniel said contentedly. 'Most cooper's apprentices take seven years to qualify – Salomon ought to do it in five.'

Like a shoot sending out new leaves. Salomon. Sometimes, when she and Anna were washing sago, or twisting rope, or teasing out coir for the lean-to, he would stand chipping away at a stave on the block. 'I'm telling you, you should look at a tree differently. You *see* the staves in the branches before you even start whetting your axes and saws. Daniel can see a whole barrel in a tree.'

'And I can see trouble if you don't wear your apron the way the master showed you!' Anna scolded.

'The apron's too hot.'

'Apron protects your clothes!'

They were constantly at each other.

'Liverwood. Daniel says Master Sven says that of all the woods on the island it's the nearest to oak. The Commander has had notices nailed up that nobody may use liverwood for fires.'

Salomon, the cooper's apprentice, at peace; he'd arranged the years ahead of him in neat rows, working out how long it would be before he could return to the Cape.

'By that time you might even want to stay on Mauritius,' gingerly broaching the possibility.

'No. This is not my home, Pieternella.'

Daniel's yard was a happy place. Daniel's yard was very often the place where the discontented came to grumble …

An angry Tant Theuntjie reproached him because an ungrateful wretch had left Oom Bart in the lurch and *she* was the one who had to stop him from swapping Katriena for a male slave.

Grieta came crying whenever Willem had beaten her. Anna brought vinegar cloths for her bruises and brazenly asked Grieta: What were you getting up to in the forest with Abraham Steen?

'Pieternella,' Grieta warned her one morning, 'this stupid slave of yours is going to stab herself in the back one of these days!'

Tant Maijke had leave from the Commander himself to come down to the river mouth on the *Europa* once every four weeks to visit Cornelia. She usually called in on her and Daniel as well. 'Our Commander's heart is bleeding to death and mine along with his. Why didn't God rather release me from this hellhole and spare Juffrouw Margaretha and the child?'

Daniel flew at her: 'Because we cannot fathom the mysteries of God and it's not up to us to question His ways! Or call His creation a hellhole when we're the ones that actually belong in hell.'

'You rat! I will not be spoken to like that!'

She stepped in: 'Just let it go, Tant Maijke.' Daniel had gone back to the garden. 'Everyone says things will be better once we're under the new governor at the Cape.'

'What do *you* know? Putting on airs since you've married Daniel, are you - I see you even piss in a porcelain pisspot now!' Anna had just come in from the privy, carrying the pretty chamber pot Daniel had bought from the English. 'But I'll tell you something: even if you piss in a gold pot, you'll still be a half-caste Hottentot, Pieternella Evas!'

'At least my mother was never banished to Mauritius.'

'You rat of a rat!'

After that Tant Maijke stayed away for a good long while.

Sometimes Willem van Deventer's Maria came. 'Willem is with Bart. He says if Lamotius won't let them move to Batavia, he will regret it.'

'Daniel says wheat won't do on the island, there's too much moisture in the air.'

'Willem hasn't got a single seed in the soil. He says Lamotius isn't going to tell him where to seek his salvation, he'll find it for himself.'

'How's Annie Bruyns?'

'Lamotius had her tied up at the lodge on the Flats, with the cows. Half the butter goes to the lower Lodge and half to the lodge on the Flats. The Sergeant says the last time he tasted such golden yellow butter was in the fatherland. The cows yield much more milk here than at the Cape. Probably because they're wild cows caught in the forest.' Maria was speaking faster and faster. 'Don't tell Daniel but Maijke has also had two cows caught and tamed. The Sergeant hasn't noticed that Annie is making extra butter. Jan Muur who lives somewhere on the other side of the island buys from Maijke. They say he supplies pirates. If Lamotius hears that, there'll be war.'

'By this time, Pietertjie must be with her granny and grandpa.'

'Yes.'

'Do you still hanker after the Cape, Maria?'

'Every day. And you?'

'No. *This* is my home now.'

'Daniel is good to you.'

'Yes.'

'I see Salomon is also here. Bart says he sacked him because he wouldn't work. I told myself I didn't believe it.'

'What you told yourself was right.'

She waited till the new year before she told Daniel she was pregnant again. He was pleased.

She didn't tell him about Anna who'd been in one of her strange moods the previous afternoon when she came down to her and Catharinatjie at the river. When it was very hot in the afternoon, she always went down to the river to play with the child.

354

'It's not far now.'

'What's not far?'

'Ship.'

'From which side?'

'Same side, same ship.'

'The *Boode*?'

'Yes. Shadow starting to fall.'

'It can't be the *Boode*. It's only February, barely half a year since it left.'

'Anna says. And Anna says it's going to be another little girl.'

'How do you know I'm pregnant?' Not even Daniel knew yet. The baby inside her was *her* secret! Her apple-blossom secret that nobody was allowed to know about! Not yet. 'How do you know, Anna? How did you know about the ship and the cyclone, how do you know everything?'

'Anna doesn't read in the book, Anna reads in the sky.'

'What else do you know?'

'That our salt barrel is empty and the supply store at the Lodge went up in flames.'

They were having lunch when the soldier arrived to say the *Boode* was out beyond the reef, asking for a pilot. Would Daniel please come immediately.

'That means Sven isn't on board,' he said and got up from the table.

And nor were the saw-blades.

What there were, were two domes and the coils for Jan Harmens's still, and a hand-mill for the Flats for milling sugar cane so that plenty of cane arrack could be distilled.

No, not for the Flats, the Commander decided. The best would be to mill the cane for the sap down at the Lodge; he was himself was the most competent distiller of arrack on the island.

'Enough will have to be distilled for us to send to the Cape to earn some income. Urgently. Till we have sufficient wood ready.'

If only there were more stills … If only the sawmill were running again …

The *Boode* meant news from the Cape.

Yes, the new governor at the Cape had been there since October. Simon van der Stel. He was actually the Commandeur.

An elegant man. And, yes, he remembered his childhood years on Mauritius very well, the frightful cyclones. He was expecting great prosperity from its ebony and enough wheat to support the Cape.

Captain Wobma, but not Maria. First Mate Berks, but a new cooper who asked on his arrival if his old friend Willem van der Hoeven was still on the island.

Lubbert was still the Second Mate.

No, the skipper and his officers would not take up residence in that shack of a Lodge, as had been the practice so far, they would stay on board the ship.

Daniel had to go aboard urgently to help with the barrels.

Supplies of rice, flour, salt, linen goods, sail cloth, dress material, nutmeg, cloves, pepper. Pewterware. There was still no porcelain to spare at the Cape. Cotton cloth for the church's ceiling, though services were still being held outside under the trees while new pews and things were being made. The Bible had also been destroyed in the fire but fortunately there was an extra one in the lodge on the Flats.

She took the ox and went to buy provisions; the salt was urgent.

'And you don't lift the stuff yourself, Juffrouw,' Anna cautioned. 'Ask someone else to load up the ox.'

'I will.' Salomon had left with Daniel well before dawn. Thomas was in the garden. 'Take good care of Catharinatjie.'

'I always do.'

In her prettiest green shift with the ox and the *caroo-coo-coo* doves and the silly little green-bodied birds, the butterflies and the forest and the river – the whole earth just for her.

Beyond the ford Oom Bart and Tant Theuntjie caught up with her and the ox, greeted stiffly and went on ahead.

She didn't let it upset her.

Daniel said the *Boode* had brought all the parts for a large boat for the island. The best man to assemble them was Bart Borms – if he and Lamotius could reach agreement on a price. One was offering too little, the other was demanding too much – plus a Company slave to help him.

The new supply shed was a new outbuilding behind the new Lodge. Oom Laurens Gabrielse heard from Jongmeyer that Lamotius had only one small, sparsely furnished room, barely enough to move about in, and that he would not allow anyone into it. Not even the slave woman who was supposed to keep it tidy.

She tethered the ox under a tree.

'Salt is a problem, Juffrouw Pieternella,' the sailor on duty in the shed told her. 'Van der Stel has sent word that we have to be frugal in the way we dispense it. The free-burghers at the Cape are no longer permitted to scrape up and waste it at will; salt now has to be collected for export to the fatherland and Batavia.'

'How can we get by without salt?'

'The *Boode* has at least brought enough for the moment. Probably took into account the fire damage and all. Free-burghers at the Cape are annoyed with Van der Stel; they now need permits to scrape up salt – for every load they take for their own use, they have to deliver two to the Company.'

'I need flour as well.'

'What about pepper?'

'No thanks.' Daniel had got some from the English. 'If you could just load up the ox for me ...'

All at once he looked past her. When she turned round, there was Lubbert. 'It will be a pleasure to help load up your ox,' he said generously and laughed aloud.

I'm no longer afraid of you, Lubbert. 'I have not asked you to trouble yourself on my behalf, Mr Second Mate. Seaman Cornelis will assist me.'

'Still just as pretty and quick-witted as ever!' he said and winked at the sailor. 'I've known her since before she even had bumfluff. Bring out the stuff.'

Pig! 'I'll manage by myself.' The sailor was scared of him, you could see. 'Or my husband can come and fetch the goods.' She wanted to escape from the shed.

'Daniel's not going to come ashore before dark.' He half sang the words as he helped to lift the sack of salt on to the sailor's back.

Something about the man made her uneasy. Outside, between the shed and the Lodge, a slave woman was sweeping. A little way away were Schoolmaster Paskij and the children. A slave was tarring the new flagpole ...

'Are you walking back to the Orange Tree Flats alone with the ox?'

'That's none of your business.' Don't let him see you're scared! The sailor was on his way with the wheat flour.

'Of course it's my business if a pretty piece of woman-flesh goes walking through the forest alone with an ox and I don't go along with her! Is Grieta still living up there?'

'She and her husband.' She saw her rescue come walking out of the Lodge with a bundle of papers in his hand. Lamotius. Without looking up. In the same clothes.

Lubbert was under the tree with the ox.

'Commander?' She walked straight in front of him and stopped. He looked up, disturbed; annoyance rose into his dead eyes immediately when he saw her. 'Commander, please ...'

'What is it, Pieternella?' Impatiently.

'Second Mate Lubbert is harassing me improperly. Please say he is not to follow me home.'

Lubbert swaggered up. 'She's making it up, Commander, she expressly invited me.'

'That's untrue!' she cried. 'I swear that's untrue!' As if pleading with him to believe her.

He did. 'Take the ox and go home, Pieternella. He won't follow you.' Curt. While Lubbert strolled off nonchalantly towards the seashore.

'Thank you, Commander. Thank you. And I am so terribly sorry about Juffrouw Margaretha and Andrea.' She wanted to lay the words at his feet, put out a hand and touch him, but he was too numb and the hate in his eyes was too strong.

A light-hearted Grieta came walking across the yard that same afternoon, wearing a new red dress with a black underdress, a red cap with an entire necklace of pearls sewn on round the edges.

'Doesn't the island just feel a little more cheerful to you, too, when a ship calls, Pieternella?' she asked gaily and sank down at the table in the sitting room.

'Daniel says it at least shows they haven't completely forgotten about us.' Pieternella was washing butter while Anna was in the kitchen baking sweet biscuits. Catharinatjie had discovered that she could climb and roll about on the kegs under the table.

'I hope he's right. Actually, I just came over to hear how you are – people gossip so, they say Daniel keeps you shut away.'

'That's not true. Daniel is a good man.'

'Willem van der Hoeven was also a good man when I married him. Men, Pieternella, are only lively while there is lust in their breeches – but they soon go limp once they've got you. You'll see.'

'Daniel says the *Boode*'s cooper is an old friend of Willem's.'

'Rik Oosthuizen. Known each other since they were in the fatherland, suffered together before the mast on the way East. Don't know what possessed Willem to get off here and become a free-burgher. There's Rik today, *behind* the mast and an important man.'

'I'm glad Daniel's not on the sea.'

'Every time I come here you've got new things – I see you've even got a wall hanging like Tant Theuntjie!'

'Mine is seamless, made entirely of knotted yarn, not cut and hemmed.'

The English women had given it to her; they said it was actually a French cloth.

'Never mind. Willem is turning a second roll of tobacco on the poles. Rik says it is now expressly forbidden for anyone to plant any tobacco at all at the Cape; it seems the Hottentots have learnt to plant it and now exchange it among themselves. Willem's got two barrels of dried beans ready, too. Van der Stel is a Mauritius man, people are hopeful, everyone is hurrying to get their tobacco and beans ready to deliver to the Lodge. It's only Lamotius who's getting more and more difficult. You can understand it, but the man can't carry on like this. They say he's like a lion with his paw in a trap; he and the new Secunde have almost come to blows. It seems Renier won't sign for the books.'

'The Commander looks really bad. He must be missing Juffrouw Margaretha terribly.'

'Rik says Van der Stel arrived at the Cape with *five* children but no wife. Brought his wife's *sister* along. What does that tell you?'

'Perhaps his wife also died.' Whenever Grieta threw back her head to laugh you could see her little tongue.

'His wife is as well as you and me, Pieternella. Johanna Six is her name; he left her, just like that, in the fatherland. Rik says the man has the attitude of a king; people are cautious, they talk behind cupped hands. His mother-in-law took him to court in the fatherland for kicking and beating her daughter and hurling her to the ground. I told Willem: His day's coming!'

'But you say he brought his wife's sister with him. How did the mother-in-law let that happen?'

'No, that I couldn't say.'

'Daniel says everyone's got a thorn festering in his flesh somewhere – it just depends on how well you hide it so nobody else notices.'

'That Daniel has become awfully good since his marriage! I'd like to know what thorn is festering in *his* flesh!'

She asked him that night. He was playing with Catharinatjie on the bed, Salomon had already gone to his room; the slaves to theirs. She was putting on her nightdress.

'Fear that I'll get home and find that something has happened to you and the child,' he replied.

'Nothing will happen to us.'

'You must let me get rid of Anna. I'm telling you, in *her* there's a pole festering, not a thorn.'

'Leave Anna alone.' She tried to put Catharinatjie down in her cradle but the child wanted to go on playing.

'And you, my love? What thorn is festering in *your* flesh?' Suddenly Daniel had become serious, concerned. 'You're always cheerful and content.'

'I am.'

'Yet there is still sometimes a worry in your eyes that makes me uneasy.'

'You're the one who says each of us hides his thorn so nobody else should know.'

'Do you want to go back to the Cape?'

'No.' He kept asking that.

'Well, what then?' Asking so nicely.

'I can't tell you.' She had to distract him, but didn't know how. 'I think the child should go to bed ...'

'Put the thorn in *my* flesh, Pieternella, let me fester it out for you.'

She went and stood at the table with her back turned so he couldn't see she was crying. But he came and stood behind her.

'Pieternella?' Tight up against her, his arms wrapped round her.

'I'm afraid I might have a Hottentot baby and you won't want the child.'

15

Deep into March and the *Boode* was ready to sail again.

Lime, tobacco, dried beans, a small load of ebony, a little ambergris – a broken still. Salted meat, salted fish, enough for the homeward voyage. Cabbages, onions, carrots, sweet potatoes.

On the Sunday Secunde Drijver and Secretary Jongmeyer conducted the customary prayers for the *Boode* and its return voyage. Also the farewell dinner that followed.

The Commander was not well.

But there wasn't enough wind to get the *Boode* out to sea.

Nor on the Monday. Woodgoose couldn't breathe.

Stiflingly hot.

Daniel came home from the ship saying the Cooper had invited him and her and his friend Willem and Willem's Grieta to have supper on board that evening.

Salomon had to bring in his mattress and sleep in the house with Catharinatjie.

Grieta arrived at the quay dressed up in her new red gown, her eyes shining and a bloom on her cheeks. Willem was dour. Daniel said the weight of four in the sampan was rather too much when there was no wind to fill the sail but with his powerful arms poling them he still managed to wiggle-waggle it across the flat silver water as the full moon rose behind the *Boode*'s masts and rigging ...

Deep within her she felt the stirring of the resentment she had felt another time when she was taken to the same ship. She with her bundles and Tant Maijke and Maria and the children and Tant Theuntjie.

She hastily banished the thought. Then everything had been dark, now all was light.

Right up to the ship, to where the lifeboat was floating, tethered like a calf beside a cow, at the side where the rope ladder hung down.

An old picture: Tant Maijke with her legs astride the water ... New picture: Grieta with her legs astride the water as her weight pushed the sampan away from under her.

'What are you laughing at?' Grieta demanded, annoyed, clinging to the ladder.

'Your turn, my love. Careful now.'

Like turning round and walking backwards ...

Except that this time there were three frightened calves and a half-grown pig in the slatted pen, not sheep or peacocks or fowls.

Like remembering an old dream. Wooden grid on the water hatch ... they beat him to death ... jackal-haired man ... 'D'ye want some nice cock, girl?' The foul-mouthed sailor among other figures on the foredeck. Bits of the same dream.

'Pieternella?' Daniel called out anxiously.

'I'm coming.'

The door to the stateroom on the stern was open; from either side of the narrow passage came the ghosts, clutching her with cold hands. Juffrouw Margaretha, the little doll, Anthonie.

The same glass-fronted cupboard.

Captain Wobma ... First Mate Berks ... Old ghosts.

The freckle-faced cabin boy was laying the table.

'How does it feel to be back on board the *Boode* after all this time?' asked Captain Wobma, sitting down beside her on the cushioned seat under the rear window.

'Good, and also not good, Skipper.'

'I can believe it. I felt very sorry for you on the voyage here.'

You didn't show it or say so. 'Is Maria well?'

'Yes.'

'And her mother, Barbara Geens?'

'Also. Daniel says Salomon is with you now?'

'Yes. It's better this way.'

'Smart youngster. He came on board with Daniel a couple of times.' He got up and walked towards his cabin.

Moments later Lubbert came down the companionway from the poop deck. Silk shirt with pleated sleeves, brown breeches, white stockings, shining brown shoes with black bows. He gave Grieta a quick pinch on the bottom as he made his way to Willem and Daniel and the ship's cooper, drinking wine on the other side of the table.

'Aha, Cooper Zaaijman! Not often we see you aboard in free-burgher garb!' was Lubbert's greeting. 'Evening, Willem van der Hoeven, not every day we have you and your wife on board ship either!' He poured himself a glass of wine and tossed it back. Poured another. Turned round and came towards her. Daniel was watching him. 'Well, well, well – and that's how life makes fools of us all!' he said and stopped in front of her. 'First smothers us down in the steerage hold, shoves us up to the stateroom for a bit to give us a taste for the finer things, and then drops us back into the hold.'

'Go away.'

'And here, believe it or not, sits Pieternella of the Cape, back in the stateroom! Let me take you down below and show you your old tracks. Come!' He put out his hand and tried to take hers and pull her up.

'No.' She put her hands behind her back.

'Come!' With the stubbornness of a man half drunk.

'Lubbert!' Daniel came and fetched him away.

She wanted to go home.

Roast leg of venison and rice and carrots and cabbage and sweet potatoes and jam pancakes and plenty of wine. Lubbert did not join them at the table. Grieta went out on deck a few times, complaining that she felt faint.

After dinner Willem and First Mate Berks started playing a game on a chequered board; Daniel and Rik went out on deck to smoke their pipes. She and Grieta were left alone.

'If I'd known it was going to be this dull,' said Grieta, 'I wouldn't have come.'

It grew late, the moon was high in the sky. Sailors were lying about all over, fast asleep, or just sitting around. The ones on the watch walked up and down, bored. The calves were bunched up uneasily in one corner of the pen, the pig in the other.

'When can we go home?' she asked Daniel.

'Tell Grieta to call Willem.'

Lubbert stuck his head out through the rear hatch: 'Daniel Zaaijman,' he called, 'come down here and drink a fine French wine with me! And bring the women along.'

'We're going ashore,' Daniel called back gruffly. She was at the starboard side already, above where the rope ladder hung, in a hurry to get home. They still had to cross the water, and then another hour on foot …

All day Anna had had a frown on her face, like someone deeply worried. Eventually she asked her: 'What is it, Anna?'

'I don't know. I just feel jittery?'

All at once she, too, felt 'jittery'. Grieta and Willem came out from under the poop deck, said goodbye to Rik and walked across the deck with Daniel.

But then Lubbert suddenly emerged above the hatch and stood in Daniel's way. 'Where are you all? I invite you, and I wait and I wait!' Thick words, wine words. Quarrelsome-words. She walked back across the deck to Daniel; some of the sailors were getting up. 'Lubbert won't let any cooper make a fool of him! Lubbert will take you by the scruff of your neck and throw you down the hatch!'

She had learnt long since not to take fright at a drunk. It was clear moonlight on deck. Lubbert's chest was bare; he was still wearing his stockings, but not his shoes. He took a step closer to Daniel, glaring at him.

'If you want to fight, Lubbert,' Daniel warned him grimly, 'come ashore where shipboard laws don't tie my hands and where you can't order me about.'

More sailors had got up anxiously. As though holding their breath. The only sound came from the waves breaking on the reef at high tide.

Then Lubbert yelled: 'You filthy dog, I'm not going to be threatened or challenged by a cooper!' He called the mate's boy: 'Boy, go and whet my knife and whet it fine!' He was out of his mind! His hands shot down to the two buttons on the flap of his breeches, undid them and shamelessly jerked his manhood through the fly, so that it hung out like a thick round tortoise tongue.

'Get into the sampan!' Daniel called over his shoulder to her and Grieta and Willem. There were sailors everywhere.

Then Lubbert uttered the most disgusting laugh, took his manhood in his hand and roared across the deck: 'Look at this, Daniel Zaaijman! Three times tonight I fucked your wife on my bunk with it!'

At that Daniel tore his cap off his head, ripped it in two and threw one piece down at Lubbert's feet. 'Bring that to me on land.'

She threw up over the side of the sampan.

Halfway to the shore the ship's lifeboat with Lubbert and two oarsmen came after them.

'Please, Daniel, I beg you!'

Willem van der Hoeven also pleaded. 'Lubbert is a swine, Daniel, he's off his head! You've got to stop him.'

They moored the sampan beside the quay and hurried off towards the Lodge. Lubbert came after them, shouting in the moonlight, brandishing his knife in the air. 'Daniel Zaaijman, your hour has come! You pig, your death is at your heels! Here, take your piece of lice-ridden cap, I'm not afraid of you!'

Her heart was hammering in her head. Daniel shouted to Willem to take her and Grieta home; she jumped aside and picked up a stick lying beside the bell-frame. Someone came out of the Lodge with a lantern ...

'Lubbert!' Daniel called out. 'You don't mean what you're doing, you're drunk.'

'You're scared, you pig!' Lubbert stopped in front of him, out of breath, still brandishing the knife above his head.

'No. But I don't want to fight with knives, I'll pleasure you with my fists.'

A second lantern was coming down from the Lodge. Lubbert lunged at Daniel, wounding him in the arm as he tried to ward off the blow. When Daniel's hand reached into his belt for his own knife, she screamed, trying to stop him.

'Lubbert,' shouted Daniel, 'I'm asking you one last time. Show some consideration for my pregnant wife – you're drunk!'

At that Lubbert sliced Daniel from high up on the chest down to his belly. She began blindly beating with the stick and screaming: 'What are you doing? What are you doing?'

'I'm going to kill him!'

In the moonlight blood is black.

Blood shining in the moonlight.

Daniel's knife was a flash of silver lightning. First he sliced Lubbert across the chest, then in the face, then under the right arm ...

A pitch-black stream.

Then they both collapsed.

Hands held the lanterns high for the Surgeon. Other hands wrapped a quilt round her shoulders.

The patch under Lubbert became a big black shadow. Somebody said he was dead.

At first light two soldiers carried Daniel home on a canvas stretcher and laid him down on Salomon's bed in the cottage.

Anna put 'strong-soup' on to boil and went off into the forest to pick pain-foil and brew it.

Laurens Gabrielse and Tant Magdalena came, Willem and Grieta, Oom Bart and Tant Theuntjie, Cornelia and Tant Maijke, Focke and his wife.

Like a funeral.

She, Pieternella, was like the long-legged water-boatmen running on the still-water pools in the river – she knew that if she stopped she'd sink, because inside her there was defiance ready to boil over. Rage. Disillusionment. Confusion.

'What are you looking at me like that for?' she snapped at Anna on the third or fourth day. They had just finished cleaning and dressing Daniel's wounds, washing him, turning him, changing his bedding.

'A little way farther into the island there's a hole in the ground,' Anna said. 'Big hole. They say there was a fire raging in the island's insides and one day it blew a hole in its body.'

'I'm worried about my husband, I don't want to listen to stories!'

'They chase deer over the edge of the hole with dogs so they fall over and kill themselves or break their legs. It saves lead and balls. They slaughter and skin them right there at the bottom of the slope. It's called the Deer Hole. A smouldering fire, Juffrouw Pieternella, sometimes breaks out in an ugly way.'

She waited till he was strong enough to walk to the lean-to and sit down there.

Salomon had gone out to cut wood for staves, Thomas was in the garden, she'd sent Anna to play with Catharinatjie down at the river.

It was no longer a fire inside her, it was a fruit ripe for the picking.

'Those words that Lubbert shouted are hanging like a stinking cloud all round me, Daniel! Grieta says every sailor on board the *Boode* has brought them ashore with him.'

'That grieves me, Pieternella, because that is something you haven't deserved.'

'How do you know?'

'I know. I know his kind. His only power is in showing off – particularly in front of common sailors.'

'Tant Barbara Geens once said every man's got a pike in his breeches and a woman is only what she's got between her legs. I look around me and, more and more, I see that it's true.'

'Pieternella …'

'It's my turn to talk, Daniel! They say Lamotius and Abraham Steen are now taking turns with Grieta. I weep for Juffrouw Margaretha and I hope she went down into her grave without knowing what she really was.'

'Pieternella, my love …'

'And I'm glad that I'm not in *my* grave without knowing it!'

'You're wandering, Pieternella. And if you wander long enough you get lost.'

'I'm not any man's pike-hole! Not even yours.'

'You're not that to me.'

'I'm not!'

'I know that, Pieternella. Believe me. God created the man as he is; and the woman as a helpmeet. If you think Grieta can remove Lamotius's grief, you're stupid. If you think I killed a man to save my own honour, you're even stupider.'

'Why did you marry me?'

'Because I wanted you for myself. Salomon's got to move back down to the cottage before sundown, from tonight I'm sleeping in my own bed.'

'Who am I?' She wouldn't let go.

'You're the lovely mother of my lovely child – and, God knows, I love you and long for the day when you will say you love me, too.'

The island Council found Daniel not guilty of murder.

16

The Sunday after that was the first when they could walk to church again.

As they crossed the Molens River bridge, they stopped in amazement for behind the reef was a three-masted ship sailing neatly through the gap without any sign of a pilot boat. Everywhere from the Lodge to the waterfront the other churchgoers were standing about in astonishment looking out over the water.

'If that isn't Sven Telleson piloting that ship, it's his ghost!' laughed Daniel.

A Dutch ship, a little bigger than the *Boode*. No greater surprise could have come up out of the sea that Sunday morning!

'It's not every day that we have two ships from the Cape come calling in the same month!' remarked Henk Karseboom.

The ship was through the Gap and the first land boat was on its way to the anchorage. The bell hadn't rung for the start of the church service, but it did ring for Jongmeyer to announce in a loud voice that the start of the service would be delayed by one hour because the Commander needed to be on the quay.

The *Quartel*. She remembered the ship; it had always called at the Cape with the fleet. The *Quartel*, whose skipper had once sold the two Robben Island chameleons to Abraham van Riebeeck and told him they lived on air!

In the first boat were an unfamiliar skipper, the coffer of money, the First Mate, Sven Telleson and a rather stout young woman in a black dress.

'I know her,' she whispered to Daniel, 'but I've forgotten her name.'

Magriet Ringels.

The wife that Master Sven had married at the Cape. Who was sitting as if stupefied on a log under a tree beside her two bundles, the forepeak of her cap completely off-centre. Fat red cheeks. Pale yellowish hair.

'Pieternella Evas!' Like one crying for help, when she looked up and saw *her* standing in front of her.

'Magriet Ringels, isn't it?' What could have possessed Master Sven? Her front teeth had rotted away.

'Jacobus sends his love, he says Salomon must think twice before he goes back to the Cape. The earth won't keep still under my feet!'

'Never mind, it will soon come right.'

'Gawd, Pieternella, you looking fine! Sven says you married, too. Have you got fat or are you preggenanting?'

'Pregnant. But why are you sitting here all alone?' Sven and Daniel were in the Lodge with the Commander and the others.

'They still got to give us a room. You still remember me, Pieternella? Our place was behind the cattle kraal.'

'I remember, Magriet. Your father was the Company's ditch-digger.' Mynheer Van der Byl used to say that nobody else could dig ditches without their sides caving in like Joachim Ringels.

'Dad bein' moved to Batavia now, we got too poor. We got caught in a terrible storm at sea, I'm purple with bruises. I dunno where I am, Pieternella.' Pleading.

'Don't worry, I'll get my husband to explain to you nicely.' Was Master Sven out of his mind? 'Once you've got a room and you can unpack your things, you'll feel better.'

'I'm so thirsty.'

'Where's your mug? The spring is nearby.'

She took out a mug and picked up her bundles to take them along. 'Leave them, just bring the mug.'

'No. Hottentots'll snatch them too quick.'

'There aren't any Hottentots here.'

'What happen to them?'

'This isn't their home.' Magriet drank like a thirsty animal. She waited till after the third mugful before she asked: 'Do you know whether Sven has brought back the saw-blades?'

'I only know he bought me a new quilt and he made me stuff a mattress. You got pretty shoes on, Pieternella.'

'Jan Yser is a freelance shoemaker here on the island. He used to work for the Company.'

'Where does Willem van Deventer live, what was married to Maria?'

'A long way from here. On the Flats.'

'Her mother give me a letter from the Cape for her.'

'She'll be very pleased.'

The saw-blades had not come.

There was nobody at the Cape who could cast them. Van der Stel had decided to send them to Batavia to be cast there.

No, not on the *Quartel*. The *Quartel* had to return to the Cape with wood and lime. There was a lot of building going on at the Cape. Robben Island couldn't keep up with the demand for shells.

Two weeks after his return Sven arrived at their home, rolling drunk. ' 'Strue's God, old Daniel, I just don't know any more. Van der Stel sends a letter to Lamotius to say we've got to have the planks cut from at least six hundred ebony tree trunks ready to send back to the Cape on the next supply ship. Seems to me Lamot's head's fallen off; he thinks I can make it happen!'

'It's not the Commander's head that's fallen off, Master Sven, it's *yours*!' She was the one who said it to him. 'Where was your head when you married poor Magriet?'

'In my breeches.'

'That I can believe!'

'If Daniel could just help me out with a small cash loan so I can take better care of her. She's not unwilling.'

One of the Post Holders on Robben Island once told her mother: Eva, the day you climb into a wine bottle is the start of a slow drowning, till you hit the bottom.

She had the feeling that Sven was near hitting the bottom. She wanted to slip her hands in under him, to stop him, to plead on her knees – anything. He was a part of her father – the only one who knew her name.

But once you have climbed into a wine bottle ...

One of the sailors at the Lodge told Salomon that Master Sven was so distracted some days that he would stand on the shore shouting across the water to the sharks in the Gap to enjoy themselves while they could, Sven Telleson was only waiting for them to finish building the new boat ...

The boat Bart Borms was building for the Company at French Church. The old shark boat, the *St Hubert*, was lying crookedly, full of water and half sunk, at one side. Like a dead thing they'd forgotten to bury. The *Europa* was no more than a floating wreck; each time they took it to Groot River and back, they had to pump harder to bale out the water that kept leaking in.

The small quantity of pitch that had come on the *Boode* on its last visit had to be kept for the new boat.

They were loading the *Quartel* for the return voyage to the Cape. Besides the provisions for the return trip, there was a little ambergris, a small amount of ebony. A few rolls of free-burgher tobacco, some barrels of dried beans. Jan Yser's request that his wife and children be sent out from the fatherland because he was now a free shoemaker. Tant Maijke's umpteenth plea to become a free-burgher.

While the baby inside her was growing and growing.

Tant Theuntjie was the first to twist the thorn deeper into her flesh. 'I see you're that way again, Pieternella. How anyone can see their way clear to bringing an extra mouth into the world on this island is quite beyond me. Lamotius is becoming nothing better than a tyrant, has no time or mercy for a free-burgher any more. Overflowing with warmth and friendliness when he got here, now all we hear about is the free-burghers' inability to make the island yield profits for the VOC. Profits out of what? Now there are rumours that the free-burghers will only be allowed to complain at the Lodge on Mondays. What are you going to do if this baby is a little Hottentot?'

'How far has Oom Bart got with the building of the boat?'

'He told Lamot yesterday to stop badgering him and interfering. And payment in cash – not one penny of credit on the account.'

Then it was Tant Maijke's turn.

'I see you've got *another* new dress. Where did you get such pretty material?'

'I've had it a long time, Tant Magdalena made it for me.'

'When is your baby due?'

'In June.'

'What are you going to do if it's a little Hottentot?'

'I hear Master Sven's Magriet is with the Van Deventers on the Flats. So where is Sven?'

'Cutting ebony with the team up on the near side of the Flats. He steals the men's rations and boozes them away, so they drop their axes and come complaining up at the lodge. I told Magriet, I said to her: Just as long as you don't have a baby with him.'

'Poor Magriet.'

'Works like a slave for Willem and Maria in the weeks when Sven can't come. He's borrowed money from Willem. What are you going to do if it's a little Hottentot?'

'Daniel says Hottentots are also God's creatures.'

'Is that in the Bible?'

'You'd better look it up yourself, Tante.'

The 'little Hottentot' was born on the tenth of June.

A fair little Dutch girl that Daniel himself took from Tant Magdalena and wrapped in the swaddling clothes and pinned tight. Himself gave her the name: Eva.

The next day he went out to shoot the pigeons that Anna kept nagging him about for her to make strong-soup with for her, Pieternella. So that Anna would have a chance, as with Catharina, to take the little thing outside and show her to the sun and the island. To greet them.

'The master wouldn't understand.'

'I don't understand either, Anna.'

'Your heart understands.'

The nosy came in droves, to see, to drink Anna's caudle, to admire and then to leave again.

She was out of bed already one morning when Grieta arrived. With two black eyes and all the skin off one of her cheeks.

'Grieta ...'

'There are days when I wish I could stow away on a ship and disappear out of this hell.'

'What did he beat you for this time?' She wanted to hear it from Grieta herself.

'You wouldn't understand. Nobody understands.' She was at the end of her tether, you could see it. 'Everyone has started kicking Lamotius, they don't see that the man is in mourning. They slander him to the Secunde. Things that are supposed to go to the Cape in sealed letters are allowed to blow about all over the place like leaves in the wind.'

'What things?'

'That he, the poor Lamotius, has to make the island yield a profit for the Company with a bunch of lazy, surly free-burghers. Who prefer to go catching cattle in the forest and taming them instead of working their fields. They keep looking out for foreign ships to deliver meat to, but when a Dutch ship arrives, it has to plead for meat.'

'Willem wouldn't have beaten you for that.' Grieta was no longer young, you could see ...

'I just wanted to offer Lamotius some comfort, Pieternella. The island is hatching plots against him.'

'Grieta says the island is hatching plots against Lamotius,' she told Daniel at table that evening.

'The island has hatched plots against every commander, my love.'

'Why?'

'It's human nature to want to have your own way; it's in the nature of commanders to try to keep the Lords Seventeen satisfied by showing a profit, because the profit you show is what gets you promotion. Two rivers in the same watercourse – flowing in different directions.'

Salomon was in his own river. Always on his way back to the Cape. 'We're going to start building the new room tomorrow, Pieternella. Your house is getting too small.' A new room for the two children. 'Daniel says when my first staves are dry he'll buy me my own cooper's axe.'

'Daniel is good to you.'

'And to you, too, Pieternella.'

'I know.'

'Don't you ever long for the Cape any more?'

'No. Do you?' He seemed so happy most of the time.

'It's what I live for.'

Thank God, Daniel was at home and not away 'catching turtles' when the Commander came walking across the yard one morning early in August. Sentry Hans Pigt, musket over his shoulder, a short distance behind.

'Why this honour, Commander?' Daniel enquired.

'Because the Lodge's walls have grown eyes and ears, Cooper. Nothing, it seems, is confidential any more.'

They sat down at the table in the sitting room. She told Anna to boil water for tea, fetch the pretty cups from the shelf and put them on the table. Spread sweet biscuits with some of the fresh butter. No, not just yet, because she overheard Daniel offering the Commander a glass of wine.

Salomon was chipping staves into shape, Catharina was playing with the wood shavings. She, Pieternella, was in the bedroom feeding little Eva, but keeping her ears tuned to what was being said next door because she suddenly felt uneasy.

They were talking about Sven, Lamotius lamenting his decline since his return from the Cape. His equipment – Company equipment – had twice been picked up in the forest where he'd left it lying. Worked for a week, disappeared for a week. Whetted the axes so poorly that before noon there were notches all over them again.

She dried little Eva and laid her in her crib.

'But that's not the reason for my visit, Cooper. The Flats have become our hope of salvation. Sweet potatoes. Plenty of them. Not just as daily fare for the soldiers but sufficient for sweet potato arrack. Plenty of it. This can only happen if I have a responsible man on the Flats to supervise things, to give guidance and set an example to the other free-burghers there. I'll see to it that he gets good land, implements, a few slaves. The only man I have confidence in is Daniel Zaaijman.'

Two steps and she was standing at the table. 'Commander, don't punish me and my children by sending us to the Flats. Please don't.'

He turned round swiftly in his chair and stared at her as if she were some repulsive apparition. Something so far beneath his dignity that he turned back to Daniel. 'You ought to be able to dispose of your land here on the Orange Tree Flats easily enough. The Company will compensate you for the house and outbuildings. Soldier Jacomo Baldini has asked to become a free-burgher and it seems as though even Secretary Jongmeyer is considering going freelance.'

Daniel had a way of frowning and slowly nodding his head like someone giving the impression that he was thinking carefully, while what he was actually doing was playing for time to get himself out of some situation.

They couldn't move to the Flats. It was too far from Black River, too far from French Church where his boat was moored.

'Commander.' She assumed the most obstinate position she could, standing at the table, drawn up to her full height, her hands on her hips. In her most sullen voice: 'Commander, my husband may move to the Flats, but I and my children are staying right here.'

He turned his head away and stared up into the roof. 'Cooper Zaaijman, tell your wife to conduct herself in a calm and proper manner.'

'Pieternella, the Commander has asked you not to interrupt.'

There are words between the words that a man and his wife say to each other and that only they can hear. Eye-words. Because though Daniel's mouth had said the words, his eyes were laughing straight into hers.

'Then kindly inform the good Commander that I will not move to the Flats. Never.' In her loudest voice before she turned and stormed out of the door. She took refuge beside the river till she saw him and Hans Pigt pass by.

Daniel came, a short distance behind them, looking for her. 'I'm afraid Lamotius is furious with you. But I think we're safe. Thank you. It was clever of you.'

'I meant it. I swear. Not just because of Black River, either, but because I'm not prepared to live in Tant Maijke's breathing space, and even less in Willem van Deventer's.'

'Lamotius says Willem has been tamed, he doesn't spend his time causing trouble any more. And Bart Borms has asked yet again to live elsewhere; he will be granted permission - as soon as he's finished building the sloop.'

'Commander's got numb eyes,' Anna remarked without concern that evening as she was laying the supper table. Daniel was busy outside.

'Why do you say that?'

'Lets Hans Pigt walk behind him with a gun, doesn't see Hans Pigt walking with hate in his heart.'

'Why?'

'Maria Mooy isn't allowed to stay with Hans in the Lodge. Has to stay hidden in the forest above Second Bay.'

'Why?'

'Ask.'

'I am asking.'

'When you've been a slave girl in the Lodge and you wouldn't do what they wanted at night, you're marked.'

'Where does Maria Mooy come from?'
'Use your eyes. East.'

A little more than a week later an unfamiliar supply ship arrived from the Cape. The *Baaren*. In her heart she was glad it wasn't the *Boode*.

Strange skipper. Strange Mate. Strange sailors.

A strange despondency that began to wash slowly over the island …

No, the saw-blades had still not come.

No, the still could not be repaired at the Cape, it had also been sent to Batavia.

Commandeur Van der Stel said the Mauritius tobacco was too strong and too bitter on the tongue, Lamotius was not to go to the trouble of sending any more.

'That's a bloody lie!' Gerrit van Ewijk from the Flats came to shout at the Lodge. 'I'll swim to the Cape and tell Van der Stel that to his face!' Fortunately the man contained himself sufficiently not to add that the English ships were keen to buy the 'bitter' Mauritius tobacco.

Lamotius should not send any more dried beans either, the Cape had enough.

'Then I'll swim with you, Van Ewijk,' said Michiel Romondt from the Flats. 'My fields are ripe with the new crop of beans. What am I supposed to live on?'

Ebony. As much as possible was to be sent to the Cape.

And lime.

And Lamotius was to place the most stringent prohibition on rendering any assistance to English or French ships that tried to anchor secretly in the island's bays.

No, the banned Maijke van den Berg could not be granted freedom.

'Oh, my agony, my agony, the darkness just keeps falling and falling all round me,' she wept to Pieternella on her way to visit Cornelia.

'You walked into the darkness yourself, Tante.'

'You miserable little half-caste! No wonder the Commander asked me the other day if you had always been so stubborn!'

'And what did you tell him?'

'I wouldn't laugh if I were you! I told him just how stubborn your mother could get.'

'Leave my mother out of it.'

'I wanted to ask Daniel if he didn't have one or two old barrels to spare, but it seems as if he's never at home any more. Not that I blame him.'

'Our Commander sent for him to go and help the Cooper on the

Baaren.'

The despondency on the island became a near recklessness. Perhaps it was sheer cussedness. Master Sven left his workmen on their own in the forest when the news came that the saw-blades had not arrived, and went off to Jan Harmens's arrack still above the Groot River. Lay there dead drunk for almost a week.

Focke Janse openly sailed his sampan out from the quay at the Lodge and headed southwards to fish out of sight – beyond Vissers Island.

On his return Lamotius had Jongmeyer wait for him to warn him, but Focke simply shrugged his shoulders and packed his catch of steenbras into bags.

Oom Bart went and told Lamotius he wasn't interested in other land if it was being offered him on the Flats, thank you, it was nothing but stones. He would make other arrangements.

The *Baaren* stayed a month.

It was under full sail on the open sea and the land boat that Daniel had taken to pilot it through was on its way back already before Lamotius discovered that Gerrit van Ewijk and Michiel Romondt had gone aboard the night before – as sailors. To go and talk to Van der Stel at the Cape themselves about the tobacco and the beans and the aloofness of the Commander.

She asked Daniel: What's going on?

He said they were like a flock of sheep breaking out of a kraal. How Lamotius was going to get them back into the kraal he didn't know.

Daniel himself was worried, he hadn't heard from Hendrik in months.

Not long afterwards they walked over to visit Laurens Gabrielse and Tant Magdalena one Sunday afternoon. Daniel still owed them for the latest clothes they had made for Salomon.

'The youngster's really shooting up now,' remarked Tant Magdalena.

They were sitting beside the house in the shade, Oom Laurens supporting his head on his hand. 'I'm not one to allow myself to be knocked offbalance over nothing, Daniel, but now the Company is pulling a man's feet out from under him.'

'Lamotius reckons the tobacco planting should continue. The climate is right, the soil is right – he'll see to it himself that the quality improves,' said Daniel.

All at once Tant Magdalena sat up. Willem van Deventer was coming along the footpath in the forest on the other side of the house. 'I don't believe my eyes!' she said. They all watched almost in disbelief as he approached. There was even something of a swagger in his step.

'Hello, hello, hello!' he greeted jovially when he reached them. 'Good to see Orange Tree Flats neighbours enjoying such a happy visit!'

'Which tree did *you* fall out of?' asked Oom Laurens curtly, getting up.

'Aah! I didn't *fall* out, I *jumped* out!'

'If you're wanting to pinch a short cut to Focke's, you may as well turn back. He and his wife have gone to Claas Wieringa at the Lodge.'

'I don't pinch short cuts anywhere, Laurens, I *take* short cuts.' Ha-ha-ha. The fellow was either drunk or spoiling for a fight. 'I'm just taking a look at the countryside round here on your side of the island – to see whether I like it.'

'Like it for what?' asked Daniel.

'For moving here.' He threw the words at their feet, defiantly.

'There isn't any land left here!' cried Tant Magdalena, alarmed.

Oom Laurens made a strange sound in his throat and got up. 'You're out of your mind, Van Deventer!' he said.

'Oh no, I'm not! Bart and I have decided to join forces. To show the whole lot of you how we're going to tame this island. The land across the river from Bart is open. We're going to clear it all for gardens, build a cattle kraal on his side of the river and everything.'

'Does the Commander know about this?' asked Daniel.

He seemed not to hear. Just stood there high-stepping and gesticulating. 'Hunting. Fishing. Salting down meat.'

'Daniel asked you if Lamotius knows about this?' asked Oom Laurens, alarmed.

'Lamotius?' Willem jeered. *'Lamotius?'* Spun round, pulled down his breeches and with his hairy backside pointing straight at them let off a loud fart and cried: 'That's how much notice I take of Lamotius! I fart up his nose!'

'Behave yourself, Willem!' shouted Oom Laurens. 'We don't need to see your arse!'

So he let off a second fart. 'And this one is for Jongmeyer's nose!' he called out and laughed. He was apparently running out of farts because the third one was just a little one. 'And here's one for the Secunde!'

He pulled up his breeches.

'You disgusting thing!' Tant Magdalena shouted at him. 'I shall see to it that the Commander hears about this! Tomorrow.'

'And what will you take as proof?' Willem taunted her. 'I'll simply say you're lying. That you're all lying!'

Tant Magdalena said she'd been to the Lodge shortly before noon to lay
a charge against Willem.

She met Jongmeyer in the passage, he said Commander Lamotius
would unfortunately not be able to see her; Willem van Deventer and
Bart Borms were consulting him on an important matter.

Their goods began arriving early in December.

Willem, Maria and the two children. Sven's Magriet. Furniture in among
the trees under sheets of canvas while Willem and Oom Bart knocked
together a one-roomed house and raised a stone kitchen with a room at
the side for Magriet and Sven.

A hutch of planks for Willem's slave.

Plus the twelve oxen and ten cows that Lamotius had granted them.
And a plough. Because they'd been allowed to join forces provided they
devoted themselves to planting wheat. Van der Stel urgently wanted
wheat.

On the second day, Magriet arrived to see her and Daniel.

'We neighbours now, Pieternella,' said Magriet, coming into the
bedroom where she was breastfeeding little Eva. 'I'm so glad.'

'Where's Master Sven?'

'Cutting wood in the Bamboo Mountains. Till the sawmill can saw,
they goin' to load the logs on to the ships just like that. He says the Cape
and the Lords Seventeen can go piss theirselves.'

'Are you happy on the island, Magriet?'

'I dunno. When's it goin' to get colder?'

'It never really gets cold here.' Magriet was on the sponge, you could
smell it. 'You must rinse your sponge regularly, Magriet.'

'Is jus' a little.'

'That doesn't matter. And I want to know from you why you're living
with the Van Deventers?'

'Where else?'

'Master Sven's got a room at the Lodge.'

'The Commander's very nasty to him. Says Sven's worthless since he
came back from the Cape. Me and Maria's maybe goin' to make butter
and cheese.'

'That will be good.'

'And you got pretty children, Pieternella. Tant Theuntjie says thanks
God they both white and Willem says I mus' ask haven' you got a pair of
old shoes for me.'

She gave Magriet the shoes when she left.

Anna was sitting under the lean-to teasing out coir; Catharina had her own little pile. Salomon was busy on the staves. Daniel and Thomas were in the garden.

Something was different. It was in the air. An uneasiness.

And as though Anna could see inside her head, she looked up and said: 'Won't be the same any more.'

'What do you mean, Anna?'

'Orange Tree Flats. The rats have moved in – wearing clothes.'

∾ THREE ∾

1

Three strange years.

One morning the Commander sent a soldier to summon her. He wanted to see her.

'Why?'

'I don't know, Juffrouw Pieternella, but I wouldn't keep him waiting.'

Lamotius could wait. 'I'll come tomorrow. I'm having trouble with my new slave woman, my children can't get used to her.'

At Lamotius's request Daniel had gone to the Groot River with Wieringa to look for the best place to build a bridge across the river. Urgently. The head gardener at the Lodge had tried to take a short cut to the Flats by swimming across the river below the waterfall and had drowned. Barely a year later Jongmeyer was trying to cross on the stones above the falls when his feet slipped and he plunged into the roaring water and eternity.

Leaving behind him slave girls with seven little orphans. So they said.

'Don't join in the gossip, my love,' Daniel cautioned. 'We live our own lives, that's our only hope.'

On the afternoon after Jongmeyer's funeral Grieta said: 'Daniel, I'm getting frightened. That mad slave of Pieternella's once said this island was going to flatten us all yet – I think it's starting to happen.'

Anna didn't say the island was going to flatten everybody, what she said was: You all just trample and trample, you don't think about the day when the island will be angry enough to start hitting back. She stood in the doorway and said it one day when Grieta was sitting at the table, telling how Willem van der Hoeven had come across the severed heads of four dumbclucks and seven tortoises that had been chopped open. North of the Groot River. He and Henk Karseboom were walking along the shore in search of ambergris when he, Van der Hoeven, had to turn inland to the Flats to try to find some extra food. That's when he came across the things.

And while he was gone, Henk Karseboom found a massive lump of ambergris, but Lamotius said the price was down and gave him only five bottles of brandy for it.

Drank for days. Master Sven along with them.

This was shortly before Sven disappeared into the forest and Lamotius and his bodyguard Hans Pigt arrived on horseback in search of him.

Hardly greeted her.

Said he'd come from Magriet, he needed to speak to Sven urgently. According to Magriet Sven was somewhere in the forest. She never saw him any more, but rumour had it that he was getting food from Daniel's house.

'Is this true, Cooper?'

She got in before Daniel, answering: 'Yes, Commander. I take him food and care for him.' The cold glass eyes seemed to shoot a beam of icy fire at her. 'My slave woman came across his hut by accident. I went and told Magriet I would take her to him but Willem van Deventer forbade her.'

'Why did you not have it reported at the Lodge?'

'Looking for a cudgel to tie round a half-dead dog's neck wouldn't help, Commander. All I've done is see to it that he gets something in his stomach.'

'Cooper ...' Lamotius was angry. 'It is clear that you have no bridle on your wife!'

Daniel lowered his head. 'It's difficult, Commander.'

Sometimes, when it had been raining, it was Daniel who took Sven his food and even fed him when he wouldn't eat on his own.

She had to get Lamotius off Daniel. 'But if you wish me to let Sven die, Commander, I shall stop taking care of him.'

He leapt up and slammed his fist down so hard on the table that the cups rattled in their saucers. 'I did not say that!'

'And I'm not trying to cause more trouble. You have been angry with me for a long time because I wouldn't move to the Flats. You barely greet me at church, and it bothers me every time.' Daniel looked up and indicated with his eyes to her to be quiet.

'Yes. And as a result of your unwillingness, the Flats lie fallow and the stills cry out for sweet potatoes!'

She kept the bridle on her tongue herself. Said nothing about the Cape that kept sending messages that they didn't want beans or tobacco from the Flats or anywhere else. That Lamotius should see to it that Mauritian free-burghers like Michiel Romondt and Gerrit van Ewijk didn't come to the Cape to waste the Commandeur's time and patience with their complaints. If there were complaints, the Commander could transmit them by letter.

Lamotius sank back in his chair, looked her straight in the eye and ordered: 'You will take us to Sven Telleson tomorrow.'

No. She didn't say it aloud.

She hid away when they came. Or had Anna say she wasn't at home.

But Lamotius was too clever for her. When he realised that she didn't want to take them to Sven, he tried a different tack ...

Master Sven was particularly unruly that day.

'How many more times have I got to tell you to leave me alone, Pernilla!'

'Get up! It's dirty under you.'

Where he always managed to get the liquor from she didn't know. Sometimes he disappeared for days on end. At other times he would sit on the stone in front of the hut, surprisingly sober, and even speak to her decently. He asked her one day: Can you at least read and write, Pernilla? Yes, Master Sven. Your dad wrote a very neat hand and read thick books. In Latin, too. They say Lamotius knows Latin – is Lamotius looking for me? Yes, Master Sven. Don't let him find me. No, Master Sven. You're a good child, Pernilla. I'm not a child any more, Master Sven.

The next day he tried to kick her away from the bed. Or sat in front of the hut like someone beyond all hope, a bottle of arrack between his feet, and pleaded with her to leave him alone.

Or quarrelled with God and the Company. 'Think they can frighten me with God!'

'Do you believe in God, Master Sven?'

'Not in *their* God.'

'Is there more than one God?' Sheer impudence.

'What goes on above my head, I don't know. But what goes on around me, I know well, and that is that man, Pernilla – *man* – is God on two legs. Or the devil. Listen to what I'm telling you today.'

'Which one are you, Master Sven: God or the devil?'

'Devil, on days that I get angry. God, on days when I'm good.'

Lamotius had her followed to the hut ...

It was one of those mornings when she had difficulty even getting Master Sven off the bed to put on a clean sheet, a clean pillow slip, to get him outside on to the stone with a napkin round his neck as a bib, to feed him some of Anna's turtle soup, to distract his attention with scraps of news: That Oom Bart had nearly finished the sloop, that they said the boat's name was going to be the *Vanger* so it could catch plenty of sharks. That the teeth of the sharks in the Gap were chattering already at the prospect. That usually got a giggle out of him.

The food was putting a little strength into his body, you could see.

No, the saw-blades had not arrived. Batavia had informed Van der Stel that he would have to order the blades from Holland. The *Baaren* had taken some ebony away, though. And another good quantity of the new season's tobacco. Lamotius reckoned this time the Cape would buy out of sheer astonishment at its fine quality.

What else?

Lamotius was furious with some of the free-burghers. They had quietly stolen down to the *Baaren* and bartered meat for pepper and were selling it to the others for much less than the Company price. Fortunately Lamotius could send soldiers to make them surrender most of the pepper. Now they were complaining that they had been assaulted.

She knew not to mention Magriet because then he would push away her hands in irritation. But he liked hearing about Willem and Bart Borms's joint farming venture. That at the start they had a field ploughed up for wheat by Willem's slave. Or rather the oxen ploughed the field and dragged the slave behind them because the slave had been so badly maltreated he didn't have the strength. That Willem had then gone hunting with the slave somewhere in the forest and come back without the slave. Said the slave ran away. So Oom Bart went and swapped Tant Theuntjie's slave Katriena for Henk Karseboom's Valentyn, but Valentyn couldn't manage the plough either. In the mean time their cattle kept straying on to the Lodge's grazing and Willem and Oom Bart were made to pay fines.

So Willem and Oom Bart waited until the church service one Sunday and then drove every head of cattle, every woman and child to the Lodge, and shouted to Lamotius as he came out of church: We don't want the cattle any more, we can't take care of the women and children any more – you take them!

She didn't mention how Magriet had stood there, crying piteously because she couldn't understand that it was all just a clever ploy.

No, they weren't flogged; the women had gone to plead for them.

What else?

Michiel Romondt and Gerrit van Ewijk came back from the Cape on the *Baaren*. Van der Stel had refused them an audience, he said if there were complaints, Lamotius could send them by letter. He was not to be bothered by free-burghers.

Really?

Yes. And Gerrit van Ewijk is getting married to Jan Harmens's daughter Hester, next Wednesday.

She was wiping his face when the man broke through the undergrowth.

'You bastard!' Sven called out, alarmed. Her whole body began to tremble. It was the new Secunde, the tall one with the red face and red hair. Smartly dressed in black, his big shining shoes smeared with mud.

'Secunde Jacobsen,' he introduced himself in a ponderous voice.

Sven got up slowly. 'May Lamotius drive you into your grave even faster than he did poor Renier Drijver!'

'I suggest that you weigh your words, Telleson,' the man warned.

'And I suggest that you turn round smartly!' Sven returned his enraged reply. 'Because I'm not having you or anyone else in the world commandeer me! I do what I want to and when I want to!'

'Then I charge you to come with me and repeat it to the Commander! Now, immediately!'

'The last commander I took orders from was Hugo! Go and tell Lamotius I wipe my arse on him and I wipe my arse on you, too!'

'I am warning you in all seriousness, Telleson …'

Foam was trickling from the corners of Master Sven's mouth. 'Pernilla,' he shouted abruptly, 'fetch my axe so I can chop this man to pieces!'

'Master Sven, please …' She tried to take his arm but he jerked free and limped up to the man. Shoved his finger almost into his face.

'You tell Lamotius the very next one who tries to commandeer me, I will chop into little pieces and give the devil my soul and body as well!'

Two days later Lamotius had her summoned. He made her stand in front of his table and expressly forbade her to go anywhere near Sven Telleson. The Council had dismissed him.

So she found herself a new way to the hut. One morning when she took some food to him, she found him lying rigid and dead on the leaf mattress.

The last little piece of her dad.

Three strange years.

That sometimes left her with the feeling that only Daniel was still on his feet. That made her cling to him to stop her own knees from buckling under her.

Despite his own despair, poor Lamotius kept on trying harder and harder to get the mutinous sheep back into the kraal. Like Focke who openly sailed out again and again in his sampan to fish out of sight of the Lodge. Eventually Lamotius sent two officials down to the shore to confiscate his sampan. Focke laughed in their faces, saying he hadn't even been afraid of Hugo who was a wealthy pirate and earned more than double Lamotius's wages, so why would he take any notice of a poor bare-arsed commander?

When they started untying his sampan he pulled out his knife and ripped the first one's shirt off his back. When he took a stab at the second one, the man spun round and sped off – with the other one following him.

Grieta came to her and Daniel in tears, saying it was a crying shame the way poor Lamotius was taunted and defied, the man wasn't made of stone! Focke Janse was actually running an illegal tavern in his house; the free-burghers and Company servants were in and out of it day and night.

'Yes,' Daniel said to Grieta and laughed. 'I hear old Maijke's been visiting Cornelia, it seems she's been able to teach Focke a whole lot about crookery.'

'It's not a joke! The Commander has had the place closed down twice, because the Company is losing income, but Focke couldn't care less! Lamotius can't carry on any more. He's already decided to ask for a transfer.'

'That would be a pity. I see there is some good progress in the construction of the new Lodge; at least he would have had a better storage room to keep himself in.'

'Are you mocking or are you pretending to be stupid, Daniel Zaaijman? Can't you see our Commander struggling to breathe? With only fifty Company servants he has to see to all the building, the office work, the felling and sawing, the gardening, the storage, the problems of the Flats, the provision of food, everything! And all the free-burghers do is pick on him.'

'You're right, Grieta,' Daniel said. 'Lamotius is doing his best.'

'And because I, Grieta, extend an honest hand of friendship to him, people make up all kinds of stories about it.'

'But he said if Van der Hoeven beat you again, he would have him locked up.'

Tant Magdalena said Lamotius had caught Abraham Steen with Grieta on the day Willem van der Hoeven went looking for ambergris. The whole of one side of Steen's face was swollen and had been beaten black and blue.

Catharina was four, little Eva two, and she was already heavy with Magdalena when Anna came in one morning later than usual. With a strange unease on her face.

'There was a thing in the sky.'

'What kind of thing?' She steeled herself not to take fright. Anna didn't say things lightly.

'Strange shining stripe where the sun comes up. It's an omen that's been sent.'

'A shining stripe in the sky?'

'Yes. Where it doesn't belong.'

Daniel had been away for almost a month at Northwest Harbour above the Black River; there were three English ships, two of which had to be careened. The third was the *Berkley Castle*, the ship whose chaplain had christened Catharina. She'd begged to go along again, but Daniel was uneasy about taking her in her condition.

She was expecting her second apple-blossom baby.

The previous time she and the two children had gone along when Hendrik came for him. Not for long because there was only one ship. On the return trip they had again spent the night beside the pretty Apple Tree River ...

In the course of the month that Daniel had been away this time he'd sent Hendrik twice to see if everything was still all right at home.

Everything was fine.

Except that she was more uneasy about Daniel. Commandeur Van der Stel had ordered Lamotius to remove all free-burghers from the western side of the island to prevent the English from finding or obtaining any comfort there. Orders from the Lords Seventeen.

'Now what?' she asked Daniel.

'It's going to be a problem. Jan and Jan and Jan walked on foot all the way from Northwest Harbour to the Lodge to ask where they were supposed to make their living then. On the Flats, said Lamotius. Where on the Flats? they wanted to know. The Company already had the best land under palm trees and sweet potatoes.'

But just when everyone thought the storm had blown over, the entire English homeward bound fleet dropped anchor in the bay at Northwest Harbour. The first thing they did was chop down the pole with the Lords Seventeen's sign engraved on the copper plaque on it.

Like a declaration of war. Like announcing: Our ships will rest where they will – chop down palms for wine, shoot deer for meat, chop wood for our fires, cut timber to take home and sell.

By the time the news reached Lamotius, the ships had left with the three Jans' and their friends' tobacco and beans and butter and vegetables – and all Hendrik's ambergris.

Then the thing appeared in the sky.

It had become their custom that when Daniel was away, Salomon would read to her and the slaves after supper, and lead the prayers.

Catharina was sitting on Anna's lap that evening, playing with the string of wooden beads that Daniel had made for her. Salomon read long and attentively; he was developing into an earnest young man. By the time he reached the recitation of the Our Father, Anna and the child were equally fidgety, and at the final words Anna suddenly prayed out louder than everyone:

'... *and lead us not into temptation, but deliver us from evil* – that thing is in the sky again!'

The thing was in the sky again.

Low in the west above the Bamboo Mountains. A star with a long, broad shining tail.

'I think it's a comet,' said Salomon in awe.

Two comets, Lamotius had announced after the lesson in church on Sunday.

'As you will have noticed, there are two comets hanging over us at present. What the melancholy consequences thereof may be we do not know, but they can only call us to humble ourselves before the Almighty Father. I ask you all to bow your heads in deep reverence.' He opened the book and read with great earnestness: '*Almighty and most merciful God, we admit and confess before Thee that we are unworthy even to raise our eyes heavenward and bring our prayers before Thee ... our consciences accuse us, our transgressions bear witness against us ...'*

At the door afterwards Focke Janse declared for all to hear: 'Lamotius couldn't scare us with the devil, so now he's trying to frighten us with the comet!'

It was Daniel's opinion that the Commander was counting the same comet twice: the one in the dawn sky was the same as the one at twilight.

And Anna went on refusing to set foot in the yard before dawn to get to the kitchen. She put the supper on the table long before dusk but refused to wait for Daniel to read and pray. 'Star-thing doesn't see Anna, Anna doesn't see star-thing.'

Daniel laughed, saying: You clod, you forget the thing is moving above our heads all day to appear again at night in the west!

She ran with her hands above her head to her sleeping place, folded her quilt again and again, and put it on her head so that it hung down like a thick roof on either side of her face. 'Star-thing can't see Anna.'

Palm-leaf hats on the children's heads.

The 'melancholy consequences' first appeared on the Flats: a sickness which no one could name. Not even Walrand the Surgeon. First headache, then fever, then stomach trouble.

Nearly twenty officials were laid up at the Lodge. Half the slaves. Old Schoolmaster Steenwyk was the first to die. Then two slaves – one was the chief cook. Then it was Jan Harmens, the Company's master distiller. Another slave. Two soldiers.

Daniel came home from the Lodge saying Claas Wieringa's wife was doing her best but there wasn't enough food for the sick. Anna said: Go and shoot me some pigeons ...

Pieternella took the first pail of soup down to the Lodge. Thomas carried it for her.

They were digging two fresh graves: a sailor and a soldier. In the passage on the way to the kitchen she met Master Walrand.

'I've brought some soup for the sick.'

'Helping hands are few, there are some of the sick who still have to be fed.' He had about him the tiredness of someone who had had far too little sleep. And he smelt of liquor.

Four sick men were lying in the room next to the kitchen. The thick hot smell of fever was in the air ...

It released something inside her. A will to help, a rage against the star and the sickness. With her own strength, she wanted to tame the fear in the eyes of the young man before whose mouth she was holding the bowl of soup. She wiped his face and hands and saw the fear in his eyes change to hope. Perhaps she was imagining it.

At the farthest bed, Walrand bent to make a small cut in the sick man's hand – a big white apron tied round his waist, a little bowl to catch the blood.

An old, old picture deep in her head …

On the way back home she met Tant Theuntjie on the footpath, a vinegar cloth to her nose. 'It's in the air. Magdalena has also gone down with it,' she said, her voice muffled by the cloth. Frightened eyes.

She got home and went to the lean-to where some of the dried yellow-bush leaves were hanging that she'd brought back from Hendrik. She took them down and pressed them against her face – felt their strength with her hands, her head and her body …

Daniel and Salomon came back from French Church with a bag of fish that they had netted on the near side of Vissers Island. Onions out of the garden. Carrots and collards.

'One of the free-burghers on the Flats has also died of it,' said Daniel, worried.

Perhaps it was her father's blood stirring within her, perhaps it was some of Juffrouw Sophia's goodness still alive in her. 'It's the little drops that we give, Pieternella, that fill the bucket,' Juffrouw Sophia used to say as she hung the pot of nasty milky stuff over the fire to take to a sick person somewhere. Stomach medicine. Anna hung the next pot of soup over the fire. Another one with fish and vegetables.

She, Pieternella, forced her head back into Juffrouw Sophia's kitchen, remembering one by one the things that she'd always had to pass to her. First the milk. Then the handful of cinnamon. Then two whole nutmegs, stamped fine on the cloth with the hammer; twenty cloves; twenty peppercorns. Instead of the handful of tree-bark that always hung in the little bag beside the hearth, she added Hendrik's yellow-bush leaves because she couldn't remember ever being told what kind of bark it was.

Boil. Stir. Sieve.

The 'star-thing' was higher and higher in the east each morning.

When day broke the next morning, the soup was ready to be taken down to the Lodge, and the stomach medicine had been sieved and had cooled down in the bottles.

Daniel had had his coffee. The children were still asleep.

She stood quietly outside for a while to watch the day breaking, to listen to the night sounds falling silent, to hear the first bird calling to say it was awake.

Daniel came out and stood beside her. 'My love, I tremble for you in your condition.'

'I am well, my dear. Send Salomon with the soup and the pot of fish so that he reaches the Lodge by midday. I'll wait for him.'

You could feel the sickness across the island. There was a haste in her to get to the sick; an impatience with Anna who was finally prepared to risk it outside – quilt-roof over her head.

She put on her own white apron and headed off down the path.

First stopped, though, to look in on Magdalena who was really very sick. Too exhausted to resist when she started wiping her face and neck and arms and legs with moist lukewarm cloths. The shutters were closed, Oom Laurens had to hold the candle for her to see, but the old man was shaking so with fear she had to tell him to sit down.

'In an hour's time, you are going to do exactly what I'm doing now, Oom. And in two hours' time give her more of the medicine.'

'Lord, Pieternella …'

Magriet succumbed the next day. Pieter van Nimwegen one day later.

Tant Maijke came down from the Flats to tell Cornelia that she wanted to be buried below the Lodge at Southeast Harbour, not on the Flats. But you're the picture of health, Ma, said Cornelia. Why didn't you rather think of bringing us something to put in the pot? If Daniel hadn't gone out and shot a deer for us, we'd have had nothing. He's rich, I'm poor, Tant Maijke countered. Shame on you, Ma! What shame is there in the truth?

Some days Grieta also went down to the Lodge to help wash and feed the sick.

Three weeks, and the tailed star was only visible in the west for a brief time in the early evening.

Then it was gone.

At Northwest Harbour three free-burghers and one woman were in their graves. On the Flats two. Four on the eastern side of the island. Eight of the Company's servants. Five slaves.

Most of those who survived were seriously weak.

But the Orange Tree Flats had not lost a single one.

'You've got the gift, Pieternella,' said Tant Magdalena, again and again.

'No, Tante. Two of the officials at the Lodge slipped out of my hands.'

They were walking back from church the next Sunday – she and Daniel and the two children; Salomon hadn't wanted to go. Lamotius conducted a thanksgiving service that day for those who had been spared and for all who had come forward in service to their neighbours in need. Claas Wieringa's Jacoba. Grieta. She, Pieternella.

In all the time that she had been helping at the Lodge, taking soup, he'd never said a word to her. Barely even greeted her.

'Does he still hold it against me that I wouldn't go the Flats? Or wouldn't show him where Master Sven was living in the forest?' she asked Daniel.

'Possibly.'

They got home. Anna was standing with her hands folded in front of her chest. She nodded her head in the direction of the cottage.

'What is it?'

'He's in his bed. Salomon.'

Four days.

In which she did everything she could. She had Daniel and Thomas carry him down to the Lodge on the stretcher, to Master Walrand.

'Don't mourn for me, Pieternella.' He was so weak already. 'I'm going back to the Cape.'

'Please don't leave!' She held him tight, *willing* her own life into him, clinging to him, realising suddenly that she was holding the last little bit of her Mamma – she couldn't let him die!

They buried him with the rest of the dead below the Lodge.

Magdalenatjie was born a month later. Another pretty little Dutch girl, at whose birth only Daniel and Anna were present because Tant Magdalena would never have made it through the storm and the rain in the middle of the night.

Anna caught the little thing. Anna bound the navel cord, washed and wrapped and pinned her into the swaddling clothes and laid her in the rocking cradle.

She complained because the storm didn't stop so that Daniel could go and shoot pigeons for the strong-soup. Because the caudle curdled.

She kept coming into the bedroom to cluck over the baby.

Magdalenatjie was three days old before Daniel could finally take the musket one morning and go off to shoot pigeons. A delighted Anna wrapped the little bundle in the baby quilt and took her outside, as she had done with the others. So that the sun and the island could see her and welcome her.

Nothing forewarned her, Pieternella. Catharina was playing outside. Eva was under the bedstead wrapping her own rag doll in cloths. Thomas was laying in sweet potato wreaths in the garden.

Fright fell upon her like a stone out of the sky. In an instant. 'Anna?' Like crying up against a wall. 'Anna?'

She leaped out of bed and ran to the door. 'Catharina, where is Anna?'

'Gone.' Without looking up from the stick she was planting in the ground.

'Gone, where?' Calmly, not to frighten the child into silence, though her own heart was beating faster and faster. 'Show Mother which way she went, Catharina.'

The dirty little finger pointed towards the forest between the work-place and the cowshed.

'Go and call Thomas, tell him to come quickly.'

The other kind of awful.

That drove her barefoot to the edge of the forest to scream and scream: Anna! Anna! Anna! Till there was no more screaming left in her and the slave behind her was saying Anna wouldn't hear.

'Best would be if I went for help, Juffrouw Pieternella.'

'Where's Anna, Thomas?' He must surely know!

'She was very restless these last two nights. Sat on the bed, rocking, rocking. I asked: Are you sick? She didn't answer.'

A different kind of awful.

Meanwhile her heart was rushing into the forest, the milk in her breasts was damming up, her hands were turning into claws ready to tear everything to shreds! She dozed off for a while in the early hours from sheer exhaustion – only to wake up from her own groaning.

Grieta was somewhere in the house. She was taking care of the other two children, cooking food … She, Pieternella, managed to keep at bay the madness that was slowly stalking her, telling herself that Anna wouldn't allow anything to happen to the child, would bring her back …

To counter the madness flaming in Daniel's eyes. 'How many times did I tell you we had to get rid of her!'

'When you find her, don't hurt her.'

'I can't believe you still want to protect her!'

'I'm not protecting, I'm just asking.'

Lamotius sent three soldiers to help Daniel and Focke search on the first day. They followed Anna's barefoot tracks in the wet forest and kept calling for her. But that night it started raining again and the tracks were washed away.

'You have to be strong, Pieternella,' Tant Magdalena came over to say. 'The baby can't still be alive.'

Her body wouldn't believe it.

Daniel, three soldiers, two servants from the Lodge, Focke and Oom Laurens Gabrielse.

'God, my love, the baby cannot possibly still be alive!'

On the day after that woodcutters heard a baby crying.

She had built a shelter of sorts out of branches. Anna. In a narrow valley at the foot of the Bamboo Mountains. And she didn't resist when they found her. Walked like a tame creature in front of them all the way through the forest and into the yard. The man carrying the baby passed her to Daniel.

Daniel to her, Pieternella.

'Have you got any shackles for us, Cooper?' asked the foreman.

Anna just stood there.

'I want to speak to her alone.' She asked. Her legs were ready to buckle under her. The baby was warm, she was still alive ...

'I will not allow it!' said Daniel. 'Thomas will tie up the slave's bundle, she's going from here straight to the Lodge.'

'I want to speak to her alone.'

'Pieternella, no!'

'I want to speak to her alone, Daniel Zaaijman!'

Tall and thin. Black otter's eyes looking down on everything as on the day when Daniel first came across the yard with her. Looking past everything. Living totally alone in a different world.

'Why, Anna?' Not a word. Not a movement of the face. 'Just tell me why.'

Nothing.

Then she saw: the two wet patches where milk was staining the old black dress round the nipples.

2

Lamotius was sitting behind a desk covered with books and papers. He glared at her as she entered.

'I sent for you yesterday morning!'

She was standing in front of the table. 'I couldn't come yesterday, Commander.'

'There is an obstinacy in you, Pieternella, which ill befits a dutiful wife. God set the man above the woman so that he might give her wise guidance and instruction.'

'Yes, Commander.' She sensed that he was clearing a path towards what he actually wanted to say.

'You undertook before God to honour and respect and in all things lawful to obey him.'

'Yes, Commander.' Say what you want to say, you're making me nervous.

'I ... I ...' He coughed loudly to clear his throat. 'I need to negotiate urgently with Daniel, but under the circumstances I am obliged to speak to you first.'

I'm not moving to the Flats. 'Negotiate about what, Commander?' He must not see she was scared.

'At present the Company is suffering serious losses as a result of the death of Jan Harmens. He was our greatest arrack distiller. At Second Bay, as you know. Since the free-burghers of that area, like those of the Flats, are increasingly processing their own sugar cane, and because of the failure of the sweet potato crop, plus other circumstances ...' His hands shifted some of the papers in front of him irritably. He must have thought she didn't know about the other circumstances: that many of the free-burghers were distilling liquor in all kinds of makeshift stills and selling it to Focke for his tavern. 'The Company needs to move its distillery to another area – provided we are able to appoint a competent and reliable man to run it there. A man like Daniel.'

'Where?' She didn't want to sound alarmed.

'Once before, when I needed him, your unwillingness to move away from the Orange Tree Flats was a sore reversal for the Company. A repetition thereof would be severely disadvantageous to your husband.'

'Where to?' Her legs had started trembling ...

'Black River Mouth.'

Her whole body began to tremble. 'Black River?'

'Yes. It's on the western side of the island.'

'On the west …' She wanted to laugh, to cry, to dance. She pressed her hands to the sides of her face and looked down so Lamotius wouldn't see she was ecstatic with joy! That a bright and shining star had fallen out of the sky and landed on her head and was sending tiny sparks into her stomach while her heart was already rushing home to start packing!

'You cannot expect to live for ever on the Orange Tree Flats, Pieternella!' It was like an exclamation of desperation. 'The Company urgently needs a man at Black River Mouth. That is where most of the palmyra for arrack grows.'

'I will go with him, Commander.'

He was like an axe already lifted for the next blow – and then the tree simply fell over in front of him. The disbelief on his face showed openly, a frown appeared between his eyes. 'Well, I must say your cooperation is encouraging, Pieternella. A woman who bows her head in humility is an ornament in the eyes of our almighty Father.'

'When does Daniel have to start there?'

'As soon as possible. Corporal Jacomo Baldini has asked to be discharged and will be appointed as his right-hand man. We are prepared to grant Daniel some slaves on credit …'

'How is Anna, Commander?' Deliberately taking the axe out of his hands.

'She gave us quite enough reason to put her in chains, but *your* interference with the process of justice prevented that from happening.'

'I only asked.' After Anna's return she had gone down on her knees before the Secunde. Lied. Said she'd sent the slave to take the baby out for a walk and that she'd got lost. No one believed her. But nor could they succeed in contradicting her.

'Anna is fine, we've put her to work in the gardens and we're watching her.'

Black River Mouth.

One day, soon after they were married, Sven Telleson had said life has four shifts: in the first you learn to crawl, in the second to walk, in the third to dance, and for the fourth you need a walking stick.

'What one am I in?' she teased him.

'You're learning to walk and old Daniel is dancing.'

'And you, Master Sven?'

'The moment the saw-blades arrive, I'll be dancing all over again!'

Black River Mouth felt like the start of her dancing time.

No, better than dancing.

As though all at once her arms had become wings for her to fly high above Oom Bart and Tant Theuntjie and Tant Maijke and Willem van Deventer and Lamotius to a fresh new world. Over the graves of Juffrouw Margaretha and Andrea and Salomon. To the other side of the sea, to the other side of the world!

Daniel and Jacomo Baldini and two slaves went ahead to build the house. Hendrik had chosen the spot: on the seaward side of his own hut. A long sturdy palm-leaf house with *four* rooms in a row – plus a stone kitchen!

Hendrik drove the oxen and cows all the way there – four whole days, taking the land route, because he had to cross the mountains with them.

A cottage for Baldini, a little farther to the south. The distillery as close to the river as safety would allow …

'Remember, every barrel of arrack has to be rolled to the shore before it can be loaded on to a boat or a ship,' Daniel explained.

The actual stills had yet to arrive. From somewhere. Lamotius had sent the late Jan Harmens's three broken ones to Batavia to be repaired. The other one, which had been brought back from the Cape on the *Baaren*, had been so 'repaired' that it was completely unusable. In the mean time Daniel and Baldini had to do the best they could with home-made stills. On a small scale. Building fireplaces. Palm wine to distil into arrack.

On the evening of the day after she had been to Lamotius, Daniel came home and stopped in the doorway with the broadest of smiles on his face, before grabbing her round the waist and spinning round and round the table with her.

'Are you happy, my Daniel?'

'So much happiness feels too much for me to contain! And you, my love?'

'This is the second biggest happiness of my life. The biggest was my wedding party.'

Slave quarters. Hendrik's little 'hospital' for Thomas and the two new slaves, Adam and Goliath. And Maria, the one who had been exchanged for Anna and whom she had had trouble getting used to. Fat and stupid – and submissive in a way Anna never was.

She missed Anna.

The first load of furniture went to Black River on the *Zeemaat*.

She and the children followed with the second load.

Her whole being sang as she made the house a home. She wished she could plant flowers at the door. Up beside the river she picked green sprigs with pretty red buds and arranged them in an earthenware vase on the table. She took the children down to the yellow-sand bay and picked up shells to set on either side of the pathway to the front door of the house. It was all so, so beautiful.

The house faced directly west – seawards. The two short sides faced north and south. Hendrik chopped away all the branches in front of the house to clear the view far over the river mouth and on to the sea. 'We don't need to hide anything any more!' he laughed.

The most incredible thing happened one morning. They must have been at the Black River about three months. She and Maria were giving the children their breakfast when Daniel appeared in the door and told her to close her eyes.

'You're not allowed to look before I say!' He was clearly very excited about something. All she could think of was that there might be a dumbcluck bird or a tortoise nearby.

He led her outside, stood behind her and then said she could open her eyes …

On the open sea, far beyond the reef, was a picture that quite took her breath away for a moment. Sails. Ships. One … two … three … four … five …

The whole ocean was covered with ships! Eleven of them. Of some of them you could see no more than their sails above the horizon.

'The homeward-bound fleet,' Daniel said behind her.

'*Our* return fleet? The Dutch fleet?'

'Yes. On their way to the Cape. It seldom happens that they pass *this* close to Mauritius. They usually sail past closer to the Madagascar side.'

Like a mystery that had suddenly appeared before her eyes. A piece of a puzzle. Which gradually drew down over her a sadness for all the hundreds of souls on board – all who were hungry, sick, flogged. All who had to sweat to get the wealth-laden wooden geese safely back to the fatherland.

A homesickness. A remembrance of the thundering of the cannons that the lookouts on Lion's Head fired across Table Bay as the return fleet came sailing into view. The joy in the little town, the bustle. The malevolence with which her mother viewed their approach – cursing, saying that if there were no such things as ships, the Goringhaiquas' cattle and sheep would still be grazing in the bowl under the mountain and drinking from the sweet-water river.

And all at once she didn't want to look any more.

Daniel sometimes read to them from the Bible about people who turned round and turned into pillars of salt. That you couldn't move forward while you were looking back ...

She turned away and went back into the house. She didn't want to look back.

Just before noon the cannon shot sounded behind the reef: *Douff!* By the time she had come out Hendrik and Daniel were already on the water in the sampan, because behind the reef lay an enormous ship and something about its heavily laden body was saying it couldn't go any farther.

She told Maria: 'Keep an eye on the children ...'

It was one of the home fleet: the *Europa*. The island's own *Europa* would look like an insect against it. She stood on the shore and knew that it was Daniel who was piloting it through the gap into the anchorage. Heard voices on the deck, saw one of the ship's lifeboats being lowered – a boatload of half-dead sailors being rowed the short distance to land. Hendrik followed with four more on the sampan. Her head was working already, telling the oarsmen to carry the sick into the nearest shade. Most of them in hammocks or sheets of canvas. Some in quilts. Those pleading eyes. But their mouths were not gaping and swollen purple on the inside as with dysentery; nor were there the usual cries of pain as they were picked up or put down ...

The next boatload was coming across the water to shore. Hendrik helped her sort out the worst cases to take to his little hospital.

'Where's the Surgeon?' she asked.

'On board, with the rest of the sick.'

'What does he say, what is wrong with them?'

'It might be food poisoning.'

'Where's Daniel?'

'On board. Something is going to have to be done urgently. They say the water that has leaked in has already filled the hold. Their pumps couldn't cope. Two have broken.'

'Where are we going to get enough food for them all?'

'They'll come, the free-burghers. Always on the lookout. Call the slaves to help carry.'

Hendrik showed Thomas and Goliath and Adam which of the sick to take to the hospital first. He himself helped them carry. Got the oarsmen to help. Had Daniel's tent pitched behind the house for the next batch, had space cleared and sails stretched between trees for the rest.

Meanwhile she hung the first pot of milk over the fire – cinnamon, chopped nutmeg, cloves, peppercorns, Hendrik's yellow-bush leaves. What else?

She saw the three Jans mercifully coming across the river with their sampans full of vegetables and meat and butter – saw the disappointment on their faces because it was a Dutch ship that would pay less than the English.

'Please, bring as much as you can. I'll write down every item and see to it that the ship's bookkeeper pays you,' she said.

'No more meat unless they pay decently.'

'And bring one of your wives to help with the food; the ship's cook can't come ashore.'

Maria at the biggest cauldron, stirring the stew.

Thomas and Goliath carried water from the river to get the stinking bodies clean.

'Mother ...'

'No, Catharina, we can't go and play down by the river today.'

'Why are they making those noises, Mother?'

'They're sick, my child. You go and play with Eva and look after Magdalenatjie.'

Hendrik came back from the ship to say the Surgeon had sent word that he'd come as soon as he could. That he, Hendrik, unfortunately wouldn't be able to help any more, he had to walk to the Lodge to take a letter from the skipper to the Commander.

'It's almost dark, why don't you wait and go early tomorrow morning?'

'It's full moon. Hendrik knows the way.'

Lamotius's reply was that the ship should be given only temporary help, enough to allow it to sail round to the Lodge where full assistance would be rendered.

'The ship is way beyond temporary help, it wouldn't have made it even halfway to the Lodge.' Daniel fell into bed well after dark that night, too tired even to wash.

Lamotius sent word that Daniel was to see to it that every nail and plank and mast-pole and anything else was accurately recorded so the costs could be recovered ...

Hendrik went back to the Lodge with letters from the skipper *and* Daniel. That the *Europa* was not in any condition to reach the Lodge, that it had sprung serious leaks, that the cargo had already been unloaded, that a great deal of damage had been caused by the water in the hold. Pumps had been repaired, as much water as possible was being pumped out – they would start the next day careening and cleaning and caulking.

Many sick.

Whom she nursed with her 'other' hands. Some other power – a different *her* that seemed to arise the moment she tied on her white apron. Patience with the sick, impatience with the half-recuperated and their foul mouths. Four of those under the canvas sheet outside she sent back with the Surgeon to join his own lot above the shore.

Impatience with the three Jans who wouldn't provide any more meat, only vegetables and butter and bread and cheese, but who were eventually prepared to go out and shoot a deer or two for her, if she could get them the lead and shot from Daniel.

Jan Muur brought his wife, Willemina, to help with the food. A truly capable woman, and a tough one – who wouldn't hesitate to take a sampan and two slaves and go out to catch a turtle. She knew their grazing spots. 'On this side of the island you learn to do everything, Pieternella.' Willemina had already sent two of her children back to the fatherland – one on an English ship, one on a French ship.

A fortnight later Secunde Jacobsen and Bart Borms and two sailors arrived in the island's new sloop, the *Vanger*. Dignified and self-important – to ascertain on behalf of the Commander that everything about the repairs to the *Europa* was being done properly.

'And remember that we'll need food and somewhere to sleep, Pieternella!' Oom Bart came up the house to announce.

'There's one place vacant under the canvas and one inside the tent.'

'The impertinence! Who do you think you're talking to?'

They slept on the shore under canvas sheets with the rest.

Next day Secunde Jacobsen was waiting for the three Jans. There had been complaints from the skipper that there was no meat for the beached seamen. That he had sent the sailors out hunting, but that they had been shot at by the free-burghers across the river.

'Secunde, have you ever seen a place when it has been destroyed by sailors? Shall we take and show you how many palm-heads they have already chopped open to make palm wine?'

'That, free-burghers, is not the issue. You were provided with cattle on very reasonable terms on condition that you supply us with meat the moment that we require it. Our information is that your stock have bred well.' One Jan was playing with his toes in the mud, one kept twitching his shoulder as though he had some affliction. The third, Willemina's Jan, stood glaring at the Secunde with naked hostility. 'This is first and foremost an island of *succour*, to rescue the ships of our fleet. *That* is why you are here! *That* is why I want to know from you why you are not bringing meat!'

'We're waiting to be rescued ourselves, Secunde,' replied the first Jan, Jan Lodewijks, aggrieved. 'Twice the Commander has told us that we have to move away from this side of the island altogether.'

'Because you apparently have no qualms about provisioning our enemies!' Jacobsen was angry. 'You will supply this ship with meat from tomorrow, or you will place your hounds at their disposal to go hunting for them.'

'Our children have not been christened or confirmed; we've asked and asked one Commander after the next to send a minister to us ...'

'Free-burgher ... what is your name again?'

'Jan Muur.' Willemina's Jan.

'It will do you no good, Free-burgher Muur, to look for an excuse that has nothing to do with this case. Do you realise that our inability to supply meat to these people will be reported all the way to the fatherland?'

The next day, they brought two barrels of meat; said they had taken them out of the mouths of their children.

It seemed that not a word had been said about the rolls of tobacco that the sampans took across the water and bartered with the sailors ...

'Came from as far away as the Flats with tobacco and beans,' Willemina let slip. 'Wanted to turn back when they saw it was a Dutch ship, but felt too sheepish.'

The *Vanger* stayed a week.

Two weeks later it was back – with Commander Lamotius himself on board. And a bookkeeper. But without Bart Borms.

'It remains a desire of mine, Zaaijman,' the Commander said that evening at table, 'to walk all the way round to here along the shore. Not only to observe the real splendour of this island but also to view the bays and rivers for future exploitation.'

'As you say, Commander.' Daniel was only mouthing the words, she could tell. He was too tired. They hadn't even finished caulking one side of the ship yet, and the captain wouldn't trust a single seam if Daniel's eyes had not seen every tar brush and hammer and piece of oakum.

She relinquished her and Daniel's room to Lamotius; put her best sheets and pillow cases and quilts on the bed. Most of the sick in her care were back at the shore. Willemina no longer came across the river every morning to help. Only on some days, to visit.

Lamotius filled his pipe for the umpteenth time. 'You know, Zaaijman, our late master woodsman once said: Even if a thousand men felled ebony on this island for a hundred years, there'd still be enough left for another thousand men for another hundred years!'

'As you say, Commander.'

'But that is not what I wish to talk about. I paid a visit to Baldini this afternoon. It is his opinion that you will soon be ready to distil – as soon as the *Europa* departs. That is the reason why I wanted you to help the ship only temporarily to enable it to reach the Lodge. As far as possible, we wish to prevent ships from obtaining assistance on this side of the island.'

'Yes, Commander.'

'As far as I am able to ascertain, Baldini is the only one engaged at present in collecting the palm sap you need for the wine.'

'Yes, Commander.' Daniel was half asleep.

'I am informed that the slaves assigned to you principally to assist with the distilling spend most of their time working here round the house.'

'They helped with the sick.' She had chipped in. He looked at her as if to say: I was not speaking to you. 'We nursed thirty-three very sick sailors here, Commander.'

'Aah ... the ship had no Surgeon?' Bitingly rude.

'The Surgeon had almost as many under the trees at Yellow Bay. Only the very worst cases were brought up here under the shelter.'

'Your husband signed an important contract to distil *arrack*, Pieternella, not to hire out his wife as a nurse!'

Daniel was fast asleep in his chair.

She borrowed his words: 'As you say, Commander. Your room is ready, I trust you will not find it uncomfortable. And kindly do excuse Daniel, he works extremely hard.'

Lamotius left the next day on the *Vanger* for the Lodge at Southeast Harbour. The bookkeeper stayed behind to make sure that all expenses were accounted for, so that all debts could be settled as soon as the *Europa* was ready to depart.

The repair work that had to be done to the ship was among the most extensive ever undertaken at Black River Mouth.

'Pieternella,' Willemina started nagging, as the work was coming to an end, 'tell Daniel to ask if among all the cargo unpacked on the beach there isn't any of that Indian cloth like we got from the English.'

'I'll ask him.'

'Some of us and our children are wearing such tatters the birds fly off in alarm when they see us.'

'Who is there on that side of the river who could teach me to make clothes?' It was something she'd had on her mind for a long time. Keeping three girls and herself in clothes without Tant Magdalena was a challenge.

'Jan Lodewijks's Aaltjie,' Willemina assured her. 'She was an orphan in a gaol in the fatherland. She can even make lace.'

'I'll come over and ask her.'

'Don't wait too long. Aaltjie and Jan are also biding their time to get away on a ship. Several others have done so already. You never know when it'll be your lucky day.'

The *Europa* left on a Sunday morning late in September, after more than two months. The *Vanger* had come for the bookkeeper on the Friday before and Daniel had spent the Saturday evening on board the *Europa* at the Captain's farewell banquet.

The next morning she took Catharina and Eva and walked down to the yellow-sand bay to see if Daniel was on his way to the shore yet. He was, with a fully laden sampan.

The *Europa* was through the reef already.

Hendrik had set off the previous day along the shore towards Northwest Harbour in search of ambergris. He was afraid some of the free-burghers across the river would beat him to it.

She watched Daniel coming across the water; he seemed not to be as steady on his feet on the sampan as usual. As though his arms, as he dropped the anchor-stone, were limp ...

'Daniel?' He was wading to the shore with uncertain steps.

In a loud sing-song voice he tried to call out: 'Morning, my wife, of whom the Word says her price is above rubies ...' His knees gave way. He collapsed on the ground, rolled over and just lay there.

Catharina started crying. Eva followed her lead.

'Is Father dead?' asked Catharina, frightened.

'No.' She couldn't contain her laughter. 'Father has just collapsed from exhaustion. Go and call Thomas and Adam, tell them to bring a stretcher.' Goliath was with Baldini.

She sat at his head so her shadow could fall over him. Her handsome 'dead' husband.

And all of a sudden everything was peaceful and tranquil again. The calm water out to the reef was shining and smooth, the droning of the ocean distant. Beyond it, the *Europa* was flying away, its wings spread wide, with all the noisemongers inside its body. All they had left were hundreds of footprints on the yellow sand waiting for the wind and the tide ...

It was *her* piece of the island again.

Her dancing floor.

Her sleeping jackal-haired husband whose feet the tide was slowly creeping up on ...

It was a long time since last they'd been alone. A long time since she'd been left alone with the things in her heart.

The children were growing. Catharina was almost six, Eva almost four. Both were Daniel's water-babies who played with him under the water quite unafraid; little hands bringing up one living shell after another to show her on the sampan. Or to make Magdalenatjie crow with delight when the little heads suddenly popped up out of the water first on this side of the sampan, then on the other. Daddy-fish always near and watching ...

Before Magdalenatjie had begun to take her first steps, Daniel had had her, too, in the water a few times. Only she, Pieternella, wouldn't get into the sea, no matter how often Daniel promised to hold her.

She waved away the fly-thing buzzing round his head and combed his hair with her fingers. All at once she had a wish in her heart that one day she would be able to give him a handsome strong son just like himself.

She hoped she'd be able to drag him out of the way if the water reached his feet ...

One day Jan Dirks's Elisabet had come across the river with Willemina – a small, grey-haired woman with a bent back – and started crying when she saw the ship lying on its side. She said God grant that she should please be back in the fatherland before the day came when she, too, would be left to lie like that.

She, Pieternella, was glad that she didn't have a fatherland to keep calling her back. That Mauritius had accepted her – given her its blood to eat.

She didn't yearn for anywhere else.

In the new year, she would start teaching Catharina to read and write. For the mean time. It was Daniel's wish to get them a schoolmaster when the time was right.

She heard the children coming back with Thomas and Adam – Baldini and Goliath behind them to unload the sampan.

They rolled him on to the stretcher and rolled him off again on Hendrik's bed.

Baldini asked if he might read the Sunday lesson for them, since Daniel was incapable of doing so.

'Yes, please, I'll call the slaves together.'

Strange little fellow, Jacomo Baldini. Thin and dark with small jet-black eyes and an earnestness about him that always made her think of Sick Comforter Heere. Only the black garb was missing.

His happiness he got from only two or three things: reading the Bible word for word; the handful of vine-stocks that he'd planted below his cottage on the slope and that he nursed like children; and his lute.

'Where do you come from, Baldini?' she asked one evening at table.

'Padua.' He ate taking little, rapid bites.

'Where's that?'

'In North Italy.'

'Our schoolmaster at the Cape used to say that was the boot-shaped land.'

'But I've been a Hollander and a Protestant for many years now. The worthiest of the Hollanders, the great divine Erasmus, left deep tracks in my mother country, because not only did he clear the path for Luther but he also translated the True Word for us from Greek and taught us not to trust any priest but to read the Word of God for ourselves.'

When Baldini was so serious it always made her long for Salomon.

Daniel gave an impolite laugh. 'They say Erasmus never went back to Holland; he said the Dutch spent too much time drinking and carousing!'

Occasionally Daniel would ask Baldini to read the evening lesson and prayer. But the slaves would get fidgety because he went on so long. But on days when he played his lute for them, they never wanted him to stop. It sounded then as if even the birds would fall silent and come to listen for curiosity; as if the straw-tails would hover lower over the forest. The most beautiful golden notes strung together in long strings.

And Baldini could also shin up a palm tree as nimbly as a monkey to chop out the crown with the cane knife, hollow out the top for the sap to seep into – and go back up to scoop up the sap with a big ladle.

Then the tree died.

Daniel slept till late in the afternoon.

Got up, went down to the river to wash, and came back to put on clean clothes. 'I admit, my love, I don't know much of what happened in the world after midnight.'

'Baldini and Goliath put the stuff from the sampan under the hospital shelter. We didn't open anything.'

'I'm sorry I arrived here like this, Pieternella. I first wanted to tell you how very proud of you I am in my heart.'

'And I of you, my Daniel.'

Flour, rice, sugar, coffee, tea, nearly a bale of pink cloth with fine blue and white stripes …

'The women across the river really need material for clothes.'

'It's yours to do with as you like.'

'They'll be so happy.'

Wrapped in a sack and tied up with string was a flat, hard thing which Daniel held out to her. 'For you, from the Skipper and the Surgeon, to thank you one last time.'

It was a huge flat round dish with pictures in painted frames all round the edge. Blue and white. In the centre, a big picture of a long-tailed bird and flowers and things, and a big VOC painted in the middle.

The most beautiful meat platter.

'There's something I want to ask you to do for me, Daniel.'

'What, my love?'

'Build me an outside kitchen somewhere. Feeding so many sick folk from the kitchen in the house is really inconvenient.'

They were still discussing the kitchen when Hendrik appeared, looking much the worse for wear.

'Two English ships lying at anchor in Turtle Bay above Northwest Harbour, urgently want *Daniel Zimon, the cooper*,' he said breathlessly.

3

On a swelteringly hot Sunday just three weeks later, the minister from the two English ships baptised fourteen free-burgher children under the trees above Northwest Harbour.

Daniel had asked him to.

The children baptised ranged from babes in arms to children old enough to crawl, to walk, and some even taller grown. Someone in the crowd of friends and relations said, irreverently but out loud: 'Lamotius would wet himself if he saw what's going on here today.'

Nobody laughed.

Daniel came to Black River Mouth in the *Zeemaat* on the Saturday to fetch her and the children and Maria. Thomas and Goliath had set off on foot along the shore on Friday to put up the night shelter on the north side of the bay beside the sweet-water stream at Northwest Harbour.

Daniel sailed northwards all along between the reef and the land with her and the children and Maria. Past the weirdest free-standing hills, like chunks of mountain left behind on the flats when all the rest were piled up on top of one another. Teat Mountain, the one with peaks that looked like an udder pointing up into the sky. Past a small level plain, another small bay. Dolphins. More chunks of mountain.

To the beautiful smooth-water bay at the foot of the basin under the red-brown mountain, where one of the peaks had a gigantic stone perched on its head that made you wonder when it was going to tumble off.

'The other Pieter Both,' said Daniel.

Tall waving green grasses between the rocks on the mountain slopes. Small herds of cattle everywhere.

Daniel had spent only two nights at home in all the time that he'd been helping the English ships. He agreed that Lamotius would have a fit if he saw how much meat there was suddenly available to deliver to the ships. And milk, butter, cheese …

Apart from tobacco and beans.

In the forest between the mountain basin and the sea at Northwest Harbour lay an extensive stretch of lush farmland where the vegetable gardens looked for all the world like loose patches of cloth stitched on everywhere.

Truly, another strange piece of the island. 'Where are we now on the island, Daniel?'

'Eleven o'clock on the watch.'

But no houses – till they saw thin wisps of smoke that betrayed the hiding places of the brown-leaf cottages.

Unfamiliar free-burghers and their wives, few of whom she'd ever seen before. She had met Jan Roelofse and his wife Martjie, though.

The three Jans lived on another small plain more towards the south, towards the Black River Mouth side. They had brought their wives and children and set up their shelters at Northwest Harbour on the Friday. After Daniel had let it be known that he had asked the ship's chaplain to baptise his two youngest, the free-burghers started coming to him one by one to ask if he would please put in a word for them, too, so that their children might also be christened. The three Jans among them.

Early on the Sunday morning, while most people were still asleep, she went for a walk along the beach with Magdalenatjie.

The *Zeemaat* was anchored in a channel close to the edge, the two great English ships much farther out.

The sun was still behind the mountains, the morning shadows lay cool and dark across the entire mountain basin.

Tranquil.

All over, chimneys were beginning to reek.

After a while Magdalenatjie fell asleep with her head on her shoulder. She turned back, it was starting to get hot.

On the near side of the spot where the three Jans had pitched their shelters she suddenly noticed a reddishness between the trees and began to laugh. It was the wives of the Jans, all in brand-new dresses made of the pink material with fine blue and white stripes. Their caps were of the same stuff. So were their girls' dresses. Where the new material had run out, they had inserted strips of old cloth among the new. Very neat.

The men and boys were in black.

The minister was already on his way to the shore when an unfamiliar man and woman hurried up, out of breath, down the footpath from the northern side: Adam Cornelise and his wife Cathrinha Kel with three unchristened children from the Flats. 'We only heard yesterday that there might be a baptism here today. If we could also please have our children baptised …'

Embarrassed.

Rather a pretty woman, Cathrinha Kel.

'A ne'er-do-well,' whispered Aaltjie, and watched the woman out of the corner of her eye.

'What's that?'

'Dutch body – Eastern soul. Born in Batavia, raised by Eastern slaves. Adam's face is often a mess, the way she beats him.'

The minister, a tall man with grey hair and a grey beard, was dressed in black. Four sailors carried a wooden chest up from the boat, placed it under the trees on the sand and covered it with a dark red cloth. Daniel read the words embroidered on it in gold thread, ALMIGHTY IS THE LORD, and translated them into Dutch for them.

A second boat came across the water from the ships with the Captains and their wives and some of the officers. Elegant women. The men lifted them out of the boat and carried them ashore. Women with the same lace-edged bonnets on their heads, tied under the chin with bows, like the English women at the yellow-sand bay that other time ...

Except that these women appeared never to have seen Dutch women before, because they stood openly staring at them, and one kept having to cover the laugh in her mouth with her hand.

Everyone with children to be baptised had to stand in a long line in front of the chest with the red cloth.

'This isn't a popish business, is it, Daniel?' asked Jan Muur anxiously.

'No.'

'Are you sure?'

'Yes.' An older sailor with a wrinkled face and lots of freckles took off his cap and stood beside the minister. 'He knows a little Dutch,' said Daniel.

Then the minister read from the Bible and prayed. Very dignified. Then each of them had to bring their children one by one. The old freckled-face sailor held the small silver basin with the baptismal water and helped the minister with the names: Hester, Ragel, Johannes, Belie, Pieter, Lourens, Maria, Breggie ...

The last were their Eva and Magdalena.

The ships sailed at first light on Monday. That night the old sailor with the freckles knocked at Jan Muur's door looking for 'mister Zyman'. Jan brought him to the Black River on Tuesday morning. 'No, Daniel, I don't understand what he wants. I think he's missed his ship.'

He had his chest on his shoulder. No, he hadn't missed his ship, he'd deserted. He'd searched all his life for a place that would tempt him to stay for ever. When he saw Mauritius, he knew this was that place. If only he could be taken to the Commander, to give himself up.

What is your name?

Robert Hendricks.

How did you come ashore?

Stole the sampan the man and woman and two children fleeing from Northwest Harbour used to row out to one of the ships ...

Hendrik took him to the Lodge on foot.

The next morning Daniel and Baldini and the slaves started building the outside kitchen between the house and the hospital. A stone hearth and chimney, side walls of bamboo and palm leaves, south side open. Two long tables, enough shelves, room for barrels.

'What you've built me is really convenient, my Daniel. Thank you.'

Soon after the start of the new year Daniel and Baldini rolled the first firkins of palm arrack down to the shore and took them to the *Zeemaat* on the sampan.

The 'stills' they had to work with were little better than the makeshift things the illicit distillers used, but Lamotius was still bravely hoping for the two large ones that he'd sent to Batavia for repairs.

And for the saw-blades.

Daniel would have delivered the arrack the week before, but a storm arose in the night that by next morning had her fearing in her heart that it was developing into another cyclone.

'This is a south-east storm, my love. Not a cyclone.'

'If only I knew whether Anna had run off into the forest ...'

'Forget Anna.'

For four days the storm raged.

By late in the afternoon of the fifth day the casks were aboard and all was ready for Daniel and Goliath to sail round to the Lodge.

No, she didn't want to go with them. Later some time, when Southeast Harbour and the Orange Tree Flats had been more firmly stored away in her mind. Not that it had been bad there, it was just that Black River Mouth was now her home.

But would he please leave something at the Lodge for Anna? A piece of cloth, a few sweet biscuits and the pretty cup whose saucer had broken. Anna always so loved the cups ...

She and Maria were packing a food basket for Daniel and Goliath's few days away. Daniel had gone off to show Thomas where he and Adam were to lay out the new section of garden for the sweet potato vines that he wanted to bring back. Hendrik and Adam and Baldini were down at the stills, cleaning up and preparing for the next distillation.

Hendrik had explained to her the essentials of the process. Of arrack. 'It's actually just sweating wine, Pieternella. Heat the bottom of a pot of wine over the fire, the steam rises up into the dome, becomes droplets and these run down and out of the long spout – the coil – and you catch arrack at its end. Nice and strong.'

The next moment a cannon shot boomed behind the reef and straightaway everyone dropped what they were doing.

The *Baaren*. Storm-wracked, its mainmast missing, the hold full of water. It was on its way from the East to the Cape with a cargo of rice poured dry into the hold in Batavia, most of which had to be jettisoned when the storm was at its worst. Terrific loss and damage.

She wondered if fish ate rice.

The seven sickest sailors were in the little hospital before dark, there was a stew on the fire, the milk with spices and yellow-bush leaves was in the other pot, and Hendrik's bed was covered with clean linen for the prostrate Captain De Hoop who came to the table in the sitting room to write the letter that had to be taken down to the Lodge urgently.

Such a dreadful loss, such a dreadful loss ...

Pack food for Hendrik, get a lantern ready – the moon rose only just before dawn. Even if he took every short cut he knew, it would still take him more than a long night of walking.

Then he had to wait for Lamotius's reply.

The reply insisted that the *Baaren* was to proceed to Southeast Harbour. That Daniel was to assist with only the most essential repairs. The distilling of arrack was not to be interrupted under any circumstances.

A month.

Then the *Baaren* was able to sail out one morning, thoroughly patched up and with a temporary mainmast. The *Zeemaat* followed shortly behind it with the arrack.

'My thanks to you, Juffrouw Pieternella,' Captain De Hoop had said ceremoniously, after the meal the night before. 'My stay with you and Cooper Daniel here in your home was extremely pleasant and therapeutic and will be brought most pertinently to the attention of Commander Lamotius.'

All the sick had recovered and were back on board.

The three Jans were highly dissatisfied because they'd been paid too little for the vegetables and the butter and the milk and the buttermilk – no, they didn't have meat to supply. It had taken a lot of trouble to catch the three turtles; the things had not yet gone back to their usual grazing places after the storm.

'Did Commandeur Van der Stel not issue instructions that you were all to be removed from the western side of the island, Free-burgher Muur?' asked the Captain.

'Wouldn't say that rumour had reached us here, Captain. Be a right mess if we weren't here to stop the bloody English destroying everything in sight.'

'There are heavy penalties for swearing, Free-burgher!'

'I beg pardon, Captain. I hope you've written down in your book how much palm wine they've made and boozed away. How many tortoises have been chopped open and grilled.'

'I gather from the sailors that there are quite a few free-burghers over towards Northwest Harbour – who, without any conscience at all, help the enemies of our Noble Company.'

'I couldn't say; we live just a little way beyond the river.'

She waited till the following morning before asking Hendrik to take her across the river in his sampan.

'Daniel didn't say a word about your needing to cross the river, Pieternella,' he said uneasily, shifting from one foot to the other.

'Then I'll get Thomas to take me. And ask Willemina to teach me to wiggle the sampan myself!'

'Willemina's arms are strong enough to row a ship! With that little body of yours, you'd have trouble rowing a turtle shell across the river.'

The three small leaf cottages were another hour's walk beyond the river. Dogs barking in the distance. She reached Aaltjie first. Hendrik went to the garden to Jan.

'I've come to ask if you will teach me to make clothes for my children. Daniel will pay you.'

'Have you got scissors?'

'Daniel had the smith at the Lodge fix a pair for me; they're good and sharp.'

'And cloth and sewing thread?'

'I've got quite a lot of cloth, I asked Daniel to buy me more thread from the store.'

'I'll teach you.'

Then Hendrik took her to Willemina. She and Jan and some of the older children were laying in sweet potato wreaths, sweat pouring off them.

'I'd like to speak to you alone,' she said to Willemina.

Hendrik took her place with the wreaths.

'Come, there's some buttermilk at the house.' Willemina wiped her face on her apron.

The house was a little bigger than Aaltjie's, but just as sparsely and decently furnished. Clean.

'I'm pregnant again, Willemina.'

'You're not showing yet.'

'I know. But I need reassurance, because my slave is no midwife. You're the closest to me, but still not really nearby. I've worked out my time, it will be towards the end of July. What I've come to ask is whether you would come and stay with me for the last week or two. Just in case.'

Willemina passed her a mug of buttermilk. There was no table to sit at, other than the coarse-grained one outside next to the kitchen. 'If your Daniel will lend my Jan one of your slaves for the outside work. My girls can take care of the house.'

'I'll ask him.'

'And my price is one of those fine young steers of his.'

'I'll tell him.' The old women in the Hottentot kraals used to charge one sheep for a girl baby and two for a boy.

They took their buttermilk outside and sat on the tree-trunk benches in the shade behind the house to drink it. Lovely and fresh, with tiny gouts of butter floating in it.

The sea in the distance; round them the small flat plain where the cottages and gardens were and the cattle grazed. Fowls. Pigs. Beyond the plain, the peculiar black-stone mountains. She and Hendrik had come along the footpath beneath them that morning. Scattered hilltops on the northern side in the direction of Northwest Harbour.

'Another three years,' remarked Willemina, like one in hope.

'What then?'

'Then Jan will have served his punishment. A fifteen-year free-burgher contract.'

'And then?'

'God knows.'

'Have you ever seen the most beautiful spot on the island, Willemina?'

'Yes. It's in the mountains up here behind us. Haven't been there for a long time. That's one thing about hard times, they take all the beauty out of things.' Her dress hung limp between her knees; she licked the last of the buttermilk out of the mug with her finger, enjoying it.

'If only we had a decent market where we could regularly sell a little. I'm always telling Jan: what with this island and the Company, God's head must be badly muddled, because we pray for storms to blow ships our way; and the Company prays for fine weather to keep them sailing past Mauritius. Perhaps we should learn to pray in English.'

'At least more English ships come here than Dutch ones.'

'Yes. It's a miracle – they arrive just when you don't know where the next penny is going to come from. Gawd. Luckily Lamotius seems to have gone quiet about us moving away from here. One day I'll take and show you that lovely spot.'

'Actually I was talking about another place, but it doesn't matter. I'd love to see *your* lovely spot. Some day.'

'Wonder if I could still get there. Seven waterfalls, falling like seven pure white veils over all the rocks. Too beautiful for words. Each one sings its own water-song, and together they're a mountain choir that sings right through you.'

'It sounds lovely. And thank you for the buttermilk.'

'Stay a little longer. It's not often I have a Hendrik to bend his back in *my* place. We also had a slave at first but he ran away, chain and all. When is Daniel expected back?'

'The day after tomorrow, or thereabouts.'

He arrived the next day. Friday.

Yes, he did go and deliver the things for Anna. No, she didn't say anything.

Rather try guessing who was sitting waiting at the Lodge for Lamotius, all dressed up and blushing with happiness? Maijke van den Berg. To hand in the banns for her and Robert Hendricks's wedding so they could have their freedom as soon as possible. You're making it up! I swear. Abraham Steen has been appointed Master Woodsman in place of Sven. Robert Hendricks is Master Gardener on the Flats. According to Lamotius the grass is knee-high in the gardens on the Flats. Of the four rows of vines, only four stems are left, and all the fruit trees have died. Lamotius says it's all a sore trial to him – all that good farmland on the Flats but the free-burghers have worked barely three morgen of it.

'How is the Commander?'

'You would say the pain is still there in his eyes, and yet there has been good progress with the building of the new Lodge and the stone packing shed.'

'Did you buy the thread?'

'It's in the bag.'

'Thank you.'

'Everyone is very happy about the unexpected opportunity to send stuff to the Cape. Forty-something big rolls of tobacco have already been delivered to the Lodge for Lamotius to send on. Fine tobacco. Beans, too.'

'Did you see any of the others? Oom Bart or Tant Theuntjie?'

'No, but from what I hear Bart is in bed most of the time. His back, apparently. He says it was the *Vanger* that broke him. Focke says Bart is scared Lamotius will harness him to help with the repairs to the *Europa*. They haven't got very far yet, but he's hiding in bed anyway.'

'When is Tant Maijke's wedding?'

'Not any time soon. Lamotius says he'll first have to write to the Cape for permission for her to get married. And in any case, she couldn't come and hand in the banns on her own, Robert had to be present as well. She said Robert couldn't come with her, he had an impossible amount of work to do in the gardens up there.'

'If I know Tant Maijke, it wouldn't surprise me at all to learn that Robert Hendricks himself knew nothing about the marriage.'

'I think Lamotius suspects the same thing.'

'How are the repairs to the *Baaren* going?'

'Slowly. The small quantity of rice that was left in the hold has been unloaded and is drying on sheets of canvas in front of the Lodge. Slave women with shovels keep turning the rice while another keeps the dogs away.'

'How is Grieta?'

'I only saw Van der Hoeven. He says Lamotius keeps pestering him about the ebony on his land because it is some of the best still standing in the vicinity of the Southeast Harbour. He wants to have it felled for the Company because it's near the mill for when the blades arrive.'

'And?'

'Van der Hoeven says he'll shoot the first man who sets foot on his property with an axe and he hopes it's Lamotius himself.'

She waited till the Sunday before telling him of her visits to Aaltjie and Willemina.

'Something's worrying you, woman. What is it?'

'The thorn in my flesh is festering again, Daniel.'

4

The little thing was born on the twenty-eighth of May. A month too early. But Hendrik got Willemina there in time.

A little girl.

With the strangest, strangest look in the two little jet-black eyes when Daniel handed her baby to her. But it was only for a moment, then they were just ordinary little eyes that closed and went to sleep.

But there was something hanging in the room. Round the bed. A silence. A knowing that grew ever greater.

She was the prettiest little Hottentot girl baby ever – whose real name had already been given away!

Eva.

Who screamed without stopping till she, Pieternella, told Willemina to unpin her and take her out of the tightly wound swathes. Then she was quiet.

But her own crying wouldn't stop, because this was no ordinary crying, it was the festering out of a thorn that had long been deep seated.

And Anna wasn't there to take the child for the sun to greet her and for the island to see her.

Only Willemina, at the foot of the bed with the pail of warm nutmeg water to bathe her feet in, to lessen the terror of an early birth that sometimes overcame a woman. Like *her*, Pieternella.

Willemina didn't understand.

Only Daniel did.

Daniel who got up in the predawn hush and picked up the tiny bundle and laid her between her and himself and held them both tightly till day broke.

'Her name is Maria,' she announced. 'My mother always said it was her desire to have a second daughter so that she could place Juffrouw Maria Van Riebeeck's name on her head.'

'Her name will be Maria, my love. And I shall love her like my life.'

Acceptance was an apparition that came slinking in through the door slowly and secretly and crept in under the bedclothes – into her very being. That made her press the eager little mouth to her breast and feel the untamed strength of an animal stirring inside her in her determination to keep the tiny thing safe.

'At the bottom of the old clothes chest that you gave me when we were married, under the spare sheets and quilts, there is something wrapped in an old dress of mine. Please go and fetch it and bring it to me.'

Hendrik had taken Willemina home that morning and had brought Goliath back.

Daniel stood beside the bed for a long time with the two pot shards in the palm of one hand. 'Where do they come from, Pieternella?'

'I brought them from the Cape with me. They are all that was left of my mother.'

And he gently laid the shards on her stomach.

5

At last the thorn in her flesh had festered out.

By the time that Aaltjie came to teach her about dressmaking, Mariatjie was everyone's little dolly who lay kicking and crowing on her floor mattress wearing only a nappy. Three months old.

'Always said a brown calf is prettier than a white one,' was all Aaltjie said. 'Bring me an old dress of Catharina's so we can pick it apart for a pattern.'

Catharina and Eva went to 'school' in the mornings – in the small palm-leaf room that Daniel and Hendrik had made for them. A low table with stools, some pictures that Baldini had drawn for them on the walls. Letters of the alphabet that Daniel had cut for them from thin laths. Of course most of it was really only play. Daniel had given Captain De Hoop a letter to take to the Cape asking for books and quills and paper to be sent on the next supply ship.

'Did you know the two who got away on the English ship, Aaltjie?'

'Yes. It was their tenth year on the island. They had long been on the lookout for a means of escaping. Like most of us. Just hoped nobody would come up behind them and betray them; you never know who's going to trot down to the Lodge to stab you in the back. I hear they're saying the next one to take ship secretly is likely to be Gerrit van Ewijk's Hester – daughter of Jan Harmens the Company's distiller.'

'I know.'

'My Jan was up on the Flats, he says she's in a bad way. Poor thing. Her mother always dressed her so prettily, even though they were poor. They say Gerrit actually locks her in the house when the fit takes him. On other days he makes her pick up a spade and dig with the slaves.'

It was enjoyable having Aaltjie there in the daytime. 'I often wonder how things are with Willem van Deventer's Maria.'

'I don't know her, we never lived at the Cape. One of the *Baaren*'s men told Jan that Simon van der Stel is stirring things up at the Cape. Planting thousands of trees and vines for winemaking, I believe. Even established a new town and named it after himself, too: Stellenbosch.'

'I can't imagine it.' She didn't want to talk about the Cape. 'Are there any dumbclucks left on your side of the river?'

'Long time since I've seen one. Have to be starving before I'd eat that thing. I've had to, though. Jan says we should perhaps start thinking of moving to the Cape. Under this Lamotius we're going backwards even faster than under Hugo.'

'And tortoises?'

'Those we still get regularly. Tell your slave to start heating the iron, we have to smooth the material before we cut.'

Aaltjie was someone whose own work was thorough and who wasn't easily satisfied; every row of stitches had to be as straight as an arrow and all the stitches had to be the same size.

'When next Daniel takes a load of arrack, get him to see if he can buy ribbon and lace. And more buttons, too. They say there are nice new things in stock at the Lodge. All the old stuff was destroyed in the fire.'

Every time Daniel had to go to the Lodge he tried again to sweet-talk her into going along. She laughed, said he must be getting old if he didn't want to get away from her and the children any more.

The children were fidgety all the while he was away. Every morning: Is Father coming back today? Tomorrow? When then?

Perhaps she was also getting old, she laughed inside herself when she found that she, too, was looking out over the water in the direction the *Zeemaat* would come from. The anxiety at night when the wind came up ... The happiness when he was home again.

With the news and the provisions.

Yes, the supply ship had come. Yes, with the children's school materials. Yes, he'd got everything on her list: lace, buttons, thread, flour, rice – only half the rice because the Cape had sent only half the amount Lamotius had ordered.

No, the stills had not arrived yet. Nor the saw-blades. Van der Stel had sent word that Lamotius was *not* to trouble himself to send any more tobacco to the Cape, nobody wanted the Mauritian tobacco, which was only taking up space in the storage shed.

The new stone Lodge was coming along nicely. Yes, he'd seen Anna, she was still working in the gardens. No, she had not looked up or greeted him. And no, Maijke was not married yet, she couldn't drag Robert down to the Lodge to hand in the banns with her.

Oh and, by the way, the *Boode* had been lost at sea in a storm somewhere in the East in among a bunch of islands ...

Boode – steerage hold – pots on ropes – barley with prunes – Lubbert – Tant Theuntjie – Tant Maijke ... like an old nightmare that came flashing through her head to pluck off the last thread between her and the Cape.

When Hendrik had gone with Daniel to deliver the arrack, *he* would bring her the gossip on the sly.

'You'll have to go easy on the rice, Pieternella. This island is going to be stuck without rice soon. The Second Mate on the supply ship says Van der Stel's household uses five wagonloads of rice a *month*.'

'That can't be true!'

'Honestly. The Lords Seventeen wrote to him from Amsterdam, they wanted to know: What kind of extravagance is this? Simon replied: three of the wagonloads get fed to the Company's hunting hounds to give them strength, because if there's no venison available, there won't be enough food for the ships. Hottentot tribes round the Cape have hardly any livestock left, the barterers have to travel farther and farther looking for other tribes.'

'I wonder which way they're heading.' She didn't really want to know, but just for a moment she'd wondered – whether the Chainouqua and the Hessequa behind the mountains on the south were still safe.

Next day soldiers on horseback arrived from the Lodge and nailed the poster to a pole at Northwest Harbour. A new order had come from the Commandeur at the Cape that all free-burghers were to leave the western side of the island forthwith.

Jan Muur and Jan Dirks told Daniel the free-burghers had trampled the thing into the ground and then pissed on it. Baldini didn't laugh. He said: You all took an oath to serve the interests of the Company faithfully and to subject yourselves to its orders. The Bible says you shall subject yourselves to the king …

'Van der Stel isn't the king, and Lamot even less!' Jan Muur argued angrily, and asked whether perhaps the Bible said you had to take the food out of your children's mouths?

As usual Daniel tried to counter. 'Don't argue, people. Go and talk to Lamotius. He, too, wants to get away from here, but the Cape and the Lords Seventeen in Amsterdam are pressing him from all sides to get the island to make a profit for the Company. And then, all the free-burghers either go complaining to him or else ignore him completely. I don't know how the man survives.'

'And I don't know how you can still come up for him!' Jan Muur lashed back. 'Comfortable behind your arrack contract and laughing while you watch the sea for Englishmen to save! Why haven't you also been ordered to leave here?'

'Because I'm supposed to see to it that you don't sell a carrot or a cabbage to the enemy.'

All their mouths fell open at once.

But Jan Muur's words stirred a fear inside her. Why had Daniel not been ordered to leave the western side of the island with the others?

She asked him. He said Lamotius was begging for every drop of arrack to try and make a guilder's worth of profit; dreaming about how much arrack he would eventually be able to export once the stills had arrived. She needn't be worried, they were the last whom Lamotius would want moved from there.

And his assistance to enemy ships?

Either Lamotius didn't have enough spies watching or else he was deliberately turning a blind eye.

Across the Black River and up towards Northwest Harbour not one of the free-burghers moved.

Eventually it felt to her as though the Lodge had mercifully forgotten about them. Each one was living his own life – while keeping their eyes on the sea for the first sign of a sail.

'Gawd, old Daniel, something had better wash up here soon now.'

Once a month Daniel went off to deliver the arrack; sometimes took some sweet potatoes with him, some beans. Brought back provisions. A little news.

Poor Lamotius. Three officials all but succeeded in poisoning him and the master woodsman. Geel and Swaanswyk and Molin. Molin the Surgeon? Yes. They'd actually intended to poison Secunde Jacobsen as well, but he'd gone off to the Flats. Matters at the Lodge were bordering on rebellion. The guilty three had jeered at the entire government of the island, calling them hirelings and knaves in sheep's clothing, before they were caught and taken to the torture chamber to extract their confessions. That same night they broke out and, inexplicably, gained access to Lamotius's office and tore up the confessions.

Geel and Swaanswyk were banished to one of the outer islands. Molin was still at large.

Baldini was chopping off and hollowing out the heads of fewer and fewer palm trees to collect the sap, because he had a talent which he seemed unaware of: teaching children their lessons. In the mornings he taught Catharina and Eva to write with a fine hand, taught them to read, to calculate. Had them sitting open-mouthed listening to his stories. In the afternoons, she, Pieternella, sometimes taught them to sew rows of neat stitches on bits of cloth while Baldini helped with the distilling.

Daniel usually conducted a service for them all early on Sundays.

Afterwards he often rigged up a canvas awning on the sampan and sailed across the inside waters to frolic with his water-babies among the fishes and coral and shells and little underwater sea-trees. She and Mariatjie stayed on the sampan.

If the weather and the wind were right, they sometimes went out on the *Zeemaat* up far beyond Northwest Harbour, to the big bay at the head of the island, the Bight-Without-End. To show the children the flamingos and the small waterfowl.

Or southwards down to Quarrel Hill – the first Both's Head – to pick up shells on The Plaat, the big sand island, or for Daniel to let the children play and dive in the green-water channel round The Plaat. Before long they would clamber wide-eyed on to the sampan to tell her about something he'd shown them under the water.

'Biting shells, Mother! Hundreds. Sitting in rows on the rocks under the water. They can bite you dead and you can't come up for breath!' Eva, back on the sampan, shaking for the first time with childish fear.

'Father poked a stick in one's mouth and its mouth just snapped shut!' added Catharina in alarm.

At just over two, Magdalena didn't know much about fear – as long as Daniel stayed with her under the water. 'Father not scared.'

And then.

It was another Sunday and the children had clambered back on to the sampan beside her. Daniel put out his arms for her to pass Mariatjie to him. When the others were six months old, he had regularly taken them into the water with him. Even, for brief moments, *under* the water.

There was a bond between Daniel and this smallest daughter of his that sometimes made Pieternella throw her arms round his neck for the sheer joy in her heart. She knew he could *hear* the feeling-words in her heart …

On other days she would simply hug the little brown-bodied creature tight and wish she knew the words to pray, so that she could ask God please to keep a wingtip over Mariatjie. To keep and preserve her.

The sweetest little thing. With a mouth and eyes that were always ready to laugh.

She took off Maria's dress and handed her to Daniel. But when her feet touched the water, she drew them up and started screaming so terribly that even Daniel got a fright and immediately put her back on the sampan.

'Maybe she's scared the biting shells will catch her, Mother,' said Catharina, trying to comfort her.

A week later it happened again.

The first time she herself saw one of the 'biting shells' she was panic-stricken. Goliath and Hendrik had prised one loose with crowbars and brought it to the yellow-sand bay on the sampan. The biggest shell she'd ever seen in her life: you could hide a small child between its two giant halves!

Yawning shell.

Except that the mouth of the one on the sampan was clammed up.

She went straight to the distilling chamber and confronted Daniel. 'How could you take the children near such a dangerous thing under the water? Hendrik says it could even grip and drown an adult!'

'Keep calm, my love, I always make sure they're safe. And just wait, tonight I'll make you the most delicious chowder with that "yawning shell".'

Black River Mouth – or rather the whole of the western part of the island – had become her world. A world unending. And the world of all the 'illegals' too.

Gratitude for four English ships at once, lying at anchor beyond the reef at dawn one morning.

Not long after that the French ship.

Shortly before the end of the year two more English ships …

'Just our luck, Daniel,' laughed one of the Jans, 'that Lamotius had all the horses shot except his own two, otherwise the soldier would have been here with his hammer and nails again.'

The horses supposedly ate too much.

Foreign captains in her house, round her table. The sick under the awning in the little hospital. She didn't seem to have inherited her mother's gift for learning a new language with ease; Daniel or Baldini or Hendrik usually had to interpret for her. But at least she could say *how are you* and *open your mouth* and *keep hands off* and a few other words. Or get by with gestures.

Foreign women. Foreign children. Catharina and Eva and even Magdalena suddenly knew about *bread* and *butter* and *milk* and *cows* and *ships* and played happily with the little strangers down at the river, building low walls with stones and pebbles, picking up shells, hiding away when Baldini came to call them for school.

The chaplain on the previous ship had christened Mariatjie, too. At home.

When that ship sailed, it had on board a free-burgher from the Flats who wasn't prepared to see out the remaining ten years of his contract.

Not that life was without its conflicts.

She was walking over to Aaltjie's one day with a roll of cloth and a small bowl of rice, soon after the last two English ships had left. She'd crossed the river on the sampan with Daniel that morning; he had to see to the slaves cutting palm-heads.

'Remember to bring home some palm-cabbage,' she said when they parted.

'I will. And don't you get back too late, my love, and get me worried.'

The 'cabbage' was at the top of the palms. It was actually the young leaves that had not yet unfurled. First you stewed your meat till it was nice and tender, then you put the palm-cabbage on top and let it cook in the gravy. Soft as marrow. Delicious.

She had been walking for more than an hour after crossing the river when she realised she was following the oddest trail. She stopped to look. Yes. It was exactly as if someone had dragged something along the footpath. A sack of wood. No. A stone. No. A fresh track. She walked faster and faster.

Following the path she dropped into a forest hollow; imagined she heard someone groaning …

The next moment she stopped dead in her tracks. She needed to get her breath back after the fright and to give her head a chance to believe what her eyes were seeing.

Willemina, straining and groaning, was dragging home a giant tortoise. Tortoise on its back, a rope wound round the huge shell and knotted tight …

'Willemina!'

'Gawd, Pieternella, what a fright you gave me!'

Willemina, sweaty and breathless, the other end of the rope tied round her waist.

The tortoise with its rough legs, tortoise with its long wrinkled leathery neck, tortoise with one beady eye open, the other full of sand.

'Willemina, what are you doing?'

'Have you gone blind?' Willemina had taken off her cap and tucked it into the front of her dress; hot red flushes on her neck spread across her face. 'It's the heaviest damned tortoise ever, but I told it: you're not going to pull me down, I told it!'

'How far have you been dragging it?'

'Far. I struck it lucky on my way over to you!'

'You do know that Lamotius has imposed a heavy fine for tortoise poaching?'

'What?' Willemina lost her temper on the spot. 'Are you telling *me*?'

'If they catch you, they make you pay.'

'Whose side are you protecting from the wind? Lamot's side?'

'It's awful dragging the thing on its back like this. Don't you feel sorry for it?'

'You're not suggesting I should *carry* it?'

'No, that you should untie it and let it go. Please.'

'Are you all right in the head?'

'Hendrik says the tortoises are getting scarce.'

'Has he counted them? Have *you* counted how many the last bunch of Englishmen took away with them on deck? Or were you too busy counting Daniel's gains and unpacking all your new goods? Go and scratch under your own bed – dresses made of prettier and prettier cloth; furnishings ever more elegant; shelves filled to overflowing with porcelain ...'

'How many tortoises did the English take with them?'

'Ask Daniel, he helped build their hutch and load them.'

She turned round and walked straight back to the river to wait for Daniel. It took almost the whole day.

Somewhere inside you there is another you that waits till you are totally alone and then starts moving, like the slimy foot slowly crawling out of a snail-shell. You chase her back, she frightens you ...

You stick your hands into the soil and delve down in search of something to hold on to, you don't know what. You feel only a vague unease slipping like sand through your fingers. A two-headed axe cutting both ways till its blows are like thunder in your ears. Tortoise on its back; tortoise in the pot for hungry children, hungry sailors. Palm-cabbage on top of the meat; palm tree dead because they've chopped its head off for wine and arrack to ease the pain of being human.

Douff! went the axe. It was wonderful to be human, it was wonderful to be alive. Pretty children, a handsome husband, fine cups and saucers and beds and bedsteads and quilts and sheets and dresses and shoes and stockings; a beautiful meat platter, earthenware basins, silver bowls, silver spoon, silver forks, her pearl necklace ...

Douff!

Anna. There's another you inside you ...

Goodperson.

Badperson.

It worried her that Sven Telleson once said man himself is God or devil. Perhaps he really meant goodperson and badperson ...

Willemina was not a badperson.

Sven Telleson was a badperson but he was not a badperson!

Khoi means person. *Khoikhoi* – people-of-people. Hollanders are not real people, Pieternella, their bodies are hollow inside, her mother said.

Douff!

Daniel, Juffrouw Margaretha, Juffrouw Sophia were not hollow people!

The tastiest of all is turtle. Female. With lots of eggs in her body. You cut off the covering of the stomach, carefully take out the guts and gall bladder, cook the turtle in its shell on its back with onions and salt and pepper and a sprinkling of vinegar. A little nutmeg ...

Mauritius was not a people-place, yet it was *her* place and her children's.

She got up and walked down along the water's edge. Her head wouldn't think straight, the other person inside her simply wouldn't lie down! She didn't want Willemina to be cross with her on account of a tortoise.

Douff!

Had they chopped off the tortoise's head yet?

Turned back again and waited above the spot where the sampan was moored.

Drew lines in the sand, creating a dream ...

One day all the free-burghers will have absconded on the ships. Lamotius will be in his grave, and the officials, too. Then only she and Daniel would be left living on the island with the children. And Hendrik, perhaps.

'Pieternella?' It was Daniel. Dirty and full of bleeding scratches. 'Didn't you go to Aaltjie?'

'No. I turned back, and now I'm turning in circles. How many tortoises did the last bunch of Englishmen catch?'

'Fourteen. They want to release most of them on the island of St Helena to breed there. Come, you're looking feverish.'

'I'm just a bit confused about being human.'

'My dear love,' he laughed and took her hand, 'you don't get confused from being human, you get confused from trying to play God! What has upset you so much?'

'A tortoise.'

He picked her up and carried her *shloof-shloof* through the water to the sampan. The children's voices sounded across the water. Maria the slave was waiting with them on the far side. Daniel took the oar and

424

peacefully began to wiggle-waggle the sampan across the water. 'Life sings, Pieternella, believe me, it sings.' He was her cheerful Daniel with bright light shining in his eyes.

'What does it sing?' she asked, playing along.

'I don't know. All I know is that it sings most sweetly when you are with me.'

'I love you, Daniel.'

He suddenly stopped poling. 'That's the first time you've said that, Pieternella.'

She waited a week before she took the cloth and the rice across the river again. Hendrik took her across; they were collecting sap and chopping firewood. Daniel had already gone through before dawn.

Sweet biscuits for Willemina.

'I'm sorry.' Willemina was splitting palm leaves for a broom.

'You didn't even put out a hand to take hold of one end of the rope to help me drag it!'

'I'm sorry. I've brought you some sweet biscuits.' Be nice, please. 'We're into a new year, we can't live at loggerheads.'

'But it was worth the sweat, I can tell you. That tortoise fed us for three days. Thank you, don't know when last we saw or smelt wheat flour.'

She got to Aaltjie's; Aaltjie said there was a kind of balance in it. Her Jan had just gone to tether a calf and then he was on his way to Black River – to her, Pieternella, with the message from Lamotius.

Message from Lamotius?

Like news suddenly falling out of the sky.

Yes. Jan had been to the Flats, and from there to Groot River Mouth when the *Vanger* was starting on its return trip to the Lodge. Took a small quantity of beans along, some dried fish. The supply ship was lying at anchor, Lamotius said he needed to get a message to Daniel Zaaijman's wife, Daniel was to bring her to the Lodge urgently.

Bring her to the Lodge?

Yes.

The walk back to the river felt as long as a day; she tripped and fell twice in her haste. There was nobody at the sampan. She called and called. Eventually Goliath swam across and fetched her home.

No, the master was still busy among the palms in the hills on the other side. In the mean time, he, Goliath, and Thomas had to chop the firewood into shorter lengths. The first sap was already fermenting, they'd be able to start distilling the next day.

When Daniel got home just before nightfall, she was almost beside herself with worry.

6

By the time Daniel dropped anchor at French Church two days later, she knew it could only be about the Flats again.

The previous year, the whole of the Flats with all its tillable land and rivers had been given to Gerrit van Ewijk and Michiel Romondt, with a contract to supply the whole settlement with fresh food like sweet potatoes and vegetables and wheat. Slaves, implements, wheat seed – whatever they wanted.

And they went off hunting and fishing and looking for ambergris instead.

Lamotius sent Master Woodsman Steen and two officials to take back possession of the land, but Romondt shot at them, though he denied it later. Said he'd shot into the air to summon the other free-burghers to help him.

'What do you want me to say to the Commander, Daniel?'

'I don't like to hide behind a woman's skirts, Pieternella, but you'll have to get us off the hook again. *If* it is about the Flats.'

What else could it be?

She and Daniel and Mariatjie.

Maria the slave and Baldini and Hendrik would care for the three left at home.

They reached the Lodge; a big strange ship was in the anchorage. The *Westerwijk*, said Daniel. He knew the ship.

Unfamiliar sailors. Strangers who greeted Daniel and came over to laugh and chat.

The quay was bustling, so was the Lodge. A new stone building; in places the palm-leaf roof was still green. Everywhere there were piles of sand and stone and lime, scaffolding up against the walls, ladders – you could see they were still building. Piles of sharpened stakes with slave women standing and peeling the bark off them with long cleavers, their eyes dead.

Anna was not among them.

'Pieternella!' It was Tant Maijke, sitting in the shade on a low bench at the side of the Lodge. She took one look at Mariatjie and got to her feet in alarm. 'Oh God ...' Half mystified.

'This is Maria, our youngest.'

'Oh God ...' The old woman had a wild-eyed look on her face. 'Pieternella, I'm looking straight into the face of your mother!' she said, frightened. And as was the child's friendly nature, she suddenly kicked her little legs straight and laughed with her whole body and mouth and eyes.

'How old is she?'

'Turned a year and a half.' She quickly shifted the child to her other hip when the old woman wanted to take her.

'Please let me just hold her,' she asked, the tears welling up in her eyes. 'It's little Eva!'

'No. It's Maria. Now go and spread it all over the Orange Tree Flats, tell them I have at last had a Hottentot baby!'

'I'll say you've had the most beautiful baby ...'

All at once she realised that the old woman had a strange sadness about her. An old cat without claws, a storm spent. 'Are you well, Tante?'

'What shall I say?' She kept her eyes on the child. 'My health is giving in. The only one who cares at all for me is our beloved Commander. God will bless him.'

'But I heard you were getting married, Tante?'

'The children I brought into the world have abandoned me. My fatherland has abandoned me; here I sit, exiled. I came down two days ago on foot from the Flats so Commander Lamotius could write out my will for me. So now I'm just waiting. He said he'd arrange for me to go back to the Groot River on the *Vanger*. No, I'm not getting married any more.'

'I'm sorry to hear that.'

'You should have called the child Eva.'

'Actually we've come because the Commander ...'

She wanted to say something more, but just then the most exquisite woman came walking towards them from the direction of the gardens – slowly, her arms folded across her chest, and clearly deep in thought. Her dress was the colour of a green parrot's feathers, tiny pleats gathered round the slenderest waist. Collar of the whitest lace. Golden ringlets hung over her ears underneath her cap, swinging lightly as she walked.

At every step the shiny black toes of her shoes peeped out under the hem of her dress.

She didn't look up.

The most beautiful woman.

Aletta Uytenbogaert.

Tant Maijke knew. It seemed her husband was one of the new exiles from the Cape who had arrived on the *Westerwijk* - one Jan Dubertin. From the way Lamotius was dancing around them, particularly round the woman, they must have been important. 'But being important doesn't help, Pieternella. Once you're banned, you're banned. I said to the Commander, I said: If only I could go back and spend my last days at the Cape.'

Like the old Lodge, the new Lodge also had a long wide passage along one side. All the shutters were open to allow the sea breeze to waft in.

The woman was leaning against the wall, Lamotius was standing with her, his back to the entrance, and the way the woman was looking at him trumpeted forth the fact that she had the *look*.

She, Pieternella, noticed it straightaway and realised that this was an inconvenient moment to have come down the passage, but they couldn't turn back. Tant Magdalena used to say that Grieta's great problem with men was the *look* she was born with. A gift - sometimes a curse. A kind of inviting, like caressing a man's face with a lock of your hair.

Daniel coughed to let Lamotius know they were there.

'Cooper Zaaijman! Pieternella!' he exclaimed when he turned round. This was a different Lamotius, a strange one with happiness beaming out of him. 'What a delight to see you both at the Lodge again!' Friendly, as though he really was glad. 'Allow me to introduce you …'

But the woman had already turned round and walked away.

'I could have been here yesterday,' Daniel said, 'but there was no wind.'

'Of course. Come, let us walk over to my office.' Something felt really odd. 'Have you come alone? Without your beautiful daughters?'

'Our youngest came with us. Tant Maijke is playing with her outside.'

'Do sit down. Poor Maijke. She isn't well. I'm considering shifting her from the Flats to the Lodge.'

'Who's the strange woman?' she asked straight out.

'Aletta Uytenbogaert - wife of Dubertin the exile. She and her husband and their slaves arrived on the *Westerwijk*. Tragic. I'm letting them stay here at the Lodge for the moment. But let's leave that topic, shall we? I have very good news for you, Cooper Zaaijman: the two stills sent to Batavia were repaired and returned to the Cape, and they, too, have come on the *Westerwijk*.'

'That *is* good news Commander,' said Daniel, surprised.

Why was *she* sent for to hear that?

'I have already given orders that the *Vanger* is to bring me a load of bricks from Klinkenburg. We shall build you a brick chamber for the stills at Black River as soon as possible.'

So it wasn't about the Flats.

'We're going to run short of barrels, Commander.'

'There are quite a few here that you can load and take with you. All still your own handiwork. I remain hopeful that you will still be able to find the time somewhere to cooper for us; the new man is not your equal, Zaaijman.'

He was speaking too fast.

'My late father used to say that to become a cooper a man had first to go grey just working on staves.' Daniel was just making words, she could tell.

'Unfortunately I cannot spare any lime to bring to Black River Mouth. You'll have to break coral out of the reef and let it lie in the sun to dry. I shall come myself to show you how to burn it.'

'Commander …' She couldn't wait any longer. 'It seems that Jan Lodewijks brought us the wrong message … that you wanted to see me.'

'Yes.' He picked up a bundle of papers and tapped them straight on the table. 'Among the exiles to have arrived from the Cape is your brother, Jacobus van Meerhoff.'

First her ears began to buzz. 'My brother?' Then her heart started beating wildly. 'My *brother*?'

'Yes. With a special letter from Commandeur Van der Stel concerning his case.'

'Jacobus?'

'That he should be placed in the care of his sister and brother-in-law.'

'Why?'

'I regret to have to inform you, Pieternella – but he has been declared a good-for-nothing at the Cape. The Church Council no longer sees its way clear to taking care of him, he is already twenty-five years old.'

Daniel took her hand. 'This news is a shock to my wife, Commander.'

'I understand, Zaaijman. You and your wife are among our most respected free-burghers. I would dearly have wished you to have been spared the task which has been laid upon you. Believe me.'

'Where is he - my brother?'

'Still on the ship. We brought him ashore to be registered, but since we still have a shortage of accommodation at present ...'

'I understand.' It had nothing to do with accommodation, Lamotius's eyes looked away too quickly.

'I shall send a land boat to fetch him for you.'

An old dress that you had taken off and thrown away, because you had outgrown it, not because you didn't want to remember. Worse. A trouble that you had buried in a deep hole but that suddenly came bursting through the clods!

To be placed in the care of his sister and brother-in-law.

'Daniel?'

'Keep calm, my love.'

They stood on the quay waiting for the boat with him on it to arrive. Tant Maijke was looking after Mariatjie.

The boat swung its nose in the direction of the shore and she began to strain her eyes to catch a glimpse of him. In among all the anxiety inside her there was just a hint of gladness stirring.

A figure with a twisted body on the floor of the boat, a bird without wings fallen out of the sky. Wobbly neck. A figure that remained seated till one of the sailors jabbed him in the back and told him to get up and get off.

When he got to his feet, it was a tall dark man. Hair like teased coir smeared with oil and combed into rat's tails, under a red cap. Old brown breeches, off-white jerkin. Shoes.

'Van Meerhoff!' the sailor called, throwing a bundle after him. He turned and picked it up, indifferent.

Daniel stepped forward and put out his hand to greet him. Said he was Daniel Zaaijman, Pieternella's husband.

The man's body offered a diffident greeting, looked past Daniel and saw her standing there. His head dropped. 'Tell my *ousis* I greet her with respect.' Although younger than Jacobus, Pieternella's status was that of elder sister.

Not an old dress, or a trouble bursting through the clods - but shards from another time: a potter's cottage, a reed flute, a bow and arrow and a dead mouse - the brother her mother had often given a 'lesson' to, on the stone in front of the cottage, when he and she, Pieternella, had been quarrelling about something. That was when her mother had taught him that a brother had to treat his sister with respect, because she was his *taras*. His *gei taras* in whose name he was never in his life to swear falsely, because if he did, she would have the right to claim the best cows and ewes in his herd. And he would argue and say: But Mamma, I haven't got a herd! And her mother would say: Just so long as you know it.

'Jacobus?' She wanted to go closer, to touch him, but something in him prevented her.

Her brother was more Hottentot than Hollander.

He had Dutch shoes on his feet and a Dutchman's cap on his head, but it seemed that in his head there was still the law that a brother and sister could play together while they were children, but that as soon as the sister became an adult - a *taras* - he was never again to speak to her directly. He would have to ask someone else to speak to her on his behalf. Or else speak up into the sky.

'Jacobus, look at me! I'm your sister, we're living in other times, you are allowed to speak to me!'

He didn't want to. He turned to Daniel. 'Tell my *ousis* it wasn't my wish to be placed in her care.'

A bird that had fallen out of the sky and landed on *her* head. He climbed aboard the *Zeemaat* with his bundle and, without a word, stared straight ahead of him the whole way to Black River Mouth - except when he had to turn his back to light his pipe.

The bird's name was cussed - and he spent almost a year leaving his droppings on everything: her house, her yard, her whole life. A bird of prey trapped in his own cage and nothing and no one could get him to break out of it. Not tears, not cursing, not Daniel who grabbed him by the throat after he'd broken into the distilling chamber for the umpteenth time and been picked up dead drunk in the forest.

'For heaven's sake, man, I give you a drink every night, but it's never enough!' Daniel was murderously angry. 'Your sister is afraid of you, my children live in fear, my slaves laugh at you, my own patience has run out!'

There were days when she hung her head in shame before Daniel. 'I beg your pardon from the depths of my heart, I would never have wanted to bring this upon you, Daniel.'

'I know, my love. Relief will surely come from somewhere.'

When Baldini put him to work hoeing in his vineyard, he went nosing about in Baldini's cottage, drank his wine and stole his watch.

Hendrik's patience lasted longest. He had Jacobus sleep in his room, shoved a spoon between his teeth when he had fits. Moistened his head. Set him to dragging coral up from the shore to dry in the sun, coral that the slaves had chopped out of the reef. As Lamotius had ordered. It wasn't a full day before Goliath came to report: the man is off his head – he walks around kicking sand over the coral. When they go and speak to him, he kicks sand over them, too.

After that Hendrik took him with him across the river and taught him to chop palm heads. The still would arrive any day and there was not enough palm wine.

Three trees, and he disappeared, cleaver and all.

'I'm sorry, Pieternella,' Hendrik said, at the end of his tether, 'he's your brother, but the man does nothing but cause trouble!'

A week later Jan Dirks and Jan Lodewijks came across the river with him, tied up and badly beaten. They'd caught him in among their cattle cutting the throat of a calf with the cleaver.

She waited till the next morning. Till the children were at school and the slave Maria had taken Mariatjie down to the river to play for a while. Jacobus was eating his porridge and milk and bread outside; he would never sit at the table with them. If Maria gave him a spoon, he would hurl it into the thickets and eat with the shell scoop that he'd brought with him in his bundle. The kind she and her mother used to pick up on Robben Island ...

'Jacobus, when you've finished, I want to speak to you inside the house where we can be alone.' She went outside to say it to him. 'Today is the day that you and I are going to have a big talk. A *final* talk!' She was angry, she was exhausted with worry, exhausted with shame. Exhausted from crying.

He looked up into the sky, acted as if he was speaking to someone above his head. 'Tell my sister her brother will not enter her hut.'

'You tell my brother,' she told the one in the sky, 'he's not in a kraal, he's on Mauritius!' The law of the kraal said a brother was never to enter his sister's hut if she was alone in it. 'Tell my brother he is trampling my heart into the ground. Tell him his *!gab kami* – his little brother Salomon – is sitting on his grave weeping for the pain that he, Jacobus, has come here to sow!'

For the very first time it seemed as though something had touched him. The shake of his head, the jerk of his shoulders, the frown between his eyes. Like one in pain.

432

Only for a moment. Then he threw down the porridge bowl, clenched his eating shell between his teeth and disappeared into the thickets beyond the little hospital.

But deep within her she suddenly knew that only *she* could break open his cage. She didn't yet know how. Or when.

Maria the slave came back up from the river and asked if she had looked out over the sea yet ...

The *Europa* from the Lodge was dropping anchor in the mouth of the river. Not at the spot where the ships normally did but far up in the river.

'Not that I take any notice of such things, Pieternella,' said Lamotius when he reached the house, out of breath, 'but that mad slave Anna disappeared into the forest last night.'

Daniel and Hendrik and the slaves were across the river collecting palm sap; Baldini had stopped school when she told him the *Europa* had arrived, and hurried to the distillery.

'Commander, if Anna has disappeared into the forest, there's a cyclone on its way,' she said.

Lamotius looked uneasy. 'One would prefer not to take any notice of the inmost darkness of an insane slave woman, but for safety's sake I have stripped the yards and secured the *Europa* with three anchors. We cannot afford to lose her.'

Her mind had to be everywhere at once, thinking: how to entertain Lamotius, give him something to eat and to drink, think where to let him sleep. Send the slave Maria to call Baldini, to tell him to bring every available rope and thong; the iron pegs that the tent ropes were always tied to ...

'How your daughters have grown, Pieternella! And they have very pretty manners. How old are they now?'

'Catharina is eight, Eva six, Magdalena four and Mariatjie two.' Please, Daniel had to get home before dark! If in the mean time Baldini could anchor the roof of the little schoolroom ... 'Catharina, go and fetch your book so you and Eva can each read a piece for Mynheer Lamotius. How many men are there with you, Commander?' She needed to know how much food and bread and wine, how many sleeping places, to get ready.

'The young assistant, Jacob Ovaer, one soldier and three sailors. If you could provide shelter for Ovaer, I would appreciate it. We brought a sampan, they are unloading it at the moment. The bricks, a few barrels, the stills. I hope enough coral has been dried; we shall have to start burning lime first thing tomorrow.'

'Of course.' There's going to be a cyclone …

'Has enough firewood been chopped and cut?'

'Daniel has everything ready, Commander.'

'Oh, what a responsible free-burgher! Truly, a rarity on this island, Pieternella. The day the three stills which I have now sent to the Cape on the *Westerwijk* return and are set up alongside the two which I have just brought, this island will make a profit out of arrack which will cause the hearts of the Lords Seventeen to rejoice!'

'There is a freshly made-up bed for you in Baldini's cottage, if that would suit you?' Where could the slave Maria be after all this time?

'That would suit me very well. Baldini is such an intelligent man, such pleasant company.'

'Children, stop being a nuisance round Mynheer Lamotius!'

They were standing on either side of him, pestering him to be the first to read or to show. Mariatjie tried to climb up on to his lap. He stopped her when she wanted to take the child from him.

'Leave her,' he said and lifted her on to his lap. 'She reminds me of Andrea. Her sunniness.'

'Yes, Commander …' As though, for the first time, the subject could be mentioned. As though the scabs had healed over the old heartache and Lamotius had got his old life back. 'Andrea was a beautiful child.' She had sat down opposite him at the table for a moment.

'That is true, Pieternella. And is it not good and gracious that one does not know in advance what life will do to one?' He wasn't really as heartless as the free-burghers liked to make out.

'Surely. And I didn't want to unpack the stone in my heart here before you, Commander, but we were so happy here at Black River Mouth – until my brother Jacobus was placed in our care.'

'Is he causing you problems?'

'Terrible. I don't know what we're going to do, I don't know how much longer Daniel is going to put up with it.' Mariatjie was playing with his fingers.

'I shall speak to him.'

'He's run off into the forest again.'

'If it becomes too much for you, I shall issue orders for him to be placed in irons.'

'I hope that won't be necessary. Please excuse me for a moment.' She needed to get out. Before the previous cyclone, there had first been small fleecy clouds in the sky and the weather was just as oppressive as today.

When she got outside, she felt an iciness run through her: the bright blue sky was full of small fleecy white clouds.

7

The first blast came just before midnight.

'That's the harbinger,' Daniel said, and got up to close the door and shutters on the front room. The shutters on the rest of the house had already been bolted shut on the inside and secured on the outside.

Lamotius, Baldini and Ovaer were still sitting at the table with the umpteenth bottle of wine between them. Supper had long since been served: beef with rice and sweet potatoes and vegetables. Sweet cinnamon dumplings. Not one of them had apparently even thought of going to bed, or taken any notice of the possibility of a cyclone.

Hendrik had come back across the river a little earlier and came to the door to say the sampan had been hauled up high and secured. His food was in his room.

The soldier and the three sailors had their meal in the outside kitchen, where they'd made themselves mattress-beds to sleep on.

It was almost dark by the time Daniel and the other palm-sap tappers got home. When he heard that Anna had run off into the forest, he started issuing orders like a slave-driver. First of all Hendrik had to take a lantern and get back across the river to warn the nearest free-burghers. Orders telling who to tie up what, what to secure, what to pack away. More lanterns! They carried up water from the river. Rocks. Orders for supper to be eaten early so the fire could be put out.

'Zaaijman, I still hope that the mad slave's disappearance is no more than sheer desertion. The week before last all Dubertin's slaves deserted into the Orange Tree Mountains.'

Orders that a sheet of canvas and stones and drinking water and food and cushions and quilts be brought into the room nearest the sitting room, so that everyone could shelter there if indeed a cyclone struck them. It was her and Daniel's room, the largest in the house. Dry clothes for the children. Every available mat was shifted in under the bedstead ...

Daniel and Goliath and Adam went down to anchor the *Zeemaat* more securely.

No, she wasn't afraid.

But the strangest excitement kept rising like a fever inside her. Expectation. As though every drop of strength in her body was preparing itself for the invisible monster that thought it could come and catch them …

Each time she went outside, the night felt darker. There wasn't a star in the sky. A pitch-black quilt cast over the earth, and where Jacobus was only God knew. The lantern in the outside kitchen had been blown out long ago, the sounds of tired men snoring rolled out from the open side.

The slaves were in the slave cottage – the last to be anchored with ropes and poles.

Was she imagining it or were the frogs more vociferous than usual? Calling more urgently? Closer? The crickets, too.

Where was Anna?

She went indoors again, lit a candle and checked on the sleeping children – four small ebony beds. Tucked in the quilts where little bare feet had kicked them off …

Monster, please not my children.

In her body, she thought, there might be another baby.

For the umpteenth time, she swept up the tobacco crumbs between the elbows on the table; took another empty bottle to the kitchen. Noticed the vigilance in Daniel's eyes.

Lamotius was sitting at the head of the table. The sultry weather had him shedding his jacket and sitting in his pleated white shirtsleeves. The rest were in their working jerkins.

'What now lies ahead of me on this island, my friends, I do not know.' A high seriousness in his voice. 'Over a thousand years ago a wise man said that we should always observe thoroughly before we bestow our trust. I assure you that I have observed Lieutenant Jean Baptiste du Bertin very thoroughly and I have reached the conclusion that Jan Dubertin – as he is generally known – is not to be trusted.'

'I am no sage, Commander, but my head tells me that no exile is to be trusted. Jan Dubertin is an exile.' At the start of the evening, Ovaer was a quiet young man, but the wine was making him increasingly bold.

'What was the reason for this Dubertin's banishment?' Baldini wanted to know.

Daniel was listening like a watchdog, she could read his body. She had long since learnt that it was when he drew a certain silence round him that his ears were listening most acutely ...

'Dubertin owed his position of power at the Cape to friendship with Commissioner Van Goens,' Lamotius informed them. 'As you know, the annual visit of the Commissioner to the Cape is the visit of the highest authority. His word takes precedence over the laws of any Commandeur or Governor.'

'A good man to be friendly with!' Ovaer's tongue was already too loose.

'Dubertin took less and less notice of our esteemed Commandeur Van der Stel. Complaints of assaults and insults brought against him by the free-burghers were simply denied. Remember that, among other things, he was in charge of the supply stores. Even Van der Stel tried to lay complaints against Dubertin before the Commissioner – in vain.'

'That's odd,' remarked Baldini.

'Not merely odd; it perhaps explains why our own free-burghers' tobacco found no market there. According to evidence that has subsequently come to light, Commissioner Van Goens himself dismissed the sentry on guard on the quay at night to make it easy for Dubertin to have the contraband tobacco from the ships smuggled ashore. The same with liquor. He grew rich through selling it all privately and pocketing the money himself.'

'Tell the bit about the slaves, Commander,' prompted Ovaer.

'He even withheld the slaves' monthly ration of fifteen barrels of fish and sold it to the ships instead.'

'How did they eventually find him guilty?' Daniel wanted to know.

'It happened when High Commissioner Van Reede arrived unexpectedly at the Cape. He was an old enemy of Van Goens' and a man of far higher importance. He ordered that the complaints be investigated. Dubertin, my friends, was a consummate robber. He stole everything he could lay his hands on: wood, iron, copper, fish, meat, bacon – anything that would sell. So they banned him to Mauritius for twenty-five years and now he is *my* problem!'

'And his wife?' It was she, Pieternella, who asked.

'A most courageous lady,' he said with undisguised admiration, 'who has voluntarily followed her husband into exile. An educated lady of the best class; her father was an influential jurist in the fatherland. Currently in the East.'

Then the wind struck. From the south.

Daniel and Baldini carried the two smallest children to the large room; Catharina and Eva could walk. Lamotius and Ovaer remained seated at the table. Perhaps they thought it was just an ordinary storm, because Lamotius was still ponderously saying that he hoped the *Europa*'s anchors would hold, the boat had only just been rebuilt at great expense ...

No one heard the rest of his words because all at once the monster burst upon them, terrifyingly embodied in wind and rain, as though it wanted to sweep them off the face of the earth, house and all! She saw the terror flash across Lamotius's face when he leapt up and hurried to the bedroom, with Ovaer stumbling after him. Daniel came back to fetch her and the lantern.

Lamotius was sitting at the foot of the bedstead with his arms round the bedpost, his mouth opening and closing. He was speaking but nobody could hear him above the infernal rush of the elements. The earth itself was trembling beneath them! Every time a tree crashed to the ground outside, it sounded like a gunshot. Ovaer was sitting on the ground, holding on to one of the legs of the bed, his head pressed against his hands. Baldini sat, upright and respectful, on one of the clothes chests, holding the lantern. She and the children held on to one another at the head of the bed.

No, she wasn't scared. She kept looking the monster in the eye with a resistance that showed she would never let her children be blown over. Nor herself.

Whenever her will to resist seemed about to rip loose, she would look at Daniel, standing completely calm beside the bed, as though it was in his power to determine every moment of the assault.

Then she'd steal some of his strength.

Just moments before the wind ripped a hole in the children's room next to hers and Daniel's, he started rolling the stones off the canvas and pulled it over the bed ...

When the lantern blew out, her hands felt for the children and made them crawl in under the heavy bedstead. Not one argued, not even little Mariatjie. Like small animals with an inborn way of *knowing*.

The monster chased its breath right through the house; in under the bed. Somewhere things were being broken and kicked over, but in all the noise no one could tell *where*.

And somewhere it had Jacobus in its talons.

By daybreak its first rage was spent. When the unearthly silence of the eye of the storm descended on them, Lamotius's voice was the first to be heard, asking Daniel to light a lantern and fetch the Bible or *Home Sermons*.

'This is only the eye, Commander.'

'I know. When it returns, this house is going to collapse on top of us. We need to pray urgently for protection!'

And again they waited.

She sent the children into the other room to use the pot. Mariatjie was getting restive, Baldini helped to soothe her while she gave them sweet biscuits and buttermilk.

Ovaer held the lantern for Lamotius to pray the words in the prayer book, and he trumpeted them to heaven: '*O Lord, punish us not in Thine anger, chastise us not in Thy wrath. O Lord, refresh our souls and lead us in the paths of righteousness, and ever be with us ...* Hold the lantern higher, Ovaer! ... *Be not far from us, for terrors are at hand, and here we have no helper ...* Cooper, what is the extent of the damage?'

Daniel had come in from outside. 'Not too serious, Commander. Mostly wind damage, so far the rain has fortunately not been too severe. It's just the hole in the roof; Hendrik and two of the slaves are trying to cover it with a canvas sheet and pack stones on it to hold it.'

'Hendrik? The ambergris thief?'

'Hendrik who helps me everywhere until the long-promised slaves eventually arrive!'

'Has the *Europa* survived?'

'It's still dark.' Curt.

The eye soon passed and then came the second assault, from the north-east. For hours.

By midday the monster was spent.

The outside kitchen had blown down, the frightened soldier and sailors were sitting stupefied under drenched mattresses, waiting for further perils.

The hospital had been flattened. The schoolroom. A part of Hendrik's house.

The *Europa* and the *Zeemaat* were still anchored firm, though rocking on the most incredible swells; the yellow-sand bay had been washed away so deep in places that two houses could have fitted into the craters.

With a pale face and a hoarse voice, Lamotius called everyone together up at the house and ordered Ovaer to read a preachment of thanksgiving. '*O Almighty and Eternal God, who punished the unbelieving and unrepentant world with the Biblical flood, yet spared and preserved Thy faithful servant Noah, we thank Thee ...*'

Next afternoon the coral was shovelled into an oven-pit and burnt, and the sampan started bringing ashore the bricks from the boat for the building-in of the stills.

The slave Maria came to say that Jacobus was sitting behind the slave house. Weak from hunger and like someone who'd escaped from the claws of a beast of prey.

'Jacobus?'

'Beg my sister to rescue her brother from this place they call Mauritius!' he said to the one in the sky and crammed food into his mouth with his hands.

After four days they put out the fire in the kiln and began to carry the lime to the distilling place for one of the sailors who was a mason.

But he could build in only one of the stills. They hadn't brought enough bricks for two.

'That is a serious pity, Zaaijman,' Lamotius shook his head and said. 'All I can suggest is that I return later and see to the building-in of the other one. By then perhaps the other three stills will have arrived from the Cape ...'

Daniel grew angry. 'Couldn't you have *seen* that there were too few bricks, Commander? I realised that as soon as I saw them piled on the shore!'

'Do you think counting bricks is all I have to concern myself with, Zaaijman?' Lamotius was angrier still. 'While these bricks were being loaded, I had to watch Dubertin and get him placed on the Flats – supervise the *Vanger* to take two loads of his goods to Groot River Mouth – arrange for them to be taken from there to the Flats by wagon!'

'Why can't Baldini and I build in the other still?'

'No. That is a task for a craftsman. If you find that the arrack tastes of copper, rinse out the still with lye and urine.'

On its rampage the monster had raced through the palm trees with a cutlass and mowed off the branches everywhere it could, so that Hendrik would go out day after day with Adam and Goliath, and come back at night with a barely decent sheaf.

The three Jans waited till Lamotius had gone before they crossed the river. 'Gawd, Daniel, we're ruined. If you could help us out with a few spars and some pieces of canvas. A little rice.'

The cyclone had knocked four of her prettiest cups, five saucers and three porcelain plates off the display shelf, Daniel's world map out of its frame, smashed the children's school things. Each time Catharina and Eva dug some unbroken object out of the debris, they laughed with happiness and came to show it off in their dirty little hands.

When the river was running clear of mud again, she and the slave Maria could start washing the quilts and sheets and tablecloths in its upper reaches.

Jan Muur's Willemina came up to their laundry place one morning, looking as if the loss and damage were still clinging heavily to her. 'Jan went to the Flats and from there to the Lodge for a few supplies. He says although this cyclone wasn't a really big one, the countryside has really been hammered. They say Focke Janse of Orange Tree Flats is dead – I thought you might have known him.'

'Of course.' That was a shock. Focke was one of her remaining links with the *Boode*.

'And Willem van Deventer was dying. He'd probably be buried by now. They say he went outside into the eye and cursed the cyclone because a piece of his roof had blown off.'

'Willem van Deventer?' That was the second shock.

'Yes.'

'I wonder if ...' She fell silent. It would be sinful to wonder if a woman was happy that her husband was dead. 'I know his wife very well. She'll probably go back to the Cape now – to her other children.'

'It'd be a stupid woman who didn't get away from this place. Jan says the most amazing people have arrived on the Flats. Rich and important. Jan Dubertin. His wife's name is Aletta. My Jan reckons if she isn't at least a princess, she's from some noble family or other.'

'Lamotius said he'd placed them on the Flats.'

'Jan says they've had a nice big house built, near the bridge they're building across the Groot River. You've been there.'

'Yes. But that was long before they started building the bridge.'

'About half an hour above the waterfall. They invited Jan in and gave him some refreshment; he says the man said it was clear the free-burghers are having a tough time on this island.'

'Has the bridge been finished?'

'Nearly. The smith has finished all the iron mountings.'

'It's a dangerous river.'

'Jan says we shouldn't start rejoicing too soon, but it looks as if this Dubertin might not be afraid to stand up for the free-burghers.'

'And his wife?' She couldn't work out why the woman kept bothering her ...

'Jan says he couldn't stop looking at her. I said to him, I said: Shame on you!'

The first to be finished was the children's room. Then Hendrik's. Daniel explained to the children that their schoolroom would have to wait for the new leaves that were already sprouting on the palm trees, and that then he would take everyone off the distilling to rebuild their school. They'd see. And a new hospital shelter for Mother.

And yes, the still did make the arrack taste of copper. Hendrik went out to pick lye-bushes and burn them; she didn't ask who peed in the still, but the problem was solved.

But it wasn't the arrack or the cyclone that remained the rock of offence, it was Jacobus. Nothing helped, no cursing or pleading or threats, from anybody.

'It feels to me that all he's doing is trampling me to pieces, Daniel!' she cried out one day in despair. The night before Jacobus had broken into the distilling chamber yet again. That morning he had been in the garden tormenting Thomas by jerking him off-balance by his ankle chain – in retaliation, because the slave had hit him on the back with a spade for deliberately stamping on the pumpkins the week before.

Jan Dirks had beaten him half-dead a second time; he'd spied on Elisabet and the girls when they were crouching over the pit-latrine. Like most of the free-burghers, Jan had placed a plank with a round hole in it across a hole in the ground behind a bush. He hadn't bothered about erecting a screen.

Daniel was fit to be tied. 'Pieternella, I'm boiling over with worry: we've got four daughters!'

'Jacobus wouldn't do my children any harm, Daniel.'

'How can you be sure of that?'

'Because I'm his *gei taras*. My children are untouchable. Believe me.'

'I don't know what you're talking about, Pieternella. It feels as though you are walking into another world where I can't follow you, and that disturbs me!'

'I'm not walking into another world, my Daniel – I'm just remembering little pieces of a world that Jacobus still seems to be lurching about in. But I'm just as disturbed as you are, I don't see any way out.'

The way out came of itself.

A man from Northwest Harbour came to say that there was an English ship that urgently needed a cooper. Daniel and Goliath left in the *Zeemaat*. Baldini remained at the distillery. Hendrik and Adam went off cutting palm heads. Thomas was in the garden. She was making Catharina a dress; the child was outgrowing her clothes. Tall like her father.

All day long Jacobus followed the shade as it moved round the slave house. The slave Maria took him his meals, and scolded Magdalena and Eva because they wouldn't stop pestering him – if they weren't clambering over him, they were pelting him with pebbles and shrieking with laughter when they hit him.

'Juffrouw Pieternella,' the slave complained, 'the master said expressly the children were to keep away from him, but they won't listen!'

'Don't worry, Maria. I'm keeping an eye on them.' She went and sat with him for a while, just to chat with him – even though he addressed his every reply to the one in the sky. She asked if Barbara Geens was still alive. Yes, but she's old, walks with a stick. How were the Van der Byls? Fine, and highly regarded. How were things on Robben Island? As usual. Except that the rabbits that were put there in Mamma's time had now taken over the place. An extra burden for the Post Holder because they were eating up all the grazing. Van der Stel asked almost every shell-boat to bring back rabbits to the mainland for the notables' table. The Commandeur got angry when the Post Holder sent word they couldn't catch the things. How were the free-burghers? Not allowed to graze their stock between Lion's Head and Table Mountain any more; now only high officials had grazing rights there. Pieter van der Byl told Jan Vlok that was against the orders of the Lords Seventeen, officials weren't allowed to own stock. But they took no notice.

Late one afternoon Jacobus suddenly disappeared.

She asked the slave Maria if she'd seen which way he'd gone. Yes. Towards the river, while Juffrouw Pieternella was trying on Catharina's dress. But he didn't cross, she'd watched him, he went down towards the yellow-sand bay.

'Watch the children.'

Sometimes something deep within you sends a message to your head. She'd remembered that it must be new moon.

The sun was sinking when she reached the sandy bay. Out over the sea in the west lay a bank of thin clouds coloured pink. The trees and the forest and the hills were slowly putting on their nightclothes.

The thin silver sickle of the moon hung like a smile in the sky.

On the shore in the distance stood the figure of a tall thin man, motionless. Jacobus. There was something about him that stopped her going any closer.

Dead still, as though carved out of wood. Black against the sky.

She suspected he might do it. Dance. First on one foot, then on the other foot. An unhurried hop ... hop ... hop. Like someone who first had to find the right steps. Had to feel for them. When he found them, he placed his hands, one behind the other, in front of his mouth and began to whistle the short one-toned sounds of a reed-flute, his feet treading the rhythm all the while.

A Hottentot dance. On this strange earth beneath his feet while a sickle moon hung in the sky and the tears rolled down her cheeks – down past her throat, into her dress, because deep, deep within her a rumble-drum was playing an accompaniment.

God – *Gounja* – Almighty Father – *Gounja Tikwa* – look down upon Jacobus, please, she prayed.

He went on dancing for a long time.

Then he sat down. When she stopped behind him, she could hear his breath racing.

'Jacobus ...' His whole body jerked with fright. 'Don't turn round.' The swish of the waves was far out behind the reef. In front of them a fish would leap out of the still water and plop back again. 'Who are you, Jacobus?'

'I don't know, *ousis*.'

'Who do you *want* to be?'

'A real person. A Hottentot. A *Khoi*.'

'Why didn't you go to Mamma's people?'

'I did.'

'To the Cochoqua?'

'No. They haven't got kraals any more, all their stock is gone. I went across the mountains to the Chainouqua. To Chief Dorha.'

'And?'

'They made me eat with the women and children. Sleep with them. I wasn't allowed into the circle of the men. The children jeered at me.'

'Why?' But she suddenly knew why.

'They said I was a *kutsire*.'

'I understand.' A boy who had not yet been made into a man was a *kutsire*. A grown man who had never been made into a man was a shameful *kutsire*. Unclean.

'I went to other Khoi people, the Namaqua at the Castle that came back with Commandeur Van der Stel after his trip to visit them. I wanted to go back to their country with them; I thought they would take me because they were a bit different.'

'And so?' Her thoughts were with the Chainouqua ...

'They threw stones at me. Said they didn't want the breath of a *!Uri San* among them.'

'What's that?'

'A white Bushman. A poor white man.'

'Will you go back to the Cape if you can, Jacobus?'

'Yes. This isn't my home. Never. But they declared me good-for-nothing, *ousis*. They won't take me back.'

'Would you allow yourself to be initiated as a Chainouqua?'

'That was what I was on my way to do when Jan Vlok caught me the last time.'

'I thought you were with Barent Backer.'

'They took me away from there the first time I ran away to the Chainouqua.'

'They said you stole and drank, too.' He didn't reply. 'Tell me the truth, Jacobus!'

'I did.'

'Swear on my life that you will go to Chief Dorha of the Chainouqua and have yourself initiated, if you are given a second chance.'

'*Ti !gas ao nu* – I swear on the life of my *gei taras*, I swear!'

8

It was May.

The palm trees had yielded very little sap; Hendrik told the children this was the trees' sleeping time. May was also the island's coldest month, although it really wasn't *cold* cold.

But Mariatjie was a little chesty and Daniel wondered whether it wasn't the dampness of the river rising up into the house.

Her problem just went on wandering round the house. Jacobus. Who wanted to know the way to the Lodge so that he could wait there for a ship to the Cape. Who didn't want to understand that she would first have to speak to Lamotius; that she couldn't simply go there on her own but had to wait till Daniel had arrack to deliver. No, Jacobus could not go with them then; it could be months before a ship arrived.

Often the fear in her heart that Lamotius would not allow him to go back had her deeply worried. As with Salomon. The only hope was that Jacobus was a grown man, while Salomon had been just a boy.

Daniel had brought the news of Willem van der Hoeven's death the previous time he'd been to the Lodge.

Hendrik quietly told her the rest of the story: that Grieta hadn't shed a tear, just stood at the graveside with her eyes shut, and Abraham Steen beside her. Hendrik heard from Tant Theuntjie. Lamotius delivered the funeral oration himself, brief and perfunctory. He was not seeing Grieta at all any more ... other stories were doing the rounds. What stories? Theuntjie's stories that would land you in court.

'What stories, Hendrik?'

'Ovaer says his lips are sealed, but his eyes saw the gifts that Lamotius showered on Dubertin's Aletta. His ears heard the laughter and whisperings.'

'Between Lamotius and Aletta?'

'Every night, apparently, while they were staying in the Lodge. Ovaer says Lamotius is openly saying that he doesn't know what such a beautiful woman could see in a boor and a thief like Dubertin. Don't let Daniel know I told you.'

'I won't. But I'm glad I'm not her, stuck on the Flats.'

'It wasn't Lamotius who put them there, it was Dubertin who demanded a place to stay as far as possible from the Lodge. He made Aletta give back all the gifts.'

All that Daniel would say to this was that Lamotius had a strange restlessness about him.

Maybe, but it definitely had nothing to do with the free-burghers living on the western side of the island any more. He'd apparently decided to ignore them, certainly hadn't sent any more posters to warn them off.

Daniel came to the door late in the afternoon with the bucket of milk; the lamp was already lit, the table laid for supper. And who should come up the footpath from the river, as though they'd fallen out of the sky? Lamotius and Secunde Jacobsen. Not a sign of a boat on the water.

'Zaaijman ...' Breathlessly. 'I've just been saying to Secunde Jacobsen: at least your good wife will give us supper and somewhere to lay our heads tonight.'

They had left from the Lodge three days earlier in the *Vanger*, sailed to the Groot River, and travelled on foot from there to the Flats, where they spent the night in the ruined lodge. They'd continued across the island the next morning to Northwest Harbour.

Visiting free-burghers all along the way.

'We're trapped with a viper in our midst, Zaaijman. There's a constant stream of free-burghers and Company servants going to Dubertin's, which makes me profoundly uneasy. The free-burghers at Northwest Harbour are felling more and more trees by the day to clear even more land for tobacco; I tell them the Cape does not require any more Mauritian tobacco, where are you going to find a market for the product? They don't answer me. We've still got thirty-two giant rolls of it in stock. And between Northwest Harbour and you here, Jan Muur and Jan Lodewijks and Jan Dirks complain that there is too much shade up here; they also want to move to Northwest Harbour to plant tobacco for a livelihood. I told them to lay it before the Council on Monday.'

Almost all night long.

About Dubertin, Dubertin, Dubertin. Have you met the man, Zaaijman? No, Commander. I'm warning you, the man is hatching a plot to challenge my authority; he will oblige me to put him on one of the outer islands yet. Yes, Molin and Swaanswijk and Geel have escaped from Tobacco Island. Dubertin hid them in his house. But they have been caught again. As soon as the supply ship arrives, they'll be sent to the Cape and brought before the court.

Maijke van den Berg is well, Pieternella, she's diligent in her care of the palm tree plantation. She's not far from Dubertin's house, she says there's a constant stream of callers. Michiel Romondt says poor Aletta Uytenbogaert has twice come to him in tears to ask for refuge; she simply cannot endure Dubertin's cantankerousness any more.

'What are you going to do?'

'I don't know. Make an attempt to get her closer to the Lodge where at least she'll have protection.'

She waited till the next morning to catch him alone. Baldini had taken Jacobsen to show him his vineyard, and also the few cattle that Baldini had acquired. Hendrik had gone off after ambergris, taking Jacobus with him.

'I need to speak to you about my brother, Commander. I want to plead with you to send him back to the Cape to stay with my mother's people, which is what he wants most. The Church Council will have no further expense on his account. Please.' She was ready to go down on her knees before him. She was prepared to read him the letter she had written to Chief Dorha. Jacobus or a soldier could read it to him.

'I have understood your problem for a long time now, Pieternella. Don't worry yourself any more about it, he will be sent back to the Cape on the next supply ship.'

Like light suddenly breaking through. 'I thank you, Commander. From my heart.'

Relief that could have lifted her feet clear off the earth – except that Hendrik and Jacobus hadn't yet got back when the slaves started rolling the barrels of arrack down to load them on to the *Zeemaat*. It was Lamotius's proposal that Daniel should take the arrack that was already in the barrels to the Lodge now, so that he and Jacobsen could use the opportunity to get back home.

It cost her a flagrant lie when he said Jacobus could go along at the same time and he would give him odd jobs to do on the building site till the ship arrived. She lied that Jacobus was doing odd jobs for the free-burghers across the river.

Luckily the children didn't hear her.

Two months.

While her time came closer, Jacobus broke in twice to steal arrack. He threw a rock at Thomas and she had to stitch the gash in the slave's head with needle and thread.

'Daniel, I just cannot carry on!'

'Be strong, my love. It's September. If the ship doesn't arrive in the next week or two, I'll take him to the Lodge myself. Lamotius may as well put him in irons.'

Light, dark, darker.

At last *light* when Jan Dirks returned the saw he'd borrowed, and said the *Baaren* had arrived at Northwest Harbour and was unloading goods for the free-burghers.

How was that possible? The supply ship always ran straight for Southeast Harbour …

Daniel laughed. He said: 'Pieternella, make that delicious beef stew with dumplings tomorrow, and send Thomas to the garden for enough vegetables; I'm expecting extra mouths at our table. And tell Jacobus to get his things ready.'

It was like spinning round and round from crying to laughing, till the *Baaren* fired a single cannon shot to ask for a pilot and dropped anchor in the mouth of the Black River.

The table was laid, the food simmering gently; Jacobus was wearing breeches and a shirt that Baldini had given him.

The ship unloaded a chest full of stuff for Daniel: tools, school things for the children, two new copper pots and a kettle, an iron bucket, another two beautiful porcelain chamber-pots …

'Skippers, Pieternella, like to trade for their own account. Remember, they work for a trading company that pays very poorly, and poor payment

448

makes for dishonest employees.'

Captain De Hoop had lunch with them that afternoon and brought them the news from the Cape. About all the dissension. That officials could now own as much land as they thought they could manage. The Commandeur had claimed a large farm for himself, *Constantia* – and spent more time there than at the Castle. The directors in Amsterdam were apparently unaware that the farm was bigger than the whole of Amsterdam!

She didn't want to know anything more about the Cape.

It was like turning back when you didn't want to. Where you were chased away when you were really still a child because they didn't want you any more! The pain of it. Salomon …

No, nothing would make her turn back. The pain had passed. Mauritius was now her home, her life, her jackal-haired husband.

But Jacobus had to go back.

She left the men at the table to talk about men's affairs and went to the bedroom. She took her letter out of the chest to read it through one last time. *Honoured Chief Dorha, I am the sister of the bearer of this letter. My name is Pieternella, I am the daughter of Krotoa whom the Hollanders called Eva. I now live far across the sea in a strange country, but in me and my brother flows the proud blood of the Chainouqua, which our mother taught us to honour because our ancestor Eijcouqua was a courageous Chainouqua. That is why it is the desire of my brother Jacobus to be initiated into your kraal as a Chainouqua and to swear everlasting loyalty to you. I ask that you will accept him …*

She folded the letter, addressed and sealed it and wrapped it in a piece of canvas. Then she went outside to give it to Jacobus. Captain De Hoop was in a hurry, he wanted to leave that same afternoon. He had on board an exile from the Cape whom he wanted to put ashore before the man breathed his last. Wouldn't eat, wouldn't speak. A Frenchman and an expert in vine-growing and winemaking whom Simon van der Stel had specially imported to the Cape. And then started mistrusting because he suspected the man of smuggling letters with all kinds of information about the Cape to France.

'Van der Stel is like a man constantly haunted by a ghost; he's convinced the French or the English are just waiting for the right moment to attack the Cape and take over. He has no compassion for their ships and little for their sick. No mercy at all for free-burghers who want to supply them with food or help, so as to put a little money in their pockets. I'm just mentioning this to you, Daniel – and to the free-burghers up at Northwest Harbour, too. When one hand washes the other, both come clean.'

'Don't trouble yourself on our account, Captain. Lamotius has shut his eyes to this side, he has far greater worries about Dubertin.'

'Can't say I blame him. Dubertin is cunning – and his wife even more so. She once smuggled a quantity of jewels to the fatherland for Van Goens, hidden in the clothes on her back.'

She remained standing on the shore until they were through the reef and Daniel and Hendrik had returned on the sampan. She felt the world gradually growing bluer and greener and bigger and more beautiful all round her. Tranquil.

Rescued.

Even though he was her brother.

✍ FOUR ✍

1

On the morning of the tenth of October, as dawn was breaking, she gave birth to a son, Pieter. Aaltjie handed him to Daniel and he just stood there with the screaming, kicking little thing in his big hands. The pride and wonderment on his face washed over her like an act of cleansing. That she could give her husband this gift, in return for all his goodness to her.

All three Jans and Willemina and Elisabet came across the river to share Daniel's joy with bowls of caudle - caudle which she taught the slave Maria to make just as Anna had taught *her* to make it.

The outside kitchen was the first to be rebuilt, then the children's schoolroom, then the hospital. The new slave house was bigger than the old, to allow room for the three new slaves that Daniel had bought from the skippers of visiting ships: Jake, Karel and Jamika. All three from Madagascar.

'Truly, Pieternella, this looks like the time of the slaves,' Hendrik said, bringing the 'other' news when he came back from the Lodge after he and Daniel had delivered another load of barrels of arrack.

Gerrit van Ewijk had taken his wife Hester to the Lodge to be placed in custody after he had caught her and one of the slaves in adultery. Two witnesses. Hester and the slave were both in gaol. Lamotius said the charge against her was so serious he would have to send her to the Cape to be tried. The slave he would punish himself.

'Why,' she asked Daniel that night, 'were the late Jongmeyer and Abraham Steen and all the others who fornicated with slave women not thrown into gaol?'

'My love, if once you start fighting the injustices of life, you find yourself struggling up a mountain that has no top.'

'That's not an answer. As far as I know, the Company laid down a law that a man who fornicates with a slave woman must work for six months for the Company as a slave himself and live on slave's rations.'

'Pieternella, don't bother your head about the Company's laws.'

'I'm bothered because it seems that hidden under the quilts there are different laws for women, Daniel.'

'Maybe you're right, Pieternella. That's why I say again: live your own life and do so as fairly as you can.'

'That's still not an answer, Daniel.'

The late Willem van Deventer's widow Maria was so destitute, Hendrik said, that Lamotius had allowed the few cattle that Willem had left to graze among the Company's herd. When she asked why poor Maria hadn't rather returned to her people at the Cape, he said: Because Free-burgher Lambert Stam's free-burgher contract had not yet expired ...

The late Sven's Magriet was slaving for Bart and Tant Theuntjie.

And yes, Jacobus had left on the *Baaren.* So had Molin and Swaanswyk and Geel. In chains.

On board the *Baaren* was a bottle of the Black River arrack and another of sweet potato arrack that Lamotius had distilled at the Lodge. For Simon van der Stel. Who would without any doubt be so satisfied with the products that he would ask for regular consignments.

A few ebony boards, sawn by hand, while they waited for saw-blades. It had been impossible to saw more; the island was caught in another severe drought, there were only pools of dirty water left in the rivers. Many Company servants were ill. Surgeon Molin was on his way to the Cape; Deputy Surgeon Wilde was hiding at Dubertin's on the Flats because it seemed he owed too many people too much money.

A few slabs of ebony. Some dried beans and a few rolls of tobacco, because they were the only source of income for most of the free-burghers. They would be completely destitute if he, Lamotius, didn't buy their tobacco.

Another still needing to be repaired. Another saw-blade pattern.

Poor Lamotius, Baldini often said.

If the man didn't have to prevent the sheep on the east of the island from breaking out, then it was the sheep on the west side he had to worry about – or leap on his horse and race to the Flats to nip things in the bud up there. Have manure delivered to the vineyard where he had placed Van der Stel's Frenchman. Forbid free-burghers to conspire with Dubertin ...

Baldini had been to the Flats. He said Dubertin was ploughing and planting with the best of them, the complete free-burgher – chastising the slaves assigned to him, entertaining every free-burgher that passed on his way to the bridge. A man with two hearts. Instead of showing remorse and modesty in his behaviour, he strutted about, showing off wherever he went!

Jan Muur came back from the Flats and told Daniel the free-burghers had only to wait till the great man in their midst received his papers from the Cape. Which great man? Dubertin, of course! What papers? His real papers. Dubertin had never been banned; Henk Karseboom said he was a secret commissioner who'd been sent to the island to investigate the complaints and other matters. We mustn't let Lamotius get to hear of it. As soon as his papers arrive, he'll assume full authority. Do you believe this, Jan Muur? Of course, why would the man lie?

She and Daniel and the children were on the sampan anchored on the near side of The Plaat one Sunday. Far from the biting shells. Pieter was a sturdy six-month-old baby with, it seemed, not a nervous red hair on his head. Daniel could dive in with him, let him go under water and each time he'd come up with a beaming face panting for breath.

Catharina and Eva and Magdalena shrieked with laughter – Daniel's three smooth-bodied girl-fishes.

She, Pieternella, and Maria stayed on the sampan under the awning. 'Mother not going under the water?'

'No, Maria.'

'Father not taking Maria under water?'

'No, Maria.'

She was nearly three. A sun child. A happy child. Whom everyone – skippers, strangers, acquaintances alike – always wanted to pick up and cuddle and kiss.

Later Daniel handed Pieter to her, climbed out of the water himself, keeping an eye on the three girls, who still wanted to play. 'Pieternella,' he said after a while, 'there's a serious matter on my heart.'

The way he said it frightened her. 'What matter?'

'In a month's time, at the end of May, my contract as a free-burgher expires. For me that means freedom.'

Her ears started humming. 'Freedom to leave Mauritius?'

'Yes. But I don't want to. I say, like Robert Hendricks: the place has called me to stay here for ever.'

She closed her eyes and felt the relief wash over her. 'So what is the matter on your heart, then, Daniel?'

'I want us to move to Northwest Harbour.'

'Northwest Harbour ...'

'Not tomorrow or the next day – but before the end of the year. I'm not an arrack distiller. I'm a cooper.'

'You've got an arrack contract with Lamotius.'

'And he with me – that we would be given slaves and enough stills. He came and had one built in, promised to bring the other one back and build it in. And three others as well. Nothing has come of it. I want to move to Northwest Harbour and be my own master. A cooper. To help ships. I want to move to Northwest Harbour because Black River is too damp for you and the children – and I want to build you a stone house.'

'Tell the girls to get out of the water.' Pieter and Maria were getting fidgety on the sampan.

'First tell me what your heart says, Pieternella.'

'We're moving to Northwest Harbour.'

They were in bed already and the lamp had been blown out when somebody came knocking at the door.

Daniel called through the shutter to hear who it was. Adam Cornelise from the Flats. The one who'd come with his wife Cathrinha Kel to have the children christened that Sunday at Northwest Harbour. The ne'er-do-well.

Daniel pulled on his breeches and opened the door.

Somewhere something was wrong, there weren't just two voices. She got up and went into the front room in her nightdress. A strange man was standing just inside the doorway, his small round face yellow with dark patches in the light of the candle. His eyes watchful. His clothes smart but spoilt, as though he had come through water and many thickets.

Jean Baptiste du Bertin.

No longer young. The dark green velvet jacket tight and flapping up over his old man's belly. The shirt and its white lace collar not quite so fresh any more. Breeches of the same stuff as the jacket, white-stockinged legs brown with mud, the bows on his shiny black shoes wet and limp.

But it was the hardness in his eyes that brought her up sharp on the other side of the table. The eyes of a hawk. Dark.

Jan Dubertin.

And beside him a drab-feathered fowl, dripping wet and badly frightened: Adam Cornelise. Jan Muur had told him where he would find the sampan in the forest so he could get the man across the river to ask for refuge at Daniel's.

She heard every word spoken at the table as she set down bottles of wine and glasses before them, revived the fire and hung a pot of water to heat so they could have something hot to eat and drink afterwards. Buttered bread. Sliced some of the meat left over from lunch, cheese ...

The stranger's voice was like the velvet of his clothes, his words rounder, softer – different. But something kept warning her that there was ruthlessness behind that velvet voice.

'I was subjected to an unjust trial at the Cape, Zaaijman; on Mauritius, thanks to the fabrications of the Commander, I have been accused of sowing insurrection and declared a public mutineer.'

She made mental pictures of his words. Watched Daniel and saw that he was listening in his guard-dog silence. Realised that behind *his* indifference there was a cunning strength concealed.

'Because life on the Flats is often lonely, I invited Free-burgher Karseboom and his wife to spend a few days at home with us. He will be able to testify to the horrors committed there in the early hours of yesterday morning.'

Abraham Steen, Master Woodsman, and fourteen Company servants, armed with muskets, pistols, axes, sabres and leg irons, had invaded his house without warning and kicked up a tremendous din. They grabbed him by the hair and pushed him around, while Master Steen shouted: 'Beat the crook to death!'

When the first rage had subsided, he and his wife were told to get dressed and accompany them. At a question from his wife Aletta Uytenbogaert, they learnt that they were to be taken to a boat waiting at Groot River Mouth. From there he would be taken to Tobacco Island – an island without any means of sustenance or drinking water – and his wife to the Lodge. He, Jan Dubertin, was under arrest. They wanted to put him in irons but his wife begged them not to. She sent Karseboom to call their good neighbour Adam Cornelise to come and take care of their goods.

After that Master Steen had the house searched for weapons and confiscated two silver-mounted pistols and two muskets.

A wagon had come up from the Flats Post; his wife was ordered to get on to it because the track to Groot River Mouth was long and difficult. He was made to walk beside the wagon, while Master Steen and the Company's men were drinking neat brandy and firing into the air to signal their victory.

After about an hour he saw his chance and disappeared into the forest. Escaped. At Free-burgher Cornelise's house it was decided that on account of his extremely perilous position he should be brought to Black River Mouth. To Daniel Zaaijman.

Foreign captains, officers, sailors; foreign women that came on foreign ships and speaking a foreign language – none of these felt alien in her house.

Jan Dubertin did.

Baldini had taken one look at him and said he was Catholic.

No, not alien because he was a Catholic but because he was cloaked in a danger that made her knees threaten to buckle under her. A trapped lion that would tear anyone apart in his need to break free.

'I see Lamot's design, Zaaijman.'

'What is Lamot's design?' Daniel was playing dumb. She was getting breakfast ready for them. Adam Cornelise had left at daybreak.

'Only Lamot and I know. That's enough.' Bluntly. 'How long do you think it will take Free-burgher Cornelise to reach the Flats and establish what the situation is there, and get back here?'

'Give him two days. Three. The man will have to rest somewhere, after all.'

Adam had slept under the awning at the hospital. Jan Dubertin at Baldini's. Wearing a shirt and breeches of Baldini's, he came in in the early morning to say that he would prefer not to stay with an Italian.

'Italians are untrustworthy – they trim their sails to the prevailing wind, no matter where it's blowing from. And in any case, his house it too isolated, Lamot's henchmen could easily trap me there.'

'I'll prepare one of the rooms in the house for you,' she said.

'Good.'

She and Daniel had lain awake for a long time the night before.

'What are you thinking?' she asked him.

'I'm wondering how early I can wake Hendrik and get him on his way to Southeast Harbour without Dubertin tumbling to it. Hendrik has friends among the soldiers there.'

'Are you going to send word that Dubertin is here?'

'I'm not a betrayer. But I'll know what to do when Hendrik gets back.'

'I'm frightened of the man, Daniel.'

'Frightened you don't have to be, my love, but careful certainly. An exile who is now also a fugitive from justice could make things on this island very uncomfortable.'

'He's sleeping on your property! If Lamotius hears of it, you'll also be in trouble!'

'I didn't invite Dubertin. You'd better pack some food for Hendrik for the road.'

Catharina wanted to know if the man was sick. Most of the time he just sat on one of the beds in the hospital staring and staring ...

The only words Dubertin exchanged with her, Pieternella, were when she went to fetch yellow-bush leaves under the awning to stew them for Goliath. The slave was poorly. Dubertin had asked the previous evening how many slaves there were on the property. Six. How many in chains? Two. He gave orders to tell the slaves that he was a ship's officer from Northwest Harbour.

'I assume that this shelter is sometimes used as a hospital?' he asked her.

'Yes, Mynheer.'

'Often?'

'No, Mynheer.'

'On what occasions? The sick are supposed to be cared for at the Lodge.'

'Just anyone who is sick, Mynheer.'

'How often does your husband deliver arrack to the Lodge?'

'As soon as the barrels are full.' She was being deliberately obtuse; he addressed her with a haughtiness she didn't like. Then he lost his temper.

'You're not speaking to a fool, Juffrouw Zaaijman!'

'Nor are you, Mynheer Dubertin.' Then he grew even angrier.

'What exactly do you mean by that?' Rapid and suspicious.

'I can read and write and do sums. I can read joined-up writing. I don't have to sound every letter first. Just some.' As though she were really stupid.

At that he was reassured again and got up to walk down to the distillery.

Baldini said he'd come to spy and eventually asked Daniel if Lamotius really expected them to be satisfied with such apparatus? It was nothing less than a disgrace.

Then he came nosing around in the house. Examined the porcelain on the shelves, the wall hangings, everything in the kitchen. Her and Daniel's bedroom, the children's room. The added room where the slave Maria was making a bed. Came back and looked at the meat platter in the cupboard in the sitting room. The one which the skipper of the *Europa* and his wife had given her.

'Arita,' he said. 'The blue used is evidence of outstanding quality.'

'It's a meat platter.'

At that he went outside again to sit under the hospital awning and wait for Adam Cornelise.

Three days.

Adam got back late in the afternoon.

Yes, soldiers were everywhere, searching for him in the forest; the Commander had declared him a fugitive from justice and an escapee. Posters had been nailed up strictly prohibiting anyone to speak or listen to him, or to succour him with food or drink. He was to present himself at the Lodge within eight days to account for himself.

Dubertin got up and went to the door, stood there looking out – and turned back again. 'What else?' Dubertin made it sound like a command.

'There's a reward of five rixdollars for any slave who reveals where you're hiding, Mynheer.'

That gave Dubertin a fright. 'Where are your slaves, Zaaijman?' he exclaimed.

'Outside.'

'Go out and see who's been listening at the shutters!'

'They wouldn't.'

'Go out and see!'

Daniel got up without haste and walked round the house. Dubertin was pacing up and down in the sitting room.

'Where is my wife?' he asked Adam.

'She was at the Lodge, but she's back on the Flats again now. Master Steen has two armed sailors guarding her at night in case you try to take refuge there. Their orders are to shoot to kill if you arrive there and attempt to resist.'

Daniel came back inside. 'No one there.'

'Where's the maid?'

'She's gone down to the river with the children.'

'How safe am I here, Zaaijman?'

'I'll move you to one of the other free-burghers if it becomes necessary.'

She went down to the cowshed to wait for Daniel, knowing that he would come and help with the milking.

'Daniel?'

'Keep calm, my love. Hendrik ought to be on his way back.'

He arrived the next afternoon.

Not at the house, but behind Baldini's. He sent Thomas to call Daniel from the distillery.

Dubertin was sitting under the awning. Daniel had to skirt the house and slip through the forest to get to Hendrik. She walked past Dubertin with an arm full of sheets and a quilt towards Baldini's cottage 'to go and make up the beds'.

Daniel was all for sending her back to the house, it was too dangerous, the man was on his guard.

No. She wanted to *hear*.

They went aside into the forest and sat down.

'This is an ugly business, Daniel. And getting a lot uglier. Karseboom and Michiel Romondt are going from free-burgher to free-burgher, saying this is the time for them to march under arms on the Lodge and rid themselves of Lamotius. The men are drunk on their own breath.'

'What do you hear of Dubertin?'

'That's the other thing. Hans Pigt was the one who helped him escape. He knew Lamotius wanted to put him on Tobacco Island while he gathered evidence to prove that the man is a danger. That there were plots being hatched in his house against the Council. To compile affidavits, force the soldiers and sailors to sign them, to admit that they heard Dubertin instructing them to mutiny. That they heard him libelling the Commander.'

'Where's Aletta Uytenbogaert?'

'Lamotius is having her house on the Flats cleared and making her move closer to the Lodge. He's getting pretty randy about her.'

'Close your ears, Pieternella!' Daniel interrupted.

'No. I'm not stupid, I want to know what's going on.'

'Lamotius wants her. He wants her badly. He's got his plans all worked out for getting her.'

'And she, Aletta? Does she want *him*?'

'She wrote him a letter only last month inviting him to visit her – a very enticing letter. Jan Yser who had to take it to the Lodge for her opened and read it on the way. Hans Pigt reckons that she swung round very quickly in fright when they went to arrest her husband. At first she probably thought a little fun with Lamotius wouldn't do any harm, just make her life on the island a little sweeter. It seems now that she's seen through his plan.'

'Seen what?' Daniel asked.

'Exactly what you suspected was Lamotius's plan.'

'What plan?' Pieternella asked.

'To assemble sufficient evidence against Dubertin to have him re-banned back to the Cape. Anyone re-banned back to the Cape never arrives at the Cape.'

She went lame with fright. Suddenly Dubertin and Aletta and Lamotius were nothing. Mere strangers. All she could see before her eyes was Jacobus ...

'Jacobus was not re-banned to the Cape.' She said it so that they should know. They just looked at her. 'Jacobus has gone back to my mother's people, he has not been re-*banned*!' She wanted to poke it into their eyes so that it would penetrate their heads and make them stop just staring at her! 'My brother was never banned!'

'He was sent to your mother's folk.' Hendrik. He picked up a twig and started playing with it.

'Daniel?'

'He's gone to your mother's people, Pieternella.'

But the worry went on haunting her like a spectre. The possibility that *she* could have sent her brother to his death. But then she kicked the spectre aside and told herself Lamotius wouldn't have gone behind her back and banned him, knowing that it was actually a death sentence ...

The next morning she heard Daniel and Dubertin arguing fiercely under the awning.

'No, Dubertin, now you listen to *me*! If Lamotius catches you, he'll ban you out of his way, and you know what *that* means!'

'I won't allow myself to be tormented by either you or Lamotius, Zaaijman. I have made more friends on this island in fourteen months than Lamotius has in his eleven years!'

'No Commander has yet made friends on this island, because no Commander has yet been able to persuade the Company to take any notice of the island's problems.'

'I have friends and relations in positions of the highest authority!'

'They won't be worth a blue bean if you're caught.'

'Lamotius is a crook and a deceiver!'

'Stop trying to fight Lamotius and save yourself, Dubertin.'

'The free-burghers want me to lead an insurrection against Lamot.'

'Stop right there!'

'I will not be shouted at by an arrack distiller, Zaaijman!'

'The only thing that can save your arse is to get away on a ship before Steen and his soldiers get their hands on you. Your only salvation will be the arrival of an English or a French ship here on the western side of the island, and for that you've got to have patience.'

'How can I stay safe till then?' With what sounded like the first note of panic in his voice. 'Who is standing ready to betray me?'

'That I don't know. In the mean time we'll have to get you hidden by one free-burgher after another. Don't stay in one place.'

Thank God, she said in her heart. At least he wouldn't be on Daniel's property when they caught him.

Baldini came down from his house and rang the school bell. For Catharina and Eva and Magdalena. Maria and Pieter were still too small.

Dubertin had never taken any notice of any of the children. One night he came to the door and snapped at her to silence the children, they were disturbing him. She was washing Pieter – the child was kicking and screaming; Magdalena was brushing Eva's hair, it was pulling and Eva kept shouting …

She told Catharina to dry Pieter and put on his nightie, dried her hands on her apron and went into the sitting room.

The outside door was closed, the shutters bolted. It was stuffy. Dubertin was seated on a chair beside the wall; no eye should be able to peer through a crack and see him.

'This is my house.' She stood directly in front of him and said it to his face. Daniel was outside somewhere. The slave Maria was in the kitchen. 'My children will make a noise for as long as *I* can stand it.' Softly. Politely.

'No woman addresses me as though I were her equal, Juffrouw Zaaijman!'

'So I have heard.'

'Pardon?'

'The island is small, Mynheer, sound travels far.' She didn't care. Dubertin was a fugitive, and a fugitive under your roof was a cyclone gathering strength. Except that she'd never been *this* frightened of a cyclone.

'I knew from the first moment that you were not to be trusted! *No* woman is.'

Grind your teeth. 'As you say, Mynheer.'

She and Maria gave the children their supper and put them to bed.

It was goodness knows how many nights since Daniel had held family prayers for her and the children and the slaves. Dubertin thought it too dangerous because they might be taken by surprise in the course of the prayers.

When she returned to the sitting room, Jan Dirks and Gerrit van Ewijk and Jan Roelofse were just coming in the door. Like robbers.

Daniel followed a little later.

They had come to say that Lamotius was going off his head. Lambert Janse, a servant working in the Company's gardens on the Flats, was summoned to the Lodge by Lamotius to report what he had been doing at Dubertin's house one night a short while before. Lambert said he'd gone to fetch a sack. Lamotius said he was lying. He knew that Laurens Gabrielse had also been there, and Kees Janse, too. He knew Dubertin had incited them against him and the Council and the Company. Lambert said that wasn't true. Lamotius swore at him, saying Kees had already confessed and signed an affidavit. Now it was his, Lambert's, turn. But he wouldn't. So they chained him to a tree outside and nailed up a poster forbidding anyone to speak to him. It rained and blew all that night and the next day. They gave him only water and sweet potatoes. The Commander came out cursing and threatening him, saying that Lambert had been eavesdropping at the Lodge windows at night and carrying the news to Dubertin. By the third day Lambert was broken. He sent for Master Steen, said he'd admit everything and sign whatever Lamotius wanted if they would please just set him free.

That wasn't all.

Seaman Kerneels Janse of the Flats Post was leading the oxen in front of the plough. Lamotius arrived and wanted to know from him how many times he had been to Dubertin's house and what was said there to the detriment of himself, Lamotius, and the Council. Kerneels said nothing was said to their detriment. Lamotius screamed at the sailor walking behind the oxen with the whip to give Kerneels a couple of lashes there and then. Again and again and again. It was impossible to endure it – bleeding, Kerneels said he'd confess to anything.

That wasn't all …

She went outside, she didn't want to hear any more.

The sleeping island. The night darkness. The stars were bright and clear – large and small; they hung so tranquilly above everything. When she was small, she believed they were the eyes of dead people …

Where was Jacobus?

What had got into Lamotius?

Hendrik said one of the guards had said Gerrit van Ewijk's Hester had been crying uncontrollably; the slave that she'd had relations with had died in the gaol. Not from all the torture. He just stopped talking and eating. The Surgeon could find no other cause of death.

'When passion becomes a fire in your innards, Pieternella, and you can't get your way, it scrapes all the life out of you.' Daniel wasn't present. 'That's what's happening to Lamotius.'

'When is the next supply ship due, Hendrik?'

'It should be on its way by now.'

'When is Dubertin going to get out of my house?'

'Tomorrow. They're going to have him hidden somewhere at Northwest Harbour for a day or two. I'm going back to the Lodge.'

'We need sugar and flour.'

When she woke up the next morning he was gone. Dubertin. He'd left with the three footpads some time in the night.

It felt as though peace had crept out of the forest and come and lain down on the yard again. The children were playing; Baldini had to ring the bell twice to get the older ones into school. Thomas had made Maria and Pieter a 'housey' out of a wooden chest and given it a canvas door.

Daniel had crossed the river with his musket to borrow hounds from Jan Muur to hunt down a deer. They were running out of meat.

Hendrik had also left.

She went outside to sit in the shade and work on a little dress for Maria. There was no sign of a sail on the sea …

2

'Be strong, my love. Life never runs only downhill – we'll make it up this slope, I promise you.'

But faith wouldn't settle in her heart any more. 'When is it going to end?'

'As soon as we manage to get Dubertin away.'

From Jan Roelofse at Northwest Harbour, to Henk Karseboom, to Jan Dirks, to Daniel Zaaijman, to Jan Muur, to Daniel Zaaijman …

'I feel safest here with you, Zaaijman.'

'You can't stay here too long. Lamotius's soldiers are causing trouble in all the free-burghers' homes. The man wants you under arrest.'

Hendrik brought back the news from Southeast Harbour: Secunde Jacobsen was dead and buried, Ovaer had been appointed in his place.

The rest was like war. On one hand Lamotius was living in daily expectation of an attack on the Lodge. He'd had additional sentries deployed at night; had four cannons positioned and loaded with saltpetre.

On the other, he was having the island turned upside down in search of Dubertin.

Aletta had had a room added at Laurens Gabrielse's and Tant Magdalena's, where Lamotius's soldiers constantly harassed her.

'A man, Pieternella, who wants the woman who has him on fire is a dangerous animal.'

The trapped woman was even more dangerous.

Aletta sent for Lambert and Kees; they came to her and made depositions to the effect that they had signed Lamotius's affidavits under duress. That Dubertin had never incited them against the Commander.

Jacob Ovaer arrived with three armed men and kicked down the door. Laurens Gabrielse got such a fright he fled. Ovaer said: It's not you we're looking for, Gabrielse, it's the false declarations the witch has taken down!

They opened her chests, pitched out everything on to the floor and took not just the depositions but all her documents. They claimed that, in addition, she owed a fine of fifty rixdollars because she and Dubertin had sold liquor on the Flats, and for the transportation of her goods. She demanded that Ovaer put it in writing and bring it to her. And with it an inventory of all her stuff at the Lodge.

That was when Daniel and Adam Cornelise built Dubertin a hut in the forest.

Barely a week later Master Steen's woodcutters caught Goliath on his way to take food to Dubertin's hideaway. In the torture chamber they extracted from the slave the information that he had led Dubertin to Orange Tree Flats a few nights earlier, to Aletta.

Daniel and Adam moved Dubertin's hut.

Ovaer and his three armed men came back to Laurens Gabrielse's house and searched through every room, shouting all the while: 'We want Jan Baptiste Dubertin!' Ovaer handed Aletta a letter for the money she owed. She demanded the names of the people to whom they were supposed to have sold liquor. Ovaer said: 'Shut your mouth and count out the money.' She said she would pay it all just to get rid of him. At that he became enraged, laid his sword to her chest and shouted: 'Tell us where your husband is!' She went on saying she didn't know. That made Ovaer press his sword even closer to her chest and say: 'You're now speaking to the new Secunde of Mauritius! I will not be lied to! Where did your husband get clean clothes? How many nights has he spent here?'

'I'm begging you, I don't know where my husband may be.'

'War, Pieternella,' said Hendrik, 'becomes a game for spies.'

Soldier Soetemeer eavesdropped outside the Lodge and took the words to Aletta at night. When they caught him, he denied it. They took and showed him his tracks and flogged him to death at the flagpole.

Hans Pigt came back from Aletta's, where he'd made and signed a declaration against Lamotius. They arrested him and beat him almost to death with a cane.

Next morning, mercifully, the news arrived: there was an English ship at Northwest Harbour in urgent need of a cooper.

Jan Lodewijks had brought the news. Daniel asked him to send his wife to stay with Pieternella and the children. Hendrik had to go to Northwest Harbour with him.

Aaltjie arrived that same evening. 'Henk and Romondt have criss-crossed the whole western part trying to rouse the free-burghers to rebel. They say they want to launch an armed attack on the Lodge.'

'And?'

'Lucky about the ship. Jan told Romondt: Rebelling won't put a penny in my pocket but the English pay for whatever we've got to deliver.'

The three armed soldiers arrived the next afternoon.

'Bring your children out of the house!' shouted the one in front.

'Why?' An icy calmness took hold of her.

'We want to search your house.'

'Search it for what?'

'Not for what, for *whom*!'

Aaltjie came and stood behind her in the doorway. 'You're looking for a turd in the dark! You've just come to upset the children.'

'We're not talking to you, we're talking to the wife of the cooper.'

She reassured the children, woke Pieter from his afternoon nap and took them outside. 'You'd better not disarrange my house.'

Two went into the house, one stayed outside.

'Where's Daniel?' he asked.

'Go and look for him, he's gone hunting.'

'You're lying!'

'Dare to shout at me again and Daniel will deal with you. That I promise you.' Catharina and Magdalena started crying.

'Where's Dubertin?'

'I don't know and I don't want him on my property.'

'You better not; there's heavy penalties for helping the swine.'

A fourth soldier came from Baldini's cottage. 'Can't find anything, Sergeant.'

The other two came out of the house. 'Don't we get anything to eat?' asked one.

'No.'

'Sergeant, Willem and I will stay behind and wait for Daniel.'

Her body began to tremble. 'You can wait for him at the river, not here where you're upsetting my children.'

Aaltjie was standing with Maria on her arm. All at once the child started screaming wildly, thrashing about to free herself. Then Pieter also began to cry. Then Eva as well.

'Clear off!' Aaltjie yelled at the soldiers. 'If Daniel Zaaijman hears his children have been molested, there'll be trouble!'

They must have been across the river already when Aaltjie admitted that in desperation she'd pinched Maria to start her screaming.

The *Zeemaat* arrived on the Sunday of the week after that and Aaltjie went home.

'Dubertin's aboard the ship already,' Daniel brought the news. 'But there's still a lot of work to be done on it.'

He knew about the soldiers that had been there. They'd searched Jan Dirks's house as well and taken Jan off to the Lodge. Jan Roelofse was caught on his way back from Dubertin and also taken to the Lodge.

'Daniel?' Her terror felt too big for her body to contain. 'They wanted to know where you were.'

'Keep calm, my love. I've got my eyes open. We got Dubertin on board last night. We're halfway done.'

'Where's Hendrik?'

'He went down to the Lodge yesterday to spy for us.'

'How will I know what he's found out?'

'I'll send him.'

'How will I know you're still safe?'

'I'll send Hendrik. You know where the little coffer is – in case anything happens to me.'

'Don't talk like that!'

Aaltjie returned on Monday.

'Jan Dirks's Elisabet is in bed with a head that won't stop aching. I wish to God they'd catch the damned outlaw and do whatever they want to with him! Everybody is under suspicion. What does Daniel say, where's Dubertin?'

'Nobody knows.' She didn't dare say.

Hendrik came on Wednesday.

Jan Roelofse had been flogged at the bell-frame and now had to spend a fortnight working as a slave.

Jan Dirks was not flogged, the Surgeon had found that he wasn't strong enough. But he also had to do a fortnight of slave labour.

'Things are in a bad way at the Lodge, Pieternella. It's very dry. There's no water. They're having to cart it in barrels with oxen. Almost half the officials are down with stomach trouble.'

'Do you think they'll arrest Daniel, too?'

'I hope not. Lamotius is now completely insane. Hans Pigt is still refusing to sign the affidavit to the effect that Dubertin incited the free-burghers to attack the Lodge. So now Lamotius has had his wife, Maria Mooy, taken away from him and she's being kept at the Lodge. Steen has given all the soldiers leave to do whatever they like with her. He will protect them. They say she can hardly walk any more.'

'No!'

'That's not all. Master Steen says he won't pay any heed to any bitch that comes to complain that a soldier has raped her. Daniel sends word that you must keep the house bolted at night and have the musket beside the bed.'

'Where's Goliath?'

'At the Lodge. In chains. Daniel says he wants his slave back.'

'When are the English going to leave?'

'As soon as possible. The skipper says he's never before seen such fear among the free-burghers.'

'When is the supply ship from the Cape expected?'

'Everybody's watching out for it.'

On the next Sunday three armed soldiers were lying in wait for Daniel at the river below the house. He'd come back on the *Zeemaat* from Northwest Harbour to see how things were at home; they must have seen the sail coming across the water.

'Don't be scared, Pieternella.' She and the slave Maria were giving the children their supper. Baldini was also at the table. Daniel was standing in the doorway, with the three behind him. Guns cocked. 'They've come with a warrant, I'm under arrest.'

She began to weep; the three elder children also started crying and jumped up to run and cling to him.

'Let go!' shouted the pimply-faced soldier.

Daniel ignored him and sat down at the table. The soldiers were treading on one another's feet in the doorway. 'We said you could just come and fetch your things and say goodbye, Zaaijman!' one of them shouted, furious.

'And I'm telling you: if Lamotius wants me, I will sail my boat round to Southeast Harbour and knock on his door myself.'

'That's not allowed – we have been ordered to come and arrest you!'

Baldini opened the Bible and began to read aloud. The children continued hanging on to Daniel. She walked over to the door with Pieter on her arm, feeling such strength surging up inside her that she could have committed murder. 'Get out of my house! You're frightening my children. If my husband has said he'll sail round to Lamotius, then that is what he'll do.'

'Listen here, Juffrouw ...' The soldier stepped forward. He smelt of wine.

Daniel was on his feet immediately. Pushing the children aside, he said: 'Touch my wife, and you're dead, soldier!' Baldini read more loudly. 'Pack some things for me, Pieternella.'

'I'm coming, too.'

'No.'

'I am going with you to Lamotius, Daniel, if I have to hang on to the back of the boat till I get there.'

She and Daniel and Pieter and Maria. And one soldier.

All three wanted to come but Daniel would only allow one.

Halfway there the sun began to set. 'Damn it, Cooper, you're going to drown us! Drop the anchor in one of these bays, the dark's going to catch us!'

'Sit still!'

She wasn't afraid. She knew the moon would soon rise because it was only two days past the full. Daniel lit a lantern and made the soldier lie on the bows watching till the moon was high above the water.

At ten o'clock they anchored at French Church.

'Go off and tell the Commander and Master Steen that I'm here and I'm staying here on the boat with my wife and children till daybreak.'

The soldier shuffled his feet nervously, not seeming to know whether he should get off the boat or not. 'You're under arrest, Cooper!'

'Get off and report!' roared Daniel. So the soldier jumped down.

Night.

Everlasting.

The mud at French Church smelt different from Black River mud. The moon was whiter. The stars on the south less bright. She could hear the swishing of the sea behind the reef and the never-ending wavelets lapping against the hull of the *Zeemaat*.

But inside her, nothing would come to rest. She was weary. Because of Dubertin. Because of her concern for Jacobus. Because of worry about Daniel. Because of the poisonous cloud hanging over the island like a pestilence.

She told Daniel only half of her plan: To take the children and stay with Oom Laurens and Tant Magdalena. He was unwilling at first, because he didn't want her going anywhere near Aletta Uytenbogaert. Afraid she might let slip that Dubertin was already on the ship.

'I'm not stupid, Daniel!'

'And nor are Laurens and Magdalena either.'

'No.' Her plan was still taking shape. First she wanted to look Aletta Uytenbogaert in the face. To see what it was in her that could get a man so fired up.

The worst was her fear that they might torture Daniel, even though he kept saying he wasn't afraid of Lamotius. Even though he kept saying they were nearly at the top of the slope now.

At first light she started walking up towards the Orange Tree Flats, and Daniel headed for the Lodge.

'Daniel ...'

'Don't cry, Pieternella. Be strong.'

The footpath had been widened and was rutted with wagon tracks. Cattle dung. *Caroo-coo-coo* doves. Little green twitterers.

'Why's Father not coming with us?'

'Father has to go and see another man first, Maria.'

Past the ford.

Her plan was becoming clearer all the while, but she didn't have all the words for it yet …

Past the turn-off to where Oom Bart and Tant Theuntjie lived. Old tracks, dead tracks. Hendrik said Tant Maijke now had a room in one of the outbuildings at the Lodge. Behind the slave quarters.

'Why's Father not coming?'

'He'll come as soon as he's finished with the man.' Pieter was a weight to carry. Almost heavier than the bundle.

The cloud of poison was spreading over the joy of her life. Over her husband. Over her children. Pieter who was becoming more of a new young Daniel by the day; Catharina who was starting to mature. Baldini regularly commented: These children are clever. Magdalena draws so well. Especially trees. Ships, too.

Oom Laurens opened the door with frightened eyes; the next moment they were filled with tears and happiness and relief. 'Pieternellatjie!' He took the bundle and the child from her. Tant Magdalena came out of the adjoining room and also began to cry. Maria crawled under the table in the sitting room after Tant Magdalena's tame cat and tried to pick it up and drag it out.

'She's my little Hottentot.'

'She's your prettiest.'

'Daniel is at the Lodge, he's under arrest because of Dubertin.'

Oom Laurens went to the door and took a quick look outside, like someone who first had to check for danger. Came back again. 'We don't know any more, Pieternella.' He had got old. So had Tant Magdalena. 'We just don't know any more.'

'Maria, let go the cat!'

'Leave her, let her play with him,' said Tant Magdalena and put out some bread and buttermilk on the table. 'You know that Aletta has added a room to our house here?'

'Yes. I'd like to see her.' She is my plan …

'She's still in her room. There were soldiers round the house all night; we heard that her husband was in hiding on your side of the island. What's going on?'

'I can't say, but I should think it can't be very long now before he gets away.'

'May that be the truth! Then maybe Lamot will calm down again.'

'No, Laurens,' said Tant Magdalena, 'Lamot will never calm down before he has her in the Lodge with him.' The cloud of poison was everywhere, even in this house.

'What's going to happen if he *can't* get her, Tante?'

'God only knows. Everything's been overturned already but Lamotius just goes on and on.'

Oom Laurens got up and went over to the door to look out again. The two old folk were frightened. Really frightened. 'Aletta asked Lamotius for leave to return to her house on the Flats. So he went there with a few soldiers on Friday and burnt her house to the ground!'

'What?'

'Yes.'

Things were even worse than she had imagined. 'What's going to happen?'

'We don't know. We just live with the fear.'

A slave woman in chains came in and walked through to the kitchen. 'Aletta's slave, she's already run away twice. She helps me in the house. Never speaks.'

'What's Aletta going to do?'

'Try to flee back to the fatherland; her father is a very important man. We hope ...' Tant Magdalena leant across the table and whispered: 'We're living in hope that when the supply ship comes the skipper will take her on board.'

'I'm scared they might do something to Daniel.'

'Rumour has it that Dubertin hid at your house, too.'

'He did. I want to see Aletta.'

'She's devastated, spends most of her time just sitting in her room. She says if her father were to hear what is going on here, Lamotius wouldn't survive.'

'I want to see her.'

The room added on for her was made of palm leaves and planks. Spacious. There were finely woven mats draped over a chest and a small table. A cupboard in dark wood with small pale pieces inlaid round the edges. A mirror in a curved frame. A painting of a copper pot of flowers, in a gold frame. A clothes chest carved with curly-tailed dragons. An easy chair with velvet upholstery and carved legs and arm-rests, gold tassels round the seat. A silver candelabrum on silver feet. A silver tray. A four-poster bed with a silk coverlet. Silk cushions. A small round table with high legs with a large glass inkpot on it – a cradle for the quill to rest in. An empty bird-cage. A chair with turned legs at the small table where Aletta Uytenbogaert was seated. Over everything hung a delicate sweet perfume.

'You're scrutinising my room, you're scrutinising me.'

'Yes.' It was the strangest moment. And the strangest thoughts came into her head. That she was standing on the threshold of a butterfly's home. Except that a woman with the green-brown eyes of a cat was living in it and looking at her, Pieternella, as though she was an old picture from the distant past. Lydia de Paape. Hendrik Lacus's Lydia. The way she used to look at her mother in the Post House on Robben Island.

'Who are you?' Like: what do you want?

'I am Pieternella van Meerhoff. I knew Lamotius's wife.' Yes, and a man could catch fire for her and burn his fingers ...

A rapid movement of the cat's eyes. 'What do you want from me – or has Isaac Lamotius sent you?'

'No. I've sent myself. From Black River Mouth where, much against my will, I had to shelter your husband.'

'Where is my husband?' Quickly, as though frightened.

She knew she was going to say it. 'On the English ship at Northwest Harbour.'

Slowly Aletta Uytenbogaert got up out of her chair. 'Why have you come to tell me?'

'Did you know Hendrik Lacus's Lydia?'

'No. When is the ship leaving?'

'Soon. In the mean time my husband is under arrest at the Lodge.'

'Who is your husband?'

'Daniel Zaaijman.'

She came round the table quickly. The perfume with her. 'The Cooper?'

'Yes. He's in custody. And if so much as one hair of his head is harmed, I shall go straight to Lamotius and tell him where to find your husband.'

A bolt of lightning flashed through the cat's eyes. Not fright – fury. 'How dare you come and blackmail me!'

'I shall also inform the Commander that you are planning to escape on board the supply ship.'

The cat showed her claws. 'Do you know who you are speaking to?'

Lydia. 'Yes. To a cat that played with the wrong mouse, and took fright when the mouse began to chase *her*!' Words that fell quite unafraid from her lips, while the vigilance in Aletta Uytenbogaert's eyes subsided and she sheathed her claws.

'I am stunned. I have received nothing but loving kindness on this island from the wretched free-burghers and their good wives. Now suddenly one of them has come here under my roof to do me harm!'

'You needn't try tears. My husband is not one of your wretched free-

472

burghers and I am not kind-hearted. That is why you are going to walk to the Lodge with me so the mouse can see we are the best of friends.' The plan had suddenly found its words.

'Never!'

'Then I shall go there alone.'

She was outside already when Aletta called to her to wait.

'You are going to pay for this, Juffrouw Zaaijman, you *and* your husband.'

The whole way to the Lodge.

She couldn't help remembering how Tant Theuntjie had prodded and shoved her all the way back home that morning after church …

Shortly before the wooden bridge across the Molens River she stopped and looked Aletta straight in the eyes. 'My mother, Juffrouw Uytenbogaert, was a Cape Hottentot who had to fight for herself against Lydia de Paape. You don't need to understand, all you need to know is that I have tough blood in me and that today I am fighting for my husband and my children. And it's you I'm fighting.'

'You will regret it!' A cat in a trap, hissing and spitting.

'I know where your husband is. As soon as we have crossed the bridge, you will link arms with me and smile.'

'You're not my class!'

'You're not this island's class.'

They met him in the passage. Lamotius. Thin. Grey. So consumed with hate or spite or something that just for a moment she felt sorry for him. She noted the undisguised fire in his eyes as he glared at Aletta Uytenbogaert.

'Mynheer, I've just come to hear whether Daniel is well.'

'The Council will decide about that in an hour or so.'

'I've just been telling Aletta how good you were to me that time. And afterwards. And to Daniel, too.' A trickle of sweat ran down her spine. 'We'll wait outside for the decision of the Council. I ask with my whole heart that you will be merciful to Daniel. He's a good man.'

He didn't once take his eyes off Aletta Uytenbogaert.

Thank you, she said to Aletta outside, you can go back to the Orange Tree Flats. I'll wait here alone.

The trembling only took hold of her once the woman had walked away. Tant Maijke was sitting in the shade of a tree in front of one of the outbuildings. Old. A peeled yellow staff for support.

'Tant Maijke …'

'What are you doing here?'

'Tante, are you sick?' The old woman sat there, shrunken, her dress limp between her knees. A dirty white bonnet on her head.

'I'm just waiting for my death. Every day. It's only our dear Commander who has any feeling for a poor widow.'

'How is Cornelia?'

'Cornelia?' As though she didn't know anyone of that name.

'Your daughter, Tante.'

'I haven't got any children.'

'But ...' Was there no sense left in her brain?

'Van Nimwegen forbade me his yard a long time ago. Lamotius understands. No child who allows her mother to be rejected like that deserves to have a mother. He says so, too.'

'But Tante, you've still got Johanna – who's married to Gerrit Visser at the Cape.'

'Has she, in all the years, once put her hand to paper to ask if her poor mother is still alive? No. No, I haven't got any children.'

'But don't you have a son somewhere in the fatherland, Tante?'

'I haven't got any children.'

Gerrit van Ewijk's Hester and a slave woman were hoeing the drought-stricken earth in the palm tree garden, her feet bare and her old worn dress covered in dust up to the knees. Her face was wet with sweat.

'Lord, Hester ...'

'Pieternella?'

'I've actually come to see if I couldn't see Anna ... I thought you'd been released already.'

'The Company never releases you. I have to wait for permission for a passage to the Cape to arrive. My sin is too serious for this island's Council.' As though she didn't care. Drifting where the stream carried her. Living because she wasn't dead.

'Do you know Anna?'

'The mad slave?'

'Yes.'

'She's not mad. She's with the team peeling hedge-stakes on the seaward side of the Lodge.'

Anna.

In whose eyes there was a sudden gladness when she looked up and saw her, Pieternella, standing there.

But she wouldn't look up again. Just went on standing there beside the huge sharp-pointed stake chipping off the bark with a chopper, chip, chip, chip.

'Your child Magdalena has turned five.'

Nothing.

She walked back to the Lodge and waited.

The tension in her body would not yield. The uneasiness in her heart about Daniel went on piling up.

The Company never releases you ...

The water inside the reef where Daniel took her that first time in the sampan ...

In the distance across the bay the smoke from the lime kiln.

How would she get home with the children if they locked Daniel up?

She would fetch Aletta Uytenbogaert and drag her back to the Lodge by her hair and exchange her for Daniel! She'd sworn it in her heart.

He came walking out of the door. Looked up into the sky like someone who first wanted to assess the position of the wind and the sun. Daniel.

Free.

Only when the *Zeemaat*'s bows had turned west below the island, with Pieter and Maria safely roped so they couldn't fall overboard, only then did he tell her what had happened. That Steen and Wieringa and Lamotius had asked him if he had sheltered Dubertin. Yes. Where was Dubertin now? Hadn't seen him for a long time. Then all at once Lamotius fined him ten rixdollars for hunting on days when hunting was forbidden, and another ten rixdollars for selling turtle-spread to an English ship last year. 'I'm still completely baffled, Pieternella! The Commander's brain has given in.'

'Turtle-spread?'

'That's what he said, my love.'

3

Two weeks later the English ship sailed, with Dubertin on board.

Like a page torn out of a book, crumpled up and thrown away.

That was in September.

At the beginning of October their slaves started carrying stone down from the hills above Northwest Harbour on pallets. Jake, Karel and

Jamika. Started breaking out coral to burn for building lime.

'Father is building you a cyclone house,' Daniel told the children, to amuse and prepare them. The schoolroom would still have to be made of palm leaves and bamboo, but one day ...

'Who's going to teach us, Father? You said Master Baldini's not coming with us.' They wanted to know.

'Aah! Your father is keeping his eyes open for a real schoolmaster!'

'Master Baldini *is* a real schoolmaster!'

Catharina had turned nine the month before. Eva was seven, Magdalena five, Maria three. Pieter was a year old but wasn't walking yet

In her heart Pieternella had dug a deep ditch down the middle of the island, from north to south. East of the ditch was where Lamotius and Aletta and Tant Maijke and the rest of them had their place. West of it was where she and Daniel and the children and Baldini and Hendrik lived. In peace.

Even Willemina, shortly after Dubertin's departure, came across the river one day and spoke a true word. Said she hoped all the serpents would now slither down away from the Flats to Southeast Harbour and keep away from the western side of the island. 'I told Jan, I said, we should also move to Northwest Harbour. No use waiting for Lamotius's permission. He's only interested in Aletta Uytenbogaert. Jan Dirks and Jan Lodewijks also want to move.'

The shutters on the cyclone house had been built in already when Daniel took her and the children on the *Zeemaat* to see it one Sunday. And to take food to the slaves.

Wine for the two free-burghers who were helping Daniel build.

A half-finished stone house. Four rooms and a kitchen. *Two* outside doors. Above the freshwater stream on the northern side of the bay. A small wooden bridge across the river to the island, where Daniel already had a kind of work-place and where he wanted to build sleeping quarters for the slaves as well.

'Where's Mother's hospital?' Eva was a proper little nurse. Adept at feeding a sick sailor and ready to be quite fierce with him if necessary.

'Mother's little hospital will also be finished.'

On the way back that afternoon she told Daniel she suddenly felt herself sawn in two. 'My body is at Black River and my heart is at Northwest Harbour.'

'I'm glad, my love. We're going to be happy.'

When they swung into Black River Mouth, the Company's *Europa* was lying at anchor.

Lamotius. With the lime and bricks and the other still.

'I know I should have come and built it in long ago, Cooper, but circumstances with that Dubertin required all my time and attention. At present we don't know *where* the man is hiding.'

Plus three of the promised slaves that he and Baldini were supposed to get.

Daniel waited till the still had been built in before he told Lamotius he wanted to return to coopering. Baldini was quite prepared to continue with the distilling.

Lamotius was standing at the door outside, thoroughly enjoying a bunch of grapes from Baldini's garden, while she had to struggle to stop the children goggling at his lip-smacking, open-mouthed delight.

'Truly, the very best grapes – I foresee unimagined future profits from this distillery!'

'If Baldini can have Goliath, my slave that you're holding at the Lodge, and these three new ones …'

'The Company would welcome having barrels of your quality again, Cooper. Truly, the best ever grapes. The three stills I sent to the Cape on the *Westerwijk* to be repaired ought to arrive on the next supply ship. I foresee a bright future for the Black River distillery.'

'I want to move to Northwest Harbour,' Daniel tried to get him off the topic of arrack.

'They're only a bunch of illegal layabouts up there, Cooper, I'd rather find you a place at Southeast Harbour. The only problem I foresee is the transportation of the arrack from here to the Lodge. Baldini doesn't have a boat and the Company seldom has one to spare.'

'That's why I want to move to Northwest Harbour; I'd still take the arrack round to Southeast Harbour. And my barrels, too.'

'Where's Dubertin?'

'I don't think he's on the island any more.'

'You're mistaken, Cooper. When we tortured Aletta's slave woman a little, she confessed that he spent a night with her only last week. I'm telling you, Daniel, that danger is still in our midst.'

'She was lying to stop the agony, Commander. Dubertin left on an English ship goodness knows how long ago.'

He flung the skeleton of the bunch of grapes across the yard. 'What are you saying? Ship that was where?'

'Somewhere in one of the bays.'

'Was any assistance given to the ship? Who helped Dubertin get aboard?' Lamotius was on his feet, the devil in his eyes. *'Who?'*

'That's the story doing the rounds, Commander.'

Lamotius remained on his feet for a moment, then sank back on to the low bench. 'I warned Aletta Uytenbogaert how many times that her husband was planning to escape without her, but she wouldn't believe me. Now I need to return to the *Europa*, I must hasten back to my duties.'

On the day after Christmas Daniel took the last load of their furniture and his tools on the *Zeemaat* to Northwest Harbour.

It was the first day for a long time that there had been enough wind to fill the sails.

It was hot, it was dry.

Hendrik came from the Lodge and said stomach trouble was still raging. Row upon row of officials lying prostrate. Four had died. The Molens River had stopped running altogether, the gardens had been scorched to death. Lamotius said it was the worst drought he had experienced in his eleven years on the island. Famine was stalking them.

The Flats were the worst hit. The deer that used to graze to the north were now coming into the gardens for food. They'd cleaned out Michiel Romondt, even eaten the fruit off his guava trees.

There was still a trickle in the freshwater stream just below their fine new cyclone house with its green-leaf roof. Daniel had taken planks and tree-stumps and built a place for them to draw water, and Thomas had made the dipper for everyone who had to fetch water on their side. The slaves and children were forbidden to play or walk or wash in the water. Towards the southern part of the bay Daniel and two free-burghers built a weir below the spring where water could seep in and collect at night ...

The river, still farther south, was no longer running at all.

The gardens were drying out in the merciless heat. She let the children, wearing sun hats, bathe in the seawater to cool off. Some of the other women came to stare in horror and predicted their deaths, but when they saw that nothing happened to hers, they brought their own children and cautiously allowed them to do the same.

Only Maria refused to go into the water. Daniel had a tub rolled down to the shore, filled it with seawater and had it carried up for her. She cooled off in that.

After dark Daniel took Pieternella to the channel beside the island, held her firmly, and walked her into the water one foot after another till the coolness covered her whole body.

478

'Relax your body, my love, I won't let you go.'

At first she kept her shift on, but later she waded in naked with Daniel and learnt to experience a part of his water-world. To become a fish-body. But always kept her oldest shoes on for fear of the poisonous stonefish or a sharp piece of coral.

Northwest Harbour was like a soft quilt slowly folding itself round her.

She waited till they had come up out of the water again one night, then carefully broached the topic: 'How much money does a slave woman cost?'

'I've been keeping an eye open for another slave for you for a long time.'

'I want to ask you a special favour – I want you to buy Anna for me again.'

He was rubbing her back dry with the towel; his hands suddenly stopped. 'Don't ask me that, Pieternella.' It was the dark of the moon, she couldn't see his face. 'Please don't.'

'Every time the slave Maria and I strip coconuts, or plait palm leaves, or render coconut oil for the lamps, or make turtle chowder …'

'No, Pieternella. Never. She nearly caused the death of our Magdalena baby.'

'Then I don't want a second slave.'

It was different, living at Northwest Harbour. Having neighbours a stone's throw or two away. Other children for hers to play with. A sense of safety. Coolness.

To walk across the little bridge to Daniel's work-place. An awning on poles. To watch him at work, to see his hands fitting the staves into the master-hoop, driving the narrow-neck hoop over that, then the wide-necked one – that made the barrel stick out like a rigid wooden dress. To see him plunging the barrel into the water. And Thomas clinking up to him in his chains to help him raise the unfinished barrel over the fire-pan for the wet wood to steam and become pliable before the bottom hoops were driven in to give the barrel its bulge …

Her old Daniel. Her cooper. Her jackal-haired man who was turning grey.

'How old are you now, Daniel?'

'Thirty-eight – you knew you were marrying an old man!' With a sly grin.

Hendrik now took a short cut to the Lodge.

479

Across the Flats to the mouth of the Groot River and from there on the *Europa* or the *Vanger* to the Lodge. If he missed the boat, then by road.

Early in February he came to say the supply ship had finally arrived. The *Baaren*. A man had arrived on it who was wandering about the Lodge saying that a certain Daniel Zaaijman was expecting him. No, the man wouldn't walk back with him – probably afraid he'd murder him on the way.

'Who could it be, Daniel?'

'I asked De Hoop to try and get me a teacher for the children. That's all I can think of.'

Hendrik brought the news that Tant Maijke had died and been buried. In her will she'd committed her soul to God and named the Commander Isaac Lamotius as her sole earthly heir, to decide all her affairs in his sole discretion. She mentioned that he had constantly supported her with acts of kindness and comfort, that he was a wonderful man ...

Jan de Wilde, the Deputy Surgeon, who had witnessed the document, said Lamotius had written out the will in his own hand.

'Why are you crying, Mother?'

'Not for Tant Maijke; for a piece of my childhood, and for my own mother as well.'

'Did she love you, Mother?'

'Very much.'

'And did you love her, Mother?'

'Very much.'

Eva was the enquiring one.

To find out about the other thing that was troubling her heart, she called Hendrik aside privately.

'You didn't hear whether my brother had arrived at the Cape, did you? They usually let you know.'

'No, I heard nothing. There was another good-for-nothing who had to be thrown overboard on the voyage here, though.'

'Who?'

'Schoolmaster Pasqual from the Cape. He'd been molesting the schoolchildren. So they banned him to Mauritius, but the skipper had orders – child molesters molest again.'

'So they threw him overboard?'

'Better that way. We've got problems enough on this island.'

The week after that Daniel went to deliver arrack and barrels and came back with the rest of the news *and* the schoolmaster.

Wilhelm Wilde from Middelburg, not far from Flushing where Daniel came from. No, he was not related to Surgeon De Wilde.

Peculiar man with a hunchback. Not old, not young. Grey-brown hair showing from under a flat black hat. Old black clothes. Face almost as pale as his white-stockinged legs.

Magdalena started crying, Eva was crying, said they were scared of the schoolmaster. Daniel had to speak to them to pacify them. Catharina said he was transparent, like the ghost crabs. Eva asked: Where's he going to get a bed? Daniel said: But you know we've added on a room to the schoolroom for him to stay and sleep in. No, Eva persisted, a bed with a hollow in it, for his hunchback!

Daniel waited till the children were asleep that night, and Schoolmaster Wilde was in his room, before telling her the other news. They were sitting inside at the table.

'Things are looking bad for the farmers, Pieternella. Van der Stel is still refusing to buy Mauritian tobacco; the last shipment of beans sent to the Cape was eaten on the voyage by the crew, in desperation. The bottles of sweet potato arrack and palm arrack which Lamotius sent to Van der Stel didn't reach the Cape either.'

'And Jacobus?' He seemed not to have heard her.

'Instead, Van der Stel has sent three leaguers of Cape wine and instructed Lamotius to develop a market for *Cape* wine on the island.'

'Is the man mad?'

'Or stupid. I suspect he's not exactly keen for Lamotius to go to any more trouble distilling arrack. And in any case the three stills sent back on the *Westerwijk* were looted by pirates off Madagascar.'

'And the ship?'

'Also. The worst is: Van der Stel wants only one thing from Mauritius and that's wheat, and wheat won't grow in our climate.'

'Did you get any flour?'

'One cask. The wheat that arrived from the Cape was full of weevils. It's been spread out to dry in the sun.'

'And Jacobus? Did Lamotius perhaps ...'

'Jacobus didn't reach the Cape, Pieternella. He died on the way.'

Sheer fright coursed through her entire being. 'Died – or was thrown overboard?'

'Don't ask, Pieternella. I am so sorry.'

She screwed up her eyes tightly and told herself: *Don't make pictures! Don't see them throwing him overboard!*

'That's frightful. And I was the one who sent him back.'

'Don't.' Daniel came up behind her and put his arms around her.

In early March Jan Dirks came back from the Lodge with more news.

That the *Baaren* had sailed a few days earlier – with Aletta Uytenbogaert and her slave woman on board. Lamotius carried on like a mad thing when Master Steen came back from the ship and reported that he'd seen her on board. The ship's crew had carried her baggage down from the Orange Tree Flats at night. Lamotius commanded her to be brought back. The skipper said *he* was the Fiscal on board his ship and he wouldn't have her sent ashore.

Lamotius said: You'll get no pilot to take you out on to the open sea before she is back on shore!

The skipper said: Then I'll sail through without a pilot, I know the way.

And he ran on to the reef.

Fortunately there wasn't much damage. But for the entire week that the ship lay in the anchorage being repaired, there was open warfare between the skipper and Lamotius. The officers took Aletta's side, saying it would be unchristian to surrender her to *such* a tyrant.

On the last day of February the *Baaren* unfurled her sails. Gerrit van Ewijk was also on board. On its way the *Baaren* had to call at Madagascar to buy slaves before sailing on to Batavia. Van Ewijk wanted to buy himself some slaves.

They said Lamotius shut himself up in his room for days on end …

All Pieternella felt in her heart that she owed Aletta Uytenbogaert was to ask that the slave traders should not beat her to death on Madagascar.

4

Northwest Harbour.

'I never want to leave here again, Daniel.'

'I'm glad, my love. I don't either.'

The rains came. The free-burghers' gardens were refreshed, the rivers ran, the springs flowed.

Two English ships. Seven sick in the new hospital.

A French ship. No sick.

The free-burghers volunteered their help in building the schoolroom; Schoolmaster Wilde had first eight, then ten, then fourteen children to teach. Patient, calm and strict.

The Cape wine had soured, so Baldini made brandy of it.

Another English ship. Fourteen sick in the hospital, and the Captain and his wife asked if they could stay with her and Daniel ashore.

They were sitting at table one afternoon when a shadow suddenly darkened the doorway. It was Jacob Ovaer with three armed soldiers come from Lamotius to see what was going on.

'Not only is the enemy's ship in the bay but the skipper is in your house, Zaaijman.'

'Yes.'

'What do you think the Commander's going to say when he hears of this?'

'I can imagine.'

'It's starting to look like a *town* here round the bay! Yet you were expressly ordered to move to the Flats so that no assistance might be rendered to the enemy here. Disobedience is mutiny!'

'Look all you can, Ovaer, and then go back to the Lodge and tell all.'

'You're going to get into trouble, Zaaijman!'

A bee without a sting.

Because not long after that some of the free-burghers went to the Lodge to ask whether Lamotius had a few cows to sell them. Their wives wanted to make cheese. Lamotius sold them twenty cows. He asked no questions and made no fuss.

Then it transpired that an English ship had arrived in one of the bays on the eastern side of the island and asked for assistance. That Lamotius had made far more of the English visitors than was proper – spent three days on board eating and drinking, sold them the best red and black ebony planks in stock, or exchanged them for liquor and cloth, which he afterwards sold to free-burghers and pocketed the money himself.

'Lamot's gone downhill fast, Daniel!'

It was late November when four English ships in dire straits called at Northwest Harbour, bringing the news that France was once again at war with Holland.

Seventeen sick. Hendrik and the slaves had to stretch canvas sheets between trees to allow them all some shade. Aaltjie and Willemina came to help; the busiest of them all was Eva in her big white apron and stiffened cloth cap that she, Pieternella, had had to make specially. Schoolmaster Wilde later complained that Eva was missing too much school. Eva, who wept most piteously when one of the sailors was buried.

The ditch she'd dug in her heart between east and west was deepening. She took less and less interest in the news Hendrik brought from the Lodge.

That Lamotius had stabbed Master Steen with a knife and that Steen had very nearly died. Deputy Surgeon Wilde had had to fight for his life for weeks. When Wilde asked Lamotius for his money, because the fee for treating knife wounds and sexual diseases had to be paid directly to the Surgeon, Lamotius swore at him and had him flogged.

'It seems that since the island has got rid of the Dubertins, Lamot is searching for demons in all kinds of other places and ways.'

'You'll need to go out and pick me more yellow-bush leaves, Hendrik. My stocks are running low.'

'People are saying that you are the healer of Northwest Harbour. I hear Aaltjie's now teaching you midwifery as well?'

'Yes. But there's only so much help I can give before I have to stop. My eyes have learnt to steal from visiting surgeons, and I beg from their medicine chests. The worst is when you have to fold your hands in helplessness.'

The other worst was when you woke up in the middle of the night with a cyclone tearing everything apart.

Without a word of warning that it would wait for the very last day of the year, when most folk were sleeping off the effects of the New Year's Eve dance at Jan Roelofse's place. Many of them in a drunken stupor.

Without the signal of an Anna who ran off into the forest.

Without anything having been tied down.

Only the stone house, the cyclone house, stood its ground.

On the big bedstead the children's eyes were full of tiny lantern flames – eyes saying: We're not scared, because Father and Mother are here with us.

Once it was light the eye of the cyclone brought the bitter news: the schoolroom had been flattened, Thomas and Hendrik had to drag Schoolmaster Wilde's drenched body out of the ruin like a piece of flotsam and carry him to the house. All that was left of the hospital were two poles. Hendrik's house had been blown awry – the eye allowed them just enough time to fetch thongs and tie things down.

For its return, Daniel made the children crawl under the bed, stopped

484

Pieter who kept trying to crawl out, and made a game of it. She felt Catharina's body trembling through her nightdress, saw Eva's lips praying in the dim light under the bed, heard Magdalena crying. Maria's arms clamped tighter and tighter round her neck.

By nightfall it was all over.

By the time it was fully dark they had calculated the worst damage. Seven roofs and houses had been smashed. Barent Meulenbroek's head had been cut open when a shutter struck him – she stitched it with needle and thread and bandaged it. Breggie Janse was in premature labour – lay the fire to heat the water …

The stone house stood firm. And was filled to overflowing with the worst of the battered folk. She and Eva had to attend to everything, and comfort everyone, and stay on their feet.

Catharina went about with the bottle and the jug that Daniel had put in her hand to give everyone a little 'strengthening medicine'.

'Gawd, Daniel, what a mercy the rain wasn't too bad this time.' Jan Dirks. He'd also suffered serious damage.

Daniel's face was grim when he came to tell them that the *Zeemaat* had pulled free of its anchor and was lying washed up on the island. Four sampans were gone. Half his work-place. There was only a hole in the roof of the slave quarters.

Exactly a full month later she stopped below the house one afternoon to rest for a moment. Daniel's two oxen were coming by with a few palm leaves and bamboo stems for the schoolroom that was almost complete again. She listened to the hammer blows and voices in the distance. All over, folk were busy rebuilding.

A cyclone is like giving birth, she thought. Once the pain is past your courage comes back redoubled.

Jake and Jamika came past carrying a pallet of stones between them. Daniel had undertaken to build a stone room for Hendrik too. Then one for the slaves. Jan Muur and Willemina were also carrying stone and burning lime. So were some of the others. For stone houses.

Looking up, she noticed that the sky was covered with small wispy snow-white clouds. There can't be *another* cyclone on the way, she said in her heart. Cyclones came every three years. Sometimes they stayed away even longer …

The air was sultry, she felt sweat trickling down her face. Daniel came walking up from the river, saw her standing there and waved with the hammer in his hand.

'Why are you standing here so far away and lost in thought, my love?'

he asked when he reached her.

'You once said Mauritius wasn't a people-place.' She noticed the immediate suspicion in his eyes. 'No, I don't want to run away, I just know it doesn't help complaining about the setbacks we suffer.'

'The answer is to be better prepared.'

'How do dumbclucks prepare themselves? Where do they take shelter?' Where does Anna take refuge?

'Not many dumbclucks left to seek shelter, I'm afraid.'

'Where do tortoises find shelter?'

'In their own shells and where the experience of the ages has taught them to.'

'I think – I think there's another cyclone coming.'

He looked her straight in the eye for a moment. Then up at the sky, across the sea, over the mountain basin. 'I think you may be right, my love.'

Midnight.

You get a strength from somewhere that allows your body to wrap itself round your children. Daniel held Pieter and Maria. Hendrik and the schoolmaster and the male slaves crouched under the table in the sitting room. Breggie Janse and her month-old baby boy were in the children's room with the slave Maria and Eva's two kittens. Three other women with their children were in the other room.

Stone house. Fortress house.

God, she later prayed out loud amid the hellish din, if You have poured the strength into this cyclone, then use that same strength to spare my children!

And the rain.

Eleven cows drowned, gardens washed away, the wooden bridge over the river to the island was gone ... All that was left of the leaf houses on the southern side of the bay when the eye came were their tops. Two families had made it to her and Daniel's place before the wind and the rain returned with renewed fury.

Night.

Day.

At Black River Mouth there were even drowned deer hanging on the treetops. Cattle lay washed up among other flotsam on the yellow-sand bay. Hendrik told of the terrible stench.

The stone house had survived but lost its roof. So had the new schoolroom and the slave house and the work-place and Hendrik's house.

Out of the mud, slowly and dejectedly, people gathered up their courage again.

By early March the stone house had another roof.

Jan Muur was the first to go down past the Flats to the Lodge. Only the stone-walled Lodge and the one stone outbuilding were still standing.

Adam Cornelise from the Flats had drowned trying to save his cattle.

It took Baldini and the slaves Lamotius had brought three days to struggle from Black River to Northwest Harbour.

'There'll be no more distilling, Daniel. The stills, everything, gone! The little I could save from my house is in these bundles. And my lute.'

Four extra mouths to feed. Hendrik and Jake went ranging as far as the Flats with the ox, hunting deer for meat.

It was towards dusk on a Sunday that a big Dutch ship of the return fleet came limping, wraith-like, across the sea: a skeleton arisen from a watery grave, without a single mast, its body listing with the water that had leaked in.

The *Berg China*. Struck on the open sea by the second cyclone.

The two elegant gentlemen who sat down at her table looked as though they hardly dared trust the ebony chairs under them. Captain Hubert Hoffe and the merchant Samuel Elsevier.

No, they had no one sick on board that needed to be brought ashore; the Surgeon and his deputy were perfectly competent.

No, they had not come for comprehensive repairs – they were hoping only for emergency aid to enable them to reach the Lodge at Southeast Harbour and Commander Lamotius, an old friend and acquaintance of Elsevier's.

They did not require accommodation either; they preferred to remain on board the *Berg China*.

'If you've limped all the way here, you could surely have limped round there while you were at it?' asked Daniel, almost rudely.

Elsevier's head jerked up like a horse's. 'We have not asked for your opinion, Zaaijman. Only a recommendation to some person on this side of the island who would be able to assist in making the required damage assessments.'

'It's unfortunate that I am the only one able to do so on this side of the island.'

'Then we shall expect you on board at first light tomorrow.'

The skipper was not quite as arrogant. 'The cyclone seems to have struck you fairly hard as well.'

'Two cyclones.'

It was two full months before the ship could risk sailing to the other side of the island.

Baldini took the Captain's letter to Southeast Harbour to make the required report. He came back with a letter from Commander Lamotius recommending that Daniel Zaaijman accompany the ship since there was no better carpenter or cooper at the Lodge.

The merchant Elsevier and some of the ship's officers spent much of their time ashore, going for walks. It seemed that they had begun to trust her house and her cups and tea and jam-puffs and pancakes, and came in for them. Long conversations with Baldini. Elsevier was astonished at Magdalena's drawing of the cyclone: trees blown awry as though the wind was still blowing across the paper. A palm-leaf cottage in tatters.

After almost a month he remarked stiffly: Your children, Juffrouw Zaaijman, are particularly nicely brought up.

The free-burghers came to complain that it was very heavy work catching *two* turtles and bringing them to the ship on sampans – if the esteemed merchant would kindly undertake to see that they were well paid for it all.

The 'esteemed merchant' sometimes questioned her at length about the Cape. He was amazed at her knowledge of the Hottentots. And even more so when she told him her mother had been a Hottentot.

'I am not at all pleased that that windbag comes keeping *my* wife company all day!' Daniel said on many a night when he came home.

'He's got to pass the time somehow, Daniel.'

'Well, let him go and do it somewhere else.'

Sometimes she questioned *him*, Elsevier.

Pretended to be stupid. 'Do you perhaps know Jan Dubertin?'

'Jean Baptiste! Do I know him? My dear Juffrouw Pieternella, I have just returned from Ceylon where Lieutenant Dubertin's cruelties and tyranny will long be remembered by those who suffered them!'

'And his wife?'

'Aletta Uytenbogaert. Impeccable ancestry.'

'Dubertin was exiled here on Mauritius.'

'So I heard. My old friend Commander Lamotius doesn't know how fortunate he is that the man escaped. Is his wife still on the island?'

488

'She also left a good while back.'

Under Daniel's supervision Baldini and Hendrik managed to get the *Zeemaat* seaworthy again.

'Here I am, cutting myself in three, and Hoffe comes complaining that we're working too slowly! Elsevier is in a hurry to get away to the Lodge.'

Two months and the *Berg China* sailed out through the reef one afternoon with Daniel on board, taking with it Magdalena's drawing of the cyclone. Elsevier swapped it with her for a comb and a cake of sweet-smelling soap.

In July the free-burghers at Northwest Harbour had some good luck: an English ship, the *Chandos*, came in for food and water. On the third day after it arrived, Daniel came back on foot from the Lodge to see if all was well at home. When he saw the ship he exclaimed: 'Now if that isn't the work of Providence ...'

He bought two barrels of pitch from the ship; the repairs to the *Berg China* were grinding to a halt for lack of tar.

With Daniel came also the news that the supply ship, the *Haantje*, had arrived in Southeast Harbour. Simon van der Stel had sent word that he was now *Governor* at the Cape, not Commandeur any more.

The *Haantje* had brought two saw-blades but they were unusable.

Hester, the former wife of Gerrit van Ewijk, was to be sent to the Cape at the first opportunity. She would sail on the *Berg China*. Permission had been granted for Maria, Willem van Deventer's widow, to return to the Cape. She would also leave on the *Berg China*.

'Maria and Lambert Stam were married at the Lodge last week.'

'Does she look happy, Daniel?'

'The best she's ever looked. He's going back with her.'

'I'm happy for her.'

The other news he held back until the *Zeemaat* was ready to leave the next morning. That after many vicissitudes Aletta Uytenbogaert was back in Holland and that her father, advocate of the court in Utrecht, had laid criminal charges against Lamotius to which he had to reply in writing. That Hans Pigt and his wife and Deputy Surgeon De Wilde and Lambert Janse and one or two more witnesses had been summoned to sail to Batavia on the *Haantje*.

The *Berg China* spent a total of seven months at the island. And then had to leave without its Deputy Surgeon, Jan Tauke: the man was all afire for the late Adam Cornelise's Cathrinha Kel.

5

It was at Northwest Harbour that she saw her older children grow into people. Real people.

Catharina, a pretty young girl with a head of coppery hair that betrayed her headstrong nature because she wouldn't ever wear a cap on her head, though she often emerged from forest dells with leaves in her hair.

'Who is this child, Daniel?'

'Someone learning to live her own life, my love.' Daniel was very proud of his children.

'Should I be worried about her?'

'No.'

Catharina, whom she had to comfort for a whole day when she first began to bleed and had to go on the sponge.

'But, Mother, are you sure I'm not going to die?'

'I'm quite sure, my girl.'

'Tant Willemina's Mina says it's the start of a girl's hell on earth.'

'Does it look as though your mother is living in hell?'

'No.'

'Well, then. When I was your age, I married Father.'

'Really?'

'Really.'

Eva.

Daniel used to say that if she'd been a boy, she would have been a surgeon. A refined child.

Magdalena.

The delight of Baldini and Schoolmaster Wilde.

Northwest Harbour saw Maria and Pieter grow from babies into children. Maria eight, Pieter six. Constantly at play on the seashore or in the hills or with the other free-burghers' children.

'Father, I'm begging you, on my tummy on the ground, please to tell Schoolmaster I don't have to go to school.'

'Why don't you want to go to school, Maria?' Daniel was so patient with her.

'It's the schoolroom's roof.'

'What's wrong with the schoolroom roof?'

'Geckos.'

'But you like catching geckos!'

'The-the-the – the sun can't shine through the roof on to them.'

Her Hottentot child, prettiest of all her children. Draw her for me, the merchant Elsevier asked Magdalena just before he left. But Magdalena said she didn't really draw people.

Pieter didn't fight against having to go to school. He simply ran away.

The spitting image of Daniel. Daniel's pride and joy. 'Captain' of the *Zeemaat*. Carpenter with his own tools in the work-place. Thomas's lord and master.

'Soon's I'm big and Father goes to the Lodge with barrels, I'm going to chop off your chain right at your leg. So's you can easily come into the forest with me.'

And then Little Daniel was born. On the twentieth of November, and Eva was the broody hen who made him her doll-child from Day One. She refused to pin him into his nappy.

'I don't know any man as happy as I am, my love,' Daniel said, holding the tiny thing's head in his huge hand.

He was at Southeast Harbour when she gave birth, but Aaltjie was with her.

He'd had to go round to deliver barrels, but also because Jan Muur had come to say that the supply ship *Duijf* had arrived. 'There's big trouble at the Lodge, Daniel, I'm telling you.'

The late Master Sven used to say that Mauritius wrapped heaven and hell together for you in one quilt ...

The supply ship had brought the island a new Commander from the Cape. Roelof Diodati. His first instructions and task were to arrest Lamotius and Secunde Ovaer and Master Steen, to gather witnesses to testify against them and to send them all to Batavia on the *Duijf*.

'It was horrible, my love,' said Daniel when he got back. 'Thank God they weren't clapped in irons. At least Lamotius was able to board the land boat with a little dignity.'

'How was Lamotius?'

'Arrogant, like an innocent offender. Steen was drunk and Ovaer was furiously angry. Diodati prevented the free-burghers from spitting at the boat as it shoved off.'

'What's the new commander like?' It was strange having to imagine the island under the authority of a new commander.

'Young. He was the bookkeeper at the Cape. I doubt whether he's up to the task.'

'Did you speak to him?'

'He questioned me about this side of the island.'

'And?' She was overcome by the old unease: that the Company would start meddling again and try to have the free-burghers on the western side moved away. 'What did you tell him?'

'Just enough. That down the years we have had to help rescue a fair number of Dutch ships ...' Daniel, with his eyes full of mischief.

'And his wife?'

'He isn't married.'

Early in the new year the *Vanger* sailed into Northwest Harbour before a blustery wind – Commander Diodati was on board.

Tall and thin. Black locks down to his shoulders, under a big black hat with a feather. Jacket and breeches of dark blue velvet, showy white silk shirt with broad lace. White stockings. Black shoes.

Darting brown eyes.

He stopped with Daniel under the tree in front of the door, took off his hat to fan his face. There was something about the man, his stance, his way of looking around, sniffing, as though he had caught an unpleasant smell. She stood watching him for a long while through the shutter on the sitting-room window – turned round, took off her house-cap, put on one of her pretty caps and went outside.

'Mynheer ...'

'My wife, Pieternella van Meerhoff,' Daniel introduced her.

'Any connection with the erstwhile Surgeon at the Cape?'

'My father.' I don't like you, Mynheer, but I don't yet know why.

Catharina came up from the riverside and apparently didn't notice the man, just called out excitedly to Daniel: 'Father, a flock of pinkbirds has landed high up in the river!' The children always called flamingos pinkbirds. They cried when free-burghers went out and shot them for the pot up near Bight-Without-End and came back, each with a bunch of them tied by their necks and slung over his shoulder.

The hat in Diodati's hand stopped fanning – on his face an expression somewhere between wonderment and disbelief.

'Commander, this is my eldest daughter, Catharina,' Daniel said. 'Catharina, this is our honourable new Commander.'

'Mynheer.'

She'd taught her children beautifully. Diodati needn't think he'd come to visit a bunch of rustics.

Or that Daniel Zaaijman would simply sit at the table with him in silence, sucking at his pipe.

'Catharina, spread a fresh tablecloth on the table.' Aside to Catharina.

'But Mother, that was a clean tablecloth only this morning!'

'Do as I say, girl. The pretty blue and white striped one that the English gave us last time they were here.'

Daniel opened a bottle of special wine – one of those he'd had from the skipper of a French ship.

'It was no easy task for me to have former Commander Lamotius arrested.' You could hear Diodati was still practising how to sound important. 'The man apparently thought he could compel the necessary respect by keeping strictly to the narrow way, but in reality it only made the free-burghers rebellious.'

'As you say, Commander.'

'What I find most surprising is that he neglected to exploit the incredible source of ebony here. The wood fetches high prices in Holland. When I look at the tumbledown state of the mill ...'

'The island has been waiting for nearly fifteen years, Commander, for saw-blades.'

'Governor Van der Stel has sent a model of a saw-blade to Holland. His orders are that in the mean time the wood is to be sawn by hand.' He made it sound so easy.

'There's a shortage of hands at the Lodge, Commander.'

'Proper arrangements ought to enable us to deliver the desired two hundred beams a year with ease ...'

Baldini came in and Daniel introduced them. They shook hands like two fighting cocks observing each other from different perches, Diodati on the higher one – without getting up. Baldini grim-faced. They spoke to each other briefly in a very foreign language. Italian, Baldini explained later, adding that Diodati's ancestors had married into some of the leading families in Italy – hence their lineage. Wealthy.

She waited till they were all at table for lunch. She saw Diodati's eyebrow lift just a fraction in surprise when he had his first taste of roast duck with her delicate crab sauce.

'We don't live only on sweet potatoes, Commander.'

'I didn't think you did. May I assume you learnt the culinary arts at the Cape, Juffrouw Pieternella? The Eastern slave women are remarkably fine cooks.'

'I was still a child when I left there.'

'Are you happy on Mauritius?'

'Yes. But it's not a people-place.' She wanted to ask him something …

'Not a people-place?' From the height of his perch, while his eyes kept returning to Catharina and he tried not to stare too hard at Maria's unlikeness.

'No, Mynheer. You'll only be happy here if, *perhaps*, the island takes you to its heart.'

'I think that depends on oneself.'

'Father says we mustn't jump too hard on the island's floor,' Maria told him with childish high seriousness, looking straight at him with her dark-brown eyes. 'Otherwise it hurts, and it cries.'

Daniel laughed and explained with a wink: 'Maria is in the habit of jumping out of trees that are too tall, Commander.'

'I understand.'

She waited till the slave Maria had cleared the table and Catharina and Magdalena had gone to fetch the jam-puffs. 'Hester Janse – Hester van Ewijk … she was sent from here on the *Berg China* to the Cape for trial. I keep wondering what happened to her, Commander.'

He frowned for a moment, then brightened up. 'Of course. The woman who, um, – with one of her husband's slaves – um …'

'Fornicated,' she helped him overcome his embarrassment. Boldly, as though it was no great matter. 'And was she tried?'

'The word I wanted is *adultery*.'

'Was she tried?'

'Immediately upon arrival. As a matter of fact, I was the clerk of the court.'

'What was her sentence?'

'She was publicly flogged and has to work for the Company for five years. At the time of my departure, she was carrying cargo from the quay to the Castle with the slave women.' As though it was no great matter.

'But that's frightful!' It felt as though everything within her was rising up in helpless rebellion; she wanted to grab something and smash it, and the man just sat there and calmly started asking Daniel why the arrack distilling had failed … 'Hester had already spent five years here in the gaol at the Lodge for her *adultery!*' She didn't care that she had interrupted him. 'Already done five years of slave labour!'

'I was not the Fiscal, Juffrouw Pieternella.'

'You're a man.'

'I don't know you like this, my love,' Daniel said, once Diodati had left, on his way to see other free-burghers.

'No, nor do I. I just want to take Catharina and tie her up in the forest.'

'Pieternella?'

'To stop Roelof Diodati getting her.'

A year later they were married.

In the Lodge. By the Captain of the supply ship *Baaren*. Catharina in the most beautiful pale blue dress, which she, Pieternella, and Aaltjie had worked on for weeks. With a wedding feast afterwards in the square courtyard.

'Now at last our luck has turned, Daniel!' the free-burghers at Northwest Harbour rejoiced, teasingly. 'A neighbour with the Commander as his son-in-law can only make things lighter for us all!'

Two fiddles and Baldini's lute provided the music at the feast.

Oom Bart fell asleep in a chair against the wall early on in the evening. 'He hasn't been well for a long time now, Pieternella,' said Tant Theuntjie and danced all evening with widower Henk Karseboom.

Oom Laurens and Tant Magdalena were deeply moved. 'How have the years fled past so quickly? I helped bring her into the world with my own two hands. And here she is today above us all – the wife of the Commander.'

'That's true, Tant Magdalena.' She laughed and chatted, and danced with Daniel, but all the while she was fighting the ghosts that wanted to come and share in the wedding. Juffrouw Margaretha and little Andrea. Salomon.

Grieta. Wrinkled and downhearted. 'Gawd, Pieternella, I've heard a rumour that they've thrown Lamotius and Master Steen in gaol in Batavia. Ovaer is under open arrest – whatever that means. There's no mercy in life. I'm telling you today, that Aletta Uytenbogaert first opened her legs for Lamotius and then suddenly pinched them shut again. I know her type. You just don't do that to a man.'

Only Hendrik wouldn't come to the wedding. 'Wouldn't know if I was supposed to sit or stand; and in any case somebody has to keep an eye on the house. Plenty of runaway slaves in the forest.'

Diodati issued orders that they were to be caught. Shot if they resisted.

The three Jans and their wives came on foot across the Flats to the Groot River and on the *Vanger* from there to the Lodge. 'We had to bale water the whole way, the boat leaks so.' The women hadn't been to the

Lodge for many years. 'I thought it would have been a palace by now,' Willemina said out loud. 'And all it is is just a four-roomed house.'

Stone-built. At the rear of the square. A storehouse, also of stone. Palm-leaf roofs. The side wall of the square closest to the sea was also built of stone, to the height of a man. But the foundations of the entrance portal had given way after the last two cyclones; the pillars were completely skew. Magdalena had some of the slave women at the Lodge haul in branches to disguise the crookedness a little in honour of the feast. Outside the portal, behind a decrepit semicircular fence of stakes, stood two cannons, listing on rotten wooden supports. The *Europa* lay on the beach like a stranded, dried-up whale; there was no pitch to caulk it with.

Everything was in a state of neglect.

The doors and door jambs and windows were all rotten with wood-borer. Daniel said it was because there was no tar to treat the wood with.

'The place depresses me, Daniel!'

'It's only because you haven't been here for so long – or because you went on hoping for too long that she wouldn't accept him. Be at peace, my love, the man is not unpleasant.'

'I suppose in my heart I probably believed that my daughters would marry men like their father.'

Daniel had a good laugh at that, he said good coopers were a scarce commodity.

In the year that had passed, fighting-cock Diodati's feathers had started falling out one by one.

He thought because he was Van der Stel's friend things would be different. He sent a large quantity of the free-burghers' tobacco to the Cape and waited hopefully for the outcome. Good tobacco, and packed as Lamotius had said it should be: open in casks, like the Virginia tobacco that was so popular at the Cape. Not spun. All the West Indian tobacco now arrived in the fatherland as young leaves, where it was dried and spun and served in a sauce ...

But then Van der Stel sent word that tobacco had little value as a medium of exchange; the Hottentots had too little livestock left to barter. They were not to send any more.

'It's pretty devastating, Master,' Diodati complained to Daniel, while his eyes kept looking in the direction of Catharina.

'That's the way it's gone for years and years, my friend.'

My friend.

'Why don't you like him, Mother?' asked Catharina, repeatedly.

'When you were little, I had a slave called Anna. She would have said his fire is too cold.'

'Oh Mother, you're silly!'

The salted meat, the butter and the soap that Diodati sent to the Cape were rejected without explanation.

'Wood, Master, wood. Our salvation lies in wood.'

'I can only agree with you, my friend.'

'Commander Lamotius noted in the diary that even if a thousand men were to cut ebony on this island for a hundred years …'

'I know. And I agree with you: our hope lies in the wood.'

The free-burghers of Northwest Harbour were selling more and more wood to English ships, but Daniel didn't mention this to Diodati.

When the two hundred beams of red and black ebony lay piled up above the quay, Daniel congratulated him. There were weeks when Diodati himself went out with the woodcutters to fell trees south of the Flats and to haul them out over the Bamboo Mountains on wagons. They couldn't bring them round from Groot River Mouth on the *Vanger*, the boat leaked too much.

Every slave and Company servant who could be spared at the Lodge had to help with the wood. They didn't complain too much. 'At least he doesn't swear at us, and he's pretty generous with the rations …'

When the *Baaren* arrived, the beams were ready. But the captain said he couldn't take them on board because he was now headed for Batavia. The wood would have to wait for another opportunity. And Van der Stel sent word that the Lords Seventeen had announced that they expected to receive at least a thousand to twelve hundred beams a year from Mauritius. Large beams. Not knotty, and not cross-grained.

Diodati was irresolute. On the day before the wedding he told Daniel he'd come to the decision that there was only one other thing that would satisfy the Company: wheat.

Catharina was *so* pretty and *so* happy.

'I love him, Mother. With my whole heart.'

They got back to Northwest Harbour from the wedding on the Friday. On the *Zeemaat*. Two English ships were waiting in the bay for repairs and meat and vegetables and 'Mister Ziman'.

Daniel said: Not before Monday, my daughter was married on Wednesday, tomorrow night I'm having a little dance for everyone who couldn't be there.

On Saturday evening both the Captains and their wives and some of the officers came to share the fun.

'Why are you so quiet, my love?' Daniel asked later that night.

'I'm missing Catharina and I'm keeping my eye on that Englishman who keeps wanting to dance with Eva!'

'My love, our daughters are pretty - like their mother!'

Northwest Harbour was heaven and hell wrapped in one cloth.

6

Hell arose at Southeast Harbour.

For two whole years, no supply ship arrived.

'Some days my poor husband sends lookouts all the way to the top of Kattiesberg, Mother.'

Catharina had been brought to bed of a son. She, Pieternella, and the Secunde's wife had been with her.

'Don't let it upset you, my child. It's not good for your milk.'

'Stay with me, Mother, don't go away!'

'I just wanted to go outside for a while.' It was pleasant to wander round the Lodge occasionally. The outbuildings, except for the small stone gaol, were all made of palm leaves: the kitchen, the slave quarters, the barracks for the Sergeant and the soldiers. A leaf house for the two huntsmen and the two wagoners and the four woodsmen. Three seamen. A smithy. A second smithy up on the Molens River near the old mill. As a child she had been fascinated by the smith at the Fort - his fire, the *shoof, shoof* of his bellows like someone with a wheezy chest, his long pliers, the piercing iron noise of his clanging hammers.

The one at the Lodge made the same noises.

There were other sounds as well - that she recognised deep in her memory. The cursing and shouting of the two seamen locked up in the gaol. Leendert and Cornelis. Who were caught when they tried to escape on an English ship and now had to wait to be sent to the Cape. Sometimes, when some of the shell carriers on Robben Island had had to be locked up, they'd also carried on like that.

Most of the officials and the Surgeon lived in a part of the stone

Lodge.

She also liked dropping in on old Jan Yser, the freelance shoemaker, in the kitchen. His task was to swat flies – when he wasn't having one of his heartbreaking coughing fits. He'd always hoped that the Company would allow his wife and children to come out from the fatherland to join him. When he couldn't make shoes any more, he asked Lamotius to send him back to the Cape. Unfortunately people couldn't just be sent. So they took him back into the service of the Company. Eventually he couldn't manage anything more than swatting flies.

'How are things going, Oom Jan?'

'They're not going, they've stopped.'

Sometimes she walked out to the gardens to say hello to Anna. Even if the slave pretended not to hear.

Daniel accompanied Diodati to the Flats. Once again rats had eaten every blade of wheat that came up through the soil. The free-burghers had delivered too little of their sugar cane to the Lodge to keep the Company's still operating. Instead they were distilling cane arrack in makeshift stills of their own and depriving the Company of further income.

She and Daniel and Maria and Pieter and Little-Daniel and the slave Maria spent a month at the Lodge helping Catharina.

Diodati had developed a peculiar twitch on one side of his face. What with all the struggling and worry, the man was exhausted. 'There are days when I feel it's all getting too much, Father.' He called Daniel Father, her Juffrouw Pieternella – there was too little difference in their ages for him to be able to call her Mother. 'The ebony is lying here cut. I've had it brought down and stacked in the square to await the ship. And now no ship comes. Shortly after I arrived here the late Oom Bart Borms said Mauritius had a way of bewitching its Commanders. I resented it at the time – now I'm beginning to wonder.'

Tant Theuntjie had married Henk Karseboom and they'd also moved to Northwest Harbour. 'That's the way life turns, Pieternella, here we are, neighbours again. Henk says the only free-burghers that are making any kind of a living on this island are the bunch here at Northwest Harbour. Thanks to the enemy. Till Van der Stel comes and drives you out completely. They say he's a devil.'

'Daniel says we're not moving.'

'Of course not, with the Commander for a son-in-law he can safely make a living out of the enemy. And you out of the sick in your so-called hospital.'

'I don't get paid for that, Tante.'

'So where do you get all the cloth and porcelain and silver from?'

'It's all part of Daniel's earnings.'

'Well, I wonder. I see you're going to have another wedding one of these days. Free-burgher Hans van Schoonhoven is wearing a path to your yard.'

'He's a hard worker.'

'Hope his backside's all right – wasn't one of Captain Frooij's slutboys a Van Schoonhoven?'

'Tant Theun!'

'Somewhere there's something wrong, Father. Either the supply ship has sailed clean past the island or else it's been lost at sea.'

'That we cannot know yet.'

'Unless the Governor didn't have a ship to send. I don't think the war is over yet; the Company needs every ship it can get.'

'We can only wait and pray, my son.'

'And what is the child's name going to be?' Pieternella, asked him. Catharina asked her to.

'Salomon.'

'Salomon?' She thought her mouth must have gaped at him for a moment.

'Yes. It's an old and respected name in my family.'

'I thought for a moment it was after my brother ...'

'No. It is not, Juffrouw Pieternella.'

His respected family hung round his neck continually.

She and Daniel and the children and the slave set off for Northwest Harbour early one Sunday. It was like being able to breathe more and more freely. At the Apple Tree River Daniel steered the nose of the *Zeemaat* into the river and turned round again up near the apple trees. Like a breath of fresh air. Even though it wasn't the time for the trees to be in blossom. Dropped anchor beside the waterfall and let the children play for a while.

'One day, my love, one day ...'

'What then?'

'When the children are grown up and have left home, I'll bring you here for a whole week. Just you and me.'

'Won't we be too old by then?'

'Never!'

There was one English ship in the anchorage when they reached home;

the free-burghers were plying the sampans back and forth to get their vegetables and meat and butter and wood and tobacco delivered.

No, the ship was not in need of repairs. Just food and water.

'That's how Providence takes care of us,' as Daniel was to say later.

Because on the next Sunday the soldier from Southeast Harbour came to say that the Lodge, with the storehouse and books and papers and supplies and ebony and everything had burnt to the ground.

She could recall hearing herself calling out to heaven – Daniel said he caught her as she fell. Your body can absorb only so much fright. When she came to, Eva was wiping her face while Daniel rubbed her feet. His face grey and grim. Eva was crying.

'Mother! Catharina and the baby were saved, Roelof got them out in time. He was burnt but is out of danger.'

Three of the Company's slaves and Van Nimwegen's slave woman had tried to burn the Commander and all the officials alive as they slept so they could take over the island and rule it. The powder cellar had also exploded.

The slaves were caught and tortured to death.

The ghost of Hans Beer ...

She and Daniel took the *Zeemaat* to fetch Catharina and the baby home. Diodati really wanted to come with them but had to stay at his post in case the supply ship arrived. He was living under a sheet of canvas in a corner between two fire-blackened walls. The Surgeon had bandaged his hands; fortunately his legs were not seriously burnt.

Daniel told him there was an English ship at Northwest Harbour that could take a report on the disaster to the Cape. The entire stock of paper, quills and ink had been reduced to ashes, said Diodati. Daniel promised to produce the necessary document.

The ship had not yet left when they got back to Northwest Harbour. And when it did leave, Free-burgher Claas Oosthuizen, his wife and child were also on board – they couldn't take it any longer.

Northwest Harbour welcomed Catharina and little Salomon with open arms.

'It's good to be home again, Mother.'

'And we're happy to have you here with us, my child.' All she had were the clothes on her back, they would have to make her some new ones.

'Roelof says he's going to ask to become a free-burgher. Then he'll get 'sixty men to cut wood and he'll run the wood business for the Company at a profit.'

'Your father says the draught animals at the Lodge have got some disease. About twenty-seven oxen have died. The woodcutters are having difficulty getting the wood hauled out.'

'Roelof is doing his best, but there are days when I wonder if he shouldn't ask for us to move to Batavia.'

'That would be a sad day for your father and me.'

'Don't you and Father ever think of moving there, too?'

'No. Mauritius is our home. Even though it beats us down on to our knees at times, we don't want to go anywhere else.'

A year later the island beat them down on to their knees yet again.

The roof of the new Lodge at Southeast Harbour blew off into the sea; the water round the lodge on the Flats was the depth of a man; the free-burghers' sugar cane was devastated; cattle and deer washed out to sea.

Umpteen houses and roofs blew away at Northwest Harbour. Gardens washed away. Cattle drowned. Only Daniel's stone house remained standing – though it lost its roof. And Hendrik and Baldini's stone cottage. The palm trees were stripped of leaves. It took them weeks to collect enough for new roofs. The schoolroom would have to wait.

It was weeks before Daniel and Jamika could go to Southeast Harbour to fetch Catharina again. They found her and Diodati and the child in a wooden hutch partitioned off in one of the roofless rooms. Diodati was sick.

'I just cannot continue, Father. I'm going to ask to be released from this hell at the very first opportunity.'

The dysentery that had been raging before the cyclone still had most of the officials confined to bed – seven had already been buried and all the medicines had been lost in the fire. There were hardly any usable axes or saws or chisels or whetstones left at the Lodge.

Catharina couldn't leave her husband behind alone. Soldiers carried him in a hammock when he had to see to outside tasks around the Lodge.

Three months.

Then, thank God, the supply ship finally arrived. The *De Swaagh*. Hendrik had been off searching for ambergris on the eastern side of the island and brought them the news: that more than a year ago, another ship, the *Standvastigheid*, had already been loaded at the Cape with the letters and all the provisions and equipment; it was ready to sail for Mauritius when a storm arose in Table Bay one night. The ship had wrenched free and run aground in the mouth of the Salt River.

When the news came that the supply ship had arrived, she and Aaltjie were making Eva's wedding dress. Her wedding to Hans van Schoonhoven would also take place at the Lodge.

The most beautiful snow-white dress with delicate lace.

Eva and Hans were properly smitten with each other. Even Daniel conceded: 'Yes, Pieternella, he *has* got the right fire for her.'

A week later, when he said he would have to go down to Southeast Harbour, she laid down her needle and prepared to go with him. Pieter and Maria would have to stay behind with the slave Maria and Baldini and Hendrik. Magdalena wanted to go along because she was worried about Catharina and was missing her. 'I'm beginning to wonder, Mother, if the only thing that Roelof Diodati is stuffed with is his important family!'

'Magdalena!' Daniel reprimanded her. 'Show some respect for your brother-in-law. The man has a heavy task as Commander of this island.'

Little-Daniel also had to go along. He was a child who had to be tied on a short leash the whole time, to keep him from falling overboard, because he seemed not to have any fear of water at all; only three years old, but he'd be over the side as soon as you took your eyes off him!

'Really, Daniel, your daughters are demure and know their place, but your sons are full of wildness!' she complained one day.

'Those boys are close to my heart, my love,' he laughed proudly. 'And I wouldn't call our Maria exactly demure!'

There were days when this child, so different from the others, had her deeply worried. She was a riddle of a child who sometimes frightened her. Always up in the hills when she could get away from school or her household tasks. Always cheerful, always running. Not one of the children from any of the other houses could catch a long-tailed lizard, but *she* could! 'It's because they don't know where he *lives*, Mother. You have to sit *dead* still so that he thinks you are a stone ...' Her hands, her eyes, her whole body would all be vigorously explaining to you at once. And there wasn't a bird anywhere in the vicinity that could hide its nest from her. 'I didn't steal the baby, Mother, I just brought him to *show* you. His mummy knows, I told her I'd bring him back now-now.'

The thing that really gave her a fright was when Magdalena made Maria a doll. The head and body were of old sheeting, stuffed with sawdust that she'd gathered wherever planks were being sawn. Even Daniel couldn't help staring at Magdalena's handiwork when he came in at night. Eyes, nose and mouth worked in coloured thread. A dress, a cap, bloomers ...

Maria protested against the bloomers 'She's not on the sponge!' She was still far from being on the sponge herself but there was nothing she didn't know about.

When the doll was finished, she put her down and covered her so she could sleep. The next morning she tied her on her back with a piece of an old quilt to be able to walk into the hills with her.

'Maria ...?' She, Pieternella, was dumbfounded. Never, after Catharina, had she ever again tied any of her children on her back. 'Why are you tying her on your back?'

'She doesn't want to stay behind at home, so she has to come along.' Completely serious.

'Why don't you carry her in your arms?'

'Then I wouldn't have hands.'

Daniel thought it was something to laugh about. 'I don't understand why it bothers you, Pieternella.'

'Where does she get it from?'

'Where does Pieter get his handiness with a hammer and saw and chisel from? He gets it from *my* blood.'

'You don't understand.'

'No, I do understand. It's the old thorn in your flesh festering again, my love. But tell me: have you ever seen any other child on this whole island who is as cheerful and happy as Maria?'

'No.'

'Well then. Leave her be. Let her carry the doll whichever way she wants to.'

That afternoon Tant Theuntjie arrived.

'Pieternella! Isn't it enough that the child is a half-caste Hottentot? Do you have to teach her Hottentot manners as well?'

'Leave Maria alone. She *wants* to carry her doll like that.'

They reached Southeast Harbour the next afternoon. The *De Swaagh* was anchored in the roadstead, and the sea and the quay were alive with unfamiliar sailors and sampans and land boats, all trying to load the last barrels of lime and what little ebony there was. The ship was in a hurry to set sail. Faithful, leaking old *Vanger* was moored beside the quay, after going round to fetch the small quantity of cut wood piled up at the Groot River.

The Lodge had a new leaf roof, the pillars of the entrance portal were now more crooked than ever – but Catharina wept with happiness. Little Salomon was walking strongly already and was too sweet.

Only Diodati was nervous and irresolute – though at least he was up and about again. He would pick something up two or three times, drop it, issue an order here, withdraw one there.

'I'm simply overcome, Father. The Cape has sent no fewer than ten new free-burghers. Embittered men, without wives. I've sent them to the lodge on the Flats for the time being; most of them were banned over disagreements with the Governor. They say the Governor and the officials are claiming more and more land for themselves again. This while I, the Commander, and the officials on this island are little more than slaves! And what's more, the Cape has sent another *seven* convicts here.'

'Exiles or convicts?'

'I can't tell the difference. I haven't even properly finished the letters that have to go to the Cape yet and there the ship is, ready to sail!'

Unfamiliar faces all about the Lodge. The only distinction between sailor and convict were the chains some of them wore. Six of them were chained in pairs, one singly.

It was the one who was chained alone that attracted her, Pieternella's, attention. The only dark skin among the seven. A straight-haired Easterling like Fair Ansiela. He stood there silently weeping, unashamed. Young. Wet streams of tears trickling down his cheeks as if from a fountain. Jantjie from Batavia. Who had got Van der Stel's daughter Adriaantjie with child. Adriaantjie said: It wasn't Jantjie. Van der Stel said: Throw him in gaol, he's a heathen who's dishonoured a Christian girl!

The new Surgeon who arrived on the *De Swaagh* told Catharina the story himself.

'I feel so sorry for him, Mother. His sadness is so deep.'

When the child was born it was obviously a white man's child. Adriaantjie said she wouldn't have the child's father, she wanted Jantjie. They were meant for each other. For ever. The Fiscal said: Flog the heathen in public and send him to Mauritius for twenty years.

But the most dangerous of the exiles was the one with the dark eyes and the sparse black beard, who was chained to the one with the red hair and the blue-striped cap.

Diodati himself told the story that night at table. The Captain and some of the officers and the new Surgeon were present. It was almost like a party. Roast venison with rice and vegetables. There was rice again, the *De Swaagh* had brought it. Three soldiers making music in the corner, two fiddles and a flute. Catharina looked beautiful in her dark-red dress with the lighter red under-dress. Fittingly modest, as the wife of Diodati.

Sparse-beard was known as De Seine. He deserted from his ship in Table Bay one day and found work with the Huguenot Rochefort at Stellenbosch. He absconded from there and strolled about the town saying he wished the French would take the Cape so that he could join them, he liked being on the strongest side, and for money he would even serve the devil!

Van der Stel had him arrested, saying: I'm charging you not only with rebellion but with blasphemy as well. De Seine said: I wouldn't bother if I were you. If God doesn't want me, the devil will take me – in any case, he's already got half of me!

They flogged De Seine, threw him in gaol and sentenced him to exile on Mauritius for ten years. Two weeks later he escaped. One of the bush rangers caught him out in the veld and brought him back. An extra six years on Mauritius and back to gaol. Heavy leg irons and a block chained to his foot until there was a ship ready to sail for Mauritius.

'I hope you've got the villain well locked up,' the skipper joked with Diodati at table.

'They're all properly chained and locked up.'

Her full attention was no longer on the stories round the table. The new Surgeon, Jan Bockelenberg, was sitting at the bottom end of the table opposite Magdalena. A tall, attractive man elegant in black with a neat white pleated shirt. The way he looked at Magdalena and spoke to her was striking.

So was the way Magdalena's eyes looked at *him*.

The skipper had news from Batavia. The court case against Lamotius and his henchmen had started. The last he'd heard was that the prosecutor had asked for Lamotius to be beheaded.

'*What?*' she exclaimed.

'Yes. Twelve years of forced labour for Steen, and for Ovaer a fine and banishment.'

Lamotius beheaded? She instructed her eyes: Don't make pictures.

One of the officers knew the Cape well, so Diodati asked him why he thought the Cape wouldn't take the Mauritian tobacco. 'Our tobacco has improved *so* much, and yet it is still rejected.'

'That's impossible. Last year the *De Swaagh* brought sixteen thousand pounds of tobacco that had been ordered from the fatherland – Van der Stel is cunning, he gives the Hottentot tribes a little tobacco free each month to ensure that the smoking habit doesn't die out among them.'

Lamotius without a head?

506

The slaves brought more bottles of wine to the table.

'How are the Chainouqua? How is Chief Dorha?' she asked the officer.

The man looked at her in surprise. 'How odd that you should ask, Juffrouw Pieternella.'

'I came from the Cape originally.'

'The Chainouqua have been virtually exterminated. When Dorha had no more livestock, Van der Stel sent the barterers past him to the … um … the large tribe beyond the Chainouqua?'

'The Hessequa.'

'Right. He sent his barterers to the Hessequa, and Dorha blocked their way for all he could. Van der Stel had no choice: the fleet was on its way, he plundered and scattered them and placed Dorha under arrest on Robben Island.'

No, she was no longer from the Cape. Nor did she wish to hear any more. It was only that she couldn't stop her ears.

Diodati wanted to know why Van der Stel was demanding so much lime from Mauritius. Couldn't Robben Island provide shells any more? Yes, Robben Island was still yielding shells, it was just that there was so much building going on at the Cape. You wouldn't recognise the place. They'd just completed a most decorative balcony at the Castle, a crown for an emperor - just a pity Van der Stel spent more time on his farms and in his vineyards than in the Castle. He was claiming ever more land for himself. In the mean time the free-burghers were making a living by smuggling - supplying foreign ships, even though it was forbidden. Bartering livestock with the Hottentots, forbidden or not; they gave more brandy, more tobacco, more beads. Van der Stel was tired of struggling with the farmers …

A sudden cry went up in the courtyard. A frightened soldier rushed into the dining room. 'Commander! Commander! They've gone! Broken out! De Seine and some of the others!'

Chairs were knocked over in haste. A bottle of wine as well. The music suddenly stopped. Two shots rang out in the yard. Another one. And another. Feet running and running. Orders given in the dark.

'Mother, come away from the window!'

Fear of a cyclone is one kind of fear; fear of escaped convicts is an anxiety that grips and holds and chokes you till you can barely swallow.

At daybreak they established that the runaways had escaped with the *Vanger*, which had been moored at the quay. The two sailors, Leendert and Cornelis, had got away with the others; Leendert claimed he knew the way through the reef.

'It's still a miracle that they got through!' was Daniel's comment.

Jantjie from Batavia had stopped weeping, but was constantly atremble. They'd wanted him to go with them, but he wouldn't. He was afraid of De Seine. How did they break out? They'd stolen a crowbar the previous day. Used it to get the chains off four of them, the other two broke out, chains and all. Where were they heading? To an island where the French were. Mascarenhas? Yes, that was the name.

'They won't get there,' said Daniel, shaking his head.

De Seine had said they were going to come back with the French and take over the island.

Seven men.

Did they take food and water?

No. They said they'd be there before they needed any.

On a very clear day long ago, she and Daniel and Hendrik had been standing on one of the hills opposite the Black River when they pointed out to her a tiny island across the sea far to the west. Mascarenhas.

'We'd better get home,' Daniel said that night. 'There's no point in having the cannons all set up and ready on this side of the island. If they survive, they'll attack from the west.'

Anxiety that grips and holds you ...

Daniel piloted the *De Swaagh* through the reef early the next morning. There was a favourable wind, but the skipper was disconsolate at having to leave the island in such a mess.

The *Zeemaat* was at the quay. Daniel and Diodati had jointly decided that Catharina and the child should not go along to Northwest Harbour, they'd be safer at Southeast Harbour.

Catharina was expecting again.

And Samuel Elsevier, Daniel told her on the way - the one who sat and talked to you in the daytime when I was at work - is now apparently the Secunde at the Cape.

Oh. That might mean that Magdalena's drawing of the cyclone was also at the Cape. How strange.

At Northwest Harbour nobody had heard anything yet.

Hendrik said every available firearm would need to be loaded. He and Jake would walk up along the coastline and spy out the bays. The villains would be sure to come ashore looking for food and water - or be washed up on a beach somewhere. He hoped it would be just the pieces of their wreck that washed up because the wind would have no mercy on a stupid convict at the helm of a leaky boat on the way to Mascarenhas. Karel and Jamika had to take a warning up to the Flats, in case the gang landed at Bight-Without-End and headed south towards the Flats.

It was like a storm cloud growing ever larger.

The first signs that the fugitives might perhaps have come ashore for food and water were found up at Turtle Bay by Free-burgher Gerrit de Boer from the Flats when he and his slave were out hunting. Turtle Bay was an inlet between Northwest Harbour and Bight-Without-End.

'Are you sure they were not the tracks of runaway slaves?' Daniel asked them when Hendrik brought them back with him.

'I'm sure, Cooper. They'd caught two deer in snares and made a fire to grill the meat. Judging by the leftover bones, they were pretty hungry. And going by the parts of the skins they left behind, they made themselves two skin bags for water to take with them.'

'They seem to have got off in the *Vanger* again,' said Hendrik. 'It looks as if they're going to have another try at getting to Mascarenhas.'

'The wind will blow them back,' said Daniel. 'We'll need to keep our eyes skinned.'

The cloud of unease grew and grew.

No children in the hills, no children in the forest. No women alone to go gathering firewood.

Three days, and a panting breathless Jake brought the rumour: They had landed in Turtle Bay *again!* With their own eyes, he and Master Hendrik had seen the *Vanger* sailing out through the reef on to the open sea. Like a deliberate taunt – sticking out their tongues. There were signs that they had come ashore for food and water again; Master Hendrik had stayed behind to watch and see what happened.

'I'll give you enough food and an hour to rest, then you trot back and tell Master Hendrik he's got to come here.' Daniel said this with his cunning look. 'By tomorrow the wind will have turned; they won't get into Turtle Bay again – unless there's a very experienced sailor among them.'

Ten days, and then even Daniel had to concede that either they had reached Mascarenhas or they'd perished.

Every bay on the western side of the Island was watched. On the fourteenth day Hendrik said he was going to walk along the shoreline to the Lodge; Daniel was worried that they might have risked going back there.

Three days, and Hendrik was back. The *Vanger* was lying in Klimops Bay. A grapnel had been lowered behind and the nose tied to a tree with a painter.

The convicts were abroad on the island.

Klimops Bay was where the mountain ran into the sea, not far beyond the corner that marked the foot of the island.

The message was sent from house to house: Keep shutters and doors bolted at night; listen carefully to exactly where dogs start barking; don't venture outside without a firearm.

Hendrik was on his way to the Lodge again, taking the short cut.

Waiting for a cyclone to turn was a quiet waiting. Waiting to hear where the convicts were going to emerge made you feel creepy all over. Lying on top of your bed sweating at night because the shutters were closed. Maria had to be disciplined twice because she wouldn't play inside the house any longer, she wanted to go up into the hills. To her *friends*!

'What friends?'

'My *friends*, Mother!' She cried and threw herself down on the floor.

'Maria, get up! What friends?'

'All sorts. The grabfootmannikins.'

Grabfootmannikins were like chameleons.

A soldier came back from the Lodge with Hendrik. Two of the convicts had been captured. A certain Claas and Willem who had been exiled from the Cape together. They had met Free-burgher Jacob Groot above the Deer Hole and asked if he couldn't give them some food and show them how to get to the Lodge. They wanted to go and plead for pardon. It was De Seine who had pushed them all into this thing.

Jacob Groot kept his head; said his house was not far away, they could come with him. He first needed to make sure that there was nobody there. If it was safe, he'd beckon to them. He went ahead, loaded his musket, and beckoned. They came. He arrested them and walked them to the Lodge.

They pleaded. Swore they didn't know where the rest were – there had been strife on the boat because they couldn't find Mascarenhas. Their food and water kept running out and each time they had to come back.

When they were taken to the torture chamber, it transpired that four of the others had gone to look for salt and pepper; the meat they'd managed to get hold of was too bad to eat without salt. What else? Tobacco and meal as well. Where? They didn't know. They swore, they pleaded. Where was the one called Plank? He'd left the group on his own.

Where was the boat?

Lost.

Bring the thumbscrews ...

Tied up in one of the bays, they couldn't say where any more because they'd got lost.

The smith who had his work-place up at the old mill came to the Lodge to report that someone had stolen four of his ducks and his copper pan. The Commander sent two soldiers to hide up in the forest near the mill. And along came Plank that evening, with the pan and the plucked ducks, to steal some fire. So they captured him.

One soldier and two of the woodcutters were in hiding at Klimops Bay, waiting for De Seine and the other three. Plank had volunteered that De Seine's intention was still to head for the French. If there were pirates at Mascarenhas, that would be good, too.

Jan Tauke, who married the late Adam Cornelise's widow, came from the Flats to Jan Muur at Northwest Harbour. With a black eye, because his wife had beaten him, said Willemina. She used to beat up the late Adam like that too, regularly. The wretched Tauke had come to say: Cathrinha asked if there was any news of the convicts yet - and please could he stay over for a night or two?

Next came the news - brought by one of the soldiers on the Flats - that the two sailors, Leendert and Cornelis who had broken out of gaol together, had knocked three times on the window shutter at Cathrinha Kel's, Tauke's wife, before she answered. They said they were dying of hunger and didn't she have anything for them to eat? She told them her husband had gone to Western Harbour and could return at any moment. They said: Please. She kept her door bolted, but gave them meat and sweet potatoes through the window. They ate the food outside. She told them she'd have salt and pepper and tobacco for them tomorrow. Where would they spend the night? They weren't allowed to say. Who all were there? De Seine and another one, Braur.

It was scarcely dark the next night when they were there again. Knocked three times on the window again. Didn't she have any salt and pepper and tobacco and beer for them? The other two had crept up on a calf and slaughtered it, they wanted to grill the meat. She told her stripling son: Bring the salt and pepper. She gave them tobacco and beer at the door herself. Just as they sat down to fill their pipes, the Company servant Jan Nys and three of the new free-burghers ran out from behind the house and shot Cornelis as he jumped up and ran away. Hit him four times. She had walked to the lodge on the Flats by herself to tell them how to ambush the bandits. Cornelis fled into the marsh in the dark; they couldn't find him. Leendert, who also tried to run away, was wounded twice, but the boy caught up with him in the banana grove and dragged him back.

At first light Cornelis crawled out of the marsh of his own accord. Weak from loss of blood. They took the two to the Lodge at Southeast Harbour.

'And De Seine?' asked Daniel.

'He and Braur must have heard the shots and fled. You'll have to sleep with one ear open – their tracks are leading straight towards the sea. We suspect they are going to follow the shoreline to try to reach the boat. Hiding up by day and moving by night.'

A few days later, not far from where the *Vanger* was moored, the two were trapped in the early morning in the dark before dawn. Braur surrendered, De Seine ran for it.

So they shot him. Dead.

7

When the cloud of unease disappeared, it felt as though peace had dropped from the sky and was streaming in through every door and window.

Aaltjie sent a child from house to house to say there was going to be a dance at Jan Lodewijks' that night. Please just bring a lantern.

Daniel came back late that afternoon from working with the barrels on the island. He called: 'Pieternella, come outside and see here!'

A sight that quite took her breath away for a moment. The sun was setting, the clouds on the horizon behind were the softest pink, and on the red water a red-winged fleet sailing slowly southwards on its way – to the Cape.

The homeward-bound fleet.

She and Daniel on the island of succour. Eva's two cats round their legs. The children inside the house. The first frogs down at the river. The whole big earth, the whole big sky ... In her heart she knew, all at once, that she sometimes forgot to be glad she was alive.

But then she was very glad. Eva and Hans were also married on a Wednesday at the Lodge. Daniel took two boatloads round on the *Zeemaat*: the meat, the wine, extra mattresses and bedding, for her and the children and the slave Maria. Schoolmaster Wilde. Baldini.

The second load brought Eva's Hans and most of the wedding guests.

Catharina was only just up and about again. She'd given birth to another fine boy. Danieltjie.

Six months later, Magdalena married Jan Bockelenberg and also moved into the Lodge. A very capable man.

'Our house is getting empty, my love.'

Maria was thirteen that year, but her 'growing up' was happening more slowly than the other girls'. Pieter was eleven. Little-Daniel five.

Two English ships.

Twelve sick to be brought ashore. Eva left her housekeeping and donned her white apron.

The free-burghers rejoiced over every penny that fell into their pockets for what they delivered to the ships day after day.

'One thing I will say for your Commander son-in-law, Daniel,' said Jan Muur after the ships had left. 'He doesn't care what happens on this side of the island.'

'It's not that he doesn't care, Jan, it's that he has too much to do on the other side.'

'Keep it that way, Cooper!'

There were fifteen children in the schoolroom in their yard.

Baldini was teaching one of Elisabet and Jan Dirks's children to play the lute. He told the children stories. Sometimes he went to the Lodge for weeks on end to help with the distilling which poor Diodati was trying to keep going.

'Father, most of the officials and I are working ourselves to a standstill, in vain. Everything gets broken. Dysentery won't let up, Bockelenberg says it's the water. But there's no other water available. The river isn't flowing. The arrack I sent on the *De Swaagh* again failed to reach the Cape.'

Three English ships.

The fine sheets and tablecloths she shared out between Eva and Magdalena, the delicate cups went to Catharina.

'And what do I get?' demanded Tant Theuntjie. She now used a stick when she walked. 'Had it not been for me and the late Oom Bart, you'd never have got here.'

'You can have some tea, Tante.'

'Got my own tea. I'm not a beggar. Aaltjie says you got dress material too.'

'Take some of the blue.'

'Hand it over. I believe there's four of the new free-burghers got away on the ships?'

They went down to Southeast Harbour to see Magdalena's pretty little girl baby. Petronella. Magdalena was up, but Diodati was in bed, a cabbage leaf to his head. The supply ship had left that morning.

'Roelof isn't well, Mother. A weird thing happened yesterday afternoon and he's taken it terribly to heart.'

It *was* weird.

All at once, the river that ran across the Flats – the Flats River – had started rising at noon and overflowed its banks. The free-burghers' sugar cane plantations were covered in mud again.

'Captain Damme and everyone on the Flats are witnesses,' said Diodati with unease in his eyes. 'There wasn't a cloud in the sky, not a drop of rain, not a tremor in the earth's crust, nothing. It was for all the world as if the water simply rose up out of a crack in the river bed and then an invisible hand closed the crack again. I'll do the humblest work at the Cape, as I wrote to Van der Stel last night, but I've got to get away from here!'

No one could explain it. Clear river water.

Baldini said it was a sign. Daniel said: Don't upset the Commander any further.

Hendrik said the Commander had been upset since the previous week, about the runaway slave that the soldiers had picked up at the top of the island and brought down to the Lodge. He was as old as the hills. There were two iron rings round his ankles that had once had chains attached. He'd been wandering for years in the forest. He told Diodati: You can go on searching, you can shoot us if you like; this island belongs to the runaways. We grow our own tobacco, we make our own wine, we set our own snares, we catch our own tortoises – and we watch you.

They opened his rucksack. In it were chicken claws and turtle bones, the combs of two water-hens, some tree bark and all kinds of twigs.

His magic charms.

They chained him again and threw him in gaol. His charms were burnt.

Jantjie from Batavia was pleased to see her, Pieternella, again. Yes, Fair Ansiela was still alive, but she was very old. Yes, there were still Hottentots at the Duintjies, but they caused a lot of mischief. The Cape was full of unrest. Watchmen went about the streets at night with rattles so criminals would know they were on the lookout. Juffrouw laughed? It was true! But he would go back, tomorrow, Juffrouw, this was not his place, here.

How could a river simply have risen like that?

Bockelenberg said: 'Mother, please come and show me again, step by step, how you mix that stomach medicine.'

'Do you still have any of those yellow-bush leaves I sent you with Hendrik?'

'Plenty.'

Magdalena came to watch. The baby had a quiet contentment about her. 'I hear Father has written to the Cape for a carpenter?'

'Yes. There are times when he has to act as both carpenter and cooper for the ships; he needs extra hands.'

It was good to see her children at Southeast Harbour; to see Oom Laurens and Tant Magdalena. Grieta. Sometimes the late Sven's Magriet, up on the Orange Tree Flats with Cornelia and her husband. Though she was nothing more than a slave.

'Are you happy, Magriet?'

'I'm here now.'

'Do you want to go to your own people?'

'Dunno where they are.'

'And if the Commander could find out for you where they are?'

'Like to see 'm agen. I dream 'bout 'm.'

'I want to ask a favour of you, Roelof Diodati.' The man's stiff-necked manner of looking at her had not relaxed an inch in all the years. Nor has yours, Pieternella, Daniel gently reminded her. Perhaps not.

'A favour, Juffrouw Pieternella?'

'Have you gone deaf?' Before she could stop herself, she'd given him a hostile reply. Catharina had spoken to her about it umpteen times already.

'Ask what you want to ask.'

'Magriet Ringels up at the Orange Tree Flats with the Van Nimwegens – her people moved to Batavia from the Cape a long while back.'

'Before my time.'

'Will you write to Batavia and ask what has become of Joachim Ringels? Whether he's still alive?'

'Why?'

'Magriet should go to her father and mother.'

'Why?'

Bridle your tongue. 'Because here she's only living because she isn't dead.'

'What a foolish statement! We're all only living because we're not dead, Juffrouw Pieternella.'

'You're wrong, Roelof Diodati, but you wouldn't understand. Do Magriet this kindness and I promise to wipe my heart clean towards you.'

'To wipe it clean of what?' He was on his high horse immediately. 'All I've ever done to you, Juffrouw Pieternella, was to marry Catharina and give her a position that she could not have achieved on this island in any other way!'

God Almighty. 'I hope she's happy.' I'm going to bite my tongue to pieces today.

'Has she any cause not to be happy?' He was angry.

'I raised her, she'll know what happiness is.'

'What do you mean?'

'Diodati, you and I have locked horns from the beginning. Some days I don't even know why any more, but today I haven't come to lock horns with you. Merely to ask a favour.'

'If Magriet Ringels has a request, she can direct it to *me*!'

'And if I had that runaway slave's magic charms today, I'd magic *you*, Diodati!' There's someone inside you and sometimes you can't tame her tongue, no matter how hard you try.

But all at once the man was cool and extra stiff.

'Before I was sent here as Commander, I read up in the Cape journals to find out more about what I was to expect to find here. Very interesting. Two children were sent here once – children of the Hottentot Eva.'

'That was my mother.'

'Why do you think, Juffrouw Pieternella, that is a topic which Catharina never wishes to be broached?'

Like the coldest cold shuddering through your being. A thousand ghosts in your head …

Which she took back to Northwest Harbour with her – to disguise every day, so no one else should realise that an old wound had opened again inside her. Deadperson. Halfcasteperson.

'Are there still dumbclucks on the island, Daniel?' Catharina was ashamed of her. Magdalena probably also.

'Hendrik doesn't think so, my love. Why?'

'I would really like Maria to see one.' Daniel had told the slaves several times to bring home a tortoise for Maria. Then she would build a stone enclosure for it, plead with it please not to go away, lie on its back. Then she'd remove the stones so it could get out; tie a bunch of leaves on its back; tell everybody the tortoise with the leaves on its back was hers; nobody was to chop it open because if they did she would cast a magic spell on them to kill them.

She didn't ask where the child got that from.

Half-caste human. Picking and picking at a scab while hollowing out with her bare hands her ditch down the middle of the island between Northwest Harbour and Southeast Harbour.

'I'll be ready to deliver more barrels next week, Pieternella. I'll send Jake and Jamika out to catch us a turtle – to make us chowder to take along.'

'I'll make some and send it along with you. I can't leave the house just now.'

'What's bothering you, Pieternella?'

'Sometimes there's a bundle in your inmost being that you have to carry alone.'

'What I feel in my inmost being is a deep unease about you, my love. I see you dragging your feet along the shore, I see your head drooping as you sit on the bench under the tree, I hear you getting up at night and wandering through the house in the dark. Talk to me, Pieternella!'

'It's something that doesn't have any words to talk with.'

Half-caste human.

8

A storm blew two English ships past to Black River Mouth, where they lay behind the reef firing their emergency cannons.

Daniel and Hendrik took the *Zeemaat* and helped them back to Northwest Harbour. Thirteen sick to bring ashore. The wife of one of the captains in bed in the house. Two foreign children up into the hills with Maria.

Another ship the next day. Ten sick.

The slaves Karel and Jamika had to help wash and feed them. Thomas in the outside kitchen helped the slave Maria at the cooking pots.

'It's hard work, Mother, but it's so good!'

'Thank you, Eva. Tell Hans, too, I thank him – that he's still prepared to lend you to me.'

'He'll always lend me to you, Mother. But I think you should first go and see what's wrong with Maria. She's chased the English children away and is sitting behind the schoolroom crying.'

Maria?

'What is it, Maria?' Though in her heart she knew …

'My stomach hurts.'

'Get up and come back to the house with me.'

'No!' Like a little wildcat. 'I'm never going to get up again! Don't let Pieter or Father or Schoolmaster know I'm here! I'll creep into the forest when it gets dark.'

'I've got a better plan. As soon as it's dark, I'll bring you a clean dress, then you and I will walk down to the river together; we'll wet a sponge for you …'

'How did you know, Mother?'

'I was a girl, too, once.'

'You're such a good mother.'

The fit of weeping the child provoked in her suddenly was a happy weeping. A weeping for the pity of it all. An angry weeping. A moment of healing.

Diodati sent word with one of the woodcutters that the supply ship had arrived and that he needed to speak to Daniel urgently, that the new Secunde and his wife had arrived, and the carpenter as well.

'I can't leave here at this time, Pieternella.'

'Send Hendrik to fetch the carpenter in the mean time, and say that you'll come as soon as you can.'

'Will you come with me this time?'

'No.' It was the fourth time she'd refused.

What distressed her most was that in the mean time Magdalena and Bockelenberg had had a second little daughter. Johanna. Pieter and Daniel said she was exactly like the first one.

On the Sunday afternoon when Hendrik came walking across the yard with the dark, shortish, stocky carpenter – toolbox on his shoulder, bundle in his hand, canvas jerkin, canvas trousers, peasant shoes – Daniel took one look at him and said: There's a proper carpenter.

Abraham de Vries from Amsterdam. Who heard at the Cape that there was a need for a carpenter on Mauritius.

'I wasn't at the Cape very long, Oom, but I just decided to head for Mauritius. There's too much strife at the Cape.'

Hendrik also brought the news that the Lords Seventeen had instructed both the Cape and *Mauritius*: only firewood and fresh water were to be supplied to foreign ships. *Nothing* more. 'This is going to make things difficult for us, Daniel.'

'Very difficult.'

Maria came in from outside and Daniel introduced Abraham to her. 'And where is he supposed to sleep?' she asked. The child had a forthrightness about her that no one could erase.

'There's room with Hendrik and Baldini.'

'You're not going to enjoy sleeping there! They snore worse than Oom Karseboom's dogs!'

Hendrik laughed.

'Maria!' she scolded. You could see the man felt uncomfortable, as a stranger would. 'Abraham can decide for himself. You go and fetch us some buttermilk and biscuits. Please don't take any notice of Maria, Abraham.'

'I'll be grateful for any bed, Tante.'

Nice manners, you could see.

It was Daniel who, in the week after that, got a stubborn obstinacy into him that drove her into a corner.

The ships had been helped on their way, and everybody had been given their tasks about the house and on the island. He came to her and said: 'Pieternella, pack for us.'

She got a fright. 'For where?'

'We're going to Catharina and Magdalena.'

'No, Daniel, don't.'

'We'll sail as far as the Apple Tree River and sleep there tonight. The children are staying at home.'

'Daniel, don't.'

'Pieternella, I will pick you up and *carry* you to the boat in front of everybody.' This was a Daniel without mercy. He wouldn't have hesitated to do it.

'Please, Daniel, I'm asking nicely.'

'Pieternella – pack!'

In all the years they'd been married, there had never been any anger between her and Daniel. Not even when they had differed about something.

But now there was a wrathfulness in her that made her go aboard with her equanimity in tatters. She didn't want to go to Southeast Harbour! Never again. Her only hope was that at Apple Tree River she might be able to persuade him to turn back – though in her heart she knew that was about as likely as putting a pot of water on a cold fire and hoping it would boil.

They'd already passed The Plaat and had almost reached the lower Quarrel Hill before he spoke a word to her.

'It won't help, filling your head with all kinds of struggles and thoughts, Pieternella. If a ship starts leaking and you don't careen and caulk it, it will sink. You've sprung a leak – between you and Catharina and Magdalena – and it worries me and it worries them. A lot.'

She gave him no answer.

When he dropped anchor in the Apple Tree River, Willemina's words from long ago suddenly came back to her, that beauty is destroyed by suffering – or anger – or the sadness in your heart. Once more the pretty blossoms were hanging on the branches like delicate waxen butterflies, pink and white, but their beauty would not drop from the branches into her being.

Daniel carried their bedding from the boat. Their food. Built them a small shelter. Lay down on his side on a mattress and lit his pipe. She just stood there and felt the trembling gradually drawing into her body.

'Come and sit beside me, Pieternella.' In his comforting voice.

'No.'

'We're not leaving here till I know what's worrying you, my love. Has been worrying you for a long, long time.'

'You don't "spring a leak" between a woman and her daughters, Daniel Zaaijman. What you get is an unending darkening that goes on hurting you even into your sleep.'

'Come and sit beside me.'

'No! Catharina and Magdalena – possibly Eva, possibly the other children, too – are ashamed of me. Don't you try to stop my words! I know what it is to love your mother but to be so ashamed of her that you want to flee into the mountains and hide in some place where nobody will ever find you again!'

'Pieternella ...'

'I'm talking! You asked for it, Daniel Zaaijman. My mother was a Hottentot – I'm half-Hottentot. You know it. Being a half-Hottentot is not that bad. When it gets really bad is when other people regard you as only half *human*. Worst of all is when you start seeing yourself as a half-human.'

'Pieternella, don't.'

'*That* is the festering sore in me. Don't get up! I haven't finished. Because there's something *I* know that you Hollanders, you pure whites, seemingly don't know, and that is that you are not better than the Hottentots – even though most of you think you are.'

He laid aside his pipe, got up and stood directly in front of her. 'Do *I* think that way, Pieternella?'

'I don't know. All I know is that there is a raw pain inside me that will not go away.'

'I don't understand it. After Maria's birth you seemed to me like someone who had been purified – you crept more deeply into my heart than ever. Someone must have put the pain back into your heart. Who was it?'

I won't tell him about Diodati. 'Pain sometimes happens bit by bit.'

He held out his arms to her – her Daniel with those eyes that looked right into your heart. 'Come, Pieternella, let me hold your pain.'

Something like a cleansing force flowed out of him – and into *her*. And then the beauty dripped off the branches and lay all around them again ...

They arrived at Southeast Harbour in rain.

Diodati stood around uncertainly, Catharina was crying so much. And Magdalena with her. And so was she, Pieternella.

'Really, what a moving little occasion of sadness!'

It was only Daniel's eyes that stopped her from answering back. 'Children,' he said, 'your mother has a deep pain within her that she doesn't deserve. Diodati and I are going to look at the cattle; the three of you are going to talk it out.'

The second purging.

No, Mother, we're not ashamed of you.

'But Maria really embarrassed us when she was here with Father the last time.'

'Why?'

'She stood watching me putting Danieltjie into his nightie; Roelof was also in the room at the time. Maria remarked that the child favoured you. Now Roelof is very particular about noble ancestry, you mustn't blame him ...'

'So what were you ashamed of?'

'Roelof disagreed with Maria. He said the child didn't take after Mother in the slightest, that he was completely white. Then Maria told him to his face she hoped he'd get the shits as a reward.'

'Oh no. I am sorry.'

'But on the next day his stomach trouble started.'

No gold could have paid for the peace that now settled in her heart.

Her gladness about Catharina's Salomon and Danieltjie. Magdalena's two pretty little girls.

Jantjie from Batavia came to show her that his legs were free, after five years in irons. It appeared that Commander Diodati had misread the letter of banishment that came from the Cape. The letter had instructed that he was *not* to be clapped in irons.

Daniel came in from outside and they went to their room to wash and dress for dinner. Diodati was very particular about the ceremoniousness of the evening meal.

'What did he want to see you about so urgently?'

'He asked whether I would buy his cattle, he's expecting his relief to arrive on the next supply ship.'

'Where would he go?'

'His real wish is to be appointed Commander in Deshima, but he realises that he might first have to spend a year or more in Batavia being prepared for such a posting.'

'Deshima?'

'In the Far East. Japan.'

'That means we lose Catharina.' Like a new burden lying in wait ...

'It's all in the hands of the Almighty, my love. Have you met the new Secunde and his wife?'

'Only in passing.'

'A good man. Abraham Momber.'

Later, at the dinner table, she couldn't help thinking of that meal at Black River Mouth when Lamotius – had he been beheaded yet? – and the late Secunde Jacobsen had sat for almost the whole night going Dubertin-Dubertin-Dubertin!

The only difference was that now it was the Van der Stels-Van der Stels-Van der Stels.

If it wasn't Simon, then it was Willem Adriaan – Simon's son who had succeeded him as Governor at the Cape. Or else Secunde Elsevier. And other names as well. The Governor and officials were appropriating ever more land for themselves – something the Lords Seventeen had expressly forbidden.

Simon encouraged them, and helped himself, too, very generously. He told Willem Adriaan: The free-burghers are a lazy rotten bunch, it's time the officials showed them how to farm.

Commissioner Heins wrote to the Lords Seventeen that he'd never encountered more obedient and more willing free-burghers anywhere. Most had been born at the Cape or had at least grown up there.

There was another Van der Stel, too: Frans, old Simon's other son. Quite as arrogant as his father and brother. Lived for pleasure. He had been allocated almost the whole of the sea in False Bay to fish in or do with what he liked.

'Truly,' Secunde Momber said, dejectedly, 'our Noble Company is being robbed by its officials and impoverished by its wars. When they're not going in fear of an English attack on the Cape, they're frightened of a French one.'

Daniel was in one of his listening silences again.

Momber was the oldest person at the table. Grey. Thickset. Short of breath. But he beamed forth an earnestness of mind that washed over the Lodge like a sense of security.

His wife was softly spoken, sincerity in her eyes when she looked at you. 'Catharina says you are very fond of Mauritius, Juffrouw Van Meerhoff?'

'Especially the western side of the island.'

'I should very much like to pay you a visit. To get to know the island better.'

'You would be welcome. My husband will come for you in his boat, my home will receive you and feel honoured.' As long as there were no enemy ships about …

'Thank you. You are most kind.'

Bockelenberg stopped her the next morning. 'I am so glad you are back with us, Mother, though I was going to come and fetch you anyway – as soon as the *Vanger* is seaworthy again. They've almost finished the caulking.'

'What are you going to do with the poor *Europa*? It's still lying there like some rubbish thrown away.'

'There isn't enough pitch for both.'

'The ointment you gave me last time is very soothing.'

'The ship brought more stock. I'll let you have another jar.'

'Thank you.'

'Promise me that, if Magdalena falls pregnant again, you will come to be with her, as has been her wish each time. Not the mad slave woman.'

'Anna?'

'Yes. Though I have to admit she was a great comfort to Magdalena each time.'

Anna?

9

They got back to Northwest Harbour. The *Zeemaat* had hardly had time to anchor or she to set her feet on dry ground when Tant Theuntjie came hobbling along with her walking stick.

'Time you kept an eye on your house, Pieternella.'

'Oh, Tante ...'

'That wild daughter of yours spends more time over on the island with the carpenter than anywhere else. There's trouble coming, I'm warning you.'

'What trouble?' She didn't feel like Tant Theuntjie's tales. Maria and Abraham had been like brother and sister from the start, she'd seen them becoming friends.

'Sleeping on the same property without any parents to watch them?'

'They're just friends.'

'There sits Jan Dirks's poor Liesbet – they've also got four daughters but yours grab all the men.'

'That's not true. In his time, the previous Commander wrote for orphan girls to be sent out from the fatherland. There are how many free-burghers and officials and soldiers without wives?' The problem was not Jan and Elisabet's four daughters, who all had squint eyes –

Hendrik said a man with nature's desires in him would marry a stick in a frock! The real problem was Jan, who set the dogs on every youngster who came by.

'What did you bring me?' Tant Theuntjie demanded.

'We've brought quite a lot of fish. Daniel and Magdalena's husband brought back a good catch from Fisherman's Island yesterday.'

'Don't want fish, enough fish in the sea. Well, I'll be off; just thought I'd come and tell you.'

When Maria came across the yard from the island, it was almost as if she got a fright. It was Maria, but she was a different person. She looked taller. The blue-flowered shift swirled round her in a dance, two little brown feet playing like small animals in and out under the hem.

'Why are you looking at me like *that*, Mother?'

The prettiest, prettiest girl. 'Haven't I watched you grow up then, Maria?'

'Mother?'

I think some part of my mother must have looked like that when my father fell in love with her. 'You're lovely, Maria.'

'I'm glad. Abraham says so, too.' Mischievously.

'So is Tant Theuntjie right?'

'Has that old woman been gossiping to you already? She was here every day, nosing around. So I told her Abraham wouldn't come to bed with me because he's scared Father will beat him to death.'

'Maria!' The child was ridiculous and completely out of her mind! 'Don't be flippant. What is it with you?'

'I'm happy, Mother.'

'I thought you were just friends ...'

'We were at first.' All at once she was completely serious. 'I'll be sixteen next month. I've always known that one day I would marry a man like Father. Abraham de Vries is the man. We love each other.'

'You're different from my other children.'

'I know.'

'You're my pot-shard child.' Why did she say that?

'Your *what?*'

'Pot-shard child.' She got up, went to the bedroom, unpacked the chest and took out the shards wrapped in the old dress – for the first time in years.

It felt as though an entire lifetime was lying in her hands, a link somewhere between her and Maria which she didn't even try to understand.

The child took the shards in her small brown hands and sat dead still, just looking at them. Then she raised them slowly to her face and laid them against her cheek.

'They feel old.'

'They are shards of a rumble-drum that your grandmother made herself. Your Hottentot grandmother.'

'Where did you get them, Mother?' She was running her fingers over the pattern of tiny beads on one of the shards.

'I brought them here with me when I was fourteen.'

'I wish it was the whole pot.'

'So do I.'

'But they don't belong here.'

'Why do you say that?'

'I don't know. It just feels that way.'

What she really wanted to say to Maria wouldn't turn into words ...

But that night she told Daniel that Maria and Abraham had better get married as soon as possible – and had to stop him leaping out of bed in a sudden fury. 'No, Daniel! She's not pregnant!'

Life wrapped up love, too, in different cloths. Abraham and Maria's love was wrapped in a beautiful cloth.

'She's completely ridiculous, Mother!' complained her Pieter-child. 'She dances around with her dress spreading wide out around her and Abraham sits staring at her. It's not decent.'

'It's the new moon.'

Daniel sent Hendrik to the Lodge to ask Diodati if he would please come and marry them at Northwest Harbour. That was what Maria wanted.

Abraham and Jamika and Thomas began to build them a two-roomed cottage beyond the schoolroom. They made a very neat job of it, too.

And one day the words just arrived on their own.

'Maria ...' They were stripping coconuts to plait mats for the cottage.

'What's on your mind, Mother?'

'Abraham is white, sure enough, but he's got a sallow complexion and dark hair. You're dark. So you're going to have brown children.'

'They'll be much prettier than pink children.'

'Does Abraham know your grandmother was a Hottentot?'

'Yes.'

'Does it bother him?'

'No.'

'Have you asked him?'

'No. Father did. Told him if he wasn't good to me, he'd drown him.'

'Maria!'

It *was* a wedding!

Daniel and Eva and Hans and Hendrik and the slaves transformed the hospital into a 'church'.

She and Aaltjie made the dress: white, with the most beautiful lace that Daniel had got from a French captain. All round the edge of the cap Aaltjie sewed matching tiny white round-bellied shells on long threads. Whenever Maria moved her head, they would swing gently and rattle quietly. Ever so pretty!

Twice, Jan Muur came to unpack his disquiet at their door. 'Gawd, Daniel, you say the Commander's coming? But what if there's a storm and the English come looking for shelter?'

'Then we'll send them round to Southeast Harbour like we're supposed to do.'

'That will be a loss, man!'

The storm didn't arrive, nor did the English. Only the *Vanger*, with Diodati and Catharina and Magdalena and her husband and children and a few sailors. Oom Laurens and Tant Magdalena. The Mombers were invited but couldn't get away from the Lodge.

Diodati was seriously distressed because yet again the supply ship had not arrived. 'Therefore we shall unfortunately not be able to linger very long, Father.'

'Don't you start getting hasty and think you're going to marry me in a hurry!' Maria warned him. 'I want to be married nicely.'

'The marriage service is prescribed, Maria, I shall perform it as written and according to my duty.'

The marriage was properly ceremonious.

The dancing went on till the sun came up.

The *Vanger* stayed another two days because the joy of having all the children at home at once was a second feast on its own.

When the boat sailed off in the morning, she said to Daniel: 'Now we've got only the two boys left at home.'

'Yes, the house is empty. It was hard for me to give away my other three girls, but parting with Maria was the hardest of all. But God knows how grateful I am that she's still living on my property.'

10

Life doesn't remain an even path under your feet.

By the time she had to go Southeast Harbour for Magdalena's third baby, the news had arrived from the Cape: Diodati was being transferred to Batavia.

Like the news of a death.

'It's God's will, Pieternella,' Daniel was trying to talk down his own heartache. 'We've been lucky to have had our children around us as long as this. Now we have to accept what comes, however hard it may be.'

'At least it's not Deshima.'

'Not yet.'

One day Baldini asked Daniel if he knew that Diodati actually wanted to go to Deshima?

Yes.

He came to her where she was nursing seven sick English sailors under the hospital awning. She could see he was disturbed from the way he was wringing his hands. Eva came to relieve her and she went aside with him.

'Diodati is convinced he's on his way to Deshima.'

'He's often said so.'

'Said what?'

'That that was his dream. That it had more or less been promised him.'

'What else?'

She had to think. 'That it had been a very important trading post for the Company for well over a hundred years. Something like that.'

'The Dutch are the only Europeans those heathens will allow on one small tip of their realm.'

'Yes, he mentioned that.'

'The whole truth?'

'What whole truth?'

That was when Baldini poured out the most frightful story.

That the people of Japan hated Christians, crucified them, burnt them alive and chopped their heads off. Once a man who was something like a king summoned all the foreign merchants to assemble before him. He said to them: You keep nagging to be given a place in my country so you can come and trade here. Right. Today you will be subjected to a test, and only the one who passes it will be permitted to establish a post here.

Conditionally.

The merchants fell over one another in their eagerness to be the first to be led to the room where the test would have to be passed in secret.

The test?

A large wooden cross, like the one on which the Saviour died for our sins, lay on the floor. Stamp on the cross! the guards ordered them. Stamp!

The Portuguese stepped forward, stopped – lowered his head when he couldn't raise a foot to do so. The Frenchman couldn't either. The Englishman lifted his foot and held it in the air till the sweat was pouring off him – but lowered it without touching the cross.

Then came the Dutchman and stamped on it without hesitation.

'You're not making all this up, are you, Baldini?'

'I swear. Even today, all weapons and Bibles and hymn books and *Home Sermons* and things have to be nailed down in a barrel, and all preaching and praying is forbidden at that trading post. So are the Commanders' wives and children – the heads are provided with heathen whores in their places.'

'No!'

'Yes.'

She walked down to Daniel on the island. He said he'd heard the story but couldn't tell if it was true. All he knew was that they had to live their own lives at Northwest Harbour – to be *able* to live.

Daniel couldn't go to Magdalena with her, there were two French ships at Northwest Harbour. One without a mainmast. So Pieter took her and Hendrik and Jamika on the *Zeemaat*.

'You can see whose hand has trained him,' Hendrik said as Pieter steered them past the lime kiln at Mud Bay on their way to the quay at Southeast Harbour.

In his heart, Pieter was a sailor, like his father, but he wasn't a cooper. Little-Daniel was. Pieter was a carpenter, like Maria's Abraham, even though he was still mostly an apprentice working under Abraham's supervision.

He made the most beautiful furniture. Chests of drawers, tables, chairs. English captains had twice bought articles from Abraham and paid him well. An ebony bedstead for Secunde Momber.

Magdalena was still walking.

Diodati was busily helping Hendrik and the slave sort out the cattle that they were to drive to Northwest Harbour. The money Daniel had sent for the cattle was carefully counted out.

'Your father-in-law sends word that a few more should be included to cover possible losses on the way.'

'At the price I'm selling them to him for, I'm already suffering a loss.'

Diodati had wanted the Company to buy the cattle from him. At first they said they would; then Van der Stel let him know that they didn't want the cattle any more.

Catharina and some of the slave women were packing, her eyes red with weeping. 'We don't even know when the ship with the new Commander is going to arrive, but Roelof is all ready to go and wait on the quay!'

What lay ahead for Catharina, only God in heaven knew ...

The week before, Eva's Hans had come to ask Daniel if he would lend him his support in his request to the Commander. He and Eva were keen to move to Black River Mouth. To farm with cattle; the ships paid well for meat.

'What did you say to him?' she asked, her heart aching.

'I told him we'd miss Eva. You, particularly. But I think it would be right for them. Aaltjie's Jan Lodewijks is also talking about moving to Black River Mouth.'

'I'll miss her sorely.'

Eva and Hans had one little boy.

When it was Magdalena's time, Anna came into the room in a clean black dress and started rubbing Magdalena's back and belly when the pains came. Without a word. Dipped cloths in vinegar water and wiped her face when the pains were at their worst. Allowed Magdalena's hands to grip her.

Another little daughter. Anna.

And she, Pieternella, swaddled the little thing herself, so that Anna could take her outside for the sun and the island to welcome her.

Like paying a debt.

There was a new life kicking inside her own body.

'Do you think I'm too old?' she asked Daniel one day.

'Pieternella!' he exclaimed and burst out laughing. 'What makes you ask a question like that?'

'If I'm calculating accurately, I must be forty now.'

'And I still have to look carefully when you are walking along with your daughters – to make out which is the mother and who the daughters!'

'I just wanted to tell you: I'm expecting again.'

Little-Daniel was twelve when Johannes was born. On the twenty-eighth of January.

'Another cooper,' Daniel predicted proudly, holding the little thing in his hands.

Tant Theuntjie came over, walking with two sticks now, to see. 'Luckily another little white one. I see Daniel is getting pretty grey nowadays – probably reckons he's making provision for help in his old age.'

She had been up and about a long time when Hendrik brought the news that the supply ship had arrived. No new Commander had been sent to the island; Secunde Momber had been appointed the new head. The new Secunde was one Philip de la Fontain.

'The Company couldn't have made a better choice than Momber,' was Daniel's opinion. The knowledge that the arrival of the supply ship meant that Catharina was leaving was a rock that each of them had to try to get round for himself.

The other news was that there was something like a war on at the Cape between the free-burghers and Willem Adriaan van der Stel. 'They say it's all darkness; not even the sun is allowed to rise unless the Governor says it may.' He was living in luxury on his farm Vergelegen, the size of ten free-burgher farms, with over two hundred slaves, not counting the hirelings. He had enough livestock in his personal possession to supply the whole outward bound fleet as well as the homeward bound fleet, *and* the hospital *and* his own table with meat for a year. Herds of cattle behind the mountains on the southern side, herds on Robben Island, herds on Vergelegen – and never mind all the livestock in the possession of Secunde Elsevier and the Minister and other officials.

Furthermore, strict posters had been nailed up forbidding free-burghers to barter stock with the Hottentots. Anyone who disregarded this decree would get a noose round his neck under the gallows, be flogged and branded, and exiled to Mauritius for life.

Daniel laughed, he said Van der Stel had better be careful that *he* wasn't exiled to Mauritius.

But, said Hendrik, all this was still nothing. The Commissioner arrived at the Cape and demanded of the Governor: But how can it be that you have not informed the free-burghers that only they, and not the officials, may barter livestock with the Hottentots?

The farmers were furious.

Van der Stel said: I didn't tell them because they go bartering deep into the interior without even taking any goods to barter with. They just murder the Hottentots and steal their stock.

The farmers said: But that's a filthy lie you're telling!

Daniel said: Hendrik, don't get yourself so worked up; the Cape isn't our concern. Our only concern is that Abraham Momber should be able to retain sufficient strength to get this island on its feet eventually.

Pieternella, Maria and her two pretty little boys and Pieter, little Johannes and the slave Maria sailed round to Southeast Harbour on the *Zeemaat* with Daniel to say goodbye to Catharina.

'If only God would tell me today whether I'll ever see my Mother and Father again!' Catharina said to them. Heartache was making the child rebellious.

That evening at table, Diodati, fired up with haste to get everything on board, and with bitterness in his soul, said: 'I'm leaving here, Father, worn out from my labours, having achieved virtually nothing! How many sample consignments of the free-burghers' produce have I not sent to the Cape, only to have them ignored? Catharina, stop crying, you're upsetting the whole table. Now Governor Willem Adriaan sends word that no more is to be sent, the Cape is getting quite enough of such goods from the fatherland and Batavia. Couldn't they simply drop some of those contracts and give the free-burghers of Mauritius a chance?'

Secunde De la Fontain was thirstily slurping up his wine and chewing with his mouth open, spilling food and wine on his square collar. His brown hair hung down to his shoulders in rat's tails. It was unpleasant being at table with him. His manners had Maria and Pieter giggling disrespectfully.

'Son,' Daniel said, 'in our hearts we all know that Mauritius was never encouraged to penetrate the Cape market. All they've ever wanted is our ebony – provided we don't expect saw-blades to cut it with. And if my daughter needs to cry because she has to bid her parents farewell, she can cry as much as she wants to!'

This was the first time Daniel had raised his voice to Diodati.

Catharina told them later that Diodati had been deeply disturbed by an accusation by Governor Van der Stel that he had been extravagant in the remuneration he paid to people who caught runaway slaves. She came to the defence of her husband: 'It was the only way that the slaves could be brought in, Father!' Diodati's personal expenses were also regarded as being too high. His household had apparently used too much sugar and soap and wax.

Next day, Abraham Momber was sworn in as the new Commander.

Magdalena was expecting her fourth.

Bockelenberg was concerned that she should have taken Catharina's departure so deeply to heart. Momber's Juffrouw Elisabet was a wonderful comfort to her, but it was still bitterly painful for her.

And for them all.

Just to see Catharina clambering aboard the land boat with Daniel who had been asked to pilot the ship out ... He came back and wouldn't look up. Didn't even see her and Magdalena and Maria and Bockelenberg standing on the shore. All the others had left already. Oom Laurens and Tant Magdalena, Grieta. Even Cornelia and Van Nimwegen. Wieringa. Michiel Romondt. Gerrit van Ewijk, who now dressed in a silk robe since returning from the East as an old India hand.

The trip back to Northwest Harbour was like returning from a funeral – except that a piece of *herself* had gone down into the grave as well. And of Daniel, too.

But her stone house was like an animal's body that she could creep into for shelter and hide in. Until Daniel said one day they ought to have reached Batavia by now.

Only then did she feel she could stand upright again.

Three English ships.

But it was dry. And hot. The vegetable gardens gave what they could. In the heat some of the free-burghers' dogs wouldn't get up to go hunting, they had to slaughter some of their reserve stock. Schoolmaster Wilde let the children out earlier in the day.

Baldini came up from the Lodge saying that there was at least a bit of an easterly breeze in the early morning and in the evenings, but for the rest it was even drier there. Dysentery had broken out again. The water in the pools stank too much to be drunk: drinking water was being brought up from Goose Brook. Momber didn't have enough Company servants working the wood, they'd had to go out and help gather food, because famine was stalking the Lodge. And the Flats as well. Van der Stel had sent virtually no wheat on the last ship, saying the island should produce more sweet potatoes for starch, that cooked in the same pot with the meat it was 'an extremely nutritious foodstuff'. As if every free-burgher on Mauritius didn't know!

They watched the mad slave every day to see if she was about to go off into the forest. It was a long time since there had been a cyclone ...

The mad slave didn't go off into the forest. She came knocking on the door of the stone house at Northwest Harbour before dawn one morning.

'Anna?'

'It's Magdalena's time. I've come to fetch you, Juffrouw Pieternella.'

'But there's still a month ...'

'It's her time.'

'Come inside, you've startled me, I've got to think and pack something. Maria is in the kitchen, she's getting the breakfast.'

Something was odd. Even Daniel said so. In all the years Anna hadn't set foot in Northwest Harbour.

'Why have you come to call Juffrouw Pieternella?' he tried to interrogate her in the kitchen.

'She's her blood mother.'

'Is Magdalena well?'

'Magdalena is well.' Anna's face gave no sign of anxiety.

To Southeast Harbour by boat.

'Can't it go any faster?' she wanted to know.

'The boat goes as fast as the wind blows,' Daniel said. Pieter offered to take her and Anna but Daniel said he would do so himself. 'I know you won't hear anything against Anna, Pieternella, but I still don't trust her. She's living in a forest of her own, you never know which way she's going to jump out.'

Johannes was nine months old and restless. She and Anna took turns looking after him. 'Why hasn't the master bought you a second slave? Is he stingy or just too poor?'

'I heard what you said!' Daniel barked behind her.

Magdalena was glowing with health when they got to the Lodge. Shortly before they moored beside the quay Anna asked her please not to mention that she'd walked to Northwest Harbour to call her, Pieternella. 'It would make her uneasy.'

'I was beginning to wonder if you weren't just looking for an excuse to visit the Lodge,' said Daniel.

And at the dinner table Commander Momber laughed in some embarrassment, saying when Anna disappeared some of the officials had convinced him that there was a cyclone on its way. To be honest, they had even begun to take precautions. Not that one would welcome a cyclone, but if the drought didn't break soon ...

Sometime in the early hours, Bockelenberg came to say that Magdalena's pains had started.

When she went into the room, Anna was there already, the bedding had been drawn back and a canvas sheet spread over the mattress.

At about midday, Magdalena gave birth to a tiny girl, and shortly afterwards, with the baby in her arms, she died. They hadn't been able to stop the bleeding.

That's what they said. But it didn't feel real. Something picked Pieternella up and bore her high above the treetops, away over the earth. She saw her tall, strong Daniel in the carpenter's work-place planing coffin planks, *shoof, shoof, shoof* while bright tears trickled down his cheeks. Bockelenberg was standing on the edge of the quay like one of the dead; Momber beside him with his hand on his shoulder. Juffrouw Elisabet, she noticed, was taking Magdalena's other three little children for a walk along the shore.

Anna was in the bedroom rocking the little bundle in her arms – rock, rock, rock. The little one pinned into swaddling bands.

While everyone waited for the wagon which had gone to the lower side of the Flats to fetch a free-burgher's wife who had also had a baby so that she could suckle Magdalena's baby, too.

Magdalena was buried the next morning. Not far from Salomon. And Momber's words were far below, down on the earth somewhere: *How impossible it is not to shed tears as, like planting a seed in the ground, we entrust our mortal remains to the earth to await the day of resurrection ...*

While she drifted downwards, ever so slowly.

How impossible it is to accord our final tribute to our dearly beloved daughter and sister and wife ... without profound sadness ...

Get up, Magdalena, don't be dead!

The Lord knows what we have lost in her, what a striking model of patience and faith, what a powerful fighter for the Kingdom of God ...

Paper words. Not Magdalena words.

Gently her feet touched the earth again, and slowly Magdalena died.

11

You crawl back into the body of the stone house until you can breathe by yourself again.

First Catharina, alive but dead. Then Magdalena dead for ever.

'Open your mouth, you've got to eat!' Anna was standing at her bedside forcing spoonfuls of food down her throat.

The Commander had said the slave could come back with them to Northwest Harbour for three months. He'd heard from Bockelenberg that there had been a close bond between her and the dead woman.

Daniel objected. Said he didn't want the child thief back on his property.

'Master Commander sent me with Juffrouw Pieternella, not with the *master*.' Taunting.

Daniel was too sick at heart to put her in her place.

'Why is the master making the boat tip like this?' On the way home Daniel had to tack in the lee of The Plaat. 'The thing's going to fall over!'

'I'm tipping it so you'll fall off.'

The banter was better than their terrible grieving silence.

On the boat, between two thin boards and wrapped in sailcloth, was a drawing of the *Zeemaat* they had found among Magdalena's things. Another of the *Europa*, when the ship was still lying, dead, on the shore. Bockelenberg gave them to Daniel, saying he only wanted to keep the drawings of the trees and the other ships.

Heaven and hell wrapped in a single sheet, and life that eventually comes knocking at your head, saying: You may mourn in your heart, but now you have to get up and live, because *you* aren't dead!

There were meals to be prepared, mattresses to be stuffed, needlework to be done; Little-Daniel had to be fetched from the island and made to go back to school. The schoolmaster had said the child was clever but very unwilling when it came to his books.

She needed to go to Black River Mouth, to see how Eva and Hans were getting on. To teach Anna to pick yellow-bush leaves. To feel the drought in the body of the island.

Hendrik and Jamika went off to see if they could catch a turtle. They came back with two fish.

'The drought has invaded the sea as well, Daniel. There's nothing to catch. They say caterpillars have eaten the last of the gardens on the Flats, and there's no fish left in the water at the Lodge either. The new Commander reads a longer prayer every night, but it doesn't help. And apparently it's just as dry at the Cape.'

There is no help for the heartache that drags behind you like a weight at your feet.

Daniel and some of the others dug open the spring at the southern end of the bay and made a catchment dam. The river near them on the northern side was running ever more slowly – Thomas had to stand guard to make sure that the water was shared out fairly.

'Tell the mad slave to go off into the forest and summon the rain!'

The *Vanger* arrived unexpectedly from Southeast Harbour with Jan Bockelenberg and Magdalena's three older girls. They had come to say goodbye.

'I can't carry on, Mother. I miss her too much.'

The supply ship had arrived, heading for Batavia. He intended to go with it. With his four motherless children.

To Batavia? Then will you see Catharina?

Yes. She'll be happy to get a letter from you.

She went into the schoolroom to write by the light of a lantern, speaking ink-words to Catharina as though the child was sitting opposite her. About Magdalena. About the drought. The heat. About Johannes's birth. Something about everyone. That her old slave Anna was with her. That father had already wanted to chase her away because she lacked respect. Anna had told Father straight to his face to go the Lodge and pay for her; she didn't want to be owed for, because she'd now moved to Northwest Harbour for good.

Daniel came and sat with her in the schoolroom, and added the last bit of the letter. That our lives belong to Almighty God and are in His hands. That she should always do her duty to her husband and children, take good care of herself and always walk in the ways of the Almighty.

The letter felt like a cleansing.

'We've still got each other, my love.'

'We've still got each other, my Daniel.'

They said goodbye to Bockelenberg and Magdalena's children the next morning.

That evening brought the storm and the rain.

Not a cyclone, because Anna didn't disappear.

But the rivers ran again and the gardens rejoiced in the seed and the wreaths of sweet potato vines that were hastily planted in the wet earth. The grass on the hills began to sprout, the thin bodies of the cattle gradually filled out. Every eye scanned the sea in the hope that the storm would have sent a ship or two their way …

Slowly you learn to walk upright again.

Baldini came from Southeast Harbour and reported that the rain had brought merciful relief there as well; it was just that the folk down there were sadly dispirited.

The ship that Bockelenberg and the children left on had been delayed for more than a week. Fortunately there was a small quantity of prepared wood that could be put aboard for Batavia – reports from the Cape said Batavia was in urgent need of mast poles.

Two English ships.

'Truly, Daniel, it was Providence that saw to it that there would be something in the gardens and that there'd be enough firewood piled up ready.'

Twelve sick brought ashore for nursing.

Plenty of coopering.

Down from the Flats they came, looking like starvelings, bringing small casks and bottles of cane arrack, embarrassed and grateful for every penny. A few beans, a little tobacco.

'The drought squeezed us dry, Daniel.' Their clothes were threadbare, some no more than tatters.

Baldini said the island was going to overflow with free-burghers yet. The Captain of the supply ship told them that Secunde Elsevier at the Cape reckoned that at the most it would be only two or three years until there wouldn't be any further need for free-burghers at the Cape. The officials would be able to supply the ships with all they needed.

Willem Adriaan had sent word that Commander Momber was to have a large quantity of lime ready for the next ship to leave for the Cape. And plenty of wood. The skipper said the houses the officials were having built for themselves all over the Cape were jewels of luxuriousness.

Unfortunately there was no chaplain on the English ship to christen Johannes and the other free-burghers' children. The man had died at sea.

By the time the *Vanger* dropped anchor at Northwest Harbour again one afternoon, all was calm and the sea was empty of ships.

Abraham Momber sat down at the table, deeply depressed. 'I dare not stay away from the Lodge too long, Cooper Zaaijman. Secunde De la Fontain drinks himself into a stupor every day; his office work only gets done if I help him with it. The man gets furious and abusive when they won't give him any more liquor.'

'Send him back to the Cape, Commander. You cannot continue like this.'

'That is my intention, Cooper. But in the mean time we have to continue in these appalling conditions. The drought did break for a while, but the river at the Lodge has stopped flowing again. Fish are lying choking in the mud. I begin to see the hand of God in everything – in the decay of man and beast. When last did you and your wife sit down at the Communion table, Cooper?'

'Lamotius asked time after time for a minister to be sent here, Commander; my son-in-law Diodati regularly submitted the same request. Only a properly ordained minister can serve Communion.'

'Exactly. But isn't there a yearning among the free-burghers to be able to practise their religion, to give their children a Christian upbringing?'

'We raise our children as best we can, but none of them has been confirmed ...'

'How then can God hold his hand over us? Rumour has it that there are even free-burghers who have had their children baptised by the *enemy*'s ministers. Isn't that treasonable?'

'I'm no traitor, Commander, but I had all mine, except the youngest, christened by English ministers.' Daniel was angry. 'And that is how I am able to say today that Magdalena met her Creator as a baptised Christian.'

'If you put it that way. But such baptisms were still not performed according to the rites of our Reformed Church.'

'Commander, for most of the free-burghers it's not a matter of the rites of any church, it's a matter of survival. Believe me.'

'It cannot continue like this. And the assistance that is still being rendered to the ships of our enemies here at Northwest Harbour must stop!'

More than a year later a new Secunde, Gerbrandse, arrived on the supply boat. And a new Surgeon, Andries Root. And an order for the component parts of fifty farm carts with precise instructions for each part. Plus a request for between six and eight hundred slabs of ebony.

Hendrik said Momber said he didn't know how that was to happen, most of their energy went into gathering food because of the new drought. But they would do what they could.

Then Hendrik took a letter out of his pocket.

A letter from Catharina from Batavia!

Her small neat handwriting, her breath, her heartache about Magdalena, her longing for Mauritius and Father and Mother. Bockelenberg was unhappy in Batavia; he'd asked to go to the Cape with his children.

Like the resurrection of the dead.

12

The two soldiers arrived in the afternoon and stopped at the door, much the worse for wear.

'You look like men who've come a long way, Sergeant,' said Daniel and invited them in. They wouldn't come in, they still had to call on many more free-burghers. 'Has something happened somewhere?' Daniel enquired.

'Can't say, Cooper. The Commander wants to speak to every free-burgher and family head at the Lodge on Saturday. It's urgent.'

'Must we come armed again?'

'No.'

Maria and Abraham and their two sweet little boys had just arrived for a visit. 'Did you notice, Father?' asked Maria. 'The soldiers looked as if something had made them really nervous.'

The only other time the free-burghers had been summoned to the Lodge was in Diodati's time, when they'd had to go armed because an English pirate ship had run aground at Black Rock, north of Southeast Harbour, and a hundred and seventy pirates were carrying all their weapons and powder and goods ashore. Diodati was consumed with unease. Daniel advised him: Negotiate with the pirate captain; I know him, he's the Englishman John Bowen.

They went to talk to the man, showed him a spot an hour north of the Lodge where the pirates could camp.

Diodati ordered the free-burghers to deliver as much food as possible to the pirates to stop them from going on raiding parties or attacking the Lodge.

Now *that* was a blessing fallen out of the sky, said Michiel Romondt. Some of the other free-burghers on the eastern side of the island and the Flats came to Northwest Harbour and told Daniel: Will you please see to it that the men from this side of the island keep their hands off the pirates? This time it's our *chance*. You never tell us when there are enemy ships here; you seldom give us a chance to make a bean. The pirates are ours.

Daniel said that was fair.

Three months, while the farmers rejoiced and kept up the supply of produce, and the money rolled in. Palm wine by the barrel. As much arrack as they could lay their hands on. The pirates paid up. The pirates bought the *Europa* from Diodati, caulked it and sailed off to Madagascar.

A year later rumours were doing the rounds that the same band of pirates had sneaked into the same bay and were again being provisioned by the free-burghers. Daniel said the men were playing with fire now.

No, this time it couldn't be pirates that Momber had summoned them for *so* urgently.

'We can only wait, Mother,' said Pieter. 'But you can't help wondering.'

Baldini and Hendrik had also gone along. Schoolmaster Wilde said it was to shoot runaway slaves in the forest. Without weapons?

She and Anna took Johannes and walked over to Tant Theuntjie to take her a bowl of turtle stew. Tant Theuntjie said Henk Karseboom had gone off with one of her walking sticks, how did he think she could walk? Henk reckoned there'd been a mutiny on the supply ship.

On the way back Anna said: 'They all reckon wrong.'

'Tell me what you know, Anna.'

'Anna doesn't know, Anna just feels the earth is overbalancing.'

'Don't say that!'

'You tell me to say, then you tell me not to say.'

When Daniel got home it felt as if it was the earth under *her* feet that was overbalancing. She'd never seen him like this before – his eyes rigid and cold in his head, his teeth clenched, his mouth a hard cleft when he spoke.

'Where are the slaves?'

'Daniel?'

'Where are the slaves?'

'Thomas and Jake are in the garden, the others are over on the island.'

'Where are Anna and Maria?'

'Maria's in the kitchen, Anna's in the bedroom with Johannes. Daniel, what's happening?'

Pieter came in from outside. The news was on his face, too. 'Is it true, Father? What Hans has just told me?'

'Yes.'

'Please, tell me!'

'It's still a secret, the slaves may not know or they'll start deserting. The Cape has sent word that the Lords Seventeen have issued instructions: Mauritius is to be closed down. We've all got to leave the island.'

Mauritius must close. You close a chest by turning a key in a lock ...

'Mauritius has to be evacuated, Mother!' Pieter was trying to get it through to her.

'Why?'

At that the words started spitting out of Daniel's mouth: 'So the English can come and occupy the island and stop threatening to take the Cape!'

And in any case the island was of no further use to the Company. There wasn't room on the supply ship for the wooden parts of the forty farm carts that were ready for loading. Don't plant or sow anything more; food will be sent from Batavia until ships arrive to take everyone away.

Where to?

The Cape or Batavia. You are to make up your minds as soon as possible and come to the Lodge to state your preference.

Surely the Company couldn't seriously intend ...

All your property – houses and outbuildings and work-places and sampans and fruit trees and farming fields – is to be set alight. The English must not find anything to their advantage on the island.

Words.

The free-burghers were to slaughter as many of their cattle as possible and salt down the meat in barrels. All hounds were to be let loose to hunt down the remaining livestock and game.

'Daniel?'

'I'm going to the Lodge. I'm going to speak up. I'll tell them we're not going anywhere. The new Secunde, Gerbrandse, has been appointed to hear all complaints and questions.'

Daniel and Eva's Hans and Maria's Abraham and Pieter and Baldini went to the Lodge together to discuss the issue.

They said they were prepared to occupy the island alone with their families. To keep it out of the hands of the enemy. To raise the VOC's flag.

Gerbrandse looked over their heads, didn't even take his pipe out of his mouth. No, you would succour pirates and the enemy with an equally generous hand and thereby endanger our fleet. All stone buildings are to be broken down right to the ground. Remember, inspections will be undertaken to ensure that these instructions have been complied with.

542

Are you the owner of the *Zeemaat*, Cooper? Yes. The boat must be burnt.

And the slaves?

Slaves that are your property go where you go. You are to supply all provisions for them and yourselves for the voyage. Sell the slaves when you get there and get some money in your pockets. And stop moaning to the Lodge. All the rest are satisfied.

Let's run away, Salomon. I don't want to go to Mauritius. We can't, Pieternella, they'll send soldiers to look for us. Please, Daniel, let's hide in the forest, they won't find us …

'Juffrouw Pieternella, you can't go on crying like this; you're weeping away all the drinking water for the baby inside you!'

'How do you know there's a baby inside me, Anna?'

'Anna sees. The master doesn't see yet. He's walking about like a prisoner: to the island, to the house, to the Flats, to the house, to the island. Looking for an escape. Your Maria-child is packing things in two piles: one to take, one to burn.'

It's not true!

'Maria?'

'Abraham and I have already chosen, Mother. We're going to the Cape.' Like someone trying to hide her joy. 'Don't blame me, Mother, I feel like the pot shards that have to go home.'

Eva?

'Hans and I have also decided to go the Cape, Mother. He's going to start slaughtering some of his cattle next week.'

Tant Theuntjie?

'What would I want in the Cape? Henk says we're going to Batavia. What are you looking so confused about? Right from the start you didn't want to come to Mauritius.'

Aaltjie?

'Jan says now at least we don't have to try and escape on an English ship.'

'What do Elisabet and Willemina say?'

'They're already packing. Remember, the day they say the ships have arrived, there's going to be a mad rush. We're all going to Batavia; the men have all been to the Lodge to hand in our names.'

Daniel?

'The first houses on the Flats are already burning. The Company servants are knocking down the Lodge.'

'What are we going to do?'

'I don't know, my love. Honest to God, I don't know.'

'Hendrik says he's not going anywhere.'

'Hendrik has only himself. Hendrik is an old runaway sailor. As far as the Company is concerned, he doesn't actually exist.'

But it was Hendrik who brought back the first speck of light from the Lodge.

A ship from the Cape had anchored at Southeast Harbour. The *Ter Aa*. It was on its way to Madagascar to fetch slaves but had orders to round up some of the slaves in the forest here on Mauritius first and to catch or shoot them. But it was the news from the Cape that was almost too good to be true! Willem Adriaan had had some of the leading free-burghers thrown in gaol. He threatened to hang them because they refused to bend to his authority and that of the officials. Elsevier had recommended: First chop off their hands. These same free-burghers and their friends were the ones who had signed an indictment against the Governor and his officials and had got other free-burghers to smuggle it to the fatherland.

At the time when the *Ter Aa* sailed from the Cape, the news had just arrived from Holland: Willem Adriaan and Minister Kalden and Elsevier had been banished from the Cape for ever – back to the fatherland. Frans van der Stel was banned from all the Company's areas of operation. They said the Cape was jubilant!

It was Willem Adriaan who had said the island had to be shut down ...

'No, Pieternella, that doesn't mean a reprieve. It was the Lords Seventeen that issued the order to *him*.' Daniel was losing heart.

'He was a liar!'

'I've decided. We're going back to the Cape, my love.'

Words she didn't want to hear.

Christiaan was born on the twenty-eighth of March. Daniel went out to shoot the pigeons for the soup, Anna wrapped the baby in the little quilt and took him outside to show him to the sun and the island. Came back and laid him in his mother's arms and said: So that he'll know where he was born.

'There will be a way out yet, Anna, I'm telling you!'

'There's a dance at Master Jan Muur's place tonight. Juffrouw Willemina says they want to be the first to burn down their house. The *Vanger* is coming next week to start lugging the people and the stuff they're taking with them away to Southeast Harbour.'

The ship that was to bring the promised food from Batavia didn't arrive.

Momber sent four Company servants to Daniel to buy back some of Diodati's cattle; folk were becoming discontented. All they had to eat was salt meat and water, no vegetables or starch.

Christiaan was two months old.

'They're going to forget about us on this island, Daniel. I'm telling you. The ships that are supposed to come and fetch everybody won't arrive either.'

'That's idle thinking, Pieternella. A vain hope. And it will leave you hanging in the air and then drop you again from a terrible height. Accept it, my love, hold on to me. If this is God's will ...'

'It's *not* God's will!' She shouted it out loud. 'It's the Company's god's will that came in and took off and ate up and chopped down and stamped out, and never cared a penny!'

'Pieternella ...'

'Didn't care about the saw-blades, didn't care about Sven Telleson!'

'Pieternella ...'

'Didn't care if we lived or died!'

Anna appeared in the doorway. 'You're poisoning your milk, Juffrouw Pieternella!'

Daniel hugged her tight and held her till her fear subsided.

The big English ship arrived in the twilight.

Maria had arrived early that morning from her and Abraham's house and sat down on the bed beside her. She was bathing Christiaantjie.

'Mother?'

'Have you and Abraham had words, Maria?'

'No, Mother.'

'What then?' The child had *something* on her mind.

'Mother, you do know that I love you more than anything else on earth?'

'No, you don't love your mother best, you love your husband best.'

'That's different love, Mother. You're tied to me. Tightly.'

Something was warning her. 'What is it, Maria?'

'They're busy loading our goods and our two slaves on to the English ship – if Abraham works as a carpenter on the voyage to the Cape.'

'Tell me it's not true.' Not Maria.

'We can't wait any longer for the ship that is supposed to come; we'll go ahead and find a house for us to live in – for you and Father and Eva and Hans and us. Please, Mother.'

'Mauritius is your home.' Like a last grasp at something.

'Not any more, Mother.'

Anna took over bathing and dressing Christiaantjie.

She walked down to the shore with Maria, feeling as though all words had suddenly fled her. A river that had dried up all at once. A mouse that saw the hawk swooping down but didn't have the will to run and hide.

She watched them loading the last chests and things on the ship's boat and rowing away with them – the sawdust doll tied on top of one of the bundles, its embroidered mouth still smiling.

All she gave Maria as they said goodbye were the two pot shards.

Secunde Gerbrandse arrived in person on the *Vanger* a week later. Stout. Red freckled face.

'Why is your stuff not packed, Zaaijman? Do you want me to set fire to the house as it is?'

'Not if you want to go on living.'

'Who do you think you're talking to? Or do you think I don't know about the English ship that was here, that your daughter and son-in-law left on it?'

'They had permission.'

'Perhaps they did. What I *don't* know is what you and the bloody English discussed.'

'What's there to discuss?'

'A traitor's always got something to sell.'

'I'm not a traitor. Get off my property. I'll bring my own things to Southeast Harbour.'

'I see you've built yourself a very comfortable living here. Got rich, thanks to the enemy. I hear your wife says you're not going anywhere. Tell her you've got one week to report at Southeast Harbour – or all hell will be let loose on you.'

Mounted soldier below the potter's cottage: The corporal is furious, you've got to come to the quay, you've got to go aboard!

If she remembered rightly, she'd thrown a stone at him.

She waited behind the shutter till the Secunde had left before she would risk going outside.

'What now, Daniel?

'Now they've got us chained up, Pieternella.'

13

The two ships dropped anchor in the inner waters in front of the Lodge. The *Carthago* and the *Mercurius*.

If you close your eyes, you see your own pictures. The footpath through the green-leaf tunnel to the Orange Tree Flats. The little flock of green chatterboxes with their white-framed eyes. The *caroo-coo-coo* doves. Pernilla. The shining fishes in the clear water of the river. Crabs. The leaf-roof house. Anna.

She opened her eyes to see where Anna was. She was standing with Christiaantjie on her arm. It wasn't their turn yet. Sailors and soldiers were loading the *Carthago*. Overloading it. With everyone and everything that wanted to go to Batavia. Among those waiting was Magriet Ringels with her bundle.

She'd cleared a space under the shelter that Daniel had rigged up for them with a sheet of canvas in the forest. Broken away small branches to give herself a clear view of the sea in the direction of the quay.

A fire burns down into ash.

She opened her eyes again and walked across the ash. Came across Tant Maijke's ghost on the Flats. Exchanged greetings. The dumbcluck birds. The tortoises. The bats. The pure-white ribbon-tailed birds high above the forest at the Black River.

'Pieternella, why are you sitting here all alone, my love?'

'I'm just walking across the island in my heart, saying goodbye, my Daniel.' She was so desperately sorry for him.

'I would have given anything to have been able to spare you this. Thank God we're not on the *Carthago*, they're overloading that ship.'

Daniel and the slaves had returned to Northwest Harbour alone to knock down everything and set it all alight. The *Zeemaat* was still waiting for him. Secunde Gerbrandse had said: I want to *see* that boat in flames, Zaaijman.

Strangely, the Lodge had burnt down on its own. The officials who'd had to stay till the end had made themselves shelters in the ruins. Another ship would be sent to fetch them.

The *Jerusalem* had arrived from Batavia and there had been a farewell dinner for the officers. When a toast was drunk to all the notables of the Noble Company, the cannons at the Lodge were fired six times in their honour. Some of the tow or soot from the barrels of the cannons had landed on the leaf-roof of the Lodge – everything went up in flames: the Lodge, the store room, the workshop, the salary books. And the last of the food.

The officials looked like derelicts emerging from the forest, dirty and patched and miserable.

'Do you remember Sven Telleson, Anna?'

'Remember him often.'

'He said life wraps heaven and hell together for you in one cloth.'

'And for him an extra bottle of arrack surely.'

'I sometimes wonder if there is any heaven left in my cloth.'

'How far is this Cape place?'

'It was more than fifty days away when my young brother and I came here. Daniel says it will now take only half that long. At this time of the year the ships take a shorter route, running before the east wind the whole time.'

She made Daniel promise her one thing: that he wouldn't sell Anna when he sold some of the other slaves at the Cape.

The *Carthago* sailed the next day and almost immediately the wind dropped.

The same thing all over again: the *Boode* hadn't been able to sail either; there hadn't been any wind …

Three weeks. Then the wind returned.

She'd only seen Daniel cry once before, when he was making Magdalena's coffin. The second time was when he had to set fire to the *Zeemaat* with his own hands.

The *Mercurius*. Woodgoose. With only three families who wanted to go the Cape: Daniel Zaaijman's, Michiel Romondt's, Hans van Schoonhoven's.

Anna was not with the other slaves in the sleeping hutch on the deck. She wasn't there when everyone was taken aboard.

They said she'd walked into the forest before the great cyclone. She never came out again.

Afterword

After their return to the Cape on 26 January 1709 Daniel and Pieternella made repeated attempts to return to Mauritius. After the shattering news at the end of that year that the French had commenced their occupation of the island, they admitted defeat.

They bought a small farm, Patrijsen Vallei, outside Stellenbosch. It seems to have been only a home for they did very little farming. Jan Bockelenberg established himself as a free-burgher-surgeon in Stellenbosch. Consequently Daniel and Pieternella had close contact with their dead Magdalena's four daughters.

One of the Zaaijmans' neighbours was a bent old man who managed Elsevier's farm, Elsenburg. The man was Isaac Lamotius. He had served six years hard labour in a salt mine in the East for his part in the Dubertin case.

Pieternella and her son Johannes died in the smallpox epidemic in 1713. Daniel a year later.

Shortly before Diodati was appointed Commander at Deshima, Catharina died in Batavia.

Sources consulted

Die Buiteposte: Dan Sleigh. HAUM Publishers. Pretoria, 1993.

Cape Good Hope, 1652-1702. The First Fifty Years of Dutch Colonization as seen by Callers: Two volumes. Cape Town, 1971.

Naauwkeurige en uitvoerige beschrijving van de Kaap de Goede Hoop: P Kolben. Part 2. Amsterdam, 1731.

The Present State of the Cape of Good Hope, or a Particular Account of the several Nations of the Hottentots: P Kolben. London, 1731.

Beschrijvinge van der Kaap der Goede Hoop met de zaaken daar toe behoorende: F Valentijn (E H Raidt, et al, eds). Two parts. (Van Riebeeck Society, Second Series, numbers 2 and 4.) Cape Town, 1971-1973.

The Khoisan Peoples of South Africa: I Schapera. London, 1960.

Krotoa, called 'Eva': A Woman Between: V C Malherbe. University of Cape Town, 1990.

The First South Africans – and the laws which governed them: Whiting Spilhaus. Juta and Company Limited, Cape Town and Johannesburg, 1949.

Briewe van Maria van Riebeeck en ander Riebeeckiana: D B Bosman. Amsterdam, 1952.

De Vereenigde Oost-Indische Compagnie: Els M Jacobs. Amsterdam, 1997.

Ordre en Instructie voor de Chirurgyns: Amsterdam, 1696.

De ontdekkingsreis van Willem de Vlamingh: G G Schilder (ed.) The Hague, 1976.

Muiterij – Oproer en berechting op schepen van de VOC: J R Bruijn and E S van Eyck van Heslinga.

Predicatiën voor alle Zon- en Feestdagen: L Hofacker. Part I and Part II.

De Huispostille of Predicatiën: Justus Bulaeus.

Kraal and Castle: R Elphick. London, 1977.

Geslagsregisters van die Ou Kaapse Families: C C de Villiers. (Revised and supplemented by C Pama.) Cape Town, 1966.

Die herkoms van die Afrikaner: J A Heese. Cape Town, 1971.

Archival Sources

Dagregister en Briewe van Zacharias Wagenaer, 1662-1666. A J Böeseken (ed.). Pretoria, 1973. (SA Archival Documents. Important Cape Documents, part 2.)

Belangrijke Historische Documenten over Zuid-Afrika: G M Theal. London, 1911.

Daghregister, 1651-1662: J A van Riebeeck. Three parts. (Edited by D B Bosman and H B Thom.) Cape Town, 1952-1957.

Dagregister Mauritius, 1.1.1685-31.12.168 (Ref. DR-M).
Inkomende Brieven Mauritius, 1679-1690 (Ref. C-IB).
Uitgaande Brieven Mauritius, 1678-1690 (Ref. C-UB).

Other Assistance

Dr Dan Sleigh, historian and fellow-researcher.

Mauritius: Dr Dan Sleigh and Michel Espitalier-Noël for days of reconstruction and discovery of the island's VOC period.

Dr Helena Scheffler, historian, for valuable contributions on interiors, clothing and women's customs during the 17th and 18th centuries.

Staff, Schreuder House, Stellenbosch.

De Gevangenispoort, The Hague.

Maritime Museum, Amsterdam.

Amsterdam Historical Museum.

Rijksmuseum, Amsterdam.

Robben Island staff.

Esther Grobbelaar, Curator: Ceramics, South African Cultural Museum.

Cooper Abie Valentyn of the Brandy Museum, Stellenbosch.

Captain Wilhelm von Schütz for his knowledge of ships and sailing.